D1572409

A LIFE SPARED

A Novel

John K. Lanphier

DORRANCE
PUBLISHING CO
EST. 1920
PITTSBURGH, PENNSYLVANIA 15238

Dorrance Publishing Co
585 Alpha Drive
Suite 103
Pittsburgh, PA 15238
Visit our website at *www.dorrancebookstore.com*

ISBN: 978-1-6393-7275-1
eISBN: 978-1-6393-7675-9

For Mom and Dad – the two angels who walk with me daily.
Thank you for saving my life.

Chapter 1

Saturday, 5 August 1972

For two reasons, it was hard for me to believe it was actually August. First, the temperature that Saturday morning was unseasonably chilly, even for northern Minnesota. When Mom, Dad, and I left Duluth early, bound for Mankato, I actually felt the need to wear my windbreaker until the inside of the car warmed up some.

Northern Minnesota in the late summer is normally hot and muggy, with temperatures that range from the high-eighties to mid-nineties. Duluthians don't mind the heat so much, but the seventy to eighty-five percent humidity, which is felt almost daily that time of year, is enough to drive people bonkers. They just get tired of constantly sticking to themselves. Nonetheless, earlier in the week, a storm front came roaring out of the northeast. It blew across the Great Lakes and cooled things off considerably. Forecasted highs for the entire state of Minnesota were only going to be in the low seventies.

The second reason for my disbelief was because I had spent all of June and July anxiously anticipating that trip. August had finally arrived and when travel-day came, I was distinctly aware that the dream I had dreamt for so long was actually coming true. And the closer we got to Mankato, the more my excitement and impatience grew within me.

John K. Lanphier

We had been on the road for what seemed to me an eternity. To make matters worse, blood circulation to my butt had stopped a hundred miles behind us. I had a severe case of deadass and it was driving me crazy! So, when we finally made our entrance into Mankato from the east, I could hardly sit still!

We had departed Duluth at sunrise and traveled south, just over 235 miles. To me, the trip should not have taken anywhere near as long as it did. I mean, the posted speed limit on Interstate 35 was sixty-five miles per hour practically the entire way, but Mom conscientiously did no faster than the ol' double nickel. She always tested my patience that way – I was always in a hurry, to get someplace, but Mom never was, or she just didn't care.

Three years had passed by since I left, or for accuracy's sake, had been taken from, Mankato. I could now scarcely believe I had been gone that long. I was desperate to control the rush of emotions that surged their way throughout my innards, but I was rapidly losing the battle.

I instructed Mom to turn left off Riverfront Drive, then turn right onto Front Street. It wasn't the most direct route to where we were going, but what Mom didn't know would not hurt her, or so I thought. As we began our drive down Front Street, Mom had to remind me once again to sit back, relax, and stop blocking her view through the rearview mirror. Then, for what seemed like the umpteenth time, she again asked for directions to the Wilsons' house. I could tell she was getting a kick out of pestering me repeatedly that way. In my eyes, she was perpetrating a crime by torturing me with my own impatience. Nevertheless, I honestly didn't mind. It was one of those rare moments, when Mom demonstrated she actually *had* a sense of humor, dry as it may have been.

"It's on Westwood Drive. Don't worry, I'll tell you when and where to turn," I assured her.

With an all-knowing smirk on her face, Mom asked, "Jacky, do you think you can sit still that long?"

Mom also knew that I positively loathed being called Jacky by anyone, but especially by her. She only did it when she wanted to get a rise out of me. But, I was in too good of a mood to let her get under my skin. So, in response, I just gave her a snotty, little look in the rearview mirror.

Dad had just finished smoking a cigarette and put the butt out in the ashtray. He then closed the wing of our red, Ford station wagon. After he secured the little, pivoting window, I heard him chuckle.

I hated it when Mom and Dad smoked in the car and because they had repeatedly done so for the entire trip, my stomach was now churning nauseously.

When it came to being me, queasiness, mixed with a heightened-emotional state, inside an enclosed space – like a car – were not good bedfellows.

Out of nowhere, Dad barked an order. "Jack, describe what you're seeing for me."

He must have done that to me about twenty times on the trip down from Duluth. It was one of many things I disliked about his blindness. He always seemed to ask it of me when I wanted to be alone with my thoughts, which, back then, was a constant state of mind for me. Providing Dad verbal descriptions of everything my eyes took in was how he trained me to be *his* eyes. My attitude may not have been the best, but I indulged him always. After all, he did volunteer to be my dad. Besides that, I knew all too well that Mom would not tolerate less from me.

As we three continued our entry into town, I swallowed hard and tried to calm my breathing. I then attempted to describe for Dad, in detail, all the sights of Mankato. That July, I had just turned thirteen years old and lacked the necessary vocabulary to articulate things clearly for him. Nevertheless, he constantly challenged me to get better at it. I patiently answered Dad's questions, all the while knowing my words could not accurately draw that mental picture for him to see in his head.

As I kept my rudimentary descriptions flowing, I was able to attach an unspoken memory to every block we traveled. The buildings on Front Street, with their Victorian architecture, looked all too familiar to me. I noticed, though, that there were far more vacant buildings than what I remembered in 1969. *What happened here?* The silent question stayed in my head and would linger awhile.

Many of the stores I once explored with my friends were now closed. The Record Shack – where I used to accompany Tony Milner, so he could look for 45

RPM recordings – was no longer open. The Rainbow Café – where my friends and I got the greasiest fries in town – no longer existed.

When I saw that The Grand, The Towne, and The State movie theaters appeared to still be in operation, I breathed a short sigh of relief. I remembered going to many Saturday matinees with Joel, Dave, Tony, and Mike at those theaters.

Kresge's Five & Dime was also still in business. It, too, was a welcomed sight. The guys and I had eaten at the lunch counter there often. I smiled and wondered if Mr. Steiner still worked the grill.

Right next door to Kresge's, its competitor, F.W. Woolworth, once operated, but it had a sign posted in the window, too. It stated the building was for sale or lease.

I next saw the old bank building and tried to describe it for Dad. Because of its old-world architecture, I always thought it was one of the finest buildings on Front Street. My next favorite was located just across the street from the bank. It was The Graif Building. Matt J. Graif's Fine Clothing for Men was one of oldest businesses still operating on Front Street. Later in life, I learned the decorative cornices that wrapped around the rooftops of both structures were a signature giveaway. The architecture was known as Renaissance Revival. However, that particular afternoon, I didn't care about any of that. I just thought the buildings still looked cool and was glad to see that not a single brick was out of place, or so it seemed.

When Mankato West High School was off to our left, I remembered that our first turn would be coming up shortly. The YMCA – where Danny first taught me to play pool – marked our turn onto West Fourth Street.

I probably should have guided Mom to a more direct route to the Wilson residence, but I just couldn't help indulging myself, by way of a zigzag tour of the old neighborhood. I was finally on my old stomping grounds and all at once, my past life came flooding into my head. My pulse quickened and my stomach flipped.

I then pointed over Mom's shoulder and described for Dad a house on Winona Street. It once belonged to the first foster family I was placed with. Their name was Matson. I had lived with them throughout my first-grade year. Because of better job opportunities, they moved to Kansas in the fall of my second-grade year, thus creating the need for new living arrangements for me, which at the time, was absolutely fine with me because there was no love lost on that family. My lack of emotional attachment to the Matsons helped facilitate an easy transition into the Wilson household.

The Matson house overlooked some train tracks, which ran north and south through that part of town. Just on the other side of the rails, the campus of Mankato West High sprawled out in all directions. I then remembered how in the fall, when I was supposed to be asleep, I stood at my bedroom window and watched the Scarlets play football on Friday nights. Back then, the noise of the games or the passing of a train always kept me awake, wondering if I would ever go to that school or be able to explore the rails, just to see where they led.

Not three blocks from the former Matson home, stood good, ol' Roosevelt Elementary School. I attended the first grade there. As we passed the school, I instructed Mom to take an immediate left. Three blocks south on Hubbell Avenue, St. Joseph the Worker, Catholic Church and Parochial School awaited me. It was the last school I attended before moving to Duluth. It was also where I met my very first, best friends: Tony Milner, Joel Brighten, Dave Lester, and Mike McDonald.

My heart was suddenly pounding. I could feel myself losing the battle being waged inside my stomach. Sweat broke out on my forehead. *Damn it*, I thought, *I'm gonna lose it!*

I needed to get outside before I vomited in the car, so I asked Mom – almost ordered her – to pull over at the church. In turn, Mom gave me a look of concern through the rearview mirror, then complied with my desperate request. She could see that I was struggling, so she pulled over and I hurriedly jumped out.

Behind me, Dad yelled, "Jackson?!"

I heard Mom say, "Brice, just give him a minute."

There on a patch of green grass, facing the front of the church, I leaned forward. With my hands on my knees and my eyes closed, I filled my lungs with the cool, clean, afternoon air. Mom then surprised me from behind by putting an arm around me. In a flash, I recoiled from her touch, which caused her to immediately jump back.

5

"Sorry, honey, I didn't mean to sneak up on you like that. Are you okay?!"

I turned and gave her a weak smile. Then, I gave her something I rarely offered back then, a half-hearted hug. I wanted to let her know that my reaction to her touch was all me and had nothing to do with her, but she was well aware of that already.

"I'm okay," I assured her. "My stomach just about got away from me is all."

"You've been an absolute bundle of nerves for days," stated Mom. "Are you really *that* happy to be here?" The worry in her eyes showed clearly.

I mumbled my response. "I've been dreamin' about it for a long time."

Truer words were never spoken. I was so hung up on the life I had left behind in Mankato. My inability to let go of it was keeping me from enjoying the vastly enriched lifestyle afforded me in Duluth. I just couldn't get that small town out of my head, or, more importantly, my heart.

Shaking her head slowly, Mom asked, "You think you can get it together long enough to guide me the rest of the way?"

"Yeah, I guess," was my simple reply.

As I walked back to the station wagon, I thought, *you idiot!*

When I wasn't in control of my emotions, my embarrassment always surfaced. I detested feeling that way. Most of the time, I was a complete rock. That was the opinion shared by Mom and Dad. They, plus various teachers of mine, said as much. Nevertheless, in the three years since I had left Mankato, there were many times when I most certainly was not the rock they alleged me to be. That's when Doc Elliot, child psychiatrist, came into my life.

At first, I was not a willing participant. Nevertheless, I soon realized that Doc Elliot was an extremely patient man. He was neither pushy nor insistent; traits that earned my trust. The trip to Mankato was actually his idea. He said it was time for me to go back and face my demons. At the time, it sounded like a bunch of psychobabble to me, but that was okay. In truth, it was going to get me what my heart most desired. According to the good doctor, I needed to put a few things to rest. Only then would I start to enjoy my life in Duluth. When he spoke those words, it made perfect sense to me. But, as I stood in front of my old church, I was no longer sure of myself. I doubted my ability to let that small town and everyone I knew there just slip away. At the same time, I was quite thankful that I had two, full weeks to figure it all out.

As Mom and I walked back to the car, I wiped sweat from my forehead with my shirt sleeve. The act garnered me one of her disappointed looks. "That's what your handkerchief is for," she mildly scolded.

"I didn't want to get a booger on me." I regretted the words almost as soon as they left my mouth. I kicked myself mentally for my immature response. *Stop being such a smartass!*

"Jackson, that's disgusting!" Mom chided. "And, is there a way to the Wilson place with less twists and turns? When your dad and I leave, I don't know how I'm going to find my way out of here."

Mom was right, I had toured the neighborhood enough for a while. There would be ample time for more, but it would have to until after I got settled. I was suddenly in more of a hurry to get to our destination, so I decided to take it easy on Mom and guide her by the most-direct route. It wouldn't be hard, either – we were only three blocks away.

When Mom and I returned to the car, Dad was leaning on the hood, smoking another cigarette. He heard us as we approached. "Catherine?" he queried.

"Yes, Brice, it's us. Finish your cigarette please. We need to get going."

Mom then walked around the rear of the station wagon to get to the driver's side. Dad took one last drag off his cigarette and then flicked the butt out into what he thought was an empty street. Instead, he nearly hit Mom with it! I was the only one who saw the act, though.

Forgetting about Dad's phenomenal hearing, I muttered, "That was close."

"What was close?" asked Dad.

"Nothing, forget it," I replied, then opened the back door of the station wagon, got in, and closed the door behind me.

I did not want to make a big deal of it right then, but in actuality, I had no tolerance for my parents' smoking habits. They were well aware of my aversion, too, but it never seemed to matter to them. I hated it most when one or both insisted on lighting up inside the car. In the past, I tried to get them to see the error of their ways. Instead, they made the boundary lines crystal clear for me to see. When their lecture was through, there was absolutely no doubt in my mind. They didn't need *my* permission or concurrence to do anything. The subject pretty much became taboo and I learned to live with the shitty end of the stick. To my way of thinking, it was a small price to pay for parents who actually wanted me.

Westwood Drive was pretty much as I remembered it, but with some minor changes. Unlike the cookie-cutter dwellings of modern-day housing developments, the well-maintained houses within that neighborhood were of various architectural designs. Each house expressed their owner's individual taste in style and ability to grow gardens. Most were painted white and had bold colors for the trim. There were a few nonconformists, who painted their house a gaudy yellow or blue, but at least they kept them neat. From the outside, most of the houses appeared to be quite small; it was a deception. The dwellings sat atop full underground basements. The square footage in living space went up exponentially, when family rooms, dens, bedrooms, and extra bathrooms were established in the basements.

Manicured lawns and hedges ran up and down the entire block. There were no fences in the front yards, only a few neighbors had them in their back yards, but none were for privacy reasons. Bursts of color from small gardens bordered sidewalks and driveways. Small shrubs, annually-planted flowers, and various perennial plants were used to accent the front of each house.

The trees were three years more mature than when I left. Elm, maple, mountain ash, birch, poplar, and various species of evergreens adorned the entire neighborhood. Here and there, a few apple trees could be found, too. They were usually strategically tucked in their owner's back yard. It was a ploy to ward off apple thieves, but that lame defense never worked.

Adjacent to the back yards of those properties located on the west side of Westwood Drive, laid the train tracks that ran north and south through that entire section of town. Looking at the steel rails, I immediately remembered how scheduled trains woke everyone early each morning and continued on throughout the day.

When the Wilson residence finally came into view, a huge smile crossed my face. Other than what looked to be a newly painted, white, clapboard exterior, the house appeared almost exactly as I had left it. Contrasting color was provided by black shutters, which hung beside each window, the front door, which was painted a rather loud shade of red, and a basic-gray shingled roof. By comparison to slightly newer and larger homes in the area, the Wilson house appeared tiny and insignificant. Nevertheless, I could not have been happier to see it, knowing that I would once again sleep under its protective roof, with a family I had been missing terribly.

As soon as Mom turned into the driveway, I started looking for Kurt Wilson's bassett hound, Barney. I thought he would come waddling from the back yard and be the first to greet us, but Barney was nowhere in sight.

As we slowly pulled up beside the house, Janet Wilson appeared quite suddenly out of their side door and leapt onto the driveway. She was at the car to greet us before Mom brought it to a complete stop. Janet leaned down by Mom's open window and peered at the three of us with a bright smile and excited, brown eyes. "Hi everyone!" she greeted. Her eyes then met mine. "Hey kid! There you are!"

I scrambled out of my car door and rushed around to where Janet waited with open arms. As I landed in her embrace, I greeted her in return with an excited, "Hi!" It was the only word I could get out. Prior to that moment, I had never been happier to see anyone.

Janet Wilson was just as I remembered her. I looked for significant changes but found none. She was still slight of figure, with boney knees and elbows – just on the healthier side of anorexic. She had a gaunt, pockmarked face from years of battling acne. Her ruddy brown hair, as always, was cropped short for convenience and did not appear very stylish. In fact, I always thought Janet to be somewhat untidy in her appearance. She wasn't exactly what one would call a raving beauty, but at that moment in time, she looked fantastic to me.

Janet wrapped me up in her slender version of a bear hug, twisting me back and forth. She then pushed me back to arm's length and eyed me up and down. Excitedly, she said, "Well, let's have a look at what your mom and dad brung me! I can see you need a haircut and you're growing way too tall. Stop that right now!"

I loved the energy in her voice and couldn't keep from laughing at her over-animated greeting.

"Look at the tan you're sportin', kid," she continued. "The neighborhood girls get a load of you and you'll be fighting 'em off your entire stay here!"

Janet then pulled me in again and with one hand, grabbed my bangs. She gently pulled my head back and looked down, taking in my facial features. I looked up into her big, brown eyes and we both just held each other, smiling.

"I've missed you so much, kiddo," Janet said softly, her voice trembling, but just a smidge.

"I missed you, too." Again, I wanted to say more, but words failed me. Janet was the first and only foster mother I allowed inside my heart. It's probably because she was the only one who actually made any attempt to win me over. All others had kept their distance to prevent any emotional attachments.

Rather abruptly, Janet then turned her attention to Mom and Dad. She asked about the trip down and whether they had any trouble finding their way. Dad showed off his hidden abilities by reciting every interstate, highway, and county road we had to take. Like most people, Janet was genuinely impressed. I knew Dad enjoyed messing with people's heads that way. Most folks underestimated him and his ability to get around. I knew from experience that he could navigate the streets of Duluth better than me. However, when Dad credited me with directing them through the streets of Mankato, I did get a small surge of pride.

Right then, I remembered that I hadn't seen the hound. "Where's Barney?" I interrupted. "I thought for sure he would meet us when we pulled in."

Janet replied, "Well, honey, there's your first piece of bad news. Barney's not with us anymore. He just got too sick, so we had to put him down."

"Oh man! I'll bet Kurt took that hard."

"We all had to adjust afterward. Barney was a member of this family before you were."

I was sincerely disappointed. When Kurt – the elder of the two Wilson boys – was seven, he got Barney for a Christmas gift. Back then, Barney was just a newly-weaned pup, tripping over his big ears. That was years before they took me in. I remembered how the thunderously loud noise of passing trains would hurt Barney's sensitive ears. He would sit in the front yard and howl mournfully until the train traveled farther down the line. When I was with him, I would cup my hands over his ears until the train passed. Almost immediately, he would stop howling, wag his tail, look at me with his big, droopy eyes, and attempt to lick my face. When there was no one else to talk to, Barney was my buddy. As long as I scratched and rubbed his belly, he was happy and didn't care what secrets I shared.

Dumb dog, I thought, becoming momentarily sad.

Janet then brought me out of my somber mood by informing us that Brad was at the store, picking up a few things for that night's dinner. "He should be here anytime now," she said, looking out at the street, as if she expected him to pull up, right then and there. "He is so excited about you coming here," she added.

"What about Kurt and Danny?" I asked.

"Well, that's your second piece of bad news, kiddo. Those two now have girlfriends, so they are off traipsing around with them someplace. But they know that you were due in this afternoon. They've been pretty excited about you coming home, too…I mean…to Mankato."

Because of her slip of the tongue, Janet shot Mom a quick apologetic look. In return, Mom just shook her head and smiled, thus signifying that no offense had been taken.

With a disgusted look on my face, I exclaimed, "They have girlfriends?! Oh, God!"

"That's funny," chuckled Janet. "At first, those were my exact feelings about them and girls. But I've kinda got used to the idea since. How about you, kid? Anyone got you wrapped around her little finger?"

Tersely, I exclaimed, "Are you kidding?! No way! Not me!"

It wasn't that I found girls revolting – my feelings ran very much to the contrary. I had been attracted by a pretty face many times, but I had no, real experience with the opposite sex. So, instead of admitting that fact, it was so much easier to sound repulsed by the idea of ever being with one; such was my maturity level.

I then caught Mom smiling. I knew she was enjoying the initial banter between Janet and me. Mom enjoyed anything and everything that gave her more insight to me, a somewhat difficult task, I'll admit.

There was a little more casual conversation between us all before Janet instructed me to get lost for a little while. She wanted my parents to go into the house for coffee and, as she put it, grown-up talk.

Knowing her intentions all too well, I said, "That means you want to talk about me behind my back, right?"

With a huge smile plastered to her face, and in her best Minnesota accent, Janet replied, "You betcha. She then turned to Mom and stated, "Oh, for sure, he don't miss much, do he?" I loved it when Janet intentionally used poor grammar. It was all a put-on.

In return, Mom chuckled and shook her head. She then replied in clear, concise English, "No, he does not."

Dad was more than happy to except the offer of coffee. I knew he was probably having caffeine withdrawals. His last cup was obtained at The Happy Chef in Owatonna, during our lunch stop. A coffee cup in close proximity to Dad was a common sight. He didn't have many vices, but coffee and cigarettes were at the top of that short list.

Before going into the house, Mom instructed me not to run off too far because they would be leaving for Faribault soon. They were not traveling straight back to Duluth. They were going to spend a few days with one of Dad's old school buddies. They hadn't seen each other since they attended the State School for the Blind, which, coincidentally, was also located in Faribault.

As Mom led Dad toward the house, walking side by side, I watched and smiled at how comical they looked. I knew they had no delusions about how they appeared to others, either. Brice Landry towered in height over his wife and when he walked, he took huge strides. Mom did her best to keep up. At the same time, she expertly guided him away from shin-skinning obstructions. Oftentimes they joked, "Together, we look just like Mutt and Jeff, don't we?!"

Catherine Landry's height was a measured five-foot, one-inch tall. she maintained a decent figure, too, for a woman in her forties. Her hair color then was that of salt and pepper. She kept it set and piled on top of her head, kind of like a football helmet – a common hair style for women back then. Mom's eyes were brown and somewhat heavy lidded, which required thick, corrective lenses. Although her appearance was quite conservative at all times, it did not make her look older than she actually was, it simply fit her. To me, Mom was rather unremarkable to look at, but that didn't matter. I had learned in three years that she had a huge heart, which captured me when everyone else had failed. That is, I had only been her son for three years, but there was nothing I would not do for her.

The daughter of a railroad executive, Mom was brought up in a time where girls were educated to be efficient homemakers, but not much more than that. Nevertheless, Mom didn't hold with such conventional ideas that women were only good for the kitchen and making babies. Instead, she initially chose to be a career woman. She also kept herself involved in the community with volunteer work. I remember her telling me that before I came along, she had convinced Dad to open their home to the less fortunate, as a shelter for unwed mothers. However, it was Dad who convinced Mom that she could have the career of a lifetime, should they adopt a child. Apparently, he succeeded in making a pretty-strong case for the initiative because Mom immediately stopped taking in pregnant women. When their last young lodger moved out, Mom began converting one of the spare bedrooms into something suitable for a little boy. Years later, I asked why she had her heart set on a boy. She replied, "I didn't! I simply believed that your father wanted someone to carry on the Landry name. Now, I wouldn't have it any other way. Someday, you'll provide me the daughter."

Mom was also the disciplinarian within the Landry household. She was an old-school Catholic, who didn't tolerate blasphemy of any kind. Dad often joked about how Mom thought Charles Darwin was a bona fide charlatan. Of course, every time he said such things in Mom's presence, she always scowled at him. But what did Dad care, he couldn't see her disapproving looks!

Prior to getting married, Mom worked in the reports and administration office of the Duluth Police Department. She left that position shortly after marrying Dad. She then became the chief bookkeeper for their business. In truth, she was the only bookkeeper back then. When the two decided they wanted a family, they didn't want to risk giving birth to a visually impaired child, so adoption became the solution to their dilemma. When I arrived on the scene, Mom took a sabbatical from the business. She hired a widowed woman, Mrs. Brown, to keep

Dad's books. Mom wanted to ensure my transition into their life went as smoothly as possible by staying at home more. At the end of our first year together, Dad asked Mom to return to work. They kept Mrs. Brown, too. Apparently, I was not the only thing to grow some in one year's time.

In the three years since leaving Mankato, I had learned to love my adoptive mother very much but was guilty of not telling her so. That is, nowhere near as often as I should have.

Brice Landry was a full foot, plus a few inches, taller than his wife. He had massive arms and shoulders from growing up and working on his parents' farm in Mahtowa, Minnesota. He was also a heavyweight wrestler in high school and college. He had light brown hair – what little there was of it – and Mom always helped him keep it neatly groomed. Because of his huge appetite at mealtime, Dad was a tad bit more than slightly overweight. He preferred suspenders to a belt, but sometimes wore both; just to be sure, I supposed. Dad constantly hitched his drawers up to belly button height, which always got a chuckle from me. At first, I thought he was just clowning around for my sake. Later, I observed and learned that it was an actual necessity for him, especially when the elastic in his suspenders began to wear out.

Dad was born with inoperable cataracts in both eyes, but he did have some vision until young adulthood. A brain hemorrhage close to the optic nerve required the surgical loss of his left eye. The right eye simply ceased to function. From that day forward, Dad could no longer see. Nevertheless, he remained a man of great vision.

Dad may have been visually impaired, but he could outwork me any day of the week. When I first met him, Brice Landry's size alone intimidated me greatly. If he ever had a mind to, I knew he could break me in two, just like a dried piece of kindling. However, I learned in no time that Dad was perhaps the most gentle, caring, and loving man on the planet. When it came to disciplinary actions, he didn't believe in the hands-on method, for which I was eternally grateful. Instead, I sat through lectures. "Words are powerful things, Jackson," explained Dad. "You may not remember everything I tell you now, but someday, when you need them, you'll remember my words."

After graduating high school, at the State School for the Blind in Faribault, Dad worked diligently and obtained a business degree from St. Cloud State University. After college, the Minnesota State Services for the Blind had him running the coffee shop in the St. Louis County Welfare building in Duluth. That's where he first met and began dating Mom. The police department was situated right next door and Mom spent her lunchtimes at Dad's coffee shop. A few years after Dad and Mom wed, he gave the coffee shop back to the state. He wanted to strike out on his own because he felt the state was holding him back. Dad had all sorts of business ideas. Nevertheless, he knew none of them would see the light of day, either, not if he kept working within the confines of the state's system, which was built for people more handicapped than he, or so was his explained figuring.

He and Mom took a huge risk and purchased a vending business from a man, who had been forced into bankruptcy. Dad's belief that customer service and satisfaction was the most important facet to any business – he hung his hat on it. After the vending business began to succeed beyond their wildest dreams, Dad branched out into industrial real estate. He also invested in up-and-coming technologies. With sound planning, patience, and a lot of hard work, he and Mom turned B & C Enterprises, short for Brice and Catherine, into one of the fastest growing companies in the Twin Ports area. I once asked Dad how he did it. "It's quite simple, Jackson," he replied. "Take your time and grow your business with the patience of the Lord, Jesus Christ."

With a confused look on my face, I exclaimed, "What?!" At the time, I simply couldn't catch the correlation.

"Don't worry about it now," laughed Dad. "Someday, I'll teach you everything you need to know. The rest will be up to you." It was his way of telling me to enjoy my youth. There would be time enough ahead for what he called, "The hard stuff."

Janet's voice then jostled me from my trance. "While you wait out here, get your gear out of the car," she directed. "After that, you can shoot baskets or something to keep yourself occupied. The basketball is right where it's always been, remember?"

Not wanting to be anywhere near the adults, while they more than likely discussed me and the events that led to my visit, I nodded and replied, "Yes, ma'am."

Mom abruptly turned and asked, "Now, why isn't it that easy when I'm giving the orders?"

In response, I just gave her a sheepish grin. Mom winked at me, then turned and informed Dad that there was one step up to the landing, and the screen door opened to the left.

When the three adults disappeared inside the house, I went to the station wagon and began digging for my suitcases and other gear. I was only going to be in town for two weeks, but Mom had me pack almost my entire wardrobe. *What is it with moms and being prepared?* The thought perplexed me to no end. The Boy Scouts of America, who I was also affiliated with back then, had it as their motto: Be Prepared. However, they were never as prepared as Catherine Landry. I once asked Mom, "Why do you always ask me if I have clean underwear on?"

"Just in case we get into a car accident," Mom had replied. "You have to be prepared for such things."

Unable to restrain my propensity for adding wisecracker inputs, I countered with, "If you get us into a car accident, I think the ambulance guy is still going to find me with dirty underwear."

Mom's way of looking at the world was something I struggled with a lot. I think Dad had much the same feelings, but he still advised me well. Dad always said, "Don't try to understand it, Jackson, just do what she wants, then press on."

For that trip, Mom helped me pack two, large suitcases. One we stuffed with knock-around clothes, as Mom called them, and the other was filled with what Dad called my Sunday-go-to-meetin's. I also brought my fishing pole, a tackle box, two baseballs, my baseball bat, and my prized baseball mitt. I got it all out of the station wagon and initially put it on the landing by the side door. I then gave it some thought and decided to move it all back out onto the driveway. When Dad exited the house through that door, I didn't want him to trip on any of it – their training was finally taking hold.

When I had my trappings all organized in a neat pile on the driveway, I headed for the garage to find the basketball. If my memory served me correctly, I knew I would find it just within and to the left of the side door. When I opened the door, I was met with the mixed aromas of oil, solvents, and dust. The mustiness of the enclosure almost made me sneeze. Then, my eyes gazed upon Brad Wilson's prized, 1966 Corvair. The exterior color was a brilliant white, but the interior was blood red, with red and white tuck 'n' roll upholstery. The mere sight of it brought a huge smile to my face.

In 1968, Brad bought the used car. Supposedly, it was as a surprise birthday present for Janet. However, she wasn't comfortable driving a vehicle with a standard transmission. She preferred an automatic, but the Corvair came equipped with four on the floor. So, when it came to figuring out who Brad truly bought the car for, there was no real guesswork to be done. In addition, there was a distinct difference between the way Brad and Janet drove that car. I preferred Brad's way. I loved riding with him, especially when he screamed through town in that powerful, little, two-door coupe. When Janet drove, it was like putting grandma behind the wheel of an Indy racecar – what a waste of machinery.

As I stood there, motionless and gawking, I could scarcely believe how well Brad had preserved the car. Sitting in the dimly lit garage, Brad's little rocket still looked brand new.

Coming out of my stupor, I quickly located the basketball, snatched it up, and then hurried back out into the fresh air. The basketball hoop was suspended, centered and just above the large, garage-bay door. As I stood directly beneath it, dribbling the ball, just to get the feel of it, I remembered some of the crazy basketball games that took place under that hoop. Usually, Kurt and Danny were teamed up against Brad and me. Brad was a notorious cheater, who did things like lift me all the way to the hoop to make the score. Sometimes, he had Danny on his back while doing it. Mostly, I remembered the laughter.

That Was Then, This Is Now. Just then, S.E. Hinton's novel, which I had just read earlier that year, came to mind. The words in the title had real meaning for me. My adoptive father couldn't do such physical things with me and I was still trying to deal with the situation. Once, Dad did try to show me some wrestling moves, but Mom disrupted that lesson. She was too fearful that Dad might accidentally hurt me. Neither Dad nor I liked the decision, but Mom won that round.

When Brad Wilson pulled up in a white, Mercury, four-door sedan, I was busy shooting baskets. As soon as he stepped out of the car, I spied him, and my heart began to pound. When I ran toward him, Brad saw me over the roof of the Mercury and a brilliant smile immediately spread across his face. "Hey! You're here!" he exclaimed loudly. "Wow! I was expecting a lit'ler guy!"

Even though I was no longer the lit'ler guy Brad remembered me to be, I launched myself into what I knew to be strong and capable arms. He held me close for a bit and then, like Janet, pushed me back to arm's length, to get a better look. "Wow, buddy, you've filled out some!"

"Yeah, maybe, a bit," I mumbled.

He, too, just had to tug on and give me crap about the uncombed mop on top of my head. "Your hair got long, too! Glad I kept those clippers I used on you and the boys. Don't you worry, we'll take care of this in no time."

I laughed and shook my head, while exclaiming loudly, "No way! I remember those hack-jobs you gave us. The hair stays!"

God, he looked good. As always, the first thing I noticed about him was his muscles. He had always impressed me as being quite strong, physically. According to him, he got that way playing football in school. Later, while serving in the Army during the Korean conflict, he was a boxer. I remembered him telling me, "I was compact, but I came equipped with a mean, right hook."

Bradley Wilson was then in his early forties but was guilty of trying to look younger by growing his noticeably-thinning hair and sideburns longer. His hair was dark brown, with flecks of grey and always neatly combed. He was only five-feet, ten-inches tall, but his barrel chest and slim waistline made him look like a force to be reckoned with. Not given to the latest fashions, his black, plastic-framed glasses left him looking exactly as I remembered him.

Brad was an engineering supervisor at the Post Office and had been so since our first meeting. He was also a not-so-dedicated Catholic, which bothered me some, but I still considered him to be more charitable than some of the most dedicated church goers I knew. Brad was the type of person who always pointed out the good in all things, even when there truly wasn't any good to point out – a trait that oftentimes frustrated the hell out of me.

When I first moved in with the Wilsons, Brad was the first one I warmed to. Prior to him, I had been afraid and standoffish toward all other father figures. During my years with them, Brad did more than just turn my fear around. He, along with Kurt and Danny's help, systematically bolstered my self-confidence by teaching me to defend myself. Brad played referee to many a boxing match, which took place in the garage or back yard. Back then, Kurt, Danny, and even a much smaller me sparred often. If Brad caught us boys bickering, squabbling, or even refusing to talk to each other, he would get out the boxing gloves. "Okay, let's go out back," he instructed us. "We're gonna get this settled." It was more or less a rock-solid rule with him. Disharmony in the house was something Brad did not tolerate, and he definitely had his way of handling us boys. Mostly, he did it with love, but I know in my heart that he truly enjoyed teaching the art of pugilism. Even though I was that lit'ler guy, when I lived with the Wilsons, thanks to Brad, when I left Mankato in 1969, I already had the makings of a pretty good boxer.

Brad and I were still standing out in the street, doing a little catching up, when a Volkswagen micro bus quite suddenly showed up on the scene. Since I had never seen that van before, I didn't pay too much attention to who occupied the inside. Nevertheless, I did notice that it did not park, nor move on down the street. The driver just stopped in the middle of the narrow lane in front of the next-door neighbor's house. Suddenly, the sliding rear door was thrown wide open and out scrambled a short, but stocky, male teenager. He was coming our way and running at a good clip. I recognized Danny in an instant and knew I had better get to softer ground. As good as it was to see him, what he had in mind would probably hurt a little.

As I bolted from where Brad and I had been standing, my heart leapt, nor could I hold back the laugh that sprang forth. Instead of running away from Danny, as he more than likely expected me to, I ran right at him. We both angled our approach, so we would come together in the front yard. I knew he would crouch some, in an attempt to tackle me, so I hunkered down lower, but it didn't help. Danny had me by weight and when we hit, the force from our collision knocked me backward. I was barely able to keep a firm grasp of his right leg, but succeeded, so we both landed in the grass in a heap, laughing like idiots.

"Jackson! Hey, little brother! It's about time you got here!" Danny's excitement was genuine.

Trying to be clever, I replied, "I could only get here as fast as Mom would drive, which is not very fast…ever!"

"Spoken like a true smartass!" returned Danny.

We just laid there for a moment, grinning, and sizing each other up. To me, Danny looked very much like Janet. He had her eyes and nose, but he had perfect skin. Also, his hair was a richer brown, like root beer. Danny's facial features had changed very little since I had last seen him. At age fifteen, he still had quite a boyish grin, for which I presumed girls went gaga. I remembered his smile and laughter as being contagious. At that very moment, I silently admitted to myself, *I wish I were Danny.*

I thought Danny would be taller, like Janet, but when we stood, we both noticed that I had caught up to him in height. "Holy crap!" exclaimed Danny. "You look tall enough to take me on…almost!"

"Almost," I conceded. "You still have me by a few pounds."

Danny chuckled, "And a lot more experience, little brother. He then looked past me and said, "Uh-oh, you'd better duck!"

His warning came much too late. No attempt to evade what came next would have been fast enough. In my excitement, I had completely forgotten about Kurt. After parking the van, he had successfully snuck up behind me. Realizing my mistake, I tried to make a move, but was immediately grabbed from behind. Kurt put me into a reverse bear hug and lifted me off my feet. With my arms pinned at my sides, I knew I was about to have my guts squeezed out.

In the past, when Kurt and I wrestled, it was his ultimate-submission hold. There and then, just like a boa constrictor, his powerful arms began to squeeze. Immediately, I could not take in a breath. With my feet totally off the ground, Kurt then shook me a few times. Joyfully laughing, Kurt asked, "You give?"

The only sound I could barely grunt out was an extremely labored, "Yeah."

Kurt immediately put me down and released his vise-like hold on me. He then turned me around and gave me a normal hug. Wearing a broad smile, which showed a mouthful of straightened teeth, he exclaimed, "Hey, Shrimp, how're ya doin'?!"

Still laboring to get sufficient oxygen into my lungs, I laughed and replied, "Better…especially now that my guts aren't being squeezed out." After a shared laugh, I added, "I see you finally lost the braces…Looks good!"

"Yeah, I got rid of those the year after you left," replied Kurt. Then, after looking me up and down some, he exclaimed, "Wow! I guess I'll have to stop callin' you, Shrimp! You've really shot up some!"

I could see then how Kurt was rapidly turning into a younger version of Brad. He was seventeen years old and about to enter his senior year at Mankato West High School. However, even with the brown hair, which he wore just past collar length, I could tell he had the beginnings of Brad's rather pronounced forehead. When I had moved north, Kurt wasn't wearing glasses. The plastic-framed lenses he now wore told me he truly was Brad's son. In addition, Kurt's entire body was rock-solid muscle, which would explain his number-one ranking in the state for high school wrestling. That is, within his weight class. Kurt was a middle weight, who had lost only one match during his entire junior year. That loss took place at the state championships. Kurt had made it all the way to the championship pairing, but he was taken down by a senior from Brooklyn Park, who arguably should have been wrestling in the heavy-weight class, or so I would hear later that evening. As a senior in the coming school year, big things were expected from and for Kurt.

Brad stepped up and joined the three of us on the front lawn. Now four, we just kind of huddled there, like we were calling a play in a pickup football game.

"All three of my boys together again," said Brad. "Is this great or what?"

We stayed huddled that way for a few moments. That is, until Danny suddenly remembered that he and Kurt had brought guests. When I turned toward the Volkswagen van, I looked upon three teenagers. One was a rather chunky-looking guy that I approximated to be about Kurt's age. The other two were pretty girls, a blonde and a brunette.

As we walked over to where the three teens stood, Kurt pointed out the pudgy, male and said, "That goofus is Larry Armstrong. He's a friend of mine." Larry and I exchanged greetings and shook hands. Kurt then took the pretty brunette by the hand and brought her forward. "This is my girlfriend, Janelle Peterson. Janelle, this is the punk kid…I mean…foster brother I've been telling you about, Jackson Harris."

Brad immediately jumped in with a reminder that my last name had undergone a change.

"Oh, yeah, sorry…It's Jackson Andrew Landry now, right?" Kurt corrected.

Without answering, I put my hand out to shake Janelle's, but she stepped inside my outstretched hand and gave me a hug instead. "Kurt's family gets hugs," she said softly. "Hello, Jackson. I'm glad I finally get to meet you!"

Feeling quite unprepared and somewhat embarrassed by her intimate greeting, I replied with a simple, "Hi."

Danny just stood off to the side, smiling. I guess he was a little too caught up in the moment. So, the other girl, a very pretty blonde, with blue eyes, stepped up and stuck her hand out in my direction. "Hi, I'm Carrie Anderson."

Picking up on the sweet tone of her voice, I was immediately enchanted.

As I took Carrie's hand, Danny woke up and said, "Oh, yeah…Sorry about that, little brother. Carrie is my…" He then paused and looked at Carrie, like he didn't quite know how to categorize her.

"Girlfriend?" I inserted the word I thought he was searching for.

They both simply looked at each other, like there was a big question mark between them. Finally, Danny broke out that charming smile of his and said, "Yeah, as a matter of fact, she is."

I then looked at Carrie. She was absolutely beaming her approval of Danny's on-the-spot decision.

Brad rolled his eyes at Danny's stumblebum way of introducing Carrie. Then, seeing that Mom, Dad, and Janet had come out to watch the reunion spectacle from the driveway, he put his arm around me and turned us toward them. "Come on," he said. "Introduce everybody to your mom and dad."

As we headed toward the driveway, I overheard Janelle talking to Kurt. In a hushed voice, she said, "You didn't tell me he was so cute."

Brad heard the comment, looked at me and then chuckled. I kept my eyes forward and simply walked on. Instinctively, I knew he was laughing at me because my face felt quite flushed. I also knew it was probably as red as pickled beets.

After introductions were made all around, casual conversation broke out. I barely uttered a word to anyone because I was content to just listen, while taking the whole scene in. When it was time for my parents to get on the road, Dad was the first to speak up. However, good-byes at the Wilsons' were something that took twenty to thirty minutes to get said, especially when Janet Wilson was involved. As Mom and Dad slowly made their way toward the station wagon, Janet peppered them with a few more questions. After twenty minutes of additional conversation, Dad made another attempt, but Janet countered with another question that was of interest to Mom. So, there went another ten minutes. Dad then put one foot inside the car door and apologized. This time, he adamantly stated that they *really* needed to get going.

Not to be dissuaded, Janet looked like she was going to pipe up again, so Brad grabbed her and playfully cupped his hand over her mouth. "They really have to go, honey," he said.

Everyone laughed, Janet apologized, and then true final good-byes were said.

Before getting into the car, Mom pulled me off to the side. "Are you going to be okay?" she asked.

"I'll be fine, Mom. You'd better get on the road before Janet starts in again."

"If you need anything, Janet knows how to reach us in Faribault. Don't forget about going to church tomorrow and next Sunday, too." Mom's rules about attending church on Sundays were concrete and not to be discarded, even when she wasn't there to supervise.

Wishing Mom would stop obsessing and just get into the car, I said, "Yes, ma'am."

Sounding a bit surprised, but happy with my cooperative response, Mom said, "There now, that wasn't so hard, was it?"

I walked Mom to the station wagon, gave her a final hug, opened the door for her and closed it after she got in. I then repositioned myself at the front of the vehicle and jammed my hands inside the pockets of my jeans. With my shoulders slightly hunched, I watched Mom safely back the station wagon out into the street. She then slowly headed down Westwood Drive.

Janet stepped up to my side and put her arm around me. "Those are some special people, aren't they?"

I continued to watch the station wagon until it disappeared on Moreland Avenue. Then, turning and giving Janet a straight look, I simply stated, "Yeah, they are."

Chapter 2

When entering the Wilson house from the side door, just up from their driveway, a person had to make an immediate decision – go straight or turn right. Situated just inside a small entryway was a stairwell, which led to the basement, with an elongated den, which took up a whole third of the floorspace. As well, the furnace room, a small workshop, a full bathroom, and Kurt's bedroom could be found down there. However, if you took an immediate right after entering, and up one step, you would find yourself in the kitchen. Just past the kitchen was a small dining area, which then led into the living room. In between the dining area and the living room was a narrow hallway. It led to a bathroom and master bedroom. There was also another stairwell. It led to an attic, which had been renovated into an extra bedroom. That's where Danny and I laid awake at night, telling newly learned jokes and stories to each other. We also fought, shared secrets, and did other things that boys do when they are growing up in the same bedroom. Sometimes, we even slept.

Upon entering the house, the teenagers immediately migrated to the basement den. Once there, they got the record player going and began to do what teenagers do best – hang out.

Janet had warned everyone that dinner wasn't going to be anything fancy. It would consist of hot dogs and hamburgers off the grill. Potato chips and canned pork 'n' beans were also on the menu – Janet didn't believe in getting too ambitious in the kitchen on Saturdays during the summer. Nevertheless, it all sounded good to me. Back then, cheeseburgers were my favorite meal.

Brad stayed outside to get the charcoal lit inside the grill. He was one of those guys who used half of a can of starter fluid and lit a bonfire, just to get a small pile of charcoal briquettes going. In years past, it was the source of some harassment for him, which always came from three smart-assed boys.

Before I, too, could escape to the downstairs, Janet caught my attention. She gestured for me to follow her into the kitchen. *Aw geez*, I thought. *She wants to go at it already?!* Feeling a bit edgy, I followed, knowing that we were about to have our first, little, heart-to-heart talk. That is, Janet would do the talking, while I sat and listened.

"You'll stay upstairs with Danny, kiddo," Janet began.

"I figured that would be the sleeping arrangements, unless he became a total hog about the place." My response was meant to be disarming.

"Before we go any further, get that mule-headed brother of yours to help you get your luggage upstairs. Then, we can talk for a bit before dinner."

"Okay, but you need to remind me...Which is the mule-headed one?"

In response, Janet put on her best are-you-kidding-me look, then said, "You haven't been gone *that* long, have you?!"

I shot her a sly smile and then yelled down the stairwell, "Danny! Mom wants you to get up here...NOW!"

Janet couldn't help but laugh. "I see you're still a little snot!"

I proudly declared, "Absolutely!"

A few seconds later, Danny could be heard stomping up the stairs. Sounding a little impatient, he yelled back, "What do you want?!"

With a straight face and emotionless tone, I replied, "Mom called you mule headed and said you're supposed to help me get my stuff upstairs."

When Danny entered the kitchen, he immediately shot Janet a look of suspicion.

Janet just rolled her eyes and chuckled. "Help the twerp, will you?"

26

With a knowing smile, Danny replied, "Yeah, okay." He knew all too well what was going on.

Danny and I put my fishing and baseball gear in the garage. Then, we were able to get the rest of my trappings upstairs in one trip. When we had my two, large suitcases properly situated on my bed, I turned to go back downstairs, but Danny stopped me. Looking as though he didn't quite know how to begin, Danny said, "Wait a minute, little brother." After a moment or two, he added, "I hear you're not doing too well up north. We don't have to talk about it right now, but I want to talk to you about it sometime. No hurry. You *know* Mom will be talking to you about it…Dad, too. And, it'll probably be soon."

Immediately feeling a bit self-conscious, I mumbled, "Yeah, I know. It's not what everybody thinks, though."

"That's good enough for me, for now anyway. I'm really glad you're here. God! I can't get over how you've grown!"

"It happens, or so they tell me."

Danny then walked over and put an arm around me. "Okay, we better get back down there. You know better than to keep *her* waiting." He then gave me a playful shove down the stairs and followed directly behind me. Together, we generated a lot of noise for just going down one flight of stairs.

When we two got to the dining area, Janet was waiting at the kitchen table, smiling, and shaking her head. "I can't say I've missed that noise much. Just now, you two sounded like a couple of horses coming down those stairs."

While I stood there, grinning, Danny pushed past me and headed for the basement stairwell. "Good luck, little brother!" He laughed, then stomped down the stairs, just as loudly as before, to which Janet shook her head, pressed her lips together, and closed her eyes tightly, what I always called her Lord-give-me-strength look.

When Danny's loud exit came to an end, Janet then turned an unreadable gaze on me. "Have a seat," she said, then got up to pour herself another cup of coffee and light a cigarette.

Elvis Presley sang softly in the background. I immediately remembered that conversations were pretty much one sided and took a while, especially when Janet put her Elvis records on. I wasn't looking forward to this part. This was the point where I expected Janet to lay down the rules and regulations. As well, I would probably have some answering to do for what few letters I had written over the past three years. More than likely, we would then move on to whatever she had discussed with my parents. I slid nervously into one of the chairs at the table but refused to make eye contact with her.

Drawing cigarette smoke deep into her lungs and then exhaling, Janet said, "So, how does it feel to be back? The old house hasn't changed much, has it?"

Feeling quite apprehensive, I mumbled, "No, not really."

"Okay, let's get to it," began Janet. "Your first instruction is to relax. We all want you to enjoy yourself. You have no idea how happy we are to have you with us again. We only have you for two weeks and we want it to be a really good two weeks. You already know I've talked with your mom and dad. There will be plenty of time for us to talk about that stuff later. I know you'll want to spend lots of time with your old friends, but you're also going to have to leave some time for Dad and me. The boys are going to want you around them some, too. But you're going to have to remember something. They have girlfriends now and little brothers sometimes get in the way. You have any problems with that?"

Smiling, I replied, "No, ma'am."

"Good! When you leave this house, I'll need to know where you're off to and when I can expect to see you again, understood?"

"Yes, ma'am," was my response again. I couldn't believe I was getting off so easy.

"Just one more thing," asserted Janet.

Of course, I sarcastically thought. *There's always just one more thing.*

"I don't think I'm going to be comfortable with you calling me Janet for the next two weeks. You used to call me, 'Mom.' Would you have a problem calling me that now?"

I had not given any thought at all to what she was asking. I had never considered for a second addressing Janet by her first name. I simply couldn't, so I quickly replied, "I don't think I could ever be comfortable calling you anything *but* Mom."

Janet smiled and reached out, with her arms wide open. It was her way of saying, "This talk is now over." It also meant, "Give me my hug and then get lost.

I have stuff to do." So, I gave her the hug she expected and then bolted upstairs to unpack.

After putting my wardrobe away, which was accomplished in a rather immature and half-assed fashion, I went down to the basement and joined the other teens. When I arrived at the den, I found it much the way it was before I left. There was an old couch, adorned in a gaudy plaid material, with matching easy chair, ottoman, and love seat. An old wooden coffee table sat situated between the couch and love seat. The easy chair, which shared an old end table with the couch, separated where the lounge area ended, and the billiard area began. Directly across from the chair and ottoman, a huge RCA color TV was placed for the family's viewing pleasure. At farthest end of the room, Brad had constructed wet bar. Behind it, a full-sized refrigerator chilled soft drinks and beer. Even then, I thought the furnishings were somewhat gaggy, therefore appropriate to be hidden in the basement den.

Immediately upon my arrival, two teenaged couples hurried to straighten themselves up a bit. They must have heard me coming down the stairs and thought I might be a supervising adult. As I walked toward Larry Armstrong, who was at the pool table taking practice shots, I acted quite casual about the whole scene.

"You want to play a game?" I asked.

"Sure," replied Larry.

While I racked and arranged the pool balls, Larry chalked his cue. At that point, Danny asked, "So, how did it go with Mom?"

"Oh, you know, she read me the rules."

Kurt asked, "What rules got read?"

"You know…the usual stuff…like…let her know where I am every minute of the day, be sure to stay out of Kurt's way because he still hates you, and don't beat up on Danny too bad, when he messes with you. You know, stuff like that."

The girls and Larry laughed. Kurt and Danny simply looked at each other with knowing smiles, while nodding their heads. Suddenly and simultaneously, they both flew from their seats and charged in my direction. The girls gave out excited, little squeals and Larry backed himself as flat against the wall as his chubby body allowed. Kurt went up one side of the table and Danny the other. I was at the end of the pool table, with a wall at my back and no escape route. When they reached me, there was some preliminary, playful sparring before Kurt expertly took control of me. He quite easily got me into a Full Nelson. I was now totally vulnerable to whatever form of torture Danny was about to administer.

Danny put on a devilish grin, cracked his knuckles, and said, "I wonder if we can still make him pee his pants."

"Yes," countered Kurt. "Let us see if it is still possible to make him do that." Whenever Kurt started using overly proper English around me, I just knew I was in trouble.

I was terribly ticklish along my ribcage, so tickling me was a common form of torture with those two. Brad and Janet were guilty of it, also, but Kurt and Danny were the worst. On one occasion, when I was eight years old, they teamed up on me. They kept at it until I laughed so hard that I lost control of my bladder, but just a trickle. Right then, they had me right where they wanted me.

Of course, I pleaded a little for them let me go, as if that would stop them, but it was all to no avail. Danny started in along my ribcage and my laughter commenced. Uncontrollably, I laughed louder and louder. Suddenly, we all heard footsteps coming down the stairs. Without warning, I was immediately dropped onto the floor, while Kurt and Danny stood by, with innocent expressions on their face.

When Janet appeared in the doorway, she looked upon the scene and then asked, "Okay, who's torturing whom down here?"

Kurt offered up, "Aw, Mom, we're just seeing if we can still make him pee his pants."

"Not on his first day here and not in front of the girls," ordered Janet. "Save something for tomorrow."

Everyone had a good laugh, but soon settled down. Kurt and Danny returned to their girls, while Larry and I turned our attention back to the pool table.

Because I had not shot pool on that particular table in over three years, Larry won the first two games. I used those two games to get used to the lay of the table again. I then beat him the next two games.

Well into our fifth game, which I was leading, Larry asked, "Who taught you to shoot pool?" I could tell he was impressed.

Nodding toward Kurt and Danny, I replied, "Take your pick."

After beating Larry that game, he and I paired off against Danny and Carrie. When Larry and I succeeded in beating those two, without much trouble at all, Kurt and Janelle stepped up to the table. They fell to Larry and I, too, just as effortlessly. It was very apparent to me that the girls were a rather large handicap to their boyfriends. They didn't know one end of a pool cue from the other.

During our matches, I paid very close attention to the patience my brothers displayed. As well, I was acquainted with the expert tutelage they provided the girls. It was strange watching them get so close to their female partners, just to teach them how to properly line up a shot. The smile on the girls' faces told me they cared more about the closeness than what was being taught. When Kurt and Danny taught the girls how to actually shoot, I paid even closer attention.

I recognized Kurt's short, choppy, back stroke, when lining up a shot. When he was ready to pull the trigger, he would pull back one last time, very long. Then, with great force, Kurt would let it fly. You could always tell when he was shooting, just by the thunderous crash his shots produced.

In contrast, Danny's was a game of finesse. He had a long, smooth, back stroke. And when he shot, he never used brute force. His delivery was always nice and gentle. It was as if he feared he might bruise the cue ball.

Because Kurt and Danny had both taken a hand in teaching me how to shoot pool, I recognized both influences in my game. It just depended on what I felt each individual shot called for. Yes, those two may have taught me the game, but they most assuredly did not use the same teaching techniques they were using on those girls. I caught myself giving them both long, hard looks. *Good grief,* I thought. *Are these really the same brothers I left three years ago?*

Suddenly, Janet called down from the kitchen, so I was abruptly brought out of my trance. Supper was finally ready.

In the Wilson house, suppertime was somewhat informal. Basically, as Janet would say, it was a game of grab it and growl. That meant, fill your plate, find a place to sit and then dig in. If you left the kitchen hungry, it was your own fault because there was always plenty of food available.

Building my favorite, double-decker cheeseburger was almost as fun as eating it. The burger consisted of two large hamburger patties, with a slice of cheese on both, placed on a single bun. I then added, onion, pickle, tomato, mayonnaise, and ketchup. When I finished constructing the enormous burger, I noticed everyone looking at me, like I was some kind of circus act.

Janet asked, "What, no lettuce?"

Without missing a beat, I replied, "Nope…Lettuce is rabbit food."

"I've got a dollar says you don't eat that whole thing," said Danny.

Feeling quite cocky, I countered, "A dollar?! Is that all you've got?! I'll take that bet!"

When I bit into my masterpiece, a mixture of grease, ketchup, mayo, tomato, and pickle juice oozed out of the bun and onto my hands. In fact, every time I took a bite, the mess just got worse. Nevertheless, I kept after it until half the burger was consumed. Right about then, the hamburger bun quit on me and turned into greasy mush. Eating the remainder of that burger was definitely a challenge. I was afraid I would get more grease on me than in me. It was then that I became keenly aware that everyone present was watching me conquer that burger with great interest.

Brad asked, "Who taught you to eat like that?"

My mouth was full, so in response, I simply nodded toward Danny.

Carrie laughed heartily. "I can believe that!"

The rest of that first meal at the Wilson table was filled with laughter. I was at long last beginning to relax and feel like I was back in my old skin. After so much anticipation, I was finally where I truly belonged, or so I thought. I honestly couldn't remember the last time I had laughed that long and hard. Suppertime laughter was one of the things I had missed most. Then, the thought that it was all going to be nothing more than a temporary pleasure crept into my head. It must have shown on my face, too, because Janet gave me a concerned look and then asked, "Jackson, are you okay?"

Absentmindedly, I replied, "Yeah, great! I think I might have ate that burger too fast, though."

"Or maybe it's the simple fact that you actually polished off that monster," Janet countered.

Wanting to keep angst to minimum that first night, I said, "I'll walk it off after supper. I want to see the neighborhood before it gets too dark."

Janelle asked, "Do you miss Mankato much, Jackson?"

"Sometimes, a little too much," I mumbled.

Brad's cheerful voice chimed in, "Well, we have you for the next two weeks and we are going to have a great time."

I couldn't help but smile. Right then, it felt so right, just being with them again. The welcome I received, the laughter, everything was as I imagined it would be and more. I couldn't remember how long it had been since I had felt that happy about anything. In fact, I was so happy that I actually volunteered to help clean the dishes after dinner!

"Nope," answered Janet. "It's probably the only night you'll get away with it, so you'd better enjoy it. Why don't you go for that walk you mentioned?"

"Kurt and I will take care of the dishes, Mom," offered Janelle. The fact that she called Janet Mom, too, still didn't ring quite right in my ears.

Kurt winced at Janelle's gracious gesture, but just the same, agreed. Right then, I knew exactly what he was feeling. Many times, Dad volunteered his services, and mine, to clean the dishes after any given meal. It was one of my least favorite chores to do. Doing dishes was right up there with cleaning the toilet – I despised both activities.

As I headed for the door, Janet reminded me that it was getting cool at night. "Better take a jacket, kiddo."

I grabbed my windbreaker, gave Janet a kiss on the cheek, and remembered to thank both of my former-foster parents for dinner. As I headed out the side door, I called behind me, "I won't be gone too long!"

Shuffling down the driveway, I tested the air and then donned my windbreaker. It was early evening and the sun was beginning its descent. The day had not been very warm, and the evening air was cooling fast. The windbreaker was a good call. *I hope it warms up tomorrow*, I thought.

Looking up and down Westwood Drive, I couldn't decide which way to begin my exploration. I didn't want to go visit any of my old friends, not just yet. Instead, I felt the need to get a feel for the place again. Wanting memories to take hold of me, I took in a few deep breaths of cool air and let them out easy. Finally,

I made my decision and took a right at the end of the driveway. I headed toward Moreland Avenue because I wanted to see the Wilsons' old house.

I first met the four Wilsons in the early fall of 1966. I was seven years old, and it was right at the beginning of my second-grade year. I had transferred to St. Joseph the Worker from Roosevelt Elementary School. Kurt and Danny attended St. Joseph's, too. My social worker, Miss Churchill, introduced the family to me, while they lived in their temporary residence on Moreland Avenue. It was a cracker-box-sized house, with cinderblock walls that were painted the most putrid shade of green I had ever seen. The whole house could be summed up with one word – tiny. It was the most unimpressive house in the entire neighborhood. It had two bedrooms, one bathroom, the smallest of kitchens, the puniest dining area, and an extremely miniscule living room. When I first came to the Wilson family, Brad and Janet were in the middle of negotiations for the house on Westwood Drive. So, for our introductory month together, quarters were somewhat cramped.

On the day I moved in, I had to say my final good-byes to the Matson family before leaving for school. While I was in class, my belongings were delivered to Janet. I had instructions to meet Kurt and Danny after school. In turn, they had instructions to walk their new little brother home. I pestered both of them repeatedly throughout that day. I even interrupted them in class. I felt the need to remind them, more than a few times, not to forget about me. Kurt told me to stop being a pain the ass about it. "We're not going to forget!" he asserted. "Now, stop coming to my classroom!"

On the other hand, Danny exercised a lot more patience. "Jackson, you have stop worrying about it. Kurt and I will meet you right in front of the school. You'll see, it'll be okay." And so it was. The two met me, just as they said. However, it was Danny who actually walked with me, while Kurt kept a hurried pace a good distance ahead of us. When we three arrived at the house, I hurriedly checked to see if all my toys had been delivered, along with my clothes, but the toys hadn't made the trip. Back then, I didn't have many personal possessions, so the toys I did own were cherished. I thought it quite heartless of the Matsons to forget about them. "What will I play with now?!" I whined.

Kurt noticed how upset I was, so he went into his bedroom and brought out a cardboard box filled with his old toys. "Here," he said sternly, placing the box in front of me, "I don't hardly ever play with these, not anymore." He then turned to walk away, but swiftly turned on his heels. While pointing a warning finger at me, he added, "But you have to give them back when I say so, okay?!" I wholeheartedly agreed to the conditions and the deal was struck.

My transition into the Wilson family was comical at best. At first, Kurt objected vehemently to another kid joining the clan. According to him, there wasn't room enough for the two they already had. Danny simply told him to shut up. He liked the idea of being a big brother, therefore, no longer the baby of the family.

Initially, I slept on the living room couch. That is, until they found out I was a bedwetter. Brad quickly obtained a cot for me to sleep on. At bedtime, it was unfolded and positioned in the living room, right by the fireplace. At night, I felt comforted by the smell of partially-burnt wood and soot. Within a week or so, the cot was setup at the foot of the boys' bunkbeds, and that small bedroom became even smaller. By hook or by crook, Brad and Janet were determined for us boys to bond.

I suddenly became cognizant that I was standing in the middle of the street, smiling and remembering how Kurt had never asked for or demanded the return of those toys.

We moved into the house on Westwood Drive just before Halloween of 1966. The new house had plenty of room for three boys to sprawl out and keep from getting in each other's way. Well, not too much anyway.

As I stood looking at the old house on Moreland Avenue, I couldn't help but laugh a little under my breath. My initial days with the Wilsons could have gone a lot smoother, but those humble beginnings made for some great stories later. The important thing for me to remember was how they successfully assimilated me into their family and taught me to adapt. For the first time in my young life, I knew what it was to be happy.

Right next door to that cramped, little box of memories, lived my friend, Tony Milner. Just then, I had to fight the urge to go ring his doorbell. I was fairly sure there would be a big welcome waiting for me there, too. It would be one that I wished to savor, so I decided to hold off.

Since I didn't want to be detected, I decided that it was time for me to move on and continue my reconnaissance of the neighborhood. Making sure that no one was watching, I slipped in between the two houses and furtively moved into the alley at the rear. The alleyway separated properties between Moreland Avenue and West Ninth Street. Using the shadows and hedgerows for concealment, I successfully made it to the alley without being discovered. I suddenly realized it wasn't going to be so easy to keep from being seen. If I happened across one human inhabitant, I stood the risk of being recognized. I knew everyone who lived in each house for a three-block stretch, provided that no one had moved away since my departure.

It seemed extremely quiet for early Saturday evening. There wasn't a soul around. I crouched in the shadows and listened for a bit. The crickets and frogs were singing, a dog barked off in the distance, but not a single human sound could be heard.

I looked back at the Milner place and saw that their back yard had been freshly mowed. I loved the smell of their freshly cut grass. When Mom put me in charge of mowing our lawn in Duluth, that smell, my allowance, plus a little personal pride, were the only reasons I didn't complain. Well, not too much.

The Milners' hedges were also neatly trimmed. Tony Sr. always took great care in keeping his property one of the neighborhood show places.

Right smack in the middle of their back yard, stood a mature weeping willow. The tree stood tall in the glow of the setting sun, with its long, slender branches cascading down, like a yellowish-green fountain. Even at such a young age, I was able to appreciate its beauty. Staring at that tree immediately launched me into the past. I remembered having fantastic adventures in it with Tony and my other friends. However, there was no greater adventure under that willow than that of my first kiss.

Julie Falkner was more than just some girl I used to go to school with at St Joseph's. She was my very first, serious crush. She had short, curly, black hair, deep-blue eyes and an extremely cute, turned-up nose. When Julie smiled in my direction, I always felt a little stab of fear and panic inside. She was the first girl who didn't make me want to barf, as my friends and I used to say. Back then, girls were entities I barely tolerated. In a word, girls were…icky! They were those creatures who usually kicked, scratched, gouged, and punched. As well, they were generally rude and obnoxious toward the guys and me. When the neighborhood kids played Capture the Flag or Kick the Can, the team with the greatest number of girls on its roster was sure to lose. That being said, Julie Falkner was the exception to all those rules. Besides being the prettiest girl in our classroom, she was actually nice!

It was during rehearsal for our fourth-grade play that I felt love's first pin prick. Literally, she poked me with a pin!

That fall, we performed Rodgers and Hammerstein's musical version of *Cinderella*. Well, it was sort of a musical. Our production had only one song in it. Julie, who was cast as Cinderella, had to sing it. I was secretly captivated every time she rehearsed the number, *In My Own Little Corner*.

My part, as one of the guests at the ball, wasn't much, but at least it was a speaking role. "Who could she be?" It was the one line I practiced over and over again in front of the mirror at night.

The day before performance night, we had a dress rehearsal. It could not have been worse. Ricky Tomlinson, who was cast as the handsome prince, was home sick with the flu. That meant, when it came time to rehearse for the royal ball, Julie was left without a dance partner. So, our director, Sister Mary Therese, grabbed me for a stand-in.

"Jackson Andrew!" screeched Sister Mary – she always used my first and middle name – "You stand in for Ricky!" She then pretty much shoved me in Julie's direction.

In front of the other guys, I played it up, like I was extremely disgusted. In truth, I was quite taken with the idea. Julie didn't seem too repulsed, either. As we stood face to face, waiting for the music to begin, she smiled angelically at me. Without uttering a single word, her smile made me feel like she was trying to tell me something.

Since the waltz was too difficult for us kids to learn, either that or there wasn't a nun who actually knew how, we were taught the most basic dance step known to man – the box step. When the music began, Julie and I began to stumble uncoordinatedly in a small square. Mostly, our lack of grace was my fault. Like most nine-year-old boys, I had two left feet.

That day, the sewing of Julie's costume dress was not entirely completed. There was still some unfinished stitching left to be done on the cuffs of her sleeves. So, for that rehearsal, the sleeves had been pinned, but in such a way that Julie would not get poked by them. Unfortunately, that did nothing for my safety.

Julie and I were giving the dance our best effort, when suddenly, I felt a sharp pain in my shoulder. The pins in Julie's dress had found their mark.

"OW!" I yelled.

Without thinking, Julie pulled back in surprise and the pins sank in deeper. I was quite literally like a fish on a hook. If Julie moved one way or another, thanks to those pins, I was more than willing to follow in her footsteps. As well, I was sure she was drawing blood.

Poor Julie, she didn't know what to do. It was clear she didn't want to hurt me, but I just couldn't get her to stand still! Finally, we got the attention of one of the other nuns, Sister Marie something or other – I could never remember all the nun's names. She successfully set me free again. Fortunately, it was decided that we needed no more rehearsal of the box step, so I went back to my normal position on stage. Julie gave me an apologetic smile.

Following rehearsal, I looked for my friends: Dave, Mike, Joel, and Tony. We usually walked home together, but on that day, they departed ahead of me. Since I was left with no alternative, I started for home alone. As I walked that afternoon, I wasn't paying attention to much of anything. There was no real activity to engage me. But then, quite suddenly, I had an eerie feeling creep through me. I sensed that I was being followed. Carefully, I peered over my shoulder to see if my suspicions were true. To my surprise, I spied Julie, along with two of her friends, Anne Hayward and Gail Paulsen. They were following me a short distance back. With my friends nowhere in sight for a support system, I began to feel a bit uncomfortable. So, I quite deliberately faced forward and quickened my pace.

Just like lionesses, when stalking their prey, girls back then looked for any opportunity to pounce on a boy. You just didn't dare get caught alone! That afternoon, I was clueless of my pending doom. That is, I didn't actually know I was in trouble, not until I heard Julie call out, "Hey, Jackson, are you a fast runner?!"

The question puzzled me enough to make me stop and turn around. "Yeah, I'm pretty fast," I replied, observing that they, too, had stopped and were keeping their distance.

"That's good," teased Julie, nodding her head confidently. "You're gonna have to be for our new game."

All three girls wore mischievous grins and were giggling, which spelled real trouble for me. Regardless, I dared to ask, "What new game?"

Being the ringleader, it was Julie who answered. "It's called, We Catch You, We Kiss You."

My mind didn't quite believe what my ears had just heard, but from the look on Julie's face, I got the distinct impression she was dead serious. Just then, I wanted to be anywhere but on that street, being confronted by those three troublemakers, so I began to back up slowly, my only thought being, *Oh, hell no!* I then turned and began to run. At the same time, the three girls launched themselves from where they stood and were now in hot pursuit, laughing their silly, little, nine-year-old laughs.

I tried to shake them by cutting through a few back yards and jumping over a couple of fences. My ego was such that I thought there was no way any girl was going to catch me. Nevertheless, that afternoon, my ego was not the only thing to suffer a minor defeat.

The three girls had split up and successfully surrounded me. Because of some miscalculations on my part, they eventually caught me under the Milners' weeping willow. I didn't want to come off like a total chicken, so when Anne and Gail grabbed me by the arms, I didn't struggle *too* hard. Still, it was a very uncomfortable situation. I wished they would just slug me in the arm and get it over with. Instead, Julie brought her face to within inches of mine. She had the brightest, bluest eyes of any girl in the fourth grade, and I was suddenly swimming inside of them. Her breath smelled of bubble gum. I was suddenly too mesmerized to even think of attempting an escape.

In a soft tone, Julie said, "I'm glad Sister Mary picked you to be my partner at rehearsal today, but I'm sorry about getting you with the pins."

I was tongue tied. I couldn't utter a single word. *Say something, stupid!* The thought went through my head, but my mouth didn't cooperate.

Suddenly, Julie leaned in and smiled sweetly. Then, she very softly whispered, "Are you ready?"

When Julie Falkner planted my first kiss squarely on my lips, my eyes shot wide open. The kiss itself wasn't much more than a peck. Nonetheless, I just about lost control of my bladder.

It was over in an instant. The girls turned me loose and ran off, giggling those sadistic nine-year-old giggles. Me? I stood there, with an idiotic look on my face, trying hard not to pee in my pants.

I was suddenly in love. Anyway, that's what my adolescent brain told me. My heart was pounding, while my thoughts dispersed in a thousand directions. I was so consumed by what had just taken place that when I turned to leave, I just about walked face first into the trunk of the weeping willow. Feeling totally embarrassed, I mumbled to myself, "Cripes, is that what love does to you?!"

Not wanting to see or talk to anyone, I walked the rest of the way home in a hurry. I didn't want anybody to know what had just taken place. I sure as hell didn't want Kurt or Danny finding out about it.

Lying wide awake in bed that night, I tossed and turned, worrying about what my friends would say if they found out. At the same time, I couldn't stop thinking about Julie's smile and that kiss. I marveled at how in an instant, she had gone from yucky to yummy. I didn't know it then, but Julie had flipped the switch, lit the eternal flame, got the ball rollin', and any other sappy metaphor that applies. From that day forward, as far as I was concerned, girls in general were no longer as icky as I once thought they were, and they would never be so again.

The next day at school, while passing each other in the hallway, Julie promised to keep the whole thing a secret. She was pretty cool that way, but Anne and Gail were a different story all together. They told everyone! For weeks, the entire fourth-grade class tormented me with that piece of information. In no time at all, the incident became known and referred to by all as… *The Kiss*. Apparently, Julie and I had broken that particular new ground before anyone else in our fourth-grade classroom.

Short, affectionate glances and smiles took place sporadically between Julie and I that school year. In the spring, we secretly exchanged our school pictures behind the church, but nothing more romantic than that took place between us. After all, we were only nine at the time. I still had no real use for girls, but I did secretly love those blue eyes, especially when she aimed them and her smile in my direction.

In the spring of 1969, just after my fourth-grade school year, I moved to Duluth. During my farewell tour of the neighborhood, I secretly walked to Julie's house to say good-bye. Her father, Gary Falkner, met me at the door and gave me the bad news that Julie wasn't home. She was visiting her grandparents and wouldn't be back for a few days. He promised to tell her that I had stopped by. I left Mankato before Julie returned, so I didn't get to say good-bye to my first encounter with puppy love. Months later, I was amazed to discover that not being able to say good-bye to Julie hurt more than actually saying good-bye to the rest of my friends.

As my mind came back to the present, I found myself wondering about Julie Falkner. *Does she still live at the same address? If I try to see her, will she even recognize or remember me? Do I even want to see her? Why am I even thinking about it? Girls just complicate things!*

In a short time, Doc Elliot's advice rang inside my ears. "Keep it simple, Jackson. You're only going to be there for two weeks. Don't take on more than you're capable of handling. When I see you next, young man, I want to see you smile."

I decided right then and there. I would not pursue seeing Julie or any other girl in Mankato. What would be the point? Besides, I wasn't ready for that kind of stuff. Still, I wondered what Julie looked like after three years. I thought she was pretty in the fourth grade. I could only imagine how pretty she had become after so much time had passed. When I first moved to Duluth, I discovered there were pretty girls in my school. After three years of growing, they just kept blossoming. I was then quite certain the same had to be true for Julie.

After clearing my head, I got back to my reconnaissance mission. By using the alleyway and heading west, I was able to make it to the train tracks and proceeded to follow them north. I wanted to get to St. Joseph's Church to check on times for Sunday Mass. Promising Mom that I would go to church on Sundays was not a problem. I actually looked forward to it. St. Joseph's was a very large part of my Mankato past. I wanted to see it again. I wanted to feel as good as I used to feel when I attended Mass there.

While balancing on a rail, I passed a few trails that branched out from the tracks. They led off into lush green wooded areas that lined both sides of the railway. The ditches between the tracks and the woods were a mixture of stink weeds, as we called them, ferns, and wildflowers. I knew the woods on both sides like the back of my hand. Taking one of the well-beaten paths, I ducked into the brush on the west side of the tracks. I stood just inside the tree line and breathed in. My nose was immediately filled with the mixed scents of pine and cedar, along with some birch and poplar. There was enough light for me to see that kids were still using the pathway to get to and from school.

I decided to stay in the woods and follow the path. The path and the wooded area ended just east of Hubbell Avenue. When I arrived, I stayed in the brush line to ensure that no one detected my presence. After all, I was on a *secret* mission, so it wouldn't pay to be discovered at that juncture. When I was satisfied that the coast was clear, I stepped cautiously from my hiding place.

As I made my way down the silent avenue, the atmosphere felt a bit eerie. Suddenly, I could see the school and church just up the block. As I got closer, I lost interest in moving secretively and simply strolled toward my destination. I slowed my pace and leisurely walked on the opposite side of the street; my eyes locked on St. Joseph the Worker the entire short distance. The sun was low enough to silhouette the school and church. The rectory stood directly between the two buildings, but further back from the avenue. In the failing light, it was a little difficult to see because it was a significantly smaller structure, and it stood in the shadow of the much-larger church. I remembered there was also a convent, which housed the nuns who taught at the school, but I could not see that building because it was located in the rear of the property.

I stopped directly across from the church and looked for signs of activity. Except for a few birds and a small cloud of flying gnats, nothing moved. Stepping into the street and slowly approaching the church, I observed a brick and glass-encased sign located on the front lawn. It welcomed all to St. Joseph the Worker and informed them of Mass times. According to the sign, church services took place at 8:00 and 10:00 AM on Sundays. I decided then that I would attend early Mass. There would be less chance of anyone recognizing me that early. There was no good reason for me to be fearful of having people recognize me, but then, understanding my fears was not something I excelled at, not back then.

Having obtained the information I came for, I purposefully turned to leave the grounds. I did not want to offend Brad or Janet on my first night by staying away too long. Nevertheless, something made me change my mind. Quite suddenly, an uncontrollable urge took hold of me – I needed to see inside of the church. I assumed the doors would be unlocked because they were always unlocked. In years past, I had taken refuge in that church, simply because it was open at all hours. So, when I gave the entry door a tentative tug, I wasn't at all surprised to find that I could walk right in.

From the outside, the very front of the St Joseph the Worker appeared as an inward-bending radius. It had large, glass, entry doors at the left and right corners of the building. They led to an open, but not-too expansive vestibule. I stepped inside, walked slowly to the center of the hallway, then stopped and took in my surroundings. The vestibule was just as I remembered it. To my right was a public restroom. To the right of that, a door that led to the outermost aisle that ran along the north wall. To my left were bookshelves with an assortment of Christian literature on them. There was also a door that led to the extreme southern aisle. I was drawn to the rich tone of the stained, oak woodwork. I knew that once I entered the main sanctuary, it would only get better. Directly in front of me, two large doors led to the church's center aisle. They were ornately carved and stained, as well. I cautiously opened one and smiled, as I was once again bathed in the all-too-familiar beauty of the church's interior.

Chandeliers, which were suspended from a vaulted ceiling, lit up an atmosphere that was serene, but with loud colors. The entire length of the center aisle was covered with a vibrant red-carpet runner. It ran all the way to the steps leading to the altar. The pews on either side of me were the same shade of stained oak as the rest of the ornately carved woodwork. I remembered the large, stained-glass windows that lined the upper portion of the north and south walls. They used to mesmerize me and keep me occupied during many a Mass, usually when I was supposed to be listening to an important sermon. Just below them, smaller, stained-glass windows separated the Stations of the Cross. I then remembered that directly above the spot where I stood, was a rather large choir loft, complete with pipe organ.

The altar area was also impressive. Long, marble steps led up to the marbled altar floor. Both were polished to a brilliant, high-gloss finish. In the right light, a person could actually see their reflection on them. Behind the altar, an enormous wooden crucifix hung from the rear wall. The sad eyes of Jesus Christ appeared to survey everything within the walls of St. Joe's.

Except for two elders, who were kneeling in prayer toward the rear of the church, I was the only soul present. I dipped my fingers in the holy water vessel, which was located just behind the last row of pews. I crossed myself and then slowly made my way up the center aisle. Without thinking, I stopped, almost habitually, when I came to the third row of pews from the front. I genuflected and then ducked in on the righthand side. There, I sat quietly and listened in sweet silence. Shortly afterward, I heard the two elders leave the church. I now had the place all to myself, but suddenly was not comfortable with the idea of it.

Sitting there alone, I foolishly allowed bad memories to wash over me. I remembered sitting in that exact spot many times before and why. I remembered the beatings I took at the hands of Linus Matson. Those beatings were the reason I had such a close relationship with a church.

Linus Matson had a hair-trigger temper and no patience for any child who wasn't his own, or so it seemed to me. Reminding me that I wasn't one of his kids was habit with him. On one occasion, when I was barely seven, he provoked me into running away. Linus was angry about something, so he took it out on me. He had a propensity for doing that, too. He told me that all I was good for was the small amount of money they received for taking care of me.

"Well, I'll just run away then," I spat in defiance.

"That's fine," Linus fired back. "Just make sure you tell us where you're going first."

Minutes later, when no one was looking, I ran from the house, and did so without an inkling of an idea where I would go. I wandered for blocks. That is, until happenstance put me in front of St. Joseph the Worker, so I crept inside to hide. I sat in the exact same pew, third row from the front. There, I prayed for God to help me. Approximately two hours later, Father Michael found me sitting there. He immediately notified Linus, who came to collect me directly. Linus was nice enough in front of Father Michael, but it was an entirely different story when we got back to the house. I wore those welts and bruises for a few weeks.

That was the first time I used St. Joe's as a hideout, but there were other times, too, and it was always Father Michael who found me. On one such occasion, I begged Father Michael not to send me back to the Matsons. Nonetheless, my pleas fell upon deaf ears; he escorted me back himself. At first, I thought I was doomed, but then I watched the kindly priest give Linus what we kids called the evil eye. It was a penetrating look that Father Michael could conjure up. He had used it on me many times, usually when he was trying to extract the truth of a matter, and it gave me the willies. By giving Linus the evil eye, Father Michael actually made that grown man cower. For all Linus Matson's character defects, he was still a bound-in-faith Catholic. Father Michael was the pastor of his church, therefore, not to be trifled with. In front of me, Linus promised to be a better foster parent and acquiesced to Father's warnings about mistreating me.

After that incident, the beatings became a lot less frequent, but wouldn't go away entirely until I moved into the Wilson home. With the exception of Father Michael, I didn't trust grownups for quite a while. I didn't believe protection for me existed, except for when I was inside that church. I was safe while inside St. Joe's. God protected me there and there alone; of that I was certain.

That first evening in Mankato, inside my sanctuary, I sat in that pew and remembered my terrible past. The ever-present, but unanswered, *why* question came to mind. *Why me?* And, like countless other times before, tears welled up in my eyes. *Damn it! Not here! Not now!* But my thoughts could not fend off the huge lump that formed in my throat. So, I stopped fighting and for a short spell, let those terrible memories take over. As I remembered things that I had prayed to God I could forget, my tears flowed freely. Once again, I felt so alone, but didn't want to be. After a short time, I pushed those terrible memories back inside and was able to, as Kurt used to tell me, dry up.

The sleeves of my windbreaker made for a lousy handkerchief. I was suddenly thankful that Mom insisted I always carry one in my back pocket. Taking it out, I dried my eyes and thought about heading back to the people I had come to visit. Just then, a short, round, little man appeared from the sacristy and walked directly to the altar. He wore the traditional black garb of a Catholic priest. What I remembered to be grey hair was now turning positively silver. His old horned-rimmed glasses were replaced with a style more fitting the times. He looked to be making preparations for Sunday morning's Mass. I knew at a glance it was Father Michael O'Reilly. Besides being the Pastor of St. Joseph the Worker, he was one of the first adults I ever thought to be a true friend. He was also one of the very few people I trusted implicitly. He had presided over my baptism, my first confession, and my first communion. When he spoke, I always got a real kick out of his thick Irish accent. No one talked to me the way he did. No matter how depressed I was, the singsong lilt in his voice always cheered me up. In the past, Father Michael always acted as though he were genuinely excited to see me. I estimated that he was now somewhere in his early sixties. I remembered him taking annual thirty-day sabbaticals to Ireland and wondered if he still did.

Remaining silent, I watched Father Michael as he moved about and placed some unrecognizable articles on the altar. He arranged them, then rearranged them until he was satisfied they were where they needed to be. He then turned and saw me but did not make a connection. He went about his business, as if I were not there at all. The priest then went to the pulpit, which was located directly in front of me. There, he fiddled with some papers, probably his sermon for Sunday's worship. He looked over the rims of his glasses and caught me smiling at him.

"Hello, Father," I greeted.

"Good evening young man, and what mischief brings you to church on a Saturday night?"

"I guess I thought I might run into an old friend."

He backed out of the pulpit, came down the steps, and stood in the aisle by the first row of pews. He then gave me a good hard look. Quite suddenly, a grand smile came to his face and his eyes absolutely twinkled. "Jacky?! Jackson lad! Saints be praised, tis really you!"

I got out of my pew and went to him. The priest pulled me in close and hugged me harder than I thought his older arms capable.

"Jackson Harris! Of all the people I expected to see here tonight, you are definitely not one of them, you rascal you! Oh, but it does this aging heart good to see you now."

I let him go on and get his excitement out before trying to get a word in. When he was finally through, we sat back in the pew.

"When did you get into town, son?"

"This afternoon, Father. I don't know if you remember the Wilsons, but that's who I'm staying with."

Nodding his head, Father Michael replied, "Of course, Jacky, I remember them. They're one of my occasional-Catholic families."

Not understanding his reference, I scrunched my face and queried, "Occasional Catholics?"

"Yes. Occasionally I see them in church, usually around the holiday season."

Naturally, I gave his light-hearted, but accurate, remembrance of the Wilson family the courtesy chuckle it deserved.

"So, I'm to believe that you just got in today, but couldn't wait until tomorrow to see your old friend, Father Michael...Right?"

"Well, not exactly, Father. Not that I'm not really glad to see you and all... but...actually, I just came to see the church."

"Is that the old friend you spoke of earlier?"

"Kinda...You both are, I guess."

"How long has it been now, four years?"

"Three, Father. It just seems longer."

He then gave me his penetrating look and said, "The eyes are the windows to the soul, son. And yours tell me that you have been crying. Either that, or you suffer badly from allergies."

"I can't lie to you, Father. It was quiet in here. I was alone and started

47

remembering things I wish I could forget. I was remembering the things that used to make me come here to hide."

"Ah yes, 'twas I that found you. In this very pew, too! More than once I recall."

"Yes, Father. That was me."

"Those were darker days for you, Jacky. I pray things have become much brighter for you since then."

"Oh, they have, Father! They really have!"

I then took the opportunity to share the better aspects of my new life in Duluth with him. I spent about fifteen minutes recapping three years' worth of news.

"So, you are Jackson Landry now. That's wonderful! It takes very special people to make a son out of a boy they did not create. Their love must be powerful, Jacky."

"Okay, Father, save some for tomorrow," I jabbed.

"You'll be here, of course?" It was more of a statement than a question.

"Yes, Father. I plan on coming to the early Mass."

As Father Michael rose up and backed out of the pew ahead of me, he said, "And you can bring the Wilson family with you."

Getting up and exiting the pew, also, I chuckled, "I'm not making any promises there, Father."

Father Michael then stated, "You'll not be minding, when I point you out to everyone in the morning, will you? I think the people would like to welcome home one of our own."

"Well…actually, Father…I'd appreciate it if you didn't do that. You see…I'm not ready for certain people to know that I'm in town, not yet anyway. Some of those people might be here in the morning."

"Such mysterious behavior from one so young, but nevertheless, if that is what you wish…"

"Thanks, Father," I interrupted. Then, before he could offer a counter argument, I blurted, "I have to go now!"

"Okay, lad! I cannot tell you how happy I am to see you again."

"Me, too, Father! See you in the morning, okay?" I then began stepping backward down the aisle.

Father Michael called after me, saying, "You'll be giving my best to the Wilsons for me...Yes?"

As I hurried my retreat a little more, I said, "Absolutely, Father...Good night." Then, I turned and made my escape through one of the large, oak doors.

It was wonderful to see Father Michael again, but I had learned years ago that if you didn't make a fast break for it, he could keep you talking for hours – I didn't have hours.

When I stepped outside of the church, there was still some lingering light, so I decided to cut my neighborhood exploration short. Wanting to make it back to the house by dark, I took off at a trot. As I jogged along, I became aware that there was a severe lack of activity in the neighborhood, especially considering that it was still early on a Saturday night. Although I thought it a bit curious, the lack of intrusive neighbors afforded me the ability to return to the house undetected.

As always, I entered the Wilson house by using the side door. At the top of the stairs, I stopped and listened to some commotion coming from the basement. Just by the noise level, I could tell that Kurt and Danny had more friends over. Janet and Brad were having a beer and playing cards at the kitchen table – another familiar sight in the Wilson home. They both looked up and smiled.

"Well, you didn't get lost after all," poked Janet.

Brad asked, "Did you have a good walk? Did you get to see anyone?"

"Yes and yes," I answered, but didn't go into any detail. With a satisfied grin plastered to my face, I joined them at the table.

"Feels good to be back, does it?" asked Janet.

"Yeah, it really does. What I've seen of the neighborhood looks good. Nothing looks like it changed too much, except..."

"Except what?" asked Brad.

"Well, everything seems smaller, like it shrunk or something."

"Jackson, you were a runt three years ago," chuckled Janet. "You've done a lot of growing, youngster. It isn't that things got smaller. It's that you got a lot bigger."

"So, who did you get to see while you were out?" asked Brad.

I told them about my walk to the school and church. I also told them about my visit with Father Michael, keeping the overall details to a minimum. However, I did tell them how Father Michael referred to them as occasional Catholics. Strangely enough, they thought the moniker was pretty humorous.

"You're going to church in the morning, right?" asked Janet.

I smiled and looked her in the eye. "Yes, ma'am. All by my lonesome, right?"

While we three laughed, we heard footsteps coming up from the basement. Shortly thereafter, Danny poked his head around the corner at the landing. "Cool! You're here!" he exclaimed. "Are you staying up here with the old people or coming downstairs?"

Brad and Janet ignored his remark and nodded for me to go. I hesitated and just looked at the two of them for a moment. Up to that point, it had been a great day. I loved seeing those two again. Their easygoing ways had always helped me loosen up and forget my fears. Never getting hostile, when we boys poked fun at them, they always found the humor where we intended it. I sometimes thought Kurt and Danny crossed the line a little, but Brad and Janet never seemed to take offense.

I then went to the stairs, where Danny waited, positively grinning from ear to ear. "What're you smiling about?" I asked.

"You'll see."

Suddenly, I became slightly nervous. *What's waiting for me downstairs?! More importantly, do I really want to find out?!* If I knew Kurt and Danny, they probably had some asinine prank ready to spring on me. I looked back toward Janet and Brad, to see if they would give away some hint as to what awaited me, but no clues were given because they had returned their attention back to their card game. So, I followed Danny down the stairs, but kept a little distance between us. My guard was all the way up. I wanted to be able to turn tail and run at the first sign of trouble.

Upon entering the den, I immediately noticed the number of teenagers had gone up dramatically since suppertime. In the bar and lounge area, the number of teenage couples getting cozy had more than doubled. Music softly played in the background to help with the mood. I then turned toward the pool table and my heart jumped. There stood my old friends: Tony Milner, Joel Brighten, Dave Lester, and Mike McDonald.

I gasped, "Oh my, God, you're here!"

As far as I was concerned, my homecoming was now complete. There was no way for it to get better than that. I had been so nervous about whether my friends would welcome me back, but there they were. Their smiles told me everything I wanted to know. I wanted to hug the four of them, but that just would not be cool. Instead, like mature men, we simply shook hands.

I then turned to find Janet and Brad standing by the stairwell, smiling. I went to thank them, but Janet waved me off. "Uh-uh, kiddo," she said. "Dad and I had nothing to do with this. It was those four." Janet then pointed to Kurt, Janelle, Danny, and Carrie. All four were sporting huge grins. "Actually, it was Janelle's idea," continued Janet, "but the four of them did all the scrambling, while you were out on your walk."

I went to where they were seated to thank them. The girls got up from where they sat because they wanted hugs. I thought, *what's with the hugging?* It felt strange expressing my thanks in such a way in front of everyone. At the same time, it also felt…appropriate.

I thought I lacked the ability to strike a kinship with anyone very fast, especially a girl. Nevertheless, I felt there was something different about Janelle. For some reason, my instincts told me I could trust her. The jury was still out on Carrie because there was far too much mischief in her smile. Janelle's was warm and genuine.

As I hugged Janelle, I whispered, "Thanks."

She replied, "You're most welcome. Now, just go have fun."

I spent the rest of the evening meeting more of Kurt and Danny's friends, plus getting caught up with mine. The guys asked so many questions and because I was habitually evasive, it was hard for me to give detailed, honest answers. For the most part, we played pool, joked a bit , and talked sports.

When conversation turned to baseball, my ears pricked up. The Minnesota

Twins had always been a shared interest between my friends and I, so I was now happy we were talking about something I knew extensively. In fact, we all talked knowingly about the Twins and what a poor season they were having. That summer, the team was struggling. It began with a slow start in the spring and as the summer got older, they were not performing any better. Early in the season, the Twins general manager, Bill Rigney, had been replaced by long-time Twins player and coach, Frank Quilici. However, the change didn't appear to help. The Twins just didn't seem to be able to get any real momentum going at all.

We also talked about how some of our favorite players were fast approaching the twilight of their careers. Harmon Killebrew – my very first and all-time favorite baseball hero – was still playing well, but he was aging. Tony Oliva's knees were shot and had limited him to just ten games that season. Nonetheless, even though the team was having a lackluster year, Jim Kaat was on his way to another Gold Glove Award. Rod Carew was the only Twins team member chosen for the American League All-Star Team. He was also on course to win his second American League batting title. Nevertheless, that August, the team was floundering in third place in the American League West, and there was little hope of them reaching the playoffs.

Grandpa Mack – short for Macintyre – was Mom's father. Thanks to him, I knew everything about the Minnesota Twins. We followed the team very closely together. The team was the initial glue that made Grandpa Mack and I instant buddies. Gramps loved all things baseball, especially the Twins. I shared in his passion for the game and the team, so we became tight in a very short time.

During our baseball banter, Dave Lester volunteered to contact the neighborhood guys and put a game together. Of course, we all thought it was a great idea. Besides the fun derived from playing ball together again, it would be a great opportunity for me to see some of the guys I used to know well.

As we chattered on, I suddenly became aware of a subtle quietness that had settled over the dimly lit basement. Periodically throughout the evening, I kept a curious eye on Kurt and Janelle. All too often, they were caught up in a passionate lip lock. Danny and Carrie were now trying to keep pace, as were other teen couples.

At a rather inopportune moment, I decided I needed another root beer, so I schlepped my way over to the bar to get one. I carefully made my way around, or over, the feet of groping teens, but almost got tangled up in a pair, which were blocking my path between the coffee table and couch. That's when Danny caught me gawking.

"Careful, little brother," Danny teased. "Kissing girls is dangerous business."

I had no doubt that what Danny said was true, but it didn't keep me from wondering what it was all about. To be so wrapped up in one girl, so that all you wanted to do is make out with her; the notion was alien to me. I also wondered if my old friends were as far behind the power curve as me. No girl since Julie Falkner had shown any real interest in me, so how was I to know? Give me sports and I was fine, but where girls were concerned, I was truly ignorant.

"Oh my, God!" exclaimed Carrie. "He's so cute when he blushes!" Of course, the comment was directed at me.

I couldn't help myself. Danny had caught me staring, so I was instantly embarrassed. I felt the blood rush to my face and knew I could not hide my redness from everyone. Danny pointed at me and laughed. When he did, Kurt and Janelle decided to take a breather. I guess they wanted to seewhat the commotion was all about. When Kurt saw my beet-red face, he let me have it. "Geez, Jackson, let some blood go to the rest of your body!"

There was an eruption of laughter from everyone within earshot. Like a puppy, with his tail tucked between his legs, I simply got my root beer from the bar and then made my way back to the pool table. As I tripped my way through the gaggle of teenage couples, I heard Janelle tell the others to layoff. I turned and looked at her. Without saying another word, she smiled and gave me a knowing wink.

When I finally made it back to my friends, Tony asked, "A little shy around girls, Jackson?"

Trying to act like it was no big deal, I replied, "I just get a little tongue tied, that's all."

"Don't worry about it," said Tony. "Enjoy your freedom while you can. There's always baseball, football, basketball, and hockey."

"Amen to that," said Mike.

Suddenly, we all just looked at Mike, kind of dumbfounded like. He had almost no athletic ability in any of those sports, but he was still always one of our gang. We usually appointed him the everlasting referee or umpire, depending on what we were playing. Mike always appeared okay with that arrangement, too. If we were short a player and asked him to stand in, he always got extremely nervous. We didn't ask Mike to stand in often, but when we did, he performed like a complete spaz.

In contrast, I was good at sports. I was at my best when playing sports, and didn't even mind crowds. In fact, I enjoyed them. The sound of a crowd cheering me on was one of the few things I truly loved. It was the only time I felt accepted. I competed hard against others and took great pride in winning. So, why was I so confident in my athletic abilities, but had absolutely no confidence in myself around girls? I had yet to learn that one has absolutely nothing to do with the other.

When it was time for my four friends to leave, I accompanied them up the stairs, then outside. We stood briefly on the driveway and promised to see a lot of each other in the coming days. Just as I expected, it was Dave who made the most magnanimous statement before leaving.

"Hey, Jackson, it's great to have you back, man. While you're here, we're gonna have a blast!"

The five of us made plans for meeting Sunday afternoon at Tony's place, to watch a Twins game, the first of a doubleheader. They then said their good-byes and departed for home, all except Mike. He lingered behind, but only momentarily. He had something to say, but I guess he wanted only me to hear it. "I…I'm not very good with girls, either," stammered Mike. "It's not that I don't like them. I just don't know what to say."

It was then that I gave Mike a critical assessment. His red hair was an uncombed mess, but I had always been accustomed to seeing it that way. I knew his mom probably made him comb it before he was allowed to leave their house. Nevertheless, in the past, just as soon as Mike was out of her sight, he just messed it up again. Even in the dim light from the porch, I could tell his chubby face and arms were red from sunburn. Mike had his mom's fair and freckled complexion. I then remembered how he never seemed to tan from the sun; he just burned. Like Larry Armstrong, Mike was chunky. I attributed that to his nervous eating habit. Mike always seemed to be chewing on something. If there wasn't anything edible in reach, he could oftentimes be found chewing on his tongue; a source of some mild-mannered ridicule from us guys, about how he looked like a cow chewing its cud.

Just then, I smiled at him because I didn't quite know what to do with the little factoid he just laid on me. I mean, it's not like I ever thought he *would* be a real hand with the girls. Mike was probably the shyest person I had ever met. It's how I remembered him, and he hadn't changed a bit. My friends and I were always protective of him. If some kid tried to take advantage of Mike's shyness, they usually had Dave, Joel, Tony or me to deal with, sometimes all four of us.

I then remembered Kurt taking care of a bully, who once tried to pick on Mike. Kurt wasn't the best older brother in the world, but I thought he was that day.

Mike had always been protected in his shyness. Therefore, I believed he became comfortable in it and never actually tried to come out of his shell. Me? I hated my shyness. I hated my fears. Kurt and Danny had taught me to face my fears. So, why were girls so difficult? Why did I even care? There were more important things for me to worry about. *I'll work on the girl thing later,* I thought. *Much later!*

When Mike finally departed, I went back inside and returned to the basement. I hung out by the bar and listened to all the banter of the older teens. I knew I could learn a lot, if I kept my eyes and ears open, but kept my mouth shut. When some of the couples danced slowly in whatever open area they could find, I watched closely. I took note of how at ease they all seemed to be with each other; a real clique. I wondered if I would ever be part of a group like that. To me, fitting in and being accepted was something to be prized and sought after. However, in the three years since I had left Mankato, fitting in was something that had eluded me.

Suddenly, Kurt turned his attention to me and asked, "So, Jackson, any girl in Duluth caught you yet?" He was trying to make me blush again, so Janelle gave him an elbow to the ribs.

Kurt winced, "Ow! Hey! What's that for?"

"Just leave him be," asserted Janelle.

I couldn't help but laugh. My tough, older brother, being bested by a girl. The mere notion of it was simply too cool! Then, remembering his question, I flatly replied, "No girl up there is interested in me."

Carrie immediately spoke up. "I don't believe that. She probably just hasn't let you know...*yet*."

I always blushed at such comments. And right then, I was true to form.

"There he goes again," said Kurt, so Janelle gave him another elbow.

The hour was now late and past my usual bedtime. Because I planned to get up early for church, I said good night to everyone. Once again, I thanked the four responsible for the reunion with my friends. "Thanks guys, it was a great surprise."

Janelle got up and held out her arms. I assumed hugs were now going to be a mandatory thing from there on out, for her anyway. As we embraced for what I hoped would be the last time, she softly said, "Welcome home, Jackson, I hope to see a lot of you while you're here."

"Me, too," said Carrie, holding her arms out.

I finished saying good night to everyone and then went upstairs. Janet had already gone to bed and I could hear Brad snoring on the living room couch. I prepared to climb the stairs leading to the attic. I tried to be quiet during my ascent, but every step creaked loud enough to wake the dead. I winced and hurried upward, so I could get the racket over with as fast as possible.

That first night, I laid in my old bed, remaining awake for I don't know how long. The entire day replayed in my head. New things were now mixed with old and it all felt wonderful. From that moment on, I wanted time to move at a snail's pace. For the coming two weeks, I wanted to savor everything and wanted to rush through nothing. As I began to get drowsy, the memory of a pretty girl, her two friends, and a weeping willow crept into my head. I must have fallen dead asleep before Danny turned in because I didn't hear him come up those creaky steps.

Chapter 3

Sunday, 6 August 1972

I was awakened quite early and rudely by loud rock 'n' roll music. It blared from an AM/FM clock radio, which sat atop an old nightstand made of pine. The stand was situated between Danny's bed and mine, so either of us could reach over and shut the loud contraption off. That morning, Danny beat me to it.

As soon as Danny released the shut-off button, he yawned and sleepily exclaimed, "Up and at 'em!"

Just as sleepily, I asked, "What gives?"

"Mom said we are all going to church this morning."

"You have got to be kidding me!" I enunciated the words for effect. My next thought made me almost burst out in laughter. "Father Michael is going to have a heart attack."

"Yeah, probably," laughed Danny. "Since you left, we don't go to church much."

Still wiping sleep from my eyes, I quipped, "You didn't go much when I lived here."

"True, but Mom thought it would be nice for the seven of us to go together."

"Seven?"

"Yeah, the girls are coming, too. They decided last night."

I had no indication from the previous evening that anyone planned on coming to church with me. Now, the whole clan was going, complete with girlfriends. I didn't quite know what to do with the information, so I just accepted it, rolled over and got out of bed.

After stretching my still-sleeping muscles some, I went right into the old routine of finding out who had first dibs on the shower. At the bottom of the stairs, I discovered Brad and Janet drinking coffee at the kitchen table. I must have looked quite the sight. When they saw me, sporting what I imagined to be a rather severe case of bedhead, they just laughed and waved me into the room.

Janet then instructed me to go down and make sure Kurt was awake. I shuffled to the basement stairwell and while keeping a cautious eye on her, playfully made it look as though I was about to yell down the stairs. As I knew it would, Janet's you-had-better-think-again look was enough to stop me in my tracks. Smiling innocently at her, I then tiptoed down the steps, listening for any sign that Kurt might be awake already. I heard nothing, so I proceeded down the short passageway to his bedroom, where I lightly tapped a knuckle on the door.

Kurt's voice boomed, "I'm awake!"

"Kurt? Can I come in?" I asked.

"Jackson? Yeah, come on in, man."

When I opened the door, Kurt's décor immediately jumped out at me. An assortment of posters adorned almost every inch of the bedroom's walls, mostly of voluptuous females and hot-rod cars. *Girls and cars*, I thought. *I should have known.*

Already showered, Kurt wore a towel wrapped around his waist. I couldn't help but be a little impressed by the toned muscles of his upper body. He was busy rummaging through his closet, trying to find something appropriate to wear. Shortly, he stepped out into the room again and held up two different colored dress shirts. "Help me out here…Which one?"

Having no opinion, whatsoever, I simply shrugged my shoulders in response.

"You're no help."

"Hey, I'm only thirteen. What do I know about making a fashion statement in church?"

Kurt snickered and then asked, "What's on your mind?"

"I wanted to ask you about Janelle."

Giving me a curious look, Kurt asked. "What do you want to know?"

"Well, how long have you two been together? How did it happen?"

Kurt's look changed to puzzlement. "You really don't know much about girls, do you? Haven't you had any come after you yet?"

"Not since Julie Falkner and two of her friends chased me in the fourth grade."

Kurt laughed, "What?!"

I was trying to impress my older brother, so I told him about Julie and my first kiss under the Milner's weeping willow. When I was through with my tale of prepubescent love, Kurt laughed even harder. Suddenly, I realized I had just made a huge mistake by confiding in him, but I remained calm about it.

"I mean in the last year or so," clarified Kurt. "Hasn't there been anyone trying to get you wrapped around her little finger?"

Regrettably, I had to honestly reply, "Not that I know of."

"Jackson, we've got to get ready for church, Bud. I think this is something we should talk about some other time."

"Yeah, you're right." I agreed. Then, still trying to maintain my coolness, I turned to leave his room.

Before I escaped, Kurt called after me, "Hey, we will be talking later." He then fixed a rather stern look on me.

"Okay," I acknowledged, adding a nervous smile.

After I closed his door behind me, I felt better knowing Kurt wasn't just putting me off, but I also knew what his last look was about. Like Danny, he had gotten the word about my troubles up north. Glad that I was clear of his intense, glaring look, I trudged upstairs, dreading the explanations I would have to give in the coming days. When I reached the kitchen, Janet informed me that it was my turn for the shower.

I rode to church that morning with Janet and Brad. Kurt and Danny went to collect their girls in the VW van. As Brad parked the Mercury, my eyes darted this way and that, straining to see if there was anyone else arriving that I might recognize. We were too early. There were but a few other vehicles present, or they were just arriving, and I recognized no one in them.

As previously arranged, the seven of us met in the vestibule of the church before going in to sit. When I caught my first glimpse of Janelle and Carrie, I couldn't help but notice how attractively they were dressed. Both wore similar looking, floral-patterned skirts, topped with a conservative white blouse. Like sisters, they also wore sweaters that morning because there was still a chill in the air. My approval of their apparel must have shown. Janelle caught me gawking and quickly maneuvered her way over to me. "What's the matter?" she asked.

Embarrassed that I had been caught staring, I did what any thirteen-year-old rookie would do in that situation; I lied. Looking down at my shoes, I mumbled, "Nothing."

Not to be put off, Janelle pushed. "You were looking at me like something's wrong. Do I look okay?" she asked.

With blood rushing to my face, I replied, "You look fine. I mean, you look real pretty."

Smiling warmly, Janelle said, "Thank you! You're very handsome this morning, too. That's quite a suit you're wearing!"

That morning, I had worn my best, dress suit. Actually, it was the only suit I owned that still fit me decently. Mom had me fitted for it the previous winter, but like others that had gone to charity, it was beginning to get tight in the shoulders. I purposefully wore no tie because Kurt and Danny wore open-collared shirts. Being cool, like them, wasn't my only reason for leaving off the tie. I simply hated getting all dressed up, but wearing a tie was simply the worst! To me, wearing a tie was for sissies. I did everything in my power to keep from looking like one of those. Besides, Mom wasn't there to supervise, plus I knew that neither Brad nor Janet cared.

When it was time for us to find a seat, we all followed Brad up the center aisle. He led us single file, about midway up, stopped and then gestured for us all to proceed into a vacant pew on the righthand side. I greatly approved of his choice. For me, being in the middle of things right then had a certain appeal.

Seating myself between Brad and Janet, the feeling was not only familiar, but comfortable. I enjoyed sitting in church and once again feeling like I was a member of their family. I was also surprised at the number of families who turned out for the early service and wondered how many I would know. I recognized a few faces here and there, but their names escaped me. It bothered me because just a few years prior, remembering their names had not been a problem. As the time drew closer to the start of Mass, the church rapidly filled to just short of its capacity.

I thought it strange that there were so many present. Usually, there was a noticeable drop off in attendance during the summer months. It was caused by families traveling on vacations, but that wasn't the case that morning. I then rationalized that some of the congregation must be guests. When I traveled with my parents, Mom always found a church service for us to attend on Sundays. Heck, even when we went weekend camping, I could not escape having to get up and go to church in some nearby town.

My mind was busy with those thoughts, when seemingly out of nowhere, the Falkner family appeared and passed us on their way up the center aisle. Gary Falkner ushered the women in his life into a pew, just two rows in front of where we sat. Lisa, the youngest, shuffled in sideways first and then Julie. As I watched Julie enter the pew, I held my breath. I thought she was going to look right at me. If she had, I just knew my heart would immediately stop beating. Still, I remained calm, but with great difficulty. Marilyn Falkner followed her oldest daughter into the pew and then Gary sat himself last, closest to the aisle.

Kurt enjoyed the coincidental convergence immensely. With a criminal smile on his face, he reached across Janet, tapped my leg a few times, and then pointed toward Julie with his thumb. As I labored to maintain my breathing, I gave him somewhat of a queasy smile in return.

It was almost impossible for me to pay attention to anything Father Michael said during the service. I was too busy looking at the back of Julie's head and wondering when I might see her blue eyes again. I was desperate to see her face. My earlier assumptions regarding Julie had been correct. To say she had grown more attractive during my three-year absence was a gross understatement. To me, she was stunningly beautiful! Her raven curls had grown much longer and hung down almost to the middle of her back. The fleeting look I got of her eyes was enough to make me change my opinion about girls entirely. I had seen and even appreciated pretty girls from a distance before, but this was crazy! I wanted her to see me and recognize me! At the same time, I wanted to slink out of that church before any such thing occurred!

Taking communion that morning was a bit tricky. Starting at the very front and alternating from pews on the left, then right, ushers invited families to form a line. Participants would then proceed up the center aisle toward the alter steps. There, Father Michael awaited them to deliver the symbolic, Body of Christ.

At the usher's prompting, the entire Falkner family stood to depart their pew. As they rose and turned to join the advancing procession, I simply looked at my shoes. If Julie were to see me, I didn't want to know it. I did, however, glance up in time to see them join the line that formed up the center aisle. For the moment, I breathed easy. One more row to go before it would be our turn. When the usher finally motioned for our pew to stand, I was the only one to get to his feet. *Great*, I sarcastically thought. *This is working out nicely!*

The Wilsons probably hadn't gone to confession in years. Therefore, taking communion would have been a rather large breach of Catholic protocol. Since Mom ensured that I attended confession regularly, I had no excuse for staying seated. Reluctantly, I stepped over Brad's feet and out of the pew, then took my place in the ever-growing procession that slowly moved toward Father Michael.

While inching forward in line, I did my best to keep my eyes on Julie. After she received communion, she made her way back to the pew her family sat in. As she gracefully walked, I couldn't take my eyes off her. *Good Lord! She's an absolute knockout!*

When I finally stood in front of Father Michael, he smiled broadly, offered the host, and said, "The body of Christ."

As I accepted the small wafer of unleavened bread, I gave the ritualistic response, "Amen."

Keeping my eyes glued to the floor, I then turned to my right and began my journey back to the pew. As I walked, I felt sweat break out on my forehead and my hands were practically wringing wet. When I was close enough to get another good look at Julie, I raised my eyes, but only for an instant. I silently thanked God because I saw that she was kneeling and looking down, supposedly saying her post-communion prayers. Upon arriving at our pew, I carefully brushed past Danny, Carrie, and Janelle. However, when I tried to get around Kurt, he gave me a little jab to the ribs. When I finally made it to my seat, the cushioned kneeler was then put down. The seven of us knelt until communion was delivered to the rest of the congregation.

My silent, post-communion prayers were quite sincere that morning, and they all had to do with getting out of that church before Julie could see me! As I stared at Julie's long, black curls, I suddenly felt Kurt's eyes on me again. When I turned to catch his look, he just grinned like the Cheshire cat in *Alice in Wonderland*.

A silent argument now raged on inside my head. *She's going to see you on the way out! So, what if she does? She won't know you! Yes, she will! No, she won't! Yes, she will! NO, she won't! YES, SHE WILL!*

I was now in a panic. Desperate to get away from Julie, I searched for any possible way to escape without her ever knowing I was there. Suddenly, my nerves and physiology stepped in and handily provided the answer to my dilemma. During final prayers, gastric fluids in my stomach growled loudly in protest. I very much needed to get rid of the cheeseburger I had eaten for dinner the previous night. So, I clumsily excused myself and then raced for the restroom located in the vestibule. Once inside, I locked myself in and there I stayed for the rest of that Mass.

There are moments in life when people believe the fates are truly against them. For me, squatting on that toilet seat, relieving my stomach of its contents, was one of those moments. After I had finished, I felt much better, not just because my stomach was no longer in turmoil, but because I was once again in control of my emotions. However, Julie was just on the other side of that door, so I was in no hurry to rejoin the world. Unfortunately, my bowel movement had created an atrocious stench, which lingered, with absolutely no promise of going away anytime soon. The smell was bad enough to make a skunk run for cover. Even after flushing the toilet, it hung in the air like a putrid, pervasive fog that refused to diminish. To make matters worse, there was no exhaust fan or air freshener available! Nevertheless, the pungent atmosphere was still not bad enough to make me move from that small, one-person hideout. I simply plugged my nose, held my breath, and stayed put.

So, there I was, locked in the confines of that smelly restroom, practically gagging on my own exhaust fumes, feeling quite cowardly and foolish. Suddenly, there came a knock at the door. Apparently, someone was having a bathroom emergency of their own. Thinking I had been rude for hogging the facilities, I hurriedly got ready to exit. For effect, I flushed the toilet again and once more washed my hands. I then mentally prepared myself for whatever and whomever awaited me. Turning the knob slowly, I cautiously opened the restroom door. As I stepped out, a tall, thin, elderly gentleman looked down at me. The smell I had left must have hit him immediately because his face suddenly became ashen. I think his eyes may have crossed, too.

Thoroughly embarrassed, I simply uttered a quick, "Sorry." Then, I hurried off to find the Wilsons.

Mass had been over for a little while and even though the crowd had thinned greatly, a few stragglers still milled about the vestibule. I quickly spotted Brad and Janet, who were engaged in conversation with Father Michael, so I casually walked over to them. As I approached, I heard Father Michael exclaim, "And here is our miracle worker now!"

I gave them all a puzzled look, so Brad chuckled and explained. "Father Michael was just telling us how he thought your being here and getting us to come to church was nothing short of a small miracle."

I laughed, but didn't say anything. My eyes nervously scanned the area for Julie.

Seemingly out of nowhere, Kurt snuck up behind me and whispered in my ear, "Too late, bud…She left with her parents already."

I immediately let out a sigh of relief, but was strangely disappointed, too. Just then, I kicked myself mentally for telling Kurt about Julie. He would now, more than likely, torture me with that knowledge for my entire stay.

"Come on," said Kurt. "You can ride home with us in the van."

I looked to Janet to see if the switch was okay.

Janet nodded, saying, "See you at the house for brunch."

I then tried to say my good-byes to Father Michael, but he motioned me aside. In his usual pleasant voice, he said, "Jacky, I was wondering if you would join me for lunch or maybe dinner sometime while you're here."

"That'll be great, Father, but you don't have to feed me. I'll stop by and visit again before I leave."

"I would like to share a meal with you, yes?" insisted the priest. It was another request that sounded an awful lot like an order. He was also giving me his evil-eye look.

I knew that accepting Father Michael's invitation would definitely please Mom. Catherine Landry taught me about a Catholic priest's vow of poverty, chastity, and all the other sacrifices they make to do God's work. She often invited the pastor of our church in Duluth to family gatherings. Spending time with Father Michael would go a long way toward helping Mom worry less. So, not dwelling on the priest's insistent invitation, I replied, "Sure thing, Father."

Before I could change my mind, Father Michael said, "That's a good man. We'll worry about the details later." He then waved me on my way and went about receiving other congregation members. In turn, I hurried to the door, gave him a wave and then exited the church.

When I stepped out into the cool, morning air, I immediately found Kurt, Danny, and the girls. As promised, they had waited for me, but seemed anxious to get moving. So, I hurried and followed them to where the van was parked.

After we all piled in, Kurt headed the microbus for home. At first, everyone was silent, but I should have known that Kurt couldn't drive the short distance back to the house without making me feel like an ass. Just as soon as I saw him looking at me through the rear-view mirror, I knew what was coming. Kurt wore a devilish grin, as he asked, "So, Jackson, how did Julie Falkner look to you this morning?"

"What's this?!" asked Danny. "Little brother, you got the hots for Julie Falkner?!"

"No!" exclaimed Kurt. "According to Jackson, she used to have the hots for him!"

Suddenly, everyone who was not driving the van, stared at me. I rolled my eyes and felt my blood start to boil. I couldn't believe Kurt had just divulged that which I confided only a couple of hours earlier. Now, I had to deal with three busy-body teenagers. I knew I was turning a bright shade of crimson because Carrie pointed at me and giggled.

In a feeble attempt to backpedal, Kurt said, "Actually, Jackson just told me this morning about something that happened when he and Julie were in the fourth grade. I just thought it was a huge coincidence that she ended up sitting two rows in front of him in church…No big deal."

Danny asked, "So, what did happen in the fourth grade?"

The bomb had already exploded, so there was no way to defuse it. With each passing second, I was getting increasingly frustrated. To make matters worse, my changing voice cracked, when I said, "Just leave it alone, okay?"

Danny thought it was all too hilarious and, of course, the girls thought it was cute. I just wanted to crawl underneath one of the van seats and hide. I thought, *I should have ridden home with Janet and Brad!*

Carrie then said, "I know Julie pretty well. We should invite her over sometime."

"Oh, God!" I exclaimed. "Just leave it alone! Please!"

The rest of the ride to the house was quiet. I tried to ignore them all by staring out the side window. Nevertheless, I couldn't help but notice Janelle looking at me with an enormous smile plastered to her face.

Upon arriving back at the house, I immediately went upstairs to get out of my dress clothes. My shoulders actually ached a little from the tightness of the jacket, so I could hardly wait to put it back on the hanger. I jumped into some jeans and donned my lucky Minnesota Twins t-shirt – the team could use the luck. Fully dressed, I was now ready to watch the game with my friends at Tony Milner's house. I was truly looking forward to it because the previous night, Tony stated that he would not tell his folks I was coming. He thought it would be a neat surprise, having me just show up on the doorstep unannounced. Now, all I had to do was wait patiently until game time.

After a well-prepared brunch, I helped Janet with the dishes. When we finished,

I went outside and then to the garage to retrieve the basketball. I wanted stay busy until it was time to meet my friends. Shooting baskets would help make the time pass quickly.

I had only taken a few shots, when I then noticed Janelle appear from the side door. She casually walked toward me and then, without saying a word, she just stood off to the side and simply watched me for a few minutes. Feeling uncomfortable by her presence, I stopped shooting baskets to see if she wanted something. I was not surprised to learn that she did. "I got the feeling that Kurt shouldn't have said anything about Julie on the ride home," she said, "I'm sure he didn't mean anything by it."

In a casual tone, I said, "It's no big deal." It was an attempt to keep her from pursuing the matter further. I then continued to shoot baskets.

Unaffected by my dismissal, Janelle asked, "Are you going to try and see her while you're here?"

"Not likely," I declared. "She probably wouldn't remember me for one, and two...I'm only here for a couple weeks. What would be the point?"

"I don't know, Jackson, but she must mean something to you. Otherwise, you wouldn't be getting so upset."

Simultaneously, I launched the ball toward the hoop, while bellowing, "I'm not getting upset!" The ball missed the basket by a country mile.

Janelle giggled and started to walk off, then stopped and turned around. "Is she your first crush?"

"Kurt told you, didn't he?"

"No, he didn't, but she is, isn't she?"

I stopped and looked at Janelle hard, trying to decide what to do next. I shrugged my shoulders, took another shot at the basket and then admitted, "Yeah, well, so what if she is?"

Janelle then asked if I would please tell her what I had confided to Kurt earlier in the morning. I decided to take a chance and gave her the abridged version of my first kiss under the Milners' weeping willow. She listened intently, but unlike Kurt, she didn't laugh. When I finished telling the story, I didn't give Janelle a chance to respond. I simply began shooting baskets again.

"That was your first kiss? That is so cool! It makes me wonder why I never thought of doing something like that years ago, with a certain guy I liked back then."

When I realized she wasn't laughing at me, my trust in Janelle grew slightly. In fact, it felt better having someone listen to me, without turning everything I said into a joke.

Next, Janelle asked if I said good-bye to Julie before I moved away. I stopped shooting again. *You might as well tell her the rest,* I thought. So, I confided in Kurt's girl once again and told of my failed attempt to see Julie. I finished the short story by saying, "So, no…I didn't get to say good-bye to her before I left. We were just little kids then. What does it matter now?"

Janelle exclaimed, "I think it matters a lot! I'll bet not only would Julie remember you; she probably still wonders what happened to you! I think she would absolutely love to see you again!"

Thinking that Janelle was stretching things a bit, I asked, "Why do you think that?"

Without hesitation, she replied, "Because a girl never forgets about the first boy she kissed."

Not to be bested, in a flat tone, I asserted, "She had her chance at church this morning,"

Janelle argued, "That's not fair, Jackson. She obviously didn't see you." She then paused, while stepping in closer. Janelle then locked my eyes with hers and said, "Look, I've seen how you are around girls. And, by the way, you shouldn't be so shy. You're too good looking and I know there are plenty of girls who would love to have you pay them some attention."

Right on cue, I felt my face burning with embarrassment.

"Carrie is right," continued Janelle. "You really are something when you blush. She's also right about inviting Julie over. You have a chance to see her and this time you can say good-bye properly. At least, think about it…Okay?"

Janelle turned to walk off, but I stopped her. "So, how come I don't have any problem talking to you? I don't ever know what to say to other girls."

"I'm safe. I'm like your sister and you can talk to me anytime you want."

After a short pause, Janelle left me with one final thought. "Just be yourself, Jackson. Girls will definitely like you if you let them."

I didn't know what else to say, and even though I didn't believe her, I muttered, "Thanks."

Janelle walked back into the house, while I went back to shooting baskets. I was pretty sure there was no way I would be making any special effort to make contact with Julie. A beautiful girl like her was way out of my league, or so I thought. Like everything else that existed in Mankato, Julie Falkner was just another item on a rather long list of things I could not have. I then remembered what Doc Elliot advised. "Don't complicate things more than you have to, Jackson. Remember, your life isn't there anymore."

In that moment, I decided to never go out of my way to see Julie. The fact that everything I had ever felt for her was now on the surface did not matter. I knew in my heart that by leaving some things in Mankato alone, I would be so much better off.

CHAPTER 4

When I rang the doorbell of the Milner residence, I could not hold back the smile, which had mindlessly spread itself across my face. I had a fairly good notion about what awaited me behind the door. The very thought of it tickled me plenty. Rather than good friends, the Milners were more like honorary family to me, and I to them. In years past, I probably spent as much time in their house as I did the Wilsons'. Three years prior, saying good-bye to them had been extremely hard. When I left their house for the last time, I struggled hard to fight back tears of sadness. Now, I was looking forward to what I knew would be a huge welcome home.

A pretty teenage girl, about Kurt's age, with sun-bleached blonde hair, answered the door. It was Tony's older sister, Cindy. I very casually greeted her, just as if I had just been there the day before. "Hi, Cindy, is Tony here?" I asked casually.

Cindy looked at me for a few seconds, then her eyes flew wide open and so did her mouth. "Jackson?! Oh my, God! Jackson, is it really you?!"

I suddenly found myself being hugged by another girl. Cindy was more like my big sister, though, so it was okay.

"It's so good to see you!" Cindy then yelled over her shoulder, "Mom! You've got to come see who's here!"

When Cheryl Milner hustled from the kitchen toward her daughter's voice, I heard her ask clearly, "Did I hear the name, Jackson?!"

With a huge grin still plastered to my face, I exclaimed, "Hi, Mrs. Tony's Mom!" The moniker was our little-inside joke. I had called her that for as long as I had known her. Cheryl Milner was another one of my former neighborhood moms.

Tearing up, Cheryl exclaimed, "Oh, by gosh, it is you! Jackson!" She then practically smothered me with her hug and made it clear she didn't plan on loosening her grip anytime soon. But, just then, the youngest of the clan, Kathy, tapped her mom's shoulder. Kathy was only eleven at the time, but she still wanted her hug, too. After I greeted and hugged Kathy, Cheryl grabbed me again and resumed her tearful welcome.

When I assessed the Milner girls, it was easy for me to tell whose looks they inherited. They both had their mother's blonde hair, which was set off magnificently by suntanned skin. All the Milner kids had the same chubby, turned-up, pug nose – a very endearing feature, not at all ridiculous looking. Even Tony favored his mom more than his dad.

Cheryl kept hugging me until Tony Sr. came from the basement. "Okay, let him breathe, Momma," he said. "He's here to watch the game, not get smothered by a flock of emotional hens."

"Watch it mister!" Cheryl jokingly threatened.

I shook hands and greeted Tony's dad; his welcome being much more dignified. We all congregated there in the entryway until Cheryl invited – more like instructed – me to sit in the living room. There, I relaxed and filled them in on some of the details of my visit. I enjoyed how they listened and seemed to hang on to every word I said. They peppered me with questions about my life up north. I did my best to give the group brief, but honest, answers. I didn't want to go into too much detail, though. After all, I was there to watch a baseball game, not give a three-year recitation about my life as a Landry.

Finally, Tony Jr. came up from their basement. He stood in the doorway and took in the scene. His straight, blonde hair was bleached even lighter from the sun. As always, it was neatly feathered and brushed back. Dave Lester once called Tony, The Primper – he always carried a comb and used it often throughout the day. I remembered that Tony's blue eyes had been called dreamy by girls in school, but Tony didn't seem to care about any of that. He just liked hanging out with the other guys and, like me, actively avoided contact with the female sex.

Tony Jr. then informed the women of how I would be in town for two weeks. There would be plenty of time for catching up. After a quick, "See ya later," he hustled me toward the basement stairwell.

When Tony and I made it to the downstairs den, the game was just beginning. That afternoon, the Twins were playing the first game of a double header against the Oakland Athletics. Dave Lester and Mike McDonald had beat me there and were now comfortably seated on a garish looking couch, which was covered in a green, blue, black, red, and white, plaid-patterned material, not unlike what one might find on a Scotsman's kilt.

I then noticed that Joel Brighten hadn't arrived, yet. "Still waiting on Joel?" I asked.

"Yeah," said Dave. "You remember how his mom can be, right? When Joe has plans to do something with us, she comes up with chores for him to do first. It pretty much guarantees that he'll be late for everything."

I smiled and shook my head. "Yep, that's his mom alright."

Mrs. Brighten was probably the only neighborhood mom I didn't get along with. His dad wasn't much better. Unlike my other friend's parents, who I loved dearly, Mr. and Mrs. Brighten weren't very friendly toward any of us. The Brightens didn't have a lot of money and they lived in a rather run-down house. Upkeep of their property, both inside and out, never appeared to be much of an ongoing concern for them. However, when it came to being friends with Joel, we guys overlooked all of that. Personally, I knew him to be probably the most intelligent of our little gang. In the past, he did a lot of reading. If I ever needed help with my math homework, Joel had always been there to lend a hand. If I still couldn't get it, he would simply tell me to copy his homework.

"If his mom doesn't keep him busy, then Gail usually does," said Tony.

"What?!" I asked, wrinkling my nose. "Who's Gail?"

"Paulsen," said Tony. "You remember Gail Paulsen from St. Joe's, don't you?"

"Yeah, I remember her from school. But, what are you telling me? Are Joel and Gail goin' steady?!"

When Tony nodded in the affirmative, I could not believe it! One of my very-first-best friends was now seeing one of the original monsters, who had chased and caught me the day Julie Falkner kissed me.

"Yeah, they've been an item since sometime around last Christmas, I think," said Dave. "I'm going out with Anne Hayward."

"What?!" I exclaimed again. *For crying out loud,* I thought. *Dave and the other monster…Really?!* "Geez!" I said, shaking my head in disbelief. "A guy leaves for a few years and all his friends go girl crazy!"

We all laughed, but I truly was astonished. The irony of my two friends being romantically linked to those two particular girls, was just a little too much for me to mentally digest. I already knew that Mike McDonald was pretty much in the same boat as me, so I looked to Tony. "Who are you going out with?" I asked.

"I'm kinda like you," replied Tony. "I'm still keeping my dukes up."

I jokingly asked, "On purpose?"

"Does it matter? Either way, I'm not tied down, not like those dweebs."

To that, Dave gave Tony a rather gregarious smile, but then shot him his middle finger.

Joel Brighten made his entry during the third inning. From that point on, it was as if I had never left. Just like three years prior, the five of us spent the afternoon poking fun at each other and laughing. The day's forecast threatened rain, with temperatures only in the mid-sixties. Even though the Twins were losing again, it was a great day to stay inside and just hang out.

We talked sports mostly, but the subject of girls kept coming up, too. Somewhere in the middle of our hubbub, Joel suddenly had a recollection.

"Hey, Jackson, someone asked about you earlier this year, when we were all at…I think it was Anne's place."

"Yeah, that's right!" chimed in Tony. "Your name did come up... when we were all laughing about some of the goofy crap we did at St. Joe's together."

"Who was asking?" I inquired.

"Julie Falkner," replied Joel. "I *know* you remember her!"

My mind raced to the words that Janelle had spoken only hours earlier, and excited I thought, *she does remember me!* Trying to sound as casual as possible, I replied, "Yeah, I remember her alright." Then, after wondering whether I should offer the information, I added, "Funny, I just saw her this morning in church."

Once again, I felt all eyes on me. I suddenly realized the chances of me not coming in contact with Julie were rapidly diminishing.

"Really?!" exclaimed Mike. "Did you guys talk?"

"No," I replied. "It was funny because I sat only two rows behind her. She never saw me, and I never got a chance to talk to her."

Tony asked, "Why's that?"

Knowing that this crew could always appreciate good bathroom humor, I told them about how I ended up in the restroom toward the end of Mass. Of course, I left out the part about how my run-away nerves put me there. When I got to the part about the old man who had to go into that little stink-hole after me, laughter erupted from all of them. Just then, what had been quite embarrassing to me was now funny as hell. So, we all had a good laugh at my expense.

Suddenly, a slight panic gripped me. I was no longer comfortable with the idea that the guys were now cozy with the very girls I wished to steer clear of. "Hey guys, do me a favor, will ya? Don't tell the girls I'm in town...Okay?"

"Why not?" asked Joel. "They'll probably want to see you."

"It's just that...I don't really want them to know I'm here," I stammered.

Shaking his head, Dave said, "Whatever." Then, smiling at my angst, he rubbed a little salt into that wound by adding, "Chicken."

We spent the rest of the afternoon getting caught up on things of absolutely no importance. We exercised our knowledge of Twins baseball and Minnesota Vikings football. Since the Twins didn't appear to have much chance at making the playoffs, it was time to start shifting our attention toward football. Persistently, Dave kept talking about getting a baseball game going for Tuesday. He had already started to make phone calls and reported that it looked good for getting enough guys to show up. So, in order to appease Dave, we all penciled in baseball for Tuesday on our mental calendars.

I then asked the guys if they still went fishing down by the train trestle at Indian Creek. Tony answered for the group by telling me that they still went there from time to time, but only when there was nothing better to do. When I suggested that we all meet at the creek early Monday morning to do some fishing, the guys answered me with bored looks. However, I did get a couple of maybes from Tony and Joel. As far as I was concerned, if I ended up fishing alone, that would be okay, too. That way, I had a better chance of actually catching fish. When we five all fished together, we rarely caught anything because we made too much noise.

During the late spring and all summer long in Duluth, fishing alone is something I did often. The city had creeks and ponds intermingled within many of its neighborhoods. My favorite trout pond was just a short, bike ride away. There, I was able to angle small rainbow, speckled, and brown trout. They were usually so small that I had to catch quite a mess of them to make a meal, but that wasn't my true purpose for fishing at all. I liked being alone with my thoughts and having no one else around to talk unnecessarily. When the fish weren't biting, I liked to relax on the bank and read books.

The Twins lost that afternoon, six-to-three. When we all went upstairs to say our good-byes, I couldn't get out the door without making a promise to return and get caught up with the Milners. It was a promise I would have no problem keeping. I loved the whole family like they were an extension of my own. Truth be told, I envied their closeness immensely. They were the best example of a Brady-Bunch family I had ever seen. I actually felt somewhat privileged because they all treated me like an honorary member. I knew saying good-bye to them at the end of my visit was going to be just as hard, if not harder than the first time.

During the short walk back to my temporary home, my head was full of wandering thoughts. They were mostly about the guys and the girls they were seeing. *We've all grown some since I've moved away, but have we really grown that much?* I still couldn't get over how strange it all sounded inside my head. *Julie Falkner actually asked about me?!* That thought put a smile on my face. Nonetheless, potentially running into her made me extremely uneasy. *What in the world would I ever say to the likes of Julie?!*

Just as I was arriving back at the house, Brad stepped out onto the driveway. "I'm heading to Pigs," he announced. "You want to tag along?"

"Are you taking the Corvair?" I queried.

In quick response, Brad replied, "Yep, I am."

Instantly excited, I proclaimed, "Oh yeah...I'm comin'!"

The Corvair was already out of the garage, so I jumped in the passenger side and found myself unable to stop smiling. I ran my hand across the smooth, red tuck 'n' roll upholstery. It was just as I remembered it. I loved that little car and knew with Brad at the wheel, I had better hold on tight. I wasn't accustomed to wearing a safety belt. Back then, not many people did. Although, wearing a belt, especially when Brad was driving, would not have been the worst idea I ever had. Even on a short straight away, Brad could go through the gears and have us flying down the street in no-time flat. Cats, dogs, squirrels, and the like had better stay out of the way. That little rocket with wheels was not about to stop, not for little animals with suicidal tendencies, anyway.

Pigs was short for Piggly Wiggly, the grocery store chain - a common reference known to many in the northland. On the short drive to the store, Brad and I struck up a quick conversation about fishing. I told him I intended to walk the train tracks in the morning to Indian Creek. He listened patiently and nodded his understanding. Since I was actually speaking in complete sentences, Brad let me do most of the talking.

We arrived at Pigs in mere minutes. Once inside their parking lot, I noticed how Brad parked the Corvair quite far from the store, away from all other vehicles. He must have read the inquisitive look on my face. "I don't want other people putting dents in the doors," he explained – Brad was well known for the way he babied that car.

Entering Pigs through the automatic doors, we then headed in the direction of the checkout lines. We had to pass them in order to get to the meat section. But we didn't make it to our destination, not without incident, that is.

Brad and I were poking fun at each other, when suddenly, I saw something that made my blood run cold. To be more precise, it was the sight of someone that made me stop dead in my tracks. It was almost as if I couldn't put another foot in front of me. Brad kept walking a short distance, but when he noticed I wasn't with him anymore, he turned to look back at me. He must have recognized the fear on my face because he then turned and looked in the direction I was staring. There, standing in the checkout line, leaning on a half-full shopping cart, was the man I feared most in the entire world, my biological father, Adam Harris.

I couldn't believe my horrid luck. It had been well over six years since I had seen him, but my recognition came immediately. With the exception of some weight gain, Adam's appearance had changed very little. His hair still looked to be almost jet black. It was from the grease he used to slick it back into a ducktail, as if he were still living in the 1950s or '60s. His square jaw and bulbous nose made his face rather unimpressive. Nevertheless, the rest of him still looked solid. Like Brice Landry, Adam grew up on a farm and had the muscular shoulders and arms to prove it. Also like Dad, Adam had thickened around the middle. Remembering Adam's past drinking habits, I naturally assumed it was a beer gut.

Adam looked right at me, but there was no telltale sign of recognition on his face. As he looked unknowingly at me, I thought I was going to piss myself, right there for all to see. I couldn't remember the last time I was that scared. I had counted on seeing certain people during my stay in Mankato, but Adam Harris was definitely not one of them.

Brad came to where I stood and nudged me out of my frozen state. Putting his arm around my shoulder, he softly said, "Come on, kiddo." He then got me started up the nearest aisle that took us away from the checkout line. When we were safely out of sight, Brad kept his arm around me and slowed his pace a bit. "You okay, buddy?"

Right then, I couldn't make myself talk, so I just nodded my head. I kept looking back over my shoulder to ensure Adam hadn't changed his mind about recognizing me.

Brad ensured we took the long way around the store to get to the meat section. Once there, he inspected the meat in the cooler and then picked out two packages of pork chops. In an even, conversational tone, he said, "The secret to good pork chops is to get them fresh. They're so much better than if you have to thaw them out."

I knew Brad was attempting to get my mind out of shock. So, in order to make him feel a bit easier about my condition, I gave him a weak smile. My heartbeat was slowing again, and my breathing was getting back to normal.

Brad continued to lead the way through the store, going up and down the aisles. He picked up a few odds and ends before deciding it was time to check out. As we waited in line, I could see no sign of Adam, but my eyes darted this way and that, constantly searching for him.

"You've got nothing to worry about, you know?" Brad insisted.

I responded by nodding my acknowledgement.

Once the groceries were paid for, we headed out of the store. When we reached the parking lot, I looked toward the Corvair and again came to an abrupt halt. Adam Harris was leaning on the trunk of a beat-up, black, '58 Chevy, four-door sedan. I recognized the car because I had ridden in it many times. I could scarcely believe he still drove that hunk of junk.

Putting a protective hand on my shoulder, Brad said, "Go back in the store, Jackson. Wait for me there."

As instructed, I turned and trotted back to the safety of the store. Once inside, I peered out the plate-glass window at the faceoff that appeared to be taking place between Brad and Adam. Surprisingly, I observed no threatening gestures between the two. Even though I could not hear a word that was spoken between them, they appeared quite civil toward one another. After what looked like a short discussion, with a few looks in my direction from both men, Adam shook Brad's hand and then headed toward his car.

They shook hands?! I was just as astonished as I was confused. *Why is Brad acting like he's friends with that monster?!*

I stayed inside the store until I saw Adam drive off. Only then did I feel it was safe to go out and join Brad. As I approached the Corvair, I said nothing. Instead of asking a lot of questions, I simply hurried to the passenger side and got in.

At first, Brad made no comment, either, but during our drive back to the house, he broached the subject by asking, "Why are you so afraid of him?"

Being my usual, evasive self, I replied, "Afraid of who?"

In response, Brad gave me a look that said, "Don't act stupid around me, mister!"

I truly didn't want to talk about it, not then, or ever, but I also knew better than to ignore a direct question from a respected elder. So, I took a deep breath and replied by asking, "Do you remember the scars on my back?

"Yes, I do."

"Well, he's the one who gave them to me. He's the one who tried to kill me when I was little."

"Kill you?! Jackson, I don't believe that. Adam's not capable of that kind of behavior. Are you sure you're remembering things correctly?"

Brad's doubt put me more on edge. "Yeah, I'm sure," I insisted. "I don't want to talk about it, okay?"

"No problem, buddy." Brad then patted my leg reassuringly and added, "I mean it, Jackson, don't let this worry you. While you're with us, I don't want anything to get in the way of you having a good time."

The rest of the ride home was quiet. The silence between Brad and I was filled with tension. I hated it. However, after seeing Brad and Adam shake hands, plus having him doubt my memory, I was no longer sure I could trust my former-foster Dad. I wanted to know how the two knew each other, but not right at that moment. I didn't want to remember, let alone discuss, what Adam had done to me, when I was so very little. Right then, I just wasn't ready to relive it all. So, I kept silent for the remainder of that short ride home. I simply continued to look out the window and labored to find one good memory involving my biological father, but nothing came to mind. There was nothing back there for me but fear and pain.

When Brad brought the Corvair to a complete stop in the driveway, I flung the door open and hurriedly jumped out. I then grabbed the singular bag of groceries and without saying a word, ran inside. Dropping the bag on the kitchen counter, I then hurried toward the stairwell leading upstairs. In my haste to reach the sanctuary of the attic bedroom, I almost didn't see Janet sitting at the kitchen table. As I scurried past, she called after me, "What's your hurry?"

When I reached the top of the stairs, I breathed easier. Plopping myself down on my old bed, I laid there on my back, waiting. *Soon, Brad will tell Janet all about what happened at the store,* I thought. *More than likely, Janet will then want to talk about it with me. I don't want to talk about it! I don't ever want to talk about that man!*

There was a heating vent located next to my bed, right where the wall and floor met. It made for a great listening post. In years past, Danny and I laid awake at night, listening in on Brad and Janet's conversations. It worked best if they were sitting at the kitchen table. That afternoon, I could tell Brad and Janet were right where I needed them to be. As I rolled over onto my stomach, listening carefully, Brad's voice came through pretty clear. "Janet, I swear, I've never seen Jackson look so scared. He was petrified."

"Poor kid," said Janet. "He lived with us for almost three years. In all that time, no such chance meetings ever took place. Now, after being gone for three years, he has to run into Adam on his second day back. Wow! What are the odds of that?"

"You know Adam and I were pretty tight in school," said Brad. "He was a little wild back then. Heck, so was I. But he never got into any real trouble."

"Not until he married Sharon Stevens, you mean," Janet corrected. "I knew that whole thing was going to end badly."

"Let's not talk about it now," said Brad. "Jackson is right upstairs. I don't want him accidentally hearing anything we aren't ready to tell him, yet."

"You're right. Before he leaves, though, he has to know the truth," said Janet. "It's time, Brad. We owe it to him."

"I know, but it's going to be so hard for him," said Brad. "He's dealing with a lot of things right now and I don't know if we should add anything to that list."

"You could be right," said Janet, "but maybe the truth can help him when he goes back home. I hate hearing about him struggling up there. We told his parents we would help."

I waited, but there was no response from Brad, just agonizing silence. It appeared the two adults in the kitchen were taking a breather, so I waited and listened intently, just in case there was more to hear. They didn't keep me waiting very long.

"Adam wants to see Jackson. He wants to talk to him," said Brad.

"Are you kidding me?!" exclaimed Janet. "He's been out of the picture now for what, six or seven years? Now he wants to talk?!"

"When the time seems right, I'm going to tell Jackson everything," said Brad. "I'm going to let Jackson decide whether he sees or talks to Adam."

Rolling onto my back, I felt an age-old anger building within me. *It'll be a cold day in hell before I allow Adam Harris to come anywhere near me! He gave up that right a long time ago!*"

I now had to bury my feelings and do it fast. I couldn't let Brad and Janet know that I had just heard every word they said. I launched myself off the bed and headed toward the stairwell. But then, I reined myself in, just short of taking the first step down. Holding back and not descending the stairs was difficult because I wanted to get out of the house. I wanted to go run somewhere, anywhere. Instead, I just stood at the top of the staircase, trying to decide what to do next. Then, I remembered something Doc Elliot taught me to do when I found myself losing control. "Just stay quiet and breathe," he advised.

I went back to the bed, laid down and curled up in a fetal position. I decided to stay there until dinner time. The old, answerless questions were now coming back and filling the inside of my head. *Why did Adam hate me, his own son? Why did he do that to me when I was so little? Why didn't anyone else in the family want me?* The biggest question I wrestled with was, *"Why didn't my mom want me?"*

I then felt tears welling up in my eyes. Damn it, crying won't change anything or make it all better. Dry up, crybaby! But fighting the emotional upheaval was pointless because my tears came anyway. Sometime thereafter, I dozed off.

"Dinner is just about ready." The words came to me in a half-dream state. When I opened my eyes, I discovered Janet sitting on the edge of the bed, gently shaking me. "Are you okay, honey?"

Not wanting to chance speaking, I simply nodded my reply.

"It would seem that you've had a full afternoon," observed Janet.

Acting as if there was no, possible way for me to know what she was talking about, I asked, "Brad told you?"

Sarcastically, Janet answered with a question of her own. "What do you think?" Then, her tone softened. "I'm sorry, kiddo. I wish that hadn't happened."

Agreeing with Janet's assessment, I added "Of all the people in Mankato, I had to run into him."

"Let's let it go for now, okay? The boys want to know if you want to go to a movie with them tonight. After dinner, they're going to the drive-in."

Putting some fake excitement in my voice, I exclaimed, "The drive-in?! Yeah, that sounds great!"

Janet then smiled and gave me a motherly hand out of bed. After helping me to my feet, she combed the mop on my head with her hands and then ushered me toward the stairs.

Brad, Kurt, and Danny were already seated, waiting for us. As I took my place at the table, I became keenly aware of their concerned looks. However, nobody ventured a single comment or question.

The pork chops were good, as was the rest of the meal, but the dinnertime conversation lacked the boisterous energy of the previous night. It was pleasant, but too tentative. I felt as though they were all tiptoeing around me. I wanted the atmosphere to be much lighter. So, thinking as quickly as I could, I nonchalantly asked, "What's playing at the drive-in and who's going besides us three?"

"We're going to see *Evil Knievel*," answered Kurt. "Larry and the girls will be coming, too."

"Great!" I laughed. "Larry and I can hold hands in the front seat, while you two swap spit with the girls in the back."

The comment had the desired effect. Everyone had a good laugh and the air was effectively cleared of all anxiety. For the rest of that meal, conversation remained lively and fun, but I could only act like I was having a good time. The thought of coming in contact with Adam Harris again dominated my thoughts. I was gripped by fear and couldn't make it stop. *Damn you, Adam Harris! May God damn you to hell!*

Seating arrangements at the drive-in theater went pretty much the way I called it at dinner. Just as soon as it got dark and close to the start of the movie, Larry and I took command of the front seats of the van, but without the handholding. Kurt, Danny, and the girls staked their claim to the back seats.

Because I often went to matinees by myself in Duluth, I had already seen that night's feature film, *Evil Knievel* – a light-hearted autobiography about the early years of motorcycle daredevil, Robert, a.k.a. Evil Knievel. So, when the back windows began to fog up, I excused myself from the van. Before stepping out, I took everyone's orders for popcorn and soft drinks. Larry said he would join me at the intermission to help carry it all.

To me, outdoor drive-in theaters were a lot like indoor theaters. Young lovers migrated toward the back, while older couples or families with kids parked closer to the huge white screen. That night, Kurt found a spot toward the very back. So, as I made my way toward the concession stand, which was located in the middle of the parking area, I had to make an effort to avert my eyes from other young patrons, as they groped and pawed at each other.

The night was cooling off, but it was also dry. As latecomers drove past me, they kicked up dust, causing me to sneeze a few times. After I blew my nose, I snapped the front of my windbreaker shut, jammed my hands into the front pockets of my jeans and continued through the many rows of vehicles.

For a Sunday night, there appeared to be a lot of nocturnal activity taking place. I rationalized that it was because summer vacation would soon be over. To me, it seemed that all kids started acting a little more desperate in August. It was as if they wanted to cram as much fun as possible into the last few weeks before school started up in September.

In front of the concession stand, rows of old, wooden, theater seats faced the huge, billboard-sized screen. I found a vacant seat away from the few people who were utilizing that area. Slouching in a chair, I tuned out the movie and let my thoughts take over. *If I had known I would run into Adam Harris, I wouldn't have come to Mankato at all! What was so important that Brad needed to wait for the right time? I haven't thought of or heard my mom's name in years. I pretty much figured I would never see her again. But then, that's what I thought about Adam, too. I wonder where she is. I wonder if she's still here in town. I don't know what to think about Brad anymore, especially since he and Adam are old friends.*

Suddenly, all of Mankato felt very strange to me. The entire town wasn't what I remembered at all. Everything had changed way too much, so I now struggled to reconcile it all in my head. Things were so much simpler when I lived with the Wilsons. Now, Kurt and Danny had girlfriends, so did my friends, Dave and Joel. *Why do I always feel so different and alone? I wish I had talked to Julie after church, but what would I have said?* Sitting there, ignoring everything that was going on around me, I wished for many things. Mostly, I wished that I could just relax and stop thinking so much.

Because I knew when the intermission would take place, I left my seat at what I thought would be the right time and made my way to the concession stand. When I arrived, I discovered that a small line had already formed ahead of me. Mom had given me quite a bankroll, so I planned to pay for the popcorn and soft drinks myself. The gesture somehow made me feel more mature. When it was my turn, I placed my order with a cheery, zit-faced, teenage boy, who scurried off to fill it. As I waited patiently, I watched other patrons in line. Friends greeted each other, making it clear to me that the drive-in was a popular night-time hangout. I searched the area for a friendly face but recognized nobody. It made me feel like a stranger in my own hometown.

When I paid the acne-plagued boy for the refreshments, I spotted Larry, as he stepped into the small concession area. He squeezed his way to the front of the line and when he finally stood at my side, offered to chip in a few bucks. I waved him off but accepted his offer to help me carry it all to our waiting party. As we walked, Larry chattered on about how dry the night was and how the drive-in dust would probably improve the taste of the popcorn. Because my mind was elsewhere,

I didn't pay him too much attention, but managed to give his not-very-funny comments a courtesy chuckle or two. Arriving at the van, with our plunder safely intact, Larry and I passed out popcorn and soft drinks. Everyone thanked me cordially for buying the goods. Then, we all settled in for the second half of the movie.

As I wedged myself down into my seat by putting my knees on the hard, metal dashboard, Janelle said, "Hey, Jackson, while you were out, we were talking."

In return, I playfully jabbed, "Oh, is that what they're calling it now?"

My flippant comment was not lost on them. When the laughter died down, Janelle continued. "We're having a get-together at my place tomorrow night...and I'm inviting you."

I immediately looked to Kurt and Danny for some hint of their approval or disapproval, but their faces were blank. Thinking that I would probably just be in the way, I said, "Thanks for asking, but you don't have to do that."

Surprisingly, Kurt piped up, "We want you to come, really."

In unison, Danny and Carrie asserted, "Yeah!"

Larry was busy stuffing his mouth with popcorn, so he simply nodded his agreement.

Something wasn't quite kosher, of that I was certain, but right then, it did not matter. I actually wanted to go. I liked hanging out with them and wanted to be counted as one of their inner circle.

"Come on, Jackson," prodded Janelle. "Say you'll come."

Knowing full well that I would more than likely regret my decision, I acquiesced. "If you really want me to...Okay."

That settled, we all hunkered down a bit and waited for the movie to resume. The evening air was now quite chilly, so I stayed in the van for the second half of the feature. When the advertisements, which beckoned patrons to visit the concession stand, ended, and the second half of the movie began to roll, the two couples behind me went back to making out. Larry and I ate popcorn and kept our eyes forward. However, I did periodically steal a peek or two over my shoulder. *Good grief! Do they ever come up for air?*

Tuning out the movie and the activity going on in the back seats, my mind began to wander again. Mostly, I wondered what it would be like to make out with a girl. I knew that I wasn't ready for such nocturnal activities, but it didn't keep me from thinking about it.

I then turned my attention back to the on-screen action, thinking how the couples in the back were missing a pretty good movie. But every time I cleared a new layer of condensation from the windshield, I would sneak another peek at the activity going on directly behind me. It was obvious that the two couples could not have cared less about anything that occurred outside their intimate, little world.

Later that night, I lay in my bed, thinking not only of events of the day, but of things to come. I was still somewhat rattled about seeing Adam. Determined to get that unfortunate encounter out of my head, I concentrated on more pleasant things. I planned to go fishing in the morning, whether the guys joined me or not. Then, in the evening, I would attend my first boy-girl party. Thoughts of a baseball game on Tuesday made me smile, too. There were good things directly ahead of me and I simply wanted to enjoy every moment. I wanted to smile, laugh, and not waste any of my precious time being afraid. Nevertheless, I was afraid. Fear had once again taken hold and I could not shake it.

Chapter 5

Monday, 7 August 1972

Shortly before eight o'clock in the morning, I headed south on the train tracks away from the neighborhood. With my fishing pole in hand, plus a daypack slung properly on my back, I journeyed toward the train trestle at Indian Creek. Although it was still somewhat early and I wasn't fully awake, my mind was already hard at work, struggling with unsettling thoughts.

Before rushing off to work, Janet had helped me prepare a brown-bag lunch. We talked a little, too, as she slapped lunchmeat on slices of white bread, then slathered them with mayonnaise. As I now took short, choppy steps, ensuring to hit every wooden tie, I remembered our short, but purposeful conversation.

"Going fishing this morning is a great idea," said Janet. "Are your friends meeting you?"

"I don't know for sure," I replied and simultaneously yawned.

"If you're there all by your lonesome, I'll bet you can get a lot of thinking done."

Janet's not-so-subtle hint was not lost on me. As I walked on, I found myself almost wishing the guys would not show up at all. Janet was right, I did have a lot of thinking to do. I had learned from prior experience that thinking and fishing were excellent companions. When the fish were biting, many times my troubles simply disappeared. But, if the fish didn't want to play nice, it still wasn't time wasted. While drowning worms in a fishpond or creek, I oftentimes got lost inside my head. If I didn't feel like thinking, I could always read a book – I habitually tucked one or two away in my daypack.

That morning, I was still undecided about what I was going to tell Brad and Janet. My troubles up north had been many. I was afraid they wouldn't understand. Additionally, I suspected that Mom and Dad had painted a rather dim picture for my former-foster parents. Nonetheless, Brad and Janet would still want to hear my version. There were things I would have to tell them, but I wasn't at all certain about how to go about it. Now, there was also the matter of Adam Harris. How was I going to tell Brad that an old friend of his was, in fact, a real monster?! Trudging along, I sincerely hoped that some answers would come to me.

The walk to Indian Creek was a comfortable one. Earlier that morning, while I was getting my fishing gear together, there was a slight chill in the air. However, as the sun began to crest the treetops to the east, things began to warm up nicely. In the past, I could never make that hike to the trestle without balancing on a rail, at least part of the way. I remembered when the guys and I had contests to see who could walk the rails the farthest and the fastest. That morning, I once again indulged myself with that simple pleasure.

The birds were in full song, as were the frogs and crickets. Just listening to their commotion helped me relax even more. As far as I was concerned, there was no better way to spend a Monday morning. While Brad and Janet hustled off to work, I got to relax at one of my favorite spots. It truly wasn't fair, of course, but who was I to complain?

It was shaping up to be a beautiful day. The temperatures were forecasted to be in the mid-seventies again. Although it was considered quite cool for August, I didn't mind a bit. I loved the new dark blue and red windbreaker I wore that morning, with the Minnesota Twins logo on the left breast. Grandpa Mack had presented it to me that very summer for my thirteenth birthday. Having a chance to wear it before the fall was fine with me.

As I neared the train trestle, I began to look for the old worn path that would lead me away from the tracks. Once I found it, I followed it through shoulder-high weeds, which terminated mere inches before a steep embankment led me down to the creek. When I walked through the tall foliage, I got fairly wet from the morning dew. I didn't mind the bath a bit. It was simply a necessary, but minor, inconvenience I had to go through in order to get to my favorite fishing hole. Besides, when I got myself situated by the creek, it would not take the warm sunlight long to dry me.

Tony Milner informed me earlier that the water level in the creek was up. It had been a rather rainy spring and summer that year, so I wasn't surprised to find that what he had reported was true. However, I remembered seeing the water level much higher in the past. For instance, the early spring of 1968, when I accidentally fell into the creek and was almost swept away by rushing waters. That day was forever engrained in my memory. I could have drowned that day, but Joel and Tony were there to pull me to safety. As I remembered the stupidity of it all, I chuckled out loud.

After conducting a quick search of the banks, I found the perfect location to set up. A gigantic cedar had fallen over and became a natural bridge, which stretched from one side of the burbling creek to the other bank. I used the tree to cross over and from the opposite bank, I was able to fish, plus keep an eye peeled in the direction my friends would arrive from, should they actually decide to join me.

Finding bait that morning had been quite easy. Before leaving the house, a quick exploration of Janet's flower garden produced many dew worms. I wrangled one from a dirt-filled, tin can, which once held pork 'n' beans, but now made for a perfect bait preserver. I impaled the slimy critter on my hook and then wiped my hands on my jeans. After tossing my line out into a nearby pool, just outside the creek's current, I set the line and then allowed my muscles to unwind. I needed to dry out from my trek through the dew-soaked weeds, so sitting with the sun on my face felt absolutely luxurious. Almost immediately, I began to relax, and remembered how much I had always loved hanging out by Indian Creek, especially when I needed a tranquil place. That is, it was extremely peaceful, just as long as a train did come along. When that happened, the very ground would shake beneath me, like a minor earthquake.

Shading my eyes from the sun, I squinted in the direction the guys would appear. No promises had been made, so there was no way for me to know if I was going to have company that morning or not. As I watched, I wondered if their being glad to see me again was just a put-on. I found myself wishing things were how I had left them, just three years prior. But then came the nagging realization that everything had changed and would never be as it once was. *I must be like a stranger to them all now*, I thought. Saddened by thoughts that I would never actually be part of the gang again, I hated how fate, God, or just plain life had taken me away from them. *Why did things have to be so different for me?* I continued to stare at the slow-moving current, allowing the hypnotic reflection of the sun to penetrate past my focus. I retreated into my inner self, that part of me I knew better than anything, any place, or any other person. The present world and its unanswered questions slowly faded away.

I was born in Saint Paul, Minnesota, on the fifteenth of July 1959. The circumstances that put my mother there at the time of my birth were unknown to me. All I had been told was that when I decided to make my entrance into this world, St. Paul is where she happened to be.

My earliest recollections were of a house off East Madison Avenue in Mankato, just up the hill from a fire station. The house was old, rundown, and was built on a steep hillside. As a toddler, I had a room to myself. There, I spent a lot of time alone, playing with my toys. The house also had a basement, which was extremely dark and dank. A fruit cellar was located down there, an especially scary place for me because it was cold, dismal, and decorated with old spider webs.

I had two older brothers, Derrick and Brian. They were pranksters, who always seemed to take delight in making me cry. As a joke, they used to lock me in the fruit cellar from time to time. There I would stay, screaming my lungs out, until my mother would finally come to rescue me. My brothers always laughed about it, as though it were truly funny. Besides the occasional torture they dealt out, Derrick and Brian didn't have much to do with me. I got used to playing in my room alone and even preferred it to spending any time with by brothers. Whenever I was allowed to join them, it usually ended up being some asinine, practical joke on me.

On one occasion, when I was four years old, I joined them and some neighborhood kids. Together, we imagined ourselves in the U.S. Army, and at war against the Japanese and Nazi Germany, both in the same geographical location. The hillside behind our house had a lot of loose sand and dirt. So, foxholes were dug for us to wage our battles against the imaginary enemies of the good ol' USA. My brothers positioned me in a hole that was way too deep for me see out of, let alone fight from or crawl out. Then, they and their friends ran off, leaving me with no way out of the hole. For what seemed liked hours, I screamed until I completely lost my voice. Eventually, my mother found me, whimpering and trembling in the bottom of the hole. For their stunt, both brothers received a severe beating from Adam. After that day, I was never again invited to play with my brothers and their friends.

We weren't a family long enough for Derrick, Brian, and I to become close. As a matter of fact, I could pass them on the street and fail to recognize them. *Has it really been that long since I've seen my own brothers?*

Next, I remembered that my mother's name was Sharon. When I was but a toddler, Grandma Harris once called her by name in my presence. So, like all mimicking kids, I tried to do the same. Of course, I was corrected immediately. From that day forward, she was simply known to me as Mom. I found it disturbing that I had lost clear recollection of her, other than to say that I loved and even missed her. I just couldn't quite understand why I felt anything for someone who left me behind. I once thought of my mom as my only ally within that home. Whenever Adam called for me to come to him, I always ran to Mom, instead. I attributed my fear of Adam to the way he disciplined me. It was usually with the buckled end of a belt or some other household utensil, so I looked to her for protection. It was to no avail because I ended up knowing the business end of Adam's belt intimately.

I vaguely remembered my mom as being very attractive, maybe even beautiful. When the two of us were together, she had a smile that made me constantly want to be around her. When Adam was home, she didn't smile as much.

I also remembered how she held me close, while seated on her lap, in November of 1963. Together, we watched President John F. Kennedy's funeral procession on TV. She wept and so did I, but only because she was so saddened by what was on the television. At the age of four, I was still too young to fully understand the significance of that event.

I then remembered the crazy little dances she and I did, when watching Dick Clark's *American Bandstand*. When we danced together, Mom seemed most happy. In short, I loved the attention she bestowed on me, whenever it was given, and the laughter we both shared.

Taking a little time off from walking down memory lane, I wondered why my mom had faded from my mind's eye. After pondering the strangeness of it all, I rationalized that it was probably due to the way she willingly gave me up and never came back to claim me. In other words, if Doc Elliott's words were true, the good stuff with her must have been fleeting.

I remembered that Adam Harris worked at the cannery, a place that had nothing to do with food production or distribution. In fact, the cannery was actually a large, privately-owned, metal-machine shop, which specialized in manufacturing tin cans. Citizens in Mankato simply nicknamed it The Cannery.

Adam seemed to have no patience for me, and I had no feelings for him, except fear. His sheer size alone was enough to scare the piss out of me. The only things I remembered with clarity about Adam were the disciplinary beatings I received by his hand. It usually involved me being draped over his knee, while he used a belt on my butt. I got back at him, though, even if it was unintentional. Whenever he would put me over his knee, I would lose control of my bladder. He spanked me and I peed on his leg. You would think that after a few wet trouser legs, the man would learn. Apparently he didn't because I remembered numerous beatings.

The worst beating I ever took happened when I was five years old. I wondered why I couldn't actually remember the beating itself or why it even took place. All I could clearly remember was waking, only to find Adam standing over me. He yelled loudly, "For the love of God! What have you done?!" I remembered how my back felt like it was on fire. I had never felt such pain, before or since. When I next regained consciousness, I was lying in a hospital bed. The room was a strangely lit place. I was terrified, and cried out for my mom, but she was nowhere around. A nurse tried to calm me but did not succeed. Then, an unfamiliar lady, who I only remembered as being very pretty, appeared in the room and tried to console me.

She whispered so softly into my ear, words I had long since forgotten. It was to no avail because Adam was there, too. I wanted to get away from Adam. I didn't want him to hurt me anymore. I wanted Mom to come take me home, but she wasn't there. *Why wasn't she there?*

I then wondered why I couldn't actually remember Adam giving me that beating. He was the only one to ever lay a hand on me in such a fashion. I just knew he was the one responsible for putting me in that awful hospital room. As well, he was responsible for the hideous scars I carried on my back.

Why doesn't Brad believe me? I pondered the question for a moment and then remembered a particular conversation I had with Doc Elliot.

"Why can't I remember that day? I mean, I have these scars and I know I got them from being beaten half to death. Why can't I remember that day?"

In response, Doc Elliot smiled knowingly and said, "Jackson, a child's mind is a wondrous and miraculous thing. It somehow automatically knows how to remember that which is worth remembering. However, it also knows how to block out that which is hurtful or not worth hanging on to. It just happens. Believe me, that beating you took is truly not worth remembering. So, you should let it go. Hopefully, in time, that memory, and the scars on your back, will disappear entirely...forever."

I had listened carefully to the good doctor's advice and at the time thought it made good sense. Nevertheless, as I sat next to that creek, remembering everything else that had led me to this point in time, I suddenly felt a strong need to remember everything, including that hideous day.

Mom never came to the hospital, but during my waking hours, Adam was always close by. He seemed to watch over me like an old, mother hen, but while I was alone with him, I was in constant fear. I truly believed he would hurt me again and was just waiting for his chance to do it, but he didn't take that chance. In fact, he never made a single move toward me. He just sat close by in a chair, never saying a word to me. That is, none that I could ever recall.

On the day I was released from the confines of that hospital room, I was terrified to leave with Adam, especially when I saw that he was not driving us home.

Instead, he immediately took me to his sister's place, my Auntie Helen. He left me there, with no explanations, other than to say, "You'll be staying here for now, but I'll come for you soon." Naturally, I cried when he left, but it wasn't because he was leaving me. It was because I wasn't allowed to go home to Mom.

I lived with Auntie Helen for the remainder of my kindergarten year, about two and a half months. She was not unkind to me, but she wasn't what anyone would describe as extremely loving, either. She cared for me with a rather delicate balance of devout-Catholic discipline, mixed with an insensitivity I could never understand. I was fed, clothed, instructed to take my bath each night, driven to and from school each day, but she never laid a hand on me. No hugs and kisses were offered, or wanted, by her. She disciplined me by having me kneel on her hard, linoleum-covered, kitchen floor. There, I was taught to recite the rosary. In the short time that I lived with Auntie Helen, I must have been a very bad boy because I remembered reciting many rosaries.

Struggling to remember more about my biological family, my mind drew a blank. When I was separated from them, I was only five years old. Sitting by Indian creek and trying to recall all that I possibly could, it felt as though one day we were together and the next, without reason or warning, we simply weren't together anymore. At the beginning of the split, there were no real answers to any of my questions. Auntie Helen simply dismissed my queries by telling me that I was too young to understand.

Maybe Doc Elliot is right, I thought. *Maybe my mind automatically knows that they aren't worth remembering.*

While I stayed with Auntie Helen, I saw Adam for what I thought would be the last time. He picked me up on a Friday evening; I was to spend the weekend with him. At the time, he was staying in an old, flop house, just off Front Street. I did not want to stay with him in that strange room because I was still very much afraid of him. That Saturday, he took me out to his parents' farm, which was located somewhere just south of Mankato. I didn't know that I was going to see my grandparents for the last time, nor was it explained to me.

The visit itself was not monumental. I chased chickens, pestered the pigs, and pretty much made a nuisance of myself to all the farmyard animals. I played outside, as I always did, but when it was time to leave, I remembered no tearful farewell from either Grandma or Grandpa Harris. Truth be told, they had also faded from my mind's eye.

When Adam and I left the farm, it was dark. On the way back to town, I fell asleep. When I awoke, I was alone in Adam's beat-up Chevy. It was parked in an unrecognizable area of downtown Mankato. I panicked and immediately thought the worst. Some teenage boys found me wandering the dark streets, crying. They took me home to their mother, an enormous woman. She held me in her massive arms and calmed me. It took a little doing, but she finally coaxed me into telling her my father's name. Immediately, the teenage boys were given orders to comb the streets, grocery stores, and bars in search of Adam Harris. It didn't take them long to find him, either. He was in his favorite bar, the Eagles Club. If there was ever a time I was actually glad to see that man, it was then. He retook charge of me, thanked the lady and the boys, nonchalantly put me back into the car, and told me to go back to sleep. Then, as if nothing had happened at all, he again left me alone and went back to the bar.

Yeah, I sure do miss him. The sarcastic thought seared my brain.

After my kindergarten year, I was placed into foster care with the Matson family. Linus, Dottie, Pam, and Jimmy Matson were a close-knit group. Love and affection were very apparent between the four of them. However, they made it abundantly clear that I was not to be included.

Dottie, the mother, was okay, I supposed, but she was no Catherine Landry. She had no maternal instinct for me, none that I ever observed or experienced. She didn't even pretend to try. She constantly reminded me that I should not get attached because my living with them was to be a temporary arrangement.

Pam and Jimmy were just spoiled brats, who constantly blamed me for household crimes they committed. I remembered how Linus collected miniature matchbox cars. One day, Jimmy maliciously pulled the wheels off of his dad's favorite car and then blamed me for the act. Disregarding my denials, Linus gave me the belt treatment, while Jimmy stood off to the side, smiling.

Like Adam, Linus worked at the cannery. When he was at work, I was able to relax and play without stress. When he came home, though, I wanted to be in any other room but the one he occupied. I feared Linus as much as I did Adam. It was probably because he had the very same disciplinary style. I guess the scars on my back were no deterrent. They didn't make a strong enough case for the possibility that a beating may not be the wisest way to discipline me.

I spent an entire summer wondering when I was going home. Linus once told me that I had no home anymore. He said, "Your real family don't want you no more. That's why you're staying with *my* family, but it won't be permanent, so don't get any of those thoughts in that head of yours." He also told me the only reason they agreed to take me in was because Father Michael twisted his arm. Linus was a real charmer. Much of what I heard from him back then was hard for me to take. It would have been difficult for any six-year-old kid.

Together, Linus and Dottie made it very clear that I would never be a member of their family. The dog received more love and affection than I did. The situation was temporary and that was fine with me. I just wanted to know where I would be going next, plus how long it would it be before I could leave because I was always ready.

Linus was only the first to tell me that my real family would not ever come back for me. As I entered my first-grade year at Roosevelt Elementary and found myself still living with the Matsons, begrudgingly, I began to adjust to the truth of it.

The Matsons attended St. Joseph the Worker church and were responsible for initiating me into the congregation. It was the one positive thing I remembered them doing. I loved the church from the first time I saw it. It was little wonder it became my sanctuary at such a young age. It was beautiful, inside and out. Hearing from my social worker, Miss Churchill, and learning that I would attend St. Joseph's Elementary for my second-grade year, was exciting news to me. When she informed me that I was also going to move in with a new family, the Wilsons, I felt more than ready to make the change. At the same time, a bout of panic took hold of me. Even with the beatings I had taken, I had gotten used to living with the Matsons. I couldn't help fearing the possibility that the Wilsons' treatment of me would just be more of the same, or maybe worse.

It didn't take the Wilsons long to figure out that I was, as Danny once put it, a pretty screwed up little dude. My first night with them, I overheard Janet tell Brad, "If you get too close to him, watch the way he practically jumps out of his skin. There's something to that, Brad." Of course, later that evening, while I was in the bathtub, Janet figured it out. That's when she saw the scars on my back for the first time.

Right from the very get-go, the rules were made quite simple for me to understand. I was told by both, Brad and Janet, "As long as you live under our roof, you're our son. You're not special or different from Kurt or Danny, but the very same. They are your brothers...period."

It was all a huge mistake because I knew better. I knew I wasn't special, but I was definitely different. However, their words sure sounded good, even though I knew they weren't true.

Brad seemed to try the hardest to earn my trust. Eventually, I learned to love him just a tad bit more than the other three. It's probably because he was the very first father figure I could relax around. When he had to discipline me, he did so with patience and words of love. He promised he would never lay an angry hand on me. It was a promise he kept.

During my second year with the Wilsons, I saw my mother for the last time. It was in the spring, just before the end of my third-grade year. I came home and heard voices in the back yard. Janet and my mother were sitting out back, talking. Janet saw me enter the back yard first, so she got up from her lawn chair and came to me. As Janet took me by the hand, I noticed that her look was anything but happy. She did manage to put on a smile, though, and said, "You have a surprise visitor."

I was overjoyed to see my mom, but she didn't return the sentiment, not with the same amount of enthusiasm. I thought she had come to take me with her, but that was not the case. In fact, she didn't even try to help me understand why that wasn't going to happen. When she spoke, her voice was flat and void of much emotion. "No, Jacky, this is just a short visit and then I have to go."

Nobody told me that day would be our last meeting. Back then, I don't think anyone could have known. That night, I cried myself to sleep. I was so tired of not being wanted and hated being left behind. I just knew it was my fault because I wasn't like other kids. I began to believe that I would always be the kid who gets thrown away. I simply wasn't as good as other kids.

By my third year with the Wilsons, I had made a significant turnaround. I wasn't afraid of absolutely everything anymore. Brad, Kurt, and Danny taught me how to box and wrestle. When it came to teaching me how to defend myself, Kurt was the greatest! He told me, "Make a stand once, Jackson, and they won't pick on you anymore."

I was involved in a singular scuffle the entire time I lived with the Wilsons. It was my very first fight and it took place in the fall of my third-grade year. Greg Dodson, a notorious playground bully, told everyone he was going to beat the snot out of me after school. I was very afraid of Greg, but I was more afraid of being looked upon as a chicken. So, I agreed to meet him when classes were let out for the day. Word of the pending brawl spread fast in that school, so I wasn't surprised that my foster brothers had gotten the word.

Just before Greg and I squared off, Danny caught my attention. Whispering in my ear, he said, "Hit him once on his nose, just like we taught you." He then gave me a get-tough look to bolster my confidence.

"Then what?!" I asked.

In a matter-of-fact tone, Danny replied, "Then, we'll go home."

Kurt and Danny also taught me how all fights start with some pushing and shoving. "That's your time to put a quick end to it," they told me. "Get the first shot in and make it count." They taught me it was never okay to start a fight, but they also taught me to never back down from one.

That afternoon, Greg stepped in with his guard down, so he could push me, just like my foster brothers said he would. It was the sign I waited for. Surprisingly, I landed a stiff jab right to Dodson's face! Even more to my surprise, he went down hard and stayed there, holding his profusely-bleeding nose. I sensed immediately that the fight was over. I was somewhat fearful of the amount of blood I saw and got very upset about what I had done to Greg.

On the way home, Danny had to calm me down. He reminded me that it was Greg who picked the fight. "He had it coming," he said.

Nevertheless, I didn't feel that way. Fortunately, Kurt ended up being right about one thing. After that day, no kid in Mankato ever tried to pick a fight with me.

My years with the Wilsons were extremely happy. I loved Janet and Brad more than I ever could my real parents. Calling them Mom and Dad felt natural, even comforting. Kurt and Danny were better brothers to me than Derrick and Brian ever were. St. Joe's and the neighborhood had provided me with fantastic friends! Dave, Joel, Tony, Mike, and I had rapidly become a small brotherhood unto ourselves. We were like *The Little Rascals*, in the *Our Gang* series of old. So, I began to have notions that I would stay in that neighborhood, with the Wilsons, forever. Nevertheless, the fates plotted against me.

In the fall of 1968, just after the start of my fourth-grade year, Miss Churchill paid me another visit. She told me about a couple from Duluth, who were looking to adopt a son. They were shown my picture and decided they wanted to meet me. At the time, I didn't understand the concept of adoption, so it was explained to me. I was then asked if I wanted to meet the Landrys.

Even though I had given up all hope of rejoining my biological family, I wasn't overly excited about meeting and possibly being turned over to another strange family. So, I stalled by asking, "What if my real family comes to take me back?"

Janet said, "Listen to me and try to understand. The family who gave you up is never going to come looking for you. They do not want you back. They want you to be someplace else, someplace where you can be happy."

I wanted to tell her that I was happy with them, but for some strange reason, I just couldn't get the words out. I immediately felt the foundations of my world begin to shift and crumble a bit. Struggling to keep my composure, I looked to Brad and Miss Churchill. They both nodded their agreement with Janet.

"Do you think I should meet these people from Da-lute?"

This time it was Brad who voiced his opinion. "It's Duluth, buddy…and yes…we do. We think this could be a great opportunity for you."

Again, all three nodded their agreement.

Two weeks later, I met Brice and Catherine Landry for the first time. They came to Mankato for a weekend and I played tour guide for them. I showed them all around town, which didn't take very long in 1968. There just wasn't that much town to show off. When the tour was through, they took me to a matinee movie at the State Theater. We then went out to eat dinner, so we could get better acquainted.

At first, I was quite intimidated by the size of Brice. In addition, his blindness gave me the heebie-jeebies. However, by the end of the weekend, I was able to be more at ease with him.

During that first-meeting weekend, the Landrys hadn't made a huge impression on me. They were not exciting people. In fact, I found them to be rather plain and somewhat boring. They didn't seem to know anything about what kids really like to do for entertainment. However, their kind mannerisms strangely attracted me. Regardless, after that weekend, I truly didn't expect to see the Landrys again. But, once again, I could not have been more wrong.

By the early spring of 1969, I believed the Landrys had lost interest in adopting me. If they had, it was okay with me. I was perfectly happy to continue my life with the Wilsons. However, just before spring break, arrangements for another visit with the Landrys were made. They had paid to have me flown from Mankato to Duluth. To be honest, when I was told that I would be taking my first airplane ride, I was immediately catapulted onto cloud nine!

When Brad drove me to the small Mankato Airport, he had to tell me repeatedly to sit still in the car. It was my first trip to any airport. I was utterly fascinated by the many aircraft I saw. As we neared the tiny terminal, I could hardly control my excitement. When it was time to board the airplane, I was so caught up in the moment that I almost missed the sad look on Brad's face.

An extremely nice and very pretty flight attendant took my hand and began to lead me out onto the apron to board the plane. When I looked back and saw

Brad struggling, I broke away from her and ran back to him. Wanting to assure Brad that everything was going to be fine, I said, "I'll be back in a few days, okay?"

When Brad knelt to hug me, I saw tears welling up in his eyes. Holding me tighter than ever before, he softly said, "Alright, buddy. You have a good time, you hear?"

I had never seen Brad that emotional before; it unnerved me.

The Landrys had a large, fancy house on the central hillside of Duluth. It overlooked the Duluth/Superior Harbor, as well as a minute portion of the north shore of Lake Superior. I wanted to explore their huge dwelling, but we didn't spend hardly any time in that house. Instead, they took me camping with a group of friends they socialized with regularly.

We camped along the shore of Lake Superior, the largest freshwater lake in the world. To me, it was like seeing the ocean for the first time. I was amazed by the enormity of it. I had never been to a lake so big that I couldn't see the opposite shore. Those days spent camping with the Landrys was a wonderful experience for me. They told me they went camping often and I was thrilled at the prospect of seeing more of such sights. The whole world seemed to open up before me.

Before returning to Mankato, I spent one night in their large house. The living room had a huge, picture window, with window seat. From there, I could see the lake and Twin Ports harbor. I was mesmerized by the panoramic splendor that window afforded them. They also showed me the room they had renovated and decorated, just for me.

"This can be yours…if you want it," said Catherine.

I was overwhelmed by it all. The Landrys then told me they wanted me to come live with them. They wanted me to move in at the end of the school year.

"We hope, very much, that you can learn to like us enough to want us for parents," explained Catherine. "We would love for you to be our son."

"For always?" I asked.

Catherine smiled adoringly and then replied, "And forever."

I didn't know what to say. As I looked around the room they offered, I saw that it came equipped with almost everything a little boy could possibly want. Brice stood in the doorway, smiling, but he didn't speak. Catherine stood at my side, but then invited me with her hand to have a look around.

I moved forward and explored what could be mine, giving the couple my back. I quietly walked around, touching the many, wonderful trappings, just to make sure they were all real. I was so absorbed with what I saw that I didn't hear Catherine come up behind me. She made a gentle attempt to put her arms around me, a harmless enough gesture. But she had surprised me, and my habitual response was to recoil from such sudden and unwanted contact. I practically jumped out of my skin!

"I'm sorry!" exclaimed Catherine, jumping back in shock.

Looking warily at her, long seconds passed, but then I decided. "I'll come stay with you, I guess, but I'd better show you something first. When you see it, you might not want me."

Facing her, I pulled my shirt over my head and then turned around, showing her my back. Once again, Catherine came up behind me, but this time, I allowed her to put her arms around me. "We know all about your scars, honey," she said, then lightly kissed the base of my neck. "We still want you, if that's alright with you."

The only word I could make myself say was a tentative, "Okay."

The Landrys came to collect me Memorial Day weekend, 1969. I didn't know that leaving Mankato was going to be so excruciatingly painful. No one had prepared me for it, either. When that realization hit me, it was too late for me to change my decision. Because I was so young, I hadn't thought about having to say goodbye to absolutely everything and every person I loved or cared about.

I didn't want to leave the Wilsons, but they hadn't asked to adopt me. Part of my pain rested in the fact that, like my biological parents, Brad and Janet seemed perfectly willing to let me go. I could never make myself ask them why.

Weeks prior to my leaving, I felt the Wilsons begin to distance themselves from me. Kurt and Danny no longer talked to me as much or spent any significant time with me. They did try to explain that they would not be there when I left. It was

Danny who told me that neither one of them knew how to say good-bye. But both of my foster brothers stated that they just couldn't be there to watch me go.

Even Janet and Brad seemed to pull away from me some. That is, until my last evening in their house. I had just finalized the packing of what few possessions I owned and was about to go see my friends one last time, but Janet stopped me from walking out the door. "I thought you said good-bye to your friends already," she said.

"I did, but…"

"Well, I want you here with us then, kiddo," interrupted Janet. "Tomorrow, your new parents will be here to take you to your new home. But tonight, you're still my son and I want you here with me, okay?"

I couldn't say a word. Sadness had begun to take hold. I knew then that I was going to have to do what none of my friends would ever have to do, what no kid should ever have to do.

Janet led me into the living room and there we lounged on the sofa together, watching some unremembered program on the TV. I leaned back against her, my head resting on her chest. Janet held me to her with one arm, while slowly and lovingly stroking my hair with her free hand. For the last time ever, I fell asleep in her arms.

On the morning of my departure, Janet gave me my last hug and kiss at curbside. No words were spoken; it was over with quickly. With her hand cupped over her mouth, she then ran back into the house.

I fought to keep my tears from coming, but when Brad scooped me up in his arms, I lost the battle and sobbed uncontrollably. As he held me tight and kissed my cheek, tears streaked his face. "Good-bye, buddy," he said. "Be a good boy, okay? I love you. We'll always love you."

When Brad tried to put me down, I couldn't make myself let go. I knew I had to, but my arms wouldn't cooperate. So, Brad placed me in the car and then gently made me relinquish my grip on him. Putting on a brave smile, he then closed the door and waved.

We drove away in the Landrys' blue Buick sedan. Kneeling on the back seat, I watched Brad get smaller in the rear window. Because I had just been given away again, I felt myself dying inside. Brice kept reaching out to me from the front seat. He spoke ever so softly, telling me that everything was going to be okay, but his words didn't help one bit. My heart had been shattered and I was scared to death of my immediate future. We were well outside Mankato before I could stop my tears.

That first night, when Catherine turned off the lights and closed the door of my room, I lay in my new bed, never feeling more scared and alone. I rolled over, put my face into my pillow, and again cried myself to sleep.

I judged that my first summer in Duluth went relatively smooth. While getting used to living in completely different surroundings, I appreciated not having to worry about schoolwork. It wasn't easy having complete strangers for parents, but the Landrys worked very hard to make me feel at home. Their attempts to win me over in a hurry revolved mostly around providing me everything I had in Mankato, plus so much more. Since my old bicycle couldn't make the trip north, they immediately had me pick out a new one. I chose a blue, five-speed, Schwinn® Stingray. Then, at my request, Catherine helped me get signed up for Little League. When I learned I would be able to play baseball, I just knew things were going to be okay. They even bought me a new baseball glove to replace the old one Danny had handed down to me. However, I continued to use Danny's lucky mitt. That is, until I got the new one adequately broke in.

That June, Catherine actually walked me down the block and introduced me to Jerry Campbell. Jerry was my age and became one of my first neighborhood playmates. He, in turn, introduced me to other kids in the neighborhood, but none of us became instant friends.

It was also in June that the Landrys wanted me to begin getting used to calling them Mom and Dad. I did as I was told, but it felt totally alien to me until at least August. They were extremely patient, though, and didn't make a big deal of my occasional slipups. Sometimes, I forgot and accidentally called one or both of them by their first name. Mom would then give me a look that clearly told me to correct myself. Not too begrudgingly, I always did.

On July 15th that year, I spent my tenth birthday with a group of my parent's socialite friends. They were complete strangers to me, too, so I was quite miserable. Mom saw how I wasn't having a very good time, so she got the idea that I might like to call some of my Mankato friends on the telephone. When I talked to Joel, Dave, and Tony, I was thrilled to hear their voices. However, when I called Mike's number, no one answered, so I felt a little bummed out. Getting to talk to my Mankato friends helped make that birthday tolerable, but not much more than that.

I thought I was adjusting to my new surroundings just fine. That is, until the beginning of the new school year. Mom arranged for me to attend a private, parochial school, named Saint Jean's. So, instead of taking a three-block walk to attend the public school the whole neighborhood went to, I had to take a thirty-minute bus ride to the west end of the city. Unfortunately, my attending a different school kept me on the outs with the neighborhood kids, too. I asked my new mom why I couldn't go to the same school as Jerry and the others. "We can afford to provide you a better education than what your friends will get in public school," replied Mom.

I then asked, "Are we rich?"

"We are fortunate," replied Mom.

Mom's three-word explanation didn't help me understand the situation any better. But I was accustomed to adults failing in their attempts to help me understand why my life had to be so different. That is, in comparison to other kids I knew. So, when I saw that Mom wasn't going to be any better at it, I simply walked away, accepting her answer as another thing that was absolutely worthless to me. I rationalized that attending St. Jean's was just another one of many things that I would simply have to put up with, regardless of how I felt about it.

From the very start, it was difficult for me to make any new friends at St. Jean's. I did my best to fit in, but the other kids made me feel like an outsider. I was, after all, the new kid in town. Mom and Dad did their best to coach me through this phase by warning me that it would take time for my schoolmates to accept me. I took their word for it and initially remained optimistic. Experience had already taught me that if I bided my time, eventually I would fit in, just like I did at St. Joseph the Worker and the neighborhood I had so recently left behind.

I played football that year; the coach using me extensively on defense. He liked how I wasn't afraid to hit someone or afraid to be hit. What did he know about fear? The truth was, initially, I was deathly afraid of being hit. Nevertheless, I remembered what Brad, Kurt, and Danny taught me about facing my fears and it served me well. In very little time, I learned how getting hit during a game or in practice wasn't the same as getting beat on. By the end of the season, I was in love with the game!

When Mom and Dad got too close or made sudden moves around me, I was still a bit jittery, but I was getting better. However, I still couldn't tolerate being touched by strangers at all. I gave tentative hugs to Mom and Dad before bed. Mostly, it was because I thought it was something I was automatically supposed to do; it wasn't heartfelt. I missed everyone in Mankato terribly, but I refused to talk to the parents I was trying on for size about it.

In the spring of 1970, Mom, Dad, and I went through legal proceedings; I was finally adopted. When the formalities were completed, the judge wrapped his gavel once from his station and then declared me Jackson Andrew Landry, a name I instantly liked very much. Anything that distanced me from the disgraceful name of Harris was fine with me.

When we left the courthouse that day, I felt entirely different. I finally had, and belonged to, parents who actually wanted me. I wasn't too sure about the extended family, though. They were polite enough, when we were all together, but sometimes I noticed different looks being aimed in my direction. Mom and Dad said it would take time to fully position myself within the family. To my way of thinking – if I had the rules correct – since I had been adopted, my position within the family was supposed to be a done-deal. Once again, I just didn't understand why things had to be so different for me.

The real trouble didn't begin until my sixth-grade year. I still wasn't fully accepted by the other kids at St. Jean's. Apparently, my last name being changed from Harris to Landry seemed to cause some difficulty for them. I rapidly learned that being adopted carried a stigma that I had not been properly prepared for. As far as some of my schoolmates were concerned, I was a mutt.

I had gone through a growth spurt during the summer and discovered that I was much larger than many of the other guys that fall. I played football again and my new size made it easy for me to excel at the sport. However, being good at football didn't win me any popularity contests. It felt as though I was accepted as part of the team, but when I was off the playing field, it was an entirely different ballgame.

A teammate from a well-to-do family, who went by the name of Brantley Hartel, liked my issued football gear better than his. So, he strongly suggested we make a trade. In return, I just as adamantly suggested he get lost. At the time, we were in the locker room following afterschool practice. Suddenly, I became keenly aware that all eyes were on Brantley and me. I got the distinct impression that my teammates knew Brantley's intentions well in advance. I guess Brantley wasn't accustomed to people refusing him because he pressed the matter by shoving me against a row of lockers. For that, I flattened him with a stiff jab to his nose. The look on his face told me that he had expected no resistance from me. Knowing that I had surprised him, I should have waited to see if he had enough, but I didn't. Not giving Brantley any chance to recover, I launched myself onto him and hit him repeatedly in the face. For the first time in my life, I had lost control of my temper. Surprisingly, I didn't feel ashamed. Instead, I felt liberated. When the others pulled me off Brantley, I saw that I had bloodied him pretty good. Because he was the one who started the ruckus, I didn't feel bad about what I had done to him. Remembering Kurt's advice to me, I figured my actions would be a good psychological deterrent to anyone having thoughts of trying my patience again.

When Coach McFall saw what I had done to his star running back, he threatened to throw me off the team. Even though I wasn't in the habit of starting fights, I learned quickly that I would be held accountable for defending myself from someone more valuable than I.

John K. Lanphier

That winter, I was strongly urged to play basketball. Once again, my athletic ability won me a certain amount of acceptance on the team, but not within any particular social group. I played well and enjoyed the cheers of the crowd, especially when I scored. At first, Mom and Dad attended all the games. But then, they stopped coming because it was hard for Dad to get any enjoyment out of the experience. All he could hear was noise. I tried to understand his dilemma and even said it was okay. However, my emotional wounds were now growing deeper. My teammate's parents came to all the home games and many of the away games, but mine were no longer there to cheer me on.

Things did not work out at all the way I expected. Contrary to what Kurt taught me, guys continued to pick fights with me. I tried in vain to ignore their insults, but they always pressed the matter by either cornering me or taking the first swing. By the early spring, I was getting into way too many brawls and my temper was constantly getting the better of me. If someone pushed or shoved me, I threw punches that bloodied their noses or blackened their eyes. If someone tried to wrestle me down, I would keep my distance and use boxing techniques. In short, I was relying on Brad, Kurt, and Danny's training way too much. Realizing that the fighting was getting out of control, I asked Mom and Dad for help. They, too, were getting quite tired of replacing my torn school uniforms, so help was definitely in order. Mom talked with the nuns and with the school principal, but it didn't help one bit. When the nuns and teachers failed to supervise closely, my schoolmates continued to taunt me.

I fell into a depressed state and lost all interest in doing my schoolwork, so my grades suffered. I felt as though I truly didn't belong at St. Jean's. I had no idea where I did belong, but I was quite sure it wasn't there. Feelings of regret for leaving Mankato rapidly set in. I wanted to leave Duluth and go back to where I came from. I even wrote to Janet Wilson, telling her as much. In Janet's return letter, she practically dismissed the whole issue entirely, but did tell me to keep my chin up. When I was alone in my bedroom, which had become way too often, I looked at photographs of my friends from Mankato. I kept them, along with other memorabilia, in an old cigar box that Grandpa Mack had given me. How I wished I could go back and be with them.

In March of that year, I met Doctor Robert Elliot at Duluth's Human Development Center. At our first meeting, I wasn't overly impressed with him. Like Mom and Dad, everything about him seemed rather plain and unexciting. His hair had a slight wave and was the color of salt and pepper. He neatly parted it on the side. The plastic tortoise-shell reading glasses, which sat way too far down his slender roman nose, made him look a bit nerdy. When I talked, he seemed more concerned with what he scribbled on a notepad than listening to me. However, it was his voice that captured my attention most. It had a calming quality to it. When he asked questions of me, there was always neutrality in his tone. He seemed neither interested nor disinterested. When he spoke, I didn't feel judged, which would have made me leave immediately. To him, I supposed, I was just another troubled kid, nothing special.

The Doc and I spent our first few visits talking about my school and about all the fights I had gotten into. Mostly, he seemed to key in on my temper. He told me that he had talked with my teachers and most of them agreed that I was like a volcano – they just never knew when I was going to erupt.

At first, I didn't trust the Doc and wouldn't talk freely with him about anything. Back then, I didn't trust anyone, with the exception of Mom, Dad, and Grandpa Mack. However, in a surprisingly short period of time, I slowly began to open up to my psychiatrist. By May that year, I was actually looking forward to our sessions. It felt good to have someone actually listen and help me understand what was going on inside of me.

With Doc Elliot's help, I managed to limp through the rest of that school year, but my last report card was atrocious. I received an abysmal grade in math and had fallen way behind in my reading comprehension. Mom wasn't about to stand for that, so she hired a distant cousin to tutor me for the summer.

Cousin Kathy was working toward her teaching degree at the University of Minnesota. She was taking the summer semester off, so she was glad for the employment opportunity. Because Kathy was family, Mom made it worth her while, financially speaking. Kathy had a happy-go-lucky way about her and was extremely patient with me. We became good friends fast. Once I focused, she was able to get me caught up in mathematics and did so quickly. As a bonus, she touched on some of the things I would study the next school year. Her objective was to put me slightly ahead of my peers.

"Next school year, you're going to blow them away, Jackson!" I loved the energy Kathy had in her voice. She always made me feel as though I could do anything. All I had to do was keep the bad stuff in the world out and concentrate on more pleasant things.

That summer, Kathy sparked within me a true desire for reading. Together, we read entire novels. She told me that I read beautifully. During our sessions, she constantly tested my understanding of more complex words. Dad succeeded in getting me into the habit of having a dictionary close by, so I could look up the definition of words I didn't understand. My vocabulary grew rapidly, plus I took secret pleasure in understanding words that normally confused kids my age.

In no time at all, reading became my favorite pastime. Even after Kathy's tutoring sessions were over, I continued on with whatever book we were reading. She even introduced me to Shakespeare and taught me how to interpret his writings. We read stories by Dickens, Hemmingway, and Robert Louis Stevenson, just to name a few. When we began reading Salinger's, *The Catcher in the Rye*, I wasn't sure I would like it. In the end, it turned out to be one of my favorites. Books by S.E. Hinton were extremely meaningful to me. I could personally relate to her portrayal of the greasers against the socials, or Socs in *The Outsiders*. I even got into the habit of carrying books in my daypack, especially when I went fishing by myself.

Kathy and I made a real connection that summer. My reward for doing well was always a trip to the Dairy Queen for soft-serve ice cream. She also bought me an edition of *The Tales of Edgar Allen Poe*. The Black leather-bound book was beautiful, with gold tipped pages. It was one of the most splendid gifts anyone had ever given me.

Also that summer, Mom, Dad, and I camped on the weekends in Wisconsin. Our camper was parked all season long at Wasko's Campground, on Lake Minnesuing. I got to know some of the other kids, whose families also parked their campers there for the summer. We all had a great time together but seemed to understand that our friendship would only last that summer.

At the campground, I had a small crush on a girl from Bayfield, Wisconsin. Her name was Sherry McGuiness and she was plenty cute. Secretively, when Sherry was there with her family, I was extremely happy. We two fished, went swimming, and roasted marshmallows by fireside, but we were never alone together. Grownups or the other kids were our constant chaperones. When Sherry's family wasn't in camp, I didn't enjoy myself as much. I spent most of those weekends reading. I still didn't know how to talk to the opposite sex and thought perhaps Sherry suffered from the same affliction.

Labor Day weekend, all of us kids got together one last time. Summer was over and so was the camping season. As we all said, "See you later," knowing full well we probably would not, Sherry surprised me by giving me a quick peck on the cheek. Before I could say a word, or return the favor, she ran off to join her family.

Standing there, turning red from embarrassment, my thoughts were simple. *That just figures! She waited until it was too late!* Still, it was a great ending to a pretty good summer.

My summer visits with Doc Elliot went very well. Apparently, by the end of August, a noticeable change had taken place in me. At least, that's what the Doc said. "You're smiling, Jackson! That's great!"

At the time, I hadn't noticed, but I suddenly became cognizant of the fact that I was happier. I was even looking forward to the coming school year. Football season was coming soon and I could hardly wait. Yeah, a change *had* taken place.

That fall, for some unknown reason, Mom made me her pet project. Her lessons were all geared toward how to properly act around women. To me, her viewpoints were prudish and unabashedly old fashioned. I was expected to open all doors for her, stand when ladies entered or departed the room, seat myself at the table, only after helping Mom with her chair, and a whole passel of other things that had to do with good etiquette. "I'll make a gentleman out of you yet, young man." The statement came out of Mom's mouth more times than I cared to count. Still, I liked how she was trying to teach me to, as she put it, interact with young ladies.

I didn't truly believe girls my age liked that old-fashioned stuff, but Mom was adamant. Most of the girls I knew had a more cavalier approach to interacting with boys. That is, none of them were anywhere near as prudish or ladylike as Mom. I could see that changing with the times was not Mom's strong suit.

I honestly hated the idea of returning to St. Jean's for the seventh grade. But I was pleasantly surprised to find that things weren't as bad as I had anticipated. The kids accepted me more and, initially, no one tried to start any fights. I played football well with the team and St. Jean's enjoyed a winning season. That seemed to garner me even more acceptance. I still didn't have anyone I could call my best friend, but I wasn't alone all the time, either. Overall, life was beginning to feel not great, but at the very least, much better.

I still thought about my friends in Mankato, but I also became keenly aware that communication between us had come to an abrupt halt. I had not received a letter from any of them in just over a year. I didn't understand why or how I let it happen, but I had stopped writing to them, too. I wrote to all my Mankato friends the previous spring, but there had been no response from any of them. I still liked to pull out the old cigar box from time to time and rummage through the photographs. I also held up and stared at a Saint Christopher medal, which I also stored in the box. Like my other St. Joe's schoolmates, I received it in the third grade. Father Michael had presented one to each of us, just before the ceremony of our First Communion. Now, the small, blessed medallion, which hung from a silver chain, triggered memories of a cute girl, with blue eyes and shiny, black curls, secretly trading school pictures with me behind St. Joseph the Worker church.

Just before the holiday season, my self-esteem took another hit. Schoolmates talked openly around me about upcoming parties and get-togethers they were throwing or planned to attend. I wasn't invited to any of those social events. I was starting to feel differently about girls but didn't really know what to do about it. Mom's teachings didn't help, either. It wasn't something I talked about or admitted to anyone, including Doc Elliot. My grades were good, which kept Mom and Dad satisfied. I hadn't been in a single fight and things were looking up, so I didn't worry too much about the other stuff. I would have liked an invitation to some of those parties, but I consoled myself with the fact that there were always books to keep me occupied. I still felt happier than I had in a long time and just knew things were going to keep getting better. As usual, I could not have been more wrong. Over the holiday break, I suffered another setback.

My cousin, Trina, was Mom's favorite niece. Many times my ears had to endure Mom's gushing, "Oh, how I miss my Trina. I wish she would come visit me." Trina lived with her husband, Gilbert, somewhere in the back woods of Wisconsin, near Chippewa Falls. Gilbert was a good enough sort, but Trina was a spoiled brat. Dad had warned me to watch my step around her. "I know she's your mom's favorite, but don't be fooled by her," he advised. Personally, I had not perceived anything bad about her. But then, I had only seen her a couple times. I had not spent enough time around her to know why Dad's opinion of her was so uncharitable.

Right after Thanksgiving, Mom seemed especially happy. The closer it got to Christmas, the cheerier she became. That year, Mom and I worked together, decorating the house with a large assortment of Christmas decorations. Throughout the entire task, Mom hummed, sang carols, and talked excitedly about how much fun we were going to have. Most of Mom's family was scheduled to be at our place for dinner and a Christmas Eve celebration. It all sounded great to me, but I knew the real reason for Mom's jolliness – her favorite niece was coming. Still, Mom's happiness somehow rubbed off on me, too. I looked forward to the event because Mom came from a large family and when they all got together, a lot of storytelling and laughter usually took place.

When Christmas Eve finally arrived, I spent the entire day helping Mom with last minute preparations. Inside, I could hardly contain the excitement that was building. Together, Mom and I bought groceries, wrapped gifts, baked pies, set the dining room table, and other such chores. All my effort was willingly given. It kept me in high spirits and in anticipation of a wonderful celebration.

That night, we had a packed house. Every room was lit with an assortment of colored lights. Tinsel and garland hung all over the place and Christmas music played in the background. The ten-foot Douglas fir, which Mom and I had decorated in the living room together, got raves from the women. Little cousins chased each other around the house and generally made nuisances of their miniature selves.

I listened, as Uncle Ted told the same, worn-out jokes he told at all our family functions, and Grandpa Mack politely laughed at them. That is, I think he laughed. Grandpa Mack had the kind of laugh that always made me wonder whether he was actually laughing or coughing up a lung. I knew Uncle Ted wasn't Grandpa Mack's favorite, but that night, Gramps seemed to be making a special effort.

Because there were so many people in the house, windows had to be cracked open to let some of the frosty December air in. The men generally congregated in the living and dining rooms, while the women stayed busy as hens in the kitchen. Mom had me walk around with a silver platter and serve our guests something called hors d'oeurvres. I thought it was a pretty fancy word for crackers, topped with salami and cheese, or pickled herring. Regardless, I did it with a smile. I loved the whole atmosphere and was more than willing to help out.

It was after a bathroom break that I heard loud talking coming from Mom and Dad's study. Even though the door was closed, the voices carried nicely down the wood-paneled hallway. I tiptoed closer to study's door and listened, just to see if there was any real trouble going on behind it. In a short while, I recognized the voices as those belonging to Mom, Auntie Janice, and Trina. It sounded as though they were having quite the disagreement. I was too late to catch the entire conversation, but what I did hear was enough set me on edge.

"What are you getting at?" I heard Mom ask.

Trina asked in a rather snooty tone, "How is he different from the other charity cases that have lived in this house with you and Uncle Brice? Why did you have to adopt him?"

I then heard Mom. "Janice, you had better get control of your daughter…and do it quickly!" It was the first time I had ever heard anger in Mom's voice. Even from the other side of the thick door of oak, I could tell that Mom was furious.

When Auntie Janice spoke next, it wasn't difficult for me to deduce who Trina inherited her snooty attitude from. "Well, Catherine, you and Brice never did discuss your decision with the rest of the family. Don't you think you should have seen how we all felt about it first? Before making such a large decision, I mean. Don't you think we should have had some say in the matter? People *are* talking you know."

Mom fired back with both barrels. "We didn't discuss it with all of you because it's none of your darned business! How you may feel about it does not matter to us one bit! Brice and I could not care less what other people have to say, either! We don't answer to any of you, nor do we need your approval of anything we do! Shame on you both! Jackson is our son, and if there is anyone in the family who has a problem with that...well...they know where the door is! And I suggest they don't let it hit them in the derriere on their way out!" Even when mad, Mom had the ability to keep from using foul language. If Dad had been in the room, he probably would have told them all to go to hell, while laughing in their faces for merely thinking their opinions, of any kind, mattered to him.

At that very moment, I realized that I had a *real* mom, but at the same time, I was also devastated by my aunt and cousin's disapproval of me. Before anyone could discover that I had overheard anything, I quickly and quietly snuck back down the hallway, then upstairs to my bedroom. There, I lay on my bed, stared at the ceiling, and tried to get control of my emotions. Now I knew, with great certainty, there was something significantly bad about me. If I was not inferior, Mom's sister and niece would never have questioned my right to be a member of the Landry family, of that I was now convinced.

Temporarily bringing myself out of the past, I again tried to relax and simply breathed in the morning air. I listened to the gurgling of the creek's waters, washing over rocks and settling into the pool that I was halfheartedly fishing in. Birds chirped and a nearby squirrel chattered away. The sun had warmed me and all but dried my clothes already. Everything about the location was tranquil. The only disturbances that registered were the troubling thoughts that raced through my mind. *What makes me so different? What is it about me that made my family not want me? Why didn't the Wilsons adopt me? Why doesn't Mom's family accept me? Why do other guys always want to fight me? What the hell is wrong with me?! Why can't I be happy, just like everybody else?!*

Returning to my memories, I picked up where I had left off and stewed some more about the Christmas-Eve debacle.

I thought about how I had been so excited in the days leading up to that holiday, but then I overheard that unfortunate conversation between Mom, my aunt, and my cousin. That same night, at dinnertime, I managed to bury everything I was feeling. I even managed to act cordial toward Trina, when she sat next to me at the dining-room table, her and that fake smile of hers. I couldn't even look at my aunt. I had nothing to say to people who thought I wasn't good enough to be part of their family. Looking around at all the seated guests, I wondered who else sided with Janice and Trina. *Do they all feel the same way?*

Although I had already been seated at the big-people table, I suddenly had an overwhelming urge to be somewhere else. I no longer cared to spend another minute around two-faced adults. So, looking directly across from me, I gave my cousin Tommy the nod and pointed toward the kitchen. In return, Tommy rolled his eyes and emphatically nodded his agreement. In unison, we rose, grabbed our plates and then headed out of the room.

Understandably puzzled, Mom asked, "What are you two up to?"

Giving the room a big, but insincere, smile, I replied, "You guys are too loud. We're gonna eat in the kitchen."

Christmas for me was ruined. Even the wonderful gifts Mom and Dad bestowed on me brought little joy. However, I didn't want to ruin Mom and Dad's holidays – I owed them too much. So, I acted as though everything in my life was perfect. Purposefully, I kept the truth locked away, deep inside me.

When New Year's Eve came, Mom and Dad went out on the town with friends. I stayed at home by myself. Of course, Mom worried that I might not be comfortable with the idea of staying alone in that big house. But I put on another fake smile, showed her the book I would be reading, and gave her all kinds of assurances that I would be just fine.

After Mom and Dad left for their party, I did something I had not done in quite a while. I sat down and wrote letters to my Mankato friends. I even wrote one to Julie Falkner, knowing full well that I had no address to send it to. Like all kids, I remembered the name of the street and where her house was situated on it, but never paid any attention to the house number. Not to be put off by any of that,

I wrote to her anyway. In the letter, I wrote down heartfelt things I wished she already knew.

When my letter writing was completed, I felt pretty good about myself. I then went to the den and lit a fire in the fireplace. In a short time, I had a decent blaze going, so I just sat there and stared at it for I don't know how long. As I watched the flames lick away at the wood, I thought more and more about running away to Mankato. Then, uncontrollably, my mind switched gears on me. I remembered that I hadn't heard from any of my Mankato friends for over a year. In fact, I hadn't heard from anyone there for quite some time, not even Janet. Now, as anger built inside me, I changed my mind about mailing the letters. Instead, in a burst of rage, I threw them into the fire and watched them turn to ash.

Reading was now out of the question because I couldn't stop my mind from spiraling into the dark abys it was now heading. I wandered from room to room, trying to control the dreadful thoughts that coursed their way through my mind. I would have given anything to be someplace else. Anywhere would have been okay, as long I wasn't all alone inside that huge house.

Standing in front of the picture window in the living room, looking at the lights of the city and the harbor, I fought back my tears. I refused to cry because I felt too old for that immature behavior. For the first time ever, I cursed God for my life. I hated knowing that because of me, Mom was no longer a member in good standing within her own family. I wanted to leave Duluth more than ever. I had no idea where in this world I belonged. I was only certain of where I wasn't wanted.

After the holiday break, I endeavored to concentrate on my schoolwork. It was the least I could do for Mom, especially after she showed her willingness to toss her family out the door for my sake. However, as soon as I heard about what a great time my schoolmates had with their families and friends, my depression grew worse. Determined to be as good as any of them, I wore a smile for a mask, and even told lies about what a fantastic Christmas and New Year's I had.

Yes, I fooled everyone for a while. That is, everyone but Mom. She was the first to notice a negative change in me. I overheard her tell Dad that I was developing a couldn't-care-less attitude. When they broached the subject with me, I couldn't deny it. But, at the same time, I just couldn't bring myself to tell them why. I couldn't even tell Doc Elliot about it because I was certain he would tell my parents.

Thoughts of running away to Mankato happened daily. The fact that I had no idea what I would do if I actually got there was not important to me. I only concerned myself with getting away from the people and the place that didn't think I was good enough. If I ran away, it would solve all my problems and theirs.

Mom and Dad began pushing for answers, so did Grandpa Mack. Apparently, he noticed the change, too. As well, Doc Elliot was beginning to get on my nerves and my teachers were trying to stick their noses where I felt they didn't belong. I also became a bit paranoid about suspicious looks I seemed to be getting from my classmates.

That winter, I played basketball again, but doing so brought me no joy. Mom and Dad still did not attend my games. The only reason I played was because it helped me hide what was really going on inside of me. If I had quit the team, it would only serve to bring more suspicion on me.

My grades began to suffer again, and everyone pushed for answers as to why. I just wanted people to leave me alone. I may have had to take it when adults pushed me, figuratively speaking, but there was no way I was going to allow someone my age to get away with it. So, it was during that winter's low point that another spoiled and overly privileged school kid just had to prove how tough he was.

Darrin Anderson had been feeling pretty good about himself. He had gone through a major growth spurt in the past year. All of us at St. Jeans noticed how big he had become, but none of us were impressed. He was a good four inches taller than me and a lot heavier. However, his weight and size had nothing whatsoever to do with muscle. Darren was not fat so much as he was downright obese. In the lunchroom, he stuffed himself like a pig. Additionally, Darrin was probably the biggest non-athlete in our class. Still, bullies who once picked on Darrin, when he was shorter and thinner, shifted their attention to much smaller targets.

Early in March, while in class, Darrin began a feeble attempt to bully me. Our math teacher, Mrs. Metcalf, had been summoned to the office for an important telephone call. Everyone knew Darrin had a crush on Sarah Caskey. I, unfortunately, occupied the desk next to her. Darrin poked at me and rudely ordered me to switch seating with him. I would have done so, too, if it hadn't been for the pitiful look Sarah gave me. Her eyes practically begged me not to move.

If I said I wasn't secretly attracted to Sarah, I'd be lying through my teeth. She had amazing, hazel eyes and long, wavy, blonde hair. The smattering of freckles she had along her cheeks were what really got my attention, though. Yes, Sarah was definitely cute enough, but like all other girls, I just knew inside that I didn't stand a chance with her. But that didn't mean I was willing to let Darrin push me out of the way, either. So, instead of doing the smart thing, I turned to Darrin and heard myself say, "Get lost, fatso."

That's all it took. Thoroughly enraged that I wasn't going to give in to him, Darrin glared. He then boasted to all present that he would be trashing me after school. I tried to ignore everyone's looks by keeping my eyes on my math assignment, but then Sarah tugged at my sleeve. When I looked at her, she smiled and whispered, "Thanks, I don't want that tub of lard anywhere near me."

Because my desk had become the proverbial hot seat, I simply rolled my eyes and turned my attention back to my book, while thinking, *I should've given him the desk. What do I care?* But I was habitually locked into a paradigm that made it impossible for me to give in to the obnoxious behavior of others.

I truly had no intention of fighting Darrin after school, that day or any other. Doc Elliot's words, "It's better to walk away from a fight before it happens, rather than after," took root in my head. Grandpa Mack's advice was valuable, too. "When you've bested a fool, you've done nothing." Kurt and Danny taught me to never back down, but I just couldn't see the value in hurting Darrin, especially since I was convinced that he, in fact, did not stand a chance against me. So, I was absolutely resolved to get away from school before anything bad happened.

When classes ended for the day, kids hurried for their lockers. Everyone retrieved their winter coats, hats, scarves, mittens, or gloves. Barely taking time to put any of those articles of clothing on, they all bolted for the doors, which led to the school yard and bus stop. I just knew they all wanted to be in position for when Darrin and I went head-to-head. However, I was in no hurry at all. My bus wouldn't leave until I was on board and I had planned to make a beeline for it. So, while standing at my locker, gathering my books and preparing to leave, I took my sweet time. I even prepared myself for all of the snide comments that most assuredly would come my way. If I didn't fight, I would be labeled the biggest chicken in school. I kept telling myself that I truly didn't care what anyone thought or said. But the honest-to-God truth was that I did care, very much. I loathed people thinking that I was somehow so much less than their selves.

When I finally stepped outside and began to make my way toward the line of waiting buses, I quickly observed that the playground was packed with young spectators. Just as I had predicted, the usual idiots – the ones who were always spoiling to see a fight – began to mercilessly goad me. As I hurried toward the bus, I didn't see Darrin anywhere, so I thought I might make a clean getaway. *If I can just get on the bus and into my seat, it will all work itself out,* I thought.

Unfortunately, when I arrived at my designated bus, there was already a line of kids ahead of me, waiting to get on. So, I stood quietly at the back of the line and waited my turn to board. Wishing the line would hurry, I concentrated hard, so I could tune out the many obscenities that the instigators yelled at me. Suddenly, I felt someone roughly grab the back of my down-filled parka. When I whirled around and saw Darrin Anderson, I was not even remotely surprised.

With a vicious sneer plastered to his smug mug, Darrin announced, "No you don't, Landry, it's time to get your ass kicked."

Facing an overconfident Darren Anderson, I shook my head and whispered to myself, "Okay, dumbass, if this is what you really want."

Whatever happened next, whatever harm I did to Darrin, in my mind, it was all justified. I had done everything possible to stay out of this fight. Now, I could hardly wait for what I knew was coming. Once and for all, I was going to show everyone what happens when you pick on me.

The behemoth sloth named Darrin came at me with his guard down. Calmly, I waited until he was just in range. Then, the familiar, metallic taste of adrenalin filled my mouth. I literally yelled, "YOU IDIOT!" In the same instant, I threw my first punch directly at his nose, putting everything I had behind it.

Darrin was lucky that day because I wore my heavily-padded mittens. When I landed the first punch, it caught him totally by surprise. I don't know if it was the force of the blow, or him simply losing his footing on the snow and ice, that made him fall. Regardless of which, Anderson went down extremely hard. The look on his face told me he that had no idea what he had gotten himself into. It should have been enough for me, but it wasn't. I had too much anger stored up inside and I was about to take it out on a fat, unskilled, and overmatched opponent.

In a split second, I was on top of Darrin, pinning him to the ground. I then unleashed a barrage of punches to the side of his face. He was absolutely helpless to defend himself, but I didn't care. I couldn't stop myself from pummeling him. It was no longer Darrin that I was hitting, but rather, some faceless demon.

I don't know how much time passed before a teacher showed up and tried to pull me off the blubbering meat sack, but I didn't know it was a teacher. I simply felt a hand grab the base of my neck from behind. Without looking, I reached behind me, grabbed someone's groin area and then squeezed...hard. I was now completely out of control and, not unlike a vampire, badly in need of more blood. Obscenities that I had heard often, but never spoken out loud, spewed forth from my lips.

As suddenly as it all began, the brawl ended, when powerful hands finally took charge of me. I was literally ripped from the fat boy and found myself in a reverse bear hug, much like Kurt used to put me in when we wrestled. However, the arms that held me now were not squeezing the life out of me. The arms simply held me in check, so I could do no further harm. I then heard a calm, familiar voice in my ear. "Settle down, Jackson. It's me, Mr. Gustafson."

Mr. Gustafson was my English and homeroom teacher. He was also one of my favorites, but none of that registered just then. I struggled to get away, but Mr. Gustafson held me fast and continued talking softly, calming me down and bringing me back into reality. Finally, I quit fighting him and like a rag doll, went limp. Mr. Gustafson then put me down and without saying another word, put his hand on my shoulder and guided me back inside the school.

The next thing I could recall, I was sitting in the principal's office, waiting for my parents to come collect me. I refused to talk to anyone in the room and when they got too close, I instinctively recoiled. When Mom and Dad finally arrived, they were, of course, furious. I had no explanation for them, either. I just wanted to get out of there. I simply wanted to leave and never come back, but that wasn't going to happen on my timeline.

I was questioned, almost interrogated, for about a half hour, but I remained committed to keeping silent. Even Mom and Dad got nothing from me. I was threatened with sitting there all night, if that's what it took, or until they got some answers. I didn't care what they wanted, nor did I budge.

Mom became frantic, "Jackson, do you have any idea what you've done to that boy?!"

I had no idea how severely I had hurt Darrin. At that particular moment, it was one of many things I could not have cared less about. *The fat-ass shouldn't have pushed me into it*, I thought, but voiced nothing. Instead, with renewed anger building and tears welling up in my eyes, I just looked defiantly back at Mom. Determined not to cry, I choked it all back and fortified myself for whatever came next. Once again, I was about to pay a dear price for finishing what someone else had started.

Screw it, I thought. I don't care anymore. Why should I? I don't belong here. I never did and never will.

In disappointment or disbelief – I couldn't be sure which – Mom shook her head. Finally, she must have figured out that they weren't going to get any immediate answers because she then announced that we were leaving. On the ride home, which seemed to take forever, Mom informed me that I had been suspended from school for three days. Her words barely registered. When we got home, I still refused to speak, so I was sent to my room. There, I changed out of my dirty, school uniform and then flopped down on my bed. When I was called down for dinner, I refused to go. Neither Mom nor Dad pressed the matter, either.

That evening, I made serious plans to leave Duluth. I would have left that very night, but I had no idea where I might go or how I would get there. Besides, it was still the dead of winter, so I postponed my decision to leave until the coming spring. I would simply use the time to formulate a better plan. Later that night, the events of the day had exhausted me to the point that I didn't even bother to get out of my jeans and sweater at bedtime. I simply fell into a deep, but greatly troubled, sleep.

The next day, I was scheduled an emergency session with Doc Elliot. As I sat across from him, I was determined that he, too, would get no more information out of me than anyone else had. In turn, he communicated his genuine concern for how quickly things seemed to have changed for me. "You were doing so well, Jackson. What happened?"

Determined not to answer, I just sat there and glared at him. Doc sat very still and just looked back at me. It was a battle of wills and one I was determined to win. Then, I let my eyes wonder and I looked around the room. It was no surprise to me that my gaze landed on his bookshelves. They were filled with what I believed to be reference books the Doc used for his practice. I wanted to ask him if he read other books, too, but that would require me to utter words. So, I simply sighed and affixed my eyes back on the good doctor. For long minutes, we simply sat in silence.

My uncharacteristic boldness would not last, though. In my heart, I knew that I was disappointing Doc and for some unclear reason, I cared about that. Then, I saw something that changed the status quo. It was simply a look the Doc gave me. Gradually, his facial features softened and when they did, something in my head gave way. Overwhelming emotions built up inside me. I didn't want to let them escape, but at the same time, I wanted to let absolutely everything out. Anger, pain, frustration, mistrust, and sadness welled up within me until I thought I might explode. I felt tears coming on and this time I could not fight them back. Finally, the dam burst, and I allowed myself to cry. Doc didn't move. He waited patiently, but then my anger took over.

Seemingly out of nowhere, I raged, "THIS PLACE AND THAT SCHOOL HAPPENED TO ME! THEY WON'T LET ME BE HAPPY HERE! NOBODY WILL LET ME BE HAPPY HERE!" I couldn't hold back anymore, so I let the words come freely, but lessened the volume a bit. "I don't belong here," I sobbed. "I never did. I don't want to stay! I don't want to stay anywhere I'm not wanted!" I sat there and cried, wishing I could just leave.

"That's good, Jackson," coaxed Doc. "Let it all out. Get it all out and don't hold anything back." Doc then got up, came over, and sat next to me. He tried to put an arm around me, but as always, I recoiled from his way-too-intimate gesture. He didn't push by trying again. Instead, he went back to his chair and patiently waited for me to calm down.

When I finally regained control of my faculties, Doc handed me a box of tissues. When he spoke, it was in his soft, non-judgmental tone. "I talked to your home room teacher, Mr. Gustafson. He told me that when he pulled you off the other boy, it was as if you didn't even know where you were at the time. Blind rage he called it. Can you tell me about that?"

At first, I didn't want to say anything, but then I changed my mind and decided to tell Doc everything. I used the rest of the session to tell him about Christmas Eve and the not-so-wonderful family I was adopted into. I told him how hard I had tried to stay out of the fight, but everyone kept pushing me toward it. I asserted, "People are always pushing me. One way or another, people are always pushing me. But this time, it was just too much. I don't want to be here anymore. I want to go home. I want to go back to where I belong."

At the end of my three-day suspension, I hated the very thought of returning to school. As I walked the halls between classes, I felt eyes boring holes into my back. Even Sarah Caskey looked uneasy, as she sat next to me in Mrs. Metcalf's math class, trying in vain not to catch my eye. *So much for being a hero,* I thought.

When I saw the damage I had done to Darrin, I never felt more ashamed. He had two black eyes from the broken nose I had given him. There were also various cuts and bruises along both sides of his face. The worst of it was the fear I saw in his eyes. Darrin refused to speak or even look at me. I couldn't imagine his humiliation and for the first time ever, I hated myself. Because of the extent of his injuries, coupled with how I had completely lost control, I couldn't forgive myself, let alone ask for forgiveness.

For the rest of that school year, the Doc and I met. He was able to help get me back into a better frame of mind, so I could at least concentrate on my schoolwork. But I don't think he kidded himself for a minute about the deep depression I had fallen into. I was no longer interested in making him believe that there was even the slightest possibility of me being happy in Duluth. I remained adamant. I wanted to leave Duluth and return to Mankato. I needed Brad, Janet, Kurt, and Danny. I needed my friends. I needed to go back to where I belonged, back to where I was happiest in my short, screwed-up life, and there was nothing the Doc could say or do to change my mind.

Inevitably, Mom and Dad found out how Auntie Janice and Trina had hurt me. When Mom realized how much damage their words had caused, she was furious with them. With the exception of Grandpa Mack and a few others, the three of us stayed away from most of Mom's side of the family. For weeks, when Janice called the house, Mom hung up on her. I learned then that Mom truly knew how to hold a grudge. Watching Mom refuse to talk to her sister did not do my heart any good. In fact, it worsened my depression. I felt that she should not have to deny her sister, not for the likes of me.

Doc Elliott and my parents teamed up and tirelessly worked on me. They continually assured me that there was no life at all waiting for me in Mankato. *Maybe so*, I thought. *But there is no life for me here, either. I guess I just don't belong anywhere.*

At school, the suspicious and disapproving looks I got from other kids kept up for what seemed like weeks. I tried to convince myself that I truly did not care anymore, but it was just another lie I told myself in order to get through my days.

For the rest of that school year, nobody dared to pick a fight with me. Additionally, because I spent a lot of time alone, I was able to get my grades back up to where they belonged. Books became my constant companions and I allowed myself to get lost in them. Unlike most of the guys in school, I had absolutely no interest in girls. I felt that girls were just a big nuisance. I thought they probably felt the same way about me. Mostly, I felt that girls in school, the ones who knew me, were simply afraid to come near me. I didn't trust anyone and saw right through any polite, but insincere, smile that came my way. My guard was up, and I was not going to let it down for anyone.

When the school year finally reached its end, I was actually able to enjoy the last few days before embarking on the summer break. At recess, I was included in baseball games, which helped prepare me for the Little League season. During my last math class, I was caught completely by surprise by Sarah Caskey. When the final bell rang, she reached across the thin space that separated our desks and slipped me a note. When I opened it, I saw that she had provided me her phone number and address. The note also asked me to stay in touch over the summer. I didn't take her request too seriously, nor did I think it made me special. I had witnessed many kids do the very same thing that whole last week of school. It didn't even dawn on me that Sarah had been the only schoolmate to make such a gesture toward me. I thought she probably slipped such notes to most, if not all, her classmates. I did, however, give her an insincere smile and nodded my agreement.

At the beginning of summer, baseball, books, and fishing by myself were the only activities I looked forward to. I hardly looked forward to camping with my parents because we were not returning to Wasco's, on Lake Minnesuing. Instead, Mom and Dad thought it would be better if we picked new spots throughout the northland. I was able to appreciate coming in contact with campground kids because they didn't know me. I had learned from experience that there would be no expectations of staying in contact. So, it truly made no difference to me, not one way or another.

At the beginning of June, Mom prodded me to go outside and play with the neighborhood kids. I tried it a few times, but I couldn't get interested in any of their silly, little games. Nevertheless, I made sure I didn't mope around the house because I knew Mom would put me to work. Instead, I went on long hikes to secret places of solitude. Usually, there was a fishpond or a creek to drop a line into. There, I would think my thoughts, read my books, and get lost in a world that only existed inside my head. I had brief moments of happiness, but when those moments came around, I was usually alone. I regressed to where it felt as though I simply walked around in my reality but looked forward to nothing. My depression was now a constant because I had nothing of any substance to share with anyone.

One night in late June, Mom and Dad sat me down in the living room for a talk. They told me of how they worried about me. They could see how unhappy I was and knew it was because I didn't have any close friends. They knew of my lingering desire to return to Mankato. They went on to tell me how they had been discussing matters with Doctor Elliott. Then, they told me something that really made me pay attention. I could scarcely believe my ears when Dad said, "Doctor Elliot recommends that we send you back to Mankato…for a visit, that is." Dad then went on to explain how they had arranged a trip for me. The Wilsons had already been contacted and were anxiously awaiting my return, which was set for August.

At first, I was so excited that I couldn't speak. If Doc Elliott had been there, I probably would have kissed him. It was like a dream come true. I felt like pinching myself to ensure that I wasn't asleep.

Mom then told me there were a couple of stipulations I must agree to. First, I had to see Doc just before leaving for Mankato. There would be another appointment with him immediately upon my return.

Whatever Doc wants, Doc gets! I was ecstatic. August couldn't come fast enough!

My thirteenth birthday came and went, as did the entire month of July. I was happier than I had been in a long time. At the birthday party, which Mom and Dad threw for me, I was able to fool everyone. I made like I was sincerely happy to see all of my parents' friends. In truth, I was indifferent to the whole lot of them. Since I didn't have any real friends of my own, Mom invited a bunch of her socialite friends and their kids. I knew them all but could not care less about them being present. The people I really wanted to be with were 235 miles south of where I stood.

The best birthday gift I received came from Grandpa Mack. He bought me the Twins windbreaker and three tickets to a Minnesota Twins ball game. At the end of the month, Grandpa Mack drove Tommy and me down to the Twin Cities. We used my birthday tickets and watched the Twins beat the Chicago White Sox, one-to-nothing. It wasn't the most exciting game we ever attended, but it was a win.

I played baseball with zeal that summer. It didn't bother me one bit that I wouldn't be able to play for the entire season. Actually, I was anxious for it to be cut short. In addition, it was okay that Mom and Dad didn't attend any of my games. Like football and basketball, they were never in the bleachers and I had become accustomed to their absence. In their stead, Grandpa Mack came to most of the games and cheered for me. He, Tommy, and I were becoming real pals. No, it wasn't hard for me to smile in those waning days of July. Every day was bringing me closer to Mankato and the people my heart truly desired.

A few days prior to leaving for my trip south, I kept my appointment with Doc Elliott. I was in high spirits that day, but Doc was not in a playful mood.

"Jackson, do you think I've ever lied to you?"

"No sir."

"Well, I'm not going to start now. There's a reason I want you to go to Mankato. In order for me to help you, I need you to go there and find out the truth. That is, I need you to go there and find out that there is nothing waiting for you there."

I immediately lost my smile, and I gave him a straight look. *Geez, Doc, are you being straight or just trying to bring me down again?*

Doc continued, "Mind you, I also want you to have a good time. I want you to see your friends and find your smile again." He then tossed a large, thick folder on the coffee table before me. "That's you in that file. It's full of pain and anger, just like you are full of pain and anger. During your trip, what I'm hoping you will learn is all that the pain and anger did not originate here in Duluth. It started in Mankato and followed you here. You've just never been able to recognize that fact…or taught how to handle it properly. I can't teach you those things until you learn the truth, believe it, and understand it. So, go to Mankato and find your smile, but also find out the truth about yourself. There's one, last thing I want you to do there and it's very important."

Considering his words carefully, I asked, "What is it?"

Doc looked me straight in eye and then said, "Say your good-byes, Jackson. Whether you believe it or not, there is no life for you in Mankato, not while you're growing up anyway. It's here in Duluth, where your parents love and care for you deeply."

Doc Elliott had some other words of wisdom for me. Mostly, that stuff was about what I should and shouldn't do during my visit. When I finally left his office, I had a lot to think about. I wanted to be happy in Duluth, but everything I had experienced told me that just wasn't going to happen.

What if Doc is right? What if there really isn't anything for me in Mankato? If there's nothing for me there and nothing for me here, where is my place in this world?

Chapter 6

Still lounging on the fallen cedar by Indian Creek, a voice called out to me. It was a vaguely familiar voice, too, but it seemed to come out of nowhere. When the voice called out to me again, it immediately snapped me out of my trance-like state. It was Tony Milner, yelling, "Hey, Jackson, are you sleeping down there or what?!"

When I looked up, I saw him carefully making his way down the same, narrow, steep path that I had negotiated earlier. Loaded down with a daypack and fishing gear, Joel Brighten followed close behind.

Feeling genuinely glad to see them both, I called out in response, "I was wondering if you guys were ever going to show up. What time is it?"

"Almost nine-thirty," replied Joel. "You catch anything yet?"

In truth, I had been so deep in thought that I never thought to check my line. But, instead of telling them that, I lied. "Naw, it's been pretty slow. I thought I had a couple of bites earlier, but he wouldn't take it."

The three of us spent the rest of that morning fishing. We kept conversation light and I pumped them for more information about the changing face of Mankato. As we chattered on, I pretty much gave up hope of ever catching a fish because we were making way too much noise.

At one point, Joel reached into a brown paper bag and produced an unopened pack of Lucky Strike cigarettes. He had swiped it from his dad's stash and threw it in with his lunch. As we talked on, Joel offered a cigarette to Tony and me.

I had never tried smoking before, not even out of curiosity. I hated cigarette smoke, especially when my parents lit up around me. In contrast, Grandpa Mack's pipe tobacco didn't smell too bad. In fact, I kind of liked it. But I was pretty sure that smoking was a habit I would never pick up. Overall, I thought it was just plain disgusting. However, that morning by the creek, I was not about to act like a wimp in front of my two friends.

I accepted the cigarette and a match. After lighting the small, white cylindrical object, I drew smoke into my mouth, but refused to inhale. I tried to appear like it wasn't my first time, so did Joel and Tony. All went well until Tony dared me to inhale. When the smoke hit the back of my throat, I thought I might actually choke to death. Joel and Tony tried to inhale, also. Both experienced much the same results as me. When my friends stopped hacking and coughing, I asked, "You guys smoke often?"

Looking at each other and chuckling, the two replied, "Nope."

As it turned out, it was the first time for all three of us. We then decided that all we needed was some practice. So, not long after we finished our first cigarette, we tried a second. That next cigarette didn't go down any easier than the first. In fact, I never actually smoked the whole thing. About halfway through it, my stomach vehemently protested. I bolted from where we sat and vomited in some nearby bushes. Joel and Tony were not far behind me.

As I wiped slime from my mouth, I said, "Yeah, we're cool alright."

When our stomachs finally settled down, we laughed. Joel crumpled the remainder of the pack and threw it downstream. We then finished cleaning up in the creek.

The fish weren't biting at all, so we quit at noon and headed back to the neighborhood. While walking on the train tracks, Joel asked what I was doing later on. I told them about the party I would be attending later that evening.

Tony exclaimed, "Older women?! Oh man! You've got it made in the shade!"

"How do you figure?" I asked.

"You're the new guy in town," explained Joel. "Chicks dig that."

"It's not that way up north. I've been the new guy plenty up there and the girls couldn't care less."

"That's big-city stuff up there," rationalized Tony. "Down here, it's a small town. Girls go crazy over any new guy who shows up. Don't worry man! While you're here, you're gonna get all kinds of attention. You just wait 'n' see."

I stopped abruptly and looked at Tony like he had gravel for brains. In return, Tony shrugged his shoulders and blurted, "You can look at me like I'm crazy all you want, but you just wait 'n' see."

Feeling confident that there was absolutely no truth in what Tony alleged, I simply walked on in silence. I mean, why start an argument over subject matter neither of us knew anything about?

The rest of the afternoon was spent hanging out with the guys in Tony's front yard. Later, Dave Lester joined us. He was pretty excited about having a baseball game all set for Tuesday afternoon.

"Some of the girls will probably show up while we're playing," said Dave.

To that, I said nothing. I had been looking forward to the game, but I was rapidly changing my mind. I still had no use for girls, let alone girls at a baseball game. They usually wanted to play, too, which just screwed things up. Then, there was the issue of exactly which girls would be showing up. I still wasn't in any mood to come in contact with any of the girls I remembered. I was afraid they wouldn't remember me and that would just make me feel worse. Nevertheless, it appeared likely that Tuesday was going to be judgment day.

Maybe it'll be okay, I thought. *The girls I've seen in town so far have been nice. I like Janelle and Carrie. They're pretty sweet. Just relax and remember what Janelle told you.*

Just then, I heard a car horn. It was Janet, returning home from work. I said, "See ya later," to the guys and headed to the house. It had been a good day thus far and I wanted to visit with Janet for a while. I was sure she would appreciate some help in the kitchen, especially since I would be disappearing that evening with Kurt and Danny.

During dinner that night, I listened closely to my foster brother's chatter. They seemed genuinely excited about me joining them for the gathering at Janelle's house.

"I'm glad you're coming with us tonight, little brother," said Danny. "You just wait, we're gonna have a blast!"

"Doing what?" I asked.

Clearly taken back by my question, Kurt and Danny looked up from their plates and then to each other. To me, it seemed that both wanted the other to come up with some kind of believable answer. Kurt finally said, "I don't know about you, but I know what Danny and I will be doing."

Smiling, I said, "Yeah, I know…You two will be playing patty fingers with the girls and I'll get to hang out with Larry."

"Aw," said Danny. "It won't be that bad. They have a pool table, too!"

Upon hearing that, I immediately perked up. As far as I was concerned, when a pool table was available, the possibilities for having a good time increased exponentially. I was now very much looking forward to the evening ahead.

After dinner, Kurt and Danny took care of cleaning the kitchen, while I washed and changed my clothes. I had no idea what the proper decorum was for attending one of those shindigs, so I winged it by simply putting on a plaid, short-sleeved button front and a clean pair of blue jeans. When I returned to the kitchen, my brothers looked me over.

"Didn't you bring anything better than that to wear?" asked Kurt.

"Yeah, but what's wrong with this?"

"Never mind," said Danny. "That'll do."

Feeling quite self-conscious, I repeated my question. "What's wrong with what I have on?!"

Kurt shook his head, gave me a disapproving look, and said, "It looks like you're going fishing again. You're going to a party, dummy. Girls like it when you dress a little better."

What do I care about what girls like? The thought of getting dressed up, just to go hang out and shoot pool, seemed a bit ridiculous to me. At the same time, I didn't want to stick out like a sore thumb.

Kurt then instructed Danny to take me back upstairs and help me pick out something more appropriate to wear. Immediately, Danny slugged my arm and motioned with his head for me to follow him.

Danny rifled through my belongings and picked out a suitable shirt and pair of dress slacks. Because both items had been sort of crammed into a dresser drawer, they were in dire need of ironing. So, Danny instructed me to go have Mom help me press them. He also told me to get a move on because we were running late.

When my clothes had been properly ironed, I changed as fast as I could. I then went to the mirror and ran a comb through the mess on top of my head. Feeling ready, I met my brothers in the kitchen again.

Giving me the once over, Kurt nodded his approval and said, "Better. Now, we're late so let's get out of here.

Upon entering Janelle Peterson's house, I was not surprised to find that it was much like the Wilsons' place. Many of the houses in that area of town had similar floor plans. Most of the living areas were located at street level. Basements were usually renovated into comfortable entertainment areas, complete with wet bars and lounges. To me, it seemed that every man had a secret ambition of being a tavern owner. Regardless, teenagers loved having such areas to hang out in, especially when adults kept their supervising eyes upstairs.

When Kurt, Danny, and I entered the basement, I watched Janelle and Carrie fuss at my brothers for being late. Unmoved by female blustering, my foster brothers just put their respective girl in a lip-lock. That quieted them right down, even if it was just for a moment or two.

Per my normal reaction to new things, I battled apprehensive feelings about being there, but Janelle and Carrie's welcoming hugs helped put me at ease. When I saw the Petersons' pool table, I relaxed even more. Then, Larry Armstrong shook my hand and proclaimed me as his pool-playing partner. "Watch out guys," warned Larry. "This kid can shoot!" He then challenged any and all takers to step on up for a game of eight ball. Having Larry put so much confidence in my ability felt great. After Larry and I beat the first set of challengers, I saw the approval in their eyes. Then and there, I just knew I was going to have a good time.

While making my way to the bar for a root beer, I listened to the music, which blared from a large, Magnavox stereo console. A couple of teens, who were dancing already, gave me curious looks as I passed by. I simply tried to act casual and hoped my anxiety didn't show too much.

I was still suspicious of why Kurt, Danny, and the girls had been so adamant about including me. At the same time, I was pretty excited about the whole scene. Educationally speaking, it was a great opportunity for me to learn a thing or two about the social niceties involving teenage girls.

There were a dozen of us teens jammed like sardines in that basement. Besides Janelle and Carrie, there were four other girls present and they were all quite attractive. As I looked them over, my pulse quickened. I was positive they would see me as some kind of spaz. So, I did my best to stay calm and simply mimicked some of the behaviorisms of Kurt and Danny.

The guys present consisted of Kurt, Danny, Larry, and two others whose names I don't recall. During introductions, I had been too busy looking at the girls and didn't pay much attention. So, their names went in one ear and right out the other.

Initially, I stuck close to the other guys. We all congregated around the pool table. The girls hung out together and chattered lively in the lounge. I caught a couple of them smiling in my direction, so I quickly averted my eyes. It didn't take long for me to figure out that I was seriously out of my element. Nevertheless, I was thrilled to be included in the festivities.

Early on, we guys shot pool, talked sports, and listened to some of Larry's ridiculous stories. The girls rifled through records, gabbed about other girls they despised, and randomly stole whatever guy they could for a dance. The first hour or so passed quickly that way. In no time at all, I was truly enjoying myself. It was easy because when I played pool, all my concentration went into each shot. When I wasn't shooting, I was afraid some girl might ask me to dance. But no girl made the slightest move in my direction; I was glad of it. After a comfortable interval, when everyone had loosened up a bit, one of the girls suggested we play a game called *Truth or Dare*.

Prior to that evening, I had never played *Truth or Dare*, but the rules seemed simple enough: A designated inquisitor calls out a poor unfortunate's name and offers the ultimatum, truth or dare. The poor soul called upon must then choose between what they believe to be the lesser of the two evils. Should they choose truth, they must give an honest answer to what is usually a very personal and/or embarrassing question. Should they foolishly choose a dare, well, let's just say that is when the game begins to get interesting. Having successfully given an honest answer, or properly executed the required actions of a dare, the poor unfortunate then becomes the inquisitor. He or she will then take their turn at torturing another poor soul of their choosing.

A special rule had been incorporated for that evening's festivities. If you were called upon twice and had opted to tell two truths, you had to automatically accept a dare, when called upon a third time.

We had been playing the game for about an hour and fortunately for me, no one had called on me. I couldn't remember the last time I had been around so much laughter. I listened to the many embarrassing truths, which were admitted by the girls, just so they didn't have to take a dare. On the other hand, the guys weren't afraid at all to take a dare. It seemed as though they would do anything to keep from admitting to anything of substance.

I was enjoying myself immensely. That is, right up until I discovered the real reason Janelle invited me.

Danny had just completed his second dare of the evening, which consisted of him drinking half a can of root beer, while standing on his head. He had Kurt and Larry hold his legs to balance him, while he held himself up with his left forearm and drank with his right hand. When Danny finished, he was allowed to stand again. Immediately upon getting to his feet, Danny let loose a thunderous belch! The guys all cheered, but the girls thought it was gross. Me, I was downright impressed!

Danny was now the inquisitor and he called upon a fairly good-looking girl named Lori. After giving her the ritualistic ultimatum, he checked himself. "Lori!" he bellowed mischievously. "This is your third time, isn't it?!"

"Yes it is," admitted Lori, wearing a look that told everyone she knew she was in deep trouble.

Danny fiendishly continued. "So, instead of truth or dare, I get to ask you… dare or dare?"

Rather snidely, Lori replied, "Yes, Danny, but you don't have to be an ass about it."

Just then, I should have paid more attention to Kurt because he got up and left his seat next to Janelle. Seemingly riveted to what transpired between Danny and Lori, Kurt casually walked over and repositioned himself at the foot of the basement stairs, stretching his arms and back all the way. There, he casually leaned against the wall and waited, like the rest of us, to hear what Lori's fate would be.

When Danny did pass sentence on Lori, I could scarcely believe my ears. Root beer almost went up my nose when he loudly declared, "You have to make out with Jackson…for five minutes…right here in front of everybody."

Of course, everyone howled with laughter. Everyone, that is, except Lori and me.

Gripped with panic, I immediately bolted for the stairs. However, there stood Kurt, smiling confidently, while blocking my only escape route. I tried desperately to get past my older brother, but he quite effortlessly grabbed me and slung me over his shoulder. Kurt then carried me over to the sofa Lori was sitting on. Without much trouble, he simply dropped me down next to her. When I landed, I almost bounced right off the plush cushion. Very quickly, I shifted myself upright, so I wouldn't look so small in Lori's eyes. I was absolutely humiliated.

Tony Milner's words about older women raced through my head. I figured Lori to be at least a year or two older than me. Sizing me up, she shook her head slightly and then gave me an understanding smile. Over the commotion of laughter, Lori asked, "Have you ever made out with a girl before?"

I just knew my changing voice would fail me and crack. So, with what I can only imagine was a look of sheer terror on my face, I simply shook my head slowly.

It was clear to me that Lori sensed my fear. She immediately went on a plea-bargaining campaign to get her sentence whittled down to three minutes. Danny was willing to cooperate, but it would have to be with the added provision that we French kiss.

Now, I may not have been the most experienced guy in the room, but even I knew that French kissing involved the use of tongues. *That's just gross*, I thought, as I fought the urge to run for the stairs again. The only thing holding me in place was the thought of Kurt catching me again. He would then throw me back down next to Lori, just like a bag of dirty laundry.

Lori rallied the rest of the girls to her. She implored them to help plead her case. Then and there, I learned how a small group of girls can be an insurmountable force. In short, Danny gave in to their tactics. Lori successfully got her sentence reduced to making out with me for three straight minutes, no breaks allowed, but no tongues were necessary! She seemed satisfied with the reduction in severity, but I didn't feel any better about my situation, not one bit.

Accepting her fate, Lori scooted in closer to me and put her arms around my neck. As I looked into her brown eyes, a single thought rifled its way through my panicked mind. *Oh my God! I'm really gonna have to do this!*

Lori leaned in and whispered, "Are you ready?"

Now, where have I heard those words before? The thought had barely registered, when Lori gently pressed her lips to mine. There on that sofa, with ten sadistic teens watching, our lips just kind of melted together.

For the next three minutes, I tried to give back everything Lori afforded me. Learning as we went along, I sincerely prayed that I was doing it right. Until then, I never knew that three minutes could feel like an eternity. My head was swimming and I lost all capacity for clear thought. Keeping my eyes tightly closed, the presence of the other teens seemed to fade away. Lori's breath was hot, but it was also sweet. Suddenly, I felt something very powerful, like electricity, shoot right through me. It was all so new and surprisingly wonderful! I never thought I would enjoy being that intimate with a girl, but there I was, doing what just moments ago, what I could barely fathom.

From seemingly out of nowhere, I heard the group give a final ten-second countdown. The three minutes ended and so did the kiss. As everyone laughed, I found myself struggling to catch my breath.

Lori gave me a sly smile and asked, "Are you sure you've never made out before?"

"Never," I admitted, but then thought, *I doubt I'll ever hesitate again, though!*

When I casually got up from Lori's side, there was still laughter going on. Trying to keep my cool, I hurried back over to the pool table. I most assuredly had enough of the whole truth-or-dare thing for a while. Now, I just wanted to hide under a rock somewhere.

Besides being thoroughly embarrassed, I was madder than hell at Danny. I should have kissed him for providing me that breakthrough. Instead, I was pissed off! The more I thought about it, the more I realized that Danny wasn't the only guilty party. There were four teenagers for me to spread my anger between, but Danny was my current target. I knew my face was beet red and I felt like the laughingstock of the entire evening.

I guess Lori and I had been the star attraction of the night because the others brought a sudden end to the game. In a rush to claim the pool table, Larry Armstrong immediately grabbed me for a game of eight ball. Because of my anger and embarrassment, my concentration was now totally screwed up. When it was my turn to shoot, I could barely sink a ball. To make matters worse, I caught Lori giving me intermittent looks. Once, she even winked at me and shot me a pretty smile. Feeling totally unsure of myself, I attempted to give her a charming smile in return. Danny caught the exchange and gave me a knowing wink. I looked daggers back at him and used my middle finger as an exclamation point. Then, after thinking about it, I knew I couldn't stay mad at him, so I smiled and shook my head. Danny just laughed.

Whatever else I was feeling at the time, I knew that kiss wasn't special. I wanted it to be, but there were no bells ringing in my ears or fireworks going off in my head. I had preconceived notions that my first make-out session was supposed to be with someone special. Instead, I shared that intimate moment with a complete stranger. Although it felt nice, the act was performed as a source of amusement for everyone else present. No emotional strings were attached. That is, I didn't feel any, not really. Nonetheless, I also had to admit to myself that making out with Lori was definitely not the worst experience of my young life.

Sultry, slow songs began to ooze from the Magnavox and couples commenced holding each other tightly. Watching them sway back and forth, it looked to me like they were actually glued to one another. At one point, while Kurt played a game of pool against Larry, Janelle took the opportunity to ask me for a dance. I told her I didn't know how, so she offered to teach me. Janelle took my hand and led me to a spot that afforded us a little room. She placed my hands on her hips and then clasped her hands around my neck. Together, we began to sway, much like the other couples were, except there was a lot more daylight between us.

Trying to put me more at ease, Janelle struck up some casual conversation by asking, "So, how did you like making out with Lori?"

When I replied, "It was okay, I guess," blood rushed to my face.

"Wait until it's with someone you really like. I bet you'll feel a lot different about it." Janelle then smiled knowingly at me and made it clear she wasn't making fun of me.

Once again, I didn't know what to say, so I just looked at her with a blank expression on my face.

"By the way, Lori thinks you're pretty cute. She also thinks we should all go out sometime. What do you think?"

Panicking again, I thought, *I don't know what to think!* Lori's interest in me had taken me totally by surprise. It was impossible for me to comprehend that she actually enjoyed our encounter.

My fear must have been apparent because Janelle chuckled and said, "Breathe, Jackson. You can think on it. But I think you two should go out. I mean, you have already made out with her."

At that, we both laughed, and I began to relax again. I realized then that I truly liked Janelle. She was one of very few girls I wasn't too nervous to be around. Now, she had me thinking that it was possible for me to date an older girl!

I then remembered what Tony Milner had said earlier in the day. *Could that stuff about being the new guy in town be true?* The very thought of it struck me as being quite funny. So, I chuckled nervously and said, "I need to think on it some. I'm not sure yet. Tell Lori I think she's pretty cute, too."

"I have a better idea, Jackson. Why don't you go talk to Lori and tell her yourself?"

At Janelle's suggestion, my anxiety level went up about twelve notches. "You know I can't do that!"

"Jackson, breathe, will you?" whispered Janelle. "Give yourself a chance."

Then, the song we were dancing to ended. The Magnavox began to go through its cycle and dropped another record on the turntable. Janelle thanked me for the dance and then made her way back to Kurt. Once again, I retreated to the pool table. I was feeling very much like a worm on a hook. I wanted to leave but knew I couldn't go anywhere. That is, not until Kurt and Danny were ready. So, I figured I would simply stick close to my pool partner, Larry.

While watching Larry take on another opponent, my mind wrestled with Janelle's advice. *Give myself a chance?! What for?! I don't live here anymore!* To me, the whole idea of dating any girl, let alone a girl in Mankato, was absolutely absurd.

As the evening went on, Lori made no attempt to talk to me. She kept her place on that sofa, where we kissed. However, I did catch her giving me occasional glances and smiles. To me, it seemed as though Janelle could be right. It looked like Lori truly wanted me to go spend some time with her. The distance between us was now frustrating me. Suddenly, I found myself sincerely wishing that I could just walk up to Lori and initiate a conversation. The more I thought about it, the more I talked myself into it. *Damn it! Here goes nothing,* I thought.

Still trying to convince myself that I could succeed, I slowly walked over to where Lori sat with her friends. When I stood immediately in front of her, our eyes met. Of course, fate worked against me and my changing voice cracked, as I said, "Hi, Lori is it? Now that we've made out, I suppose I should probably introduce myself…I'm Jackson." I was going for funny, so when everyone in earshot erupted in laughter, I felt better.

"Have a seat," laughed Lori.

I spent the next thirty minutes or so learning to make small talk. Mostly, I just let Lori ask me questions. In return, I did my best to give interesting or witty responses, but truly did not feel adequate to the task. I learned that Lori's last name was Mudd. She had an easy going way about her and seemed genuinely interested in getting to know me. I felt myself slowly beginning to relax around her. She asked me about Duluth, so I did my best to describe it for her. When I talked about our house on the hillside, overlooking Lake Superior, I marveled at how she seemed to hang onto my every word. Lori told me she had never been farther north than Minneapolis and St. Paul. As far as she was concerned, Duluth and Lake Superior might as well be on an entirely different planet. In relation to Mankato, I had to concede the point. Many were the times I felt that Duluth might as well be on the other side of the globe.

At Lori's request, I attempted to dance a few times. When I confessed that I wasn't any good at it, she understood and didn't make fun of me. I felt as though she appreciated the fact that I was willing to try. By watching Lori and some of the other teens, I was able to mimic some of their movements, but I was most definitely in dire need of practice.

When the music slowed down again, Lori caught my arm and kept me from walking away. She coaxed me to stay by softly asking, "What's your hurry?" Lori then clasped her hands around my neck.

Initially, I rested my hands on Lori's waist. Together, we slowly swayed, as the recording group, Climax, sang, "Precious and few are the moments we two can share..."

During that dance, Lori moved in closer. She took my hands from her hips and placed them around her back. Suddenly, there was absolutely no daylight between us. I was more than a little nervous, but her warmth also created a new sensation. I was thrilled that she was making a play for me, so I relaxed and just let nature take its course.

Lori whispered in my ear, "I like you, Jackson. We should go out sometime."

In response, I sweated some and stammered, "Well...I'm only here for two weeks...and um..."

Lori interrupted me with a chuckle and then said, "Relax, I said we should go out. I didn't propose marriage."

True to character, I was nervous again, but managed to speak without my voice cracking. "Sure, that would be great."

The rest of the evening went by in a blur and I truly did not want it to end. Hanging out with that group was fantastic! I emphatically wished that they would continue to include me in their gatherings. That night, my confidence got a huge boost and I began to feel much older than my actual years.

When it was time for everyone to leave, Lori looked me in the eye and asked, "Do I get a good night kiss?"

Once again, my blood pressure rose, but I managed to say, "Do you...want one?"

With both hands, Lori gently grabbed the front of my windbreaker and pulled me in close. The kiss was a lot more intimate than earlier because this time, it was her idea. However, for some baffling reason, it still didn't ring any bells in my head.

Before heading the van toward Westwood Drive, Kurt drove a few of his friends home. When he, Danny, and I were the only souls left onboard, Danny turned around and smirked from the front seat.

"So, little brother, how do you like Lori Mudd?"

Unable to hide my embarrassment, I replied, "She's very...friendly."

The three of us laughed all the way home. Of course, I took some good-natured ribbing from both of them, but I didn't mind a bit.

As that evening came to a close, I felt things were getting better for me. I was happier than I had been in years. I could not stop the rush of excitement within me. I had only been in town for two and half days, but it all felt so natural. *Mankato is where I truly belong,* I thought. I was with my brothers again and it all felt stupendously right.

When we got home, the three of us went to bed immediately. Danny and I lay in our beds, quietly talking before sleep took us. He continued to poke fun at me about Lori and how she had taken a shine to me. It had been years since we were able to talk like that. It was one of the things I missed most about him. For all his mischievous ways, Danny had always been my confidant, my confessor, and the one person I shared practically everything with.

After Danny had drifted off to sleep, I stayed awake, replaying the entire evening in my head. I had finally discovered that girls could really be cool. *Janelle said they would like me...if I let them. Dave and Joel already know how this feels. So, is this my time?*

Chapter 7

Tuesday, 8 August 1972

Like many sibling relationships, regardless of the love and bond that exists between two brothers, there are times when one would simply like to dropkick the other into the middle of next week. That morning, I had a very strong urge to do exactly that to Danny.

Because Kurt and Danny had kept me out quite late the previous evening, I was still sleeping soundly late into the morning. Danny had already risen and prepared himself for work – he had a summer job working for a lawncare service. Normally, he would have been gone already, but that morning, his employer apparently did not need him to come in as early. However, just before Danny did depart, he stealthily crept up to my bed. Then, bringing his mouth to within an inch or so from my ear, he shook me vigorously and practically yelled, "Wake up, man! It's ten-thirty! Don't you have a ball game today?!" He then ran for the stairs.

Understandably irritated, I yelled, "YOU BUTT HEAD!" For emphasis, I also threw my pillow in his general direction, but did not come remotely close to hitting him.

As Danny disappeared down the stairwell, he called back to me, "I gotta run! See ya later!"

I did have a baseball game to get up for and was glad of it. That being said, it was also a good thing the game was scheduled for later in the afternoon; I was in no shape to jump out of bed and go play ball. Even though I felt groggy, my mind was still charged from events of the previous night. Slowly, I rose from my bed and then stretched my still-sleeping muscles. After shuffling down the stairs, I looked around the house and discovered that I had the whole place to myself. I then took a nice, long, shower. The hot water helped my muscles unwind and bring my whole person back to life.

While I ate a bowl of cereal, the phone rang. It was Tony Milner, wondering when I would be coming over. "Mom's makin' lunch before we go play ball. She wants you to be here, too."

"Thanks," I replied. "I'll be there right after I clean up the kitchen here."

That morning, all the Wilsons must have been in quite a hurry to get to work. A small mess had been left in the kitchen, so I decided to clean it before disappearing for the day. Mom would have been both proud and jealous of my willingness to do that one chore. It was something I silently pledged to work on when I returned home.

As I scoured a greasy fry pan, I thought more on the previous night's festivities. A change had taken place within me and I was quite cognizant of it. I suddenly felt more ready for whatever came along. When I went to the garage to retrieve my baseball gear, I was still thinking about the great time I had in Janelle's basement. *When I tell the guys about what I did with Lori Mudd, they'll think I'm a god!* Tony would be especially impressed, but mostly about him being right. I could already hear him gloat, "See, I told you chicks dig the new guy in town!"

Why is that? I asked myself. *Why would any girl in this town want go out with me?! I don't live here. I'm only in town for two weeks, but that didn't seem to bother Lori one, little bit!* I should have been happy with the revelation. Instead, I was absolutely perplexed.

When I finally left the house and headed down the block to Tony's, it was almost noon. The sun appeared to be out in full force, but the temperature was only in the mid-seventies. Except for a few wispy clouds, the skies were clear. A light breeze blew lazily from the southwest, giving the day an extremely comfortable feel. A sense of wellbeing bubbled up within me and I simply allowed myself to enjoy the moment. *Perfect ball-playing weather*, I thought.

I arrived at the Milner house, just as Cheryl was about to serve lunch. Although I had eaten a bowl of cereal not long before, as soon as I caught a whiff of the wonderful smells emanating from their kitchen, I instantly became famished.

Cheryl hugged me and said, "I hope you're hungry because I made plenty."

I knew Cheryl Milner was no slouch in the kitchen, so I exclaimed, "You bet I am!"

As it turned out, Cheryl was serving up a special lunch in my honor. She had fried some chicken and prepared a big bowl of coleslaw. Pork 'n' beans were also served, another favorite of mine. And, as if the aforementioned wasn't enough, freshly sliced, homemade bread was available. As I looked upon the spread before me, my stomach growled loudly. Everyone heard it and looked at me with comical faces. Cheryl instructed me to take a seat at the table and then asked, "Aren't Janet and Brad feeding you over there?"

Once again, I found myself in familiar and greatly missed surroundings. Eating and laughing at the Milners' kitchen table was not a new experience for me at all. Many times, in years past, I had been invited for lunch and sometimes dinner. If I just happened to be with Tony at mealtime, an invitation had always been extended my way.

That afternoon, Tony Sr. was at work and so was Cindy. Mr. Milner taught English and American Literature at Mankato State College. Cindy was a carhop at Robby's Drive-In. That left Cheryl, Kathy, Tony, and I together at the table.

Just like so many times in the past, table conversation was lively. Mostly, I satisfied more of their curiosity by telling them about my life in Duluth. At the same time, I felt challenged to get the meal eaten, while it was still hot. I could barely get a mouthful down before someone would fire another question my way. All their attention was focused on me and I enjoyed it immensely.

When lunch was over, I hugged Cheryl – she would not have let me get away with less – and thanked her for the wonderful meal. I even offered to help with the dishes. Tony, of course, looked at me like I was deranged.

"No thanks, Jackson," said Cheryl. "You boys run off and enjoy yourself." As an afterthought she added, "I don't suppose it would do any good to tell you to stay out of trouble."

"We're playing ball this afternoon, Ma," replied Tony. "How much trouble can we get into?"

Giving her son a rather stern look, Cheryl replied, "Tony Milner, if anyone can figure out a way, it's you."

After giving Cheryl's comment the courtesy chuckle it warranted, Tony and I made our retreat toward the basement stairwell. It was our intent to hang out there and wait for Dave and Mike to arrive.

Just before disappearing through the doorway, I looked back at Cheryl. While flashing a mischievous smile her way, I said, "Thanks again for lunch…Mrs. Tony's Mom."

Cheryl rolled her eyes back at me and said, "Oh, get out of here…and you're welcome."

Once Dave and Mike showed up, we left Tony's house and walked to Joel's place. Picking him up last was intentionally planned that way. It was one of our oldest tricks. With the four of us standing on the Brightens' doorstep, Joel's mom would be less likely to invent more chores for him to do. Our strategy usually worked like a charm.

Joel met us at the door, looking much the same as he always did back then. His extremely wavy, dark, brown hair was a tangled mess. Long hair was in style, but even I had to admit that Joel could really use a haircut. The only time I could recall seeing him with his hair looking remotely combed was at our First Communion ceremony. Even with the use of some pomade, his hair just didn't cooperate. Joel's tanned face was freckled a little, just under his eyes, which were also dark brown. He truly was quite the sight, standing there in a rumpled T-shirt and blue jeans that were so faded, a person could hardly tell they were ever blue.

His black canvas tennis shoes had holes in them and would soon have to be replaced. However, even if he did get a new pair, I doubted that Joel would ever actually throw the old ones out. He had a reputation for never throwing anything away. If an article of clothing became old and worn out, Joel didn't care, he just kept wearing it.

In order to help save Joel from possible, last-minute chores, I volunteered to prey on any charitable feelings Mrs. Brighten might have. I did that by going in to greet her after my three-year absence. Joel led me through their cluttered entryway filled with strewn shoes, jackets that couldn't find a hanger or a hook, old newspapers, and some magazines. Carefully tiptoeing through the mess, I followed him into their living room. There, Joel stopped us at what he guesstimated was a safe distance from where his mom slouched in an old recliner.

Putting what I can only describe as false excitement into his voice, Joel called out, "Hey, Ma, look who's here! You remember Jackson, don't you? He moved away a few years ago and is back for a couple of weeks to visit."

Mrs. Brighten was not what anyone would call an attractive woman. She sat in their living room looking rather disheveled. She appeared to be engrossed in a soap opera that she had tuned in on their old black and white TV. She wasn't wearing makeup and her face looked a bit pasty, like she hadn't seen sunlight in quite a while. Just then, I couldn't recall if I had ever seen her outside of their house. Her dark brown hair was streaked with grey and looked like she hadn't bothered to take a comb or a brush to it. It was easy to tell where Joel got his grooming standards from.

Mrs. Brighten looked at me and I saw what I thought to be disapproval in her eyes. "Jackson? Jackson Harris?" Her speech was slurred somewhat, but just a tad.

"Hi, Mrs. Brighten. It's Jackson Landry now. I moved to Duluth and was adopted a few years ago."

"Landry you say?" Mrs. Brighten's face was expressionless, and her eyes appeared unable to focus clearly. "Well…You still look like your mother." She then turned her attention back to the TV, thereby dismissing Joel and me.

Even though I couldn't remember clearly, I had always heard that Sharon Harris was beautiful. Nonetheless, Mrs. Brighten's delivery sounded more like an insult. My heart instantly sank a bit and an emotionless, "Yes, ma'am," was all I was able to muster for a response.

Mrs. Brighten's acceptance of Joel's friends had never been very warm, but it seemed that she maintained a special, emphasized disapproval of me. Suddenly, I couldn't wait to get out of that house.

Just then, Joel motioned for me to follow him. He grabbed his baseball mitt, which was waiting on the stairway leading to the second floor. We then slipped out the front door and just about tripped over the guys, who had been waiting on the steps. Each of us hurriedly made sure we had all our gear, then we all made a run for it down the block, not bothering to slow down until we were out of shouting range of the Brighten house.

It was a seven-block journey to the ballpark and one we guys could never trek in silence. Excited chatter broke out between Dave, Tony, and Mike. Joel, however, noticed me bringing up the rear and not joining in the fun. He must have known what was on my mind because he fell back to join me.

"You're not thinking about what my mom said, are you?"

"Kinda."

"Don't waste your time, man. An hour from now she'll probably forget you were even there. That wasn't just a glass of orange juice sitting next to her. It's usually half full of vodka, too."

I looked at my friend with a questioning expression.

"She's okay sometimes, but once she starts in on the early-afternoon screwdrivers, it's a good day to be someplace else."

Genuinely surprised, I replied, "Wow! That's not good."

Temporarily forgetting about my bruised feelings, I considered Joel's circumstances. I never thought he had what anyone would consider the most solid family life, but I wasn't prepared to hear that it was actually worse than I had previously surmised. Not only did my friend live in that dilapidated and dirty house, but now it appeared as though his mom had effectively turned herself into an alcoholic.

"The real fun won't start until Dad comes home from work," continued Joel. "I'll bet you'll be able to hear the two of them all the way up at the Wilson's."

I was suddenly embarrassed that I had even briefly felt sorry for myself. "I'm sorry, Joel. I didn't know."

Joel countered, "Yeah, and what could you have done if you did? I'll tell you something, Jackson. There's times I wish I was you. At least you got the hell outta this town."

Seeing that Joel was dead serious, I replayed in my head, everything I had just experienced inside his house. I then realized, even after everything I had been through, Joel had it much worse. He was stuck in a terrible situation and had no escape. At that moment, I made a silent vow not to feel sorry for myself anymore. That is, anymore that day.

"Let's just forget about that crap," asserted Joel. "Let's just go play ball, okay?" Wishing I could easily forget about things that bothered me, I replied, "I'm with you."

When the five of us arrived at the ballpark, we discovered that we had beaten everyone else. While waiting for the others to arrive, we hung out by the old, wooden bleachers, which appeared to be recently painted a dark, hunter green. Dave and I then decided to loosen up a bit by playing catch. Joel and Tony took the hint and did the same. Because Mike was not a player, he entertained himself the only way that was available to him, by making snide comments about our occasional poor throws and missed catches. That is, until Dave just about threw his mitt at him.

When the rest of the guys finally showed, I wasn't surprised to find that I already knew a few of them. They remembered me, too, but there were also some that I hadn't met. Doug Haines was the only one who remembered me well. Although we had not been close in the past, he surprised me by greeting me like a long-lost friend.

When all the players were in place, we quickly chose teams. Of course, I was one of the last to be picked. I wasn't surprised, though, because no one there knew how good I was, except maybe Dave. However, even he only had his memories to work with. It was all perfectly okay with me because I simply planned to be the secret weapon for whichever team I landed on. I was a good infielder and a better-than-average hitter. But I was also a decent outfielder, too, if there be a need. Apparently, there was a need because the team I landed on asked me to cover right field. I hated playing as a right fielder. Everyone I knew hated playing in that defensive position because the action was usually sparse. Nevertheless, I thought I had better earn my wings again before insisting on a better position. I reconciled my disappointment by reminding myself that it would just feel good to be playing ball with the guys again.

The teams ended up being a little lopsided. Most of the batting talent appeared to be on my team. I figured that out during our first at bat. Dave Lester pitched for the other side, so that was enough to keep things interesting. In the first inning, my team went through two-thirds of the batting order and scored two runs. Dave's team scored one run from a single-shot homer he ripped over the left-field fence. As I watched the ball sail over the chained links, I shook my head and smiled, remembering how between all of us, Dave had always been the best.

At the top of the second inning, two of my teammates hit singles to get on base. So, when I stepped up to the plate for the first time that day, there were two players already in scoring position. I had to keep myself from literally licking my chops at the opportunity. Dave smiled cunningly at me before delivering a fast ball, right down the pipe. I threw my shoulders and hips into the swing, but the connection wasn't as sweet as I'd hoped for. I ended up hitting a triple that scored two runs and solidified our lead for the remainder of the game.

After I held up on third base, Dave gave me a dirty look from the pitcher's mound. Snidely, he said, "I see you've been practicing." Then, just like I had done earlier, he shook his head and smiled.

By the bottom of the fifth inning, I had become quite bored standing around in right field. Because there had not been any balls hit toward my assigned area, I was probably the first to notice the girls show up and sit in the bleachers. I was busy gawking at them, when suddenly I heard someone yell, "RIGHT FIELD!"

Just in time, I came out of my stupor and easily caught a rare pop fly. It marked the third out, so it was now my team's turn at bat again. At the end of five innings, my team was ahead, six-to-two.

As I jogged in toward the dugout, I looked toward the girls to see if I recognized any of them. By my count, there were seven or eight present, but as I ran, I couldn't get a good look at them. So, after tossing my mitt in the dugout, I went outside the fenced-in diamond to get a drink. The water fountain was located very close to the bleachers and provided a much better vantage point to look the girls over. As I bent down to take a drink, I turned my head slightly and snuck a peek. Suddenly, my eyes recognized and locked onto the very girl who had ruthlessly kissed me in Tony Milner's back yard, Julie Falkner! Astonished, I just about stuck my whole face in the fountain before pulling back and reminding myself to keep my cool.

Absentmindedly dribbling water down my front, I got a much better look at Julie than what I saw in church on Sunday. When she smiled, her blue eyes seemed to shimmer in the sunlight. That afternoon, she wore denim shorts and was sporting a pair of nicely-tanned legs. Her raven-black curls were pulled back into a ponytail, and tied with a blue ribbon, which, in my opinion, matched her eyes perfectly. Bending over the fountain, with water practically going up my nose, I thought Julie looked absolutely gorgeous!

Although I couldn't hear a word Julie was saying, I could see that she was having a lively conversation with Gail Paulsen and Anne Hayward. Some of the other girls present looked familiar to me, but at that moment, I couldn't remember any of their names.

From the quick look I got, it appeared Anne had also transformed into a very attractive young lady. She had long, flowing-brown hair and the hint of a freckled face.

I had always remembered Gail as a cat-eyed little snot, but right then, I had to quickly alter my opinion. Her sun-bleached, blonde hair framed a pair of pretty green eyes and a very cute smile.

I was busy gawking at the three girls, when Julie gave a short glance in my direction. Sharply, I spun around and headed for my team's dugout, hoping upon hope that she had not seen me, let alone recognized me. I needed many things right then but having Julie Falkner in my head wasn't one of them.

When I made it safely back into the confines of the dugout, I silently thanked God that the girls could not see inside. I then watched Tony step up to the plate to take his turn at bat. Immediately remembering that I was supposed to be on deck to hit next, I grimaced. Trying to act as casually as possible, I took hold of my lucky bat, which I had leaned just inside the doorway, and stepped back into the sunlight. Keeping my back toward the bleachers, I then took a few warmup swings. I overheard some of the girl's idle chatter and felt good that none of it was in reference to me.

That afternoon, my dress was quite deliberate. I wore blue jeans, a white cotton t-shirt and a plaid, short-sleeved, button-front shirt. I left my shirt untucked and unbuttoned, so I could swing the bat easier. Back then, one of my favorite movies was *Cool Hand Luke* – I was a huge Paul Newman fan. Right then, I imagined that I looked a lot like him. I was also wearing my brand-new Converse® blue-canvas tennis shoes – we called them bumpers. Mom would have killed me if she knew I was wearing them to play baseball, in lieu of the older, rattier pair I had brought. But she was 235 miles north, so I was confident that I was safe.

After Dave got Tony to swing at and miss a fastball, he delivered a careless off-speed pitch. Tony threw himself into his swing, but it only netted him a bouncing ground ball that headed toward second base. The second baseman missed the grab, but the centerfielder brilliantly backed him up. It was to no avail, though, because the throw to first base was just a tad late. Tony beat the throw by a smidge and was awarded a single-base hit.

Now, it was my turn at bat. Doing my best to get the girls out of my head, I slowly walked toward home plate. From previous innings, I had learned that Dave's skills as a pitcher were rapidly developing. However, he still had not mastered his curve ball, which meant that if I were to allow anything to disrupt my concentration, I would probably not be able to duck in time. I would likely take a ball in the mouth or maybe an ear. So, clearing my head outside the batter's box, I sized Dave up. He stood on the mound, with those steel-gray eyes of his, boring holes into me. *Was he actually trying to intimidate me?* The thought made me chuckle for a moment.

I then remembered how Dave's dad used to coach us both in their back yard. Go figure, besides being a gym teacher, Jim Lester was also the baseball coach for the Scarlets at Mankato West High. Dave's pitching ability had been amplified. It took no stretch of the imagination for me to know that his dad's teachings had played a large part in his development.

I also noticed how Dave was beginning to look more and more like his dad. Unlike my other friends, who were either chunky, like Mike, or long and slim, like Joel and Tony, Dave was beginning to fill out. Like me, his musculature was developing nicely. I always thought of Jim Lester as being muscle bound. It wouldn't be long before Dave would be the same. If there was a large difference between Dave and his dad, it would have to be the hair. Dave's hair was dirty brown, with a pronounced and distinctive wave to it. Like many of us, he wore it just below collar length. Jim Lester's hair was plentiful on the sides and back, which he kept closely cropped and neatly trimmed. Up top, though, he was as smooth as a baby's butt.

When I felt ready, I stepped into the batter's box, took a couple additional swings with the bat and then waited for Dave's first pitch. When the ball came zinging past my head, I ducked out of the box and put a hand up to my ear, just to ensure that it was still attached. The pitch was high and inside.

"Ball one!" called Mike.

When I stepped back into the box, my attention was all on Dave. As I dug in and waited for his next pitch, a single bead of sweat traced its way down my nose and just sort of dangled at the very tip. Not bothering to wipe it away, I stared back at my friend on the pitcher's mound.

Like all serious, young ballplayers, Dave's confidence rested in the fact that he worked harder at the game than his peers in Mankato. However, so did I and I was out to prove it. So, even though Dave delivered a blistering fast ball, I tagged it with everything I had. The connection felt pretty sweet, so I was sure it was headed out of the park. Jogging toward first base, I watched the ball in flight. To my disappointment, the ball landed just short of the fence, bounced once, and then went over the top rail. It was a ground-rule double.

"Crap!" I exclaimed. It was my favorite cuss word. It was a word I had heard Kurt and Danny use many times, especially when they were frustrated. Just then, I was frustrated because I badly wanted the home run.

I took my bases and looked over at Tony, who was now stuck on third. With the two of us on base and nobody out, I felt more than confident that someone would get another hit. I was anxious to score, especially with the girls watching. It was then that I snuck a little look toward the bleachers. All the girls were still sitting there, gabbing. They didn't appear to be paying any attention to the game at all. That is, all but one. Julie Falkner had left her seat and was now standing at the fence, looking in my direction.

Oh God, I thought. *Not now!* Quickly, I acted as though I had not seen her. In turn, Julie made no gesture that told me she recognized me. She just stood there, hanging onto the chained-linked fence, seemingly scrutinizing the occupant on second base – me.

I got my head back in the game and did so at just the right moment. Doug Haines was stepping up to the plate. I learned previously that he, too, was a good batter. I readied myself and made sure that Tony was, also.

Dave threw two balls before he got one across the strike zone. Haines just watched it go by. Dave then threw another careless off-speed pitch and Doug unloaded on it. Unfortunately, he didn't hit the sweet spot. The ball became a worm burner, which I had to jump over on my way to third base. Tony made it safe to home plate.

The short stop made an excellent grab and an even better throw to third. The ball beat me there by a mile, so I slammed on the breaks and headed back to second, with the third baseman close behind me. They had me in a pickle and I truly didn't have much hope of getting back on base successfully. However, the third baseman must have got a little too excited because his throw to second sailed over the baseman's head.

Cool! I thought, as I slammed on the breaks again and ran back toward third. Tony was giving me the all-clear sign to round third and run for home, so I trusted him and stepped on the gas.

Unfortunately, I was only halfway to home plate when the ball arrived there. Once again, I skidded to a stop, changed directions, and headed back toward third base.

Great, another pickle! The sarcastic thought flew through my head, as my lungs began to labor. I was now absolutely certain that I would not be lucky enough to get out of a double pickle. Nevertheless, not trying simply was not an option, not with all those girls watching.

Because the catcher had more than enough time to set and carefully aim, his throw to third base was right on the money. So, I reversed direction once more and headed for home. I guess the third baseman didn't want to chance another wild throw because he attempted to catch and tag me all by himself. With the third baseman right on my heels, I kicked it into high gear and raced for home. Luckily, I stepped on home plate a mere fraction of a second before he tagged me.

"SAFE!" called Mike.

Immediately, a rather large argument ensued. The opposing team was positive their third baseman had made the tag, but Mike held his ground. Tony was there, too, adding his support to Mike for making the right call. It was so close. In fact, had I been asked to swear on a stack of bibles that I beat the tag, I would have had to refuse. Thankfully, nobody asked.

Because I wasn't positive that I was, in fact, safe at the plate, I decided to stay out of the heated argument. I was exhausted and parched, so I left the embattled group and headed to the water fountain.

Taking in water and swallowing in large gulps, I listened to the seemingly never-ending commotion at home plate. No side appeared to be giving way. Suddenly, from the corner of my eye, I caught Julie looking at me. So, as one might say, I decided to test the waters. Finishing my drink, I then stood up straight, turned, and looked right at the prettiest girl my young eyes had ever seen. With no discernible expression, Julie just looked back at me. In fact, she gave no sign at all that she recognized me. In my head, the encounter could not have gone worse. Feeling quite dejected, I wiped the excess water from my chin, then turned and headed for the dugout. *Damn it! She doesn't recognize me! Have I changed that much?!*

Mike's call at the plate was firm and the argument finally ended. We then continued on with the game, but I was no longer having any fun. I refused to look in Julie's direction and my heart was no longer happy to be playing baseball with the guys. We played out the remaining innings, but there was no more excitement before Mike called the final out. That day, I was on the winning team, but I could not have cared less. My mind was on a pair of pretty, blue eyes, which obviously had forgotten what I looked like.

As we gathered our gear from the dugout, I very intentionally stuck close to Joel. I was hoping to make a clean getaway, without having to come face-to-face with Julie or any of the other girls. So, in a casual tone, I asked Joel, "Are you headed for home?"

"Naw, we're gonna cool down here and hang out with the girls for a little bit. Are you in a hurry?"

My mind exploded, *ABSOLUTELY!* But my mouth coolly stated, "Nope."

When Joel and I shuffled out of the dugout, I immediately took a seat at the bottom row of the bleachers. I was glad that the girls were all seated higher on the tiered, wooden benches. Determined not to acknowledge any of them, I leaned forward and kept my eyes on the dirt. I was sweating bullets and fighting an overwhelming urge to leave without my friends.

At first, the chitchat was easy going and of no consequence, just stupid teenage prattle. Tony Milner was the recognized clown of the group and his antics got laughs from everyone. A few comments were made about the game and how the sides had been too lopsided to make it interesting. Then, I heard Joel say, "Yeah…and how about that double pickle Jackson got into!"

I closed my eyes, clenched my teeth and then looked up at Joel. There he stood, wearing a rather large, shit-eating grin. His not-so innocent comment was the dead giveaway. Just then, I could have strangled him for outing me that way.

For a moment there was silence. Then, a female voice I had not heard in three years said, "So, Jackson, it looks like you're still a fast runner."

When I heard Julie Falkner's words, I immediately understood her reference. Suddenly, a switch flipped inside of me, and I couldn't keep myself from laughing. I stood and turned around, just in time to watch Julie come bounding down the bleachers. When she reached the bottom, she literally threw herself at me! I had not counted on having to catch her, so when Julie gave me a huge and unexpected hug, she practically knocked both of us over!

Julie joyously exclaimed, "I knew it was you! I just knew it!"

When Anne and Gail also came bounding down the bleachers toward me, I could not keep the smile from my face. Taking turns, they both delivered hugs of their own.

Hugs?! I thought. *They're really that glad to see me?!* My heart was now practically coming through my chest. I never imagined that being greeted by those girls, in that manner, would ever feel that fantastic! A moment earlier, I wanted to slink away undetected, but in what seemed the very next instant, I could hardly contain my joy!

The guys all had puzzled looks on their faces, so Gail retold the story of how they had tested my speed in the fourth grade. They also reminded everyone what resulted from me losing that footrace. When everyone remembered, *The Kiss*, and how they had all made fun of me that year, more laughter commenced.

Sitting back down on the bleachers, the girls commenced asking me questions, mostly about where I lived and what it was like. For the first time in my life, I concerned myself with impressing girls. For the most part, I told the truth. That is, I didn't bother to embellish any details. I talked about the Landry house and gave vague, but informative, details about Duluth. I also told them about my school, the sports I played, and even talked about some of my casual friends, but I didn't dare share information about any of the troubles I had been going through. In my heart, I greatly desired to tell the entire group how much I had missed them, but that simply would not have been cool, so I left those details out.

Julie asked, "Any girlfriends, Jackson?"

"Nope," I almost happily admitted. "No girl is interested in me up there."

To that, I heard Anne Hayward mumble sarcastically, "Yeah, right."

When I heard Anne's comment, I must've had a stupid look on my face.

Straightforwardly, Julie stated, "Jackson, all girls think new guys are dreamboats, they just don't say anything."

I was positively blown away by her frankness.

We all hung out at the bleachers and for that short time, it appeared that I was the star attraction. Tony winked at me approvingly. I then looked beyond where Tony stood. Off in the distance, I spied a familiar, beat-up, black, '58 Chevy. It was parked in a lot across from the ballpark. Immediately, a chill went up my back, but I remained calm. Warily, my eyes darted this way and that, looking for Adam Harris, but he was not in sight. I then strained my eyes to see if he was watching from behind the wheel. But, because the sun glared off the car's windshield, I couldn't tell if Adam was sitting there or not. In a short while, I felt satisfied that I was in no danger. So, I relaxed and returned my attention to the gang.

Having caught my searching eyes, Julie asked, "Whatcha lookin' at?"

"Nothing much," I replied. "Just that car over there. It looks familiar."

Julie looked toward the Chevy, then back to me again.

Good Lord, I thought. *Those eyes are killing me.*

Julie then smiled, stood up and announced to the group, "Hey guys, I've gotta get going. See you later. It's great to see you again, Jackson." She began to make her way down the bleachers but stopped and turned around. "See you guys this Friday night at my place…Okay?"

Shortly after Julie disappeared up the street, everyone began making preparations to depart, also. As I grabbed up my bat and mitt, I heard the guys say to the others, "See you Friday."

On our walk home, Gail and Anne joined us. As they walked hand in hand with Joel and Dave, I watched, thinking how strange it all looked. Tony, Mike, and I brought up the rear of that gaggle.

While we made our way back to the neighborhood, I wasn't sure of the ground under my feet, so I retreated inside my head. I had just finished having the time of my life, playing baseball with my old friends. Being reunited with old St. Joseph's schoolmates had also been a blast. Seeing Julie, talking with her and the other girls, and being welcomed back with heartfelt hugs was fairly surreal. Regardless, a familiar feeling crept over me. Just as in Duluth, the whole group would be getting together that Friday, but I wasn't invited because I wasn't part of the gang anymore. Although I had vowed earlier in the day that I wouldn't feel sorry for myself, disappointment filtered in anyway.

It's probably just as well, I thought. *I'm not good enough for her. I'm not good enough for anyone, so why worry about it? I'll be gone at the end of next week and none of this will even matter.* Unfortunately, my heart had a different opinion.

Just before suppertime, our little group arrived in front of Joel's house. The noise emanating from within was unmistakable. An extremely loud argument between Joel's parents was taking place. At first, I didn't know what to do. Then, almost instinctively, I suggested to Joel that he come home with me for dinner.

"Naw, it'll be alright," said Joel.

"Don't go in there now, Joel," I insisted. "Come have dinner with us and let them cool off."

Joel looked doubtful, but asked, "You sure it'll be okay with the Wilsons?"

Glad that I was getting Joel to change his mind, I assured him by saying, "Come on, you can call home later and let your folks know where you're at."

Gail chimed in, "Go with him, Joel. Please don't go in there."

Finally, Joel agreed. At that moment, any alternative had to sound better than walking into *that* house.

Gail and Joel said their see-you-laters, as did Dave and Anne. Before leaving, though, Gail turned to me and whispered in my ear, "Thanks, Jackson." I could see in her eyes that she seriously appreciated my gesture.

Joel and I arrived at the Wilson house in time to catch Kurt, Danny, and Brad shooting baskets before dinner. I suggested Joel join them, while I went in the house for a few minutes. After I explained the situation to Janet, I apologized for putting her on the spot. Janet developed a look that was all too familiar, the one that told me she was listening and hanging onto every word, but was prepared to say, "No," regardless. To my surprise, Janet didn't say no. Instead, she simply smiled. Then, without saying a word to me, she casually went to the side door and stepped out onto the landing. "Hey, Joel!" she yelled. "I hope you like pot roast and veggies. It's all I'm serving, but there's plenty of it. You interested?"

When Janet came back into the kitchen, I didn't say a word. I just stood there, with a thankful grin on my face.

Not wanting me to make a big deal of it, Janet squinted at me and said, "Oh, shut up." She then gave me a wink and turned her attention back to peeling potatoes.

Shortly after dinner, I walked Joel back to his house. We sat on his front steps and listened for two screaming adults. Fortunately, all was now quiet within the Brighten residence.

"Thanks, Jackson. I really didn't want to go in there after the ball game."

"Who would?"

"Mom's been struggling with booze for a few years now and I think Dad is getting ready to leave."

I couldn't think of anything to say. Instead, I remembered all that I had been going through for the previous three years. There was no comfort I could offer.

"Gail has been great," continued Joel. "If it weren't for her, I'd probably go crazy."

"Gail is so different than how I remember her," I said thoughtfully.

"We've all changed some in three years, haven't we?" Joel's question was more of a statement and it seemed to carry a certain burden with it. Then, he said "Hey man, when you leave again, I'm gonna miss you. But, when it's time, don't even think about it, just go. I know I will...someday." Joel then got up from the stairs to go inside. Just before stepping inside the door, he turned and looked back at me. He had tears in his eyes and his voice trembled slightly. "You know, if it weren't for my little sister, I'd be gone already."

I was unable to provide my friend any solace, but I felt every bit of his pain. As I watched Joel disappear into his house, a sadness took hold of me. It was then beginning to get dark, so I turned to go back to the Wilson's, but then I changed my mind and my direction. I needed to go for a walk, so I could think. I needed Front Street.

My walk took me past the ball fields and Mankato West High. I also walked past Robby's Drive-In – Home of the Gut Bomb – on Stoltzman Road. I then took a left onto Front Street and from there headed east. Once I was on my favorite street, I slowed my pace and took in everything.

I remembered getting into a lot of trouble with Janet, when I got caught walking Front Street alone after dark. Back then, I was only eight and nine years old, but I was never afraid to take those walks after sunset because it was all so friendly. When a body walked downtown Mankato, it was unlike the impersonal streets of a big city, where nameless people just got in each other's way. If you bumped into someone on Front Street, you were more likely to know them than as not. It was one of my favorite things about living in that small town. People actually knew each other. Perhaps not intimately, but at the very least, they were likely to be a neighbor or an acquaintance. Anyway, that's how I chose to remember it, even if I was just overly romanticizing the place because I had missed it so much.

I was hoping to see all the shops I used to frequent with the guys. However, many looked to have closed their doors long ago. Janet informed me earlier, the change was all part of an urban renewal project taking place on the top of the hill, at the south end of town – Mankato is one of those backward towns where north is down, while south is up. Many of the businesses that used to operate on Front Street were no longer just a short walk away. They either relocated to the south or just closed their doors for good.

After leaving Joel at his door, I was feeling more than a little depressed about my friend's predicament. I was also feeling somewhat sorry for myself because I hadn't been invited to Julie's party. As I walked along, taking in the depressing sight of empty stores, my mood wasn't getting any better. The sidewalks were almost deserted. There weren't many people milling about at all, so accidentally bumping into an old friend or neighbor was unlikely. It wasn't what I expected at all. I could see the lights of The Grand and The State movie theaters ahead of me, but most of the other buildings had no lights in their windows at all. Red-bricked, Victorian buildings that once invited customers to come in and have a look around, now just stood vacant and foreboding. A sinking feeling went through me because Front Street was dying what appeared to be a rapid death.

Although I was only thirteen years old, I suddenly felt my childhood slipping away. Shops that I once explored often, no longer existed. It felt like a part of me had died with them. Feeling more than a little melancholy over the unwanted discovery, I changed my direction and slowly walked back to the neighborhood. *Why does all the good stuff in my life have to disappear?*

I got back to the house in time to watch the last few innings of the Minnesota Twins game, as they took on the Texas Rangers. Brad lounged in the downstairs den, watching, so I joined him there. As we sat and watched the game together, he asked me about that afternoon's ballgame. I told him about the hits I had gotten and the double pickle I blundered into.

Brad listened patiently and then smiled, saying, "It seems like only yesterday that the boys and I were out back teaching you to throw and hit. Now, it sounds like you've grown into quite an athlete."

I didn't know how to respond, so I shrugged my shoulders, but said nothing.

Brad asked, "Do you play a lot of sports up there in Duluth?"

I then talked excitedly about how I loved playing football in the fall, then basketball and hockey in the winter. He already knew my favorite sport came every spring – baseball. I told him how Grandpa Mack and I followed the Twins religiously and how we had attended some of the games together.

Brad divided his attention between the game on TV and the energetic recitation I was delivering. When I finally took a breath, Brad gave me his full attention and changed the subject on me.

"You get along with all your family up there?"

"I thought I did, at first, but not everyone wants me in the family."

Brad gave me a sour-grapes look and then asked, "Now, what in the world would make you say a thing like that?"

I told him about the previous Christmas Eve and the conversation I had overheard. Brad listened intently, nodding his head knowingly. When I told Brad how Mom had almost thrown my aunt and cousin out of the house because they didn't like me being in the family, he seemed to be quite pleased with Mom's solution.

"It sounds like your mom is a pretty strong and special lady."

I nodded my affirmation and said, "It doesn't help me know where I do belong, though."

"Struggling with that are you? Well, here's something for you to consider. Out of the thousands of kids needing families out there, who did your parents choose?"

I smiled at his logic and knew it to be the truth.

"Jackson, not everyone's heart operates the same way. You're a great kid. Sooner or later, the rest of your parent's kin will come around."

I nodded, as to agree, but in my heart, I truly didn't. *They've already had three years. How much time do they need?!*

That night, the Twins beat the Rangers, six-to-five. Immediately after the final out, I said good night to Brad and then traipsed upstairs. I found Janet in their bedroom, reading. I bent down and kissed her, then thanked her again for allowing Joel to stay for dinner.

"It was no problem at all, kiddo," said Janet. "Sleep tight."

Lack of sleep from the previous night, combined with baseball and girls that afternoon, not to mention the walk downtown in the fresh evening air, had taken everything out of me. Lying in bed, I listened to the breeze outside the screened window, as it rustled through the leaves of the neighbor's birch and poplar trees. Feeling totally relaxed, my thoughts gravitated toward the wonderful way Julie had welcomed me home. Shortly thereafter, I fell into a deep sleep.

CHAPTER 8

Wednesday, 9 August 1972

Mid-morning, I found myself running errands with Janet. First, it was off to the bank. During the short drive it took to get there, I figured she would use our outing to begin her inquisition. Instead, she surprised me by keeping all conversation light and casual.

"Did you have a good time playing ball with your friends? Brad told me you played well."

"Yeah, I had a blast yesterday. So far, every day's been really cool."

"Well, it's supposed to heat up pretty soon."

"What?!" I then gave Janet a look that said I thought she was a real square.

"You said it's been cool. Next week it's supposed to heat up."

"Uh, I wasn't talking about the weather. I meant that I've been having a good time!"

With a fake smug look on her face, Janet declared, "I knew that."

Janet's little game had always been to act, and even speak, like she wasn't very educated. In fact, most people would never guess that she had obtained a master's degree in Human Relations from Gustavus Adolphus College, in nearby Saint Peter. I even found myself falling for her down-home shtick from time to time.

In actuality, Janet had a very quick wit, and she had an enormous capacity to keep me in stitches. Often, her demeanor toward us boys was that of an old mother hen, but she was mostly easy going. Looking back on it, I would have to say that her opinions were quite liberal, especially for that town. She wasn't a died-in-the-wool women's libber – she liked her bras just fine - but she definitely wasn't a staunch conservative, either. While other kids had stay-at-home moms, who cooked and cleaned all day, Janet worked as an Assistant Personnel Manager at Immanuel Hospital.

I knew Janet loved her career, but she rarely talked about anything or anyone from the hospital. At age thirteen, I wasn't interested enough to ask, either. I was more afraid of her actually telling me about her work. I would then become bored and it would show. I didn't want to insult anyone that way, but I especially would never wish to insult Janet. Nevertheless, when it came to listening to others drone on about their work, I had the attention span of a two-year-old.

That morning, Janet had rearranged her schedule. She had to go to work later in the afternoon, so she could meet with some of the hospital's nightshift personnel. The morning provided we two a great opportunity to spend a little time together, plus get some personal errands knocked out.

As we pulled into the bank's drive-up service area, I was still waiting for Janet to begin asking me questions about my troubles in Duluth. Fortunately for me, she seemed determined to leave any heavy discussion alone.

As we sat, waiting for our turn to move up to the bank teller's window, Janet asked, "Where do you want to eat lunch today?"

"How about Robby's?" I suggested. "We can get a Gut Bomb!"

Nodding her agreement, Janet said, "Okie-dokie!"

Hating the two-word bastardization of the English language, I snapped, "That is so retarded!"

Unshaken, Janet said, "Danny tells me the same thing."

"But you still use it, don't you?"

"Yeah, it's a neat little mother's-revenge thing, knowing how it drives you boys bonkers."

I didn't doubt her motivation one bit. I should have remembered not to let her know how I felt about such things. *Great, now she'll spend the rest of the day using those words every chance she gets.* The thought of it caused me to roll my eyes, while shaking my head.

The Mercury needed gas, so when we finished at the bank, Janet drove to a nearby service station. Kurt worked there as a grease monkey, as he called himself. When Janet pulled in front of the pumps, Kurt hustled out of the garage, where he had been working on someone's old Pontiac.

When he arrived at Janet's window, she playfully instructed, "Fill it up and check the oil and check the air in the tires and wash the windows and whatever else you think needs attention...please."

In return, Kurt gave her his best, give-me-a-break look, but immediately went to work on the car.

As Kurt washed the windshield in front of me, I made silly faces at the grease monkey. Kurt simply laughed and when Janet wasn't looking, he shot me his middle finger. I then stepped out of the car and chatted with him while he finished servicing it. Kurt asked if I had plans for Thursday evening and I told him that I did not. He then informed me that the girls and some other friends were coming over that night. He then invited me to hang out with them.

Remembering how I had been set up at Janelle's soiree, I was now immediately suspicious of Kurt's motivations. Even though I enjoyed hanging out with my older foster brothers and their friends, I was in no mood for any of their shenanigans. So, trying to sound like I wanted to keep my options open, I replied, "Thanks...Maybe after the game. The Twins are playing the Angels that night and I want to watch."

"Baseball over girls?!" teased Kurt. "Man, have you gotta lot to learn!"

I had no doubt that what he said was the absolute truth. I just didn't want to be instructed in the asinine way he, Danny and their girls were probably planning.

When the car was ready to go, I climbed back inside, just in time to hear Kurt give Janet the tally for the services rendered. Her gut-shot reaction was enough to make both Kurt and I laugh.

"Eight dollars?! Just for gas, window washing, and some air in the tires?! You have got to be kidding!"

While Janet rummaged through her purse for her wallet, she asked Kurt if we could bring him something for lunch.

"No thanks," replied Kurt. "I brought a lunch. Just pay up and scram, will ya? I've got work to do."

Janet's over-animated look brought more laughter from my foster brother and me.

The morning seemed to pass quickly. After our stop at the gas station, Janet indulged herself in one of her favorite pastimes – shopping. I simply tagged along, hoping the activity would get more interesting, but feeling quite certain it would not.

First, we ducked into a well-known boutique on East Madison Avenue. In fact, it was so well known that I have since forgotten its name! The shop itself was much like any boutique. It catered to the female gender and was filled with all sorts of artsy-craftsy wall hangings, candles, bric-a-brac, knick-knacks, curio, and other such womanly junk. Before entering, I silently prayed to God, in hopes that none of my friends would see me walk into such a place.

While we both milled around the joint, Janet spied and then ogled a rather strange ceramic statuette. The figure was the likeness of books, which were somewhat haphazardly stacked atop one another. The book at the very top, entitled, *Darwin's Theory*, was opened wide. Squatting on its pages was a chimpanzee. The ceramic simian peered thoughtfully into the eyes of an anatomically-correct skull of a human being.

Acting a little more shocked than usual at her taste in décor, I asked, "You want that thing for where?!"

"I want it for the living room coffee table! I think it makes a rather profound statement."

"Yeah…It says, 'Strange lady lives here.' It'll go nicely with the Don Quixote silhouette wall hanging and the ceramic mariachi band figures."

Immediately, Janet gave me a look of mock indignation.

Much of Janet's taste in interior décor could be blamed on the times, I supposed. The late sixties and early seventies were very much about gaudy, loud, large, and downright strange. Janet was also a slave to the color wheel of the times. It seemed to have been limited to pea green, rust red, brown and gold. Nothing conservative could be found in the Wilson house. Pictures and paintings had gaudy gold painted frames. Large ceramic figures adorned the floors of the living room and den. Smaller statuettes were set on coffee tables, light stands, and sofa end tables. Janet once said she wanted the house to look unique. At the time, I thought the word, "bizarre," was a more accurate descriptor.

"That will not get you a cheeseburger, mister!" Janet playfully scolded.

"In that case, I think it looks great and would make a wonderful addition to the living room."

We both laughed and then Janet changed her mind about the purchase. I think she could tell that I was getting bored with the place, so she suggested that we move on to someplace that might hold my interest more.

"Where?" I asked.

"You'll see," she replied. "It's a new place I've been wanting to check out ever since it opened. I just haven't got around to it until now."

Understanding that I was not going to get a direct answer from her, I took it on faith that I would appreciate checking out the so-called, "new place," too. So, when we arrived at the car, I opened Janet's door for her, closed it after she got in, then hustled over the passenger side.

After I, too, was in my seat and ready to go, Janet smiled at me and said, "Thank you! That was gentlemanly of you."

I shrugged my shoulders and replied, "Thanks to my mom, it's becoming a real habit. I think she could be a bad influence on me."

As Janet backed the Mercury out of the parking slot, she chuckled under her breath and said, "You little snot."

The new place Janet spoke of ended up being Falkner's new department store. Like many other businesses, Falkner's was once located on Front Street. Their new store was now located at the south end of town and to me, it appeared enormous. I had mentioned to Janet how disappointed I was to see that their old store, in addition to all of the other shops located on Front Street, had closed. Now that we were in front of Falkner's newer and much larger department store, I hesitated to go inside. As I exited the car, I must have had a rather apprehensive look on my face. Janet shook her head and chuckled. "I doubt she's in there, kiddo."

"Who?" I asked, pretending I didn't know who or what she was talking about.

"Give me a break, will ya?" she asserted. "Come on!" Then waved me forward with her hand.

For fear of running into Julie, plus tiring rapidly of Janet's aimless wandering through stores, with no identifiable purpose in mind, I truly did not want to go into that particular store. Nevertheless, I begrudgingly followed Janet and kept my eyes peeled for any sign of the girl I had just seen, hugged, and spoken to the previous day. I figured that if I did spot Julie, it wouldn't be too hard to evade her by hurrying to another department, or perhaps hiding in one of the many aisles located within the vast confines of the store.

Falkner's store on Front Street had been a fixture in Mankato since the late 1800's. Gary Falkner's grandfather opened the very first store along the banks of the Minnesota River, when the town was not much more than a German settlement. Since that time, The Falkner Corporation had diversified and grown, with vast holdings throughout the state. The Falkners were one of Minnesota's older and more affluent families. The new department store on the hill was their newest expansion endeavor within Mankato.

Gary Falkner was well thought of in the community at large. Besides being the oldest son to August and Harriet Falkner, he was the reigning Chairman of the Board for the Falkner Corporation. As a member of the church council at St. Joseph the Worker, he involved himself in many charitable activities and outreach programs. I suppose he could be described as ruggedly handsome and athletic. Before I moved to Duluth, I played T-Ball, then Little League baseball. Gary was my coach for both activities. I remembered him as being extremely nice, fair, and calm at all times. Even with the most untalented little leaguers, his had patience abound.

His wife, Marilyn, was supposed to be a different story. Janet once told me she went to school with Julie's mom. According to her, Marilyn was pretty snooty back then. "She's just another middle-class girl who married well," said Janet. "However, the way she looks down her nose at everyone, you'd think she was born to royalty."

Talk within town limits labeled Marilyn Falkner as the type of woman who wore her affluence like an entitlement. I had no opportunity to meet her prior, but I thought any woman who gave birth to the likes of Julie, certainly could not be all *that* bad.

It was also rumored that Gary's standing within the extended Falkner family was somewhat tarnished. Supposedly, it was due to him marrying beneath his status. All such gossip and talk of social standing was lost on me. At age thirteen, I didn't care about having status out in society. I was still trying to find my place within a family.

Janet wandered through the different departments within Falkner's, ensuring that just about every aisle was thoroughly canvassed. I followed but kept a somewhat liberal-reactionary gap between the two of us. I had learned quickly not to follow her too closely. She had the annoying habit of stopping suddenly in the middle of a narrow aisle and changing her mind about which direction she meant to go. I, of course, kept my eyes moving at all times, trying to locate anyone who might look familiar. Suddenly, Janet caught my attention because she had, once again, stopped abruptly. This time, she stood still and snickered at me. "Jackson, relax, will you?"

"I'm fine," I lied. In reality, I was on pins and needles.

"According to Kurt and Danny, you're supposed to be over your fear of girls."

"What?!" I was incredulous. "What did they tell you?!"

Janet laughed again and then replied, "Enough to know that you truly have been having a *cool* time since you got here, kiddo."

"It's not what you think."

"Jackson, what's the big deal? You saw Julie yesterday, didn't you?"

"Yeah."

"And?"

"And…I wasn't prepared for how much she's changed."

Wearing a knowing grin, Janet then asked, "That bad, eh?"

"No, that good," I shyly admitted.

At that, Janet lost her smile and shot me a concerned look. "Be careful there, kiddo."

"Don't worry. I know…I'm not in her league.

"That's not what I meant at all, honey. It's simply that you'll be going home soon."

"Don't remind me."

"Hey, don't start up with me, kiddo. You have a good thing going up there with your folks…And you know it."

"I know. I guess I'm just a little frustrated is all."

"If you want, we can talk about it at lunch. Are you hungry yet?" I could tell she was getting a little impatient with me.

"I could eat."

Janet's clever smile then returned. "Never a problem in that department, is there?"

Robby's was another fixture in Mankato. The popular drive-in was located directly across the street from Mankato West High School. We arrived just before noon and almost as soon as the Mercury came to a halt, a carhop rushed out to greet us. I instantly recognized her as Cindy Milner, Tony's older sister.

"Hi, Mrs. Wilson! Hi, Jackson! Are you having a good time here in town?" The question was directed at me.

"Yeah," I smiled back at her. "It's been pretty *cool*, so far." I replied, giving Janet a devilish grin.

"Great! Are you two ready to order?"

Janet requested a regular cheeseburger with fries and a Coke.

"Got it…Jackson, what about you?"

"I'll have a gut bomb, with everything, fries, and a root beer please."

"You remembered!" Cindy chuckled and then sped off with our order.

People lovingly referred to Robby's burgers as gut bombs. The moniker had a double meaning. The first being their size - Robby's burgers were huge. However, they were also quite greasy and usually sat on your stomach like a rock. In my opinion, they weren't the best burgers in town, but eating at Robby's felt familiar. Just then, I truly needed familiar because I was tiring of seeing all that had changed or gone away.

While waiting for the burgers to arrive, Janet didn't waste any time starting in on me again.

"So, what are you so frustrated about?"

I sat there, looking at my feet and thought for a minute. I wanted to tell her about Julie's party and how I hadn't been invited. I also wanted to tell her about how bad my life seemed in Duluth, but she probably already knew some of that. Actually, there were many things I wanted to talk to her about. But right then, it just didn't seem like the right time or place. So, I asked, "Do we have to talk about it right now?"

"No, we don't, but I do think we should sit down soon and discuss a few things."

"I know…and we will…just…not right now…Okay?"

"Okay, kiddo…Relax."

Janet then switched gears on me and started a long-winded narrative about how Mankato had changed since I had left. Old businesses were closing, and new businesses were opening up all over town. I listened with interest, especially when she talked about some of my favorite places and how they had relocated. *At least they aren't closed and gone forever,* I thought.

One of the newest attractions Janet talked about was a new roller-skating arena. Because I was a closet, roller-skating enthusiast, I took particular interest in hearing about Mankato's new rink. In past summers, I had spent many evenings roller skating at Duluth's Curling Club. During the winter months, there were curling lanes on the first floor and a hockey rink on the second floor. However, between the Memorial Day and Labor Day weekends, the second floor became a roller rink.

I first tried roller skating when I attended my cousin Tommy's tenth birthday party, which was held at the Curling Club. That skating party was so much fun that it kind of got under my skin. I secretly admired the dance skaters. When a couple's-only skate was announced, I sat and watched both young and old couples twirl gracefully around the rink. How two people could move as one on skates was a mystery to me. So, I secretly vowed to learn all those skating maneuvers and dance steps.

Biff, an older man in his mid-twenties, frequented the club. He sort of took me under his wing and taught me everything I wanted to know. Madison, a lady who worked there, taught me how to dance skate with a partner. Like so many other older women did back then, I was given orders to call her, Mom, too.

I ardently enjoyed skating at the club because I rarely ran into anyone from school or the neighborhood. In three years, I had become quite a bit more than just a pretty-good skater. I didn't let any of my casual friends know about my abilities. It was my little secret. It was another one of those things I emphatically felt would not have been looked upon as being *cool*. Mom and Dad didn't even know how good I was. As I listened to Janet drone on about Mankato's new attraction for young people, I found myself hoping for a chance to try it out.

Janet then moved on and talked about the construction of a new shopping mall. Like most new businesses, it was being built up on the hill, on the southern part of town. It was one of the main reasons that Front Street appeared so dead. Front Street had seen its heyday, but it now appeared that it would no longer be the shopping hub of Mankato.

In order to participate in the lunchtime conversation, I told Janet about Duluth's brand-new shopping mall. It had been completed in the past year and I loved wandering around inside it with Mom or my cousin, Tommy. Often, Grandpa Mack chaperoned Tommy and I there. When he did, he always threw money our way and told us to get lost. While Tommy and I ran off to squander our loot, Grandpa Mack would rest his bones on one of the many benches that were located in the center of the mall.

I then let my tongue loosen a bit more. I informed Janet that little outings, like going to the mall or the zoo, were how Gramps first got Tommy and I acquainted. After a short while, we both looked forward to being with our grandfather. Our favorite outings were the Minnesota Twins baseball games he took us to. In a very short period of time, the three of us became close pals. Unfortunately, Tommy lived in another part of the city and it was too far for me to see him on a regular basis. He and Gramps were the two main reasons I looked forward to the large, family gatherings.

Janet listened to me with great interest. I knew I wasn't talking about things she really wanted to know, but she seemed grateful that I was sharing any information at all.

Just then, Cindy returned with our lunch and skillfully hooked the service tray on Janet's window. She greeted both of us again and then looked right at me. "Jackson, I'll bet you have no problem eating that whole burger now. I can't believe how much you've grown."

Janet laughed and said, "Believe me, Cindy. He'll probably have it down his throat before you get back inside."

Cindy laughed at the look I gave Janet. I then mumbled, "Give me a break."

"You two enjoy your lunch, okay?" insisted Cindy. "I'll be back to check on you after." Before we could properly thank her, Cindy was off and running again. She was in a hurry because the lunch hour rush was noticeably underway. Otherwise, she probably would have stayed and talked our ears off. I remembered she had a gift for it.

"I always thought Cindy was one of the cutest and sweetest girls in the neighborhood," said Janet. "It's a wonder she and Kurt never got together. They're about the same age."

With a mouthful of burger I said, "Kurt always thought she was a busy body…And she talks too much."

Janet was indignant. "Oh, is that so?!"

Instantly, I realized that I had just let a little too much cat out of the bag. Janet didn't stand for her sons acting standoffish toward people she approved of. It was a tightrope I had to walk a few times myself. In the past, if Janet spoke charitably about someone we boys could not stand to be around, we knew it was best to just nod our head and agree with her.

Janet then looked at her watch and said, "Hurry up and finish your lunch, kiddo. I still have to get to work this afternoon."

I bolted the rest of my lunch down, feeling grateful the whole time that I didn't have to utter another word. I was also glad that Janet was in a hurry, therefore, distracted. She would be far too busy to broach the subject of Cindy Milner with Kurt. Even if she did, it would serve him right for tattling on me. Besides, I really liked the girl Kurt was seeing. Janelle was great and I knew Janet thought so, too. Nevertheless, I did give Janet's question about Kurt and Cindy a brief thought. To me, it would be like my older brother dating my older sister. That seemed just a little too weird, even for me and my mixed-up circumstances.

We finished our lunch and because Janet was now in a real hurry, I got out, grabbed the service tray, and handed it to the first available carhop. Cindy was busy chatting with some girls in an old, Ford Galaxy, so another pretty carhop took the tray from me. I then waved good-bye to Cindy. As I did, a thought crossed my mind. *If she wasn't so much older than me, and I didn't think of her as my big sister, I wouldn't be afraid to date Cindy, even if she does talk too much!*

On the drive home, we left the car windows down. The early afternoon temperature remained unseasonably comfortable. In fact, it felt more like spring than summer. The breeze coming in the window, combined with the gut bomb I had sitting on my stomach, made me extremely drowsy. I thought about taking a nap when we got back to the house. Unlike Janet, I wasn't in a hurry to go anywhere that afternoon. I laid my head back on the seat and gazed out the window at passing houses and trees. As the scenery sped past my eyes, it had a hypnotic effect. I rapidly became heavy lidded. However, in a split second, Janet brought me out of my drowsiness, when she asked, "So, you think Julie has grown into a rather cute young lady since you last saw her?"

"Yeah…Huh?!" I immediately recovered from my semi-slumbering state. "I mean, I guess so…Whatever." It was a weak recovery.

Janet kept her eyes fixed on the road ahead and just smiled from ear to ear. She had me right where she wanted me. "Relax, Jackson. It's perfectly okay that you think Julie is cute. As a matter of fact, it really is about time for you to start looking at girls through different eyes."

Oh great, I sarcastically thought. *I'm really gonna have to listen to this! I'm trapped!*

"I know girls are looking at you. I also know they like what they see," continued Janet. "You may find yourself playing catch-up in that department, in comparison to other kids your age, that is."

"Yeah, well, it's not all my fault," I mumbled.

"There isn't any blame to attach, Jackson. Sometimes kids are late starters and with all that you've been through, it's perfectly understandable."

"Yeah, I suppose." *God, please hurry up and get us back to the house!*

Janet kept up with her line of banter about the birds and bees and how I shouldn't be afraid to accept a girl's attention. I nodded my head a lot and tried to be polite about all the good advice she thought she was giving me. After all, she did buy lunch.

As we approached the turn onto Westwood Drive, I noticed the guys playing basketball in Tony Milner's driveway. Janet must have seen them, too. When I shot her a quick look and opened my mouth to speak, it was as if she had read my mind. Before I uttered a word, Janet hit the brakes and swerved toward the curb. When I say that Janet hit the brakes, I mean that when the car came to a complete stop, my teeth were almost in the dashboard. However, since I was still fully intact, I said nothing. Instead, I settled for giving her my best are-you-out-of-your-mind look.

In response, Janet chuckled and cavalierly said, "Sorry about that."

We said our good-byes there. Janet then hurriedly reminded me that Brad would be home after five o'clock. I jumped out and barely got the door closed before she pulled away from the curb. She gunned the engine and continued up Westwood Drive.

As Janet sped off, Tony laughed, "She don't drive too good, does she?"

Absentmindedly shaking my head, I replied, "Nope...but you gotta love her anyway."

The guys were short one player, so my arrival was quite fortuitous. Tony and Dave teamed up against Joel and me. Mike McDonald wasn't there to officiate, so we were on our honor.

We knew from past scrimmages that the teams were about as even as we could get them. Dave and I were the two biggest jocks of the group, so we were always on opposite sides. Dave's problem was Tony. It was Tony's basket and his ball, but I remembered that he had no real talent for the game. Joel was better at baseball than he was at basketball, but he still didn't suck as bad as Tony.

Athletically speaking, Dave and I had always been neck and neck. We pursued sports with the same vigor. That was his dad's influence at work. In years past, Mr. Lester had included me many times, when privately coaching his son. I loved it but was also aware of the true reasoning behind it. Back then, most adults in the neighborhood felt sorry for the poor, homeless boy, who lived with the Wilsons. But Jim Lester was so very different. He had a talent for making me believe there was no pity involved. As a result, not only did Dave and I become natural competitors against one another, but we also became the best of friends.

From the get-go, Dave and I were hitting shots from all over the place, thus keeping the score close. Joel was also good for a few points, which gave us a slight advantage, or so I thought. To my surprise, Tony had gained in skill and was making quite a few shots from outside the lines. It was another one of those changes I hadn't prepared myself for.

As it turned out, we had a real contest on our hands. That is, right up until the girls showed up. Almost as if they came out of nowhere, Anne Hayward, Gail Petersen, and Julie Falkner walked up the driveway. Upon spying them, Tony yelled, "Water break!"

When I first saw Julie standing there, smiling right at me, I almost choked and agreed a water break was definitely in order. My heart immediately began to race. It wasn't caused by exertion, either.

Casual greetings circulated around the group, but Julie gave me what seemed to be a little-extra something, when she turned to me and in the sweetest voice I ever heard, said, "Hi, Jackson!"

I locked eyes with Julie and immediately felt blood flooding to my face. *Say something, dummy!* But an awkward smile and a not-so-smooth, "Hello," was all I could manage.

"What are you three up to?" asked Dave.

"Oh, you know, girl stuff," replied Anne.

I thought, *"What exactly does that mean?"* I don't think any guy actually knew, but back then, we never bothered to ask, either.

As casual banter started up within the group, I paid attention, but didn't have anything to add to their discussion. I began to feel slightly invisible. So, after a short while, I unceremoniously backed away from the gaggle. While waiting for our interrupted game to resume, I decided to stay warmed up by shooting more baskets.

As I dribbled the ball, I noticed Julie watching me and not paying much attention to the others. *Great, I'll give her something to watch,* I thought.

I began my shooting exhibition by taking a few close shots, but they were too easy. I intended to impress Julie further by backing up each time I put one through the hoop. Shooting in rapid succession, from approximately ten feet away, I made four shots in a row. I then decided to back up even farther away. Preparing to shoot from approximately thirteen feet away, my concentration was locked on the hoop. Just as I was about to release the ball, Julie yelled, "Hey, Jackson!" The ball missed the basket completely, ricocheted off the garage, then bounced into the neighbor's hedge. When I gave her a mock annoyed look, she busted out laughing.

"Sorry," giggled Julie. "Can I talk to you a minute?"

First, I retrieved the ball and then went to where Julie stood, slightly away from the others. I saw Tony paying attention to us, but he kept a respectable distance.

"It was really neat seeing you yesterday," offered Julie.

I caught myself getting lost in her blue eyes, so I forced myself to blink and look away, saying "Thanks."

"Did you hear I was having a party Friday night?"

"Yeah, I heard."

Looking down at her shoes and smiling shyly, Julie then said, "Well, it occurred to me yesterday that maybe I didn't make it too clear. Everyone who was at the ballpark is invited."

Speak, you idiot, speak! I thought frantically, but at the same time, I was desperately trying to keep my cool. "So…you want me there, too?" I managed to ask.

Her expression brightened dramatically. "Yes! Absolutely! Do you remember where I live?"

Tony was suddenly at my side and threw an arm around my shoulders. Grinning from ear to ear, he said, "Don't worry, we'll get him there."

Julie then began to back away toward the others, but added, "Great! So, I'll see you then?"

Stammering greatly, I replied, "Yeah…um…that'll be great…and thanks."

Dave then suggested we get back to the game. *The game?* I thought. *What game?* I suddenly wished I had actually lost the basketball.

When I saw that the girls weren't leaving, I tensed up even more. Instead of leaving, so they could go do more of their *girl stuff*, they just stepped off the driveway and onto the front lawn. There, they sat in the grass, while we guys got back to our scrimmage.

Once again, I intended to put on a shooting exhibition for Julie, but just then, my concentration was totally screwed up. For the rest of that afternoon, I couldn't hit the broad side of a barn from the inside! Just about every ball I put in the air refused to go in the basket.

During another water break, Joel asked, "So, what's got into you all of a sudden?"

"I don't know. My concentration is off, I guess."

"Really?!" replied Joel, wearing the same shit-eating grin he wore the previous day at the ballpark. "I wonder who caused that?!"

Joel and I lost that game badly and, of course, Dave and Tony gloated. It was nowhere near the shooting exhibition I needed to impress Julie. Nevertheless, when I looked in her direction, she always seemed to be smiling at me. Was it my imagination or was Tony's theory about being the new guy in town becoming fact? The only thing I truly hoped for was to rapidly develop the ability to talk to her without tripping over my tongue.

Janet Wilson hit the nail on the head, when she said it was time for me to start looking at girls through different eyes. That afternoon, I most certainly looked at Julie in a different light. She was truly something to behold. Long, black curls hung down around her shoulders. She wore a pink pullover top and blue denim shorts. Her tanned and toned legs reminded me of those I had seen in magazines. From the approving looks Julie gave me, I came to the conclusion that Janet appeared to be right about that, as well.

The group then decided to go down into Tony's basement, so we could cool off and listen to music. As we all filed through the front door, I took note of the question-mark look on Cheryl Milner's face. As she looked up from vacuuming the living room carpet, her expression was quite comical.

As I passed, I gave Cheryl my customary greeting. "Hi, Mrs. Tony's Mom!"

Clearly confused by the small army marching toward the basement doorway, Cheryl simply mumbled, "Hello."

While the rest of us made our play for what chairs were available, Tony got the record player going. I scored a comfortable lounge chair and the couples took up the couch. Seeing that Julie was left standing, I decided to be the gentleman Mom was training me to be.

"Sit here, Julie. I don't mind the floor."

Julie graciously accepted my offer. As I repositioned myself on the floor, Tony cranked up the volume on the record player. Dave, who sat at one end of a large couch with his arm around Anne, threw me a couch pillow to sit on. Instead, I sprawled out on my back and situated the pillow under my head. Joel relaxed at the other end of the couch with Gail. When he thought I wasn't looking, he chucked another pillow in my direction. In one fluid motion, I foiled his plans by easily snatching the pillow from the air with one hand, then adding it to the other pillow already behind my head.

"Smooth," said Joel.

Wanting to get in on the act, Tony grabbed a huge, overstuffed, floor pillow and heaved it in my direction. I caught it with both hands and then positioned it against a nearby corner. I used it to cushion my back while sitting on the sofa pillows.

In mock dismay, I whined, "What's with the pillow throwing?" Laughter was what I was shooting for; our small group rewarded me nicely.

In the soft light of that basement, I repeatedly caught Julie staring at me. At one point, I thought she was absolutely beaming in my direction. It reminded me of the look Carrie gave Danny, when he admitted that she was his girlfriend. Julie now wore that look and it made me extremely nervous, especially since she was aiming it directly at me. *Whoa! I've seen that look before, but she can't be serious! Not now!*

Tony sat on a bar stool, which he had positioned by the record player. I could tell he really was getting into the new music of the '70s. He seemed to have a 45-rpm recording of the current top 40, plus cases of 45s from recent years gone by.

"Is there anything you don't have over there?" I joked but was actually impressed by his collection.

"I spend most of my allowance on records," he replied. "That and gut bombs."

"Tony, can you bring some of your music Friday night?" asked Julie. "I don't have as much of the new stuff as you do."

"Yeah, no problem," Tony replied coolly.

Suddenly, Gail got up from the couch, then practically ordered Tony to put on something slow. She then turned and held out her arms toward Joel, a signal for him to get up, also.

"Aw, come on, not now!" protested Joel.

Gail simply gave him a look that said, "Get up now, mister!" Of course, Joel acquiesced and promptly got up from his comfortable seat.

Tony played Michael Jackson's new hit single, *Ben*. As Joel and Gail held each other close, slowly swaying back and forth, a thought entered my head that almost made me break out in a sweat. *Geez, if Dave and Anne join in, Julie will want me to dance, too!"*

In an attempt to ignore the couple dancing in the middle of the floor, I laid my head back and closed my eyes. Then, I heard Tony's voice call out to me. "Hey, Jackson, do you skate?"

Trying to remain cool in Julie's eyes, I replied, "Only every winter, when I play hockey."

"No...do you roller skate?" asked Tony.

"Oh yeah!" exclaimed Anne. "Jackson, we have a new roller-skating joint that just opened up here. It's a blast!"

I looked at the guys. They were all nodding in agreement.

"We should get a group together and go," said Tony. "Jackson, are you in?"

I nonchalantly replied, "I guess I could give it a try."

It was then decided that we would bring the subject up Friday night at Julie's party. That way, we could get more people to go and then figure out when would be the best day and time.

Trying to break the awkwardness between us, Julie asked, "Do you have a skating place where you live?"

I then proceeded to tell them all about the Curling Club and how it transformed from a winter sports arena to a roller rink in the summer.

Tony asked, "What's curling?"

"It's like shuffleboard on ice," I answered. "Only, they slide big, polished rocks and use brooms for some reason or other. I've never played it, but I've watched it a few times after playing hockey."

Our little group spent the rest of the afternoon listening to records and comparing the differences between Mankato and Duluth. When I talked of Duluth, I noticed Julie giving me her undivided attention. I never had a girl so interested in what I had to say before, except maybe Lori Mudd. It was another new sensation that I didn't quite know what to do with. Still, I felt myself beginning to relax within that co-ed circle of friends, even if it was just a little. I figured if I was going to Julie's party Friday night, I had better work on my social skills. Julie was actually making it easy for me. I still wasn't quite at ease with her, but at least I didn't feel like the burger I had for lunch was stuck in my throat anymore. As the afternoon went on, interaction within the group began to feel more natural.

When Dave announced that he had to get going, it was close to suppertime. He then offered to walk Anne home. Imitating a southern belle, she replied, "Why, thank you kind sir!"

Immediately, Joel gave Gail a look. "I suppose you want me to walk you home, too."

Gail chuckled, "Well, okay, but only if you insist." With a sly smile, she then looked at Julie and me.

Julie gave me one of her amazing smiles and then asked, "Jackson, are you going my way?"

Knowing full well that I had just been set up, I was determined not to overreact. My insides felt like they were about to explode. Fortunately, I was able to keep my outward appearance composed. But I overcompensated by making a lame attempt at being funny, when I replied, "Yeah, I guess I am, whether I actually am or not."

Picking up on my clumsiness, Julie said, "I mean, if it's too far out of your way…"

I cut her off by exclaiming, "You don't have to talk me into it!"

My words were too hurried and came out way too desperate. The comment got raised-eyebrow looks from the others, that is, all but Julie. She simply smiled as though she was getting exactly what she wanted.

My immediate goal was to walk with her, without totally embarrassing myself. *If I can do that, there might actually be some hope for me, yet,* I thought.

Julie and I said our good-byes to the group on the driveway. Of course, before we left, I had to give Tony's mom, Cheryl, her special hug. She explained to everyone that it was because I had been away for so long. According to her, I was in the rears on the payment of hugs. When Cheryl relinquished her hold on me, Anne came over and playfully put her arms around my neck. She asked, "Does that actually work with him?"

Laughter broke out and I allowed myself to temporarily be the center of their attention. For the first time since returning to Mankato, I felt truly reconnected with my friends again.

After saying final good-byes to the gang, Julie and I began our journey up Westwood Drive. I said a silent prayer, hoping that no one at the Wilson residence would see us when we passed by.

Telling Julie that I would walk her home because it was on my way was quite funny. She lived on Sunset Boulevard, which was a good seven blocks past the Wilson house. We laughed about that very thing.

"Yeah, I'm going your way alright…for about a block!" I joked.

Julie laughed. "I'm sorry. I just didn't want to walk all the way by myself. I really hate living so far away from all my friends."

"I know exactly how you feel." I regretted the words as soon as they left my mouth. *Crap, did I just say too much?* If I had, Julie didn't let on.

"It's amazing to see you after all this time." Julie's tone was sincere. "I'm surprised you even remember me."

"It hasn't been *that* long, Julie,"

We kept walking and casually talking for about three blocks. Her smile and the sound of her voice had me mesmerized. I was in unchartered waters, but thankfully, I didn't feel like I was drowning.

"If you don't mind me asking, what do you miss most about Mankato?"

"That's easy…the Wilsons and everybody I ever considered a friend."

I knew Julie was fishing for something when she asked, "Am I in that group?"

Trying my hardest to be witty, I replied, "Umm…let's see…you *were* the first girl I ever kissed. So, what do you think?" I had just delivered my first serious line to a girl and didn't even know it. In turn, Julie answered with her laughter.

Just then, I heard a vehicle coming up behind us. Thinking on it later, I should have recognized the sound of Adam Harris's old Chevy. When he eased his old clunker up beside us, I could not believe my eyes, and my bad luck. With his muscular arm hanging out the driver's window, he nodded at me in acknowledgement. In a flat tone, he greeted me by simply saying, "Jackson." The "Hello" was inferred.

Just as flatly, I replied, "Sir." Then, I proceeded to look daggers at him.

"Who's your friend, son?"

Before I could utter a word, Julie spoke up, "It's Julie Falkner, Mr. Harris. I'm Gary Falkner's daughter."

Adam smiled at her and said, "Nice to meet you, young lady." Nonetheless, his delivery lacked warmth. He then turned his attention back to me. "Jackson, I was hoping we could talk sometime, while you're still in town."

The very sound of his voice grated against my nerves. I felt anger welling up inside of me. At the same time, so was my age-old fear of him. My mind replied, *"I'd love to, like when hell freezes over!"* But all I could actually get my mouth to say was a mumbled, "Sure, I guess so."

Adam then asked, "Can I offer you two a lift somewhere?"

Before Julie could react, I blurted, "No, but thanks."

"In that case, I'll leave you to your walk. I'll be in touch, son. It was nice to meet you, Julie." Adam then eased the Chevy away from the curb.

Julie and I stood there for a long moment, watching Adam's car proceed up the block. She then turned to me and said, "I sometimes forget that Adam Harris is your dad."

"I don't know what you're talking about. My dad's name is Brice Landry."

"I'm sorry, Jackson. I don't really know what to say."

Sensing her uneasiness, I quickly rebounded by offering, "No, I'm the one who's sorry. He's just the one who caused it." I then nodded in the Chevy's direction. "It's funny…NOW he wants to call me son." I then turned to Julie and asked, "How do you know him?"

"He does odd jobs for my dad from time to time. I also know him from church." The look I had on my face must have been that of disbelief because Julie felt the need to explain further. "Really, Jackson, he does a lot of work to help people who go to St. Joseph's."

I couldn't believe my ears. There was just no way for me to get my mind wrapped around that idea. The nightmare I used to call, Dad, was now supposed to be a pillar in the church community?! *My church!? My sanctuary?! No way!*

Becoming enraged and afraid that Julie would see it, I swiftly turned away, praying she wouldn't notice. It was to no avail, of course.

Putting her hand on my shoulder, Julie softy asked, "Hey, are you okay?"

I lied by replying, "Yes." Then, after a few moments had passed, I added, "I just can't believe that man was ever my dad."

A dark cloud descended over the two of us. I didn't know what to say or do. I tried to put the encounter behind me, but at that moment, I didn't have the coping skills. I was then worried about what Julie must be thinking.

"I'm sorry that just happened," I began. "I think it'll happen again, too. That is, if I don't actually agree to see him. Maybe you would be better off steering clear of me until I get this sorted out."

Julie's reaction told me more than her words. With a shocked look on her face, she gasped, "Don't you dare…Don't you dare avoid me! You hear me?!" Her soft eyes were now wild.

"Yeah…I hear you." Because of her overreaction, I couldn't stop the smile that spread across my lips. My only thought being, *WOW!*

In an instant, Julie regained her composure. I could tell she was embarrassed. "I'm sorry…sometimes I get too excited and things just…kinda…fly out of my mouth."

Facetiously, I returned, "No kidding…Really?!" I kept smiling, so she would know that everything was still cool between us.

As we resumed our walk to Julie's place, she now seemed totally unsure of herself, like she was searching for something to say, but could not land on any particular thing. Inside my head, I was pretty much doing the same thing. Taking the initiative to re-break the ice, I asked her about school, a harmless enough subject, or so I thought. Julie immediately launched herself into an energetic barrage about how she liked most of her teachers from the previous year, how time consuming, but fun it was to be on the cheerleading squad, and how she wished she had more time to practice the piano. Julie explained that she loved to play but felt there were more important things going on in her life.

Next, I clenched my teeth and asked, "Are you goin' out with anyone?" I was almost afraid of her answer.

"I'm not really allowed to go out on dates, Jackson. I don't know what my mom would think if she found out that I liked a guy. I think Anne and Gail keep secrets about Dave and Joel from their parents, too. That's why we always try to get groups together when we go out. Our parents don't seem to mind that. That's why I'm really looking forward to having the gang over on Friday. We have a great basement and my parents will stay upstairs…I hope."

Breathing somewhat easier, I said, "That didn't really answer my question. I guess what I'm asking is…Is there a guy here in town you're interested in?"

191

Again, Julie stopped, turned, and looked me in the eye. With no identifiable expression on her face, she softly said, "Yes." Then, without further ado, she turned and continued walking.

Before following, I paused and thought... *Oh, gee, thanks for clearing that up!*

I managed to walk Julie the rest of the way home without spazzing out too badly. The hardest part came when we got to her front door. I was now truly out of my element. Mad thoughts rushed through my head. *What are the ground rules here?! What's expected, a handshake, a punch in the arm?! What?!*

"Okay, so, I'll see you Friday, right?" Julie queried.

"Uh, Friday?" My mind went suddenly blank.

"Yeah...Remember? Friday night? Here? My party?"

Chuckling nervously, I stammered, "Uh...Oh yeah! I almost forgot."

Before I knew what was happening, Julie threw her arms around my neck and whispered, "You'd better be here, Jackson." She then gave me a quick peck on the cheek.

After Julie disappeared behind her front door, I just stood there, barely breathing. *Holy smokes! What just happened?!*

The entire walk back to Westwood Drive was a blur. I couldn't wipe the smile from my face, nor could I believe what was going on inside of me. It was that first kiss under the Milner's weeping willow all over again. This time, I didn't feel the need to run because I had already been caught.

Chapter 9

As I moseyed up the driveway, I observed Brad, Kurt, and Danny playing some before-dinner basketball. When they saw me, the three of them paused the game to catch their breath.

"Hey! There you are, buddy," greeted Brad, sounding a bit winded. "Where ya been?"

Rather absentmindedly, I replied, "Just hanging out with friends."

"You want to team up against these two, just like we used to?"

"No thanks. I've played already today. I'm kinda pooped out."

"Hope you like spaghetti. It's what I'm fixing for dinner."

"Great!" I exclaimed, hardly hearing a word. I was still very much inside my head.

"Did you have a good day?" asked Brad.

"Yeah, you could say that." There must have been something in my voice I hadn't intended because the three of them exchanged raised-eyebrow looks.

Brad recovered first and instead of pursuing the matter further, he simply stated, "Okay then, dinner will be in about an hour." He then headed for the side door, leaving me to face my former-foster brothers.

Kurt and Danny were both wearing mischievous grins. Their demeanor wasn't anything I wasn't already accustomed to, but when they directed those looks my way, it always paid for me to be wary. I thought it best to make a hasty retreat. So, I left them standing there and hurried into the house. Not wanting to answer any unwanted questions from Brad, I immediately rushed down to the basement. My plan was to shoot pool until suppertime and leave them all to speculate to their hearts content.

After carefully lining up and taking my first shot, I heard a stampede coming down the stairs. Kurt and Danny, acting quite nonchalantly, entered the den and took up positions on either side of the pool table. It was an effective tactic they used when they wanted to prevent my escape. *Ignore them*, I thought. *Maybe they'll just go away.* Unfortunately, ignoring those two was next to impossible.

I was busy lining up another shot, when Kurt leaned over and snatched the very ball I had been aiming at. Giving them both a blank look, I came up from my shooting stance and leaned on the cue.

"So…Jackson," Kurt began smugly, continuously tossing the billiard ball from one hand to the other. "Where were you and Miss Julie Falkner heading, when you passed the house?"

"You saw that." I feverishly tried to think of a defense strategy that would throw them off track.

Danny piped in, grinning from ear to ear. "Yeah, we saw that."

Suddenly, an idea hit me, so I answered them with a question of my own. "You gonna tell Mom, like you told her about the other night?"

Immediately, I saw that my question had the desired effect. The looks on Kurt and Danny's faces told me that I was now on offense and *they* were on defense.

Kurt asked, "Mom talked to you about that?"

"Only all morning long!" I made it sound as though they had betrayed me in a major way. I didn't mind exaggerating, either. What they didn't know wouldn't hurt me at all.

"Sorry, man. We didn't mean to." Kurt sounded truly ashamed, then he had a thought. "Wait a minute. Did she finally give you her looking-at-girls-with-different-eyes speech?"

There was no way for me to hide my surprise at Kurt's accurate guess. I exclaimed, "How'd you know that?!" Then, I couldn't help myself and burst out laughing. "You've had that talk with her, too?!"

"Oh my God, yes!" Danny laughed. "Did she also tell you how the girls are definitely looking at you differently?" He mimicked Janet quite well.

Absolutely enjoying the irony, I stated, "Wow! She needs to get some new material."

"Heck yeah," said Kurt. "Otherwise, our kids are gonna have to listen to the same speech."

We were now laughing freely, and I wasn't sore at them anymore. The fact that I had to listen to *The Talk*, the very same speech, which had previously been delivered to Kurt and Danny, now seemed more like a rite of passage than anything else.

"So, back to the original question, little brother," said Danny. "What about you and Julie?"

"Yeah, man, spill it," coerced Kurt.

"I don't know what to tell you. I was playing basketball with the guys, and the girls just, sort of, showed up. We hung out in Tony's basement for the rest of the afternoon and one thing led to another. Next thing I know, I'm walking her home."

"Were there any sparks?" asked Kurt.

Unclear of his meaning, I asked, "Any what?!"

Kurt gave me his don't-play-stupid-with-me look and said, "You know, did anything happen?"

Not wanting to admit anything, let alone give details, I mumbled, "Kinda… I guess."

Danny chuckled and then pried further. "What do you mean, kinda?"

"I mean, I don't really know if she likes me or if she's just being polite."

Danny then asked, "What happened, hugs, kisses, anything?"

"Hugs yes…and one kiss, but just on the cheek."

"Yeah, she likes you," asserted Kurt.

Danny exclaimed, "Dang, Jackson, you're a stud! First it was Lori Mudd, now Julie?! Who do you got on the line for tomorrow?!"

Knowing that I was going to have to put up with more of their immature crap, I simply shook my head and rolled my eyes. Then, I remembered my encounter with Adam and stopped smiling. Giving them a straight look, I said, "There's something else I need to tell you. I think Adam Harris is following me around town."

Danny shrugged his shoulders and then said, "He was here looking for you shortly after you and Julie went by."

"Did you send him our direction?"

Kurt, who was now looking down at his feet, replied, "Well...we told him you had walked by not long ago. So, yeah...I suppose you can blame that one on us, too."

Danny asked, "What's the big deal?"

"I don't know just yet, but it's starting to feel creepy."

"What do you mean?" asked Danny again.

"Well, ever since Sunday, I seem to be either seeing his car off in the distance or like today, he came up behind Julie and me."

"Maybe you should talk to Dad about it," suggested Kurt.

"Normally, I would. But now, I don't know if I can."

"Why not?" asked Kurt.

"I overheard him tell Mom he went to school with Adam and they were pretty tight. I'm not sure he would believe me or help me with this."

"Bullshit!" growled Danny. "You know damned good and well he would."

"SHHHHH!" hushed Kurt. Then, in a whispered yell, he said, "He's only right above us! Hold it down!"

"I shouldn't have brought it up at all," I said.

"Yeah, but you did," said Danny.

I could tell I had offended Danny greatly by voicing distrust in his dad. It was too late; I couldn't take it back. Later, I would have to find a way to make it up to him. My more immediate concern was finding an opportune time to talk to Brad about it.

When we were called up for dinner, Kurt cautioned me about bringing up the subject of Adam Harris. "I don't know what Dad's gonna think about all this, so watch it."

Brad's spaghetti was an unsophisticated concoction of ground beef, mixed with jarred, Italian-seasoned, tomato sauce, ladled over spaghetti noodles. After playing basketball that afternoon, plus taking a long, but unexpected walk, I should have been starved. Instead, I had a sinking feeling in my stomach, so I just picked at the tangled mess on my plate. Brad noticed that I wasn't attacking the meal with my usual fervor. "Either you're not hungry or you really don't like my spaghetti," he jabbed.

"No…I like your spaghetti just fine. I just have a few things on my mind."

"Like what?" asked Brad.

Kurt kicked me under the table and cleared his throat.

"It's nothing major. You know…girl stuff," I lied.

"Girl stuff?! You?! Really?!" Brad looked genuinely surprised. "Maybe we should wait until there's a *girl* present to help you out. I'll guarantee you this…A table full of *guys* will never figure out a girl problem."

"It's not so much a problem with the girl. It's more of a timing thing." offered Kurt.

Giving his oldest son an overly-animated-perplexed look, Brad asked, "In plain English please…What does that mean?"

Danny jumped in. "It's simple. There's a girl who's making a play for Jackson. He kinda likes her back, but he knows he'll be leaving next week."

Feeling like it was my turn to do some kicking under the table, I sarcastically thought, *Oh, great… Thanks, Danny!*

"Does this girl have a name? And, by any chance, would it happen to be Julie Falkner?" queried Brad.

I hesitated and then sheepishly replied, "Yes…and yes." I figured that he must have seen Julie and me, while he shot baskets with my loose-lipped brothers. *We should have gone a different way!*

Keeping his eyes on his plate, Brad considered my answer for a minute or two. While he continued eating, he nodded his head, as if he were in serious thought. Then, he looked at me and in a clear, but calm voice, said, "Look, buddy, the only thing I'm going to say at this time is…I think you need to be careful there."

I didn't understand what he was suggesting and quite frankly, I didn't care. Because of Julie's kiss, my mind was made up. So, I took a deep breath and rather forcefully announced, "I've been invited to a party at her house this Friday night. If it's okay with you and Mom, I'd like to go."

I could tell I had greatly surprised all three of them. Their faces were frozen with pure astonishment.

"Stop looking at me like that. I'm not doing anything wrong. These are my friends. They're all getting together, and it just so happens that it will be at her house Friday night." I then pointed at Kurt and Danny. "It's no different than hanging out with you two and your friends. It's just that…besides coming here to see all of you, these are the friends I came here to see. I didn't plan on the boy-girl thing. It just happened!"

Brad chuckled and said, "Calm down, buddy. That's usually the way that stuff goes, it just happens. There's nothing wrong with wanting to be with your friends."

With their eyes glued to their plates, Kurt and Danny snickered uncontrollably. They were probably remembering how it all began for them.

Brad continued, "How about if we talk to your parents about this and see what they think?"

"Fine with me," I replied.

If I gave Mom the proper assurances, I knew she wouldn't have a problem with me attending the party, or so I presumed. I also knew that Dad wouldn't feel one way or another about the whole thing. When it came to social considerations, Dad always deferred to Mom's judgment.

"I can only imagine what your honorary mother is going to say when we tell her about all this," said Brad.

Danny chuckled and then said, "Well, considering that he got her looking-at-girls-through-different-eyes speech this morning, I think he's probably in like Flint."

Again, I truly wanted to kick Danny. Instead, I gave in and joined them in their laughter.

Later that evening, the Minnesota Twins played the Texas Rangers again. The four of us bachelors decided to make it a guys-only night in the den. From the start, the Rangers took an early lead because the Twins' pitcher, Dick Woodson, was having an off night. The Rangers seemed to be teeing off his every pitch. That was the story for most of the season. By the fifth inning, I had no faith that the Twins were going to mount a serious comeback. I think the four of us lost interest in the game at the same time. It seemed like we were watching the game simply to be watching baseball.

My mind started to wander, and I found myself thinking about Julie. What a change one day could make. If I were watching that game one day prior, no girl would have dominated my thoughts. The events of the day were too significant, and I couldn't get my mind back into what was happening in the den. I must have had a far off look on my face.

"Jackson!"

"What?" I asked, my mind snapping back into my present surroundings.

Brad said, "I asked you whether you think they will make a comeback tonight or not?"

"Who?"

"The Twins, of course, remember? The TV? The game? We're losing?" Brad was now grinning. "Where did you go?"

"I guess I was daydreaming."

Kurt snickered and said, "I bet I know who you were daydreaming about."

"Yeah, well, you'd be wrong," I replied defensively.

"Are you gonna try and tell me you weren't thinking about Julie?" asserted Kurt.

I lied, by replying, "Actually, I was thinking about Adam Harris."

Immediately, Kurt lost his smile. He was now looking daggers at me.

Brad asked in a calm, straight tone, "What about Adam?"

"I saw him again today, when I walked Julie home."

"You did, eh?" Brad's eyes told me nothing.

"He said he wants to talk to me before I leave next week."

"I know that. Are you going to?" The three of them were now looking at me with interest.

"I might have to in order to get him to stop following me."

Brad's interest seemed to perk up a bit. "He's following you?"

"Well, it feels like he is."

"Look, Jackson, he doesn't want to hurt you," Brad stated. "He only wants to clear the air about a few things."

"How do *you* know that?"

"I talked to him at Pigs, remember?"

The anger in Kurt and Danny's eyes was clear. I knew they wanted me to let it go for the night, which wasn't a bad idea. I didn't want to bring the subject up at all, but I wasn't in the mood to get razzed about Julie, either. So, I simply looked to Brad, hoping to get more out of him, but his eyes were glued to the TV again. Slouching deeper into my chair, I turned my attention back to the game, also.

An uncomfortable silence settled on the den. There was a noticeable tension hanging in the air. I knew Kurt and Danny were upset with me, but that wasn't the real reason for the tension. It was as if there was a big secret between those three and I wasn't in on it. Nobody wanted to talk anymore, so I continued my pretense of being interested in the game. While we watched the remaining innings, not one of us said another word.

The Twins lost that night, three-to-two. Even though the Twins had won the two previous games against the Rangers, they did themselves no real good in the standings. A three-game sweep would have felt better.

When the game was over, Brad motioned with his head for me to accompany him outside. We went up the stairs and out the side door into the night air, which felt chilly and it raised goose bumps on my forearms. There was a gentle breeze rustling through the leaves of the mountain ash in the front yard. Someone on the block had been barbequing that evening and the aroma of something grilled was still in the air. Normally, I would have been quite comfortable with the atmosphere. But, on that particular night, the air felt heavy.

"Jackson, there *are* things for us to discuss and we will, real soon, too. There's plenty of time for that. You have my promise. A serious talk will take place before you leave here, but for now, I wish you would try to relax. I want you to enjoy your time with us and your friends."

"Okay, but what about Adam? Do you think I should talk to him?"

"Yes, I do. I think it may help you and it may help my old friend. I know you are very afraid of him because of things that happened in the past. But those times are done and over with. People need to move on. You need to be able to move on, too. I think he can help you do that. Hopefully, we can just get past all of this."

While delivering his final words, Brad kept his eyes on the ground and wouldn't look at me. He didn't wait for me to respond, either. He just turned and went back inside the house.

Of course, I did not understand Brad's last words, but I could tell he was speaking from the heart. Nonetheless, I knew he was hiding something. That evening, Brad was guilty of doing the same thing I had done earlier. He was waiting for the right time to talk about important things. Recognizing that fact, I came to the conclusion that I was just going to have to trust Brad and wait until he was ready. In the past, he had never truly let me down. As far as I was concerned, he was one of few people who hadn't. *Danny is right,* I thought. *Not trusting Brad is stupid. I'm just acting like a kid again! Grow up and stop thinking about yourself so much!*

I still needed to find the courage to face Adam, but right then, I didn't want to think about that. I wanted to think about more pleasant things, like the wonderful afternoon spent with my friends, the prospect of attending another party, and getting lost in a pair of blue eyes that were liable to haunt me forever. Mostly, I wanted to figure out Julie's unclear answer about a guy she was interested in. *Was she talking about me? No way, I'm just not that lucky...ever.*

After spending so much time convincing myself that I didn't want to see Julie, I found it befuddling that I now could hardly wait to see her again. There were many questions about her milling around inside my head, but I would just have to be patient in order to get answers.

So much had happened in such a short period of time. I felt like major changes in my life were just now beginning. All of which were impalpable, but just the same, major. In addition to everything else, I had assurances from Brad that there would be honest discussion in the days ahead. I decided to take his suggestion – relax and enjoy my time in Mankato. I stayed outside, contemplating my immediate future, until the chilly-night air got the better of me.

At bedtime, I immediately tried to fall asleep, but couldn't. I was plenty tired, but my head was simply in the wrong place. There was something I needed to take care of immediately. If I didn't, I would never get to sleep that night.

"Danny, are you awake?"

"Yeah, what's up?"

"I'm sorry for what I said earlier...about not trusting Dad."

"I know, forget it."

"I can't. Are we okay?"

"Hell yes. By the way, I don't think any of this is easy for you. So, don't go thinking that I don't understand."

"I'm worried about what's going to happen next. I'm afraid of Adam, but Dad thinks I should meet with him."

"Are you gonna do it?"

"I can't believe it, but yeah...I think I am. What do you think?"

"Why are you so afraid of him?"

I then told Danny some of what I remembered about Adam. I reminded him of the scars on my back and how those wounds got there. I told him of the fear I kept inside.

Danny patiently listened to me. When I was through, he thought for a moment and then said, "I understand why you're afraid of him. Hell, I would be, too. But, if Dad thinks it'll be okay, don't you think you can trust that? Dad would never let anything bad happen to you."

"That's why I'm just now deciding to see Adam. Dad says he thinks it will help me *and* help Adam."

"When're you gonna do it?"

"When I decide I have enough guts, I guess."

"Well, I don't know if it means anything, but I think you have plenty of guts."

"Thanks, I hope you're right."

Danny then propped himself up on his side. "Now, tell me more about what I really want to know."

"What's that?"

"I want to hear all about how you ended up walking Julie home and gettin' yourself kissed."

We both buried our faces in our pillows and laughed like idiots. Then, like so many times before, Danny and I stayed up late, talking.

CHAPTER 10

Thursday, 10 August 1972

I awoke to what sounded like someone speaking into a large, tin, coffee can. I looked around the room and slowly became cognizant that I was alone. *Danny's up already?*

I then looked at the clock radio. The large rolodex-style numbers told me it was 7:08 A.M. Remembering that I had stayed up late, talking with Danny, I groaned, "Oh man, it's way too early!"

At first, I thought the noise I had heard must have been a dream, so I decided to close my eyes a while longer. I was lying on my back and began to doze off. Suddenly, I heard the same noise again. I rose up and propped myself on my forearms. *Where the heck is that coming from?*

I distinctly heard Janet's voice, but it sounded tinny. I then heard Danny's voice and thought it had a metallic quality to it, as well. I rubbed my eyes, then stuck a finger in one ear and rattled it around. I wanted to loosen up whatever blockage was causing my afflicted hearing. Just to be sure, I performed the same procedure on the other ear. Then, I heard Janet's voice again. It was a little strained and still had the metallic tone to it. It sounded almost like it was coming from under my bed. That's when my half-asleep brain remembered the heating vent.

Once I figured out where the noise was coming from, I concentrated more on what was actually being said. I was in no hurry to jump out of bed, so I decided to lay back and give a listen to their conversation.

Because I could decipher their words with clarity, I was certain they were sitting at the kitchen table; Danny should've known better. From what I could make out, they were well into their exchange and Danny was sounding rather passionate about his side of things.

"All I'm saying is that you shouldn't give him a hard time about it, Mom."

Janet asked, "Don't you have any faith in me?"

"I lost it when you found out about *my* first serious crush on a girl."

"So...now you're saying it's serious. A moment ago you were telling me it was no big deal."

I had to stifle a laugh because I recognized Janet's verbal-Judo tactics. It sounded like Danny was falling for them, too...hook, line, and sinker. He always was an easy target for her.

"Will you please just listen," Danny pleaded. "When he talks to you about this...and he will be talking to you about it...don't give him a hard time, like you did me."

"I don't understand. Why all the concern if it's no big deal?" Janet was not letting him off the hook.

Danny was now in a full court press. "I just think she may be kinda important to him and we shouldn't make a joke of it, like you did with Kurt and me. Remember, when we first started liking girls?

Upstairs I shook my head and then thought, *What an Idiot. She won't ever fall for that!*

Danny continued, "Remember, he's only going to be here for another week. You don't want him acting all self-conscious for the rest of his time here...Do you?"

"Yeah, you're right," agreed Janet, "But, if I don't torture him with it now, when will I get the chance?"

Danny's frustration with Janet was now clear. "I can't talk to you anymore! I'm outta here!"

Janet called after him. "I'll be sure to tell him how concerned you were for his welfare. I mean, to come talk to me like this, on his behalf. It's pretty touching."

I then heard hurried footsteps and in a semi-hushed tone, Danny pleaded, "Mom, you can't let him know we talked. He probably doesn't trust me already, because of the crap Kurt and I already gave him."

Janet egged Danny on further. "So, you and Kurt get to give him crap, but I have to be the one who lays off? That don't sound too fair to me...or like it would be any fun."

I was now fighting hard to keep from laughing out loud. I thought, *Danny, just give it up! All you're doing is digging that hole deeper!*

Suddenly, I decided that Janet had enough fun. It was now my turn. So, I got out of bed, put on my best just-opening-my-eyes look, and started for the stairs. When I reached the bottom, I greeted them both by letting out a big, fake yawn and then said, "Morning."

"Morning, kiddo, it's about time you got up," said Janet.

"Yeah, well, I would have got up earlier, but someone kept me up all night, talking."

While Janet chuckled and got up to fetch another cup of coffee, Danny whispered, "Bite me!

Janet then asked, "While I'm up, do you want me to cook you some eggs or something?"

"No thanks. I'll just have some cereal or toast, after I wake up a bit." I then very nonchalantly asked, "So, what do you think about Friday night?"

Janet turned and I saw her questioning look. Danny had a big question mark on his face, too. *Gotcha both...right where I want you,* I thought.

Janet asked, "What about Friday night?"

"You mean to tell me that you don't know about Julie Falkner's big party this Friday night?" I had led them both in and was now ready to spring my trap.

"As a matter of fact...I do know about it, but how do *you* know that?" asked Janet.

I looked right at Danny and said, "Just a guess, but I figured bucket mouth here probably told you before I could get a chance."

Janet giggled and Danny's look turned to disbelief as he exclaimed, "What?!"

I waited until Janet wasn't paying attention. Then, while pointing at the heating vent, I looked Danny in the eye and grinned. The look of realization on his face was priceless. He put his face in his hands and shook his head. Janet was the only one I left hanging. It was my preemptive strike for the torture I knew she wanted to bestow on me about Julie. She didn't waste any time, either.

Thinking she was now going to do the verbal-Judo thing with me, Janet said, "So, Jackson, a couple of days ago you wanted nothing to do with girls. Now, you're walking them home and making out at parties. What gives?!"

Listen, Danny, and learn, I thought. Then, acting as though I was seriously considering my words, I said, "I know what you mean. Creepy, isn't it? But…I got to thinking about what you said in the car yesterday. You know, about looking at girls with different eyes and all that. It turns out that you were right. They really do want me!"

Janet's look now changed to that of astonishment, so I laid it on a little thicker. "Since they seem to want me, like you said, I think it's only right to give 'em what they want. I mean, I'm only going to be here for another week, so I'll try not to spread myself too thin. I figure, with Lori and Julie already on the hook, I'll probably only have enough time for one more. What do you think, Danny?"

Danny said nothing, but his face was red, as he desperately held back his laughter. Janet looked as though she had just created another Frankenstein monster.

I then turned toward Janet, gave her my most innocent look, and then said, "You're not actually buying all that, are you?"

Danny finally let go and busted out laughing. I couldn't help it and joined him.

When Janet realized she had just been bested at her own game, she joined in, too. "You snot! For a minute there, you actually had me going!"

Still laughing, I said, "I figured I'd better get mine in before you start in on me."

That morning, the three of us hung out in the kitchen for a while and enjoyed some laughter together. Danny pulled out some stories about how I used to intentionally get him into trouble. I had matured enough to admit doing it, too. Besides, those incidents were, in fact, quite funny…to me. The flip side of the coin was that I had a few stories to share about Danny, as well. To say the least, Janet's knowledge of her sons and their early dirty dealings was greatly expanded.

While I showered, Janet took a telephone call for me and then ran off to work. After dressing, I went back to the kitchen and discovered the note she had left for me. It instructed me to call Father Michael at St. Joseph's. There was a phone number included, too. When I returned his call, Father Michael invited me to join him for lunch at noon. At first, I honestly didn't feel like accepting his offer, but thought I had better go through with it. After all, I had committed myself the previous Sunday. Since I had no solid plans for that day, having lunch with my older friend seemed the right thing to do. After thinking about it some, I actually began to look forward to seeing him again. We were to have lunch right there, in the church rectory. It would be another first for me.

I checked the clock and saw that I had plenty of time, so I decided to make a short phone call home. I hadn't talked to Mom since Saturday, so she was probably worried to death about me. I didn't like her to worry but knew she would anyway. At that time of day, I knew she would most likely be at Dad's office, so I called her there. After our initial greetings to each other, I gave her a quick rundown of my activities. She sounded honestly relieved that I was enjoying myself. However, I intentionally neglected to tell her of my run-ins with Adam. There was no doubt in my mind that those encounters would immediately throw her into a panic. Besides, nothing had actually happened, yet. Knowing that I had to butter Mom up some, to make her feel better about allowing me to go to the party on Friday, I decided to let Father Michael unknowingly pave the way for me.

"Hey, Mom, guess what I'm doing here in just a little bit?"

"I'd rather you just tell me, honey."

"I'm going to church to have lunch."

"Really?! And no one had to point a gun to get you to go?!"

I gave her lame attempt at wit the courtesy chuckle it deserved. "Yeah, well, I found it hard to turn down the invitation of a Catholic Priest, especially since he's more like an old friend."

"It's refreshing to hear you say that."

I could almost hear her smiling over the phone. I knew my ploy was working, so there was no better time to spring my request on her. "I have a favor to ask. I've been invited to a party tomorrow night and I really want to go. Brad and Janet thought I should run it past you to see if it's okay."

Of course, Mom's first question called for clarity. "What kind of party are we talking about, Jackson?"

I took deep a breath and said a silent prayer before diving in. I then heard myself tell her it was a boy-girl thing and that Julie's parents would be on hand to properly supervise it. I gave her all the necessary assurances, but still expected her to have a small fit. Instead, it was me who went into mild shock, when Mom, in the most nonchalant manner, replied, "I suppose it'll be okay."

"What?! Really?!" I exclaimed. *Are my ears working okay today?*

"Yes…really. Is Janet or Brad available for me to speak to?"

"No, they're both at work now, but I can have them call you later."

"That'll be fine, honey."

"So, the coast is clear for tomorrow night?"

"Yes, it is, with reservations, of course."

"With what?"

"It means I have some concerns, but while you're down there, I trust you to behave accordingly."

"Mom…don't worry. I won't get into any trouble and I won't embarrass you or Dad."

"Jackson, I'm not worried about that at all. I've always been proud of how well you handle yourself, especially when you are a guest in someone's home. I'm more worried about…your heart."

"What do you mean?"

"Oh…never mind. There are a thousand questions that I'd love to ask right now, but we'll save it for the trip home next week."

"Just don't worry, Mom…Please?"

"Okay, honey, I miss you."

"I miss you back…And Dad, too. I gotta get going now. I don't want to keep Father Michael waiting."

"Okay, you be sure to call if you need anything. We love you."

"Love you, too…bye…and thanks."

Before Mom could utter another word, I quickly put the receiver back in its cradle. Actually, I had time to spare before I had to leave for my lunch date. But I hated Mom's lengthy good-byes, so I hung up before she could stretch it out. Besides worrying, she had a knack for that, too. I then stood there, looking at the phone for a moment. Suddenly, I felt terrible for being in such a hurry to get off the line. Just then, it dawned on me that I truly was missing the two of them…a lot. The realization brought a smile to my face.

My walk to St. Joe's was extraordinarily cheerful. The sun was shining magnificently, but the temperature was still only in the mid-seventies. The mildness of it all added greatly to my high spirits. While enjoying the jaunt, I also marveled at how easy it was to get permission to attend Julie's party. Mom didn't even bother to try a blocking move. It was quite a departure from her normal behavior in the recent past. Usually, it was a small coup, just to get permission to go to the movies. *She must be having a very good day,* I thought, *or she's just getting soft."*

My Timex, self-winding watch told me I had arrived at the rectory five minutes early. Regardless, I rang the doorbell and waited patiently. Suddenly, the tallest woman I had ever seen in my young life answered it. Dad stood six feet, four inches tall and the woman in front of me was only an inch or two shorter. Her hair, which quite noticeably was once carrot orange, was now mostly silver with only flecks of orange remaining. Her gaunt facial features reminded me of a character I had once seen in a late-night, horror movie.

"Mr. Landry?" the macabre figure before me inquired.

"Yes, ma'am," I replied tentatively.

In a rather disciplinarian tone, the gruesome-looking woman stated, "I'm Mrs. Patterson, the housekeeper. Father O'Reilly is expecting you. It's nice to meet a young man who knows how to tell time."

"Yes, ma'am," I repeated.

Father Michael then appeared in the entryway and, as usual, was in full voice. "Jackson! Come in lad! Come in and welcome. Lunch will be ready in just a bit… Right, Mrs. Patterson?"

"Shoes left at the door please, Mr. Landry," instructed Mrs. Patterson.

I immediately looked down at Father Michael's feet to find him wearing some well-worn bedroom slippers. It was the first time I had ever seen him without hard-sole shoes, so I felt better about having to walk around without mine. Just then, I wanted to do many things, but arguing with that oversized, female beanpole was not one of them. *Thank God, I remembered to put on clean socks,* I thought.

Father Michael led me down a hallway until we came to what appeared to be a clean and neatly organized living room. The room reeked of aromatic pipe tobacco, just like Grandpa Mack's house. For inexplicable reasons, I found the odor comforting.

The hardwood floors appeared clean enough to eat off, a testament to Mrs. Patterson's dedication, I presumed. The furnishings were rather plain and outdated, but not worn or tattered in any way. There were Christian-themed paintings hanging all about the room. The one thing that looked absolutely out of place was a large RCA color television set. It took up a little too much space across from the couch.

I spied and immediately loved the room's built-in bookshelves, which took up almost an entire wall. They were completely filled with books from a wide assortment of writers. *Wow,* I thought. *He has his own library!* I moved to the shelves and marveled at the many authors in his collection. I was familiar with most of them. There were various books by Hemmingway, F. Scott Fitzgerald, Homer, and Edgar Allen Poe. Herman Melville's, *Moby Dick* was there and much of Shakespeare's work was present, as well. There were many contemporary works in his collection, too, but I wasn't as familiar with those authors.

Still gawking at Father Michael's books, I asked, "Do you think it's true that Shakespeare's family were practicing Catholics at a time when it was against English law?" My question was meant to impress him, rather than get his honest opinion.

Acting totally indifferent to my query, Father Michael replied, "I think that is a rather lofty discussion for one so young. Do you like Shakespeare?"

"He's not my favorite. I spend half the time trying to figure out what his characters are actually saying, but I do like his comedies.

"You like to read?" asked the priest.

Enthusiastically, I replied, "Very much, Father! I've already read a lot of what you have here."

I then explained how my cousin had helped me with my reading and math. I went on about how reading had become, more or less, a passion of mine and how I hoped to one day have a collection much like his.

"That's wonderful, Jacky! You must come over sometime and we can discuss literature."

He then led me to a couch and made a genial gesture for me to sit. He, in turn, sat at the other end. He turned himself toward me and sat upright, almost at the front edge of the cushion. He placed his hands on his knees and exhaled heavily.

"So, tell me lad, how has Mankato been treating you thus far?"

The excitement in Father Michael's voice was always infectious. Truth be told, I was just as happy to see him. I intended to keep my visit with him quite casual. So, without giving up any details that I wouldn't want a Catholic priest to know, I gave him a brief rundown of my many activities. Because I didn't wish to divulge anything that might cause concern in his mind, I neglected to tell him about coming in contact with Adam Harris. Mostly, I talked of baseball, basketball, fishing at the creek, and being glad to be with my friends again. He listened to me with great interest and kept a very bright smile on his face. He also nodded his understanding at all the right times. I knew it was his way of telling me he approved of the information I was sharing greatly.

When I was through, Father Michael leaned back and heaved a heavy sigh, as if he had done the talking and was now out of breath. "Where do you find the energy, lad? You better save some of that. If memory serves, you still have another week to get through."

"Yes, Father, I'll be here for another week."

Just then, Mrs. Patterson came in to inform us that lunch was ready. She then asked, "Do you wish to eat in the kitchen or in here on TV trays?"

Father Michael looked to me to see if I had a preference. I then remembered how Mom taught me not to make a host or hostess go through too much trouble.

"In the kitchen is fine with me, Father."

"Then in the kitchen it shall be!"

For lunch, Mrs. Patterson had prepared a tuna-noodle hotdish, which is not to be confused with a casserole in any way, shape, or form. Minnesota women were funny about such things. Grandma Carol, on Dad's side, taught me that a casserole is the thing you cook a hotdish in. I took it in stride when I discovered that Mrs. Patterson was no different than any other women in the state. I did have to stifle a laugh, though, when I saw that it had crushed potato chips on it, as a topping. It was exactly the way Janet Wilson, both of my grandmothers, and even Mom made theirs. *Isn't there any other recipe for tuna hotdish?*

"I'll let you two enjoy your lunch together," said Mrs. Patterson. "Don't bother about the cleanup. I'll take care of it later."

"Aren't you going to join us?" I asked.

Mrs. Patterson wrinkled her nose slightly and said, "Young man, I don't even like tuna hotdish. It's his favorite!" For effect, she pointed a long, boney finger at Father Michael.

My friend just peered over his glasses and wore a rather fiendish grin. I then got the impression that he requested the casserole to facilitate Mrs. Patterson's departure. If that was his intent, it worked like a charm.

"Would you like some milk to go with your lunch, Jacky?"

"Water will do, Father."

"Nonsense, you're still growing. Have some milk." He then poured a glass for himself, as well.

Back then, I sometimes got a real kick out of adults, especially when they asked *my* preference, then gave me what *they* intended me to have, whether I wanted it or not.

During lunch, we kept our conversation friendly and pleasant. I talked lively about the church Mom and I attended in Duluth, which, coincidentally, was also named St. Joseph's.

Father Michael queried, "You said your mother and you attend church together. What about your father?"

"He comes with us every now and then, but he prefers a Lutheran Church. It has something to do with all the kneeling we do." I then thought about my words and hoped Father Michael didn't take offense.

Dad coming to church with Mom and me at all was somewhat a waste of time. He slept through most church services. I always attributed that behavior to his blindness. To Dad, there was no distinction between day and night, so he simply napped whenever he got drowsy. Often, he goaded Mom by saying, "Nothing makes me drowsier than a Catholic Priest who loves the sound of his own voice." Father Michael didn't need to know any of that, though, so I kept such details to myself.

I then asked Father Michael if he still took his annual month-long sabbaticals to Ireland to be with his family. He said that he did and would be going again soon. As he spoke, I remembered him telling me about Ireland in years past, mostly when I was hiding in the church. I think he used the subject to help get my mind off my troubles; it was a very effective tact. I had always been fascinated by his stories about growing up in the small harbor village of Balbriggan. There, he was raised and worked until his mother convinced him he should go into the priesthood.

I then asked my friend if he ever had dreams of being something other than what he was. His response was simple, "A fisherman." He then proceeded to talk about how most of the men in his family were either fishermen or worked in the cotton mills. Brought up in a family of hard workers, he felt it was his duty to pursue the path his mother laid out for him. He even admitted that he hadn't actually received the calling – as he put it – until he was a seminary student. Nevertheless, to him, how and when he got the calling was nowhere near as important as the fact that he did.

Father Michael also reminisced about how he had always been close to his mother. Because he was missing her terribly, he very much looked forward to that year's trip to Ireland.

"Wait a minute, Father. Your mother is still alive?!"

"Oh…yes lad! She will be ninety-three this coming October. I am hoping ever so much to be there for the celebration."

At that moment, my mind couldn't quite fathom the idea. To me, Father Michael was ancient, yet he was still able to travel to the other side of the world, just to see his ninety-three-year-old mother! I then thought about Mom and somehow felt I would never feel the same pull toward her. I loved Mom, of that I was sure, but it wasn't anywhere near as deep as Father Michael's love for his mother. My adoptive mother just didn't fit into any of the preconceived notions I had about what a mom was supposed to be. I also thought about my biological mother, but immediately came to the conclusion that I could not care less about her. Somehow, a loving relationship with a motherly figure seemed totally out of my grasp. I felt it was just another item that other people got to have, but not me.

Father Michael and I continued lunch with a short discussion about things I wished to do, while I was still in town. I told him I had already done most of the things I wanted to do. Of course, I didn't bother to tell him about some of the unexpected things that had never been on my agenda but happened anyway…and were pretty great to boot. No, as far as Father Michael knew, if all I got to do was more of what I had already done, it would be fine with me. I became aware of my successful evasiveness and was quite pleased with myself. I had never thought that I was all that clever before, but keeping secrets was something I was getting comfortable with.

When we finished what was left on our plates, I stood and took our dishes to the sink, saying, "Maybe we should clean up a bit, Father, instead of leaving it all for Mrs. Patterson."

"Don't you worry about it, lad. You are my guest here."

We then left the kitchen and went back to the living room to relax, digest our lunch, and visit some more. This time, I selected a comfortable looking chair, with a table and lamp next to it. Father Michael went to a desk, located just to the right of his book collection. There, he selected a pipe from a small, ornately-carved, wood pipe rack. He then carefully packed it with tobacco, which he stored in a leather pouch.

"Will this bother you, lad?"

"My Grandpa Mack smokes a pipe. I love the smell."

My friend chuckled and said, "You don't say. Well, Jacky, I don't recommend you picking up the habit."

In one, almost fluid, motion, he lit his pipe while sitting down on the couch. Within arm's reach, a brass standing ashtray awaited the wood match he used. I could tell the seat was where he liked to sit in the evenings to watch TV. When he crossed his legs and his pant leg rode up, I smiled to myself. Above his sock, his skin was paler than any skin I had ever seen before. At the sight of it, my mind wandered for a moment.

Dad sat like that often and it always struck me as funny. It's hard to take a man in long pants serious, especially when he is showing his ugly leg that way. In my dad's case, ugly wasn't the proper word. Hideous was a better descriptor. It was because both of Dad's shins were scarred and discolored terribly from years of banging into furniture or other such things at shin level.

"Did you get enough to eat, Jacky?" asked the priest, thus bringing me back to earth.

"Yes, Father, plenty." I replied, wondering when he was going to get to his main purpose. He had a look on his face, like he was pondering how best to proceed. He chewed on his pipe a bit and nodded his head slightly.

"You look like you have something on your mind, Father."

"You always were the perceptive one, lad. In the past, you and I have always been straight with each other, have we not?"

"Yes, Father."

"Do you trust me?"

"I guess so. You're one of the few people I do trust. Why?"

"Jacky, I'm going to ask you to do something and you're probably not going to like it."

"Okay, shoot."

When he heard my reply, his look became that of puzzlement, so he asked, "Just like that?"

"Yeah, I figure I owe you, Father…for all your help when I was little."

"Okay then," he said, sitting up straight and giving me his penetrating stare. "I want you to see and speak to your father."

217

I thought carefully for a moment before responding. "When you say, 'my father,' I guess you mean Adam Harris, right?"

"Yes, of course."

Sitting quietly for a moment, I prepared myself to battle any negative emotion that might surface. Surprisingly, I didn't feel much of anything. The fear was not there, neither was the anger. Brad had already convinced me to speak to Adam. So, at that moment, Father Michael's request didn't feel like a big deal. Nevertheless, there was a nagging question tugging at me, so I asked, "Why is it so important that I talk to him?"

"I believe, lad, it is an important opportunity for the two of you."

"Opportunity?" I repeated. "For what?"

"It'll be an opportunity for the two of you to heal."

I considered his words for a minute. I wasn't at all convinced I owed Adam anything, let alone the opportunity to heal from whatever afflicted him. Nevertheless, I greatly desired to put certain things behind me. And, if Adam could be one of those things, then it would be worth spending a little of my precious time with him.

"Okay, Father, I'll do it. I'll see him and I'll listen to whatever he has to say, but I'm not making any promises about forgiving him or anything like that."

Father nodded his approval and said, "That's a very wise and mature decision, lad." He then relaxed his wrinkled brow.

In that moment, I was absolutely uncertain about how wise of a decision I had just made, but things did seem to be improving. Maybe the meeting could honestly be a good thing. I knew it was wrong to hate and I had hated Adam for so very long. In fact, I didn't know how else to feel about him. There was no other emotion in my heart for him. If there was a chance for me to get rid of that hate, then the meeting was absolutely the right thing to do, or so I had just convinced myself.

I then wondered how Doc Elliot would advise me. I remembered his words, "Don't take on more than you can handle." *Am I ready for this?*

Wanting more details, I asked, "Will you be setting up the meeting, Father?"

"I can, if you wish."

"Will you be there with me?"

"If having me there will help you, I will. When would you like to do this?"

"I wouldn't *like* to do it at all, but early next week maybe, Monday or Tuesday?"

"Not sooner?"

"No, Father. I'm going to be busy for the rest of this week."

"As you wish then."

"Just one more thing, Father, when you talk to him, will you please ask him to stay away from me until we meet? I don't want to see him following me. I don't want to see him sitting off in the distance, watching me. And I don't want him coming around the Wilsons' house, looking for me."

I knew I was being far too bold, but just then, I didn't care. As far as I was concerned, Adam should be glad I was agreeing to see him at all.

Father Michael frowned but didn't pursue the issue further. "I will ask him to keep to your wishes. I don't want you to worry about this, Jacky. I will pray that this meeting will make things better for the both of you. The only thing I will ask of you is that you give him a fair chance."

I may have been bold moments before, but that was gone now. I was not about to tell my friend that I did not want to give Adam a chance at all. I would never want to see him, and I could not care less if he benefitted from such a meeting. The words were all there, waiting for me to spit out, but I bit my tongue and allowed the matter to be settled, even if it was just for the rest of the week.

Now that the main purpose for our lunch had concluded to Father Michael's satisfaction, it seemed he had no more time for me that day. He stood and said, "Well, I suppose you're in a hurry to get a move on, so you can go play with your friends."

Not really, I thought. *What's your hurry?!* However, even then I could take a hint, so I said, "I guess I'll be going then."

As we made our way to the door, I heard Mrs. Patterson cleaning up in the kitchen. I poked my head in to thank her. "It was nice to meet you, Mrs. Patterson. I liked your tuna hotdish very much. Thank you for lunch."

"Thank you, young man. It was a pleasure meeting you, as well. I hope to see you again soon."

I would have returned the sentiment, but it would have been a lie. Her appearance gave me a slight, unearthly chill. To be frank, I didn't care if I ever saw that tall, ghostly, Irish lady again!

Father Michael escorted me to the door. There, he stood by while I knelt to put on my shoes. He then opened the door and we both stepped out into the afternoon sun.

"Thanks for having me over, Father. I'd like to visit again before I leave."

"You are most welcome, lad. You can come see me whenever you wish. When I have things arranged with your father, I will contact you at the Wilson residence."

I should have let his last comment go, but I just couldn't. "Father Michael… Please stop calling Adam that. He's not my father. My Dad's name is Brice Landry."

I then turned and hurried away before Father Michael could respond. I didn't mean to be rude to him, but to be completely honest, I was extremely offended by the incorrect reference. Adam Harris willingly gave up the title long ago. I saw no reason to let others continue crediting him with it.

CHAPTER 11

When I left the grounds of St Joseph the Worker, I felt neither pleased nor proud of how I had left things with Father Michael. However, I wasn't very penitent, either. When it came to Adam Harris, anger and fear were the only emotions I had ever felt. In my mind, I would never be wrong to correct those who still referred to Adam as my father. Mom and Dad had been through a lot with me and were still in the fight. Adam had simply tossed me away, putting a convenient end to what must have been an inconvenient problem.

As I trudged along, dragging my heels a bit, I immediately recognized the darkness that was trying to overtake me. So, I pushed all thoughts of Adam Harris and our pending reunion way to the back of my mind. Because I didn't know how long lunch with Father Michael would take, I had made absolutely no plans for that afternoon. Also, I had no idea what any of my friends were up to, but I didn't actually care about that, either. The weather was positively gorgeous. That alone began to change my otherwise sour mood. Since I was already afoot and heading in a good direction, I decided to go for a walk and simply enjoy what was left of the day. Wandering around the neighborhood would give me a chance to mull things over and hopefully bring everything into a better light.

At first, I had no planned direction of travel. That is, until I reached the railroad tracks. More from past habit than anything, I got on the railway and headed south. It was a route I had traveled many times. It was the way I used when walking home from school. Back then, the guys had practically always been with me. During those walks, we had always shared a lot of excited chatter and laughter. *Those days are all gone for me,* I thought. Once again, sadness threatened to ruin my otherwise good mood. Then, I remembered what Doc Elliot taught me to do, especially when negative emotions were getting in my way. "Breathe, Jackson," he said. "Allow yourself to relax, be quiet and simply breathe. Close your eyes and listen to the world around you."

During one of my sessions with Doc Elliot, he had taught me a few meditation techniques. At first, I thought it was just a bunch of mumbo-jumbo. However, I tried it once by myself, while fishing at one of my favorite trout ponds. I discovered that the subtle sounds of nature had a calming effect on me. After approximately fifteen minutes, I opened my eyes and found that I could focus and think more clearly.

Just then, while I still stood in the middle of the railroad tracks, I decided to give Doc Elliot's little trick a whirl. So, I closed my eyes and breathed in deeply a few times. Then, I slowed my rate of breathing and simply allowed my mind to relax. I listened to everything around me. The breeze, as it rustled through nearby trees. Birds sang and called out to one another. Way off in the distance, I heard the sounds of small children, playing and laughing. A dog barked, crickets sang, frogs croaked, and squirrels chattered. Next, I heard the sound of a car passing on a nearby street. I listened closely, as its tire noise faded away to nothing, leaving me with birdsong again. I thought of nothing at all, just listened and continued to allow my mind to relax. Suddenly, I felt a subtle vibration under my feet. At first, I thought I had reached some new, Zen-like state that I had not previously experienced; it made me smile. However, as I continued to listen, it didn't take very long for me to realize that my early assumption was totally wrong. My relaxed state immediately went away and my whole body tensed, when I realized that a few, short blocks away, a train was moving toward me.

I should have stepped off the tracks and let the train go by, but quite suddenly, a different, more delicious thought entered my brainpan. *Race it, Landry! Let's see if you're as fast as you think you are!* The very thought made my heart speed up.

The train was not in sight, but it blasted its air horn, causing me to tense even more. I checked my distance from where I stood to West Ninth Street. I guesstimated that I was approximately three quarters of a block away. *Not much of a run,* I thought. *But, if I wait until the train is closer and make myself run on the ties, that'll be a better test.*

My foolhardy plan now had me totally focused on waiting until I could actually see the train. There was a slight bend behind me that the train had to round. It, too, was approximately three quarters of a block away. *That's where I'll see the engine! When I see the engine, I'll start running!*

My heart was now pounding, and I became aware of a strange taste in my mouth. Suddenly, the engine appeared, so I launched myself down the tracks in the opposite direction, heading toward West Ninth Street. Again and again the engineer blasted the air horn at me, which only added to the thrill I was experiencing. Sure of my footing, I ran at full throttle, but knew the train was gaining. After I had covered half the distance to my makeshift finish line, I snuck a peek over my shoulder, which was a big mistake. Momentarily taking my eyes off the tracks caused me to stumble on the uneven ties, but I was able to make a rapid recovery. Convinced that I could still make it, with plenty of distance to spare, I refused to get off the tracks. Instead, I poured every bit of speed I could muster into my stride and just kept running. The engine was now mere yards behind me, its air horn pleading with me to get clear of the tracks. But I was now too intent on winning. *I can beat that beast! I just know it!*

When West Ninth Street was but a few paces ahead, I knew I had won my race. Using a tall, standing spruce as my finish line, I pulled up as soon as I passed it and casually got off the tracks. I was feeling pretty, darn good about myself, too. That is, until the engine passed me. As I stood by, taking in large gulps of air, the engineer leered at me from his window and yelled, "YOU DUMB-ASSED KID! ARE YOU TRYIN' TO KILL YOURSELF?!"

Feeling a bit embarrassed, but unapologetic, I simply gave him a wave and then headed down West Ninth Street. Racing the train had done more for me than I realized. Besides the surge of pride I felt for besting a steel locomotive, I had completely forgotten all the negativity I had been feeling after leaving St. Joe's.

My footrace with the train had caused me to heat up more than I expected, so I untucked my shirt and then unbuttoned it. Jamming my hands into the pockets of my Levi's, I then walked onward. A slight breeze from the northeast cooled my heated and somewhat sweaty T-shirt. Slowing my pace a bit, I began to relax and felt a lot more comfortable. Suddenly, a squirrel chattered loudly because I had come too close to the tree it occupied. It immediately sent out an alarm to all the neighborhood wildlife. *Oh no,* I thought, *I've been discovered!* That thought, plus the scolding that little rodent was handing out, made me chuckle.

Dave Lester lived on West Ninth, but just then, I didn't wish to see him. So, hoping I wouldn't be detected, I hurriedly scooted to the other side of the street and then past his house. Once that obstacle was successfully negotiated, I exhaled and relaxed again. Thinking about things that lay ahead of me in the coming days, the thought of meeting with Adam Harris again popped into my head. But those thoughts were too dark for such a beautiful afternoon, so I made an effort and simply pushed such concerns aside.

My thoughts transitioned to my friends and how they had changed. I wished I had stayed and been there to change with them. I would have naturally been part of their group. Instead, I felt as though I were nothing more than a temporary interest. I'd soon be gone again, and their lives would return to normal. I was nothing more than an object to break up the monotony of their small-town life. Then, my mind switched gears on me again. *Knock it off, Landry,* I thought. Haven't they all welcomed you back? *Haven't they all treated you special enough? What more do you need them to do?* Realizing I was inviting misery, where none should exist, I decided to move on.

Next, I thought of Brad. After the previous night's talk with him, I could see how my troubles with Adam weighed on his mind. I just couldn't stand the thought that I was in some way responsible for his heavy heart. *He'll be glad that I'm going to meet with Adam,* I thought. *I'll tell him today, so he can stop worrying about it.*

I then thought of Julie. I knew my thoughts would come around to her. She had only been on my mind at least once every day since I hit town. Since our reunion at the baseball game, it had become more than once a day. Just then, I thought about adding some distance to my walk, but then, almost in the same instant, chickened out. *You'll see her tomorrow, Landry. Just leave her alone for now. If you were real smart, you would leave her alone...period! Damn it! I just wish I could...*

"Hey, Jackson, are you just gonna walk by without even saying hello?" a familiar female voice called out.

I was immediately pulled from my trance to discover Gail Paulsen, lounging on a front-porch swing, slowly swaying back and forth. Dave Lester was not the only person I knew living on West Ninth. Just then, I could have kicked myself for carelessly forgetting.

"Hey, Gail," I greeted. "I forgot you lived right down from Dave." *Damn it! Three more houses and I would have escaped to Baker Avenue!*

"That's okay. Come on up. I'm lonesome," chuckled Gail.

As I stepped up the front walkway, I asked, "Where is everyone?"

"They're probably at home, being on their best behavior. Nobody wants to screw things up and miss the party at Julie's tomorrow night. I'll bet everyone is volunteering to clean house, clean their room, mow the lawn, whatever they have to do to get in good with their parents."

Attempting to make a quick escape, I said, "You know, I should actually go do that, too. The Wilsons' lawn does look like it needs to be mowed."

Letting out an impish giggle, Gail said, "Relax, Jackson, you just got here. I don't bite. Well, not anymore anyway."

I chuckled nervously and then stated, "My hands remember differently. You used to kick, too."

There was once a time when Gail Paulsen could put a very mean bite on a guy. When she got upset or downright mad, you didn't know if she was going to take a chunk out of you with her teeth or deliver a solid kick to the shins. It usually happened after she got caught during a game of Hide 'n' Seek or Kick the Can. Back then, she sure hated to get caught. Her unsportsmanlike conduct was widely known throughout the neighborhood.

"You really *do* remember, don't you?" asked Gail.

While Gail moved the swing with the toes of her white-sneakered feet, I gawked from the porch steps. Her blonde hair was pulled back into a ponytail and her green eyes were filled with mischief. I couldn't actually remember a time when they weren't. Denim shorts showed off her tanned legs and a clingy, powder blue, pullover top accentuated the slight bulge of her growing, but still small breasts.

For the first time since our reunion, I gave Gail a good hard look and realized that she was definitely growing up. Her features had softened extensively, and she had distinct female curves. As well, Gail's manner had grown exponentially more feminine. She most assuredly was not the tomboy I remembered.

Because I didn't have a lot of experience talking to girls, I couldn't think of anything to say. Besides, I never thought of Gail as someone I would sit around chitchatting with. However, I did remember that Gail was never at a loss for words, so I left it to her to break the silence.

"I imagine we must all look really different to you, compared to when you left. *You* haven't changed that much, though. You're still one of the cutest guys. And I can tell that you're still really shy around girls."

Right on cue, I felt blood rushing to my face and was not at all certain how to respond. Nevertheless, I figured since she had no problem laying things on the line, I too should give it a shot. "You said, 'I'm *still* one of the cutest guys.' You didn't used to think that at all, did you?"

Gail smiled warmly and then said, "Let me put it to you this way. Why do you think there were three of us chasing you after school that day, instead of just one?"

I must have had my clueless look firmly affixed to my face because Gail laughed heartily at me. Now, thoroughly confused, I asked, "So, how come only Julie kissed me?"

Gail exclaimed, "Jackson, don't you know anything?! Just about every girl in our class thought you were adorable, but Julie liked you the longest. So, she kinda had first dibs! She's always been that way."

My mind was now busy trying to capture and remember all the little looks Julie used to give me in school. *Was it true?*

Gail giggled again. "Speaking of Julie, how was your walk yesterday?"

From behind me, another familiar female voice exclaimed, "Yeah, I'd kinda like to know the answer to that, too!"

I immediately spun around to discover that Anne Hayward had snuck up behind me. She was giving me two raised eyebrows and what I can only describe as a fiendish grin. Her flowing brown hair was down her back and she was chewing on the end of one of her locks. Anne was also wearing denim shorts, but her top was a plaid, sleeveless button-front. Like me, she had left her shirt tails out.

I was now in trouble and I knew it. There I was, faced with two of busiest busybodies I had ever known, and they wanted answers. My discomfort with the situation must have shown all over my face because it got laughter from both.

"Relax, Jackson, we're not going to torture you or anything," chuckled Gail. "Well, not too much anyway."

So, you're still that cat-eyed, little snot, I thought.

Anne repeated Gail's unanswered question, "Did you two have a good walk?"

"Yeah, we did, I guess."

"I happen to know that she's pretty impressed with you," said Anne.

"Right," I replied cynically. "What exactly does that mean?"

"It means, she likes you, dummy!" asserted Gail.

"How do you two know?"

The two exchanged a look and then turned their eyes back on me.

Gail asked, "Does your phone work, Anne?"

"It was working right after dinner last night, for quite a while, too! How about yours, Gail? Was it working last night?"

"Yeah, mine was working shortly after yours, I think."

"Okay, okay, I get the picture," I laughed. "What all did she tell you?"

"We really shouldn't say. That would be gossip," chuckled Gail.

"Trust us, Jackson, she likes you and is hoping you like her, too," offered Anne.

I thought about Anne's words for a minute. I should have been thrilled, but I wasn't.

Anne pressed, "So, do you?"

Trying to remain casual, I admitted, "Yeah, I guess I do, but so what?"

Immediately, Anne became indignant and her demeanor somewhat hostile when she blurted, "What do you mean…so what?!"

"What good does it do me…or her? I don't live here anymore. In just over a week I'll be gone again. I don't know when or even *if* I'll be back. Yeah…I like her. I guess I always have. So, all I'm sayin' is that I just don't want her to get hurt."

When I saw them both grinning, I stopped explaining myself rather abruptly. Right about then, I remembered who I was talking to. I remembered who had spread the news of *The Kiss* around the entire fourth-grade class. Quite suddenly, I realized my tongue had been waggling around inside my head a little too much. I was being far too loose-tongued, with no assurances of confidentiality.

"I suppose you're going to tell Julie what I just said."

They looked at each other and smiled.

"We won't say anything," Gail insincerely assured.

Not believing a word of it, I rolled my eyes and sarcastically said, "Great… thanks."

"You and Julie really need to talk," asserted Anne. "I think you'll get the chance tomorrow."

Then, Gail jumped in. "Jackson, just so you know, both Anne and I warned her about you not living here anymore."

"Yeah, we did," Anne agreed, "but she doesn't seem to care about that right now."

"I hope you two understand, that's not exactly good news. I honestly do like her. And I would probably spend every possible minute with her if she wanted. It wouldn't be the smartest thing I've ever done, but I'd probably do it anyway. My problem is that I *will* be leaving again. It wasn't easy the first time I left. I don't think it's going to be any easier this time. Even though I don't really feel like I'm a part of things here anymore, it's still going to be tough. All of you have been great since I've come back, but I know I'm not really part of the gang anymore. Three years of being away took care of that."

"I don't feel that way," said Anne. "Do you Gail?"

"Well, he isn't exactly the new guy in town, but then again, he kind of…is. I guess the thing that makes it easy for us is that you really were one of us. This is where you're from."

"And, in case you're wondering, Jackson," inserted Anne, "I think all of us thought about you every now and then, while you were gone. I know I did. I'm pretty sure we will again when you leave this time, too."

"Yeah," Gail agreed. "I don't think we'll be forgetting you. Will you forget us?"

I gave them a weak smile and then admitted, "I haven't been able to…yet."

My heart was already feeling the weight of their words. I hadn't expected them to say such things. I was more than pleasantly surprised to find out how they felt. Nevertheless, the moment had become way too serious for me, and I wanted to get the heck away from them. Feigning sincerity, I said, "I hate to break this up, but I really do have a lawn to mow. I'll see you two later?"

Anne replied slyly, "Oh, you'll definitely be seeing us." Her eyes showed just as much tomfoolery as Gail's.

As I hurried down the Paulsen's steps and walkway, I just had to smile. *The more things change, the more they stay the same,* I thought.

I intended to continue on with my extended walk, but then an idea suddenly took a strong hold of me. *Mowing the lawn for Brad and Janet is actually a great idea!* The afternoon was not too warm, and the yard wasn't very big, so I could be done in no time at all. Plus, I could get some pretty good mileage out of the gesture. Not that I needed it, of course, but just the same, I felt it was something I should do. Besides, Mom would probably love to hear how I pitched in during my visit.

I immediately backtracked and took a more direct route to the house. I cut through a few yards without being stopped by anyone. When I got to the Wilson residence, I found the house unoccupied. That afternoon, everyone in the Wilson clan was working. So, I decided it should be no different for me.

When Brad arrived home from work, I was just finishing up the yardwork by sweeping grass clippings from the driveway. He had beaten the others home that afternoon and initially made a big deal of the job I had done. He said he wished some of me would rub off on Kurt and Danny. According to him, neither boy would ever volunteer to do anything around the house. Getting them to do dishes, clean their rooms, or mow the lawn were things that had to be coerced, or at the very least, bartered for.

"Don't give me too much credit," I told him. "Mom and Dad would tell you the same thing about me."

Brad asked, "So...what's the deal then?"

"I just wanted to show you guys how much I appreciate you letting me be here."

"Appreciation acknowledged. Now, what's up?"

"I'm not after anything, if that's what you mean."

Brad countered in a cynical tone, "Really?"

Clearly showing my annoyance, I replied, "Really!" I then returned my attention to sweeping the driveway.

In that instant, my good mood soured. In fact, I was downright pissed off! Brad just stood there and watched me for a minute before retreating into the house. I finished the chore but stewed the entire time. I honestly felt offended by Brad's insinuation that I had ulterior motives for mowing the lawn. In truth, I did have some of those. I just didn't like him challenging me the way he did.

Just as I finished my work, Brad reappeared at the side door. He had changed out of his work uniform. He was now wearing blue jeans, a white cotton t-shirt and a blue plaid, short-sleeved button-front shirt that he left partially unbuttoned. In one hand, he held a can of beer. He squatted down on the landing, dragged a cigarette from his shirt pocket and then cracked open the beer. As I walked past to put the broom away, I tried to ignore him.

"Hey, buddy, come have a seat for a minute," said Brad.

I did as I was told but refused to look him in the eye. He slid over to give me some room on the step. After I sat, he said, "I'm sorry, kiddo. I know I sounded like a horse's ass a little while ago. You did a great job on the yard. I really do appreciate the effort. I didn't have a very-good day at work and sometimes I find it hard to put it all away before I get home."

"It's okay...I understand," I said, accepting the apology and allowing my anger to subside.

Brad then asked, "Are we good again?"

"Yeah, we're good." I knew I couldn't stay mad at him for long.

"After all that work, you must be thirsty. Want a drink?" asked Brad, holding the beer out to me.

Until then, I had not tasted beer. I didn't know if I would like it or not. I had previously listened to other guys talk about how they had shared a beer with their dads. For a few reasons, Dad and I had not gone through that rite of passage, the most important reason being Mom. She would have conniptions if she ever found out.

My curiosity was getting the better of me, so I took the beer from Brad and executed the old cliché of making sure the coast was clear, just to ensure no one was spying on us. I then took a tentative sip from the sweating can. It wasn't at all what I expected; it caused me to scrunch my face up a bit. Regardless, I took two, additional, large gulps before handing it back.

Brad cautioned me with a hearty, "Whoa! Easy there, buddy!" Then, after snatching the beer away, he asked me about my day.

Since it was just Brad and I sitting there, I told him about my lunch with Father Michael and my decision to see Adam Harris.

"That's great, I'm glad that you're coming around. However, before you meet with Adam, Janet and I really need to talk to you.

"Can't *you* just tell me what it is?"

"I promised Janet and she promised me that the three of us would be together when we talked. I'm sure there is still time. When are you meeting with Adam?"

"Not until early next week. Father Michael is going to set it up."

"Jackson, I don't want you to worry about this at all. We're coming into the weekend. There are plans for all of us to spend some time together and have some fun. You have a party to go to tomorrow night and we're planning a barbeque for Saturday. The temperatures are going to start shooting up, so we're thinking about going to the lake this Sunday.

"All that sounds great, but…why haven't you and Mom told me whatever it is you need to tell me already? You know, I have a few things I need to tell you guys, too."

"I'll tell you what, buddy, let's set a time for Monday evening. What do you think? That'll at least give us a few days to relax and enjoy the good stuff."

I nodded my agreement, but alarms were going off in my head. *What's so important? Why don't they just tell me and get it over with?* I truly wanted to know what all the secrecy was about, but it was also apparent that I was just going to have to be patient. At the same time, I knew all the pleasant distractions in the days ahead would help take my mind off the more troubling thoughts.

Gently shaking his beer can, Brad asked, "You want to finish this?"

"No thanks. It wasn't what I thought it would be."

"Don't like it?"

"Let's just say…I'd rather have a *root* beer."

We both chuckled and agreed that I would possibly develop a taste for beer when I was older. I then got up and walked slowly to the garage to put the broom away. While I did that, Brad quickly ducked inside the house. When he reappeared, he had another beer for himself and a root beer for me. We stayed in the front yard and lounged in the shade of the mountain ash tree. I asked him to tell me about his bad day at work. He said it wasn't any one thing that made it bad, just a lot of little things that didn't go very well.

"Combine a lot of little things like that and it makes for one bad day," Brad explained. "But, sitting here in the shade and relaxing can make it all go away."

When Janet arrived home, we were still relaxing out front. I hurriedly got up to go get another folding lawn chair from the garage, so she could join us. Brad caught my attention before I left. "Remember our deal, kiddo," he cautioned.

I simply nodded my acknowledgement.

The chair I grabbed from the garage looked a bit rickety. The noticeable make-shift repairs to it were a telltale sign that Brad was getting his money's worth. As long as he could fix a thing, it would never be thrown out or replaced. It was more or less a law within the household.

When I got back to the shaded front yard, I noticed Janet had commandeered the better chair I had been sitting in. So, I gingerly sat down in the chair of dubious-structural integrity and the three of us relaxed together. That is, until Kurt and Danny got home. Janet then left us and went inside to prepare dinner. The four of us guys stayed out and enjoyed the cool, early-evening air. As the three of them talked about their work, I just listened and smiled.

Danny thanked me for mowing the lawn because it was his week for that particular chore. I made a tentative promise to do it for Kurt in the next week if it needed it. I had learned long ago, when it came to those two, what I did for one, I had to be willing to do for the other.

I then caught Brad smiling at the three of us. I saw that same smile the day I arrived in town. I knew he was simply enjoying the moment. I was too, but there was also an underlying feeling. Just then, I knew the happiness that I was feeling would be very short lived.

Kurt then reminded me about his invite to hang out with the two of them and their friends. Company was coming over again that night, but I still preferred to watch the Twins baseball game. So, I simply gave them both a tentative maybe.

After dinner, Kurt and Danny left to pick up their girls. Brad adjourned to the garage to do some tinkering. He wanted to get a few things done before that night's baseball game. So, I got stuck with helping Janet clean the kitchen. I truly didn't mind because it was another reminder of when I was a member of the family. In years past, while doing the dishes together, Janet and I talked about many things. However, I wasn't always ready for her chosen topic of discussion or line of questioning. When Janet's tongue got rolling, I just never knew what she was going to bring my way. That night was no different.

As Janet handed me a plate to rinse, she said, "You're quite the helper today... What's up?"

"Nothing's up. Why is it so suspicious to help out a little around here?"

"Probably because the only time Kurt and Danny volunteer to do anything around here is when they want something."

Smiling at the truth of it, I said, "I already got what I want. So, you can consider my helping out as payback."

"Really? And what did you get that you think you need to kick in around here?"

"Two weeks."

Janet smiled and carried on a bit about how I was growing up to be a thoughtful young man. I also got a small lecture on how my good manners would always serve me well. According to her, they would help make a great, first impression, especially when I was at some girl's house, meeting her parents. At that, I gave Janet a look that said she was being weirder than her usual self.

"You can look at me like that all you want, mister, but you just wait until tomorrow night."

"What do you mean?"

"You don't think you're going to get out of Julie's house without meeting her parents, do you?"

"No, but that's not a big deal."

"You're not nervous about it?"

"Nope, Mr. Falkner used to be my T-Ball and Little League coach... Remember?"

"Gary always was a good sort, but Julie's mom is a different story."

"How well do you know her?"

In a tone void of emotion, Janet replied, "We were schoolgirls together. In grade school, we were friends. We even grew up in the same neighborhood. In high school, our friendship ended, more or less. It's not an uncommon story in a small town like this. Brad and I went to school with most of your friend's parents."

As much as I wanted to ask her more, I decided to leave it alone. So, I just continued to rinse and dry dishes.

Janet then added, "If you plan on seeing Julie again in that house, I recommend you don't forget your manners tomorrow night."

I nodded my understanding, but I wasn't too concerned. All I truly cared about was making it through Friday night, without making an ass of myself. After that, I really could not envision getting another invitation.

When Kurt and Danny showed up with their girls, I was lounging in the upstairs living room, watching the ballgame. The Twins were in Anaheim, California that night, playing the Angels. The Angels had taken an early lead by scoring one run in the first inning and two in the second. Rick Renick's single shot home run for the Twins in the third inning didn't make me feel better.

The Angels' pitcher that night was Rudy May and his arm was like a bolt of lightning. By the end of the sixth inning, I was sure the Twins had nothing more to give. Thus far that season, coming back from deficits was not their strong suit. Suddenly, Danny poked his head in the room to get the score, or so I initially thought.

"Three-to-one...Angels in the lead," I said in a low tone. "Top of the seventh." I figured I might as well answer the next question before Danny even asked it.

Danny leaned in the archway of the kitchen staring at me, but I pretended to be fully engrossed in the game. Realizing that he wasn't in a hurry to leave, nor come into the living room to join me, I finally turned my head and whispered, "What?!"

"Are you coming down?"

"I'll be down after the game."

I had planned to join them for a little while, but only because I wanted to talk to Janelle – I needed some sisterly advice. However, I figured all that could wait until after the game. I was still holding onto a weak hope that the Twins were going to wake up.

Brad wasn't paying attention to Danny, me, or the game. He had fallen asleep on the couch. Danny crept over to me and tugged at my shirt sleeve. I looked up at him and saw he had a finger over his lips. He motioned with his head for me to follow him.

Uh oh, I thought, *this can't be good.* But I got up anyway and followed him into the kitchen. Janet was reading in the bedroom, with the door closed, so we were able to whisper.

Wearing a devilish grin, Danny said, "There's someone here to see you."

"Danny, what did you guys do?"

"*We*...didn't do anything. She said she wanted to see you again." Danny then broke away from me and quickly disappeared down the stairs to the basement.

I stood there for a minute before it hit me. *Lori Mudd is down there and wants to see me?!* "Oh cripes, now what do I do?!"

Prior to coming to Mankato, no girl wanted anything to do with me. Now, it seemed there were two girls wanting my attention. The fact that I was only interested in Julie presented a real dilemma. Well, it did in my mind anyway.

Leaning on the kitchen counter by the sink, frozen-like, I thought about what my next move should be. Suddenly, I heard light footsteps coming up the stairs from the basement. I held my breath, just for an instant, and wondered if I had time to escape to the upstairs bedroom. Just then, Janelle poked her head around the corner. Seeing that I was alone, she came up the rest of the way and joined me in the kitchen. Her greeting came in the form of a sweet whisper.

"Hi, Jackson!" Then, she gave me her customary hug. "Aren't you coming down?"

Unsure of how I should answer, I replied, "Lori is down there…Isn't she?"

Janelle laughed under her breath and said, "Yeah, she is. Is that a problem?"

Trying not to think about it *too* much, I replied, "I hope not."

Janelle then took my hand and gently tried to pull me toward the stairs. "I know what you're worried about."

My resistance was subtle, but I stayed put. "You do?"

Janelle pulled a little harder. "Kurt told me."

My weight was now fully engaged. I had to use some muscle to resist her tugging, but I was still able to stay anchored. "So, what did the bucket mouth tell you?"

With a slight strain in her voice, Janelle replied, "He said that you and Julie made a connection." She then gave one good tug, but her stocking feet slid on the linoleum floor; we went nowhere. Janelle was genuinely surprised, so in a whispered yell, she exclaimed, "Cripes, you're as strong as Kurt!"

Although I thoroughly enjoyed Janelle's comparison, I had to disagree. "Not yet, but I'll get there."

"You're as stubborn, too."

"You're probably right about that," I admitted, but then decided it was time to get down to business. I had planned to consult her on what I thought was a rather sticky matter. Since we were relatively alone in the kitchen, I figured there was no better time to talk to her. "I'm going to a party at Julie's tomorrow night and I need your help."

Janelle stopped tugging on me long enough for me to tell her all about how I had walked Julie home from Tony's place. She also heard about my conversation with Gail and Anne. Lastly, I admitted to her my apprehensions about going to Julie's party.

Wearing a perplexed look, Janelle said, "I still don't understand the problem."

Feeling my face turn flush, I said, "Anne and Gail said Julie was impressed with me. Well, I'm not impressive at all, not when I dance."

Janelle's look immediately went from confused to absolute surprise. Nevertheless, she contained herself nicely and in her whispered yell, exclaimed, "Oh my, God! You're looking to knock her socks off! Aren't you?!"

Timidly, I admitted, "Well…yeah…I guess I am."

Janelle then grinned from ear to ear, as she again began to pull me toward the stairs. "The music is downstairs, Jackson."

"And so is Lori."

"I still don't see the problem."

"Oh, I get it. This is one of those times where what Julie doesn't know won't hurt *me*?"

Slyly, Janelle said, "You're catching on. Don't worry so much. Lori won't do anything to get in Julie's way." Halfway down the steps, Janelle turned around suddenly and whispered, "Of course, don't be surprised if Lori doesn't let Julie get in her way, either."

When Janelle and I reached the bottom of the stairs and entered the den, we were both laughing. All eyes locked on the two of us. Danny exclaimed, "There he is! It's about time, little brother!"

Carrie came over and gave me what had also become her ritualistic hug. Janelle then led me to the couch and delivered a very deliberate, yet gentle, motivational shove for me to sit next to Lori. She then hurried to her place next to Kurt on the loveseat.

After being seated, I turned to Lori and with what I can only imagine was a very dopey look on my face, gave her an enthusiastic, "Hi!" Lori just chuckled and returned my greeting.

Small talk broke out between the six of us, with a smattering of Danny's stupid jokes included. I refused to make any moves on Lori, mostly because I didn't have any. Instead, I watched and wondered how Kurt and Danny could confidently cuddle with their girls. I thought about putting an arm around Lori, but almost immediately chickened out. Sitting in close proximity to her was enough. In fact, it felt as though I shouldn't even be doing that. Then, I wondered. *If Julie was sitting next to me this way, would I do something about it?* Just then, Lori moved in closer, took my hand, and casually put my arm around her. I wasn't shocked by her forwardness, but I got no particular thrill from it, either. I simply looked into her eyes and smiled, like I was truly happy that she had taken the initiative.

After a comfortable interval had passed, Janelle got up and went to the record player. She refreshed the stack of forty-fives on the turn table and increased the volume a bit. "Come on guys, let's dance," she urged. Janelle then began to move her hips to the first song that played.

Surprisingly, neither Kurt nor Danny voiced any resistance, when their girls pulled them out of their seats.

Lori stood, too, and held her hands out to me, asking, "Are you game?"

It was my cue to get off my butt and join in. I spent a few uneasy minutes wondering if Janelle was going to spill the beans about my asking for help. When she gave me a discrete wink, I knew my secret was safe.

I tried to relax some and simply watched the way Lori danced. In comparison to me, she was quite good, but I was able to mimic some of her movements. Carrie, however, was the most impressive dancer there. Janelle manipulated the situation beautifully by saying, "Carrie, show me how you do that. Hey, Lori, Jackson, you gotta try this!"

Within the next hour or so, more of Kurt and Danny's friends showed up. They just trickled in and before I knew what was happening, a full-fledged, dance party seemed to be going on. By nine-thirty there had to be at least a dozen of us in that den. There was practically nowhere to stand anymore. To make matters worse, it was getting downright hot from too many people and not enough air circulation. During slow dances, it was almost steamy.

Both Janelle and Carrie snatched me up once or twice for a dance, but other than those two, I danced almost exclusively with Lori. She appeared quite happy with the arrangement, too. I suddenly had the feeling that Lori was having expectations of me. What those expectations might be, I had no idea, but right then, I truly didn't care because I was having a great time. Still, I couldn't help but think, *"Good God, it's hot down here!"*

After a series of slow dances, Lori and I were literally sticking to one another. So, I suggested we go outside to cool off.

Rather seductively, Lori said, "Lead the way."

Lori and I worked our way through the mob and quietly crept up the stairs. We then went out the side door and onto the driveway. The cool night air was positively intoxicating. I remembered that we had left the folding lawn chairs in the front yard, so I walked over and plopped down in the first one I came to. It almost groaned under the sudden burden of my weight. I had unwittingly chosen the old, rickety chair that I had used earlier that afternoon.

Offering one of the other chairs to Lori, I said, "Have a seat." I figured as long as I kept a little distance between the two of us, I was in no danger. But I figured wrong.

For a moment or two, Lori just stood in front of me. Then, with little warning, she leaned over and put her hands on the arm rests of my chair. Adding her weight to the chair, she brought her face to within inches of mine. I tried to keep my cool, but even as inexperienced as I was, I knew what was coming next.

Lori breathed, "Relax, Jackson…I don't bite."

Upon contact, her lips felt so very warm on mine and her breath was that of Juicy Fruit gum. Once again, I found it hard to concentrate and temporarily lost all cognitive thought. Not knowing what to do with my hands, I kept them clasped over my stomach. Since I was the one sitting, there was no escape, not that I cared to just then. I then tried to pull my head back slightly, so I could take a breath, but her lips simply continued to search mine out. I felt myself give in and melt like a stick of butter. *Yikes!* I thought. *This girl really likes to kiss!*

We made out that way for I don't know how long. Suddenly, right in the middle of our lip-lock, that old, decrepit chair called it quits on us. Our combined weight was too much for it to handle; the legs simply folded underneath it. We toppled to the ground and hit with a solid thud. I imagined we looked fairly ridiculous because Lori's face was nearly in my lap. As I scrambled to my feet, she laughed uncontrollably. When I looked down and saw how Lori could not stop laughing, I imagined how the whole scene must have looked to the neighbors; I joined in the laughter.

"Lori, has that ever happened to you before?"

"Jackson, the earth literally moved!"

As I helped Lori to her feet, I added, "Yep, I think it'll be a long time before I forget *that* kiss."

Lori then looked down at the ruined chair. "Sure don't make 'em like they used to," she joked. "What are we going to tell everyone?"

"Well, I don't know about you, but I'm gonna say the neighbor's dog did it."

We both broke out laughing again. That's when Kurt and Janelle showed up. They looked at us, then at the busted chair, then back to us. The looks on their faces were enough to make Lori and I laugh even harder.

Without offering the slightest explanation, I took Lori by the hand and led her away from Kurt and Janelle. We went back inside and joined the dancing that was going on in the basement den. Danny and Carrie had observed us rejoin the group, so they worked their way over to us.

Danny asked, "You two having fun?"

Still laughing, I replied, "I don't know about Lori, but I'm having a blast!"

That's pretty much the way the rest of that evening went, dancing and laughing. Up until that evening, I couldn't remember having a better time. I had lost all my inhibitions and no longer cared what I looked like on the dance floor. Lori, Janelle, Carrie, and all the other teens had given me more than enough examples to operate from. I suddenly smiled at the revelation that I wasn't as big a spaz around girls as I previously thought I was. Things were changing and I liked it! I liked it a lot!

At eleven o'clock, Lori announced that she needed to get home. Kurt, Janelle, and I transported her in the Volkswagen van. During the drive, I thought about what would be expected of me, when I walked her to the door. I couldn't help but smile at what I knew was coming.

When we arrived on Lori's doorstep, she turned abruptly and, just like at Janelle's party, grabbed the front of my windbreaker. She then pulled me in close. The kiss lasted longer than I was comfortable with, but who was I to complain? Lori had a different look in her eyes, and it made me more than a little nervous. I felt that kissing her was okay, but there was still something missing. I mean, it was intimate, yet not. Then I thought that maybe I shouldn't be kissing her at all. I figured that it was because Lori had led me to believe things would remain casual between us. Nevertheless, that long, slow, hot, wet kiss, there on her doorstep, with the porch light inviting everyone to watch, felt like many things, but casual wasn't one of them. At the same time, I could not help but admire her tenacity. When the kiss was done, Lori whispered, "Thanks, Jackson, I had a great time."

As Lori disappeared behind her door, I found myself unable to define how I felt. There was an extremely nice, warm glow going on inside me, but there was something else, too. Then, like someone slapping me upside my head, it hit me. *Confident...That's how I feel!* I was no longer worried about how to act around girls! As it turned out, Janelle was absolutely right! *Holy smokes, so that's what that feels like!"* Then, with a shit-eating grin plastered to my face, I sauntered back to the van, jumped in, and smugly said, "Home, James."

Janelle and Kurt both gave me curious looks. "Jackson!" exclaimed Janelle. "Didn't you just tell me tonight how you and Julie made a connection?"

"Nope...Bucket mouth up there told you that," I replied drunkenly. "Didn't you tell me Lori wouldn't let Julie stand in her way? Well, I can't fight 'em all off...Can I?"

"Oh my, God!" cried Kurt. "We've created a monster!"

We three laughed all the way home. I couldn't help but feel slightly self-conscious about having a little too much fun with Lori. I did, however, reconcile it all in my head because none of that evening's activities were my idea. I just did what was expected of me and went with the flow. In addition, I had learned that going with the flow can be a lot of fun. I realized that I could truly enjoy myself with a girl. As well, Lori had a rather graphic way of demonstrating that she enjoyed being with me, too. *Hey, Doc...I found my smile!* The thought almost made me laugh out loud.

When we arrived back at the house, I refrained from going downstairs. It was late and I knew my fun was done for the evening. I said good night to Kurt and Janelle in the kitchen. Janelle, of course, needed her hug. I was now getting used to it and even looked forward to it. There was a bond building between us. I was not only beginning to trust it but enjoy it as well.

As Janelle hugged me, she whispered, "You looked like you really had a good time tonight."

Unable to wipe the smile from my face, I replied, "I did. Thanks for your help."

Janelle gave me a knowing smile in return. She then winked and said, "Yeah, I think you're gonna be just fine tomorrow night."

Janelle and Kurt then disappeared down the basement stairwell. I turned and headed for the upstairs and my bed. I knew it would be a while before I got to sleep, but that was okay, too. I had no plans for the morning, so it would be okay if I slept in.

Lying in bed, trying to get to sleep, I marveled at how everything was changing. I wasn't worried anymore about Julie's party. As a matter of fact, I could hardly wait for Friday night to arrive. I wasn't worried about finding my smile, either. As far as I was concerned, it was found. Kissing Lori had been nice, but there was no doubt in my mind that I'd rather have Julie kiss me. At the same time, I knew I wasn't supposed to want any of that stuff. I wasn't supposed to want anybody in Mankato, but I just couldn't suppress what was going on inside of me. I wanted Julie and that was that.

I then remembered Janet's words about making an impression on Julie's parents. *That may take some doing, but I've never had any problems meeting adults before,* I thought.

Mom and Dad taught me to always be respectful and show people my best. "Smile, give a firm handshake to men, a gentler one for women, and when you greet someone, speak up." Mom had relentlessly hammered that lesson into my head. Her teachings hadn't failed me up to that point, so I saw no reason why they would fail me at the Falkner's. In a short time, I stopped worrying about it.

Before closing my eyes, I remembered something Doc Elliot said to me, during our last meeting. "You need to figure out there is nothing waiting for you in Mankato."

I contemplated Doc's words for a little while but concluded that he was only half right. *Sorry Doc,* I thought. *There're all kinds of things for me in Mankato. They may not have been waiting for me, but they sure don't seem to mind me being here now.*

CHAPTER 12

Friday, 11 August 1972

I awoke to the throaty-exhaust sound of the Corvair backing out of the driveway – Brad was heading off to work. I immediately looked over at Danny's bed, saw a big lump with covers pulled up almost over his head, and heard him quietly snoring. My first thought was to roll over and go back to sleep, too. However, I wanted to pack as much activity into each day as possible, so I made myself get out of bed.

As quietly as possible, I stepped into my jeans and pulled a T-shirt over my head. I then looked back over my shoulder to ensure I had not wakened Danny. Nevertheless, when I went downstairs to the kitchen, I wondered how anyone could sleep through the noise of the creaking steps. Painstakingly making my way down, I remembered how bad they were three years prior. *Cripes, do they think those steps are going to get better with age?*

"Good morning," said Janet, as I shuffled into the kitchen. She was preparing herself a lunch, so I figured, like Brad, she would be heading out for work soon, too.

"Morning," I returned sleepily.

Genuinely surprised, Janet asked, "What are you doing up so early?"

I lied by saying, "Couldn't sleep."

"It sounded like you guys had a good time last night."

243

"Yeah, it was fun."

Janet stood at the sink, rinsing her hands. Suddenly, she turned and directed a stern look my way. In a disapproving tone, she said, "Last night, I heard some commotion out front, when it was pretty late. So, I peeked out the window. Guess what I saw?"

Oh man, here it comes, I thought, then said, "I know, we were being stupid."

"Well?" insisted Janet.

"I accidently broke one of the lawn chairs."

"How did you do that?"

"I sat in it."

"Yesterday afternoon, they supported your weight just fine. Did you gain that much weight from my dinner last night?"

"No. A girl sort of...added her weight to mine...and the chair just kinda... collapsed."

"Oh brother!" moaned Janet, as she rolled her eyes and then glanced at the clock. "I'm sure there's a fascinating story coming my way, but I have to get to work. What are you doing today?"

I gave Janet a squeamish look and then tentatively replied, "Shopping for a lawn chair?"

"You're a good man, Jackson, but that won't be necessary. I'm willing to bet it was the chair that Brad has been piecing together for years."

"Are you sure?"

Janet finally dropped her stern outer appearance, smiled and then said, "Yeah, keep your money in your pocket, kiddo." Then, as an afterthought, she added, "Hey, I know you have the party to go to tonight, but Brad and I will be getting home early from work this afternoon. We want to take you and the boys out for burgers before everyone goes their own way. I'm sure the girls will be coming, too. They're pretty much attached at the hip these days."

When I realized I was no longer in trouble, I brightened up immediately and replied, "Great idea! Where are we going?"

"Where is the best place in Mankato to get burgers?" challenged Janet.

"That's easy...The Hill Top Tavern! At least, it was the best. I don't know anymore."

"As far as *this* family is concerned, it still is the best. Tell the boys for me, will you? I really have to get out of here."

Janet rushed over and gave me a quick kiss before practically sprinting out the door. Just before exiting, she turned on her heels. "Oh, Jackson?"

"Yeah?"

"Go brush your teeth, kid. You have terrible puppy breath!" Cocking her head back, she let out a huge laugh and then disappeared out the door. As Janet walked to the Mercury, I heard her announce to the entire neighborhood, "Sometimes, I just crack myself up!"

I went to the door and watched Janet back out of the driveway. I couldn't help but laugh at her early-morning humor. Next, I prepared myself some toast with peanut butter and strawberry jam. The kitchen radio had been left on and it was playing some decent, but old, rock 'n' roll tunes. I turned up the volume a little and listened to Roy Orbison sing, "Pretty woman, walkin' down the street. Pretty woman, the kind I'd like to meet..."

As I waited for the toast to pop up, I practiced some of the dance steps the girls taught me the night before. Yeah, I was truly getting into it. I was a shakin' and a shimmyin', when suddenly behind me, Danny exclaimed, "Go, Jackson, go!"

I practically jumped out of my skin and my face must have turned three shades of red. I felt like I had literally been caught with my pants down. Letting out an embarrassed laugh, I asked, "How long have you been standing there?!"

Grinning from ear to ear, Danny replied, "Long enough, little brother. You can relax, though, because Kurt caught me doing the same thing a few years back. So, it won't do me any good to tell on you."

His admission did little to ease my humiliation, but I played it off by asking, "Did you ever catch him doing that stuff?"

"Naw, he doesn't do that stuff out in the open, but I know he practices."

"Why do you say that?"

"Because his bedroom door is locked all the time and he blasts his radio. Besides that, have you seen his moves? He dances pretty good for a grease monkey.

245

Don't ya think?" We both laughed, then Danny asked, "Did you like dancing with Lori last night?"

"Yeah, I guess I did. I'm just learning, but it was pretty cool."

"When you're with the right girl, the slow songs don't suck. Do they?"

I shyly admitted, "I like slow dancing just fine, Danny. I just don't think it's been with the right girl...yet."

While I finished preparing my toast, Danny continued to razz me about the previous evening. After I smeared enough peanut butter and strawberry jam on the two pieces of toast, I set my plate on the kitchen table. I then went to the fridge to pour myself a glass of milk. When I returned to the table, I discovered my toast was missing. I then turned my gaze on Danny and immediately howled with laughter. His cheeks were ballooned outward, like a chipmunk's when gathering food to store for the winter. Before he could swallow, Danny began to laugh, too. Crumbs flew from his overstuffed pie hole.

Because he didn't have to work that day, Kurt was still sleeping soundly in his room. Like all teens, he enjoyed sleeping in on his days off, especially after staying up late the previous night. With the racket Danny and I were making, I felt sure he would be joining us soon.

"We'd better be quiet," I cautioned. "If Kurt hears us, he'll come up here and kick both our butts!"

"No he won't," replied Danny. "He can't take both of us at the same time."

After thinking about it some, I agreed with Danny's theory, but I would never willingly go up against Kurt to test it.

Just as I predicted, shortly after Danny and I quieted down, we heard Kurt stomping up the basement steps. When he entered the kitchen, his crankiness was very apparent, so Danny wasted no time telling him what had just taken place. Kurt's demeanor lightened some, but Danny and I both knew more time was needed before he would fully appreciate being awake.

Kurt then surprised me somewhat by immediately putting me on the spot. He turned his still-groggy gaze on me and said, "I never did hear what happened with you, Lori, and that chair last night.

"What chair?" asked Danny.

"The old, broken, lawn chair," replied Kurt.

When I shared the story with my two older brothers, I don't know if I garnered any coolness points with them, but I do remember our laughter. The three of us hadn't laughed like that since I moved away. We continued to poke fun at each other, while I made more toast for Kurt and myself. Not surprisingly, Danny was full already.

As we ate, the three of us enjoyed a brotherly-bullshit session. That is, right up until Kurt put an end to our fun. He always did have a propensity for being a wet blanket. Sometimes, it was pretty difficult to downshift, just to keep up with his mood swings. In the drop of a hat, Kurt could take us from laughing and having a great time, to arguing and fisticuffs. That morning was no different. He caught me totally unaware, when he very suddenly lost his smile and exchanged it for an angry look.

"Mom told us you've been getting into some trouble up north."

"Yeah? What all did she tell you?"

"She said you've been fighting...a lot," said Danny.

"Yeah, she said you beat up some kid pretty bad last winter," added Kurt.

"I was going to talk to you two about..."

"We didn't teach you to be like that." Kurt interrupted.

"It's not what you think," I offered.

I could see they both were in no mood to listen. Instead, they meant to take turns working me over, verbally. They hadn't changed a bit. I remembered them tag-teaming me that way in the past. When I was younger, all I could do was sit there and take it because they wouldn't let me get a word in to defend myself. However, that morning was the worst. I mean, they really let me have it.

"No bullies allowed in this family!" yelled Danny. "Maybe if someone were to kick your ass, you'd understand."

I did not have to take their verbal abuse long to assess that they thought I had turned into a schoolyard bully. Even though I was not guilty of what they alleged, I could not escape the truth about what I had done to Darrin Anderson. Shame set in, and I could not look them in the eye. Since I could not get a word in edgewise to explain. I sat there, looking down at my feet and just took their ridicule. In turn, they continued to heap it on me. My shame was coming on like gang busters. To me, it was clear that I had lost their respect and possibly even their love. Right then, it was more than I could handle.

Danny was the first to notice the tears welling up in my eyes. His demeanor changed immediately, and he softly spoke. "Hey, Jackson…Ease up, man. Take it easy, little brother. It's okay."

No longer in control, I exploded, "NO! IT'S NOT OKAY! YOU HAVE IT ALL WRONG!" Unable to stop my tears, I left the table and headed for the living room. There, I sat on the couch, and fought to regain my composure.

Danny came in and sat next to me. He put his hand on my shoulder and waited for me to calm down.

Kurt pulled a chair in close, then said, "Jackson…slow up, man. We didn't mean to be so rough. You go ahead…tell us what's going on up there."

After I calmed down a bit, I told them all about the fighting. I told them how, from my perspective, things were terrible for me in Duluth. I droned on about how I didn't fit in and how other guys wouldn't give me a chance. I explained how it seemed that, for no good reason, someone was always picking a fight with me. When I told them how I hated myself for what I had done to Darrin Anderson, I bowed my head and cried some more. They also listened to how scared and unsure of myself I was. I even told them that when I lost control of my temper, I *wanted* to hurt someone. After explaining all that and more, I looked up at Kurt and said, "It's not like you taught me at all. No matter how many times I've put a beating on some guy, there's always someone else picking a fight with me."

"Yeah," admitted Kurt. "I guess I might have been wrong about that. I guess it's more like my wrestling. No matter how many matches I win, there will always be someone ready to take me on."

"So, what do I do?! I don't wanna fight anymore! I'm sick of it!"

"Do nothing," said Danny. "I think you're getting to that age where it all just goes away."

"Yeah," Kurt agreed. "As we get older, I think we all just figure out that fighting is stupid."

"Really?" I asked, drying my eyes. "I mean it. I really don't want to fight anymore. I think that's why no girls are interested in me up there. They're all afraid of me."

Attempting to lighten the moment, Danny smiled and said, "Oh…I think you've got the *girl thing* figured out now."

"Not really," I replied. "No girl down here has seen me, not when I fight. They haven't seen me when I lose my temper."

"Things change during the summer, Jackson," said Kurt. "I'll bet there will be some girl up north who will be glad to see you again."

My mind drifted briefly to Sarah Caskey and I wondered if she would even give me the time of day. Unconvinced that Kurt's words were true, I asked, "What makes you say that?"

"Since you hit town, you've done some changing," said Danny. "You're definitely not as shy around girls, not like when you first got here."

"Yeah," added Kurt. "Don't you think the girls in your school have been doing some changing, too?"

"I suppose," I admitted. However, I didn't believe there was the remotest possibility that any girl in Duluth would look at me the way Julie and Lori did.

Kurt and Danny continued to reassure me about how things were going to change for the better, after I returned to school. I patiently listened but wondered the whole time whether they actually knew what they were talking about.

I was ashamed to have cried in front of them. That is, part of it was shame. Mostly, I had been missing them and the way they had always looked out for me. I didn't have that up north. I didn't have anyone who could understand like those two. So, as I continued to wipe tears from my eyes, I said, "Cripes, sorry about the crying. It's just…I really haven't been very happy since I moved. Everything has been great since I got here. I'm afraid I won't be able to say good-bye to it all again."

"You don't really have a choice about that," reminded Kurt.

"Yeah, but nothing says you have to stay gone for so long," added Danny.

It was time to level with them about that, too. "I don't think I will be coming back."

To that, they both looked at me and sneered, like I had just uttered the stupidest words they had ever heard.

"Bullshit!" exclaimed Danny.

I then came clean about my sessions with Doctor Elliot and the whole purpose of my trip. They listened closely to my words and I watched their faces, as I told them everything, including what was expected of me. "I'm supposed to be saying good-bye to this place. They tell me there is nothing waiting for me here. I say they're wrong. So far, *everything* I want is right here! I don't know how I'm supposed to leave it all again."

"I know it sucks right now," said Kurt. "But I'll bet you'll come back. It'll be sooner than you think, too."

I then informed them about how secretive Brad and Janet had been acting. I also told them about the *serious* talk that was supposed to take place after the weekend. At that, Kurt abruptly got up from the table and headed for the basement stairs. I asked, "Why are you leaving?"

Kurt answered in a somewhat emotionless tone, "I want to get showered before the girls get here."

My eyes popped wide open. "The girls? How many girls?"

"Don't worry," chuckled Danny. "Lori won't be here."

"Look, Jackson," said Kurt. "If it really is going to be a long time before we get to see you again, I say we should try to have as much fun as possible."

Kurt was hiding something. I was certain of it. At the same time, his words made perfect sense to me.

"I think you have a big night coming," said Danny, trying to break the mood again. "Stop worrying about all that other crap for a while."

"Yeah, I guess you're right. You really think it's going to be a big night?"

"Only if you don't screw it up," laughed Kurt.

"Thanks," I said sarcastically. "You're a big help."

When Janelle and Carrie arrived, I was sitting comfortably in the front yard, reading the sports page from the previous night's newspaper. The morning was so beautiful.

I didn't want to waste any of it sitting in a stuffy house. I watched Janelle park her old Ford sedan and and then watched some more, as they walked up to greet me. I made a mistake by keeping my seat.

"You had better get your skinny butt out of that chair and give me my hug," ordered Janelle.

"Sorry," I said, as I begrudgingly obeyed.

"As long as you're up…" said Carrie, with her arms wide open.

After both girls were properly greeted to their satisfaction, Janelle pointed to the busted lawn chair. I hadn't bothered to hide it. Instead, I simply propped it against the side of the house.

Janelle asked, "When am I going to get to hear *that* story?"

Gesturing toward the house, I replied, "I'm sure your boyfriends in there will be happy to tell you all about it."

The two of them looked at each other and then bolted for the door, giggling like little girls. I stood there, shaking my head and smiling. "Kids," I facetiously muttered to myself.

After the foursome had left in the VW van, I continued reading in the front yard until late morning. I had switched from the sports page to a Louis L'Amour western I had been working on. After a short while, I looked up from my reading and saw Tony, Joel, and Dave coming up Westwood Drive. I figured that I would play like I did not see them, just in case they weren't coming to see me. As they cut through the next-door neighbor's yard to get to where I was seated, I kept my eyes in my book.

Upon their arrival, Tony asked, "Hey man, you busy?"

With a straight face, I looked up at the three of them and replied, "Yeah, can't you see I'm working my butt off here?"

Dave snickered and pointed at Tony, saying, "Burn!" He then turned to me. "Can you get out of here for a while?"

"Yeah, no problem."

Joel spoke up next. "We're headed downtown. We're gonna eat lunch down there, so bring some dough."

"I've seen Front Street," I asserted. "There ain't much open anymore. So, besides lunch, what do you guys plan on doing?"

Joel asked, "Right now, do you really care?"

"No, not really," I admitted.

Joel pounced, "Well then, let's go."

I moseyed inside to grab some cash, which I had stashed in my suitcase. I hastily stuffed some bills into my wallet and then turned to leave. As I started back for the stairwell, I noticed something on Danny's dresser that looked out of place. At first, I thought it was a weird looking pack of gum. I had thoughts of stealing a stick, but then I read the label and immediately changed my mind. It was a package of condoms. *What the hell is he doing with these?* I knew their purpose, but Danny was only fifteen years old! The condoms insinuated, to me anyway, that Danny had some clandestine plan or had already acted on one. I didn't quite know what to make of it at the time. When the guys yelled up from the driveway for me to hurry up, the package of condoms almost immediately left my mind. After all, it was none of my business and I didn't want to come off like a nosey little brother. So, I decided to leave the subject matter alone. I quickly turned, ran down the stairs and out the side door to join my friends.

The walk downtown was filled with excited chatter about the coming night. As I listened to Tony talk about how he planned to be the disk jockey, I smiled. "You wait and see, Jackson. I'll have everyone dancing, even Mike!

Acting clueless, I asked, "Dancing?"

"Yeah, man," said Tony. "Don't they do that up north?"

"They dance," I replied. "I just didn't think *you* guys went in for that sort of thing."

"When we all get together at someone's house or at a school dance, it's pretty cool," added Joel, "especially the slow dances."

"Oh, I don't doubt you have a good time," I said. "I'm just having a hard time picturing Dave cuttin' a rug."

"Cuttin' a what?!" asked Dave.

Tony jumped in. "I heard it from my mom and dad. It means burning up the dance floor."

"Oh, I get it," said Dave. And, as always, he played right along. "Hey, my grandma taught me all my moves. You wait and see."

All the way downtown, there was a lot more of what we considered witty banter. I loved being with those guys, especially when we were cuttin' up. When we were together, we weren't the most mature group, but we didn't really care, either. We were young and we were idiots!

As I expected, there wasn't a lot of activity on the sidewalks of Front Street. Vehicular traffic was light to moderate, and it sped along unfettered by pedestrians. I had hoped there might be a little more hustle and bustle, especially since it was coming up on lunchtime. Nonetheless, I was disappointed to find that my earlier assumptions were all correct. There just wasn't a lot to do on that street anymore.

C & N Background Music Sales was our first stop. Since The Record Shack closed shortly after I moved away, Tony did his shopping for music at C & N. The company stocked most, if not all, the juke boxes in Blue Earth County with the latest and greatest tunes on 45-rpm records. When the records spent enough time in the juke box, C & N rotated them out. The company then sold the used records for a fraction of what you would have to pay for them brand new. That day, I learned how Tony's record collection got to be so expansive, especially on a meager allowance.

Once inside the store, Tony began to comb the racks, hoping to find tunes he didn't already own. I had never taken much of an interest in music, but with the dancing I had recently learned to do, that was all about to change. I had discovered that I truly enjoyed Top 40 Pop, the Motown sound, and rock 'n' roll tunes of that time period. I had no plans to buy any music while in Mankato, but I definitely wanted to begin a collection of my own when I returned home.

We had been looking through bins of music for about fifteen minutes, when Dave suddenly announced that he was getting hungry. "Let's go to Kresge's and get some lunch." His suggestion sounded more like an order.

"Let's go to Robby's instead," countered Tony.

"Naw, why go all the way up there, when Kresge's is just down the street," Joel insisted.

"Because the food is better at Robby's," asserted Tony. "We can get a gut bomb!"

I stood off to the side and chuckled a little at their cheesy, little disagreement. It continued for a time, too. When I tired of their antics, I headed for the door. I didn't bother waiting for any of them, either. I just stepped outside, leaned on a parking meter, and waited for them to figure out that I was no longer in their midst. While the guys finished up in the music store, I watched traffic and passersby.

People watching was a thing I loved to do when I was bored. When I shopped with Mom, I did it all the time because of how long it took her to make up her mind about anything. I watched people and imagined what their lives must be like. It wasn't hard to figure out in Mankato. People who spent their lives in that little town didn't differ too much in the way they lived. I figured Mankato was the same as any small town I had read about. In my ignorance, I thought people there were born, grew within their families, and went to school. Later, some would leave, but most stayed and served their community. They got married, started families of their own, became grandparents and then died without ever leaving Mankato. Their lives probably seemed small and obscure to people who lived in large cities, but I always thought there was a wonderful symmetry to small-town life. I liked the idea of living in a place where everybody knew you, whether you wanted them to or not. I had no such romantic notions about Duluth.

"There you are," said Joel, snapping me out of my trance. "We thought you just ran off and left us for better company."

I chuckled and said, "Well, there was this one pretty girl who…"

"Very funny, Romeo," interrupted Joel. "You ready for lunch, yet?"

"Yeah, you girls figure out where we're going to eat, yet?"

Almost shouting his response in Tony's ear, Dave exclaimed, "Kresge's!"

Tony winced and sheepishly gave in. "Okay, okay, I get it!"

Just then, we heard Mike McDonald's voice. He called out to us from down the street, "Hey guys! Wait up!"

We waited and upon Mike's arrival, he came to an abrupt stop, totally out of breath and sweating.

Wrinkling my nose a little at the slight stench of perspiration, I asked, "Did you run all the way down here after us?"

"Yes…I did," huffed Mike. "I stopped at your place to see ya, but you weren't there, so I checked Tony's place. His mom told me you guys were headed downtown. I just figured…I would find ya someplace down here."

"We're just headin' for lunch," I said. "You wanna come?"

"Yeah, come on Mike," added Tony.

"I can't eat," said Mike. "I don't have any money."

I didn't hesitate. "No problem, I've got you covered."

Mike asked, "Are ya sure? Ya know I'm good for it."

"Let's go, I'm hungry," I replied.

The cost of a cheeseburger was a small price to pay for including my friend. I thought about how many times his mom had fed me lunch years ago. A small debt would be partially paid that day.

No one was seated at the counter at Kresge's, so we five took it over. It looked just as I remembered it. Chromed-metal stools with red vinyl-covered cushions stood in a line in front of the white linoleum-covered counter. The counter was also trimmed in chromed metal. Shiny napkin holders, glass sugar dispensers, matching salt and pepper shakers, red ketchup and yellow mustard dispensers lined the countertop. Three similar looking tables, with matching chairs, stood a few feet behind the counter's stools. Just away from the tables, a row of booths were situated. They served as a demarcation point between the eatery and the rest of the store.

I thought it strange that there weren't many customers present on a Friday during the lunch hour. But then, there were a lot of things on Front Street that had changed. I decided the lack of patrons in the diner was just part of it all.

I didn't recognize the waitress but assumed she could possibly be one of Kurt's classmates. The nametag pinned to her uniform blouse identified her as Brenda. I estimated her to be seventeen or eighteen years old. Her long, chestnut hair was pinned up in a bun, making her look older than she actually was. The excessive makeup she wore was quite unnecessary. Brenda appeared a little too painted for my liking, but I still had to categorize her as pretty. She delivered glasses of ice water, tossed out some menus, then gave the five of us all a look of indifference, as she asked, "You guys eating today?"

I asked in return, "Is Mr. Steiner still working the grill?"

"Yes, he is," she replied, noticeably bored.

"Then, we're eating today," I answered.

Old man Steiner had been manning the grill at Kresge's for as long as any of us could remember. He knew all of the kids who came in and swore he never forgot a face or a name. The five of us used to hang out there regularly. Mr. Steiner would always take time to come poke fun at us.

I wasn't going to call attention to myself, but I just had to see if Mr. Steiner remembered me. So, when Brenda arrived to take my order, I said, "I'll have a fried-egg sandwich with ham, cheese, mayo, and horseradish."

Brenda immediately peered up from her notepad. The sour-lemon look she gave me was enough to make me snicker, but the comical looks of my friends made me bust out in laughter.

Kurt was the guilty party, when he accidentally initiated my twisted appreciation of horseradish – he had slipped me some on a fried-egg sandwich as a prank; it backfired on him. I loved it then and still do. I was the only person I knew who liked it with eggs, which should have helped me understand how different I would always be from others, but, of course, it did not. In the past, ordering that exact sandwich, with its weird inclusions, drove Mr. Steiner crazy.

I added fries and a Coke to my lunch request. Brenda wrote it down, looking visibly grossed out by it all. She then moved on to Tony.

When Brenda finished taking our orders, she went to the other end of the counter and placed our tickets on a spinning ticket wheel at the window. I kept my ears tuned in to the idle chatter going on between the guys, but I kept my eyes focused on the kitchen doors. Mr. Steiner did not keep me waiting long.

Suddenly, the swinging doors to the kitchen flew open and out stepped a little man. He appeared older than I remembered, but still robust. I could not approximate Mr. Steiner's age because he had always appeared somewhat ancient to me. It was probably because of the way he constantly played with his dentures. As well, I always chuckled inside about the way he wore his hair. Like Dave's dad, Mr. Steiner was bald up top, but there were plenty of greasy, salt-and-pepper-colored curls on the sides and back. In addition, he wore it too long and it was always a mess. Tony once joked that if Mr. Steiner dyed his hair red, he would look exactly like Bozo the Clown. Like his hair, the apron Mr. Steiner tied around his middle was always greasy, too. It made me wonder if he ever wore a clean one.

Mr. Steiner stood momentarily motionless, assessing the line of boys at his counter. He received various greetings from the guys, but I stayed quiet and just looked at him. He slowly strolled in my direction, giving me a stern, penetrating look. He stopped right in front of me and then smiled broadly. While shaking his head, he scolded, "There's only one person I know of who would put horseradish on one of my fried-egg sandwiches. Jackson! Am I right?"

"Yes, sir! How are you, Mr. Steiner?"

"Well, I'm still here, that's how I am. But, like most of the other shops downtown, we'll be closing here, also. Real soon, too! The owners want to get this last summer in. Then, I guess I'll just have to figure out what comes next."

As Mr. Steiner spoke of the impending closure of the store, I saw what I thought was sadness in his eyes. Nevertheless, when we went through the customary small talk that goes with such casual reunions, he wore his usual, big smile. We spent about five minutes getting caught up. That is, as much catching up as two people can do in five minutes. Before disappearing back into the kitchen, he spent a few additional minutes poking fun at the rest of the guys.

I then noticed Joel and Dave glancing at their watches, then over toward the front door. I asked, "You two have someplace to go?"

With a suspicious grin, Joel replied, "No."

Dave couldn't keep a straight face, either. So, I pressed the issue. "Okay, what's up?"

"Nothing, I swear," replied Dave.

Dave and Joel's behavior was such that I was convinced they had some asinine prank up their sleeves, but when Tony tapped on my shoulder, it distracted me. Tony asked if I wanted to see the great tunes he had scored at C&N. I simply nodded in the affirmative.

When our lunch orders finally arrived, I was still checking out some of Tony's records. As Brenda put my sandwich in front of me, I had to chuckle again at the squeamish look on her face. "Get you anything else?" she asked.

"No thanks."

"In that case...enjoy," she sarcastically said.

Suddenly, I noticed all eyes were on me. I also noticed that, like magic, our group had grown. Gail and Anne were now standing by their respective guys. Directly behind me stood Julie. I spun around on my stool and looked up into her eyes. Immediately, I attempted to give her a nonchalant "Hello," but my changing voice cracked loudly when I spoke. Laughter erupted from everyone. Right on time, blood rushed to my face.

We all hurriedly rearranged seating to accommodate the girls. I was more than a little surprised, when Julie asked Tony and Mike, who were seated to my right, if they would scoot down a seat. They politely obliged and Julie took up the stool next to me. The other two couples were to my left. I felt a little apprehensive about the arrival of the girls, which had to be anything but impromptu. At the same time, I could not have been happier.

Facing Julie, I asked, "What are you up to today? I thought you'd be busy getting everything ready for tonight."

Julie explained how she was being driven crazy by her mom. She just had to get out of the house, so the girls concocted their little scheme for all of us to meet at the lunch counter. In addition, it was also meant to be a surprise for me.

"So, are you surprised?" asked Julie.

Trying to be cool and praying that my voice wouldn't crack again, I replied, "You could say that."

While I listened to Julie go on about this and that, I nibbled on one of my diagonally-cut, sandwich halves. She told me how the preparations for the evening's festivities had all come together nicely. As Julie talked, she faced me and leaned on the counter. She rested her chin in the palm of her right hand and her smile never left her face. The look in her eyes and the energy in her voice led me to believe that she was exactly where she wanted to be. At that point in time, so was I.

After her recitation on party preparations, Julie eyed the plate in front of me and asked, "Whatcha eatin'?"

I waited until I could swallow and then answered, "Fried-egg sandwich."

Because I was totally enthralled by her presence, there wasn't time to stop her, when she reached for the other half of my sandwich, exclaiming, "Oh, I love those! Can I have a bite?"

The other half of my sandwich was already in her mouth, when I said, "Sure, but you're not gonna like it."

To this day, I don't believe a word has been invented to accurately describe the look on that poor girl's face, when the horseradish kicked in. Horrific is close, but it still falls a bit short.

As I watched Julie's face transform, I nonchalantly pushed my water glass toward her. Hastily, she grabbed the glass and downed its entire contents, ice and all, thus giving herself a temporary case of brain-freeze. Just as nonchalantly, I then pushed my Coke in her direction. Julie looked at the glass and then at me. She then laughed and said, "Cripes, Jackson, that was awful!"

Her not-so-subtle reaction caught the attention of the others, who were now understandably curious about what had just taken place.

"She'll be fine," I said coolly. "She just had a little run-in with my sandwich."

The guys immediately busted out laughing. Anne and Gail still looked confused, so Dave explained it to them. Then, we all had a good laugh. Thankfully, Julie joined in.

When it was Julie's turn to order lunch, she almost made another mistake. Pointing at my sandwich, she said, "I'll have one of those please, fries, and a Coke."

Brenda was about to turn and go, but I stopped her. "Brenda, skip the horseradish on that sandwich please."

"Oh, God…yes…please!" Julie exclaimed, then laughed some more.

When our laughter settled down and Julie had finally gotten the awful taste out of her mouth, by drinking half of my Coke, she inquired, "So, what have you been up to since I saw you last?"

I told her about my visit with Father Michael and how I thought his private book collection was extremely cool. Julie didn't need to know about the upcoming meeting with Adam Harris. Wanting things between us to stay light and casual, I didn't bother mentioning my talk with Gail and Anne on Thursday, either. Even though they said they wouldn't tell anyone about our conversation, I figured they did anyway. Therefore, Julie probably already knew my feelings for her, hence her sitting there with me. I definitely wasn't going to tell her about the previous evening spent dancing with Lori Mudd, or the broken chair, or the kiss on Lori's doorstep. As a matter of fact, there were too many things I didn't want Julie to know. The diner suddenly seemed a claustrophobic place to me. Frantically, I searched my mind for something I could share, but didn't come up with very much.

"Last night, I watched the Twins game with Brad," I said, hoping to satisfy her curiosity.

"You know, Dad and I are huge Twins fans. Maybe, you could come over and watch a game with us sometime."

I smiled and slowly nodded my head. "Me? Come watch a game with you and your dad?"

"Yeah, that would be okay, wouldn't it? I mean, he doesn't bite, Jackson."

Trying to be witty, I mumbled, "Do you?" *Stupid,* I thought, *stop trying so hard!*

"No!" Julie laughed, then said, "Relax, I'd like you to come over, but only if you want to."

"That sounds okay," I lied, my awkwardness getting the better of me again.

"You're cute when you're nervous," observed Julie.

I felt the blood rushing to my face and my voice cracked again when I asked, "Who's nervous?"

There was a lot more laughter during the remainder of that lunch. I couldn't imagine having more fun at Julie's party than I was having right there at Kresge's. When the tabs arrived, I offered to pick up the cost of Julie's lunch, too.

"Really?" asked Julie, like I had just made one of her dreams come true.

"Yeah, really," I replied, thoroughly aware that I had just foolishly given Julie more reason to be *impressed* with me.

Julie's smile, the sparkle in her eyes, and her angelic, "Thank you," was more than enough evidence for me to know that she was, in fact, as Gail and Anne had alleged the previous day.

Besides paying for lunch, I also purchased a pack of Wrigley's Doublemint gum. I remembered Janet's accusation that morning about me having puppy breath. So, I figured the horseradish wasn't doing me any favors, either. I offered Julie a stick and then, as discreetly as possible, crammed three sticks into my mouth, just to be sure.

When we all left Kresge's, the eight of us must have looked like quite the gaggle. Excited chatter came from all of us. That is, all except me. I was still unsure of myself within the group, so I did a lot of listening, some laughing, and for the most part, simply kept my mouth shut.

It was a long walk back to the neighborhood and I looked forward to every minute of it. The afternoon sun had finally come out with some force, so the heat radiating off the concrete sidewalk made it feel much hotter than it actually was. Julie walked next to me and talked excitedly about how she hoped the heat wave would stay around for a while. If it did, an afternoon pool party would be possible before I left.

I got a little nervous about all the plans Julie seemed to be making. A short list began to assemble itself inside my head. *First, there's the party tonight, then she wants to watch a ballgame together. Now, she wants a pool party, too?! What's next?!* As those uneasy thoughts rolled around in my noggin, I didn't bother to slow Julie down because I was too taken in by the excitement in her voice. Moreover, I was feeling pretty special because Julie was making it crystal clear that it was me she wanted to be with. I felt myself falling for her fast and had no idea how to stop the plummet.

Julie's appearance that day wasn't helping matters, either. She was quite exciting to look at in her white shorts and red short-sleeved pullover top. I felt sweaty, but it wasn't so much from the heat as it was from what was going on inside of me. *So, this is what it feels like,* I thought.

I then wondered if Dave and Tony had felt as awkward as me, when they first started up with their girls. As we walked on, I wanted to be brave and reach out for Julie's hand, but then I looked to see what my friends were doing. Neither Dave and Anne, nor Joel and Gail were touching in any way, so I chickened out and changed my mind.

The group took a short cut across the parking lot of Mankato West High School. We then headed for the ball diamonds on West Pleasant Street, where the guys and I had played baseball earlier in the week. That had happened just a few, short days before, but it suddenly felt like a lot of time had since passed.

When we reached the ballpark, we all decided to sit in the shaded bleachers and escape the heat for a spell. The water in the fountain was a little warm and had a metallic taste, but it was wet and safe to drink.

As the others made their way up the wood benches to sit, Julie grabbed my hand and quickly led me behind the bleachers. In a shaded area of her choosing, she abruptly turned to face me. Feeling a bit self-conscious, I quickly look around to see who might be watching, but no one from our group seemed interested in where we had disappeared to.

For the first time, it was Julie who looked edgy. She grabbed one of the bleacher's metal crossbars and supported herself. I watched restlessly, as she balanced on one foot and drew lines in the sand with the toe of her white canvas sneaker. Julie's hair had been pulled back into a ponytail that afternoon. Of course, I thought it was a great look for her. There were noticeable beads of sweat on her upper lip, too. Everything about her demeanor told me she was working up the courage to speak. The longer I waited, the more uncomfortable I got, so I decided to break the ice. Apprehensively, I asked, "Something on your mind?"

Just as uneasy, Julie said, "Geez, Jackson, I can usually say whatever comes into my head. But right now, I'm so nervous."

Wishing she would come to the point, I said, "Yeah, I kinda picked up on that."

"So...I guess I'll just spit it out." Julie then looked me right in the eye and asked, "Do you like me?"

I thought about the question for a moment but understood exactly what she was fishing for. Worse yet, I had no idea how to answer her. How do I let her down?! *How do I get out of this pickle?!* Suddenly, something inside told me that I couldn't lie to her. I didn't want to lie to her, but I still wasn't comfortable with being as direct as she was. So, attempting to be somewhat witty, I replied, "No, I always buy lunch for girls I don't like."

Julie smiled, but it quickly faded. She then looked down at her feet. I could tell my response wasn't quite the answer she was hoping for.

Just tell her you idiot! The thought rifled through my head, but I didn't know what to say next. That is, I remained clueless until Julie looked up into my eyes again. My pulse was throbbing in my ears and I wondered if she could hear my heart beating, too. So, I took a deep breath and let it out. Summoning up what courage I could, I let the words, "Yes…I do," escape my lips.

Still not satisfied with my earnest confession, she asserted, "No…I mean… do you *like* me?"

"Yes."

"You do?!"

"Yes."

"Really?!"

Okay, which word doesn't she understand? The thought made me snicker, but I managed to rein in my facetious side. Instead, I replied, "One last time…Yes, I *like* you…Okay?"

Julie then moved in closer, reached out and began to fiddle with one of the buttons on my shirt. I now thought my heart was literally going to come through my ribcage. Everything about her was telling me that she wanted to kiss! *What do I do now?!*

Right about then, something in my peripheral vision caught my attention. I suddenly looked up and found our friends spying on us. I nodded upward toward them. "Hi guys."

Julie whirled around, looked up, and with a slight whine in her voice, exclaimed, "Aw…you guys!"

The moment was ruined, but I was never so relieved. Surprisingly, Julie didn't seem too put off by it, either. I think she and I shared the same angst about what almost happened. I concluded that there would be time for all that mushy stuff later. That is, if it was actually going to happen at all. For the time being, Julie appeared satisfied with me admitting my feelings for her. As well, there was some satisfaction for me. I had just spilled my guts to the first girl I ever liked and managed to do it without passing out. Additionally, I had learned that Julie was no more experienced at that age-old game than me. One thing became absolutely clear to me, Julie was definitely no Lori Mudd.

Immediately following my friend's intrusion, I knew there would be some good-natured ribbing coming my way and it would come at their earliest, possible convenience. However, right then, they seemed content to just leave the situation alone. *God help me if Kurt or Danny ever find out about what just happened*, I thought. It was something that would never escape my lips in their presence.

I then told my friends that I needed to get home soon, so we had to get moving. After gathering ourselves, we all headed up West Pleasant Street and then turned left onto Baker Avenue. When we arrived at the intersection of Baker Avenue and West Ninth Street, our gaggle had to split up. Dave, Anne, Joel, Gail, and Tony left us at that point. As they prepared to go their way, we said our see-you-laters. Because the Wilsons lived closer to the direction they were all traveling, I could have gone with them. But I was darned sure Julie would not have let me get away with it, so I didn't even try.

"Hey, Mike!" yelled Tony. "Aren't you coming with us?"

Mike answered with nothing but a confused look on his face. Tony's weak attempt to provide Julie and I some privacy was way too obvious. Everyone there knew Mike lived closest to Julie.

"It's okay, Mike," said Julie. "You can walk with us."

Mike finally realized what Tony was driving at and asked, "Are you sure?"

"Yeah, it's fine," insisted Julie.

Two, short blocks later, Mike split off from us. As Julie and I watched him hurry down Ridgewood Street, I suddenly felt more than just a bit nervous. Even though being alone with Julie was exactly what I wanted, I could not calm my nerves.

The two of us stood and watched Mike until he disappeared from view. Then, without saying a word, Julie simply held her hand out to me. It was the signal I had been waiting for. I had wanted to hold her hand since we left Kresge's! I had wanted to hold it the entire walk back to the neighborhood! Now, we were only a few, meager blocks from her house! Nevertheless, at that moment, no disappointment registered. Julie standing there, silently inviting me to take her hand, felt like such a monumental moment in time. As I gently took her hand in mine, I felt an electricity that I had never felt before, and it surged right through me. As wonderful as it all felt just then,

I was still afraid that she might want to kiss, right then and there. Instead, she just stepped back and got my frozen feet moving by giving me a gentle tug. I found myself hypnotized by the look in her deep blue eyes.

"We better get moving," Julie said softly. "I don't want you to be late getting back."

I had more than enough time, but for some reason, I didn't want her to know that. So, with the afternoon sun beating down on us, we continued on toward her house.

Hand in hand, we slowly walked, our palms sweating profusely. Thanks to Sister Mary Vincent's health class, I knew what that was all about and took it as a good sign. As far as I was concerned, Catholic traditionalists, like Mom and Aunt Janice – the ones who insisted that sex education in the schools is inappropriate – had no idea what they were talking about.

I could have bet money that Julie would be the one to break the silence between us and won. She turned those gorgeous pools of blue on me and softly said, "There's so much I want to ask you, Jackson, so much I want to talk to you about. I hope we get the chance tonight. What do you think?"

"I have another whole week here," I replied. "If it doesn't happen tonight, I'm sure it will sometime later."

Right then, Julie appeared to be more than happy with my answer.

We continued on until we came to Sunset Boulevard. Stopping on the corner, she reluctantly turned to face me, saying, "I think we should say good-bye here."

A new confidence had built up inside of me, so I replied, "I don't think so. I was raised better than that."

Thanks to Mom badgering me all the time, I knew it was considered bad manners not to walk her to all the way to her door. But, in that instant, Mom's tutelage wasn't my true motivation. Quite frankly, I just didn't want that short walk to end.

"You're not afraid to come up to the house?" asked Julie.

"If that were the case, you wouldn't be seeing me tonight."

As we walked the short, remaining distance down her block, Julie's smile never left her face. When we reached her doorstep, she coaxed me to linger for a few minutes. There, we chatted about nothing important. That is, Julie talked and I stood there, smiling, while trying to keep up with her rate of speech. In rapid succession, Julie informed me that people would begin showing up for the party at seven o'clock. She then pressed me to find out my intended arrival time. Before I could answer, she moved on to wondering what I planned to wear that night and then immediately pleaded with me not to be late. As Julie twittered on like a Magpie, I picked up on the tone in which she spoke and suddenly realized that she was nervous. In fact, she was exceptionally nervous. I smiled about the revelation and thought it was absolutely adorable.

Julie then took a step forward and closed the distance between us. She had the same look in her eyes that she had at the ballpark. However, I didn't dare move a muscle because something, or rather, someone, appeared in the window directly over Julie's shoulder.

In the softest tone, Julie asked, "Jackson, are you ever going to kiss me?"

Without shifting my gaze from the window, I replied, "Yeah, probably, but not right now."

Looking a bit put out, Julie asked, "Why not?"

I leaned forward and whispered, "Because your mom is watching us through the window behind you."

Without turning around to verify my claim, Julie closed her eyes tight and clenched her teeth. "Please, tell me you're kidding."

"Okay...I'm kidding," I said, but truly wasn't. An attractive woman, who I assumed was Julie's mom, peered at us through curtain sheers.

"I'd better go now," I said. "I don't want to get you into any trouble. I'll see you in a little while."

Before I could move, Julie threw her arms around my neck, gave me a quick hug, and my second peck on the cheek. She then disappeared inside her house.

Wow, I thought, *with her mom watching and everything!*

Yes, I admired Julie's gumption and how special she made me feel inside. But suddenly, I was not looking forward to later that evening, when I would have to meet her mother.

As I walked back to Westwood Drive, my head swam laps, back and forth, with all kinds of thoughts. *What are you doing, Landry? You shouldn't be allowing yourself to feel this way. Doesn't Julie understand that I'll be gone in a week? Why does my heart feel so full and what is it full of? How can something that's bound to end badly feel so…right?!"* Even though I was convinced that I was making a huge mistake, I knew then that I would spend every possible moment I could steal with Julie.

When I arrived back at the Wilson's, it was almost three o'clock in the afternoon. I saw Brad and Janet's vehicles and knew they had beaten me home. Kurt and Danny were shooting baskets in the driveway, while Janelle and Carrie sat close by in the shade, gabbing. Janelle was the first to notice me sneaking toward the side door, so she called out, "Uh-uh, Jackson, get over here!"

Damn! Not now, I thought. I truly was not in the mood to have them give me the third degree, so I took my time about walking over to them. As I approached, both got up to get their hugs.

I poked at them by saying, "You know, you two are really getting weird about that."

With both of them giving me devious smiles, Janelle asked, "What's your point?"

I rolled my eyes and then turned to walk away, saying, "Never mind."

"So, tonight's the big night at Julie's party…Right?" asked Janelle, stopping me in my tracks.

I instinctively knew that she and Carrie had their caps set for an interrogation. They started asking me about what went on between Lori and me the previous night. I shrugged my shoulders. Then they began asking questions about Julie. So I put on my best blank face and gave them no more than a "yep" or a "nope" to all their nosey little inquiries. My flat refusal to answer any direct questions produced the effect I greatly desired – they gave up.

"Geez, Jackson, you're no fun," said Carrie. "Getting anything out of you is like trying to get water from a rock."

I smiled in response and simply walked toward the house. Just then, Brad came hustling out the side door. "Hey, buddy, what do you say we take Kurt and Danny on in basketball, just like we used to."

"Sure, just let me get some water first. It got hot today."

While I rehydrated myself in the kitchen, I gave Janet vague details of my activities that afternoon. She smiled and gave me a look that said, "I know better and can fill in the gaping holes of information myself."

After satisfying my thirst, I ran back outside, just in time to hear Danny proclaim to his dad, "Alright, it'll be two-on-two. The Teams are you and Jackson against Kurt and me." Then, as an afterthought, he added, "No cheating this time."

Brad exclaimed in mock dismay, "Hey! That's not nice! I'm sure Jackson doesn't cheat anymore. Do you, buddy?"

Kurt kicked in with, "He's not exactly the one we're worried about."

Brad exclaimed loudly, "Are you calling me a cheater? Why...I've never been so insulted."

I just smiled and shook my head. *Who's he putting the act on for?*

The truth is, when the four of us played basketball, Brad had a history of being the biggest cheater on the planet. There were times when his fouls were so flagrant, someone would have to pick himself out of the neighbor's hedges. It was all in good fun, of course, but then I remembered how it especially got under Danny's skin. After being pushed aside with ease, time after time, Danny would get mad, call Brad a cheater, quit the game, and then go stomping into the house. I almost laughed out loud at the memory.

The scrimmage began and in a short time, Brad realized that he and I could play those two straight up – no cheating necessary. I had grown and become skilled enough to go up against either one of my foster brothers. That is, on a basketball court. I was able to steal from Kurt a couple of times and blocked two of Danny's shots. I was also responsible for better than half the points Brad and I made, helping to keep the score close throughout the match.

Brad's game had become a bit rusty, but as we played on, I noticed some of his old agility return. It was as if he were back in school and giving it his all. I then wondered how long he could keep pace with us younger guys.

Kurt and Danny played with their usual zeal and had forgotten none of their old fake-out tricks. Their passing was noticeably practiced and watching them operate was a blast, but as well, frustrating. They were extremely hard to stop. As we played on, it occurred to me that those two weren't just brothers, they were best friends.

Although our playing area was well shaded, we were only able to stand the late afternoon heat for about forty-five minutes. Kurt and Danny won the game, so Brad and I demanded a rematch in the near future. We four stood there in the driveway, red faced and out of breath. Drenched in sweat, we shook each other's hands and called it a good game. I smiled because in their eyes, I could see that I had gained a new respect. After we spent a short period catching our breath, the six of us went indoors.

Before going out to eat, showers for the ball players were definitely in order. While Brad showered upstairs, Kurt bathed downstairs. The rest of us retreated from the heat by relaxing in the basement den. On hot days, the den was always the coolest room in the house. As soon as I plopped into the easy chair with a big glass of ice water, I became very drowsy. So, I closed my eyes and drifted, feeling uncharacteristically happy inside.

Chapter 13

In Mankato, the Hill Top Tavern had been a popular eating establishment for many generations. When I was but seven years old, the Wilsons took me there for my very first Tap Burger. Of course, mine always included cheese and fried onions. Soon after, I learned that getting burgers at the Hilltop was a regular occurrence in the Wilson family. It was the smallest restaurant I had ever seen, but I immediately became a huge fan of the place. Like everything else in Mankato, I missed it greatly after moving to Duluth. So, as far as I was concerned, eating at my favorite burger joint was a wonderful addition to an already fantastic day.

Upon entering the teeny-tiny establishment, the first thing I noticed was that it had been remodeled. The old mahogany bar that I remembered had been replaced with something more modern. It was surfaced with an off-white, ceramic tile. New cushioned bar stools took the place of the old wooden high-backs that used to line the bar. New tables, chairs and re-upholstered booths filled the minuscule seating area. The old hardwood floor was covered with ceramic tile, which matched the bar countertop. All the rusticity had been removed from my favorite eatery. I recognized nothing about the place, except for how it was still claustrophobically-tight quarters inside. Mentally, I frowned a little because it appeared almost too antiseptic. It was another change I had not been prepared for; it just wasn't the same.

"I suppose they also scrape and clean the grill," I mumbled to nobody in particular.

Sensing my disappointment in the altered appearance of the tavern, Brad replied, "Not too often."

It was Brad who taught me that if a grill gets cleaned too often, an inferior burger will be served. His contention was that most of the flavor gets thrown out with the old grease. I didn't know if his belief had any truth to it, but for me, there had been no better place in Mankato to get a cheeseburger with fried onions, fries, and a Coke.

I spent that dinner being fearful that I might accidently spill something on my clean clothes. If the waitress had a drop cloth available, I would have asked her to deliver one to our table, so I could use it as a bib. That evening, I wore my favorite long-sleeved, wide-collared, royal blue, button-front shirt. I had it tucked into a pair of bellbottomed, khaki dress slacks. Janet was nice enough to press them for me while I showered. I wasn't too sure about the dark brown dress shoes I wore, but Janelle and Carrie said they worked perfectly with what I was wearing. Before that night, I never worried too much about my appearance. But right then, I looked at the ketchup and mustard dispensers like they were some kind of enemy to fend off.

Conversation within our group was boisterous, maybe even a little too loud. Nonetheless, nobody was in the mood to be serious. Thankfully, none of the other patrons complained or even seemed to care. For the sake of keeping it lively, I was encouraged to tell the story of how the lawn chair collapsed on Lori and me. At first, I thought Brad and Janet were going to disapprove, but they got quite a kick out of my misfortune.

"That serves her right," laughed Janet. "She shouldn't have been so forward with you."

"Don't worry, she made up for it on her front doorstep," said Janelle. As soon as the words left her mouth, her face registered that she had said too much.

Janet exclaimed, "Jackson! What have you been up to?!"

"Hey, I was just being a gentleman and walked her to the door. She's the one who grabbed me and started kissing me! What was I supposed to do, spit in her face?!"

Frightful, Janet said, "I'm beginning to wonder what kind of condition we're going to send you home in!"

"Aw, Mom, let him have a little fun while he's here," countered Danny.

"I have no problem with *a little* fun, as you put it, just as long as it stays a *little fun.*" Janet then turned her faux-stern look on me, but couldn't hold back the smile waiting to escape. "It makes me wonder what other kind of mischief you've been up to."

Chuckling a bit, I then replied, "Funny you should ask." I then told them how I accidentally introduced Julie to horseradish. Of course, I felt victorious when everyone howled with laughter.

The rest of that dinner was filled with more stories of life's little embarrassing moments. When everyone took a turn sharing something, I no longer felt like the Lone Ranger. The stories and our laughter continued until well after dinner.

Although I was having a great time and didn't want to seem like I was in a hurry to leave their company, I couldn't keep from constantly checking my watch. Brad caught me and stated, "Don't worry, buddy, we'll be leaving pretty soon. We'll get you to Julie's in plenty of time."

Carrie asked, "What time are people starting to show up to the party?"

"Fifteen minutes ago," I replied.

Brad promptly turned in his chair, faced the bar, and yelled, "Check please!"

When Brad headed the Mercury toward Tony's house, he tried his best to make up for lost time. Speeding along at his normal pace, which Janet always thought was way too fast, Brad expertly weaved in and out of traffic. In the back seat, I simply held on for dear life. Even though I could swear I saw my extremely-short life flashing before my eyes, I was greatly appreciative of Brad's sense of urgency.

Before being dropped off at Julie's, we had to collect Tony, Joel, and Dave. They were waiting at Tony's, getting his record collection together. I was certain that Julie would be reaching a boiling point because we weren't there already. As we sped along, my anxiety level kept a steady climb.

When Brad finally pulled into the Milner's driveway, we found the trio waiting by the garage. I jumped out of the back and switched to the front seat. As

I made Janet move over to the middle, I took note of how the guys looked. When I saw they were dressed very similar to me, I breathed a sigh of relief. *Good, I won't stick out like a sore thumb,* I thought.

After the guys piled into the back seat, Brad put the Mercury into motion again. I was now extremely nervous because we were now slightly more than fashionably late. Moreover, I didn't know Julie's tolerance for such things. To add fuel to that fire, I would soon be standing in front of her parents. After witnessing her daughter kiss me on the doorstep that afternoon, I could only imagine what was going through Mrs. Falkner's mind.

Janet picked up on my tenseness, so she leaned into me and whispered, "You'll be fine, kiddo." She then placed a calming hand on my jittering leg, which felt like it was keeping pace with each cylinder of the Mercury's V-8 engine.

That evening, Brad's prowess behind the wheel alone made him my hero. As soon as he left the Milner's driveway, I stared at the dashboard clock. Janet glared at Brad but said nothing. She clearly disapproved of how fast he was driving. It took him less than one minute and thirty seconds to transport us seven blocks. As he pulled up in front of the Falkner residence, he was a little heavy on the brakes. When the car came to a halt, I looked over my shoulder and discovered that my friend's faces were pale white. I thought we were going to have to pry their hands from the backrest of the front seat.

"Okay, there you go," Brad said in passing, as if no big hurry had been necessary at all. "Have a great time, guys."

Tony asked, "Mr. Wilson, can we go back a few blocks?"

"Why's that, Tony?"

"I think my teeth flew out the window back there a ways."

Our laughter helped calm my nerves, but just a tad. As I prepared to exit the car, Janet kissed my cheek and then inspected the spot to ensure she hadn't left any lipstick. It was the old-mother-hen routine I remembered from years ago. I gave her a cockeyed smile, grimaced, then hurried out the door.

"You boys have fun," Janet said, as we piled out of the car.

The four of us stood at curbside and watched until the Mercury was out of sight. We then turned and looked at each other. There seemed to be an unspoken question floating between us – *Who's gonna ring the doorbell?* The thought registered in my head and I immediately wondered if the others were thinking the same thing. Of course, Dave took the lead. He simply rolled his eyes at us and then trudged up the Falkners' walkway, with the rest of our little group in tow.

When we arrived at the doorstep, Dave jumped onto the landing. He was within inches of ringing the bell when Tony yelled, "Wait a minute!" Tony then put down the two record cases he had been carrying, reached into his back pocket and produced a small comb. After running it through his hair a few times, he returned the comb to his pocket, then said, "Okay, I'm ready now."

Dave looked at me, smiled and shook his head, saying, "Have you ever seen such a primper?"

I laughed, of course, but when Dave turned to ring the doorbell, I looked at Tony and in a hushed tone said, "Let me use your comb real quick, will ya!"

When the Falkner's front door opened, a breathless Julie greeted us with a huge smile. "Hi guys! Come on in!" Tony, Dave, and Joel returned her greeting as they entered. I brought up the rear and as I stepped in, Julie leaned in toward my ear. Whispering playfully, she said, "It's about time you got here…Hi!"

"Hi," I returned. Then, as Julie closed the door behind me, I added, "Sorry we're late. The Wilsons got a little carried away at dinner." I then took my first good look at her. Trying to find just the right words, I exclaimed, "Wow! You look…amazing!"

Julie's smile and sincere, "Thank you!" told me I gained much favor with that compliment.

That evening, Julie was most assuredly dressed to kill, and I was the dead man walking. Her ensemble consisted of black, bellbottomed dress slacks and a pink, short-sleeved, cashmere, pullover top. She wore her radiant curls down and they fell about her shoulders. Her tresses were set off nicely by silver hooped earrings. In addition, her finger and toenails had a fresh coat of vibrant pink nail polish. Sandaled high heels completed Julie's outfit and gave her a more grownup appearance. I was glad to see that she wasn't wearing lipstick. In my opinion, that would have been a little too over-the-top and detracted from her natural beauty. In actuality, Julie wore very little makeup. To be honest, I didn't think she needed any.

After our casual greeting at the door, the guys and I followed Julie into their rather expansive living room to meet her parents. As we slowly filtered into the room, I took note that the décor was much more impressive than my other friend's homes. In the Falkners' living room, hardwood floors were set off magnificently by Persian-style area rugs that gave the room an aura of dignified luxury. A couple of antique, Queen Ann chairs were strategically positioned along one wall, as was a tasteful antique hardwood lamp table. More toward the center of the room, sat a large, leather sofa, accompanied by a matching lounger with ottoman. The leather was richly textured and dark chocolate in coloration. An oak coffee table and matching end tables gave the furnishings a nice, finished look. There was also a small, antique, writing desk tucked in behind the sofa. Built-in bookshelves at the rear of the room showcased a leather-bound set of encyclopedias, various other publications, family photographs, small plants, and tasteful ceramic figurines.

I was not surprised by anything my eyes took in. I had become accustomed to that standard of living in the Landry home. Moreover, I pretty much knew that all the houses built on Sunset Boulevard were a bit more palatial than other homes on neighboring streets – they all smelled of money. Back then, we teens could not have cared less. When it came to friendship, differences between the haves and the have-nots were not much of a consideration.

Once we were all present, the Falkners made a show of standing from their comfortable seats in order to properly greet their guests. Julie made the introductions.

"Mom, Dad, you remember Joel, Dave, and Tony…Right?"

Gary Falkner offered his hand to my friends and greeted each of them by name. But Marilyn Falkner stood fast, eyed the three of them suspiciously and said, "Nice to see you again boys."

Each of my three friends returned a mumbled hello or hi, their discomfort with the social formality was very apparent.

When Julie stepped next to me and gave my arm a squeeze, she beamed and announced, "This is Jackson Har…I mean…Jackson Landry." Julie giggled, as she corrected herself. "He went to school with all of us but moved away a few years ago. He's back visiting for a couple of weeks."

Gary Falkner had a friendly smile and an easy going way about him. As he took my hand in his huge, bear-like paw, I was immediately overcome by the thought that if he had a mind to, he could have easily crushed my hand. Nonetheless, I gave as solid of a handshake as my much-smaller hand could give.

"How do you do, Jackson?"

"I'm fine, sir, and you?"

As I greeted Julie's dad, I watched his eyes to see if there was any recognition from my old coach. But there was nothing in them just then, so I took a step toward Marilyn Falkner and offered her my hand, just like Mom taught me. "It's nice to meet you, ma'am," I then offered up what I hoped was a decent smile.

In return, Julie's mom smiled warmly, grasped my hand daintily and replied, "Hello, Jackson. You have no idea how nice it is for me to meet you. I knew your mother very well. We were…well…we used to be great friends."

It wasn't the greeting I expected at all. Her warm smile and words put me at ease almost immediately. Suddenly, an image flashed through my head, but just for an instant. I was momentarily catapulted into the past. When and where I could not tell, but I was left with the strangest sensation that I already knew Marilyn Falkner. *I know her. I've seen her before. It was long ago, but where?*

"Jackson, did I coach you in Little League?" asked Mr. Falkner, bringing me back to the present.

"Yes, sir! You were my coach for T-Ball and then for my first year of Little League.

Suddenly, recollection caused Mr. Falkner to exclaim, "Oh, for crying out loud, you're Adam's boy…Of course I remember you!"

Julie and I exchanged a quick uncomfortable glance. I shook my head subtly, as a signal to let the comment go uncorrected. Fortunately, she understood.

Mr. Falkner continued, "Didn't you stop by here shortly before you moved? It was something about wanting to say good-bye to Julie. Am I right?"

"Yes, sir, I'm surprised you remember that."

Julie's astonished look told me much. Then, she laughed nervously and practically yelled, "Daddy, you never told me that!"

In mock embarrassment, Mr. Falkner replied, "Didn't I? OOPS! Nice seeing you again, gentlemen. Have fun and make yourself at home." He then retreated to his chair and hid behind his newspaper.

As Mr. Falkner made an act of being afraid of his daughter's pending wrath, we all laughed. Mrs. Falkner chuckled and said, "I hope we get a chance to talk before you leave town, Jackson. Now you kids get outta here and go have fun." She then waved us on our way.

Before leading us through the kitchen to the basement stairwell, Julie shot a disgruntled look in her dad's direction. She then ushered the guys through the doorway, but stepped in front of me, saying, "You handled that beautifully." Julie then followed the guys cautiously down the steps in front of me.

"I can handle adults, no problem," I boasted. "Pretty girls are a different story." *Oh, God! That sounded so stupid,* I thought. *Relax, dummy!*

Turning around on the stairs, Julie gave me a raised-eyebrow look. "Girls?" she asked smugly. "What girls?" When she slowly let her smile return, it was the giveaway that she was teasing.

The Falkners' basement was very much like the rest of their house – impressive. It was easily three times the size of the Wilsons' and geared exclusively toward entertaining the family and their guests. The spacious den sported a tastefully furnished lounge area, with a large Magnavox color TV and stereo console. The lounge also came equipped with a full wet bar. However, the liquor had been locked away somewhere for the evening. Instead of cheaper vinyl or Naugahyde material, their polished chrome bar stools had seat cushions covered in tanned leather.

Unlike many of my friend's basement walls, which usually consisted of painted cinderblock or cheap plywood-like, wood-grained Formica, the Falkners' walls were covered with oak paneling and was stained a rich, golden brown. My eyes also noted that all the wall hangings were in stark contrast to those found in the Wilson residence. Although they were somewhat large, they were more tasteful in character and not at all gaudily framed.

Instead of tile or linoleum, the entire basement floor was covered with plush, but durable, brown-and-tan patterned carpet.

The recessed, incandescent lighting on the ceiling throughout the basement was all controlled with dimmer switches, perfect for setting whatever atmosphere a gathering required.

There was also a billiard room. It sported the same oak paneling on the walls. However, the green, felt-covered pool table, green shag carpeting on the floor, and a decorative sign, which hung above the doorway, left no question as to why it was called, The Green Room.

The guys and I weren't the last to arrive, but darned close. Anne and Gail were already present, as was Mike. Earlier in the week, at the ballpark, I had already met many of the others, but Julie insisted on reintroducing me again to everyone. I felt like I was being put on display for their approval.

As I was being introduced, I took note of how everyone had dressed similarly. The girls were either in neatly pressed bellbottomed jeans or dress slacks with colorful tops. Long hair was in style that year and the girls were all wearing it down. As I looked them over, the word, *wow*, came to mind. They were all quite attractive.

The guys had on a variety of lively colored, patterned shirts, but similar bellbottomed jeans or dress slacks. I also noticed dress shoes were worn by all. I breathed easy when I saw how my attire fit right in. For a bunch of amateurs, we all cleaned up fairly well. Even Mike left his hair combed for that evening's soirée.

Bowls of popcorn and various other snack items were strategically positioned throughout the basement. I noticed some of the guys attacking them, like they hadn't eaten in a week. However, I could not have eaten a bite. Besides being too nervous to munch, I was still stuffed from the cheeseburger and fries I had eaten at the tavern.

Everyone seemed to be immersed in conversation, but the volume on the stereo was a bit too high, so we all had to practically yell in order to be heard.

I began to make my way toward the billiard room, but thought to ask Julie, "Do you mind?"

"No problem," she replied. "I still have to answer the door a few more times."

Most of the guys then followed Tony, Mike, and me into The Green Room.

However, Joel and Dave stayed in the lounge with their girls, but in a very short time, they, too, joined us. It seemed the girl's brand of chatter got to be a bit much for them.

The evening was young, and all the guests hadn't arrived yet. So, while we all waited for the entire guest list to be present, there was a noticeable separation between the sexes. We guys shot pool and talked sports in The Green Room, but the girls huddled up in the lounge and talked about who knows what. Both genders snuck cautious peeks over their shoulders and smiled at each other playfully. When the last guest had finally arrived, the total count was sixteen of us in that basement, a nice round number. I was amazed at how it didn't seem crowded at all.

When Julie suddenly breezed into the room, Tony and I were in the middle of a pool game. She asked Tony if it was okay to open his record cases, so they could preview the music he had brought. Of course, he cordially gave his permission. As Julie left the room, she gave me a sly smile and then asked Tony, "Is he any good?"

Tony moaned unhappily, "Yeah, he's good."

After I had successfully beaten two more opponents at eight ball, Julie reappeared. She strode directly up to me and took the pool cue from my grip. After setting it on the table, she grabbed my arm and gave a playful tug toward the lounge. Julie wore a familiar mischievous grin, as she said, "Okay, we know he can play pool. Now, let's see if he can dance!"

I must have had the most ridiculous look on my face because all the guys burst out laughing. That is, right up until the other girls started grabbing dance partners, too.

Leading me into the lounge area, Julie leaned in close to my ear, so she could be heard over the music. "You do dance, don't you?"

Embarrassed, I replied, "That's what I call it, but you might call it something else."

The Hollies belted out the song, *Long Cool Woman*, and we all began to move to the beat. I noticed others were dancing like it was simply normal behavior for them, no angst at all. Some partners seemed to have their dance steps pretty well synchronized. I then keyed in on my friends and did my best to keep from laughing. The music was moving them alright, but it wasn't a pretty sight. At first, I felt a little clumsy myself, but found the rhythm and remembered the moves I had learned the previous night. *Thank you, Janelle, Carrie, and Lori!*

Halfway through that first song, I just sort of relaxed and went with it. I realized I wasn't embarrassing myself too badly in front of Julie, who moved quite well. She had a great sense of rhythm and to my untrained eye, was a fantastic dancer. I most certainly had my work cut out for me to keep up with her.

"You're a good dancer, Jackson. Did you learn those moves up north?"

"Pretty much," I lied. I wasn't about to tell her where I did learn them.

After we had danced to a few songs together, Julie insisted that everyone switch partners. That way, nobody would be left out. There were a few wall flowers present that evening, but even they were invited to dance by someone. At one point, Julie coaxed me to ask a rather shy girl named Peggy. She wasn't the prettiest girl I had ever seen, but she wasn't a train wreck, either. The Good Samaritan in me obliged Julie by doing as she requested, but I did it begrudgingly. As we danced, I observed that Peggy's lack of rhythm, ability, and confidence, made me look like I had been formally schooled at some dance studio. Nevertheless, I did my best to get her to loosen up.

After a long set of fast paced music, Tony took over as the disc jockey. He immediately moved us into a session of slower, more romantic tunes. Right about then, someone also dimmed the lights…a lot. So, as the Chi-Lites sang, *Oh Girl*, I headed for a bar stool. I had just danced with a girl, whose name I couldn't catch because of the loud music. I tried to read her lips, but rapidly learned that I had no talent for that, either. I wanted to sit the first slow dance out, but Julie was having none of it. Almost as soon as my butt hit the cushion, she came and pulled me off it. "Oh, no you don't," she giggled.

With her high heels on, Julie and I were almost the same height. So, she kicked them off and was now noticeably shorter. She was now able to rest her head almost perfectly on my shoulder. I was immediately overwhelmed by the way she held me. Julie didn't seem at all afraid to pull me in close. As we swayed to the music, there was absolutely no daylight between us. At first, Julie turned her head away and just sort of hugged me. But then, she slowly turned to face me and laid her head back on my shoulder. Julie's breath on my neck was hot, but sweet. I could tell she had been chewing gum. Right about then, I wished I were doing the same.

While I concentrated on Julie, I also scrutinized other dancers in my immediate vicinity. I made an immediate discovery. There were distinct differences between how couples going steady danced and those who showed up merely because they were invited. Exclusive couples held each other close, like they were afraid they might come apart. Everyone else kept more distance between their bodies. The realization that Julie saw us as a couple alarmed me a little, but at the same time, I liked the very idea if it. I simply allowed every fiber of my being to feel whatever it seemed destined to feel.

Even with her eyes closed, Julie was graceful. The sensation of having her in my arms was greatly electrifying my brain. I was in a dreamland and couldn't believe my luck. I finally understood what Danny had talked about that very morning. It truly was important to be with the *right* girl. As the music continued to move us in slow, intimate circles, we didn't speak a word, which was fine with me. I was perfectly happy acclimating myself to our closeness, without spoiling it with unnecessary talk.

When a third slow song began, Anne Hayward tapped her way in. "May I?" she asked.

Julie gave Anne a curt little look but relinquished her dance partner. She then walked to where Dave sat and stole him from his momentary comfort on a sofa.

Anne and I danced much less intimately. I found myself hoping that Dave was paying attention to how I kept a respectable amount of distance between me and his girl.

"She's on cloud nine tonight," said Anne.

"It's her party," I rationalized.

"Yeah, that's not it," chuckled Anne. "Before you and the guys showed up every time the doorbell rang, you should have seen her practically fly up the stairs."

That explains her being out of breath, I thought, but played it off by saying, "And you think it was because of me?"

Anne replied, "Yeah, I do." She then paused briefly, like she was thinking about what to say next. After a few uncomfortable moments passed, she surprised me greatly by saying, "You really haven't changed that much, you know? Except... maybe you got a little better looking."

Good grief! Where do these girls come up with this stuff?! "Thanks," I said. "Have I told you how great you look tonight?"

Anne smiled broadly and exclaimed, "No! Thank you!"

"Well, I didn't want Dave to think that I'm hittin' on you."

We both shared a nervous laugh. Then, Anne started in on me again. "I do understand, you know? I mean, why Julie wants to be with you so much."

Blood immediately rushed to my face. Anne saw it and giggled. "Oh my, God! Are you blushing?!"

How can she tell? It's so dark down here! The only response I could muster was, "You talk too much."

Anne teased, "Hey, anything to help your little romance along."

I pulled back a little and gave her a stern look.

Seeing that I was clearly not comfortable with her jab, she said, "Jackson, I'm sorry. I shouldn't have said that."

Slightly irritated by her insensitivity, I queried, "Little romance?"

In an attempt to explain, she said, "Well, I saw what was going on behind the bleachers this afternoon...and I thought..."

Before she could say another word, I interrupted. "We were just talking." I was now embarrassed, but I was also getting a little upset. "Look, both Julie and I know we like each other, but I don't think either one of us knows what to do about it. I leave in a week. And I've already told you that I don't want to hurt her. That's why I don't want to go too far with whatever it is that's happening."

Anne put on an almost wicked smile, nodded her understanding and then said, "Jackson, I know her better than you. Julie's not gonna give up. So, why don't you just give in?" Anne paused again, then added, "You're a good guy. I wish there were more like you around here." She then held me a little too closely.

I was now uncomfortable and hoped that Julie and Dave weren't watching us. I tried my best to appear like I was still enjoying myself, but I sure would have appreciated it if Dave had come over and reclaimed his girl.

I struggled through a total of two slow songs with Anne before I heard Julie's voice ask, "Can I have him back?"

Anne promptly thanked me for the dances and then traipsed off to find Dave.

After Anne moved off, Julie stepped in and put her arms around my neck. Instead of laying her head on my shoulder, she looked directly into my eyes. The look she gave me, coupled with what Anne had just told me, had me all confused inside.

My head was swimming and so was my heart, but the two could not agree on anything. I tried desperately to think of something witty to say, but the only thing that came to mind was, "No pins this time, right?" Immediately upon delivering such lameness, I mentally kicked myself again. *Okay, that sucked! Relax!*

Julie gave me a puzzled look, so I reminded her. "The fourth grade, play rehearsal, the pins in your costume, the so-called dance we did."

Recollection showed on her face and she politely laughed, saying, "I promise…No pins." As an afterthought, she added, "Oh, by the way, I think you look pretty amazing tonight, too."

Once again, I was in Julie's hot embrace and felt certain that she could feel my heart trying to escape my chest. I needed to do something to break the heat, something that would help slow my pulse.

"I'm thirsty. Wanna get a pop?" I asked.

"Sure," she replied. "We have a bunch on ice at the bar."

Taking me by the hand, Julie led the way through the maze of slow-dancing teens. Once we reached the bar, she grabbed a couple of root beers. Handing one to me, she then stood in front of me, looking a bit impatient. I nervously looked at her, then at the other on-looking guests. I wanted to converse with her, but the music was too loud, plus it was just too-damned hot in that basement. "Can we go outside and cool off?" I asked.

Julie exchanged her impatient look for something resembling delight. She then blurted, "That would be great! I've been wanting to get you alone for a while! Let's go!"

Again, Julie led the way through a cluster of dancers toward the stairs. Up we went, through the kitchen and then outside, stopping only once to turn the swimming pool lights on. Across their flagstone patio we walked, with Julie holding my hand and leading me the entire way, until we finally stepped onto the concrete deck by their swimming pool. We positioned two patio chairs, so we could face each other, then seated ourselves. The coolness of that evening's breeze immediately began to relax me.

The Falkners had the only swimming pool in the neighborhood. Some thought it was an extravagance that Gary and Marilyn used to flaunt their money under everybody's nose. Personally, I didn't care about any of those negative opinions because at that moment in time, Julie looked absolutely breathtaking, sitting within the aquamarine glow of the dimly lit pool.

Our conversation began by Julie asking me simple questions: Was I enjoying myself? How did I like the changes in Mankato? What was it like being with the Wilsons again? Heck, Julie even commented on how she always thought Danny was a total dreamboat. Nevertheless, she also made me promise that I wouldn't tell him, like that was ever going to be a problem. Danny's head was big enough, without any help from her. So, Julie's secret was safe with me.

Julie then got me to talk a little about Duluth. I wanted to open up to her, but I was afraid of giving her any details that might lead her to think I was some sort of troubled psychopath. I gave no hint that I spent most of my time missing everyone in Mankato. Instead, I told her about our house on the Duluth hillside, how it had a huge picture window and the scenic view it provided. I told her how I loved sitting on the window seat. From there, I watched the Great Lake's iron ore boats and ocean-going cargo ships move through the piers, to and from the Twin Ports harbor. She listened intently, as I described Canal Park, the aerial lift bridge, and the sandy beaches of Park Point. Her ever-changing expressions told me that she was getting lost in my words. At the same time, I found myself getting lost in her eyes. The more I talked, the more at ease I felt with her. Her acceptance of everything I said gave me the confidence to continue. I could scarcely believe I was talking at all. Julie just let me prattle on.

We then talked about some of our school days together. We even talked about the day of *The Kiss* and laughed heartily.

"Why did you three pick on me that day?" I asked.

Julie laughed and replied, "Oh, that's easy. Back then, you were the cutest boy in our class."

"Is that all it takes to turn your head?"

"Back then...yeah...probably," she giggled. "It takes a little more than that now, though."

"Like what?"

Looking as though she couldn't quite find the right adjective, Julie replied, "Well, he has to be more...charming."

Facetiously, I responded, "Charming?! Oh yeah, that's me alright."

Julie leaned slightly forward, took my hand and softly said, "Jackson, you have no idea."

I was completely overwhelmed by her straight-forward compliment. When she saw me squirm, she, of course, giggled.

Totally absorbed in the moment, I asked, "You like torturing me like that, don't you?"

With a mischievous laugh, she nodded enthusiastically. Then, her demeanor changed. She lost her beautiful smile, bit her lower lip and then asked, "Did you really come here to say good-bye to me before you left?"

"You heard your dad, didn't you?"

"That was sweet of you. I really wish I had been here. I've always hated that I didn't get to say good-bye to you."

"Yeah, me too," I mumbled.

The topic was now officially open, so Julie asked, "What was that like? I mean, leaving here. What was that like for you?"

I truly didn't want to talk about any of that stuff, but at the same time, I wanted her to understand. So, after thinking for a moment, I replied, "I sometimes think it was the most unfair and hardest thing I've ever had to do. It's kinda why I had to come back. I mean, I pretty much wish I had never left. Now that I've seen how the town and everyone has changed, it makes me feel like I've missed out on everything!"

Julie didn't pursue the subject further. Inside, I was extremely grateful. She simply nodded her understanding and then changed the subject to something cheerier. We casually talked a little while longer, until Julie thought it best to get back to her other guests. When we reentered the kitchen, we discovered Julie's parents preparing to bring pizza, more chips, and pop downstairs.

Mr. Falkner exclaimed, "Oh, good! You two can help bring some of this stuff downstairs! Jackson, grab some of these pizzas, will you please?"

I went to Julie's Dad, who was precariously trying to manage eight, flimsy, cardboard, pizza boxes; I rescued the top four. I was astonished by the total amount of party provisions we were about to deliver. When I turned around with my load, I noticed Mrs. Falkner giving me a knowing smile and a raised eyebrow. As I passed by and headed for the stairs, I tried to ignore her. *What is it with the raised-eyebrow looks I've been getting lately?*

With our arms full, the four of us made our way down the basement stairs. We then negotiated a small obstacle course of girl's purses and shoes, which had been dropped and/or kicked off and haphazardly strewn about. Thankfully, someone had brightened the lights for us, as we came down the steps. I would have hated to trip and make someone wear the pizza I was carrying.

Trying to be as unobtrusive as possible, Julie's parents placed their arm load of items on the bar and then tried to make a beeline for the stairs. But, before Mrs. Falkner could escape, I tugged on the sleeve of her blouse. Teens saying, "Thank you" could be heard sporadically throughout the basement. I felt I should add mine.

"Thank you for all of this."

"You're most welcome. Are you and Julie having a good time?"

Attempting to be as charming as Julie alleged, I smiled and said, "Yes, ma'am, we are. But, not too good of a time."

"Oh, good answer young man!" exclaimed Mr. Falkner.

The two adults then turned and made their way back to the stairs. As soon as their supervising eyes were no longer present, the lights were immediately dimmed again.

After most of the pizza had been ravenously devoured, Tony began playing rowdier music and we all returned to the makeshift dance floor. That night, a switch had been flipped on inside of me. I discovered that music and rhythm really did move me. I realized that I loved to dance. All in all, I was having a fabulous time in a social environment that a mere week ago was alien to me.

When I watched Mike McDonald dance, I had to laugh out loud. Like so many other things he was not good at, I had to add dancing to that list. Nevertheless, I was happy to see that he seemed to be enjoying himself immensely. Through the course of the evening, Mike was even coaxed to slow dance with a few girls. I had seen the look of fear in his eyes enough in the past to know that I was seeing it again, when he was held closely by this girl and that. Still, I had to admit, Mike was bravely holding his own, when he clearly wasn't comfortable at all.

The girl who seemed to be taking up most of Mike's time was Nancy Carter. She was a red-haired, green-eyed schoolmate, whom I vaguely remembered from St. Joe's. She now wore braces on her teeth and smiled very self-consciously. Throughout the evening, I noticed Nancy throwing googly-eyed looks Mike's way and wondered if she was making a serious play for my shy friend.

Inevitably, I had to dance with Gail. It was a difficult task because she was so much shorter than me. In addition, she wouldn't stop talking. I found myself nodding my head politely and smiling. Thanks to the music, I could barely understand a word she said. Still, I caught the gist of what she yammered on about. Mostly it was about how excited she was that Julie and I were getting together. I thought about correcting her, as I did Anne, but the more I thought about the words, *getting together,* the less I felt like denying it.

That evening, I believe I danced with just about every girl. I enjoyed the attention they directed at me very much. When I considered what little contact and interaction I had with girls in Duluth, it was an extremely new and thrilling sensation.

Throughout the night, if I danced with someone other than Julie, I found myself constantly looking in her direction. With just a look, Julie was able to let me know that the other girls had taken up enough of my time. When I was back in her arms, dancing, she held me almost too close. It was like dancing inside a sauna. At times, I felt the heat was almost unbearable, but it was a heat I never wanted to escape. It was during one such dance that she lifted her head off my shoulder and looked deep into my eyes.

"So, you've been missing us down here?"

After thinking for a moment, I replied, "Only every other day, it seems."

I was immediately conscious of sounding a little too serious, but Julie didn't seem to mind at all. She nodded her understanding and then put her head back down.

Keeping her head on my shoulder, Julie breathed on my neck and then stated, "You're not leaving here tonight without kissing me. Are you?"

It was the sweetest and most sincere request I had ever heard. Fearing that my changing voice would fail me and crack, I just smiled and slowly shook my head in the negative.

Julie's perfume was intoxicating and the whole setup was now more than I could fend off any longer. I knew it wouldn't be a smart thing to do, not at all, but just then, I never wanted anything more in my life than to kiss that girl. So, while Roberta Flack sang, *The First Time Ever I Saw Your Face,* I kissed Julie, just as tenderly as my inexperienced lips knew how.

As Julie's lips and mine pleaded with each other, she held me even tighter. My mind reeled with a new excitement and we melded together in what felt to me like the perfect kiss.

When our wonderful, first kiss was through, Julie kept her eyes closed and she touched her forehead to mine. In a voice barely loud enough to be heard over the music, she breathed, "I knew it would be like that."

"Not me," I softly replied. "I had no idea."

Julie then looked up into my eyes and gave me an adoring look. Instantaneously, my mind staggered. *Oh man,* I thought. *I've seen that look before! Landry, you idiot!* Nevertheless, there was no turning back for me now. I had broken my own rule by doing that which I had vowed not to and could not have cared less. I didn't know what had come over me or what to do about it. I somehow felt certain that nothing in this whole world would ever feel that special again. So, throwing all caution to the wind, I simply kissed her again.

After hours of dancing, eating, holding each other close, and sweating, the entire group needed to get some air. Sixteen teenagers in a single basement can generate a lot of heat, even in one as spacious as the Falkner's. Someone suggested that we go out by the pool to cool off. Julie, with me in tow, went upstairs to clear it with her parents first. After promises were given, to keep the noise level down to a dull roar, Mr. and Mrs. Falkner reluctantly gave their permission.

We all filed out the back door and took up seats wherever we could find them. Julie claimed their two-person, glider rocker, with plush seat cushions. There was no question where I was expected to sit. Lying down in the dew-soaked grass would have felt a lot better, though.

The evening progressed with a lot of teenage nonsense. We listened to some of Tony Milner's anecdotal stories and rolled with laughter. However, he wasn't the only one to act up. Many took turns telling jokes and satirical stories.

Suddenly, all eyes shifted to me, when Gail asked, "What about you, Jackson? You're being way too quiet over there!"

"I don't have any stories that match Tony's," I replied, "except maybe the time I fell into Indian Creek."

I watched Joel and Tony, as they looked at each other and then, almost in unison, exclaimed, "Oh yeah, tell it!"

As I began my story, the winter of 1968 came into focus and I remembered how especially hard it had been. From November of '67 to late March of '68, there were heavy snow accumulations throughout Blue Earth County. It was expected in the northern part of Minnesota, but not to that degree in the south. At the onset of early spring, the sun burst forth and an unseasonable warming trend melted the snow and ice too fast. The Minnesota River threatened to overflow its banks, while neighborhood tributary creeks appeared more like rivers.

In early April of that year, Joel, Tony, and I did exactly what our mothers told us not to do. We hiked down the railroad tracks to the trestle at Indian Creek and played by the rushing runoff waters. We wanted to float some homemade boats that we had hastily cut and hammered together from scrap wood.

The ice-encrusted banks appeared solid to us boys. So, I – feeling the need to be first – stepped onto what appeared to be a very thick bank of ice that jutted out over the creek. I knelt down and leaned forward to launch my boat. I had just turned loose of it, when the ice under me suddenly gave way and I was pitched headfirst into the rushing and excruciatingly-frigid water. When I broke the surface, I could hardly catch my breath. I had never felt such shockingly cold water, before or since. As I was carried downstream, my mind scrambled to get its bearings. I suddenly spotted my boat in the water and saw that I was catching up to it. I needed to get to the bank, as fast as possible, but I had no idea how I was going to accomplish that.

At first, Joel and Tony howled with laughter at my misfortune. That is, until they both realized that I was in serious trouble. I watched them, as they stood, frozen in place, while I called to them for help. Then, they both bolted and began to run after me. Joel tripped, fell on his face, swore loudly, "Shit," recovered and then continued the chase. Tony was all-out running, but couldn't catch up because of all the obstacles, like downed trees and crusted snowbanks that were in his path.

I was scared plenty, but amazingly, I didn't panic. Attempting to mimic swimmers I had seen on TV, I madly kicked and paddled my way toward the steep embankment. Once I made it, I frantically searched for something to grab onto. Luckily, I came in contact with some tree roots and held on for dear life. Holding myself in place for I don't know how long, Joel and Tony finally made their way to me. They both grabbed an arm and counted to three. By pulling together, they were able to get me safely onto the bank.

Everyone at the party knew that creek, the train tracks, and that trestle. Everyone also knew what the banks of that creek were like in early spring, when the water level was up.

Gail asked, "Did you even know how to swim back then?"

"No," I replied comically, "but I sort of learned how pretty quick!"

Laughter erupted from everyone, especially Joel and Tony, who then added to the story. They told everyone how they had to run alongside of me, as I tried to swim to the bank in the strong current. We also laughed about how I had to walk home soaking wet, with water squeaking and sloshing in my boots the entire way. When the laughter died down and someone else in the group volunteered to tell a tale, I thought about that day a little longer and suddenly stopped smiling.

There was more to my story, but I had intentionally left that part out. What everyone did not hear that night was how I had been in danger of succumbing to the effects of hypothermia. By the time we three reached the Wilson house, my lips had turned blue and I was shivering uncontrollably. At the time, Danny was the only person home. When Joel and Tony delivered me to the side door, Danny took one look at me and immediately sprang into action. He told the guys to get lost, grabbed the front of my drenched, winter coat and then dragged me inside. After closing the door behind me, Danny quickly stripped me naked, right there in the entryway. He then ran upstairs and grabbed the comforter from my bed. After wrapping me up in it and sitting me down at the kitchen table, he rushed to the bathroom and drew me a hot bath. He made me stay in the tub until my color improved and I could speak coherently. While I soaked in the heavenly, hot water, he took all of my wet things to the basement and put them in the dryer. After I had properly thawed out and redressed in dry clothes, Danny advised me, "Don't tell Mom or Dad about any of this. You'll get into big trouble if you do."

That should have been the scariest day of my life, but it wasn't. I somehow knew I was going to be okay. For all intents and purposes, I should have drowned that day. By pulling me out of that freezing water, Joel and Tony had literally saved my life. However, as far as I was concerned, Danny was the real hero.

Julie caught me in deep thought. She nudged me out of my trance and asked, "You okay?"

I gave her a smile and replied, "Yeah, fine."

"Where did you go?"

"Oh, back there for a minute."

Julie gave me another understanding nod, snuggled in a little closer and returned her attention to the group.

When the hour had grown quite late, parents began arriving to pick up their teens. The guys and I lived close enough to walk, which was the deal we had struck with our parents and/or temporary guardians. Tony's parents had some doubts, but we successfully bartered our way past any reservations they had.

Before going to say good-bye to some of her departing guests, Julie asked if it would be a problem for me and the guys to hang around until everyone else had left. Anne and Gail were spending the night with Julie. So, Joel, Dave, and I were more than willing to chance getting into a little trouble, just to linger with the girls a little while longer. Mike wanted to stay behind, too, so he wouldn't have to walk home alone. He only lived three blocks away, but we rationalized that there was greater safety in numbers.

Back in the basement, Tony put a stack of older, but smooth tunes on the record player. To help set the mood, he also turned the volume down to just the right amount of decibels. He and Mike then graciously retreated to The Green Room to shoot pool. While Julie showed the last of her departing guests to the door, I hung out with Tony and Mike.

Dave and Anne had already staked their claim to one end of a large sofa. Joel and Gail found another corner to cuddle in. Both couples were immersed in soft spoken conversation, with some making out mixed in. Of course, it could have been the other way around, too. It was hard to tell.

Witnessing that kind of intimacy between my friends felt strange. *What do they talk about?* After growing up together in the same neighborhood, attending the same school and classes together, what could they possibly talk about that wasn't already understood?

When Julie returned to the basement, I was paying a little too close attention to the game that Tony and Mike were playing. So, I didn't see her enter the room and approach me from behind. Without saying a word, Julie took my hand and beckoned me to join her in the dimly lit lounge. When I stepped off the tall billiard chair, I caught the smirk and wink Tony directed at me, as he aimed for his next shot.

Julie led me to a soft loveseat, with overstuffed cushions. There, she had me sit at one end. She then placed two large couch pillows to my right. Instead of sitting next to me, she sort of leaned across my lap and propped herself up with the pillows, so she could face me.

Help me, Lord, help me, Jesus! The thought raced through my head, as Julie made the first move. We kissed as tenderly as before. Right then, I couldn't think of a single thing to say, but it didn't bother me because I truly did not feel like talking. Nevertheless, Julie had something on her mind. So, like the other two couples, we spoke in hushed tones.

"I'm a little afraid of this," she confided.

"What, making out?"

"No, silly, I mean what's going on inside me."

"We're gonna have to talk about it, aren't we?"

"Yeah, we should, but I guess it doesn't have to be right now. I can't help thinking that this whole week, today, and especially tonight has been so…"

"Perfect?" I inserted the word I hoped she was looking for.

Julie smiled broadly and then whispered, "I don't know if it's been perfect, but I know I love how things seem to be turning out." Before I could say another word, she continued. "I know I'm not being very smart right now, but I just can't help how I feel about you. As soon as I knew for sure it was you at the ballpark, I started having feelings for you again."

"Again?"

"Jackson, I've liked you since the second grade. You know that…Don't you?"

Since Julie was now making confessions, I thought I had better try to keep pace. "If anyone had told me a week ago that I would be here with you, like this, I would have said they were crazy. But now that I'm here…I don't want it to end."

Once again, Julie's perfume worked its magic on me. I could tell she had freshened it, most likely after she finished ushering guests out the door. Her eyes and her smile were also sending me signals. Her look, her scent, her demeanor, every bit of her made me feel as though she did it all for me. Most assuredly, Julie and I needed to have a serious talk, but right then just wasn't the right time. More talking was unnecessary and would have ruined the moment. So, like any inexperienced first-timers, we kissed softly and continuously.

Allowing those special feelings to course through me, Julie and I continued to make out, as did the other two couples. I believe none of us wanted that evening to come to an end. However, the inevitable did come about, when the upstairs door opened, and the kitchen light filtered down to the basement. Quite suddenly, Julie scrambled from my arms and went to the foot of the staircase.

Mrs. Falkner softly called down, "Time to say good night to the boys, honey."

"We were just doing that, Momma."

Burying my face into a couch pillow, I heard stifled laughter from the other two couples, also.

We all pitched in and conducted some rudimentary cleanup. The industrial-strength version would have to wait until daylight. After we collected Tony's records and were ready to depart, the others slowly made their way, single file, up the stairs. Julie and I brought up the rear. However, she stopped on the first step and then turned around to face me. Stepping back down into my arms, Julie gave me one more memorable kiss. We then made our ascent to the kitchen.

When Julie and I finally appeared, Mr. and Mrs. Falkner were saying goodbye to the others. Slightly embarrassed grins were worn by our friends. Struggling to keep a knowing smirk off his face, Mr. Falkner stared holes into the kitchen floor. Mrs. Falkner was probably best equipped to handle the situation. "Did you two get lost?" she asked.

Julie squeezed my hand a little tighter and then replied, "You might say that, Momma."

"Hmmm," said Mrs. Falkner. She then turned and addressed me directly. "Jackson, I do hope we are going to see more of you before you have to leave town. I have a sneaking suspicion we will." Her smile was sly, but warm, and her invitation felt sincere.

Knowing that my face was beet red, I replied, "Yes, ma'am." Laughter then broke out from everyone.

One last time, we all thanked Julie's parents, as they waved and departed the kitchen. We teens then said our final good-byes for the evening.

Julie asked, "Call me tomorrow?"

"I'll need your number."

Julie slipped her fingers into the breast pocket of my shirt and pulled out a neatly folded slip of note paper. "You mean…this number?" She then gave me a clever, little smile.

"When did you…" I began, but Julie's lips cut me off.

When the kiss was over, Julie whispered, "It was magic. Good night, Jackson."

The walk home was quiet for the first block or so. That is, until Tony broke the silence. "So, what were you two doing down there all by yourself?"

Joel gave Tony a shove. "What do you think they were doing, moron?" He then turned to me, grinned, and said, "Geez, Jackson, you sure do work fast. Do you think if I came to see you up north, I'd get that lucky?"

I just smiled in return. *How should I know? He'd probably be luckier than I've been up there,* I thought. I then turned my attention to Mike. "I noticed you having a pretty good time tonight with Nancy."

Timidly, Mike admitted, "Yeah."

"So, anything going on there?"

"I don't know, yet."

"Yet?"

"I don't know, yet," Mike repeated.

The rest of us exchanged surprised looks and then snickered. We knew better than to poke too much fun at Mike. If he was ever going to come out of his shell, it would be best to just leave him alone and let it happen.

Our first stop was at Mike's house. After we safely delivered him to his door, we headed for Westwood Drive. All the way to the Wilson place, Tony, Dave, and Joel rode me pretty hard about Julie. I didn't mind a bit. I suddenly felt a lot older than the tender age of thirteen. I didn't know what had taken place within me or even why it had happened. All I knew for sure was that in one evening, I had undergone a drastic change. I didn't know what to make of how I was feeling, but neither did I want it to go away anytime soon.

I said good-bye to the guys on the front lawn and they continued on their way home. Using my house key – the one Janet had given me to carry for my entire stay – I quietly unlocked the side door and then silently slipped inside the entryway. For a change, there was no activity going on in the basement. I was going to leave my shoes at the entryway but thought better of it. I had them in hand, as I stepped into the kitchen and then immediately saw Janet sitting at the kitchen table.

Oh cripes, I thought. *Here we go!* There was only one reason I could think of for Janet to still be up. *It must be way too late for me to be showing up from a party!*

"Hi," smiled Janet, catching me totally by surprise. "Did you have a good time?" There wasn't even a hint of anger in her demeanor.

"Yeah, I did," I replied tentatively. "Sorry I kept you up waiting."

"You didn't, I just couldn't sleep is all."

"Is there something wrong?"

"It's nothing for you to worry about, kiddo. Hey, it really is late. You should get to bed. Danny went with Kurt to take the girls home. So, you don't have to worry about waking him up when you go upstairs."

Thinking I had just got away with a major coup, I kissed Janet good night and headed for the stairwell. When I heard Brad snoring down the hallway, I stopped.

Janet said, "You can tell me all about the party in the morning," Then, as an afterthought, she added, "Oh, and Jackson?"

"Yeah?"

"The next time you see Julie, please tell her for me...I really like her perfume."

With newfound confidence, I smiled back and said, "So do I."

As I prepared for bed, I hung my shirt on the bed post, close to my pillow, so I would be able to enjoy Julie's lingering scent. Because of the crazy and amazing feelings that coursed through me, I was not remotely drowsy. When I laid my head down on my old, goose-down pillow, I let my mind take me back to the Falkners' basement. I wanted an instant replay of every dance, every look, every smile, and especially every kiss exchanged with Julie. I don't know when or even how, but I did fall asleep. I didn't even hear Danny come up those noisy stairs.

CHAPTER 14

Saturday, 12 August 1972

I awoke in the middle of a great dream, but immediately could not recall what it was about. Blinking my eyes, trying to wake up, I heard Danny's voice ask, "You okay over there?"

"Yeah, I guess I was just dreaming, but it's gone already. I hate it when that happens."

When I was able to focus, I saw that Danny was sitting up in bed, propped up by pillows, and thumbing through a Sports Illustrated magazine. He momentarily looked up and rather absent mindedly replied, "Me, too."

Sitting up in bed myself, I tried to rub the sleep from my eyes. Danny's clock indicated that it was 8:48 A.M; I could scarcely believe I was awake. I noticed that, like me, Danny was in no hurry to get out of bed. He just sat there, flipping through the weekly magazine's pages too quickly to actually extract any information from them. Suddenly, he looked up and simply stared out in front of him. My eyes followed his gaze to other end of the room. There was nothing of great interest there, so I looked back at Danny and wondered what was going on inside his head. It was then that I saw a large, ugly hicky on his neck.

"Oh man!" I exclaimed. "Did you have a run-in with a vampire last night or what?"

"Naw, Carrie just got a little…carried away. No pun intended."

I laughed anyway. "Mom's gonna kick your ass when she sees those bruises on your neck."

"Boy! You *must* have been tired last night."

"Why's that?"

As we locked eyes, Danny's look was that of worry. He replied, "She saw them when Kurt and I got back from taking the girls home." He then shook his head for emphasis. "But that's not the worst of it. She caught Carrie and me up here last night. Needless to say, she is so beyond being pissed off. I hope she doesn't take forever to get over it. You know how she can be."

Imagining the scene that Janet walked in on, I asked, "Did you and Carrie… do it?"

Without hesitation, Danny replied, "Naw, but when Mom caught us, we were kinda on our way there."

For a moment, I just looked at my foster brother, who, because of his age, I thought was supposed to be smarter. Then, I heard myself ask, "What were you thinking?!"

"Thinking had nothing to do with it, little brother. Someday *you'll* find that out."

"I kinda know what you're talking about already, but man, oh man, I'm surprised you're still breathing."

"Yeah, well, the day isn't over with…yet."

"How did it happen? Weren't Mom and Dad here?"

"Not at the time. After they took you to the party, they went out to have a few beers. Kurt and Janelle dropped us off here, so they could go to a friend's house. We just didn't count on Mom and Dad getting home earlier than usual."

"Well, that explains the rubbers I saw on your dresser yesterday, which, by the way, was pretty stupid. Doesn't Mom ever come up here to clean?"

"Hell no, that's my job! He paused for a moment and then shook his head in anger. "Damn it, Jackson, it's not fair! Kurt never gets caught doing anything! Me? I get caught every time I screw up."

I didn't know what to say. I wished I could help make Danny feel better, but even I thought the act was so stupid that he deserved to get caught. I just wasn't going to tell *him* that. Besides, Danny was already doing a pretty-good job of beating himself up. He didn't need my help at all.

Danny then put on a weak smile and asked, "So, how did it go for you last night?"

"I screwed up, too. I spent the night dancing with Julie and then…we made out." I rolled over and yelled into my pillow, "AAAHHH!"

Of course, Danny laughed and then said, "I don't understand the problem. I thought you liked her?"

Pulling my face back out of my pillow, I said, "When I'm not with her, I think clearly and know I shouldn't get involved with her at all. But, Lord Almighty, when I'm with her…You know what I mean?"

"Uh-oh, you've got it bad, little brother."

"Danny, what am I gonna do?"

"You gotta week to figure it out, so relax. I'll tell you this much, there are worse problems to have than falling for a girl, especially if *she* really likes you back."

"Yeah, but if I don't stop it now, what happens at the end of the week? She's gonna get hurt."

"What about you? You gonna get hurt?"

"Probably, but what else is new?"

"Oh man, now look who's feeling sorry for himself. Right now, I'd gladly trade problems with you."

I thought about Danny's predicament and then said, "You're right. You win. I'll take the girl."

We both laughed, but I still wasn't convinced it was a smart course of action. As a matter of fact, I knew it wasn't. But right then, I just didn't care about being smart.

It bothered me that Danny tried to break ground I knew he wasn't ready for. I had always looked up to him as my older brother. He was supposed to be able to use better judgment. In the past, no matter how hard the problem, Danny always seemed to know the right thing to do. He usually succeeded at whatever he put his mind to achieving. But the thought of Carrie and him in bed, doing the big nasty, while still being kids, registered as just, plain wrong to me. I thought I had enough of my own problems to keep me occupied, but now I was worried about Danny, too. I thought, *enough already!*

Danny then switched gears on me and got a little serious. "You really do like Julie, don't you?"

"I didn't count on her at all this trip, Danny, but she's really something. I've never felt this way about a girl before. It just figures it would happen here, where I don't live anymore."

"If I were you, I'd enjoy the ride and do it while you can. What makes her so special? I mean, she's cute enough, I suppose, but there are lots of cute girls out there."

After thinking about it momentarily, I decided to tell Danny about the history between Julie and me. I told him how Julie was my first kiss, how it hurt when I didn't get to say good-bye, and how she told me she started having feelings for me again at the ball game. Most important, I admitted to Danny how I never stopped having feelings for Julie, even after being gone for three years.

Danny listened patiently and when I finished, he restated, "Yeah, like I said, you've got it bad, little brother. I still say you need to enjoy it while you can. From the way it sounds, you couldn't ignore her now if you wanted to."

"I think I could," I replied. "It would suck, but I think I could."

While shaking his head, Danny said, "Uh-uh, she wouldn't let you, especially since she knows you're here in this house. Besides, why would you do that to yourself? If what you say is true and you don't come back for a long time, you had better make everything count, while you're here…now."

At that moment, Danny's huge rationalization made perfect sense to me. In actuality, I knew I was just kidding myself. After everything Julie and I had experienced together, I truly wasn't going to be able to make myself stay away from her. In fact, I could hardly wait to see her again.

When I went downstairs, I found Janet in the kitchen. As usual, she was drinking coffee and smoking a cigarette. Danny was in no hurry to come down and I didn't blame him one bit. I sat at the kitchen table and acted like I still needed to wake up, which wasn't too far from the truth. Janet leaned on the counter, acting like she didn't know I was there, but I knew better. I watched her tentatively, as she looked out the window above the sink.

"Morning," I said flatly.

"Hey, you, I didn't hear you come down."

"Then you really do need a hearing aid. Those stairs are terrible."

"Yeah, they are. And they're going to stay that way until someone is old enough to move out."

I already knew what was coming, but I just had to verify it. "Why's that?" I asked.

"So nobody can go sneaking upstairs, with a girl mind you, without being heard!"

Yep, she's pissed. I knew right then I should probably keep my mouth shut, but it was such a beautiful morning, I hated to see it go to waste.

"Hey, Mom, do me a favor, will ya?"

"What?"

"Wait to kill him until I leave next week. I don't want to be implicated in his murder."

At first, Janet gave me the raised-eyebrow look – I hated that look. Then, she smiled and said, "Implicated? That's kind of a big word for a thirteen-year-old. Isn't it?"

"Well, you know how it goes. Read books, learn words."

Janet chuckled, "Get over here. I need a hug."

I went to her and she quite suddenly grabbed me. She held me just a little too tight for just a little too long. I suddenly felt there was something else going on inside of her. I felt awful because I realized that she was sad and I didn't know how to help, so I just let her hold me.

After a little while, she released her death grip on me and looked into my eyes. "You really love him like a brother, don't you?"

"Yeah, of course I do, why?"

"Never mind, I'm just feeling a little melancholy this morning. I guess I'm not ready for you boys to grow up so fast."

I then understood that Janet was actually more worried about Danny than she was mad at him. I didn't bother to tell her how I was worried about him, too. It would have just dragged the moment out, which was the last thing in the world I wanted.

Janet then did what she always did in those situations. She put on a big, fake smile and then changed the subject. "Brad and I have talked about it. We thought maybe you would like to have some of your friends over for the barbeque this afternoon."

"Really?! How many friends can I invite?"

"Well, let's keep it to a small army, okay?"

"Um…girls included?" *Oh man, is it too late to pull that one back?!*

At first, Janet gave me a surprised look, but I was the one who ended up being surprised. Instead of hitting me with a barrage of her usual witticisms, she just nodded her head casually and then said, "Yeah, I guess it'll be okay.

I knew she was exercising *great* restraint to keep from making fun of me, so I decided to give her an out. "Just like that?!" I asked. "No torture first?! I know you're dying to say something."

Janet then laughed and replied, "Yes, I am, so don't look that gift horse in the mouth."

"Okay, but I have one more favor to ask."

Chuckling again, Janet said, "I don't know that I owe you one, but go ahead."

Knowing that Danny was probably listening at the vent by my bed, I said, "I'd like Janelle and Carrie to be here, too."

"Oh, kiddo…You're sure asking for a big one there. I have no problem with Janelle, but right now isn't a good time for Carrie to be around here."

Just then, I heard Danny coming down the stairs. When he appeared in the kitchen, he looked at the two of us with expressionless eyes. "Thanks, Jackson," he said, "but don't waste your time."

Janet looked me in the eye and said very frankly, "Right now would be a good time for you to be somewhere else."

Taking Janet's not-so-subtle hint to get lost, I didn't hesitate to disappear from the kitchen. When I got out of the shower, their argument was still going on at a fever pitch. As I dressed upstairs, it continued, and I had to hear everything. When I came back down from the bedroom, I discovered Janet and Danny had moved their heated conversation to the basement. Their voices still carried quite well, so I decided to skip breakfast and do as Janet suggested – be somewhere else.

I hurried out the side door into the late morning air. The Pepsi-Cola thermometer, which hung just inches from the door, informed me the temperature was a comfortable seventy-six degrees. While dressing, I had listened to Danny's radio and the weatherman said the temperatures would be climbing fast that morning. It was projected to get into the mid-eighties by the afternoon.

I sat on the step and immediately swore under my breath because I had forgotten my book. I did wish to read, but I didn't want to go back inside to retrieve it, so I just sat there and attempted to think of something happier. It wasn't too hard, either. I simply thought about Julie and silently prayed that she would be able to attend that afternoon's gathering.

"It's a little noisy in there, isn't it?" The voice was Brad's, but I couldn't see him. I looked toward the open bay door of the garage. He then appeared from the darkness of the rear.

"Yeah, a little," I replied. I got up from the step and walked toward him. "I can't believe Danny thinks he's going to win this one."

Brad gave out an elongated, "Oooh…I don't think he believes that. I think he's arguing just to make noise. He's at that age, where it seems anything and everything has to be argued."

I just looked at Brad and nodded my understanding, even though I truly didn't. *What did Danny really hope to accomplish?* From my viewpoint, he was way out of line to even try standing up to Janet. Since back talk had never been tolerated in the Wilson house before, why did he think he was going to get away with it now? Brad must have seen the worry on my face.

"Don't worry about what's going on in there, buddy. Danny will survive this one, too. How about helping me put up the volleyball net?"

"Sure," I replied. Right then, I would have done anything to take my mind off the argument going on inside the house.

Brad had retrieved the volleyball net from the garage attic. It had been neatly rolled and put into a large, cardboard, mover's box for storage. As we unpacked it, to me, it looked as though it had not been used in years. The net had been purchased the summer after we moved into the house. When it was set up in the back yard, we had many great times. The net was regulation size, but the poles were a different story. Brad had sunk two steel poles midway in the backyard. When the net wasn't attached to the poles, a clothesline was stretched between them, making the poles functional on laundry day. When the net was raised and stretched, it never actually reached regulation height. In the middle, it usually drooped quite a bit. The dip helped little guys get the ball over the net, especially when they wanted to spike it.

When Brad and I had one end of the net successfully tied onto a pole, my stomach suddenly growled loudly.

"Didn't you like your breakfast?" asked Brad.

"What breakfast? I was in too much of a hurry to get away from the noise."

"After we hang the net, we need to go get stuff for the barbeque. How about you and I go get us some lunch?"

"That sounds great, but first I have to make a few phone calls."

"Why's that?"

"It's hard to get friends to come to a barbeque they know nothing about."

Brad laughed and said, "Ask a stupid question, et cetera."

Shortly before I went inside to call my friends, Janet and Danny's bickering had come to an abrupt end. I didn't know the results of the battle of wills between the two, but I could make an educated guess – Danny lost. And to my way of thinking, that's just the way it was supposed to be.

For a few reasons, I was glad their squabbling had finally ceased. I wanted to use the telephone in the basement. It was the coolest place in the house, plus it afforded me some semblance of privacy. In addition, the quiet that settled within the house was also greatly appreciated. As I settled into the easy chair and put the phone in my lap, I hoped Janet and Danny's attitudes would change for the better as the day progressed. It would be hard to enjoy a barbeque with those two at each other's throat.

I called all the guys first. Mike had previous plans with his family and said he couldn't make it. Dave and Joel were able to come and offered to take care of contacting Anne and Gail. I told them the girls were probably still at Julie's. Since I would be calling her soon, I'd have them contact their guy if they were coming. Tony Milner was a hold out and said he would have to get back to me. Julie was the last call I had to make. So, I crossed my fingers, said two Hail Marys and then dialed her number. The moment it began to ring, I held my breath. I reminded myself to use my best telephone etiquette.

"Hello, Falkner residence," said Julie's mom at the other end of the line.

"Hi, Mrs. Falkner, this is Jackson Landry. May I please talk to Julie?"

"Well, hello Jackson. Just a moment and I'll see if she's available."

That was painless, I thought.

After a few moments, Julie's excited voice came across the line. "Hello… Jackson?"

"Yeah, it's me."

In her most angelic tone, Julie said, "Hi!"

Nervously, I greeted her back, "Hi."

"You called!" The surprise in Julie's voice sounded genuine.

"You asked me to call last night, remember?" *Is this how this stuff is supposed to go?*

Giggling, Julie admitted, "Yeah, I guess I did…Didn't I?! What's up?"

"Well, we're having a barbeque at the house here…I mean…at the Wilsons' house…late this afternoon. I wanted to know if you could come…I mean…would you like to come…with me…for the barbeque." *Smooth, Landry…real smooth.*

Julie giggled on the other end of the line. "I'd love to come, but I'll have to ask my parents first. Can I call you back?"

"Sure…No problem."

"Okay then…"

Before Julie could go on, I interrupted, "Wait a minute! Are Gail and Anne still with you?"

"Yeah, they're still here."

"Well...could you please tell them they're invited, too? Tell them the guys will be here."

"Cool! Sure, I'll tell them. Let me coax my parents a little and I'll call you back."

"Okay."

"Okay then, I'll talk to you in a little bit. Bye!"

I really need to work on the telephone thing! The thought went through my head and I almost laughed at myself out loud for acting like such a spaz.

Just then, Kurt came into the den from his room. While shaking his head, he gave me a disapproving look and said, "I didn't hear everything, but just now, I'll bet any money you were talking to a girl."

"I know! I really suck at it!" I also snickered to cover my embarrassment.

"Yeah, you really do, but you're gettin' better. Just relax and let them do most of the talking. It's what they're good at. All you have to do is listen, smile a lot, and occasionally laugh at their stupid jokes, which are never really all that funny."

"Was it hard for you, when you first started calling girls?"

"Not really. Not if it was someone I liked a lot. Plus, I rarely ever called girls. They always called me."

I didn't know if Kurt was telling the truth or just trying to act cool in front of me. Regardless of which, I nodded my understanding.

Kurt then grinned knowingly and then said, "You must have had a good night."

I smiled from ear to ear and replied, "Yeah, I *really* did!"

Just then, the phone, which was still in my lap, rang. It surprised me and I almost jumped out of the lounger. It was Julie, calling to tell me she would be coming to the barbeque. I could not have been more excited. I felt like the day was going to be great after all. Julie also informed me that Anne and Gail would be coming, too. She then wanted to know all the details. I told her people would begin showing up at four o'clock. I then suggested I come get her at three and we walk to the barbeque together. It would give us a chance to talk.

Julie exclaimed, "I love it! That's a great idea!"

"This may go on into the night some," I said. "What time do I need to get you home by?"

"I'll let you know when you get here. Do you have a few minutes to talk?"

"Well, I have to go with Brad to get stuff for the barbeque, but yeah, I've got a few minutes."

Shortly after Julie energetically began recapping highlights from the previous night, I discovered that Kurt was absolutely right. Mostly, I just slouched in the lounge chair, with a huge smile on my face and the phone receiver stuck to my ear. I let Julie prattle on about her party and how everyone seemed to have a great time. She even touched on how she thought Nancy Carter had a thing for Mike. Julie then said she wanted to talk about us but would wait until the afternoon to do so. She thought it would be better to talk face to face. But then, Julie must have changed her mind because she began to talk about us anyway. Mostly it was a recap of how great the previous night was and how much sleep she lost. I didn't have the heart to tell her that I slept beautifully. As a matter of fact, my end of the conversation was mostly comprised of an "uh-huh" here or "uh-uh" there, mixed in with an occasional "yup" and "nope." Sometimes there was the need for a "kinda," along with my personal favorite, "I guess so." After we said our good-byes and hung up, my first thought was, *Wow! That girl can talk!* Still, I was very excited about the prospect of seeing her again.

Just before going to run errands with Brad, I noticed the house seemed awfully quiet. As we walked out the side door, the silence was almost deafening. I fully expected Janet to be playing her Elvis Presley records. It was sort of a tradition with her when she made preparations for a family cookout. However, the house was taking a rest from any noise, whatsoever.

As Brad drove us downtown, he must have seen the worry on my face. He asked, "Now on a beautiful day like this, what are you frowning about?"

"Mom's pretty worried about Danny. So am I."

"What do you think the problem is?"

"Danny idolizes Kurt, wants to be just like him, but he doesn't feel like he measures up."

"Wow! That's a very astute observation for someone your age! How did you figure that out?"

"It's easy. I feel the same way about Danny sometimes. I always wish I were more like him…and Kurt."

"Well, I think you hit the nail on the head, buddy. But doesn't that end up being Danny's problem to figure out? Don't you have enough issues of your own to work through?"

"I guess, but it doesn't keep me from caring about the people I love."

Brad nodded his head and gave me an approving smile. "You really have grown some since you left us. Don't you worry too much about Danny, I'm sure he'll find his way, just as I'm sure you'll find yours. You know, you're more like Kurt and Danny than you may think."

Brad then changed the subject and started asking me about Julie's party. I filled him in on most of the details. I told him how much fun I had playing pool against the guys and dancing with all the girls. I even confided how it appeared that Julie and I appeared to be a temporary item.

Understandably surprised, Brad asked, "How did that happen?!"

Facetiously, I replied, "Oh, you know, I slow danced with her…It was hot… We kissed. By the end of the night, I was making out with her."

Through his laughter, Brad said, "That probably wasn't the smartest thing to do."

"I know, but it sure seemed right at the time."

"It usually does. Are you sure you know what you're doing?"

Brad's posing his question was like him pulling the trigger of a gun. My true feelings on the subject came forth and I almost yelled my response. "Are you kidding?! Of course I don't! I'm thirteen and I've never liked a girl like this before! I have no idea what I'm doing or how this happened in the first place! What's gonna happen at the end of next week?!"

Brad laughed heartily. "Whoa! Okay, slow down and breathe! You sound just like Kurt when it was his first time."

That tidbit of information did not make me feel any better.

We pulled into Bob's Big Boy restaurant on Riverfront Drive. It was advertised as "The Home of the Original Double-Decker." It was also where I got my inspiration for making my own double-cheeseburger creations. The hostess seated us in a booth next to a large picture window. The scenery afforded us consisted of nothing more than the parking lot and traffic that flowed along Riverfront Drive.

A rather dull-looking waitress arrived and put water glasses in front of us, then handed out menus. When she came back to take our orders, I was more than ready. Because I had skipped breakfast, it didn't take me long to decide what I wanted. Since we would be grilling chicken and ribs that afternoon, I didn't want to ruin my pallet by ordering something too heavy. So, a BLT with chips and a Coke felt just about right to me.

"Hey, that sounds good," said Brad. "I'll have the same please."

When the waitress left, I decided it was time to ask Brad about something that had been bothering me.   "Kurt and Danny sure do party a lot. I mean, it seems like every other night, they either have a bunch of friends over to the house or go to someone else's place. Up north, I haven't been invited to any of the type of parties I've been to here."

"I'll bet that all changes for you real soon," said Brad. "I can't believe how much you've changed, right in front of us and in only a week's time. Last Saturday, you could hardly talk to a girl without tripping over your tongue and turning three shades of red. Now, look at you, you're not only talking to them, but you're dancing with them, too. For crying out loud, you're even making out!"

We shared a good laugh, but then I thought about what he said and had to agree. I was changing and I knew it. Still, there was a question perplexing me. "Why do you and Mom let Kurt, Danny, and their friends take over the basement the way they do?"

"Jackson, we want them to feel comfortable having their friends come over to hang out. When they're at the house and we're there to supervise, they can't get into any trouble. It's only when they're away from the house that Mom and I wonder what they're up to." He then stared out the window, with a far off look on his face. "I want them to enjoy what they have left of their youth. Things will be changing soon enough for those two." He then returned his gaze toward me. "Things will be changing for you, also. I just want us to enjoy this time together. God only knows if, let alone when, it's going to happen again. I really have missed you, buddy."

I gave him a weak smile of understanding. At that moment, I too was feeling the same winds of change he alluded to. I then reminded myself of my true purpose for coming to Mankato. *How am I ever going to say good-bye to these people? I love them too much.* I had said good-bye once already, back when I didn't understand the full weight of the decision. But now, there was no decision to make at all, just the reality that I would once again have to leave everyone I held dear to me.

After lunch, we headed to Pigs to get the shopping done. During the drive Brad looked to be in deep thought.

"Whatcha thinkin'?" I asked.

"I've been thinking about your dilemma with Julie. What you may not know is how young people have been involving themselves in summer romances for generations. I've always thought it was just part of growing up."

"You mean, it's okay to like a girl for a short time, then hurt her when you have to leave?"

"What I'm saying is…I don't think it's a question of morality or intent. It's natural at your age to like what you see and want what you can't actually have. This is just the beginning for you. Enjoy your feelings for each other. The feelings are going to be there whether you want them or not. Girls are definitely part of your life. They are now…and in your future. When you leave here, Julie's head will one day be turned by someone else. You'll be attracted to someone else, too. When you're as young as you are, it's just what happens. One thing is for sure, though, for as long as you live, you'll probably never forget Julie."

"Why's that?"

"No man ever forgets his very first girl." Then, Brad added, "I've discovered recently that you have a very large capacity for love. Don't lose it, buddy. The world is a much darker place without it."

Brad had never talked to me in that fashion before. Having him share those insights with me made me feel somewhat more mature. I liked him being frank with me. However, I did not like the thought that someday, someone else would get Julie's attention. In addition, I refused to believe that I would ever be interested in another girl. *No way,* I thought, *not with what I have going on inside of me!* Of course, I didn't dare admit any of those thoughts to Brad. I simply enjoyed the rest of the ride to Pigs, feeling that I was somehow older in his eyes.

While Brad and I wandered around the grocery store, picking out provisions that would be necessary for the cookout, I still worried about Janet and Danny. Their being at odds had the potential for putting a real damper on the day. It didn't take me long to figure out a solution, though. The question in my mind was whether I could get a certain, stubborn teenager to cooperate. By the time Brad and I returned to the house, I was absolutely convinced that my idea was a good one. So, after I helped Brad get things settled in the kitchen, I found Janet. She was relaxing with a magazine in the living room.

"Where's Danny?" I asked.

"I think he's upstairs, pouting."

"Thanks."

Turning on my heels, I then walked quietly to the stairs, but then bounded up them noisily, taking two steps at a time. When I reached the top, I found Danny lounging on his bed, reading my Louis L'Amour western. When he looked up and saw me standing there, slightly winded, he smiled, waved the paperback at me, and said, "Hope you don't mind me borrowing this. It gets a little boring up here."

"No problem. Look, Danny, I want you with us today."

"I'm not going anywhere, Jackson. I'll be right here."

I was now adamant and stated, "No! I want you outside and *with* us this afternoon! Go say you're sorry to her!"

Danny gave no observable sign that helped me know whether he had taken me seriously or not. So, when he tossed the book on my bed, then got up and without offering a single argument, walked toward the stairs, I was more than a little surprised. Just before Danny went down, he turned and gave me a look of embarrassment. He then said, "I was gonna do this anyway." Danny left me there to go do what he absolutely loathed – he admitted that he was wrong and apologized to his mom.

CHAPTER 15

By two o'clock that afternoon, nervous energy, mixed with excited impatience, coursed through me. As I waited for the appointed time for the barbeque to begin, I could barely sit still. I could hardly wait for my friends to begin showing up. However, before I could be in place to receive them, I still had to go collect Julie. That meant coming in contact with her parents again. When that scene played out inside my head, I wasn't overly excited, but I trusted that I would, at the very least, survive the encounter.

Brad seemed to perceive my anxiousness all too well, so he helped by keeping me busy. As I helped him clean some folding chairs, card tables, and the redwood picnic table, he just smiled knowingly and shook his head.

I, too, couldn't help but smile, especially when I heard Elvis Presley in the background singing, "You ain't nothing but a hound dog, crying all the time..." The music blared from the living room's RCA, console-stereo phonograph. Janet had turned the volume up and I could see her head bobbing in the kitchen window. Danny had done the right thing, so there was at least a temporary truce between the two of them.

At that moment, I couldn't be happier. The day seemed to be equalizing itself nicely. It was almost as if God decided that whatever I wanted was mine to be had.

As I scrubbed on a card table, trying to clean off what appeared to be petrified ketchup, I heard Janelle's familiar voice behind me, "Hi, cutie!"

I turned and gave her a sly smile. "You must be talking to me." I then gave her a little bit better than our usual hug.

"Wow! You're in a good mood," Janelle observed. "I'm thinking that someone had a good time last night."

"Yeah, I kinda have to thank you for part of it."

In an excited voice, Janelle asked, "Did you knock her socks off?!"

"I don't know about that, but she's gonna be here with me today."

"That's so cool!"

"Yeah, pretty soon I have to go get her."

Janelle wore an impish grin as she said, "I'm really happy for you, cutie."

"Cutie?!" I repeated the word, thinking she was acting a little weirder than usual.

"Get used to it, Jackson. I just call 'em like I see 'em!"

I laughed at her playfulness. At that moment, I could truly picture having Janelle as an older sister. She seemed as practiced at it as Kurt and Danny were at being big brothers. We may not have been related by blood, but she compensated for that fact effortlessly.

Suddenly, Janet called from the kitchen window, "JACKSON! TELEPHONE!"

Thinking the caller might be Julie, I left Janelle standing by the card table and ran for the side door. When I entered the kitchen, I was slightly out of breath.

Wearing a devilish grin and covering the telephone's receiver with the palm of her hand, Janet whispered, "It's your mom! What are you going to tell her about last night?"

While shrugging my shoulders and giving Janet a terse look, I took the receiver from her and spoke cheerfully into it, "Hi, Mom, what's up?"

"Hi, honey. I just missed you and wanted to see how you were doing."

"I'm great…You don't have to worry about me here."

"So, did you have a good time at the party last night?"

Janet must have overheard the question because I caught her stifling a laugh. In retaliation, I pursed my lips and squinted back at her. I then took a few minutes

316

to feed Mom minor details about the previous evening. At the same time, I kept a watchful eye on the kitchen clock, so I would know exactly when to terminate the call.

Mom actually sounded pleased that I had a good time, but not so when I told her that she called in the middle of barbeque preparation. When I told her I couldn't stay on the line much longer, the happy energy in her voice immediately disappeared. I didn't like the thought that I might have offended her, so I hurriedly promised to call her Sunday evening.

Luckily, Mom got the message that I was in a hurry to get off the phone, but disappointment still registered in her voice. "Okay, honey, I understand if you have to go. I'll look forward to your call tomorrow night. We love and miss you very much. You have fun today."

"I love you, Mom. I miss you, too. I promise to tell you everything tomorrow night, okay?"

"Okay then, I'll talk to you tomorrow. Good-bye for now."

I put the receiver back in the cradle and just looked at the phone for a minute. It dawned on me that I was beginning to feel comfortable telling Mom I loved her. In fact, the feeling was great! *I do love and miss her...and Dad, too,* I thought. *It should feel good to tell them.*

Janet jarred me from my trance. "Someone looks like he needs a hug."

"I'm okay, but I'll take one anyway."

When Janet let go of me, she wore a rather disappointed look. "You didn't mention anything about Julie to your mom."

"I'm saving that for tomorrow night."

"Why's that?"

I chuckled, "Because, it's going to take a lot longer than five minutes to break the news to her."

In truth, I had absolutely no idea how I was going to tell Mom about Julie or how my whole mindset on girls had changed. I knew that I would have to give it a decent try, but I would rather be a fly on the wall, listening to my attempt.

Suddenly, Janet and I heard Brad yell from the driveway. "Jackson! Let's go, buddy! You don't want to be late picking up your girl!"

Janet made a little too much of trying to stifle another laugh. "Last Saturday, I could have bet money that I would not hear those words in reference to you!"

I had to laugh, also. The notion struck me as a little funny, too. At the same time, it was all so incredible. The idea of it caused a minor debate inside my head: *Is she really my girl? Did last night make her my girlfriend or was she more like Lori Mudd? Was it all just casual attraction for her? Naw…it couldn't be that. She even said she had feelings for me.* Finally, I decided to put such thoughts to rest. *Relax, Romeo, and just go get…your girl.*

Brad dropped me off at the end of the Falkner's driveway, but before I climbed out of the Corvair, he asked, "Are you sure you don't want me to wait and drive you two back? It's pretty hot out and …"

"And we'll be out in it all afternoon and evening," I interrupted. "Thanks anyway, but we just want a chance to talk without having everyone else around."

"Alrighty then…I'll see you back at the house in a little while."

Brad used the Falkners' driveway to turn around and then sped off in his usual hurry. I stood and watched him leave before proceeding to the front door. I stepped up onto the landing and was about to ring the doorbell, when suddenly, almost of its own accord, the door opened. It startled me a little. That is, until I saw Lisa, Julie's younger sister, smiling shyly at me. As Lisa opened the screen door and gestured for me to come in, she giggled and said, "Hi, Jackson, come on in."

Lisa was two years younger than Julie, but well on her way to becoming like her older sister. Although Lisa's teeth seemed just a tad too big for her mouth, it wouldn't be long before she would have the same great Falkner smile. Unlike Julie, Lisa's hair was sandy brown, straight, and worn rather short. Quite noticeably, her facial features favored Gary's more than Marilyn's.

Stepping inside, I said, "Hi, Lisa, do you remember me?"

Lisa giggled shyly again and then replied, "Yeah, I remember you. Julie's not ready yet, so I'm supposed to have you wait in the living room."

As I followed Lisa, I felt a chill from their central air conditioning. The drastic temperature change, from the outside heat to the coolness of the inside, made me shudder a little.

Suddenly, Gary Falkner appeared from the kitchen with a bowl of potato chips. "Hey, Jackson, how are you? Come on in and make yourself at home. Julie will be ready in a couple of minutes, I think." He then led the way into the living room and offered me a seat on the couch. After putting the bowl of chips on the ornate coffee table before me, he settled into his leather lounge chair and picked up the *TV Guide*. As he thumbed through its pages, he chuckled lightly and said, "You might as well get used to this, young man, because for the rest of your life, it isn't going to change."

"What's that, sir?"

"You will go through great pains to be punctual and not keep a girl waiting. She, however, will go through great pains to ensure she is never ready on time."

I gave his comment the courtesy chuckle it warranted. I was too inexperienced to know that he was actually sharing an age-old truth.

Mr. Falkner must have sensed my nervousness, so he changed the subject by asking, "Are you a Twins fan, Jackson?"

"Oh, you bet, sir, even though they aren't having a very good season."

That immediately launched us into an in-depth discussion. We talked about the release of the Twins' General Manager, Bill Rigney, and compared him to his replacement, Frank Quilici, who was a former Twins player. I didn't know enough about the circumstances that led to Rigney's release by the Twins. So, I just listened to Mr. Falkner express his opinion on the matter. He felt Rigney had lost whatever it was that made him attractive to the Twins organization in the first place. Professional baseball was more of a business than a sport, so because the Twins had such a terrible start that year, Rigney paid the price by losing his job.

Mr. Falkner then asked for my opinion of Quilici. I didn't really have a personal opinion on the Twins' new general manager because I didn't know enough about him. However, like all nervous, young men, trying to make a good impression, I didn't want to sound uninformed. So, I simply repeated what Grandpa Mack had told me. "Quilici took the ball club over too late in the season to do any good.

"That's a pretty shrewd observation. So, do you think we'll do better next season?"

"The roster is getting a little old. My all-time-favorite player is Harmon Killebrew, but I don't think he has many seasons left in him. I think if we pick up some younger talent, we're still going to have a tough season next year."

Mr. Falkner appeared surprised. To me, it was obvious that he was impressed with my knowledge of the team.

"We'll have to have you over to watch a game or two with Julie and me. You know, Julie is a big fan, also."

"Yes, sir, she told me."

Suddenly, Marilyn Falkner entered the room from behind me and asked, "She told you what?"

Genuinely surprised, I immediately shot up from the couch, like someone had just lit a match and held it under my butt.

"Hello, Jackson. Relax, honey, and sit." Marilyn Falkner smiled warmly and took a seat on the opposite end of the couch. "You were saying something before I rudely interrupted."

"I was just telling Mr. Falkner that Julie already told me about her being a huge Twins fan."

"Yes, she is," conceded Mrs. Falkner. "Twins baseball is something she shares with her father. I always get too bored to sit through an entire game."

"Yes, ma'am," I politely replied, but then I had a sarcastic thought. *What do women know about baseball?*

"Don't worry, Jackson," said Mrs. Falkner, "Julie should be down in just a minute."

"Yes, ma'am," I replied again, as pleasantly as I could.

I then wished I had more to say to Marilyn Falkner, but I had no experience talking to the mother of a girl I was interested in. I had read about such social interactions, but never pictured myself being caught in one. In a word, it was... agonizing.

Just then, Julie breezed into the room, as if she were punctual and had not kept me waiting a single minute. In actuality, it was closer to fifteen, but who was counting?

As soon as I laid eyes on her, I forgave the wait. She wore a satin-finished, royal blue, sleeveless top, which was tucked into blue denim shorts. Her hair was pulled back into a ponytail and tied with a blue ribbon, which matched her top perfectly. Silver hooped earrings, much like she wore the previous night, dangled from her ears.

"Hi, Jackson, you're here already?!" asked Julie, sounding as if my timely arrival was truly unexpected.

"Jackson is a gentleman," asserted Mrs. Falkner. "He was here, right on time. Weren't you, honey?"

What's with this "Honey" stuff? The thought of Mrs. Falkner being as superficial and informal as certain family members, on Mom's side, made me even more uncomfortable. But I remained polite by again replying, "Yes, ma'am."

I couldn't take my eyes off Julie. I was pretty much in awe of her appearance and hoped that my jaw wasn't in my lap. I then reminded myself to stand in the presence of a lady. Julie looked a little surprised by my awkward gesture.

"Relax, Jackson, it's just me."

It sure is…and then some! The thought came and sort of got stuck there, like a great dream you wish would never end.

I direly wanted to be on our way, so when Julie made her final preparations to go, I felt greatly relieved. "Okay, I'm all set," she announced. "How about you?"

I imagine to this day that I must have looked rather imbecilic, standing there with a stupid grin plastered to my face, nodding in the affirmative, but not uttering a single word. Nevertheless, I was able to snap out of it and say my proper good-byes to Julie's parents.

Before leaving, we had to go through the customary exchange of instructions. "Remember you have to get up early for church," followed by, "Take a sweater because it's going to cool off tonight," et cetera and so on and so forth. I fully expected her parents to give me a few warnings, too. For example: "You had better respect our daughter, young man," and "Don't get fresh!" I expected all the things I had seen parents do in the movies or read about in books. To my astonishment, none of that took place. Julie's parents simply instructed us to have a good time and don't stay out too late. *Wow,* I thought, *Julie's parents are really cool!* Instead, I was the one who felt the need to give them some uncoerced reassurance.

"Don't worry. I'll bring her home safe."

Mrs. Falkner gave me a knowing smile and that suspicious, raised-eyebrow look.

"And, at a decent time," I added.

To that, Mrs. Falkner's smile became more genuine. "We trust you, Jackson. You two have fun."

Walking outside the Falkner's door was like stepping into a blast furnace. The heat, although not apocalyptic, was immediate and a little overwhelming. As Julie and I slowly walked down the driveway, I intentionally kept a respectable distance from her. I don't know about Julie, but I could have sworn that I felt three pairs of eyes on us.

When we turned and began our jaunt down Sunset Boulevard, Julie remained silent. That is, until we came upon a small stand of concealing, scotch pines that grew at the end of her block. Just as soon as we were behind the trees and away from any potential spying eyes, Julie came to an abrupt halt. I turned around just in time for her to grab my hand and gently pull me to her. Without saying a word, Julie let me know exactly what she wanted. She smiled sweetly, right up to the point our lips met.

Quite lovingly, Julie said, "Hi you." It was the *real* greeting she wanted to deliver earlier, but couldn't because of watchful, parental eyes.

Unable to keep from smiling, I whispered, "Hi."

"I had a very hard time waiting for three o'clock to get here," she admitted.

"That makes two of us. You look great!"

"Thank you! It took me forever to pick out what I wanted to wear for you."

"For me? You wore that for me?"

"Yes."

"Kinda like you would if…we were…"

Julie stopped me from saying more by hurriedly putting her hand up to my lips. She then lowered her eyes and touched her forehead to mine. "We need to talk about that, Jackson, but we also have a barbeque to get to. Let's walk, okay?"

I gently took Julie's hand and we stepped from the curb into the empty street. She looked at our clasped hands and smiled, like her mind had just been made up for her.

"I've been wondering if you're feeling the same as me," Julie began. "I don't know why I feel the way I do, especially since I know that you'll be gone in a week, but I do."

"The heart wants, what the heart wants." I recited the vaguely remembered line but couldn't recall where I had read it.

With an astonished look on her face, Julie gasped, "That's exactly what Momma said! Who did you hear it from?!"

"Nobody, I read it in a book somewhere. I've never really understood it, though, until just now."

"So, you do feel the same."

Julie was trying to get me to say something I truly didn't want to admit. She was definitely better at *the game* than I was. So, I thought for a second and then replied, "I don't know, you haven't actually told me how you feel."

Julie hesitated for a brief moment and then said, "No, I guess I haven't. You're gonna make me say it, aren't you?"

"You got me to say it yesterday."

Julie squeezed my hand and smiled nervously. "I've liked you for years, but you know that already. After last night, I think what I'm feeling is more than just…like."

Yep, she's definitely better at this than I am, I thought. Trying to keep pace with her ability to be truthful, I offered, "Well then, I guess we do feel the same."

"You feel that way, too?"

"Yeah."

"Really?"

"Oh, no you don't. I'm not going through *that* again." Once again, we both laughed nervously.

Julie then stopped walking and stood in the middle of the street, facing me. "Well then, I guess I should tell you that I've pretty much made up my mind.

If one week is all I get with you, I'm taking it. I don't think I could stop wanting to be with you anyway. I guess I'll just have to worry about next Sunday when it gets here."

"Can you do that?"

"I don't know, Jackson, but I'm gonna try. I do know that the one thing I can't do is ignore you for a whole week. Do you want to stay away from me?"

"No!" I exclaimed, just a little too emphatically, hoping Julie didn't pick up on my desperation. However, her look not only told me she did pick up on it, but that she wholeheartedly approved. Suddenly, I felt the need to expand and clarify my meaning. "When I first got to town, I told myself that seeing you would be a bad idea. I actually meant to stay away from you, but now I know I was wrong. I want to see you every day.

Julie nodded in agreement, saying, "So, we'll just try to make it as good as we can...Okay?"

Her eyes were hypnotizing me again and I heard myself say, "You already have. You've been my biggest surprise since I came back." *Whoa! Where did that come from?!*

"I like the way you talk, Jackson. You make me feel kinda special."

As we slowly walked on, we continued to talk. Her smile was so engaging, and I was amazed at how easy it was becoming for me to converse with her. I felt totally at ease with Julie and knew I could trust her implicitly.

When we were still blocks away from the Wilsons' house, Julie caught me looking around, like I was in search of something. "What are you looking for?" she asked.

"I was kinda hoping there would be another big tree to hide behind before we get to the barbeque."

Laughing sweetly, Julie pulled me toward her. "Do we really need one?"

"I guess not. But, you have to admit, we do pretty well around trees."

We both laughed nervously and held one another close, but just for a moment. Even though the street was deserted, I was afraid that someone might see us. At the same time, I didn't want to waste the moment. Finally, I decided that I didn't actually care if anyone saw us at all. So, I pulled her in close again.

Apparently, Julie didn't care, either. That first *real* kiss, out in the open, was positively thrilling. When it was over, I could hardly believe my good fortune. I marveled at the very idea of that beautiful girl actually wanting to be with me. It was even harder for me to comprehend how she was getting me to open up. I was now saying and doing things I never thought possible.

When Julie and I finally arrived at the Wilson's, my stomach was somewhat in knots. I just wasn't sure of the reception Julie and I would get. However, during introductions, Brad and Janet were great. Like the Falkner's, they were genuinely warm and welcoming, which helped put Julie at ease almost immediately. In return, Julie's outgoing personality served her well. In fact, when Julie wasn't looking, Brad and Janet gave me exaggerated approving looks and two thumbs up. Their approval of Julie was so animated that I had to stifle a laugh. While the four of us stood around, chatting, I was on cloud nine because Julie had a rather tight grip on my arm the whole time.

Next, Kurt and Janelle stepped up. When I introduced Kurt, he acted almost dismissive toward Julie. I knew it was his I'm-too-cool-for-primetime act and wished he would stop. All too often, Kurt's arrogance came out at the most inappropriate times. However, Janelle compensated nicely for her boyfriend's social deficiencies. She was quite charming, while complimenting Julie's outfit and earrings.

Almost as if he had been cued, Danny came out of the house to join our small group. I could always count on him to be his charming self. I watched Julie in his presence and knew they would get along famously. I also discovered that Danny was a notorious flirt, especially when his girlfriend wasn't around. I remedied that in a hurry by asking, "Is Carrie coming?" I then looked like the proverbial cat that swallowed the canary.

Danny noticeably squirmed a bit and then said, "Uh, I doubt it, little brother"

Just then, Janet excused herself and headed for the house. Julie called after her, "Can I help with anything, Mrs. Wilson?"

Janet stopped abruptly and turned on her heels. "No thank you, sweetie, but you would be doing me a big favor if you would call me either Janet or Mom."

Julie was taken slightly by surprise. She whispered in my ear, "Mom?!"

I chuckled and explained, "Just about everyone calls her Mom...You'll see."

After Janet disappeared inside, the rest of us found some shade to relax in. While we waited for the other guests to arrive, we talked on, keeping the chatter lighthearted.

Tony Milner was the first to appear and he immediately made a show of thanking me. Apparently, the barbeque was a justifiable reason for getting him out of doing some chores that he had been putting off. "Mom said it's only right that I spend as much time with you as possible, while you're in town. When you leave, though, I think I'm going to owe her...big time!"

"Glad I could help you out," I chuckled.

Dave and Anne were next to arrive. As they sauntered up the driveway, Tony said, "That just figures. Joel and Gail will be last again. I wonder who's waiting for who?"

"My money is on Gail waiting for Joel...Any takers?" I asked.

"That's a sucker's bet," chuckled Dave.

"His mom probably had him clean out the whole garage before she let him out of the house," said Tony. As an afterthought, he added, "Wait a minute, they don't have a garage!"

For the next ten minutes, we all poked fun at Mrs. Brighten's propensity for ensuring Joel's late arrival to absolutely every social gathering. At half past four, he and Gail finally showed and immediately voiced their apologies.

Now that everyone expected was in place, Brad made preparations to start the charcoal grill. Danny was the first to see him, so he offered a few words of caution. "If you guys like your eyebrows where they are, when he lights that match, you'd better stand clear."

Of course, everyone laughed. That is, until they saw Kurt, Danny, and I move our lawn chairs to the other side of the back yard. Then, in unison, we sat down, crossed our right legs over left and crossed our arms across our chests. In years past, it was the old comedy routine we three always went into come barbeque season.

Danny looked at me and laughed. "I knew you would remember."

Brad just shook his head. He was used to such shenanigans.

Just then, Janet came out of the house with car keys in her hand.

"Where you off to now?" asked Brad. "I'm about to start the grill."

"Well then, I want to get as far away as possible," laughed Janet.

Brad put on his best dejected look, lower lip dangling and all. "Everyone's a comedian today," he whined.

"I have to make a quick run," said Janet. "I'll be right back." She then hurriedly jumped into the Mercury and brought the engine to life.

When Janet cleared the driveway and then sped off, the girls suggested the rest of us work out teams for volleyball. Since there were ten of us available to play, we set about dividing the group into teams of five. No couples were allowed to be on the same team; it was the rule of the day.

As we played, I was surprised by the girl's competitiveness. I was especially tuned in to Julie's skill on a volleyball court. Janelle and Anne weren't bad either, but Gail seemed to lack the necessary coordination. Her demeanor was far too passive, possibly even squeamish. I thought it strange because I had always remembered Gail as quite the tomboy. In the past, she had always tried to best all we boys at any game. So, her docile act had to be a put on, but for whose benefit? It was another change in one of my friends that I found somewhat puzzling.

Considering the male jocks we had in the group, I was initially concerned that maybe some of the guys would get a little carried away and be ball hogs. To my surprise, the games stayed quite friendly and the laughter plentiful.

After playing two games, both teams were tied at one game apiece. However, before we launched ourselves into a tie-breaking game, we all decided to take a rest and have a pop. The girls were all flushed from the heat and exertion, so were the guys, but I didn't pay much attention to them. I took a good look at Julie, then had what I thought was an excellent idea. Running into the house, I grabbed a bunch of washcloths from the linen closet. I then ran them all under cold water from the kitchen faucet. Hurrying back outside, I began handing them out to the girls.

"Hey, what about us?" asked Danny, gesturing to all the red-faced guys. "Where's ours?"

"In there waiting for you," I replied, nodding toward the house.

When I handed Julie a cool, wet cloth, she beamed at me and said, "Thank you. This is sweet."

Janelle observed the exchange. So, when I brought a washcloth to her, she had me bend down, so she could speak into my ear. "Score one for Jackson!" she whispered, "And, thanks for the cloth."

Just then, I looked up to see the Mercury pulling back into the driveway. When it came to a halt, Janet exited the driver's side. Then, the front passenger door opened and out stepped Carrie.

"Aww, cool!" I exclaimed, then immediately walked over with Danny to greet her. Janelle wasn't far behind. As always, hugs were delivered.

When I finished welcoming Carrie, I noticed Janet had quite suddenly disappeared. So, I quickly ducked into the house to find her. Upon entering the side door, I found her at the kitchen counter lighting a cigarette. At first, Janet gave me a startled look, which then turned into apprehensiveness. I immediately went to her and gave her a big hug. "You're so cool," I whispered.

"Thanks, kiddo," she said, wiping tears from her eyes.

I heard the side door close behind me and turned to find Danny standing there smiling, but then tears welled up in his eyes. As I stepped back from Janet, Danny almost lunged at her. They hugged each other tightly.

"I'm sorry, Mom! I'm sorry!" sobbed Danny.

"I know, honey. But we're going to be okay, right?"

"Yeah, we are," said Danny, sniffling and wiping his nose.

I was extremely happy to observe the exchange. At the same time, I had a deep sense that there was something else going on than just a few hours of tension between those two. Danny was too upset, and it had nothing to do with getting caught being too intimate with Carrie. Still, whatever was going on between those two, I was sure it none of my business, so I let my suspicions die right there.

I left Janet and Danny inside to be together for a few minutes. As I stepped out the side door and onto the driveway, Carrie stopped me and threw her arms around me. She was absolutely elated. "Thank you," she said, her voice dripping with sweetness.

"I didn't do anything."

"That's not what Mom told me."

"I don't know what Mom told you, but one thing I do know, that lady doesn't do anything she doesn't really want to do."

As Carrie continued to smile, her eyes glistened. She then reached out and brushed her hand along my cheek. "You're so cool," she said softly, "And you don't even know it." Carrie then quickly jogged to the side entryway to join Janet and Danny inside.

As I walked to where Julie sat, I took note of the peculiar look on her face. It was as if she had a huge question mark on her forehead. When I pulled up a chair next to hers, I couldn't stop smiling.

"You look very pleased with yourself," Julie observed.

Sounding a bit smug, I asked, "You ever have one of those days where it seems like you can do no wrong?"

Julie replied, "No, not really."

"Me neither, but today is darn close," I said.

Without saying another word, Julie leaned over, put her hands along my cheeks and kissed me softly.

Yeah, I'm having a great day, I thought.

I bowed out of the tie-breaker volleyball game. We put Carrie in my place and traded Danny for Tony Milner. Instead of playing, I opted to help Brad at the grill. He had been quite busy cooking the chicken and ribs, so I thought he probably missed most of Janet and Carrie's arrival. He was sweating profusely, too, so I decided that he didn't need a washcloth as much as he needed a swimming pool. Hustling back inside, I grabbed a hand towel and like the washcloths, soaked it in cold water. I then grabbed a beer from the refrigerator and scampered back outside. Casually offering both to him, he smiled and nodded his thanks.

"Your parents are doing a great job," said Brad. "Who taught you that thing with the washcloths?"

"Mom...and my little league coach."

"Your little league coach?"

"Mom wears me out on how to be a gentleman around women. My coach taught me there's nothing like a cold, wet towel to help you cool down on a hot afternoon. I just sort of put the two together."

As he continued to watch over the sizzling meat, Brad nodded his approval. We also kept an eye on the volleyball game that unfolded before us. I couldn't keep my eyes off Julie or wipe the smile off my face.

"She's really something, Jackson," said Brad.

I didn't even have to look at him to know he was complimenting *my* girl.

There was more than enough chicken, ribs, potato salad, coleslaw, and baked beans to satisfy our hungry crew. When we all finished gorging ourselves, I was glad to see everyone lending a hand with cleanup. It was then time to relax in the shade and let our over-stuffed bellies digest the fruits of Brad and Janet's labor. A cooling breeze had kicked up and made for an extremely pleasant atmosphere.

Janet and Brad went to sit in the front yard, so they could smoke their cigarettes away from the rest of us. Dave and I immersed ourselves in talk of baseball. We made tentative plans for putting together another game before I left. Kurt and Danny relaxed close by but were content to just let Dave and I do the talking. Julie was off talking with Carrie, Janelle, Anne and Gail. Occasionally, I caught Julie looking my way, giving me reassuring smiles. Joel and Tony were shooting baskets in the driveway. Suddenly, I noticed Anne depart the group of girls. As she walked toward us guys, she gestured for me to join her.

I nudged Dave and pointed toward Anne. "Hey Dave, your girl wants to talk to me. Do you mind?"

Nonchalantly, Dave replied, "Naw, go for it."

As I walked in Anne's direction, I heard snickering behind me. At the same time, Anne looked at me in a curious fashion.

"What did you just tell him?" she asked.

With a straight face, I replied, "I told him you were over here hitting on me."

"What did you tell him that for?!"

"Weren't you?"

"NO!"

Struggling to keep a straight face, I exclaimed, "Oh…Sorry…My mistake!"

Anne now wore the most bizarre look, then she next asked, "By the way, what did he say?"

"He said, 'Take her, she's all yours.'"

At that, Anne scrunched up her face and squinted, like she was really going to let Dave have it. "Oh, he's gonna pay for that," she said.

I could no longer hold back my laughter, so I let it out.

Finally realizing that I was just messing with her, Anne playfully slugged me in the arm, while yelling, "JACKSON, YOU SNOT!" But she, too, broke out in laughter.

"OUCH!" I playfully yelled. "See, you are hitting on me!"

After Anne and I finished sharing a good laugh, I asked, "What did you want?"

"Oh, that! I was just going to say that I'm really glad you and Julie worked things out. It's going to be great hanging out with you guys while you're here. Yesterday and today have been more fun than we've seen around here in a while!"

"Having a good time are you?"

"Yeah, everybody is!"

We continued to talk for a little while. That is, Anne went on and on about how great she thought it was, now that Julie and I were together. Me? I pretty much just listened, smiled, and nodded my head a lot. Still, I was appreciative of Anne's excitement for Julie and me. As randomly as possible, I stole glances in Julie's direction and tried to give her my best come-save-me look. In return, Julie just laughed and stayed put with the other girls.

We have got to get our signals straight, I thought.

By dusk, everyone had grabbed a chair or sat at the picnic table. Those with chairs, formed a semi-circle at one end of the table, so everyone could be seen and heard. Brad and Janet left the front yard and joined the group, also. I loved listening to all the stories and laughter. A very comfortable feeling came over me.

Julie was being a little showy about staking her territory – me. Our lawn chairs were side by side, without an inch between the two of us. While we sat and laughed at more of Tony's antics, both her arms were wrapped around my left bicep. I could not have been prouder than to have her there with me. In between some of the laughter, she leaned in and spoke softly. "Janelle told me they're going inside to play records later."

"Cool! The girls can play records and the guys can shoot pool."

"You're right," Julie replied slyly, "the guys can shoot pool if *they* want to." She then gave me an exaggerated sweet smile. "I'm just not sure how much pool playing you're gonna be doing."

In return, I gave her a surprised look. "What am I gonna be doing?!"

Even Julie's Lord-help-me look was captivating, as she exclaimed. "Please tell me you're not that dense! Boys…Geez!"

Just then, I noticed Janet trying to get my attention. She gestured for me to join her in the kitchen. So, I excused myself and followed her inside.

"Have you invited Julie to the lake tomorrow?"

"No," I replied. *Was I supposed to know to do that? Who wrote these rules?*

"I think you should ask her, especially since it's clear that girl has got it bad for you. What happened? I thought it was no girls for you." Janet then picked up her cigarettes from the counter and went through the preparations of getting ready to light one.

Knowing there was no sense in arguing Janet's point, I said, "Julie kinda took care of that plan. I wish I could tell you how it happened, but I'm still trying to figure it out myself."

"Stop wasting your time," said Janet. "It's simple…The heart wants, what the heart wants." After lighting her cigarette, she looked at me and asked, "What's that shit-eating grin all about?"

Tony Milner bowed out early that evening. Since he hadn't brought a date, he felt the need to leave us couples to whatever we were going to do. Before he left, he and I agreed to meet in the morning, so we could go to church together. Dave and Anne overheard our plans and wanted to join us. As well, Joel and Gail wished to join the group. Julie was used to going to church with her family. She had no idea what her parents would think of a request to sit with the rest of us. If she couldn't, it would still be okay. I was more than happy to settle for her coming to the lake with us in the afternoon. I had taken Janet's advice and invited her. Julie immediately asked if she could go inside and use the telephone. When she came out again, struggling to contain her smile, I knew before she spoke that Sunday was going to be another wonderful day.

When we teens adjourned to the basement to play records, true to Julie's word, I played no pool. In fact, nobody did. Instead, I took a seat on one of the two bar stools and Julie claimed the other one at my side. As much as I wanted to get comfortable and make out with her, I didn't want to assume that she was open to that idea. So, I let the others in our party have the more comfortable seating.

Janelle rifled through a pile of forty-fives and put together a mix of soft tunes. She carefully put the stack on the record player and when the first song began, she played with the volume until it provided just the right amount of romantic, background noise. She then dimmed the lights to a nice, soft glow.

While surveying the room, I couldn't help but smile at all the intimate little goings on that were taking place. Kurt and Janelle had seniority, so they took their usual place on the loveseat. Once there, they seemed to be able to simply tune the rest of us out. It was like they were in their own little world.

Danny and Carrie wasted no time nuzzling at one end of the couch. Danny never impressed me as the type of guy who would get too serious about a girl. But, when I looked at him with Carrie, I could swear I saw love written all over his face.

I laughed at Dave and Anne, who were busy trying to get situated in the lounge chair together. It wasn't built for two, but Dave pulled her down onto his lap anyway. Anne's protests lasted only as long as it took him to get her into a lip-lock. Anne calmed right down.

Gail and Joel looked to be discussing something important in the farthest corner of the den. Gail sat in one of the tall billiard chairs and Joel blocked her escape by leaning on the arms of it. *Where have I seen that before? I hope the chair doesn't break.* The thought made me almost laugh out loud.

While I smiled at the others, Julie made it clear that she had plans of her own. She scooted off the bar stool. Then, gently taking me by the hand, Julie led me to an open space between the lounge area and the pool table. "Dance with me," she softly insisted.

As we held each other close, swaying to the soft music, I thought, *I'm supposed to say good-bye to this?* While Julie and I danced on, we kissed to Marvin Gaye and Tammy Terrell singing, *Your Precious Love.*

Julie spoke softly into my ear. "I love dancing with you." She then looked deep into my eyes. "You have gorgeous eyes, Jackson. Momma says you have your mother's eyes."

Julie's compliment immediately struck me as strange. After thinking about it for a minute, I realized that I had no clear memory of my mother's physical appearance. "That's funny," I said. "It's been so long since I've seen her. I don't remember what she looks like anymore."

"Momma said that she was the most beautiful girl in school, if not the whole town."

"I've agreed to see Adam this coming week. I can only imagine what kind of stories he's gonna tell me. I suppose I should see if I can find her. That way, I can get her side of the story, too. Then, maybe I can put all that junk behind me."

In an instant, Julie's face went from serene to alarm, but then she tried to hide it by putting her head down on my shoulder.

"What's the matter?" I asked.

"Nothing," replied Julie, refusing to look up, but her distress was too noticeable.

Thinking I had screwed up already, I pressed the matter, but just a little, "That's not true, is it? Did I say something wrong?"

Julie softly replied, "No, not at all."

"Then, what is it?" I asked.

Julie then lifted her head off my shoulder, looked into my eyes and whispered, "Jackson, please, not now."

She's right, I thought. *Why ruin the mood?* However, my curious nature wouldn't allow me to let go of it entirely, so I asked, "Will you tell me later?"

Julie reluctantly nodded her head. She then touched her forehead to mine and we continued to sway to the soft music.

It was clear to me that something I had said or done had shaken Julie. The thought of it bothered me, so I lifted her chin and looked into her eyes. "Hey, whatever it is, it'll be okay." I then kissed her forehead. I had watched that particular love scene in numerous old black and white movies. Just then, it seemed quite surreal to be acting it out. In return, Julie gave me a grateful smile and then poised her lips for the kiss she really wanted.

We continued dancing and making out until my head told me to sit down for a while. Actually, it was my feet that did the talking. They were aching from all the activity of the day.

Taking up the other end of the couch, Julie and I continued to nuzzle one another. I loved the way she curled up, almost like a kitten, and held me like she was going to take a nap right there. At that moment, I had never felt more content. Just the way we held each other produced an almost intoxicating effect within me.

Kurt and Janelle stopped kissing long enough to give me approving smiles. From the other end of the couch, Danny gave me a knowing wink. I knew then that I had finally turned a major corner, not just in my eyes, but in theirs, as well. Still, there was a dim cloud hovering above me. It came from knowing the closeness I felt with Julie would be fleeting. I had dismissed whatever it was that bothered her earlier because my mind was sweetly distracted. I simply wanted time to stop. It was another night I didn't want to end but knew it eventually would.

When I announced that it was time for me to start thinking about getting Julie home, the others took the hint and made preparations for their own departure. Because Anne lived farther away than the others, I asked Kurt if he would give her a ride home.

Carrie then decided she had better get home, also. Janet had been so gracious about forgiving Friday night's foolishness, so she didn't want to press her luck.

Kurt offered to have everyone pile into the micro-bus, but there wasn't room enough for us all. Gale and Joel then decided to walk their short distances home.

The evening had cooled off more than expected. In fact, it was way too chilly to walk the seven blocks to Julie's house. Since she lived in the opposite direction from everyone else, plus there was only so much room in the van, Kurt cleverly suggested that Julie and I stay behind. He would take everyone else home first, then return and help me get Julie home. Personally, I thought it was a masterstroke on Kurt's part. With everyone gone, Julie and I would be alone, even if it would be just for a little while.

I went upstairs to thank the others for coming and to say good-bye. Julie stayed behind in the warmth of the den. When the VW van was off and away, I went back inside and checked to see where Brad and Janet were located. Brad was snoring on the living room couch and I saw a light under their bedroom door. I assumed Janet was doing some reading, plus keeping an alert ear directed toward the floor, so she could hear the goings on in the basement.

It was just a few minutes past ten o'clock and there was a beautiful girl waiting for me in the basement. *When I get home, who is ever going to believe this story? For that matter, who am I going to tell?* The thought made me chuckle to myself.

When I walked back down the steps to the basement, I couldn't help but get a little nervous. When I entered the den, I heard the music softly playing and noticed the lights had been dimmed again. Julie sat crossed legged on the couch, nervously kicking her top leg out and back. Because it was so dark, it was difficult to interpret the look on her face. I figured she was just as nervous as me. As far as I knew, neither one of us had been in that particular situation before.

Initially, I stayed by the archway that led into the room. I didn't want to take anything for granted. So, once again, I forced Julie to take the lead.

"Do you want to shoot some pool?" I asked.

"No thanks."

"You want to dance some more?" I asked, but immediately thought, *Please say no.*

"My feet are kinda tired," she replied.

I began to walk toward her and watched, as Julie then uncrossed her legs and put one of the large couch pillows on her lap. I wasn't at all sure what my next move was supposed to be until she smiled, patted the pillow, and said, "Stretch out, relax, and put your head here."

Trying to be cool about it, I slowly laid down on my back, resting my head on the soft pillow. I then casually crossed my ankles and waited for whatever came next.

I had seen that particular scene in the movies, too, but it wasn't nearly as comfortable as they made it look. *We may need to practice this one a bit,* I thought.

Julie began to lightly run her fingers through my hair. Softly, she cooed, "Close your eyes and relax. I just want to talk to you."

Doing as she instructed, I closed my eyes and let the sweet smell of her perfume, coupled with the light touch of her fingers, take me to a place I had never been before. I then let my thoughts roam. *Is this love? Is this what Shakespeare wrote about?* In no time at all, I felt my muscles relax and all tenseness leave me. *That's better,* I thought, as my eyelids got very heavy and I rapidly became drowsy.

I was barely awake when I heard Julie say, "Thank you for today, Jackson. You may not look at it this way, but as far as I'm concerned, today was my first *real* date. It was with you and it was wonderful."

Becoming more alert, I chuckled, "Was? Are we done already? Darn, I was just getting comfortable here."

Julie giggled and then continued to talk softly. "I can hardly wait to see you again tomorrow. But I already know it won't be as good as today."

"Why's that?" I inquired.

"We'll talk about it tomorrow, okay? Tonight, I just want to be like this. I just want to make you feel as special as you've made me feel."

"You are special," I said drowsily. "You have no idea." *Good Lord, what is she doing to me?!*

"There's something I really want to say to you, Jackson, but I'm afraid."

To that, my eyes popped open and I sat up. I then spun around, so I could see her face. "Julie, you can tell me anything you want."

Julie looked down for an instant, then back into my eyes. She had the most angelic look on her face. "Please, lay back down and relax," she whispered. I gladly obeyed and when I did, Julie's massaging fingers went back to working their magic on me. "Jackson, something happened today. I realized you're not like any other guy here in town. You're very different. You're not like the Wilsons, either. You're not like any of us anymore. It's like you actually know more than any guy from here. No one has ever made me feel the way you make me feel. You know? I don't think this would feel as special if you had stayed here. I think you would have been more like...Dave or Tony."

Suddenly feeling somewhat offended, I asked, "Being like them would be a bad thing? What's the matter with them? They're my friends."

"Please don't take that the wrong way. I love all our friends and you know it. I just mean...Oh, I don't know what I mean!

Once again I got up from my comfortable position. All I could think to do was smile, pull her in close, and kiss her as tenderly as I knew how.

"I don't know what's going on with me, Julie. I don't really know much of anything. I *do* know that I've never felt like this before. For some reason, I don't think I'll feel this way again...ever."

To that, she leaned in for another kiss and I felt tears on her cheeks. I gently pulled away from her. "Did I say something wrong again?"

Julie gently sniffed and said, "No, you're doing just fine."

I took my handkerchief from my back pocket. *Thanks Mom!* Then, remembering a love scene from yet another movie, I gently dried her eyes and then offered it to her. Julie accepted it and again wiped her eyes. Then, she blew her nose into it! When she tried to hand it back to me, I was more than a little confused about what to do next, to say the least. Desperately, I tried to hide my disgust. *What the heck am I supposed to do with a used booger vault?! Mom didn't cover this! What does the rule book say about this one?!*

Suddenly, Julie began to snicker. "Jackson, do you really carry a handkerchief?"

Like so many other things Mom made me do, I knew that carrying a handkerchief in 1972 was definitely *not* considered cool by my peers. I was suddenly left with no recourse but to fess up the truth. I replied, "For the past three years, Mom hasn't let me out of the house without one." Then, as an afterthought, I added, "But, don't worry, I promise...It was *clean.*"

When I heard the familiar sound of the van pulling into the driveway, Julie and I were still doubled over laughing. We quickly got a hold of ourselves and then I went to retrieve her sweater. As I held it up in front of her, I put a mock puzzled look on my face and asked, "Who was it that wouldn't let you out of the house without this?"

"That's not fair," giggled Julie.

"Maybe not, but at least I'm not going to blow my nose in it and give it back to you!"

When Kurt and Danny came downstairs, they most certainly did not interrupt a tender moment. Julie and I looked at their puzzled faces and laughed even harder.

When I walked Julie from the van to her doorstep, it was shortly before eleven o'clock. I smiled because Kurt turned off the lights and the engine to wait for my return; I didn't keep him long.

As soon as Julie and I were on the landing, we didn't hesitate to kiss. When we came up for air, Julie reached for the door handle.

I asked, "Are you cold?"

"Just a little, why?"

"You seem like you're in a hurry to get inside."

"This was such a great day. I want to get it all down in my diary before bed."

"Well, I guess I can't get in the way of that...Can I?"

Julie put her arms around my neck, and we kissed again. Then, Julie said, "You're making it too hard for me to say good night."

Not wanting to push my luck, I said, "In that case, I'll do it for you. Good night. I'll see you in the morning."

While Julie fumbled around in her purse for her house key, I opened the storm door for her. When she found her key, I gently took it from her and unlocked the door. It was another one of those old-fashioned gestures that took Julie by surprise. "You're such a gentleman," she kidded. Julie then gave me one more kiss, but just a quick one, before entering the house. As she slowly disappeared behind the door, I stood there, watching her eyes until the door was completely shut.

On the way home, Kurt did not drive like he was in a hurry. Instead, he took his time, so we could talk.

"Yeah…I think you got that fear-of-girls thing licked."

I laughed, "I knew you weren't gonna let it go."

"Are you kidding?! No way!"

I thanked him for driving everyone home. I also thanked him for providing me the alone time with Julie.

"Regardless of what it looked like when you and Danny came in, the time wasn't wasted.

"It all just kinda comes natural, doesn't it?" Kurt joked.

"I don't know about that," I replied. "I've never been here before."

Kurt immediately put a disgusted look on his face. "Oh God, you're not falling in love with her…Are you?!"

"Well…kinda. I don't know. It's my first time." All of a sudden, I didn't feel as confident as I did a few minutes prior. I looked down at my lap and fidgeted with my hands. "How am I supposed to know?"

Kurt was silent for a moment and then said, "I think you are." His tone told me he wasn't making fun of me. "When it's your first time, I think you're supposed to fall head over heels. But if you tell anyone I said that, I'll call you a liar."

I felt better knowing Kurt understood, so it wasn't difficult making the promise. I figured it was a small favor to ask, just to help preserve his overly-inflated macho image.

I spent the rest of that ride home in a daze. Kurt kept making fun of me, but I barely heard a word he said. Instead, my mind was on Julie. I suddenly remembered how she reacted to my idea of trying to find my mom.

Kurt parked in front of the house and set the parking brake. However, before he could climb out, I stopped him.

"Kurt, what do you know about my real mom?"

At first, Kurt just looked at me with an expressionless face. Then, sounding a little peeved, he said, "I'm not going to talk to you about her."

"Why not?" I insisted.

"Because I promised Mom and Dad that I wouldn't. Listen, sometime while you're here, Mom and Dad are gonna talk to you about some things. Some of those things might be hard for you to hear. Mom and Dad feel they should be the ones to tell you, not me or Danny. I'm okay with that, too. That's why we keep dodging your questions. Why can't you just relax for now and stop worrying about that stuff. Everything's gonna be okay. Tomorrow at the lake, let's all just have a good time and save the serious crap for later. Just think about the good stuff for now. Think about Julie." When Kurt opened his door to exit the van, the domed light on the ceiling revealed his sincere smile.

When I finally got to bed that night, my mind was still traveling at Mach-one. Too many things had happened that day and from Kurt's words, so much more was going to happen in the days ahead. I didn't have enough information to know whether I should be worried or not. *What's gonna be so hard for me to hear?*

I rapidly got tired of pondering the unforeseen, so I switched my thoughts to Julie. Just a few days prior, I could barely speak two words to her without turning red. Now, I had kissed her out in the middle of the street! *How did she do that? How did she make me want to do that?* I then heard Danny roll over in his bed.

"I can hear you smiling from over here," he chuckled. "Knock it off and go to sleep. You have to get up early for church."

Getting up early for church and spending another day with my girl. How am I supposed to get to sleep? *How am I going to explain all of this to Mom tomorrow night? Will I even try? Maybe I should wait until the long drive home. Lord, right about now, any help you can give me would really be appreciated.* Sometime in the wee-morning hours, my brain finally shut down.

Chapter 16

Sunday, 13 August 1972

Father Michael looked a little sleepy during early Mass. I was fighting that same battle myself and his lengthy sermon wasn't helping. Julie noticed my drowsiness before the service even began. As seven of us piled into one pew, she observed, "You didn't get much sleep last night…Did you?"

I gave her a fake disgruntled look and whispered, "No, not really. And it's all your fault."

She smiled and whispered back, "I get to blame you for some of that, too."

Julie may have lost some sleep, but she sure didn't look it. That morning, she wore an attractive white, short-sleeved blouse, tucked into a powder blue floral-patterned skirt. Instead of knee-high stockings, Julie wore pantyhose. Brown, moderately-heeled pumps completed her ensemble. Her look was conservative, but I was still taken in by her youthful beauty.

I was proud to be seen with Julie in church. In addition, I wasn't the slightest bit surprised that her parents allowed her to join the gang and me, just grateful. Like the previous Sunday, Julie's family sat just a few rows ahead of us. Throughout the Mass, Lisa kept sneaking looks over her shoulder, making sure she wasn't missing out on some sort of fun.

I was determined to be mature and act respectable in church. I thought it was enough that Julie and I simply sat next to each other. That alone was never aloud at St Joe's, not when I schooled there, anyway. As the St. Joe's nuns used to say, "No hanky-panky allowed." However, it became very apparent to me that Julie had other thoughts.

During Father Michael's sermon, my loss of sleep from the previous night, coupled with the rising heat within the church, seriously led me into temptation. That is, I was tempted to take a nap. I was struggling mightily to keep from nodding off, when suddenly, I felt Julie gently slip her arm through mine and take my hand.

Okay, I'm awake now! The thought raced through my head, as I gave her a questioning look. The look she gave me in return was subtle, but I could tell she was quite content to be sitting in church that way. Her closeness made me feel slightly self-conscious, but I was now getting used to her bold maneuverings.

For the rest of Father Michael's sermon, I stayed somewhat alert. I just never heard a word he said because my mind kept wandering elsewhere. I remembered sitting through other church services with my friends, but those memories already seemed old to me. It was as if they had happened ages ago, when in fact, it had been but a few years – a mere blink in time.

During my days at St. Joseph the Worker Elementary, when attending any church function, we boys sat opposite from the girls. Girls on the right, boys on the left, it was an unbroken rule that no kid challenged. When we kids attended Mass together, intermingling of the sexes was simply not allowed. Joel, Dave, Mike, Tony, and I always sat together during school day services. We loved going to church back then. Anything that got us out of class was fine with us. More times than not, though, a supervising nun had to split us up. It was generally due to us horsing around during service and lacking any attention span to whatever Father Michael might be preaching.

Suddenly, I remembered how Tony used to indiscreetly fart in church. He always seemed to have gas brewing and would then let it rip, right when we were supposed to be praying in silence. BBBRRRAAAPPP could be heard from wall to wall! Because his flatulence reverberated off the wooden pew, Tony proved many times that St. Joe's had phenomenal acoustics!

When that memory popped into my head, it was all I could do to keep from laughing out loud. To keep from bursting out, I held my breath and closed my eyes. I even pinched myself to help keep my laughter contained. I don't know why passing gas in church seemed so funny, but just then, the thought of Tony's inappropriate behavior tickled me plenty.

Julie saw me struggling to keep my composure and looked at me like I was from outer space. "Are you okay?" she whispered.

In response, I simply nodded and smirked. Since Tony was sitting just to my left, I didn't dare look at him for fear of what I might do. Luckily, I was finally able to get that particular memory out of my head.

My mind moved on to when we all were in the third grade and preparing for the sacrament of our First Communion. For that particular ceremony, the girls had to wear little, lace veils on their heads. It was a source of mockery for certain girls. Gail was always my target. She once kicked me in the shins after practice for telling everyone that her veil looked like a used snot rag. Back then, it seemed like Gail was always giving me a well-deserved kick for some asinine prank or comment. With that memory firmly planted in my head, I looked down the line of us at Gail. She caught me and gave me a questioning look in return. All I could do was smile at her.

I remembered many other activities that took place in the school yard, usually during recess. Baseball wasn't allowed to be played on the asphalt school yard, but softball was. My favorite nun was Sister Marie Patrick. She was younger than the other nuns in her order and played softball with us often. She usually stayed inside the white painted pitcher's circle and pitched for both teams. It was during one such game that I hit a ball directly into Sister Marie's stomach. "OOOFFF" was the noise she made when the ball struck her middle.

Immediately dropping the bat and running to her in a panic, I cried, "I'm sorry, Sister, I'm sorry! Are you alright?!" I was frantic with worry.

"I'm alright, Jacky," said Sister Marie, but she stayed slightly bent over, like she was trying to catch her breath. She then nonchalantly reached over, picked up the ball, and with a criminal smile, tagged me with it, loudly exclaiming, "You're out!"

When my mind returned to the present, melancholy feelings set in. Allowing those wonderful memories to flood into the forefront of my mind, reminded me of my true purpose for coming to Mankato. *How am I going to say good-bye again?*

Suddenly, Julie squeezed my hand and then let it go. Father Michael had ended his sermon and it was time for a hymn. We stood and the congregation belted out, *Faith of Our Fathers*. Because of my changing voice, I kept my eyes on the hymnal and just followed along. Standing there next to Julie, you could not have paid me to chance a single note. In comparison, I remembered how I once thought Julie had a very pretty singing voice. That morning, I learned it, too, had improved, just like everything else I remembered about her.

When our small group received communion, Father Michael smiled and nodded approvingly at all of us. As we slowly stepped forward to receive the body of Christ, I could only imagine the memories running through his mind.

On my way back to our pew, I was careful not to look at Julie's parents. I didn't want to see any look that Mrs. Falkner might be giving me. So, I lowered my eyes and slowly walked with a very solemn look plastered to my face.

Once we teens were all back in our pew, the kneelers came down and my friends and I knelt to pray. As the rest of the congregation stepped forward to receive communion, I said a silent prayer for the gang. I prayed for their continued happiness, just the way Mom had taught me years prior. Like so many other things we would not do together in the years ahead, I knew we would probably never be together in church that way again. The thought saddened me and once again my heart ached for what I could not have.

A few more prayers, a closing hymn, and the service finally concluded. Since the ushers emptied the church from front to back, Mrs. Falkner got her chance to give me a suspicious-mom look. However, as they passed by on their way down the aisle, I relaxed when she just smiled warmly and informed Julie they would wait for her by the church's entrance.

I was beginning to like Julie's mom. Her dad presented me with no big concerns and Lisa was barely a consideration, but I was warned about Marilyn Falkner. I was grateful that Janet's warnings were unsubstantiated. After Mom and Janet, I was beginning to think that Marilyn Falkner was one of the nicest ladies I had ever met.

The gang and I greeted Father Michael on the way out, but as he shook my hand, I held my breath. I was afraid he would let too much information fly freely in front of the others. But, like Mrs. Falkner, Father Michael helped put me at ease.

"Good morning, Jackson. I'll be contacting ya soon, lad."

"Sure thing, Father…and have a nice day." I then exhaled and looked around to see if Adam Harris was anywhere in the vicinity. He wasn't, so I relaxed even more and made for the exit.

True to her word, Marilyn Falkner, along with Gary and Lisa, waited just outside the entrance door. They all greeted Julie and I with bright smiles. Before parting ways, we engaged in a little small talk.

"So, what time will you be by to get Julie?" asked Mrs. Falkner.

"We'll be there around eleven thirty, ma'am. We'll be going to Lake Crystal."

"Well, the day is definitely going to be hot enough for it," piped in Mr. Falkner. "Can you believe it's supposed to be almost ninety today?"

I asked, "Are you staying inside and watching the game this afternoon?"

Mr. Falkner chuckled and said, "I sure am. It'll be way too hot, so the yard work can wait another day or so. Are you two going to catch the game on the radio?"

"Yes, sir! I have a small transistor radio my parents gave me. It comes in handy when I can't catch the game on TV."

Mrs. Falkner asked, "Jackson, can we offer you a ride home, honey?"

Pointing at the five teens standing off a ways, waiting for me, I replied, "No thank you, ma'am, I'm walking with those guys." I then turned to Julie. "I suppose I'd better get going before it gets too hot. See you in a little while?"

Smiling beautifully, Julie replied, "Okay." She then gave my hand a squeeze, but I knew what she really wished for.

Sorry Julie, not in front of your parents. No way! The thought almost made me laugh out loud. Instead, I simply squeezed her hand, too, and then ran off to join the gang.

At first, our walk home was filled with laughter. Gail asked what I had been smiling about during Mass, so I shared some of the memories I came upon during the sermon. Everyone laughed and added more stories I hadn't thought of. But, when they started telling stories about things that took place after I had moved, it was difficult for me to join in the fun. Because I hadn't been with them, I couldn't get the mental pictures. So, when they were all laughing, I was only able to put on a fake smile or give them a courtesy chuckle. I was too busy wishing I had been part of those times.

It was just after nine o'clock when I got back to the house. I noticed the VW van was already missing from its normal parking spot on the street. As soon as I stepped in the side door, the smell of fried bacon filled my nostrils. Brad and Janet were still at the kitchen table drinking coffee.

"Hey, kiddo," said Janet. "Did you eat?"

"Yeah, I ate before I went to church, but is there any of that bacon left?"

"Yes, there is," replied Janet. "Would you like some eggs to go with it?"

"Sure!"

Janet grinned and said, "Well, there's the pan and there's the stove. Go change your clothes first."

I immediately ran upstairs and did as I was told. Outside, it had already heated up drastically and the upstairs bedroom was beginning to get stuffy. It was going to get a lot hotter before the day was over. The bedroom would then be unbearable. An afternoon at the lake was definitely in order. Since lake swimming was on the agenda, I dressed accordingly.

Back then, guys didn't really wear swim trunks, unless you were going to a public swimming pool. For lake outings, we just wore cut-off jeans and a t-shirt. Many times, girls wore the same, with one proviso, of course; they wore a swimsuit underneath, too.

After changing, I immediately felt a lot more comfortable. I headed back to the kitchen to make myself a second breakfast. Even though I had a bowl of cereal before going to church, the eggs and bacon sounded great.

While I was frying eggs and making toast, Brad came back to the table. He asked, "Are you ready for a full day?"

"Yeah, I guess."

"This is going to be one for the books, you three boys *and* your girls. I remember when it used to be five of us. Now there's going to be eight."

"Yeah, it seems a little strange to me, too."

"It's not strange, Jackson. It's just the way things change and how fast they seem to do it."

"Where are Kurt and Danny now?"

"They and the girls are probably halfway to the lake by now," replied Brad.

I turned and gave him a questioning look.

"We sent them out there early to get us the good spot. You remember...that shoreline, with the tree and the rope, where we always used to picnic and swim." Brad then pointed to his thinning hair and added, "I need shade and there's plenty of it there!"

As Brad talked on, Janet came back into the room and sat down at the table. Suddenly, it got awfully quiet. There seemed to be something on both their minds, but neither one volunteered to speak up. It had a very uneasy feel to it.

"What's up?" I asked.

Janet just looked at me for a moment and then said, "Kurt told us you were asking about your mom last night."

"Yeah," I said flatly. "He told me you made him and Danny promise not to talk to me about her."

"Yes, we did," said Brad. "We feel we should be the ones to talk to you about her."

My curiosity was now beginning to peak, so I decided to press the matter. "So, what about her?"

"Jackson, please, not now," replied Brad, his patience with me noticeably dwindling.

As far as I was concerned, that was the last straw. I was tired of being put off. In a somewhat exasperated tone, I said, "You know, that's exactly what Julie said last night, when I mentioned that I should try to find my mom. Kurt and Danny can't talk because they promised. Now you two don't want to talk. Everybody knows something about her except me. Why is everyone so afraid to talk to me about her? Are you *that* afraid to tell me?"

"YES!" Janet almost yelled, making me jump a little. She must have realized she startled me because her tone then got calm. "We're terrified."

"Why?"

"Because we're not sure how you're going to react when you hear it," replied Janet. "We're not sure how you may still feel about her."

"I don't think I really have any feelings for her anymore, if that helps you out."

"It doesn't," countered Brad, "but since you seem determined to do this right now, we'll tell you."

I put the fried eggs, toast, and bacon on a plate and joined them at the table. I started in on the eggs and shoveled it in as if I were starved. In actuality, my stomach was in knots, but I didn't want them to know. I needed them to tell me about my biological mother, so I could finally stop thinking about her. However, at the same time, I wasn't totally convinced I was ready for the news. There had been too much suspense leading up to it. As I chewed on a strip of bacon, I alternated between the two, looking them both in the eye. I wanted them to believe I could handle the information, whatever it was, like it was no big deal. I wanted to play it straight and unemotional. I could then digest it all later in private. Then, I noticed tears welling up in Janet's eyes. So, as Brad prepared to speak, I held my breath.

At first, Brad's gaze seemed to be fixed on the ashtray in front of him. Then, his eyes found mine and in a flat tone, he said, "Jackson, your mother is dead. She died the year after you were adopted."

For a moment, I let the words sink in and felt somewhat strange that there seemed to be no immediate shock. Nevertheless, my stomach was now churning from all the suspense, but I didn't want Brad or Janet to think I was upset in any way. So, before I spoke again, I finished eating what was left on my plate. Then, as nonchalantly as possible, I asked, "Was she sick?"

Janet answered, "In a manner of speaking, honey, I suppose you could say she was. You see, she killed herself."

I finished my glass of milk and sat for a few seconds, blinking and concentrating on my breathing. Now, my stomach was not cooperating at all. Suddenly, I became extremely queasy, like the milk I drank had just gone sour. When I realized the food I had just consumed was not going to stay down, sweat broke out on my forehead. *Damn it!*

In a flash, I bolted from the table and ran for the bathroom. In the same instant, I heard Janet yell after me, "Jackson! Brad, go after him!"

When I emptied the contents of my stomach into the toilet bowl, Brad was right behind me with his hand on my back. When I was able to calm down and keep from retching further, Brad began to massage my stomach muscles, to keep me from cramping further.

I was barely cognizant of the fact that I was also crying. "I'm okay," I sobbed.

Janet tried to hand me a cold, wet washcloth. I took in huge gulps of air trying to recover. Brad held me to him tight and Janet's hand was on mine. There, we three crouched for a little while. They held me until I regained control. In a short time, the anvil lifted from my chest and I was able to think clearly again.

"I'm okay now," I said, as I continued to calm my breathing.

Janet asked, "Are you sure? Do you think you can get up?"

Forcing a smile, I said, "Yeah, if a couple of grownups get off me."

Brad and Janet left me there, so I could clean up and brush my teeth. While washing my face, I tried to keep my mind blank. The cold water had a healing effect. It helped me regain my wits. After I finished cleaning up, I went to the kitchen and sat back down at the table where Brad and Janet awaited me.

Choosing my next words carefully, I said, "I'm sorry I put you through that. I honestly didn't know I would react that way to any kind of news about…her. I don't know why it hit me that way, but I'm okay now. I actually feel better. Now, I know why Julie looked at me so weird last night."

Janet asked, "What do you mean?"

It had all become very clear to me. So, I told them about the look Julie gave me, while dancing in the basement, and about her reluctance to tell me what she knew. Even Kurt's evasiveness made perfect sense to me now. However, I hated that they all felt the need to keep the truth from me. So, I took a deep breath and said, "I'm not going to run around acting all torn up about this. She doesn't matter to me anymore. She did once, but not anymore."

"All evidence to the contrary," said Brad, as he nodded toward the hallway, where the bathroom was located.

"I don't know what that was all about," I said. "Nerves maybe, but I'm done with it."

"Remember what I told you at lunch yesterday," Brad instructed. "Don't harden your heart, buddy. Take some time with this. We'll help if we can. Just... think about it."

I simply nodded my head and looked up at the clock. Soon, it would be time to go get Julie. I needed to get my portable radio and beach towel from the bedroom, so I got up and headed toward the stairs. As an afterthought, I turned and gave them a straight-faced look. "You can tell the others I know now. But would you also tell them I don't want anyone feeling sorry for me. I'm going to treat this the way it should be treated. It's no big deal. What she did, she did to herself. It's in the past and it has nothing to do with me."

Their looks of concern were not wasted on me, so I flashed them a smile, then turned and flew up the stairs.

The short ride to the Julie's house was way too quiet. The air was thick with tension, so I decided to break the silence. "Will someone please say something?"

"If you're okay, then so are we," said Janet. There was no emotion in her tone.

I leaned forward from the back seat and kissed her cheek. "I'm fine Mom... breathe." It was a lie, of course, but there was no way I was going to blow a perfectly good day at the lake. I was ready to do anything to keep from letting myself drown in self-pity, especially over a woman who had freely given me up years ago. There would be plenty of time to figure out how I truly felt, but it would have to wait until later. What I needed was a sweet distraction. She was getting closer every second.

We picked Julie up promptly at eleven-thirty. I was surprised to find that she was actually ready and waiting for our arrival. When she squeezed between the cramped space between Janet's seat back and the door opening, to get into the back seat of the Corvair, I held her beach bag. After handing it to her, I, too, labored a bit to get back inside.

Once we were both seated, Julie leaned over, kissed me, and then exclaimed, "Hi!"

Almost immediately, I felt my day was about to get back on track. At that moment, Julie's smile and the sparkle in her eyes were fully appreciated.

Brad asked, "You two set back there?"

"All set here," I replied.

I wasn't sure how Julie felt about rocket sleds, but we were about to find out. In a restrained display of safe vehicular operation, Brad carefully backed out of the Falkners' driveway.

"You might want to hang onto something," I advised Julie.

In return, she gave me a sly smile and almost whispered, "Like you, for instance?"

As soon as we were out of sight of Sunset Boulevard, Brad dumped the clutch and pinned Julie and I a little deeper into the cushion of the back seat – he was showing off again. I thought Julie would be horrified. Instead, she looked absolutely exhilarated.

The hot wind blasting us through the open windows was better than no wind at all. Between the throaty-exhaust noise of the car and the sound of the wind, it was impossible for any meaningful conversation to take place. Although, I did hear Janet, once or twice, try to get Brad to slow down.

As we sped past New Ulm – a small township directly to the west of Mankato – I remembered other drives to Lake Crystal. Julie held my hand, but her attention was taken up by everything that passed outside her window. I relaxed and let my thoughts drift. That trip felt totally new to me. Mostly, it was because of the beautiful girl sitting next to me. Periodically, I snuck short glances her way. I saw how she appeared thoroughly at ease, like nothing could possibly bother her. Once again, I found myself wishing I could be a little more like her. I still hadn't fully recovered from that morning's news about my mother's suicide, but I didn't want to dwell on it. I wanted to keep that all inside and away from Julie. I then looked down at the dainty hand, which seemed to fit so perfectly in mine, and wondered how something so simple could electrify me so. When I looked up, Julie turned and looked me right in the eye, but said nothing. She simply swiped some windblown strands of hair from her face and smiled, like she was feeling exactly the same thing as me.

CHAPTER 17

By anyone's standards, Lake Crystal is not a large body of water. It is very small and has a tiny, resort town situated along its western shore. Of course, the town goes by the same name. Just east of the lake itself, Brad turned off Highway 60 and headed us onto County Road 114. We traveled south on that dusty, gravel road for a couple of miles. It then curved around to the west and became Englewood road. Englewood took us to the south end of the lake and to the area where we had, in the past, spent many leisurely days, picnicking and swimming.

Brad spotted the VW van, which was parked near a stand of trees, but Kurt, Danny, and the girls were nowhere in sight. When Brad finally brought the Corvair to a complete stop, close to the van, a surge of anticipation ran through me. The ride out had been quite warm, so I was in a hurry to get into the water and cool off.

As I climbed out of the car, then helped Julie with her bag, I remembered the sandy shoreline at that location. It was perfect for wading and hunting freshwater clams. So, after stretching a bit, to get the kinks out, Julie and I jogged toward the beach. As we approached the water, I notice the lake had a subtle chop on the surface. It had been created by the warm, afternoon breeze. I then saw four heads bobbing up and down in the water. Their laughter traveled well across the low-level swells.

Not wasting any time, I pulled my t-shirt over my head and tossed it off to the side. When I turned my back toward Julie, I heard her gasp behind me. Without having to give it much thought, I knew that she was reacting to the sight of my scars. For the first time in a long time, I had actually forgotten about them. Not wanting to give Julie time to ask any uncomfortable questions, I quickly discarded my tennis shoes and then ran into the lake, loudly crashing through the shallows. As soon as the water was deep enough, I dove under. The lake was colder than I had anticipated, so relief from the noontime heat was immediate. When I surfaced, I allowed my body to relax and take in the deliciously soothing coolness. Floating on my back, I observed a few wisps of clouds in the afternoon sky. Then, it occurred to me that Julie was taking her sweet time about getting into the water.

Wondering what was taking my girl so long, I looked back toward the shore. When I did, it was just in time to see Julie toss her denim shorts next to our tennis shoes, which lay in an unorganized tangle. She had already removed and discarded her t-shirt. I was suddenly seeing Julie as never before. I don't know if it was the chill of the water or seeing her in a swimsuit for the first time, but the experience was breathtaking. My eyes drank in Julie, daintily testing the water temperature with her toes. She wore a bright yellow, single-piece swimsuit, which, in the afternoon sunlight, accentuated her tanned body beautifully. In an instant, I was able to assess that her physical development was ahead of other thirteen-year-old girls I knew. Julie already had ample breasts, which gave her a slight voluptuous appearance, and her musculature was well toned. It was now clear for me to see that she was no longer that flat-chested girl I remembered from elementary school. To me, Julie appeared quite sexy, but I was also surprised at the revelation. I simply had never thought of her in that vein before. My eyes were now locked on her and I couldn't stop staring; the laws of attraction were definitely in play. As well, Julie acted as though she was in no big hurry to join me in the water, almost as if she actually wanted to give me a good look. I didn't mind at all the seemingly excessive amount of time she was taking because I was, most assuredly, enjoying the scenery.

Watching Julie had kept me so distracted that I didn't see or hear Kurt sneak up behind me. When I did sense his presence, it was far too late. He immediately grabbed me from behind, pinning my arms to my sides. I was about to become fish bait and I knew it. I had just enough time to take in one big breath of air before Kurt very forcefully took us both under.

Anytime Kurt and I wrestled, he always overpowered me and got me into some unbreakable hold. However, there was a key to unlocking those holds. I simply let my body go limp and refused to struggle. Kurt always hated it, too, when I refused to put up a fight because it ruined his fun. So, as Kurt held me under the water, I thankfully remembered that key. I let my entire body relax, then, just as I predicted, Kurt let me go and we both came to the surface, laughing.

"You need to grow eyes in the back of your head," laughed Kurt. "What were you looking at anyway?"

I discreetly motioned toward shore and asked, "Any more questions?"

When Julie was finally ready to join us in the water, I had visions of her entry being a lot daintier than mine. I pictured her slowly wading out into the cool water until it was up to her waistline. She would then dive gracefully under, causing barely a ripple in the water. However, my girl destroyed that daydream in a heartbeat. When Julie ran into the water, she screamed loudly, splashing and causing a great disturbance. When she dove under, I continued to look in that direction. Suddenly, Julie broke the surface directly in front of me and playfully spit a mouthful of water in my face. She then put her arms around my neck and laughed loudly.

Kurt winked and nodded at me. "Yep, you definitely got that fear-of-girls thing licked."

Just down the shoreline from where we parked, a monstrous mountain ash tree tilted out over the water from a small rocky cliff. Years prior, a large rope had been tied to one of the upper limbs. From a washed-out embankment along the shore, a person was able to swing way out, let go at the apex, and fall approximately twelve feet into deep water. I was glad to see an old rope still suspended from that tree. That afternoon, we introduced Julie to the thrill it provided.

In 1968, it took me almost ten minutes to work up enough courage to swing from that tree for the first time. I was only nine years old then and had just completed swimming lessons. However, I still didn't have a lot of confidence in my aquatic abilities. Danny had to triple-dog dare me, and Kurt had to actually put me on the rope before I gave it my first try. So, when Julie didn't hesitate one second before swinging out for the first time, you could have knocked me over with a feather. I couldn't help but be impressed by her fearlessness. Everything about her seemed to take my breath away. While watching her enjoy the rope swing, I simply shook my head, feeling absolutely stupefied.

During a quick lunch of cold-cut sandwiches, chips, and pop, Kurt and Danny took the opportunity to tell embarrassing stories about me. They even told the girls about the time I spent almost an entire day pretending to be Danny's servant robot. I was only eight years old then and unsure of whether there was a real bond between we three boys. Brad and Janet were gone that entire day and had put Kurt in charge. He spent the day trying to order Danny and me around, so we made a game of it. I became Danny's robot and whenever Kurt would give Danny an order, Danny would direct me to carry it out. After hours of watching me move about the house, impersonating a rigid-metal man, Kurt decided that enough was enough.

I had literally been waiting on Danny hand and foot, so Kurt instructed me to stop. But Danny had already told me that my programming only allowed me to accept orders from him. So, I ignored Kurt's instructions.

I was busy retrieving a plastic drink glass from Danny. My orders were to take it to the kitchen. Intending to put a stop to our nonsense, Kurt stealthily crawled up behind me. He intended to take me down, pin me, and then tickle me until I gave in to his demands. After taking Danny's glass and holding it out stiffly, I performed a rigid about face, just like a soldier. Right when Kurt made a grab for me, but my outstretched hand with the glass struck him harmlessly on the side his head. In exaggerated surprise, Kurt toppled over and laid there on the floor, laughing uncontrollably. Without breaking character, I simply toddled off to the kitchen, leaving Kurt and Danny in hysterics behind me.

Over the years, I laughed about that incident to myself on several occasions. It was the one time that Kurt did not get his way at my expense. We all laughed about it again that afternoon.

As we all digested lunch, Kurt and Danny told a few more stories. It was clear their objective was to embarrass me in front of Julie. The only thing they actually accomplished was to validate the brotherly bond between the three of us.

When Kurt and Danny showed no signs of letting up, I noticed a look of concern cross Janet's face. Her frown told me she thought they were going a bit too far, but I just smiled and waved her off. Nevertheless, she interrupted Danny and threatened to start telling stories about the two of them. Immediately, Kurt and Danny turned their attention back to their sandwiches. They knew, as did I, that Janet had way too much ammunition to use against them.

While we all relaxed in the shade, Brad did what he was famous for. He just sat back and laughed at the antics of everyone else. I got the feeling that, sometimes, it was what he enjoyed most. He was also trying to pay close attention to the baseball game that he had tuned in on the car radio. At the time, the Minnesota Twins were maintaining a one-to-nothing lead against the California Angels.

Suddenly, Julie decided she had heard enough from Kurt and Danny. Giving me a playful shove, she said, "Let's grab that radio of yours. We can go down by the water, get some sun, and listen to the game."

Because of Julie's request for alone-time, smiles spread across everyone's face. Feeling a little self-conscious, I did as she asked and retrieved the small transistor radio that I had left in the Corvair. Besides the radio, I also grabbed Brad's old, olive-drab, government-issue blanket from the trunk of the car. Julie grabbed her beach bag and with a quick, "See ya," to the others, we made our way toward the sandy beach.

Letting Julie pick a decent spot for us to set up, I then went to work, trying to find the game on the radio.

As Julie spread the blanket out on the sand, she stated, "Kurt and Danny like to pick on you a lot...Don't they?"

More interested in tuning in the game than answering Julie's query, I absent mindedly replied, "They weren't picking on me. They were just having a little fun. Believe me, if they had actually been picking on me, you'd know it."

When I had the game satisfactorily tuned in, Julie and I spread our beach towels on top of the scratchy, wool blanket and then sat on them. Then, Julie almost ordered me to take off my shirt and lie down on my stomach. She wanted to put suntan lotion on my back.

Truly astonished, I asked, "Are you kidding?!"

"No," Julie replied confidently. "How else are you going to get lotion back there?"

Feeling that Julie was putting on a show for my benefit, I hesitated, but then I did as she instructed. Thoroughly uncomfortable with putting my back on display, I could only imagine the squeamish thoughts going through her mind.

Julie, disregarding anything she might have actually felt about my scars, knelt beside me. She then squirted lotion onto my back and began to massage it in. She took her time and rubbed the lotion deep into my already tanned skin. As she did, I relaxed and enjoyed her attentions. Slowly, I became less and less concerned about what Julie might be thinking. That is, until I heard her voice above me.

"Jackson?"

"Yeah."

"How did you get these scars?"

Not wanting to give any lengthy details, I replied, "They're just some souvenirs left from when I was little."

"They look like they were once very bad. Does it still hurt?"

I lied by saying, "All that pain went away years ago."

"You're not going to tell me...Are you?"

"Someday, maybe, but I don't want to ruin a good day with that kind of talk." I then turned my head in the direction of the parked vehicles, but couldn't see through some tall grass, so I asked, "Is everyone still up by the car?"

"Yep, they're all still there."

"Great," I replied sarcastically. "They won't be poking fun at me anymore today."

"Why's that?"

"Because right about now, Mom is making sure they won't want to. They're finding out that I now know about my mother committing suicide."

Julie stopped massaging my back long enough to bend down and kiss my cheek. She then resumed kneading the muscles in my back. Shortly after, I heard Julie sniffle and knew she was crying. In a hurry, I sat up and then knelt, so I could see her face. Tears streamed down Julie's cheeks and were welled up in her eyes. So, in my best soothing voice, I said, "Please don't…I'm okay…really."

"Last night, I was so afraid when I realized that you didn't know," cried Julie.

"You don't have to worry about that. I'll have to take some time to figure it all out, but not today. There's no way I'm letting any of that junk ruin my visit here. I'm definitely not letting it ruin my time with you."

To that, Julie sniffled once more and then wiped the tears from her eyes. Putting on a big smile, she gave me a quick kiss and then exclaimed, "Race you!" Julie then jumped up and ran for the water.

As I got up and followed Julie into the lake, my only thought was, *Cripes, she just put all this lotion on my back!*

After Julie and I had sufficiently cooled off, we returned to the blanket and the ball game. This time, I put lotion on her back. It was nowhere near as therapeutic as her application, but I tried. As I massaged the oily, white cream into Julie's muscles, she seemed quite pleased with my efforts. She moaned softly, "God, Jackson, that feels great."

We lay in the sun for another hour or so, turning over every now and then, so we didn't burn too bad on either side. We didn't talk too much, just dozed and listened to the Twins beat the Angels, four-to-three. Not far away, Janelle and Carrie played badminton. Kurt and Danny had also been sunning themselves and Janet napped on a blanket in the shade. As soon as the ballgame was over, I should have guessed that Brad would want to get some activity going.

As I turned over onto my stomach, I spied Brad, walking toward the beach with a football. Instead of coming all the way, he stopped in a grassy area and yelled, "Jackson! Let's get a game of two-handed touch going! Julie, will you play?"

While pointing at me, Julie asked, "Do I get to be on the opposite team from him?"

Brad replied, "That's usually the rule. No boyfriend and girlfriend on the same team."

Wearing a fiendish grin, Julie slyly said, "Oh yeah, I'll play."

In mock arrogance, I fired back, "You're not gonna be happy about that decision."

Everybody was game to play, including Janet! I was almost shocked to see that she wanted to get into the act. However, before she was able to get too rambunctious, we did have to give her a few minutes to wake up from her nap. While she did so, we all tossed the football around for a spell. It gave us a chance to loosen up. It also gave us guys a chance to see if any of the girls had any skills with a football. We knew Janet was no threat but were surprised at the agility and willingness to hustle by the other three.

During our warm-up session, Julie wanted me to throw to her while she went out for a medium-distance pass. I didn't throw the ball very hard, so she had no problem catching it. As Julie jogged back to our group, she snidely said, "That was a pretty wimpy pass. You want to try that again? This time, put a little something on the ball, will ya? That is, if you can."

As a result of Julie's good-natured jab, there were plenty of snickers and cat calls aimed at me.

I was no quarterback, but when called upon, my arm *was* capable of putting some heat on a football. So, as Julie looked at me with an impish grin, I simply said, "Go again."

Julie took off running and when I let the ball fly, there was a lot more muscle behind the throw. It had good speed, but it sailed on me a bit, so Julie had to jump in order to catch it. Admittedly, when she made the midair grab, I was quite surprised. Nevertheless, the ball had a little too much steam on it. In fact, it appeared as though the football would keep going and take her with it! When Julie came down with the ball, I cringed because she landed squarely on her butt! She then appeared to perform a perfect back somersault. When she did that, I covered my eyes. *Oh God! That had to hurt!*

Thinking that my throw may have caused Julie injury scared the bejeezus out of me. However, when Julie came up on both feet, my fears were soon put to rest. And, like everyone else, I was astonished to see that she still had the ball in her hands! As Julie once again jogged back to us, we all yelled and applauded. Upon arrival, she took an exaggerated bow. She then gloated some by saying, "Close your mouth, Jackson. You'll get sand in there."

Thoroughly amazed, I trotted to her, applauding as I went. When I got close enough, I discreetly said, "That was great, but are you okay?" I was afraid she may have hurt herself and was hiding the injury.

Julie put her arms around me, then spoke softly in my ear, "I'm fine, but I'm gonna get you for that one, Dreamboat."

Did she really just call me Dreamboat?! I fought to keep from laughing at her embarrassingly ancient term of endearment. Instead, taking it all in stride, I coolly said, "We'll see."

The eight of us split into two teams. Brad, Danny, Janelle, and Julie, lined up against Janet, Kurt, Carrie, and me. While on defense, I was assigned to cover Danny. I loved the matchup. I knew I had enough speed to stay with him, but I wasn't sure I had enough stamina to keep it up all afternoon. Because of some rather ridiculous play calling, there was a lot of laughter during that game. For my part, I just wanted to show off for my girl.

At one point during the game, while my team was on defense, I lined up across from Julie and taunted her with more arrogance. "Are you ready for this?" I asked.

Quite confidently, Julie replied, "Bring it on!"

When the ball was snapped, I bolted past her, practically untouched, and tagged Danny for a ten-yard loss.

As I walked back to my team's huddle, Julie yelled, "JACKSON…YOU BOOGER!"

On their next offensive play, I once again blew past her, but this time the joke was on me. Julie let me pass her by and then took off downfield. When I realized that I had been suckered in, I turned around to pursue her. Danny, who was playing quarterback, threw a quick pass to Julie. While the ball was in flight, I got a bit cocky and jumped up for it too early, so I came down emptyhanded. Julie caught the ball and scrambled for an easy touchdown. *Oh man,* I thought, *there'll be no living with her now!*

We continued our scrimmage for the next hour or so, but neither team had a clear advantage. After a while we didn't even bother to keep score. We were having too much fun to even worry about it.

When the heat had taken a little too much out of us, everyone jumped into the lake to cool off. The football came with and we attempted to carry on the game while in the water. But that became too ridiculous, so we switched games. We guys put the girls on our shoulders and had chicken fights. The object of the contest was simple, topple the other couples over and be the last team standing.

Janelle and Carrie both wore bikinis that day, but it was Janelle who had the first swimsuit malfunction. When one of her top strings accidentally came undone, I got my first real-live glimpse of a young lady's breasts. To say the least, I was thoroughly embarrassed. It was definitely an awkward moment, so I acted as though I hadn't seen a thing. Shortly after that, Kurt and Danny made a game out of trying to untie bikini strings. Sporadically, they made their attempts when Janelle and Carrie weren't paying attention. When I became too uncomfortable with Kurt and Danny's asininity, I looked toward Julie, to see how she was reacting to what I thought was bizarre behavior. I was amazed to find that she seemed to find it all quite hilarious. However, I wasn't taking any chances, so I invited Julie to join me and go swing from the rope again. In actuality, I just wanted one more chance at the rope before leaving. That, and some alone time with Julie, wouldn't be bad.

Julie and I waded to shore and then slowly walked down the beach to where the rope was staged. I grabbed it and offered it to my girl, but she insisted, "You first."

Before getting on the thick hemp, I spit out the stale gum that I had been chewing for the past hour. I then pulled way back on the rope and took a running start toward the jump-off point. At the perfect release point, I let go of the rope and attempted to do a back flip. Unfortunately, I wasn't able to get full rotation and ended up executing a horrendous belly flop. When I came to the surface, I yelled, "OUCH!"

On shore, Julie laughed uncontrollably. She then retrieved the rope. Just before swinging, she, too, forcefully spit out her gum.

I laughed and called out, "That was very ladylike!"

She giggled and then jumped on the rope. Her entry into the water was nothing like mine. She let go of the rope and straightened her body. She barely made a splash. When she came to the surface, we made our way toward more shallow water. When the water was chest high, Julie grabbed me, climbed onto my back, and demanded a piggyback ride. Acquiescing to her demand, I walked around a little, with her legs locked in place, so she couldn't get away. Then, I fell forward, taking us both under. When we surfaced, Julie laughed and exclaimed, "You're a brat, you know that?!"

"Hey, what did you expect? I'm a guy!"

Julie then came to me and, sort of, jumped into my arms. I cradled her, much like I would a load of firewood. I then asked, "Now what?"

Softly, Julie replied, "Guess." She then gently brought my face toward hers and kissed me.

Since the others were farther down the shoreline, we were, more or less, alone. The two of us lingered there and enjoyed a little make-out session. Figuratively speaking, when we came up for air, Julie's eyes absolutely sparkled. She then asked, "You ever try that under water?"

Not wanting to appear lily-livered, I replied, "Oh heck, I guess I'm game for anything." I gave Julie just enough time to take a deep breath. I then quickly moved in and began the kiss before I took us under. I don't think we were underwater for as long as it seemed, but when we came up for air, our need was literal.

Putting Julie down, so I could wipe the water from my eyes, I facetiously said, "That was interesting."

Julie asked, "How come it always looks so cool in the movies?"

I replied, "I'd be happy to stay with what's been working."

Smiling her sweet smile, Julie whispered, "Me too." She then moved in for another kiss.

Once again, I totally gave in to her lips and my heart pounded.

In just above a whisper, Julie said, "God, I love kissing you."

So, I am doing it right! The thought registered as quite comical, but then I verbally admitted, "I'm always afraid that I'm still a little clumsy at it."

Rather seductively, Julie said, "Nope, you're doing just fine."

We stayed out in the water, making out until Danny came to inform us that it was time to start drying out before the drive home – Brad was more than a little squeamish about letting wet or dirty things into his baby.

I carried Julie toward shore until she was no longer buoyant. Even though I was strong enough to continue carrying her, Julie was adamant. "Jackson, put me down."

"Okay, but it will cost you."

Julie just smiled and offered me her lips.

After I gently put Julie down, she kissed me again and a powerful feeling suddenly rocked me to the core. I had remembered other trips to the lake with my former, foster family, but I was now overwhelmed by the thought that none of those memories would ever stay with me as long as that particular Sunday would. Everything had changed. The scared little boy, who had always gotten in Kurt and Danny's way, was forever gone. The last remnants of him had been swept away by the warm touch and delicate kiss of a beautiful girl, who, like a thief, was stealing his heart. I no longer needed my foster brothers' prompting or prodding. I was now that older teen I wished to be. And, I had a girl. Kurt and Danny would never look at me quite the same way, of that I was certain.

Then, a pang of sadness hit me. I suddenly realized that time had changed everyone so much and it would again, after I left. I wondered if I would ever enjoy a day at the lake with this group again. Knowing the odds were against it, I pushed the sadness back by squeezing Julie's hand. Together, we waded in ankle deep water, walking slowly back to the others. While we took our time, my thoughts became resolute. *I don't care if I live to be one hundred years old, I don't ever want to forget this day. I want to remember everything!*

As we walked on, Julie talked excitedly, but I barely took in a word. My head was too full of thoughts about our pending departure. *Is this our last time together here?*

Julie tugged on my arm and jostled me into reality. "You haven't heard a word I've been saying…Have you?

"Sorry, I was just wondering if I'll ever see this place again."

"For you, it always comes down to that…Doesn't it?"

"Yes."

"Jackson, remember what I said yesterday. Let's just make this time as good as we can."

"Absolutely."

Although I had agreed with Julie, I knew that keeping such thoughts out of my head would be next to impossible. Every day was now becoming too important and when I left, I wanted to remember them all. However, even if I did forget some details, as I had forgotten other past events in my life, I was certain I would never forget Julie. I just knew that I would forever remember her look, our laughter, but especially the intimacy we shared at Lake Crystal.

Chapter 18

Our ride back to town was a complete blur. As I looked out the small, rear window of the Corvair, watching everything speed past, my eyelids became like lead. Julie had situated our folded, beach towels onto my lap. Using them as a pillow, she laid her head down, curled up, and fell asleep. Regardless of the heat that our bodies generated, exhaustion from the day's activities had taken its toll; we both slept almost the entire way home.

When we arrived at Julie's house, it was shortly before dinnertime. As Brad set the parking brake, Julie groggily thanked him and Janet for the wonderful day. I remembered to grab her beach bag and also made a gentlemanly show of giving her my other hand to help her squeeze out from the back seat.

As I walked my girl to her door, my mind began to dread the coming evening. I had promised Mom I would call and update her on *all* my activities. I still didn't have a clue about how I was going to explain Julie, but thanks to Janet, I knew I had to try. After all, a promise is a promise. In addition, I didn't know how I would divulge the news about my biological mother's suicide. That was something that was sure to send Mom into a panic, so I had little time to come up with some way to put icing on that cake. It wasn't something I wanted to talk about at all. Mostly, it was because I wasn't sure how I truly felt. That would take some time and thought. I still maintained that my immediate reaction to the news was purely a reflex action, which was brought on by the Wilsons' secrecy and the dramatic buildup. Brad and Janet probably thought I was devastated. In addition, I would probably have to reassure Kurt and Danny that I was okay. Then, there were their girls to consider. When I put it all together, I was fairly sure that I would be spending considerable time reassuring everyone that I was, in fact, okay and not traumatized. *Damn it! Now they're all going to tiptoe around me!*

Julie stopped at her doorstep and turned to face me. "Am I going to see you tonight?" Her eyes pleaded with me a little.

"I don't know. I have to talk to my folks back home and I don't know how long it will take. If I get everything done and it's not too late, will it be alright with your parents if I show up?"

"I have a better idea," said Julie. "I think I'm going for a walk after dinner."

"In that case, don't take too long to eat."

Julie gave me a quick kiss, said, "See you later," and then hurried inside. I stood there on her doorstep, smiling. I then rang her doorbell because I was still holding her beach bag.

When Julie opened the door to retrieve her property, she looked quite embarrassed. "Thank you," she giggled. Then, she gave me another quick kiss before saying, "I'll see you in a little while."

As I turned and walked back to the car, I took note of Janet, as she shook her head, all the while wearing the most peculiar look. I couldn't tell if it was approval or disapproval. Ignoring her, I squeezed into the back seat and kept my mouth shut.

Janet then turned around in her seat and grinned. "So, did you have a good day?"

"Nope," I replied. "I had another great day. Thank you two very much for everything you've been doing for me."

"Well, you're welcome very much," chuckled Janet. I could tell she was genuinely pleased with my sincerity.

"That includes this morning," I added. "I'm glad you told me about her. It's good that I know the truth."

With a subtle smile on her lips, Janet just looked at me. She then reached back with her left arm and held out her hand. I took it and held it but said nothing. Instead, I looked out the window at everything that passed by.

"You're a pretty tough kid," said Janet. "I guess you've needed to be… Haven't you?"

While Brad pulled into the driveway, Janet and I just looked at each other for a moment. Then, I remembered Julie's plans for that evening, so I asked, "Do you mind if Julie comes over later?"

Smiling slyly, Janet replied, "Julie will always be welcome, kiddo, within reason."

When we finished unloading lake stuff from the Corvair, Janet grabbed me and hugged me for a minute. "Are you sure you're okay about this morning? She was your mom."

I thought about it for a moment and then said, "The way I see it, you've been more of a mom to me than she ever was. If something happened to you, I'd have a *big* problem with that!"

To that, Janet squeezed me so very tightly.

"Hey! Loosen up," I grunted. "I've already thrown up once today!"

While we guys showered and changed, Janet prepared dinner. We sat down to a fried chicken dinner with all the fixins – as Dad would say. After a day at the lake, the five of us had powerful appetites. As we began to dig in, I looked around the table. In the glow of the small decorative light, which dangled above the kitchen table, I saw that a fresh layer of sun had been added to our already-tanned faces. Janet was a bit sunburned, but she didn't complain. That wouldn't come until later – she loathed being burnt and having to deal with it for days.

Dinner conversation began as a boisterous recap of the day's events. However, I knew that sooner or later, someone would want to talk about my feelings toward my mother's death. Of course, it was Danny who brought it up. So, I gave assurances to the four of them I hadn't been permanently damaged by the news. I told them I would have to do some thinking on it, but I wasn't going to let it get me down.

"That's probably smart," said Kurt. "I wouldn't dwell on something like that."

Until then, obsessing about or dwelling on things had been a large part of my many problems. So, I decided to take Kurt's advice and simply put it behind me. After all, as far as I was concerned, my mother's death truly did not have anything to do with me. I couldn't change the outcome, so why worry? Then, quite suddenly, I was absolutely certain that when I talked to Mom on the phone, I would be able to tell her everything and put her mind to rest. It had been a whirlwind week and I had plenty to share with her. I just had to be careful about how I put it. I didn't want to hurt Mom's feelings with thoughts that I would be happier in Mankato, even if it was exactly how I felt. When talking to her, I would just have to bury those feelings. As my confidence built, so did my appetite. So, I finished what was on my plate and dished up seconds.

"I'm glad we don't have to feed you on a regular basis," said Brad. "I'd have to get a second job to help pay the grocery bill."

"Hey, I'm a growing young man!" I declared.

"You are definitely that," said Janet. "It's probably a good thing Barney isn't with us anymore. There wouldn't be any table scraps left for him, not while you're here, too."

Conversation immediately switched to remembrances of the family basset hound. Barney was an obstacle who, for years, waddled around the house, getting under foot. I couldn't remember how many times I had accidentally stepped on that dog before I learned to check the floor before walking. He always appeared, right where I never expected him to be. If I was fixing something to eat in the kitchen, I immediately became his newest best friend. Barney was spoiled with attention by everyone and was hardly ever alone. When he was alone, you could visually see that he was not a happy puppy. When I moved away, saying good-bye to Barney was every bit as hard as saying good-bye to the rest of the Wilson family.

Just then, I was sadly missing Barney. Ironically, I found it strange that I felt more sadness for the passing of a dog than I did my own mother.

After dinner, Danny and I cleaned the dishes, while everyone else went to relax. Kurt was impatient to get out the door. He and Danny were taking the girls to another Sunday Drive-in movie. They invited Julie and me, but Julie was pretty sure her mom would not allow it. I didn't mind not going, especially since she would be coming over later. Just then, Danny decided to get his digs in on me. "So... what're you and Miss Julie gonna do?" he asked, "I mean, you'll have the basement all to yourselves and everything."

"I don't know," I said in my most innocent tone. "Maybe we'll just watch some TV or shoot some pool."

Simultaneously, Danny and I turned to looked at one another, then in unison, shook our heads, then gave each other an elongated, "Naw!" After which, we both laughed liked idiots. That is, until Kurt yelled for Danny to get a move on.

"Get out of here," I said. "I've got this."

"Thanks, little brother. I owe ya," he said, then threw the dishrag in my face.

Danny hustled off to change his clothes. As he practically ran up the stairs to the bedroom, I yelled an obnoxious threat to get him back. I then turned back to the task at hand. There weren't many dishes left, so taking over for Danny wasn't a very big gesture. When I finished, I found Janet to see if the coast was clear for me to tie up the phone, so I could call home. When she gave me the all-clear, I schlepped my way to the basement den.

Seating myself on the end of the love seat closest to the end table, where the phone was located, I took a deep breath before picking up the receiver and dialing. When Mom heard it was me at the other end of the line, I couldn't help but smile at the energy in her voice. "Oh, honey, I was just sitting here waiting for your call!"

"You sound like you actually miss me or something," I facetiously said.

"We do! We really do! The real question is, do you miss us?"

"I do Mom. I wish you and Dad were here."

"Really?"

"Yeah, that way you wouldn't worry because you would see that I'm having a great time."

"That's good, honey. Now, you might as well start telling me everything and don't leave out any details!"

"Geez, Mom, I'll be here all night.

"Well, you had better get to it then."

I began my recitation with a quick recap of what I had already told her about Julie's party. This time, however, I added more details that were purposefully left out earlier. I told her how Janelle and Carrie taught me some dance steps. I even told her how those lessons came in handy at the party.

"You danced?"

"Yes, Mom, I danced."

"With a girl?"

"Yes, Mom, with a girl. Actually, I've danced with quite a few girls."

"Wow! I guess I'm going to have to get used to that."

The topic moved on to the barbeque and what a great day that was. I even included dancing with Julie in the basement.

Mom exclaimed, "What?! More dancing?!" She clearly intended to torture me with the information I was relating.

"Yes," I laughed. "I'm getting pretty good at it, too."

I then told her about going to church with my friends.

"That's great, honey. To be there with your friends must have felt pretty good."

"Yeah, it really did," I happily admitted, but was plenty nervous about what I needed to tell her next. "Mom, I have to tell you something, but I don't want you to freak out."

"Okay, I'll try."

"Brad and Janet gave me some news about my biological mother this morning." I hesitated and almost decided not to proceed.

"Okay...and what might that news be?" Mom asked impatiently.

"She killed herself shortly after you and Dad adopted me."

"Oh no, that's terrible! Honey, are you okay?!"

"I'm fine, Mom. I was a little shocked at first, but I'm okay now. I know who my *real* mom is now, so I'm okay. Please don't worry about it."

"Oh, Jackson, I was afraid there would be bad news waiting for you down there."

"I'm sure there's going to be more bad news while I'm here, but it's okay. I'm handling it just fine."

I then decided to tell her about my upcoming meeting with Adam Harris, but Mom wasn't at all convinced the meeting was such a good idea. I admitted that, at first, I had shared those very same feelings, but then I also told her how I had changed my mind. "I think it's something I need to do."

"Be careful."

"Mom, stop worrying. Father Michael will be there with me."

"Really?! What's his interest in all of this?"

"He's doing it as a favor to me. I asked him to be there with me."

I continued to reassure her how everything would be on the up and up. I then wanted to change the subject and start talking about the day at the lake. As I started giving her details, I heard someone coming down the stairs. I looked up and saw Julie enter the den. She smiled, walked over, and plopped down next to me. Instead of leaning over, she pulled me to her and mischievously kissed me. I pointed to the phone and silently mouth the word, "Mom." I then continued to give Mom details of the day.

"So, Julie was with you again today?" asked Mom.

"Yes, ma'am, she was there."

"Would it be safe to say that you now have a girlfriend?"

"Yeah, I guess you could say that."

"Wow, something else I'll have to get used to. I hope you're being careful, Jackson."

"I am…I think. Right now, I don't really know what that means."

"Well, just don't get too serious. Remember, you don't live there anymore."

"It's funny you say that. We've talked about it and we both understand it, but here we are anyway. I still haven't figured out how it happened."

"I suppose it's natural at your age. It just happens. So, when do I get to meet her?"

"If you want to say hi, she's sitting right here."

To that, Julie practically ripped the receiver out of my hand. Giggling, she greeted Mom with, "Hello, Mrs. Landry?!"

Immediately, I began to squirm because I hadn't actually intended to turn the phone over to Julie. Now, all I could do was sit, listen, and sweat a little. On the other hand, Julie handled the conversation like she was talking to an old friend.

I wondered how her informal demeanor would set with Mom. As they talked on, Julie kept smiling and giggling, so I took it as a good sign.

"Truth is Mrs. Landry...Jackson and I have known each other since the second grade. I recognized him the second I saw him."

Because of Julie's comment, I gave her a suspicious look. *No, you didn't!*

Julie continued, "It's so cool having him down here again." Then, there was a pause, while she listened to whatever Mom was saying. However, when Julie spoke next, my eyes practically popped out of their sockets. "I think you should know, Mrs. Landry, all the girls down here think Jackson is an absolute dreamboat!"

Aw man, don't go telling her stuff like that! The thought raced through my head and I made a mad grab for the receiver, but Julie held me off and continued to embarrass me greatly.

"What makes him a dreamboat? That's easy...it's his eyes. He has gorgeous eyes!"

I now wanted to crawl under something and hide. Mom was going to torture me all the way to Duluth with the information Julie was giving her. I had heard enough, so I gave Julie a pleading look for her to stop and give me the phone back.

"Jackson wants to the phone again, Mrs. Landry. It was nice talking to you. I hope I get to meet you at the end of the week. Bye!" Julie then handed me the receiver. It was all she could do to contain her laughter.

Taking the receiver from my so-called girlfriend, I then hesitated a moment before putting it to my ear – I already knew what was coming my way.

"So...Dreamboat...she sounds like quite a girl," chuckled Mom.

"You have no idea."

"I know it's probably a stupid question...but are you really having a good time?"

"No...I'm having a great time, so please stop worrying."

Before we ended the call, Mom shared her and Dad's tentative plans for traveling to Mankato the coming Saturday. They planned on arriving in the early afternoon. We would then spend one last night in Mankato and then leave for Duluth Sunday morning. With that information tucked away, I promised Mom that I would call in a few days, just to keep her from worrying, knowing full well she would anyway. It's what Mom did well.

"Good night, Mom...I love you."

"Wow! I definitely don't hear that enough! I love you, too. Good night."

As soon as I hung up, I gave Julie a mock dismayed look. "You snot!"

Julie just laughed, put her arms around my neck and then in a whispered voice said, "This should shut you up...for now anyway." She then lightly planted her lips onto mine.

When the kiss was over, I said, "You know, I'm probably going to fall for that trick, but only every time." After that, we dove right in.

When our lips began to feel a bit chapped, we figured we had made out enough, for the time being anyway. She suggested that we get up and go for a walk. Begrudgingly, I acquiesced. Hanging out in the cool basement would have suited me just fine, but I didn't want to disappoint my new girlfriend.

As we stepped out onto the driveway, I immediately noticed that everything looked extremely different. The sun looked like a massive pumpkin hanging low in the sky. It created an orange hue and changed the appearance of all that my eyes took in. The evening was no longer oppressively hot, either. Instead, a nice breeze had kicked up and made the air pleasantly warm.

Standing there in the driveway, Julie looked radiant in the dwindling light of dusk. Her Raven curls were down and spilled about her shoulders. Even in the changing light, Julie's piercing, blue eyes showed their brilliance. Novelists, screenwriters, and poets have written pages and pages of words about such beautiful sights. However, I thought words could not do justice to the girl standing before me. Foolishly, I was falling in love for the first time and couldn't stop it from happening. In truth, I didn't want to stop it. At that moment, Kurt's wisdom from the previous night suddenly came to mind. *If this is how it's supposed to feel the first time, so be it,* I thought.

Momentarily prying my staring eyes from Julie, I remembered that we were supposed to be going for a walk. I asked, "Where do you wanna go? Do you wanna go see if the gang wants to hang out?"

"I hope you don't mind," replied Julie, "but I kinda want you to myself."

"That's why we left the basement den, right?" I facetiously asked.

Julie giggled and replied, "I meant that I don't want to go hang out with the others. I want to talk to you, but not at the Wilson's. You don't mind walking with me, do you?"

Immaturely, I tried to be funny and replied, "Not at all, I need the exercise." But my head immediately delivered a reminder that I was acting stupid. *Relax and stop trying so hard, dummy!*

"We have to hurry a little," said Julie. "It's going to be dark soon and I want to show you something."

Setting a comfortable, but hurried, pace, Julie got us started up Westwood Drive. It was quiet between us for a minute or so, but I knew that wouldn't last long. The concerned look on Julie's face told me that more questions were coming my way. Uneasily, she queried, "I was wondering how you're feeling. I mean, after finding out about your mom's death."

"Listen, I'm okay about that. There was some shock this morning, but I've gotten over it. I am a little disappointed, though. Her being gone means there are a lot of questions that won't ever get answered.

"I told Momma about it, while we did dishes tonight. She said that if you ever want to talk to someone who knew your mom, she would be more than happy to talk with you about her."

"Thank her for me please. I'll have to wait until I meet with Adam and hear what he has to say. Maybe there won't be a need for it."

"Well, just keep it in mind, okay?" Julie then took my hand. "Jackson, I have to ask you. You really don't have a girlfriend where you live?"

"Nope."

"It's just that…I find it hard to believe that someone who looks and acts like you doesn't have a girl already."

Of course, Julie's words made me blush a little, which made her giggle. I explained, "Well, thanks, but things are different for me in Duluth. Down here, I get to be myself because you and the others have known me since we were little. Up there, nobody seems to really want to give me a chance, so I don't fit in."

"So, you really do miss being down here?"

"Mom and Dad say I spend too much time thinking about this place. They hope someday I can put it all behind me."

"If that's so, why did they let you come down here now?"

"That's a long story. I hope you don't mind if I don't tell it right now."

"Jackson, you've got a lot of secrets."

"It's not that. It's just that it's been such a great weekend. I don't want to ruin it by talking about a bunch of stuff that ain't so great."

"I'll leave you alone about it right now, but you have to promise to actually talk to me before you leave here."

I knew I wouldn't be able to hold Julie off forever, but that night, I wasn't about to talk about my troubles in Duluth. Still, I wanted to open up to her, so I heard myself say, "I promise."

We continued walking, but it got quiet between us again and I hated the silence. So, I said, "Okay, my turn. In a town this small, I know someone must have caught your eye before I came back."

For a tense moment, Julie looked as though she were considering her answer very carefully. Then, she said, "There have been a couple guys in school I thought were cute, but then they tried to talk. Some are real jerks, but mostly, guys in this town don't come around me too much. Mama says it could be because they're afraid. They're afraid because I'm Gary Falkner's daughter. You don't know what that means...Do you?"

"The only thing it means to me is that he has a very pretty daughter." *Holy smokes! Did I just think that out loud?!*

"You see! That's exactly what I'm talking about! No guy in this town would ever have the guts to say something like that to me." Then, in a very soft and almost sad tone, Julie said, "When you leave here again, I have no idea what I'm going to do."

I found myself wondering much the same thing but didn't voice it. I just looked into her sad eyes. Just then, it occurred to me that we were walking in the direction of her house. "By the way, where are we going?" I asked.

"It's kind of a secret. You'll see when we get there."

We walked until we came to the rear of the Falkners' property. Julie then led me down a fence line. It separated her parents' property from a wooded area. Suddenly, I recalled how following the fence line would lead us to a beaten path. The path wound down a hillside and ended up by Indian creek - the creek bed paralleled the entire neighborhood. When we reached the bottom of the hill, I stopped and looked back toward the hillside. Memories immediately began to flood in.

Julie asked, "What's the matter?"

"Nothing, I'm just now remembering. The winter of our third-grade year, a bunch of us sledded down that path. You, Joel, and I wrecked on a toboggan going down that hill."

I turned and looked at Julie. She had the sweetest smile affixed to her face.

"You remembered! I had such a huge crush on you back then, but you would hardly ever talk to me."

"I didn't know. Even if I did, I wouldn't have known what to do about it," I admitted.

Julie then led me to an old cedar tree. It had been uprooted by high waters and winds. The massive tree now lay on its side. At its base, where the weathered roots branched out in an entangled mess, lay a large, flat rock. Julie asked, "Will you move that rock for me please?"

I looked at the size of the rock and feared I would look like a total wimp if I couldn't move it. It was flat and the approximate size of a small car tire. Julie showed me where to grab it and heave. It must have weighed seventy pounds, but I managed to pull it up without straining every muscle in my back. I then looked underneath and saw a small, square, weathered, and rusted cookie tin. I couldn't make out the writing on the cover, though. Julie took a stick and pried the tin from where it was stuck in the dirt. After she successfully retrieved the tin, I lowered the rock back in place.

"Do you remember in the fourth grade, when we made that time capsule in Sister Mary's class?" she asked. "Well, that summer I kinda did the same thing."

Julie knelt, then opened the tin and presented it to me. Kneeling in front of her, I took the rusted canister and looked inside. There was a wide variety of meaningless articles: buttons, bows, ribbons, and notebook pages, with illegible scribbling on them. I recognized a Saint Christopher medal. Mine was in my cigar box in my bedroom. We received those medals on the occasion of our first confession, just before our First Communion. *Girls sure do hang onto a lot of stuff,* I thought. But then, I suddenly realized that I was looking at some of Julie's most cherished memories.

I then spied a clear, plastic sandwich bag, with photographs sealed inside. Picking up the small bundle of photos, I asked, "May I?"

Julie sadly replied, "It's why I brought you here."

I gingerly pulled the photographs from their plastic protection. Julie identified the first likenesses as that of her great grandparents. She spoke briefly of how she missed them. Next, I looked at a few pictures of her grandparents.

"I know that, someday, I'll be missing them, too," Julie offered.

The next picture in line was my fourth-grade school picture. In it, my hair had been cut very short – one of Brad's famously-hideous haircuts. In addition, my teeth seemed way too large for my mouth. My brown eyes seemed larger than I ever remembered them. I also saw that I wore only the faintest hints of a smile – I didn't like smiling for the camera…ever.

When I looked up at Julie, I wore a look of astonishment. Tears welled up in her eyes and she said, "Maybe now you'll understand what you coming back here means to me."

I was at a tremendous loss. I didn't know what to do, think or say, so I just knelt there, with my mouth hanging open. Suddenly, Julie lunged forward. When she landed in my arms, I barely had time to catch her. I had no words that might help, so I didn't even try to speak. As she wept, I simply held her close.

When Julie finished her little, crying spell, she hastily pushed away from me and started placing articles back into the tin box. As Julie put her photos back in the plastic bag, she appeared almost angry. "I'll bet you don't even remember us trading our pictures in the fourth grade," she accused.

I stopped her hand from placing anything else in the box and made her look at me. I couldn't help but smile, as I said, "We did it behind the church in the spring, just before recess was over. Your picture and my Saint Christopher medal, along with pictures of the others, are in an old cigar box in my bedroom. I didn't bury it like you did because I want to be able to see you, whenever I need to."

"Jackson, I could have cried at the ball game on Tuesday. When you came out to get a drink, you looked right at me! You didn't even recognize me…Did you?!"

"Julie, I knew exactly who you were. I recognized you last Sunday when I sat two rows behind you in church."

"You were there? Why didn't you say something to me then?"

"I was afraid you wouldn't remember me. I would've looked and felt like a dork, kinda like I do right now. At the ball game, I looked directly at you, hoping *you* would recognize me."

Julie flared, "That just figures, the girl always has to make the first move."

"I didn't come down here looking for you, Julie. You're something I didn't count on."

Her frown then turned to a smile. She then finished putting her keepsakes in the small, rusted tin. Again, I raised the rock for her, at which point she put the tin back into its resting place. I then let go of the heavy rock and watched it fall back into place with a very pronounced thud. When my eyes met Julie's, I gave her an inquisitive look. At the risk of sounding insensitive, I asked, "So, I've been buried in a hole all this time?"

With new tears forming in her eyes, Julie explained, "I didn't know you left Mankato for good. That summer, I walked past your house all the time, just hoping to see you outside, but you were never there. One day, I saw the guys shooting baskets at Tony's place. I asked them why you weren't with them. That's when I found out you had moved away. I cried all the way home that day, Jackson. I added your picture to the box because, like my great grandma and grandpa, I didn't think I would ever see you again."

I was speechless. I tried and tried, but no words came to mind. I couldn't get my mind wrapped around the idea that Julie held me in her heart that way.

Julie continued, "So, like I said before, when you leave here again, I have no idea what I'm going to do."

Later, when we arrived at Julie's doorstep, the porch light was on. However, there was more than enough light for me to see her pleading eyes, as she said, "Before you leave town, promise me we'll stay in touch. I know I'm going to lose you again, but do I have to lose you completely?"

Once again, hardly believing I was talking to a girl in such a fashion, I heard myself say, "You're too important to me now. I'll probably end up begging my parents to let me come down here more often. I'm supposed to be saying good-bye to this place. I know now that I won't be able to do that…ever."

As if my words had immediately put her worries to rest, even if it was only for a little while, Julie smiled. "It's still early. Do you want to come in?"

"Yeah, I do, very much, but I'd better not. I have some thinking to do, and I don't do that too well when I'm with you." To that, Julie moved in and put her arms around my neck. I immediately got a little nervous and said, "Don't you think we're being a little showy? I mean, your mom and dad are right behind that door."

"You don't have to worry. They both like you…a lot. I told Momma about us. I also told her that this is probably the only chance we'll have to be together. She told me to be careful, whatever that means. Once she saw how different you were from the other guys, she told me she wished I could find someone like you here in Mankato. She said that she likes your mannerisms."

"Do *you* wish you could find someone?" I asked.

"I thought I just did."

"You're making it hard for me to leave."

Julie then whispered, "Yeah, that's because I don't want you to go, yet." She then kissed me tenderly.

"I'll call you tomorrow," I said, trying to make my escape.

"Are you sure you won't change your mind and stay awhile?"

"No, I'm not sure at all!" I laughed. "That's why I'm getting out of here now."

Julie giggled, then kissed me goodnight.

When I went to bed that night, the room was hot, but it was beginning to cool. Danny had a fan running in the window at the opposite end of the room. It was drawing cool air from the window by my head. I lay in bed, with no covers on, waiting for the heat to fall off to a more comfortable degree.

Once again, I found myself replaying the entire day in my head. Things were getting more complicated, but I didn't seem to care. I felt my heart loosening and opening to new possibilities. I knew there was a painful good-bye coming my way in a week, but right then, none of that mattered to me. I was determined to hold Julie close for as long as I could. She had made it clear she intended to do the same. What alternative did I have? I always had feelings for her, even when I was too immature to admit it to anyone. Secretly, I always knew she was special. *How am I supposed to get her out of my heart now?* How wonderful it all was, knowing she never forgot about me. I would never have had the courage to share a secret as large as the one she shared that night. As I lay there, sweating, I marveled at the epiphany I had. For the first time in my life, I was *truly* in love. *So, this is what it really feels like.* I then wondered if I would have the guts to tell her before I left town.

CHAPTER 19

Monday, 14 August 1972

They call it "Blue Monday," whomever *they* are, but that particular Monday did not start out bad. In fact, it began quite pleasantly. I awoke to Brad and Janet making noise in the kitchen. They were preparing to leave for work. I should have risen and got an earlier start to my day. Instead, I simply enjoyed lying in bed, listening to their banter. My entire body felt totally relaxed, but my mind was alert. The sound of their milling about sent me into the past. Remembering how content I once was, waking up in that bed, made me smile. Then, I sort of mentally kicked myself for not getting up, but not too hard. I wanted to wish them a good day, but I wanted to stay put even more.

The fan had been running all night long, so once the room had cooled off, it became fantastically comfortable. I had slept soundly and felt extremely rested. I was content to be lying there, with a cool morning breeze coming through the window. At the same time, there was also the nagging realization that I was beginning the downside of my two-week stay.

In order to fend off any negative feelings, I began to think about all the wonderful things that had taken place in the previous week. I couldn't help but smile at all the fantastic changes I had undergone. But then I felt my mood begin to slip. I started dwelling on thoughts about having to leave. When I thought about Julie and what she shared with me the night before, my mood worsened. I struggled with the knowledge that I had allowed myself to fall in love with her.

There wasn't going to be hardly any time for us, just the coming week. I found myself wishing I could be more cavalier about the situation. *Enjoy it, get out of town, then forget the whole thing.* Unfortunately, my heart would never allow me to adopt such an attitude. I then remembered Brad's words to me from Saturday, about remembering Julie for the rest of my life. *Is she really going to haunt me that long? Doc, I think I've dug myself into a real hole here!* I closed my eyes again, breathed in deep, then told myself I was just overreacting.

After I heard Brad and Janet drive off for work, I made myself get out of bed. I trudged downstairs and while in the bathroom, I examined myself closely in the mirror. Between the spring and summer, I had gone through another growth spurt. New muscle was something else I enjoyed. Mom and Dad wouldn't let me start lifting weights for a few more years. They said it was too hard on my developing bones and joints. Nevertheless, in the privacy of my bedroom, I did a lot of push-ups, pull-ups, and sit-ups. Every morning before school and evening before bed, I worked out. When I learned of the trip to Mankato, I worked even harder. I wanted to impress Kurt and Danny by no longer being the skinny runt they remembered. While being around them and their girls, I had observed the way Janelle looked at Kurt. She always looked like she got a great deal on a used car and wanted everyone to know it. Because of his muscular physique, it wasn't hard to believe he never had to call girls.

I then remembered our Friday dinner at the Hill Top Tavern. I had overheard Carrie ask Janelle what attracted her to Kurt in the first place. Janelle had exclaimed, "Are you kidding? Look at him!"

While flexing my muscles, I examined my physique in the bathroom mirror and wondered if Julie was impressed. Of course, I wasn't anywhere near as big as Kurt, but what there was of me looked pretty solid. I liked the way I was beginning to take shape. That is, until I saw the scars on my back. I was impatient for them to continue to fade and then, someday, just go away. They were most prominent in the summer when my back was tanned from the sun. *I'm supposed to forgive the guy who did this to me?! He's probably the reason my mom killed herself,* I thought.

Just then, there was a knock at the side door. So, I quickly pulled my T-shirt back over my head and then hurried to go answer it. It was Dave Lester.

"Hey man, want to go running?" he asked.

Seeing that he was all decked out in running gear, I asked, "Now?"

"Yeah, it's cool enough right now, but it's going to get hotter the longer we stand here. Aren't you starting to get ready for football?

"Yeah, I guess you're right. Give me a minute. I'll be right out."

Dave was right. Football practices would begin soon, so I had better start conditioning myself. I loathed the thought of hard workouts in the August heat, especially in the first week of practice. That's when the aches and pains from out-of-shape muscles were first felt. Simply getting out of bed in the morning would be a real chore. That approaching football season, I wanted to be in good shape at the very beginning. Coach could always tell who kept in shape and who didn't have the discipline. Those of us who did, were always awarded with extra playing time on game days.

Running was the work I hated most, but I knew it was the only way for me to increase my speed and agility. I liked being quicker and faster than most guys my age. The only person I could think of that might workout harder was Dave Lester. Of course, he probably had his dad pushing him half the time. All my motivation came from inside me, plus a little from reading about some body builder named Arnold Schwarzenegger in Muscle Mag.

Although the early-morning temperatures had been cool, the rising sun was warming things up fast. I hoped that the heat and running with Dave would help clean the garbage out of my head. So, after a decent warm up, we took off down Westwood Drive. Not caring which direction we went, I let Dave lead us wherever he wanted.

As Dave guided me toward Baker Avenue, he set a good pace. When we reached Baker Avenue and then turned north, I figured out that we were heading toward the high school. We ran at a good clip until we came upon a hill on West Pleasant Street. Dave then eased up the pace a little for the downhill leg of our run.

I asked, "What position you playing this year?"

"Dad has me trying out for quarterback," huffed Dave.

That just figures, I thought, but said, "That's cool." Then, as an afterthought, I asked, "By the way, where are you taking us?"

"To the track at the high school," Dave replied, as he once again quickened his pace.

At the bottom of the hill on West Pleasant Street, the campus of Mankato West High opened up to our left. The running track was situated around the football field and as soon as we got on it, I could tell it had been recently resurfaced. The smooth asphalt oval was already warm but would be unbearably hot by that afternoon.

As we ran, I imagined what it would be like to train with Dave, the team, and play football someday as a Mankato West Scarlet. But I immediately put that thought away because it was never going to happen.

Dave and I were natural competitors against each other, but not that morning. We were simply working out together, or so I thought.

"Let's do four laps here on the track, then we can walk home and talk," suggested Dave.

"Done," I said, then figured it was my turn to quicken the pace a little.

Four laps around the track was a measured mile and we intended to run it together. Neither of us jockeyed for the lead. For the most part, I simply enjoyed keeping pace with my friend and by the end of the third lap, knew that I would finish the run strongly.

Into the fourth and final lap, we remained neck and neck. That is, until Dave suggested we sprint the last one hundred yards. To my surprise, when I poured every bit of energy into that sprint, I left him in the dust. Even though Dave crossed the line a mere couple of seconds behind me, I was extremely pleased with the result of our footrace.

As we both labored to get enough oxygen into our lungs, Dave exclaimed, "Jesus, Jackson, where did you get those wheels?!"

I was too winded to talk, so I just huffed, "Thanks." After I was able to catch my breath, I said, "That was for those pitches you burned past me last Tuesday."

I may have been quicker on my feet, but I felt that because of the coaching Dave was getting from his dad, one day he would have a real cannon for a pitching arm. That opinion was based on all the stories and interviews I had read in Sports Illustrated Magazine. Big-league pitchers were always making statements about their growing years and how they appreciated their father's coaching. I, of course, felt that I would never amount to much, athletically speaking, because my dad was incapable of coaching me at any sport.

After getting a drink at the water fountain, we began our walk home. As we left the campus and headed back up the hill on West Pleasant Street, I noticed a peculiar look on Dave's face.

"What's the matter?" I asked. "You're not mad because I beat you back there…Are you?"

"No, that's not it. I mean, I'm not too happy about getting beat just now, but that's not what I was thinking about."

"So, what were you thinking?"

"I really miss having you around, man. You're the only one who could keep up with me."

"What about Tony and Joel?"

"They're good, but it's not the same since you left. You know what I mean?"

"Yeah, I know."

"You remember how my dad used to line the four of us up against each other? We'd be running plays in our back yard, banging heads…

"Yeah, I remember. You and I always lined up against each other." I paused for a moment then said, "I miss it, Dave. I miss you guys a lot."

"Like I said, 'it hasn't been the same since you left.' Dad always said you were a natural athlete. He said you would be good at whatever sport you played. I used to think he liked having you around to coach more than me. I sometimes still wonder if I'll ever be good enough for him."

I immediately got irritated and exclaimed, "Your dad used to include me because he felt sorry for me…and that's all! He's a good guy, dummy!" I then calmed myself some and continued, "He coaches you so much, you'll probably always be better than me. My dad is blind. He can't do things with me. At least, not the same things you do with your dad. So, if I'm going to be good at anything, I have to train myself. I love my dad, but sometimes I wish I had what you have."

"Sorry, man…I didn't think. It's just that, sometimes, I wish I could be good at something else, besides sports."

"Like what?!" I blurted, still a bit agitated.

"Like, knowing what to say to a girl and how to treat her."

Giving Dave my best are-you-crazy look, I exclaimed, "What?! I don't understand. What about Anne? You guys talk all the time."

"Yeah...I...I know. We've been together for a while, but lately, I think she'd rather be with someone else."

"Yeah, like who?"

"Well, like you."

"Bullshit!"

"No...really! She's been telling me how she wishes I would act more like you. She wishes I would treat her and talk to her like you do with Julie. I guess Julie tells her everything."

At first, I didn't know what to say. Who was I to give advice about how to talk to or treat a girl? I was still very much a rookie in that department. Although I knew I had undergone some serious changes, I still considered myself clueless, especially when it came to dealing with the opposite sex. But, at that moment, Dave made it clear that he was plenty worried. I had no idea how to help him.

"Jackson, I think she's gonna dump me."

My mind searched for any kind of made-up advice that might help, but the only thing I could come up with was the truth.

"Look, is Anne your first girlfriend?" I asked.

"Yeah, pretty much."

"Well, it's the same with me and Julie. Before coming down here, no girl would even give me a look. I'm learning everything for the first time...right now...with Julie."

I thought he was going to laugh his ass off at me. I even prepared myself for that very reaction. Instead, he just looked at me and nodded, as if he truly understood.

"So...how do you know to do that stuff you do?"

"What stuff?"

"You know, stuff like bringing the girls cold towels, when we played volleyball."

"I don't know, that just came to me. Look, I can't tell you how to act with Anne and stuff like that. I doubt your dad can, either. But I'll bet your mom can. What little I know about how to treat a girl, I learned from Mom."

"Your mom taught you how to talk to girls?"

"That one I'm kinda learning on my own. Julie always wants to know how I feel about her and other things. I've been forcing myself to tell her what's in my head, but somehow...she also gets me to tell her what I'm feeling, too."

"You can do that? Man, when Anne and I talk, I'm thinking of all kinds of things I'd like to say, but I can't ever seem to get the words out."

"Like I said, Dave, 'I've been forcing myself.' I think it's different for me. I don't have a lot of time left here. So, when Julie and I talk, it's like I need her to know the truth. I need her to know how I feel. I guess...I just feel like I don't have time to screw around. When I first got here, I didn't count on any of this happening. For some reason or other, it now feels too important."

"You actually think my mom can help with Anne?"

"All I know is...it never hurts to ask," I chuckled.

We walked the rest of the way, talking about the differences between our girlfriends. In a word, it felt...weird.

"Dave, do you love Anne?

"I don't know...maybe...I guess."

"Have you told her?"

"Hell no!" Then after a slight pause, Dave asked, "You think I should?"

While shrugging my shoulders, I replied, "How should I know?"

Dave asked, "What about Julie? You seem to be fallin' for her kinda fast."

"I know. It's like I said, 'It's my first time and I didn't count on any of this stuff happening while I'm here.' It's screwing with my head pretty bad, too."

When we finally made it to Dave's driveway, he mentioned how I hadn't been to his place to see his parents. So, plans were laid for me to come back after lunch. He said he would also try to get the gang to show up, so we could hang out in his basement. It all sounded good to me. I then thought we were just going to say our see-you-laters. That way, I could go get a badly needed shower. But Dave had something else on his mind and he decided that moment in time to clue me in. "I don't know if I should tell you this or not," he said. "I'll probably get in trouble with the girls if they find out."

"What is it?"

"Julie may be your first girl, but you're not her first guy."

"What?"

"Jackson, listen man. It didn't last long, and she's been regretting it ever since. The guy's a real jerk. They started up last fall and it lasted maybe three weeks. But every now and then, the guys and I find out that he's been bothering her...Ya know?"

"Who's the guy?"

"Greg Dodson."

"Oh man! You've gotta be kidding me! That moron?! I had to fight him in the third grade, gave him a bloody nose, too."

"I don't think you would find it so easy now," warned Dave. "He actually likes to fight!"

"I suppose he's gotten pretty big."

"Not really. I mean, he's about our size, but man can he hit. You know that small scar by Joel's eye? Dodson gave it to him last year. He wears rings."

"How did Julie ever end up with a goon like him?"

"He's smooth, Jackson. He thinks he's a lady's man or something like that. He had Julie fooled for a little while, but she caught him two-timing her. She dropped him like a hot rock, and he didn't like that at all. So, every now and then, he likes to make her miserable. You know...says some pretty mean stuff to her. Hey man, remember, you didn't hear any of this from me."

I smiled slyly and said, "Yeah, I did. But I guess nobody else needs to know that."

Dave chuckled, "Thanks, man." He then started up his driveway toward the house. "See you later?"

Rather absent mindedly, I replied, "You bet." My head was already swimming with the information Dave had just laid on me.

While I finished my trek to the house, I wondered why Julie hadn't told me about Greg, not that it mattered. According to Dave, Dodson was nothing but Julie's three-week mistake from the previous fall. With the way things currently stood between her and I, Greg was no big deal. Still, I couldn't quite get my mind wrapped around how she could ever take up with the likes of him. It seemed there were all kinds of skeletons popping out of my own closet. Was I going to have to possibly deal with some of Julie's, too?

When I walked in the side door, Danny sat at the kitchen table, eating breakfast. As he hunched over his bowl of cereal, he still looked half asleep. With his mouth full, he asked, "Where've you been?"

"Out running."

Looking at me like I was crazy, Danny asked, "On purpose?"

"When I get home, football practices start up. If I don't get my act together now, I won't do well, and the coach won't put me in as much."

Danny finally swallowed his mouthful of cereal, nodded his understanding and then asked, "You gonna show them some of that speed you showed us yesterday?"

As I filled a glass of water from the faucet, I replied, "That's my plan."

Using his foot, Danny pushed a chair out from the table and then instructed, "Have a seat."

"I better not. I'm sweaty and I'm sure I stink. I wouldn't wanna curdle your milk."

When Danny shoveled another spoonful into his mouth, my reply took him by surprise. He snickered and almost spewed milk and cornflakes all over himself. When he recovered, he said, "Sit down anyway."

While Danny finished eating, we talked about girls, sports I played up north, and then girls again. We then talked about how he and I used to box upstairs. Since fighting was on the table, I decided to pick his brain.

"Danny…you ever thought about how weird life can be sometimes?"

"How do you mean?"

"Well, do you remember how you kinda coached me in my very first fight? It was in the third grade, and I ended up giving Greg Dodson a bloody nose."

"Oh, yeah, I remember. What about it?"

"Well, I just found out from Dave that Greg and Julie went out for a few weeks last year."

"You have got to be kidding me! Julie?!...And that ape?!...No way!"

I chuckled and then said, "When Dave told me about it, I pretty much said the same thing."

Danny blurted, "You know I work for his dad...Don't you?"

"No! I didn't know that! Wow!"

"Yeah, his dad owns the lawn-care service I work for. I know Greg pretty well. He's a real jerk. He thinks he's hot stuff because his dad owns the business."

Danny continued to tell me bad things about Greg, which normally would have worried me. But, since I didn't actually plan on running into the guy, none of what Danny said gave me much reason for concern. Still, there was one thought that bothered me.

"You know, Danny, if I hadn't left here, Greg wouldn't have stood a chance with Julie. It would have been me."

"Jackson, don't think that way. What happened to you is just the way it is. Don't drive yourself crazy by playing the what-if game."

"The what?"

"The what-if game. It's where you sit around thinking about all the stuff that might have happened if you hadn't left. But you still have to deal with the fact that you did leave. And you're gonna leave again."

Before then, Danny had never bestowed any real wisdom on me. To tell the truth, I was pretty shocked that he came up with that insight. I was so surprised by what sounded like absolute truth that I couldn't say anything more. I just sat there and let his words sink in.

After I showered and ate breakfast, I retreated to the coolness of the basement den to do some reading. I figured I could finish the Louis L'Amour western I had been working on before going to Dave's that afternoon.

I had only been reading for about forty-five minutes, when suddenly, the phone rang. It was Julie. She began a long-winded explanation of how she had been contacted by Anne about going to Dave's after lunch. She wanted to know if I minded coming all the way to her house to get her, then walking all the way down to Dave's together.

With the run I put in this morning, I'm definitely getting some exercise today, I thought.

Julie then started bending my ear about what a great weekend we had together. I almost had to laugh because Kurt's words were coming true again. I just sat in the lounge chair, smiled, listened to her excited voice and gave her more one-word answers that consisted mainly of "uh-huh," "yeah," and "cool!"

"Wait a minute, Jackson, Momma's calling me."

There was a short pause, so I examined my fingernails and found dirt underneath them that needed to come out. Mere seconds went by and then Julie's voice came over the line again.

"Okay, I'm back. Momma wants to know if you want to join us for lunch."

"Really?"

"Yeah, really. She says it's only proper that she get a good look at the boy who's dating me. I agree. Please say you'll come. We can walk to Dave's together afterward."

"What time do you want me there?"

"Now."

"What?! It's not lunchtime yet. It's only ten o'clock."

"You didn't ask what time lunch was," giggled Julie. "You asked what time I wanted you here."

"Very funny."

"Really, Jackson, if you're not doing something more important, I'd love to see you."

As I looked at the book in my hand, I acquiesced, "Well...alright...I'm on my way."

"Great! See you when you get here. Bye!"

Continuing to stare at the paperback in my hand, I muttered to myself, "Well, Louie, some other time, I guess." *Dang it,* I thought. *I was in the middle of a good part, too!*

I was just about ready to leave the house when the phone rang again. I knew Brad, Janet, and Kurt were at work, but wasn't too sure of Danny's whereabouts, so I answered it. It was Father Michael.

"Are you busy, lad?"

"I was just about to walk out the door, Father."

"Well then, I won't be taking up much of your time. Are you free tomorrow afternoon for lunch again?"

"Is this about meeting with Adam?"

"Yes it is. I thought the three of us could sit down to lunch, while we meet."

"If you don't mind, Father, I'd rather meet before or after lunch, but not during."

"Well, he'll be here at noon for lunch, so why don't you show up at, oh, let's say, one o'clock?"

I hesitated to agree, but heard myself say, "I guess that'll be okay, Father."

"We'll see you then, lad. Have a blessed day."

For a moment, I just stood there in the kitchen, taking stock of myself, emotionally. Surprisingly, I didn't feel one way or the other about seeing Adam Harris. I had already obligated myself to the meeting, so just then, it didn't feel like a big deal. Mostly, I just wanted it to be done and over with, so I could enjoy the rest of my visit. After dealing with the news about my mother's suicide, I figured I could handle, with little or no problem, whatever news Adam Harris had to dish out. Resolved not to worry about the meeting, I headed out the side door, smiling. I was off to get looked over by my girl's mom. At least there would be lunch in it for me, that and a beautiful girl's smile.

Chapter 20

While Mrs. Falkner prepared lunch, Julie and I played Gin Rummy at the kitchen table. She was beating me by a rather large margin, too. While Julie seemed to draw every card she needed, I couldn't draw one that would help my hand. She playfully poked fun at me about how bad I was losing. "Jackson, this beating is for the football you threw to me yesterday…Gin!" Julie then laid her cards down and let out a sadistic laugh.

Pretending to be frustrated, I whined, "Let me know when you think we're even. Good grief, this sucks!" Then, I chuckled and asked, "By the way, how's your butt?"

"Jackson!" exclaimed Julie, as if she were truly shocked at my query, but then in mock smugness said, "A gentleman never asks a lady such a question."

"I'll have to remember that. So…how's your butt?"

When we stopped laughing, Julie's demeanor suddenly changed. Instead of her sweet smile, a noticeable frown appeared. I caught the look and wondered if she was thinking the same thing as me. *I could really get used to this, but I'm not gonna get that chance.* I then gave her a weak smile and she brightened up some. She then reached out and laid her hand on the tabletop, palm up, as a signal for me to take it. I checked to see if her mom was watching and then laid my hand atop hers. She caressed it with her thumb and just smiled that mesmerizing smile of hers.

"Okay you two, stop with the googly eyes and make room for lunch," said Mrs. Falkner. "Julie, go upstairs and get your sister please…And I don't mean yell from the bottom of the stairs."

Without acknowledging her mother's instructions, Julie obediently got out of her chair and went to retrieve Lisa. When she had left the room, I kept busy by getting the cards organized into a proper stacked deck and then put them back into their box. Julie's mom then started putting place settings on the table for four people.

I asked, "Can I help with anything, Mrs. Falkner?"

"Yes…You can start by calling me Marilyn. Can you do that?"

"Sure…Marilyn," I replied. Her name didn't exactly roll off my tongue, but I figured I would get use to the informality.

"It's very easy to see why my Julie is attracted to you. You favor your mother, Jackson. You have her gorgeous eyes and skin."

Adult women were always gushing over my brown eyes or how attractive they thought I was becoming. Normally, I despised such obligatory tributes because they never felt sincere. Marilyn's compliments were somehow different. When she looked at me, it was as if she wasn't seeing me at all. It felt more like she was seeing her old friend and simply stating a fact.

"I'll have to take your word for it ma'am…I mean…Marilyn. I don't clearly remember what she looked like anymore."

"Julie told me you're not ready to talk about her and I understand. But, if you ever change your mind, I'll be here. Even after you leave again, you can always call and talk to me about her. Whenever *you* are ready, okay?"

I thanked Marilyn for her offer, but secretly wished she would simply drop the matter. I wasn't comfortable with the idea of discussing such personal things with a complete stranger. I suddenly wondered if I would ever be comfortable enough to have such a talk with the mother of my first girlfriend.

Lunch at the Falkner's consisted of a cup of tomato soup and a grilled-cheese sandwich. It was a lighter lunch than I was used to, so I was left wanting more. *That ought to last me…for about an hour,* I thought. However, when Marilyn asked if it was enough for me, I could see there were no leftovers, so I lied and told her I couldn't eat another bite. Then, there were the comical looks I got when I offered to help with the dishes. Three females looked at me with gaping mouths. They were probably wondering if their hearing needed to be checked.

"Thanks," said Marilyn, "but don't you and Julie have someplace to be this afternoon?"

Julie then rushed upstairs to finish getting ready for our afternoon together. Lisa, not wanting to get stuck with doing dishes, also bolted for the stairs. Marilyn and I stayed in the kitchen and shared a few more words.

"Thanks for lunch. It was very good," I said.

"It was very simple," Marilyn shot back, "but you're most welcome."

Suddenly, feeling the urge to be up front and honest, I said, "You're not what I expected at all. I think you're pretty neat."

"Thank you, I think. If you don't mind my asking, what *were* you expecting?"

"Well...someone more...standoffish...you know...smug maybe."

Marilyn gave out an elongated "Ah," then stated, "You've been talking to Janet Wilson."

"Yeah, well, she did pretty much warn me about you. Did you two really used to be friends, when you were younger?"

"Yes, we were very-good friends when we were girls in school. Later, we had a falling out. Sometimes, Jackson, grownups aren't very smart, especially when it comes to letting bygones be bygones."

"Man! You live so close to each other, too. It's kind of a...shame."

At that, Marilyn looked at me, like she just had an epiphany and then agreed by saying, "Yes...it is."

Looking at Marilyn, was like looking at an older version of Julie. Her piercing blue eyes hadn't lost any of their intensity. Because of her age, which had to be the same as Janet, she probably dyed her hair black. She wore it shorter, yet quite stylish for that time period. Her skin seemed perfect and needed very little make-up. She had what Mom would have called, "Natural Beauty." I found her to be the exact opposite of how Janet described her. Genuinely warm and caring, she was easy to like.

When Julie was finally ready, we said our good-byes and made our way to the door. Just before stepping out, Lisa actually spoke to me. Wearing an unabashed, adoring look, she said, "It was nice seeing you again, Jackson."

I was slightly taken by surprise but managed to be civil. "Thank you, Lisa... it was...nice seeing you, too." I then turned and must've had a ridiculous look on my face. Julie just giggled at the exchange.

At the end of Julie's block, we stopped behind our favorite stand of scotch pines and kissed. If it hadn't been so hot outside, I would have preferred to spend the entire afternoon right there. When we came up for air, Julie said, "We better get going. We have to pick up Mike on the way."

Giving Julie a dumbfounded look, I asked, "We do?"

Wearing her sly smile, Julie replied, "Yeah, didn't I tell you?"

"Uh...no...You must have forgot," I chuckled.

"You don't mind if Mike walks down there with us, do you?" Once again, Julie sounded like she was telling me, rather than asking.

"No...I don't mind at all." My reply was a big, fat lie.

Julie was up to something, but it wasn't worth pursuing. I did what most clueless thirteen-year-old guys did back then – I just went with the flow.

There was no joyous welcome waiting for me at Mike's house. Mike's mom was always nice enough, but her attitude toward me had always been more of tolerance than affection. Patricia McDonald had always been a lot more reserved than any of the other neighborhood moms. Still, she sounded cordial enough when she said, "It's nice to see you again, Jackson." However, unlike Tony's parents, there were no follow-up questions about what I had been up to for the past three years. I wasn't put off at all by her lack of enthusiasm. Her almost dismissive demeanor was simply her way and one in which I remembered well.

Upon seeing Mrs. McDonald again, it wasn't hard for me to deduce who Mike got his looks from. I saw that she still had fiery red hair and a fair complexion, which, like Mike, freckled terribly in the sun. The vibrant red lipstick she still wore never quite seemed to look right on her. However, it was actually comforting to see that she hadn't changed a bit.

Mike was Mrs. McDonald's baby. She doted on him, but with some restraint. She wasn't one of those moms who drooled on her kids in front of their friends. In many ways, Mrs. McDonald reminded me of Catherine Landry. Prior to the three of us walking out the door, her only instruction to Mike was for him to watch how much time he spent in the sun.

During our walk to Dave's house, Julie peppered Mike with questions about his weekend.

"Saturday, we were in Waseca to visit my grandma and grandpa," said Mike. "Sunday, we went to Minneapolis to visit my aunt and uncle on my mom's side."

"Wow, Mike!" I chuckled. "That sounds really...boring."

"Jackson!" Julie exclaimed, giving me a playful swat.

"No...he's right," said Mike. "I was bored out of my brains. I really wanted to be here for the barbeque on Saturday."

"It's okay, Mike," I replied. "There's still plenty of time for us to get together."

"Mom promised she wasn't going to put anything else in the way while you're here," Mike said. "As a matter of fact, she's letting me have a cookout this week!"

I noticed Julie smiling and could almost see the wheels turning in her head. "What's the grin all about?" I asked.

With an innocent smile, Julie replied, "Nothing much."

"I'm starting to know what that means," I countered.

When the three of us arrived at Dave's house, I somewhat hesitated in the driveway.

Julie asked, "You coming?"

"Yeah, but I should probably warn you, Dave's mom might get a bit carried away."

Julie gave me a curious look and asked, "What do you mean?"

"You'll see."

Dave answered the door and led us into the kitchen. I let Julie and Mike enter first. As we filed in, I saw that Dave wore a huge grin. He then yelled over his shoulder, "MOM...HE'S HERE!"

In mere seconds, Sylvia Lester came rushing into the kitchen from the living room. When she made a beeline for me, her arms were splayed wide open. The other three teens had to literally step aside before they got knocked over. "JACKSON!" screeched Mrs. Lester, as she wrapped me up in her arms and kissed me on the cheek repeatedly. "Oh, honey…it's so good to see you again! Shame on you for taking so long before coming to see me!"

"Hi!" I exclaimed in return. "I'm sorry I didn't get here sooner. Everybody's been keeping me pretty busy."

Conceding the point, Dave's mom said, "Oh, I'll bet they have." Then, after giving me the onceover, Mrs. Lester said, "Look how tall and handsome you are!"

Normally, I would have blushed at the compliment, but I was too busy enjoying the warmth of her greeting.

Sylvia Lester was only about five-feet, four-inches tall. Like Mom, her hair color was salt and pepper. However, it was piled on top of her head, and resembling a beehive, with strands hanging down the sides and back. She had gained a few pounds from what I remembered, but physical changes in her made little or no difference to me. I discovered that she was still a joy to be around. Another one of the neighborhood moms, everyone present knew Sylvia Lester quite well, including Julie.

Sylvia caught Julie smiling at our reunion and asked, "What do you think, Julie, is he better looking than before?"

Julie let out a giggle and then almost adoringly said, "Yes, he is."

When Sylvia was done squeezing me half to death, I promised to bring her up to date on things at a later time. We teens then headed for the basement. Anne and Tony were there already. Surprisingly, so were Joel and Gail. *Joel's mom must have run out of chores,* I thought.

Then, I noticed we had an extra in the group. Nancy Carter was there, chatting with Anne. I looked at Mike and immediately had to stifle a laugh. Quickly getting Julie's attention, I then whispered in her ear, "Is he blushing or is that sunburn?"

The basement of the Lester home had been totally renovated during my three-year absence. What once had been plain, white, cinderblock walls, now was covered with a dark brown, imitation, wood-grained paneling. The once cold, concrete floor was now covered with plush brown and tan patterned carpeting. A bathroom had been added, too. There was also a business work center, complete with built-in bookcases, multilevel desk, and typewriter station. The desktop was covered in loud orange Formica. Dave's bedroom had always been down there, but it, too, had taken on a more mature appearance than what I remembered it to be. While Dave showed me around, I purposefully developed a questioning look. Dave saw it and immediately asked, "What's the matter?"

Trying to keep a straight face, I asked, "Where'd the Superman blanket, sheets, and curtains go?"

In return, Dave shook his head, rolled his eyes, and snidely replied, "Shut up, Landry."

In its entirety, the basement layout efficiently maximized the use of all available space, yet appeared neat and uncluttered. There was plenty of space for all of us to relax and simply hang out.

Tony didn't waste any time getting the record player going. I took a seat on a rather comfortable couch and Julie curled up next to me. I remembered how nervous I once was to be in such close proximity to her. I was now quite comfortable with the way she cuddled up to me. I marveled at how I now *desired* it. I loved the sensation that went through me, when she slipped both her arms around my bicep and just, sort of, hugged it. It was as if she were telling the world, "This is *my* guy...BACK OFF!"

I watched Mike, as he sat and smiled uneasily. Teetering on the arm of a lounge chair, he rocked slightly and looked to be trying to rub the blue dye off the legs of his jeans. It appeared as if he was trying to talk himself into something but wasn't convinced that he was ready.

Julie must have made the same observation because she turned to me and whispered, "I'm going to ask Mike to dance. Will you please go dance with Nancy?"

"What?! No way!" I exclaimed. I most certainly did not want to get involved in whatever scheme Julie was now concocting.

With rather evil looking eyes, Julie insisted, "Jackson, just do it...Okay?"

I haven't seen that look before, I thought.

While Julie went over to Tony, who was busy rifling through some of Dave's records, I sat and watched her. I just knew she was giving him instructions to play some slow tunes. When Julie then asked Mike to dance, the others gave her strange looks, too. As Tommy James and the Shondells sang, *Crimson and Clover,* Julie gave me the evil eye again, so I begrudgingly got up and went to ask Nancy Carter for a dance. The others were already filtering onto the floor to join in.

While I led Nancy out onto the make-shift dance floor, I took note of her self-conscious smile. She was trying very hard not to display her braces. As we danced, she gave quick glances toward Mike and Julie.

Feeling a bit sorry for her, I discreetly nodded in Mike's direction and then asked, "You like him, don't you?"

Nancy didn't bother to act like she didn't know who I was talking about. In fact, she even looked a little forlorn, when she replied, "Yes, I do…the big dummy."

I couldn't help but smile and assure her by saying, "Don't worry, he likes you, too."

Nancy looked back at me and smiled broadly, displaying a mouthful of braces. Just then, I took a good look at the girl I was dancing with. I envisioned her without all that metal inside her mouth. I was suddenly able to see that when the railroad tracks finally came off Nancy's teeth, she was going to be a bona fide knockout!

"Guys are such dopes," said Nancy. "If he likes me, why won't he ever call me or even talk, when he's around me?"

"Are you kidding?!" I replied in true surprise. "This is Mike we're talking about, right? He's always been the shyest person I've ever known. You know that, too, don't you?"

"Yeah…I know. Why couldn't he be more like you? It didn't kill you to come ask me to dance."

"I guess I should tell you that absolutely nothing would have happened between Julie and me if she hadn't made the first move."

"Really?!"

"It's like you said, 'guys are dopes,' when it comes to this stuff."

Chuckling, Nancy said, "Yes, they are!" Then, her voice took on a more serious note when she said, "Thanks, Jackson."

When the record was through, I thanked Nancy for the dance and then walked over to Tony. I whispered instructions for him to keep the slow stuff going for a little bit. I also told him why and tried to nod in Mike's direction without getting caught. Unfortunately, Mike did see me and came over to where we stood.

"What?" asked Mike.

"What, what?" I returned.

"You nodded at me."

"Actually, I didn't. I nodded toward you. There's a difference. But, since you're here, go ask Nancy to dance."

In a whispered yell, Mike exclaimed, "You know I can't do that!"

"Why? You know you like her and she's just waiting for you to get up the nerve. Don't wait anymore, Mike, just go for it."

Tony nodded his agreement and then turned back to the record player. Feeling quite pleased with myself, I returned to the couch, sat down and once again relaxed.

When Julie plopped down next to me, she took my arm, put it around her and leaned into me. "So?" she queried.

"So what?"

Looking rather intense, Julie then asked, "Does she like him?"

In my best innocent tone, I said, "Oh, was I supposed to find that out? Excuse me, I'll go ask." I then made a feigned move, like I was going to get up again.

Julie giggled and held me in place. "Jackson, stop it."

"Yeah, she likes him, but you knew that already. That's why you girls set this up, isn't it?"

"Well…yeah…I guess," she giggled.

"So, if you get Mike and Nancy together, are you going to start working on Tony?"

"Not a chance!" she exclaimed. "He's hopeless."

As the other couples danced, Julie and I made out on the couch. I tried to give her my complete attention but found myself also trying to keep a discreet eye on Mike, wondering if he was actually going to make a move. As it turned out, Mike only let one song go by before he got up the courage to ask Nancy for a dance. Tony didn't fail with the music, either. As Donny Osmond sang *Puppy Love*, Mike and Nancy swayed in slow, methodic circles. Their connection was successfully made that afternoon in Dave's basement.

There were now four couples and one disk jockey present. I couldn't help but wonder if Tony felt awkward in any way. He never seemed to care about being the odd man out. Thinking of my own past experiences, I wondered if there might be something else going on under his good-natured façade. Many were the times I wore a smile to secretly mask pain or disappointment. I now wondered if the same might be true of Tony.

While eyeing the others, I took note of how close and comfortable they all were as a group. Sadness rapidly overtook me because I realized how much I was going to miss them again. The past three years had taught me well. Once I was gone, it would no longer be practical to remain part of their clique. Then, I remembered that I would also be losing Julie. At that very moment, I realized Brad was right. Someday, someone else really would be taking my place in her life. As these thoughts played out inside my head, I suddenly found that I was the one who needed to throw up a façade.

As if she were cued, Julie jostled me out of my trance. I heard her inviting voice softly ask, "Would you care to dance, Mr. Landry?"

I forced a smile and formally replied, "Why, of course, Miss Falkner. I'd love to."

Once again, I held Julie close, but felt myself heading for the dark place inside my head. Not wanting to give in to it, my brain reached for all the good advice Doc Elliot had given me and held on tight, but it was too late. My future was set. I knew all too well the emotional train wreck that was coming my way. But, in that same moment, none of that mattered to me. *I don't care, Doc. If this is all the time I get to have with these friends, I'm going to soak it all up now.*

I had convinced myself that if Julie was willing to bear whatever heartache came after that week, then so was I. Pain and sadness were emotions I had become accustomed to and they hadn't destroyed me, yet. In fact, I actually knew that in time, I would be okay. Even though I would lose Julie, the heartache I would experience was a price I was willing to pay for a moment's happiness. My bout of depression didn't last long, either. Julie's smile was some of the greatest medicine

I had ever known. I found it impossible to stay moody, especially when her attention was riveted on me.

After a few more dances, Dave suggested a game of Spin the Bottle. The girls all enthusiastically agreed, but some of us guys weren't overly thrilled by Dave's idea. I had never actually played the game, but I had heard stories from some of the kids in school, so I knew what it was all about. Not wanting to be a wet blanket or appear cowardly in front of Julie, I coolly went with the flow. However, true to his nature, Mike was white as a sheet.

While we all got ourselves situated on the floor in a circle, Tony grabbed an empty pop bottle. He then tossed it to me, winked, and said, "Get it started, Jackson."

True to *my* character, I protested some about not wanting to be first, but Julie fixed that by giving me a kiss, then saying, "I'll give you one for free, but the rest you have to earn. Now spin it!"

I laughed with everyone else and tried to give the bottle a spin. It didn't work well because of the carpet, so Dave got some cardboard and instructed me to spin it on that. It worked like a charm. When the bottle came to a halt, it pointed directly at Anne. After Anne and I leaned forward and gave each other the customary peck on the lips, I gave Julie a smug little look. For my audacity, Julie gave me a light jab to the ribs.

I then saw Dave give me a curt little look. I knew what was on his mind but didn't care. After all, it was his idea to play that stupid game.

"You probably just made Anne's week," chuckled Dave. For his comment, Dave also took a playful shot to the ribs from Anne.

By the end of the game, I believe every girl had been kissed by every guy and vice versa. It was then that I noticed how Mike was rapidly becoming more relaxed around Nancy. The change seemed to instantaneously take place when she spun the bottle and it pointed at him. Instead of the usual peck on the lips between friends, Nancy gave Mike a very passionate kiss. The aggressive act got hoots and hollers from everyone. That is, everyone but Mike. His look told me that he could not have been happier.

Tony joked, "Careful, Mike, I wouldn't wanna see you two get stuck like that."

In jest, I exclaimed, "I would!"

I believe we were all equally amazed when Mike shyly said, "Yeah, me, too."

For the rest of that afternoon, no one saw Mike blush. In fact, he seemed to laugh a lot more freely. I could easily see that he was pretty pleased with himself. As I witnessed my shy friend begin to come out of his protective shell, I honestly felt joy.

When *Spin the Bottle* had lost its allure, we all just sat around talking. Mostly, we reminisced about when we were all much younger and about the games we played within the neighborhood. We rolled with laughter, when Tony reminded everyone about the time Joel jumped into McCaskey's rose bushes. It happened during a game of Capture the Flag. He had forgotten about the thorns. Joel literally had to take his pants off to get free of them.

Acting as though he was looking for a pity party, Joel whined, "Hey, I got ripped up pretty good that day."

"I remember that," I said. "I had to let you borrow my jacket. You wrapped it around you, so the girls didn't see you wearing nothing but your underwear. By the way, can I get my jacket back now?"

We created a lot of noise in that basement with our laughter, remembering how we used to play little-kid games together. Not quite so little anymore, we realized we were still together. However, the games were just a bit different. Quite suddenly and unintentionally, Gail changed the whole mood of the afternoon.

"Has anyone ever noticed how this group has always been together?" she asked. "Jackson, remember when you, Anne, and I talked the other day? Well, even though you don't live here anymore, you're still one of us. You've always been one of us."

"Hey man, you always will be," said Tony.

The sudden sincerity expressed by Gail and Tony took me completely by surprise. My friends meant well, but I knew their sentiments weren't possible. Three years of living so far away had taught me that already.

Julie smiled and nodded her agreement, but I could see tears welling up in her eyes. Immediately, my heart felt like it was stuck in my throat. I swallowed hard and smiled back at her. But I could see that the dam was about to burst, so I whispered, "Please don't…"

As Julie struggled unsuccessfully to hold back her tears, I could only watch. She slowly shook her head from side to side, whispering "I can't help it." She then buried her face in my chest and the waterworks commenced.

Gail rushed over and sat next to Julie. She then said, "Jackson, I'm sorry. I didn't think."

"It's okay," I replied.

I let Julie have her little cry, which she surprisingly recovered from in a very short time. When she regained her composure, no one uttered a word. We all just sat there, each in our own way, I supposed, feeling bad. The atmosphere had suddenly become dim, so I desperately thought, searching for a way to lighten the mood again.

Seeing that Julie was in dire need of something to wipe her eyes, I broke the somber silence. "Hey, Dave, you got any Kleenex or something for Julie? I'd let her use my handkerchief, but last time, she blew her nose in it and then tried to give it back to me."

Laughter through tears looked good on Julie. I then had to explain to the group why I actually carried a handkerchief. A thirteen-year-old carrying a handkerchief in 1972 was many things, but cool was not one of them. I ended up taking more than a few insults about being a mama's boy. Intentionally making myself the target of their good-natured jabs had the desired effect. In no time whatsoever, we were all laughing again.

Later that afternoon, as I stood with Julie on her doorstep, she felt the need to apologize. "I'm sorry about crying at Dave's, but maybe it's better you know how I really feel about you having to leave again."

"Just because I didn't cry, doesn't mean I don't feel bad. But I don't want to spend this whole week thinking about what comes at the end of it. I don't want to be reminded every day that I don't live here anymore."

Sounding a bit distrusting, Julie said, "So, you just want to have a few laughs and then run off at the end of the week. Is that it?"

"That's not what I meant at all. I just want to be able to look back on this summer and be able to smile about our time together. I don't want to think about what I already know is going to happen."

In a rather challenging tone, Julie asked, "What do you think is going to happen?"

I hung my head, wanting to tell her how I already knew that someday, someone would be taking my place in her life. Instead, I heard myself say, "I'm going back to live in Duluth, knowing you live 235 miles away and there's nothing I can do about it. I don't get to stay and, like Tony said, 'always be part of the gang.'"

Julie leaned into me and softly asked, "It's gonna hurt a lot, isn't it?"

I felt as though I was acting out another scene from an old, black and white film-noir. I gave Julie a tender kiss and then delivered my line perfectly. "It already does, Jules…every time I have to do this." I then turned abruptly and dramatically walked off, leaving her to stand alone on the doorstep.

As I hurried away, Julie called after me, "Jackson, don't be like that!"

Disregarding her plea, like an immature idiot, I just kept walking.

Chapter 21

My walk back to Westwood Drive was a troubled journey. To say the least, my brain walloped me good! *You idiot! What do you think you're doing?! You're in love with her! How could you let that happen?! What good does being love do you now?!*

However, my heart sang a completely different tune. *Don't you dare leave here without telling her how you feel. After this week, you won't get another chance...ever!* Trudging along, I tried unsuccessfully to swallow the huge lump in my throat and then whispered to myself, "This whole thing sucks!"

When I arrived back at the house, I discovered the basketball lying out in the driveway. Picking it up, I decided to blow off some steam by shooting baskets. However, as I launched the ball toward the rim, I didn't care if the ball went in the hoop. Instead of aiming and shooting, I more or less just threw the ball at the basket. I was now livid and getting madder by the second, so I continued the action, over and over again. As my anger reached a boiling point, I lost sight of where I was. In fact, I was completely unaware that Kurt had stepped outside and was now watching my little meltdown.

"Hey, knock it off! What do you think you're doing?!" yelled Kurt.

Startled, I turned around and fought to regain control of myself, but it was too late. Kurt's facial expression told me he saw exactly what I wished to keep hidden. To my surprise, he didn't even ask what was wrong. Gesturing with his head for me to follow, Kurt simply walked toward the garage. We went to the rear of the car bay, where the old, heavy bag was still suspended from a rafter. There, he rummaged around some storage bins and brought out some old, padded training gloves.

Tossing the gloves to me, Kurt instructed, "Put 'em on." I did as I was told. Kurt then grabbed the bag, holding it in position for me. "Hit it," he ordered.

Remembering what I was taught, I positioned myself the proper distance from the bag. Squaring off against it, I jabbed with my left a few times and then gave it a roundhouse with my right.

"Again," said Kurt. "Show me a combination."

Once again, I did as Kurt ordered. I showed him that I hadn't forgotten a thing they had taught me. In fact, I showed him I was actually pretty good at it.

After a short while, Kurt stepped away from the bag and said, "It's hot in here. I'm going inside. Keep hitting the bag, Jackson. Get rid of whatever it is that's got you so pissed off. Do it before it eats you up…and before anyone else sees it." Kurt then turned and walked out of the garage.

I stood and watched Kurt walk away, then turned and looked at the bag. I began hitting it again, just light jabs at first, but then they slowly began to build in intensity. Remembering what Brad and Kurt taught me, I went through all kinds of combinations.

As I continued to hit the bag, my anger grew. I badly needed a release and Kurt had just led me to the perfect outlet. So, I didn't hold anything back. I simply let my anger build until it became absolute rage. I was now like an ocean crashing onto a rocky shore. My rage came on in huge waves and then ebbed. Another wave came upon me and then it receded. It came on when I thought about how much I wished I still lived in Mankato. Then, I calmed some when I thought about how my friends still accepted me. Still, another wave hit me, when I thought of the scars on my back and the man who gave them to me. The thought that Julie didn't care I bore those marks calmed me some more. I then thought of a mother and father who threw me away like a piece of garbage. The rage flowed for everyone who never wanted me to be part of their family. I then remembered my adoptive parents. I knew how much Mom and Dad loved and wanted me, but I continued to hit the bag, while picturing those within the family who didn't think me worthy. On and on I went, doing as Kurt instructed. I took every-last bit of anger out on that bag. I kept it up until my arms felt like lead weights. Finally, I stopped, but only when I could not hit the bag one more time. I had finally run out of gas. With tears in my eyes, my thoughts rested on Julie. *Why did I have to fall for a girl I can't have?*

The heat in the garage was stifling and I was soaked with sweat. When I exited, I filled my lungs with the cooler outside air. Thoroughly exhausted, my anger back in check, I could now think clearly again.

Kurt must have seen me exit the garage because he came back outside holding a large glass of water. He coolly walked to where I stood and with a concerned look affixed to his face, handed me the water. "You were in there quite a while. Cripes, Jackson, what're you so mad at?"

Still slightly out of breath, I huffed, "Everything…absolutely everything… and I'm so tired of it. The four of you are here and I'm not. All my real friends are here and I'm not, but mostly…"

Kurt interrupted and filled in the blank. "Julie is here and you're not."

Nodding my head in the affirmative, I waited for Kurt to make some rebuke about how stupidly I was behaving, but the expected admonishment never came. Instead, his look told me he wasn't going to make light of how I was feeling. In fact, I could see that he was genuinely concerned. In the past, Kurt's attitude toward me had always been somewhat dismissive, especially when he thought I was acting like an immature brat. Nevertheless, his demeanor was now totally different. It was something entirely new and something I had never seen before, which made it automatically suspect.

Nodding toward the house, Kurt said, "Go take a cold shower and cool down. When you're ready, come downstairs and see me."

"Why?" I asked.

"You'll see," replied Kurt. "Now, go de-stink-a-fy yourself."

After showering and changing, I felt much better, but my mind was still heavy. Brad, Janet and Danny were all home from work and relaxing before dinner, but I was able to slip down to the basement without anyone noticing.

When I knocked on Kurt's bedroom door, I heard loud music coming from within. He let me in, then walked to his nightstand and turned down the volume on his radio. Wearing a rather intense look, Kurt then said, "Before I tell you anything, you have to promise not to repeat this to anyone…And I mean anyone!"

"I promise."

"I mean it, Jackson, shake on it," he insisted, while thrusting his hand out to me.

Taking his hand, I repeated, "I promise." *Kurt wants me to shake on it?! Whatever it is, it must be huge!*

Holding my hand in his vice-like grip, Kurt said, "Jackson, if you tell anyone what I'm about to tell you, I'll come after you." He then let my hand go. "I know how you feel about Julie, and I know what you're going through." Kurt then walked to his bed and sat down. "When I was about your age, there was a girl I went to school with. Her name was Gwenn. She was the first girl I looked at with different eyes, as Mom would say. I fell for her pretty hard. I guess she fell for me, too. We spent the eighth grade together, going steady. Then, right after that school year, she and her family moved to the Twin Cities. Oh man, when she left, it really hurt. It hurt for quite a while, but I finally got over it."

"But you never forgot about her…Did you?"

"I didn't have to." Kurt then reached behind him and produced a shoe box.

He held it out and instructed me to take it and open it. When I removed the cover, I saw that it was filled to the brim with greeting cards and letters. I was astonished to discover how every envelope I previewed bore the name Gwenn Johnson on the return address. I looked up and saw Kurt smiling, almost warmly – a significant departure from his usual mischievous grin.

"I keep every letter, birthday card, and Christmas card she sends." Kurt then chuckled, "It's almost time for me to get another box."

Keeping my volume down, I exclaimed, "Wow! She must really be something."

"Here's her latest picture." Kurt then handed me a wallet-sized photo of a beautiful brunette with sparkling brown eyes and amazing smile.

"Wow!" I said again. "Do you write her as much as she does you?"

"She's my best friend. I write to her all the time. When I need to hear her voice, I call her on the phone. She's the person I want to talk to, especially when I can't talk to anyone else."

"What about Janelle?"

"Yeah, she's great, isn't she?" Kurt stated it like it was simply a matter of fact. "You might not understand this, but I really like going out with Janelle. I think I might even be in love with her. But I'm driving now, so someday soon, I'm taking me a trip to the Twin Cities."

I asked again, "What about Janelle?"

"Let me ask you something," he replied. "Would you disappoint Lori Mudd to be with Julie?"

"Yeah, I would."

"So, now do you understand?"

"Yeah, I think I do. I like Lori...but..."

"It's okay," Kurt interrupted. "You don't have to say the rest. My point is that you don't have to walk around this week thinking this is all you get. You're gonna see Julie again. The same way I'm gonna see Gwenn. All you have to do is wait a little while. I mean, geez, in only three years, you'll be driving! Then, in Kurt's usual and quite-sudden way, he dismissed me from his presence by stating, "I have stuff to do now, so get outta here."

Before opening the door to leave the room, Kurt once more reminded me of my vow of silence. We now shared a secret. To me, it was a colossal one. I even had to shake on it, so now I truly was on my honor to never tell anyone, including Danny.

After leaving Kurt's room, I stayed in the basement to shoot pool until dinner time. I thought about everything Kurt had said. *Would that be Julie and me? Would we really be best friends for years to come? Would she be the one I would talk to, no matter what?* I liked the idea of keeping Julie in my life the way Kurt kept Gwenn in his. I then remembered Julie's question: "Do I have to lose you completely?" *No, Jules, you don't have to lose me at all!* Suddenly, I became quite excited about the idea forming within my head. I wasn't going to worry anymore about having to leave. I was already daydreaming about future visits to Mankato. I fantasized about how

I was going to stay attached to the Wilsons and all my friends. As far as I was concerned, I truly could stay part of the gang! *If Julie can wait, we can be together every summer! After I leave, there really doesn't have to be someone else for her. Julie and I really can stay together!*

Following dinner that night, I went into the living room with Brad and Janet. The promised talk with them was about to take place. I figured they had already dropped their bomb on me that past Sunday. After my workout in the garage and my talk with Kurt, I felt ready for whatever was going to happen. I was confident I could talk to them and get them to understand about my unhappiness in Duluth. I wanted them to know all about what had been happening up there, but I also wanted them to know how things were turning around for me.

Brad asked, "How are you doing, Jackson? How do you think your stay here is going so far?"

"Great!" I exclaimed. "I actually feel like things are really changing for me. You said you've noticed a change."

Janet asked, "Do you think Julie did all that?"

"No! All of you did it! All of you have been fantastic! I can't remember the last time I've been this happy."

Taking the next thirty minutes or so, I explained how, from my perspective, each of them in one way or another helped me to get over some problem or hang-up. I also talked about how great it was to have friends who still cared, especially after a three-year absence. I even expressed my surprise about Julie and her willingness to risk a lot of pain, just so she could be with me for the week. It was all so astounding to me. "I know I'll be coming back here! If I can, I'll come back every year. I don't know exactly how just yet, but I know I'm coming back. At the end of this week, I'm going back to Duluth and I'm gonna be happy, too. I have some really great parents, but I'm gonna see all of you again. We're gonna be together again! I just know it!"

Tears welled up in Janet's eyes. The false smile she wore wasn't enough to keep me from knowing something was terribly wrong. I got up from the couch and went to her. Kneeling in front of her, I added more assurances, "You'll see, I'm gonna be fine! I promise that you'll see me again!"

Quite abruptly, Janet stood, so I did likewise. She then grabbed me, held me close and sobbed. When she regained control, she pushed away from me. Looking straight into my eyes, she said, "When you leave here, kiddo, don't come back... Please don't!" Janet then cupped her hand over her mouth and ran for the bedroom.

Stunned, I looked at Brad and saw tears in his eyes, also. "I don't understand," I said. "Don't come back?!"

As Brad spoke, his voice trembled. "You weren't supposed to come back, Jackson. You were supposed to stay with your new family.

"What?!" I couldn't believe what I was hearing.

"You have no idea what it took for us to let you go the first time. We never wanted to go through that again. We hoped and prayed that you would be happy up there and never come back here. Then, we got the call from your parents. They told us about the problems you were having. They told us how unhappy you had become. Then, they asked if we would be willing to help. Jesus, Jackson! Of course we wanted to help, but we knew then how none of this was going to be easy. We love you so much, but you had better start understanding that there really isn't anything for you down here. When you leave, you need to let this place go. I don't want to keep having you here, just to lose you again. I barely made it through the first time. I don't know how I'm going to get through it this time!" Like Janet, Brad then hurried out of the room.

I was now paralyzed. Totally confused, I could not think straight, nor did I did know exactly what to feel. I, too, remembered the pain of leaving. I was also convinced that leaving again would be excruciating. I just hadn't counted on Janet and Brad feeling the same level of pain. Over and over, a question kept repeating itself inside my head. *If you loved me so much, why did you give me away?!*

In the early evening, the mountain ash in the Wilsons' front yard gave no shade. The shadows were too long, but a cooling breeze came in from the northwest and compensated nicely. Sitting in a lawn chair, like a stone statue, I tried in vain to collect my thoughts. I felt the familiar weight of my emotional-anvil resting on my chest. In my mind, I owed someone an apology. For what, I didn't know. *What did I do wrong? What did I do to deserve all of this crud?* Right then, a singular answer came to mind. *You were born."*

Once again, I felt myself spiraling down into the dark place that all too often plagued me. How was I supposed to know not to come back? I should have taken your word for it, Doc. You were right. There's nothing for me here.

Sitting there, with the cool early-evening breeze on my face, I was convinced that I would never be happy again.

Just then, Danny bounded out the side door and grabbed a folded lawn chair, which had been carelessly left leaning against the house. He opened it, plopped it next to mine and very abruptly sat down.

Unable to control my tears and being in no mood for any of his shenanigans, my voice trembled and cracked when I pleaded, "Cripes, Danny, not now…Please?"

To my surprise, Danny spoke in a very soft and sincere tone. "I think you're just now starting to figure out how crappy this town really is. I can't wait until I'm old enough to leave here."

"You were upstairs listening again, weren't you?"

"Yeah, I heard some of it. Mostly, I heard the important stuff."

"Do you think I should have stayed away, too?"

"Jackson, you know I'm glad to see you again, but I wouldn't have blamed you a bit if you *had* stayed away. Dad's right, there's nothing for you here. There's nothing for any of us here. It just feels like this town is dying. And I don't plan on dying with it."

I then remembered Joel's words to me from the previous week, "If it weren't for my little sister, I'd be gone already." *Do they all want out of this town? Kurt wants to go find a girl. Danny just wants out and so does Joel.*

Danny was the first to notice my friends coming up the block. "Hey man, dry up. You got company coming. You look like shit, so you'd better run inside and wash your face." His smile went a long way to helping my heart feel less wounded.

After spending some time in front of the bathroom mirror, ensuring I didn't look like Danny alleged, I went back outside. Dave, Anne, Joel and Gail were talking with Danny. Of course, he was being his usual, crass self.

I put on a weak smile and I greeted my friends. "What's up guys?"

Anne asked, "Are you and Julie fighting already?"

"Not that I know of," I replied.

Joel asked, "We're on our way over there. Are you comin'?"

"What's going on?" I asked.

"She's been crying, Jackson," said Gail. "She thinks you don't want to see her anymore."

"What?!"

"Something about it being too hard for you two," said Anne. "You having to leave at the end of the week and all. She thinks you want to end it now...before it gets too rough."

Damn! Is anything gonna go right today? The thought screamed through my head. I looked to Danny and said, "Let Mom and Dad know where I am, will you?"

As Danny slowly nodded his head, he stated "Geez, you're not having a very good day. Go ahead, take off."

On the way to Julie's, Gail tried to claim responsibility for all the drama that seemed to be taking up so much of that day. "I'm sorry, Jackson. This wouldn't be happening if I hadn't said that stuff in Dave's basement."

"You didn't cause this, Gail," I said. "It's not your fault."

When we arrived at the Falkner residence, Marilyn greeted us at the door. She seemed very pleased to see us, especially me. As Marilyn ushered us to the basement doorway, she said, "The girls are downstairs. Go make yourself at home."

The others went down ahead of me. Before I could follow, Marilyn tugged at my sleeve and smiled. "I have a rather upset daughter on my hands. She didn't think she was going to see you again."

"I'm sorry. I don't know where she got that from. I wouldn't do that to her."

Marilyn's smile broadened. "That's just what I told her. Now, go make my girl smile again, will ya?"

When I got to the bottom of the stairs, I surveyed the lounge to locate Julie.

She spied me first and got up from the couch she had been sitting on. As she hurried to me, I spied tears in her eyes.

When Julie reached me, she threw her arms around me and cried softly, "Don't you even think about letting me go just yet." So, I held her until the waterworks ended. When Julie finally loosened her death grip on my neck, she simply said, "Hi," then commenced to wiping tears from her eyes.

For the first time in my life, I actually attempted to be charming. Speaking as warmly and softly as possible, I smiled and said, "Hi."

"This afternoon, at my door, I thought..." Julie began, but I put my fingers up to her lips to stop her from saying more.

In a hushed tone, I said, "I know what you thought, but you're wrong. Until I leave, you're going to see me every day. I've got it all figured out. Later, I'll tell you all about it."

Julie smiled sweetly and asked, "Are you still a momma's boy?"

"What?"

Giggling, Julie asked, "Do you still have the handkerchief your mom makes you carry?"

I laughed and took the clean hanky from my back pocket, handed it to her and said, "You might want to keep that."

As Julie dried her eyes, she facetiously said, "Oh, shut up."

Girls and crying, I thought, *Geez!*

Shortly thereafter, Julie led me to the couch, where she had sat earlier. Together, we plopped ourselves down. Julie then clutched my arm and snuggled in close. I eyed the others and they watched us with great interest, but nobody said a word.

After a few moments of uncomfortable silence, Gail voiced another apology. "Julie, I'm sorry. I got all this started by saying those things in Dave's basement."

Again, I interrupted. "Gail, I told you, none of this is your fault; it's mine."

Joel asked, "How do you figure?"

Speaking matter-of-factly, I said, "I came back. I wasn't supposed to do that."

In genuine surprise, Anne exclaimed, "What?!"

I then proceeded to inform my friends about some of what had transpired in the Wilsons' living room that very evening. Listening intently, they all shook their heads in disbelief.

"Oh, man, that sucks!" said Dave.

"I didn't know I wasn't supposed to come back," I said. "Part of me says I'll never make that mistake again."

Julie's look turned extremely serious, as she blurted, "I hope there's another part that tells you something else!"

I smiled and replied, "That part tells me I'll definitely be coming back."

To that, Julie smiled, but I could see she wasn't totally convinced.

For a little while, our little group got quiet, as if we were all caught up in our own thoughts. Then, Joel broke the silence. "Hey, Jackson, why'd you want to come back here so badly?"

"Well, I missed the Wilsons really bad for one. They were the first real family I ever had. Two, there's you guys. I missed you all like crazy. I will again, too…I know it. You see, I don't have this up north. I don't hang out with anyone up there. I don't have a group of friends who know me, like you guys do. I've tried to fit in, but it's not easy. I don't think I'll ever have this in Duluth. I don't have my two big brothers watching out for me up there, either. I honestly feel like all I have is me, my mom, my dad, and that's it. I can't count on anyone else."

Dave asked, "You don't have any friends up there?"

"Not like you guys. I have casual friends up there. I can take 'em or leave 'em. They don't matter too much to me. We're not close. When I go back to school in the fall, I don't think there will be anybody saying, 'Hey, good to see you again,' or, 'we missed you this summer.' I haven't been lucky enough to find a group like you guys."

At that point, Gail attempted to lighten the mood. "That's it; Duluth is full of stupid girls." She then shot me a huge smile.

"Personally, I'm glad of that," giggled Julie. "There's nothing like having no competition!"

"What about you guys?" I asked. "When you're old enough, do you all want to leave here?"

One by one, they all expressed their interest in leaving Mankato. Joel didn't necessarily care where he went. He just wanted to get away. Dave wanted to go to college and play football for Notre Dame. After that, he wanted to play professional ball for the Minnesota Vikings. Anne wanted college, also, but she wanted to attend the University of Minnesota. As a Golden Gopher, she would be able to get home to see family and friends during the holidays and summer breaks. After college, Anne wasn't sure what she wanted to do. Gail wanted to go to New York. She said she had been to Minneapolis and saw all the tall buildings. Then, she looked at pictures of the skyscrapers in New York City and just knew that's where she wanted to be.

The whole time the others spoke, Julie stayed quiet, so I asked, "What about you?"

"Right now, I think the first chance I get to leave..." Julie hesitated to think. She then took in a large breath of air, let it out easy, and continued. "I wanna go north, to a city this really cute guy told me about. It has a lake you can't even see across. There's this house on a hillside, with a big picture window that overlooks the lake and the harbor. Yeah, I wanna see that. If he's still there, that's where I wanna go." Julie smiled kind of slyly at me and then said, "After that, I'll come back here. I love my family and this is where I'm from. I may move to the Twin Cities someday, but I doubt I'll leave Minnesota." She then gave me a serious look and then said. "I mean, I don't see that moving far away has done you any good."

Dumbstruck, I didn't know how to respond. Julie must have sensed it because she smiled, shook her head, and then whispered, "You didn't count on that, did you?"

I simply admitted, "You're hitting me with too many things I didn't count on."

My heart was once again trying to escape the confines of my ribcage. *How does she do that?* I was suddenly tempted to utter some very important words, but my head got in the way again. *Don't do it, Landry!* Before I could open my mouth, Julie saved me.

"Hey guys, it's supposed to be really hot again tomorrow. Let's all hang out by the pool in the afternoon.

The suggestion got excited affirmative responses from the others. I stayed quiet, so Julie asked, "What about you? Can you make it?"

"I can, but I'll be late." I explained how I would be meeting Father Michael and Adam Harris after lunch. Then, attempting to be funny, I said, "I'd much rather be here, especially now that I've seen you in a swimsuit."

Giving me a playful swat and a shocked expression, Julie exclaimed, "You're terrible!" She giggled, but then got a concerned look on her face. "Are you worried about seeing Adam tomorrow?"

I thought about her question for a moment because I hadn't taken much time to think on the meeting. I had been dealing with too many other things. "No, I don't think so," I replied. "He doesn't matter much to me now. You see, there's this really-pretty girl who has been taking up a lot of my brain these days."

To that, Julie kissed me, very tenderly. I truly didn't want to stop, but we both noticed that we had an audience. We had forgotten that Lisa was still downstairs with us. I looked to a nearby lounge chair and found her staring in our direction. Julie quickly gave her a get-outta-here look, to which Lisa smiled and without argument, graciously left the basement.

"I think she has a crush on you," whispered Julie. "I don't blame her."

Jokingly, I responded. "What's it been, fifteen minutes since I last turned red?"

The others were already busy making out, so I thought, *I guess it's time to put that smile on Marilyn's daughter's face.*

Saying good night to Julie was becoming more difficult. Nevertheless, ending our days, with her kiss on my lips, had become absolutely exhilarating. Just a few days prior, I was self-conscious about holding her hand in public. But that night, Julie and I kissed good-bye right in front of Marilyn. Of course, it wasn't my idea. To me, it seemed that nothing Julie and I did ever was of my design, but I didn't mind going with the flow, either. To tell the truth, it was actually beginning to feel...natural.

Surprisingly, Marilyn didn't seem to mind. I suppose you could say that we were all learning something new at the same time. Julie was testing the comfort limits of her parents...and me. I was learning to deal with a whole bunch of new feelings, which I had previously only read about in books, or saw in the movies. Marilyn was learning that her little girl was not so little anymore. I adjudged she was handling it beautifully.

That night, the walk home was not a comfortable one for me. The others talked excitedly about the prospect of hanging out by the Falkners' pool, but I stayed quiet. I was too busy thinking about what the climate would be like, when I stepped back inside the Wilsons' door. It must have shown on my face.

"Jackson, are you gonna be okay?" asked Anne. "I mean, when you get to the Wilsons', will there be trouble?"

"I think it'll get worked out," I replied. "When I left here, I never thought much about how they all felt. I didn't know it was so hard on them because I was too busy feeling sorry for myself."

With all the sensitivity of a rock, Dave said, "Well, I'm sure they'll get over it. You will, too, right?"

I was neither surprised nor offended by David's assertion. I was used to his brand of bluntness and knew that insensitivity was not his intention, especially toward his friends. Dave's approach to dealing with life's dilemmas was the same as you would a minor football injury – rub some dirt in it and get back in the game. He got his when-the-going-gets-tough-the-tough-get-going mentality from his dad. I remembered that he applied it liberally, too, especially when he had nothing else to offer, which was practically always. So, to Dave's candor, I simply replied, "I guess I'm gonna have to, aren't I?"

When I let myself in the side door and stepped into the kitchen, it was almost ten o'clock. Janet and Brad were seated at the table, playing cribbage again. The noise emanating from the basement told me that, once again, Kurt and Danny had a bunch of their friends over.

I didn't care to join the partying teens in the basement, nor did I want to talk to the supervising adults. I simply wanted to escape to the upstairs, so I could go to bed and put the day behind me. However, when Janet and I locked eyes, I knew that wasn't going to happen right away.

In a not-so-sorrowful tone, Janet muttered, "I'm sorry I said those things to you."

Sarcastically, I replied, "Yeah…And I'm sorry that you giving me away didn't work out the way everyone planned." I then rushed past them and hurried up the stairs.

As I lay down on the bed, I held my breath, hoping they wouldn't follow me. *Enough for one day!*

I was ashamed of the words I had just spoken. It was way too bold of me. I had never taken such an attitude with my elders before, especially elders I loved and respected. Lying on my stomach, I listened at the heating vent by the bed. My ears searched for any sign that Brad, Janet, or both might want to continue the discussion.

For a few, tense moments, no words emanated from the vent. Then, I heard Brad's voice come through the small metal grill. "Let's just sleep on it tonight. He's upset and so are we, so let's not make it worse. I made a huge mistake tonight. Now he thinks all of this is his fault."

"Brad, what the hell were we thinking back then? How did we ever let her force our hand that way? Look what it's done to us."

"I know, but I don't regret the decision to let him go without a fight. This God-damned town would never have given him a chance to be happy."

"It doesn't sound like he's been very happy up there, either," said Janet.

"The opportunity is still there for him," countered Brad. "All the opportunities for him are with the Landrys."

"What do you think Adam is going to tell him tomorrow?" asked Janet.

"I don't know…the truth probably…as much of it as he knows," replied Brad.

"You know, we're going to have to tell him everything, don't you?" insisted Janet.

"If it keeps him from wanting to come back to this dirty little place…then yeah…we'll tell him…we'll tell him everything."

"God help us, Brad. He's been hurt so much already. I can't stand it."

After a short pause, I heard Brad's voice again. "When it's time, I'll do it. I'll tell him. Now, come on, let's forget the game. I'll put you to bed."

With a prominent tremble in her voice, Janet asked, "Will you…stay with me?"

"Do you want me to?"

Another pause and then I heard Janet finally say, "Yes, yes I do."

Rolling onto my back, my mind began to work overtime, as it began analyzing new information. *What the hell is going on here? Who's this woman who "forced their hand" and how did she do it? What did Brad mean? "Let me go without a fight?" What is it about this town that makes them want me to stay away?*

After thinking on it for a while, another revelation dawned on me. *Great!* I sarcastically thought. *Brad and Janet have been fighting again. How did I miss the signs? Him sleeping on the couch or by himself in the room, Janet reading late into the night with the bedroom door closed. I should have known!*

In the Wilson house, not fighting in front of us three boys was a steadfast rule. However, in the past, there had always been clear-enough signs to tip us off. We hated it when Brad and Janet were not getting along, not because of any additional noise, like yelling or screaming; there wasn't any. It was because of the way the house felt. Laughter is what we boys were accustomed to, but when the house became quiet for days or weeks, we knew something was wrong. I had always feared they would one day go too far and decide not to make up. For the past week, the signs had all been there. I rationalized that I was just too wrapped up in my own problems to notice. Now, I was afraid that Brad and Janet's marriage was in trouble again.

I then decided to stay awake, so I could talk to Danny. He would know a thing or two. If I was patient, I'd get my answers from him. While waiting, I tried to read, but couldn't concentrate. I thought about going down to the basement and joining the teens there. But I was afraid Lori Mudd might be there and I was in no mood, whatsoever, to tangle with her. I then began to think of Julie and our evening together. Through all the turmoil that appeared to be rising, Julie and my friends seemed to be the ones to keep me grounded. I looked forward to hanging out by the pool with them.

While my thoughts were on Julie, I allowed myself to relax. Because of all the exercise I had gotten that day, plus the emotional roller coaster I had been on, I suddenly felt quite exhausted. My eyelids became lead weights and my thoughts were no longer focused. Sometime before Danny came to bed, I lost my battle and allowed myself to drift off to sleep.

Chapter 22

Tuesday, August 15th 1972

Once again, when Brad left for work that morning, I heard the Corvair pull out of the driveway. I woke up, but just for a moment. My next cognizant thought came much later, when the breeze coming through the bedroom window was no longer cool. The upstairs had heated up fast and I began to sweat under the covers, so I kicked them off. Rolling over, I looked at Danny's clock radio and when 10:55 A.M. appeared before my eyes, I groaned. I immediately felt robbed. I had wasted practically the entire morning. Disgusted with myself, I drowsily rolled out of bed and got into my blue jeans. Not bothering to put on a shirt, I stumbled down the stairs and immediately felt cooler, but also embarrassed. There at the kitchen table sat Janelle, grinning at me, like I had just made her day.

As Janelle got up to claim her ritualistic hug, she said, "Well, look who finally got out of bed."

Wanting to turn right around to go retrieve a shirt, I awkwardly replied, "Hi."

"Kurt is still downstairs, getting ready to go, so have a seat and keep me company," insisted Janelle.

The previous Sunday at the lake, Janelle had already seen my back, but I was still self-conscious about my scars, especially around girls. So, doing my best to keep from putting my back on display, I slipped into a chair opposite her. Then, in a feeble attempt to minimize my upper-body nakedness, I folded my arms across my chest. Trying to hide my awkwardness, I coolly asked, "Where are you guys off to today?"

"Kurt is taking me out to lunch and then we're going shopping."

Genuinely surprised, I asked, "Kurt is going shopping?"

Janelle giggled a little and then said, "As hard as that is to believe, yes, he is. He's so good to me. I guess that's why I love him the way I do." She then looked me directly in the eye. I could tell she was looking for some type of response from me, but I just kept my face blank and nodded my understanding.

I then asked, "Does he know it?"

"I hope so. I mean, I've tried to tell him, but sometimes girls get tongued-tied, too. I guess I'm afraid he might not feel the same way."

Enjoying the fact that Janelle was taking me into her confidence, I smiled and gestured for her to come closer. I then leaned forward and spoke softly in her ear, "Don't be afraid. You're safe."

Janelle immediately brightened and asked, "Has he said something?"

I gave her nothing more than the slightest of grins, while I carefully considered my answer. I wanted to tell her what Kurt had divulged to me the day before, but a promise is a promise. Also, I could see that satisfying the question in her mind was going to be difficult. Additionally, I felt bad for her because I knew she only had a portion of Kurt's heart. I then wondered what chance another girl had with me, when Julie had such a firm grip on mine. *Why does all this guy-girl stuff have to be so complicated?* I thought. But Janelle still needed an answer.

"Remember all the great advice you gave me?" I asked.

"Yeah."

"You should follow some of it. You gotta excuse me now, I have to go shower." I immediately got up and moved toward the bathroom.

Janelle impatiently called after me, "Jackson!"

Abruptly turning on my heels, I returned to where she sat. I bent down, kissed her cheek, and then whispered, "I *will* talk to you later. I promise, but I really have to go shower now. I have someplace to be soon."

Janelle smiled and said, "Okay, later, but remember, you promised."

After showering, I felt much better, but my mood still wasn't the greatest. I had a lot of confused thoughts bouncing around inside my head and wasn't quite sure what to do with all of them. There were too many questions that needed answering, plus I was beginning to get nervous about meeting with Father Michael and Adam. At the same time, I was anxious to be done with Adam entirely. I wanted nothing to get in the way of enjoying myself with the gang later.

When I picked out my ensemble, I did so for the entire day. I donned my cleanest pair of blue jeans and light blue t-shirt. I didn't want to wear dress slacks or anything that formal, not for a meeting with Adam, but I didn't want to look like a total slob, either. I could just imagine what the ghostly Mrs. Patterson would think if I did. In addition, I didn't want to waste any time getting to Julie's after the meeting. So, instead of wearing my normal tighty-whitey briefs under my jeans, I put on my swimsuit. As I dressed in the late morning heat of the bedroom, I heard Kurt and Janelle leave the house.

When I finished getting ready, it was lunchtime and I was quite hungry. But I knew that if I ate anything heavy, while being so nervous, it would be a huge mistake. So, I opted for peanut butter and jelly on toast.

While I ate, the phone rang. It was Julie, calling to wish me good luck. "I hope the meeting goes well for you," she said. "I think you could use some good news for a change."

"I'll take that," I said. "Right now, I just want it to be over with."

"Jackson?"

"Yeah?"

"I wish you were here already. So, I hope this meeting ends up being worth your time."

Funny…I was thinking the exact same thing, I thought, but then said, "Thanks, I'll make it as quick as I can."

We talked a little while longer, but then, quite suddenly, Julie apologized and said she had to go – some of the gang was at her door already.

Please don't hang up, I thought. *I have nothing else to do until the meeting.*

Instead, I let her off the hook by saying that it was okay.

"See you later?"

"I'll hurry...Bye."

I had thirty minutes to kill but had no idea what to do with the time. So, I went down to the basement and turned on the TV. I checked all four channels and found nothing other than soap operas to watch. I had about as much use for that brand of drama as I did a meeting with Adam Harris. So, I tromped back upstairs and decided to read the previous night's newspaper. The main headline read: "Hijackers get life sentence." As I read the story about an ongoing trial in Israel, what caught my attention was not the fate of the hijackers themselves, but their accomplices. Two Arab girls, who helped hijack a Sabena Airlines flight of Belgian origin, got a sentence of twenty-five years in prison. The accused apparently had weapons and explosives with them and planned to use them. Their pleas for clemency were ignored by military officials.

As I digested the disturbing story, I shook my head. *They brought weapons and explosives on board and planned to use them. Their pleas for the judge to go easy on them were ignored. Gee...ya think?*

When I left the house and headed toward St Joseph's, the heat was already becoming unbearable, especially as it radiated off the asphalt-covered streets. With the sun so high in the sky, there wasn't much shade to protect me, either. Hurrying along, I hoped that I wouldn't get too sweaty before getting to the rectory.

I was now in more of a hurry for the meeting to be done. My friends were already gathered around the pool at Julie's and I was impatient to join them. At the same time, I was still curious about what information Adam intended to divulge.

Upon arriving, I took in a large breath and let it out. I then rang the doorbell and prepared myself to see the tall, Irish lady again.

When Mrs. Patterson answered the door, she wore what I'm sure she thought was her warmest smile. To me, she appeared more like a dog, when baring its teeth. "Hello, Jackson," she said. "It's good to see you again."

"Hi, Mrs. Patterson, how are you?"

"I'm good, young man. Punctual again I see; very good."

"Yes, ma'am."

After taking my shoes off, Mrs. Patterson led me into the living room. The air was permeated with the smell of whatever she had cooked for lunch. Suddenly, my stomach growled loudly from lack of sustenance. I was sure Mrs. Patterson heard it, too, but she politely gave no indication that she had.

When I entered the living room, I saw that Father Michael was sitting at his favorite end of the couch. Adam sat in a comfortable lounger.

Father Michael jumped up to greet me, exclaiming, "There you are, Jacky. Welcome and come on in, lad." He then extended his hand, so I took it.

Giving Father Michael a solid handshake, I tried to make my greeting sound mature. "Hello, Father, it's good to see you again." I then turned to Adam. He didn't stand up to greet me, but I went to him anyway, hand extended. *The moron doesn't even know enough to stand up when greeting someone,* I thought. Mom always said there was never a justifiable reason for rudeness, but right then, I could think of a few.

Adam took my much smaller hand and gave it a gentle squeeze, then in a flat tone said, "Hello, Jackson."

"Sir," was the only greeting I wished to return. For emphasis, I used the same flat tone he did, and I looked him dead in the eye, without blinking, just to show him that I was no longer afraid of him. I then turned, walked back to the couch, and positioned myself at the opposite end from Father Michael. The seating arrangements were fine with me. With Father Michael between Adam and me, I felt a lot less threatened by my used-to-be father. Still, I kept a wary eye on him.

Adam was dressed differently than any time I could recall in the past. He wore a white short-sleeved dress shirt, combined with a not-too-distasteful necktie, light grey dress slacks and black dress socks. He too had to leave his shoes at the door. Adam's ensemble made him look more like an educated businessman, than a lowly, machine-shop worker.

"Well then," began Father Michael, "Let's go ahead and get started. Jackson, would you like to begin?"

"This wasn't my idea, Father. I think he should go first."

Adam smiled slightly and nodded his agreement. He nervously pulled at the knot of his necktie, cleared his throat, and generally looked as though he were searching for how to begin. When he finally spoke, his nervousness was all too obvious. "Um, I suppose I should start by telling you how good you look. You look…um…extremely healthy and strong. You…ah…appear to be growing up well. Your parents, are they good people?"

I thought about my answer carefully. Then, speaking confidently, I replied, "My parents are *great* people. They take very good care of me." *Much better than you ever did,* I thought.

"That's good. I'm glad," countered Adam.

A less than cordial, "I'll bet," was my retort.

Condescendingly, Father Michael whispered, "Jacky, give him a chance."

Insincerely, I replied, "Sorry."

"It's okay, Father," said Adam. "I was prepared for a certain amount of animosity from Jackson. I am partly to blame for everything he's been through." As an afterthought, Adam asked me, "Do you know what I mean by that?"

"My animosity? I queried. "Yeah, it means you're prepared for how much I really do hate you." I then thought him ridiculous for trying to talk over my head.

"Very good," said Adam. "I'm glad you're not as afraid as you once were, but that's not why we're here. I wanted to offer you an apology and…maybe an explanation."

Glowering, I asked, "For what?"

"For my part of how your mother and I failed you. Jackson, I've never been proud of how everything turned out, but I am truly glad you're in good hands now."

Reminded of the newspaper article I had read earlier, I thought, *"Your pleas for clemency shall be ignored."*

Adam continued, "When I married your mother, I wasn't ready to be a dad. All I really wanted was…your mother."

"What?!" I exclaimed. I was now totally confused. *He wasn't ready to be a dad but had three sons?!*

"Please, let me explain," pleaded Adam, his tone a little desperate. "I was in love with your mother. I had loved her since we were kids in school. Hell…half of the men in this town were in love with her. You see, Jackson...back then... Mankato was even smaller than it is now...and your mom was this..."

Sarcastically, I interrupted by blurting, "Beautiful creature?! Yeah, I've heard this one before. She was the most beautiful woman in town." My courage was now building and so was my anger.

Adam countered, "Yes, she was, but beauty is only skin deep." His tone was almost remorseful.

I've heard that one, too, I admitted to myself, but showed no sign that would afford Adam hope.

"Your mother never loved me. I think it's because I couldn't give her what she really wanted."

"And what was that?"

"Her freedom."

"Her freedom? So...what...you took it out on me?!" My anger was still building.

"What?" Adam's confusion showed all over his face.

I sneered and said, "You weren't ready to be a dad, but you had three boys. Mom didn't love you, so you took it out on me."

Father Michael's presence had acted as a security buffer, which only served to fuel my audacity. So, I fired the accusations at Adam and felt ready for more verbal combat. In return, Adam simply relaxed in his chair and thought for a moment. He became calm, like he had just reconciled his will for what was to come.

In a calm and clear voice, Adam said, "I was hoping you would have remembered better, but it's clear to me now that you know very little about what really happened. Of course, you don't remember. You were too little."

"What do you mean?" I asked.

"You think I'm your father."

"Well..." I began, but Adam interrupted.

"That is...you think I'm the man who got your mom pregnant with you."

"Well...yeah...of course."

"Jackson, I'm not your biological father. I never was. I'm just the guy who tried to bail your mom out, when she had gotten herself into trouble. I hoped, in time, she would learn to love me for it. But, I realized, too late mind you, that was never going to happen."

I had now heard enough. To me, Adam's words made absolutely no sense. My temper wasn't helping matters, either. Now seething, I asserted, "So, you beat me half to death and tore us all apart. Is that it?"

Adam exclaimed, "Jackson, no! That's…That's not the way it was at all!"

I didn't want to hear another word. My anger was spilling over into every response I gave, and I knew I would not be able to stop. I was losing control and now felt a desperate need to leave. So, I jumped up from the couch and said, "I have to go now, Father. I knew this wouldn't work out."

Father Michael pleaded, "Jackson, please, wait now! You're getting yourself all worked up."

I ignored his plea and continued toward the entryway to get my tennis shoes on. *Damn Mrs. Patterson and her clean-house rules,* I thought.

"Jackson!" called Adam. "I'm not the one who put you in the hospital. Don't you remember? Your mother did that!"

It was now too late. His accusation against a woman who could no longer defend herself sent my temper past the boiling point. I looked at him and with hatred in every fiber of my being, I exploded, "YOU LIAR!" I then pulled my t-shirt over my head, took it off, and wadded it up in my clenched fist. Displaying my back to the two of them, I yelled, "YOU DID THIS TO ME!" Then, in a slightly calmer, but still primal tone, I continued. "She never touched me! It was you! It was always you and that belt! It just figures you would try to blame her. If she was still alive, I'll bet she'd have a different story." I then bent down to finish pulling my tennis shoes on, yelling, "YOU'RE A COWARD! YOU'RE A LYING COWARD!"

"Jackson, no! That's not the way it was!" Adam insisted.

From the kitchen, Mrs. Patterson hustled into the middle of the confrontation, scolding the two men, "You leave him be! Can't you see he's upset?!"

When I stood, Mrs. Patterson grabbed me and attempted to calm me, but all I wanted was to see the other side of the door. Totally out of control, I pulled away and fiercely fought with the doorknob until the door opened.

I then heard Father Michael behind me. "Oh no, dear God," he said, his voice slightly trembling.

I turned momentarily to look at him and saw that he had tears in his eyes. I then bolted out of the door with my t-shirt still wadded up in my hand, scarcely aware that I was running in the wrong direction.

I ran around the rectory and instinctively bolted toward the front of the church. It had been a few years, but I needed my safe place, my sanctuary. Barely slowing down enough to open the heavy glass door, I fumbled uncontrollably, trying to grasp the handle. When I finally obtained a firm grip on it, I heaved backward. Once inside, I didn't even bother to assess my surroundings.

Thinking that I was totally alone, I ran up the center aisle and practically threw myself into the third pew from the front, on the right side. Safely there, I hit my knees, but didn't pray. In my head, I simply shouted at God. *I'm losing my mind!* In a desperate attempt to stop my tears, I closed my eyes tightly. I was afraid to open them. *Is this nightmare ever going to end?! Where do I belong?! Why can't it be here?! Why can't someone in this God-forsaken town tell me I belong to them?!*

Just then, the most soothing voice I ever heard said, "What's this now? Are ya okay in there? Aw, look at ya, boy. Yer shakin' like a leaf."

I slowly looked up to find an aged, but somehow familiar face. The man before me was clearly in his seventies or older. His facial features bespoke of years in the hot sun. Liver spots dotted his cheeks and brow. Deep lines creased his face, giving him an extremely weathered appearance. Wavy, snow-white hair was brushed back atop his head. His smile was warm, and his eyes were a brilliant shade of blue. Like Grandpa Mack's, the man's eyes seem to hold the wisdom of the ages.

The grandfatherly figure knelt in the aisle at the edge of the pew. From there, he tried to coax me from the kneeler. He then cautiously sat on the bench next to me. As he sat, I backed away some to keep a safe distance from him. If gramps tried anything funny, I wanted to be able to bolt and get out of there.

Speaking softly, the man said, "Come on up from there now, son, and let's have a look at ya." His thick Irish accent had the same calming effect on me as Father Michael's.

Unable to take my eyes off the elderly gentleman, I slowly got up from the kneeler and sat on the bench but still kept a little space between us. His gaze, though totally benign, was almost hypnotic. In a nonthreatening manner, he slowly and carefully reached toward me, gently placing his hand on my all-but-forgotten t-shirt. The whole while, he kept smiling, so I felt fairly sure that he meant me no harm. As he gently pulled at the shirt, I simply allowed it to leave my grasp. I then watched as he straightened my t-shirt and prepared to put it on me.

The man again spoke, ever so softly. "I know it's hot outside, lad, but let's get this on ya before ya catch yer death of cold in here." Then, he instructed, "Arms up."

It was like being a toddler again and my mom was dressing me. I simply did as I was told and he gently pulled the soft, cotton garment down over my head.

I took care of the final adjustments and then managed to speak. "Thank you, sir. I'll be fine now." I then wiped tears from my eyes, trying to hide my embarrassment.

"What's got ya so upset, boy?"

"It's a long story, sir."

"What's your name?"

"Jackson...Jackson Landry."

"That's a crackerjack of a name! Well, Jackson Landry, it sometimes helps to trust a stranger with yer troubles, especially someone who is willing to listen. I'd like to help, if ya let me."

"Who are you?" I asked. "You look...familiar."

"Do you know Father Michael here at St. Joseph's?"

"Yes, sir."

"Well, I'm his oldest brother, Patrick, come to visit him from Ireland."

I smiled and asked, "Are you from Balbriggan?"

Genuinely impressed, Patrick exclaimed, "Aye, lad, are you familiar with Ireland?!"

"Only what Father Michael has told me about it. It sounds like someplace I might want to visit someday."

"Ahhh…to be a world traveler…is that what you want to be when you grow up?"

"No, sir. I don't even want to leave this town, but I'll have to…and soon."

Patrick's mannerisms were enchanting. In a very short time, he got me to relax and smile. I felt compelled to give him a brief history of my troubles, right up to what had just transpired in the rectory. He patiently listened and nodded his understanding.

When I was finished, he paused thoughtfully, then said, "Ya have more scars than the ones I've seen on your back, lad. I hope…no…I'll pray…that someday you are able to find out the truth of the matter…and that it brings ya peace." He then put his hand on my shoulder. I never felt such warmth. His smile literally pierced my heart. In that very moment, it was as if he singlehandedly dissolved all my pain and despair.

Patrick then asked, "Now then, don't you have someplace yer supposed to be?"

"Yes sir. There's friends waiting for me, but…thank you for listening. You were right. It helped."

"That's good," replied Patrick. "I'll take my leave from ya then."

"Yes, sir."

"You are well met, Jackson Landry. Now, smile and be off with ya. And have a blessed day."

Patrick then exited the pew and when he walked down the center aisle, I turned to watch his departure. As he walked, the old man was slightly hunched over. I assumed his poor posture was the result of many years of hard work. I continued to watch until he disappeared through one of the large wooden doors, which led to the vestibule.

For a few minutes longer, I sat, staring blankly at the wooden door my new friend had just exited. When I snapped out of my momentary trance, I marveled at how much better I felt. It was as if Patrick had pulled my heart from a vice. Just then, I remembered that a pretty girl and some good friends were waiting for me at a swimming pool. So, I got out of the pew and turned toward the altar. Simultaneously, I crossed myself and genuflected. Then, I began my walk toward the rear of the church. From a pew, several rows back from where I had previously sat, an elderly woman gestured to me. I was in a hurry, but I didn't wish to be rude, so I smiled and went to her. Yes, ma'am?" I queried.

With a worried look on her face, the woman asked, "Young man, just now, who were you talking to?"

"He was Father Michael's older brother, Patrick," I replied. I then smiled, nodded politely, and left her sitting there. However, before I continued down the aisle, I noted her look of what I could only assess as being that of sincere bewilderment.

Wow, I thought, *you'd think she just saw a ghost!*

Chapter 23

As I approached the Falkner residence, I heard loud music and shrill laughter coming from the rear of the property. More than Patrick's words of encouragement, the cheerful sounds immediately lightened my mood. My mind switched gears and I was temporarily able to put away all troublesome thoughts. Since I was expected, I let myself in the Falkners' side gate, which led to their backyard and pool area.

The Falkners had a splendid backyard, which was taken up mainly by their large inground swimming pool. The neighbors could gossip all they wanted about the Falkners waving money under everyone's nose, just by having that pool. I could not have cared less. In fact, in that afternoon heat, I was rather glad they had it.

A four-car garage was located to the south of the pool area. Next to it stood a small cabana. Attached to the cabana, a large outdoor sauna bath was available.

The mortared Flagstone patio was quite large. It extended out from the house and then connected to the pool deck. It was partially covered by a gabled roof, which extended off the kitchen. It provided much needed shade during peak daylight hours.

At the far end of the pool's deck, a horseshoe-shaped semicircle of rose bushes butted up against ultra-white fencing. Vibrant reds, subtle pinks, and basic white spoke of a woman's touch. Various species of red and pink rose bushes stood tall, with variegated hostas directly beneath. The borders were comprised of red begonias. Where the Falkners' property terminated pink and red snapdragons stood erect against the backdrop of a cedar fence, which was also painted an ultra-white. Against the house, pink and white clematis vines climbed decorative lattice panels.

After taking in the entire backyard, I looked to my friends. The girls were sunning themselves on patio loungers, while the guys horsed around in the pool. Tony, of course, was up to his usual antics. I watched him attempt to splash the girls by performing a cannon ball off the diving board.

Dave was the first to notice my arrival and alerted everyone else by yelling, "Hey man, it's about time you got here!"

Julie looked up and broke out a huge smile for me. She got up from her lounger and sauntered toward my direction. *Wow!* I thought. *She's wearing a bikini!*

To me, Julie was positively stunning in her floral-patterned bikini of pink roses. As she approached, I tried to hide my surprise.

Julie exclaimed, "Like Dave said, 'it's about time you got here!'" She then planted a kiss on my lips. Even though I was rapidly getting used to Julie's fearlessness, her showy way of greeting me caused me to immediately look to see if Marilyn was in the vicinity. "You can change into your swimsuit over in the cabana," continued Julie, as she looked around me to see if I had actually brought one.

Innocently, I asked, "You mean, I can't just strip right here?"

"I don't mind," laughed Julie, "but Mom is probably watching right now and would have a fit."

Giving Julie a sly smile, I kicked off my tennis shoes and pulled off my socks. Keeping our eyes locked, I unfastened the top button of my jeans. When I pulled down the zipper, her eyes shot wide open. I slowly pulled my jeans down around my knees and then let them drop to my ankles. When I stepped out of my pants, cat calls and whistles erupted from Gail, Anne, and Nancy. When Julie spotted my swimsuit, she laughed and breathed a sigh of relief. Swiftly, I picked up my jeans and hung them haphazardly on a nearby patio chair.

As I turned to head toward the pool, Julie stopped me by pulling at the back of my t-shirt. She asked, "Aren't you forgetting something?"

Julie then watched me look at the others uneasily, then back to her. I opened my mouth to speak but was sweetly interrupted. In a flash, Julie closed the distance between us. Before I could voice my discomfort about putting my back on display, Julie's hand covered by mouth. She then put her lips by my ear and softly whispered, "It's okay, they know already."

"Julie, I don't think…"

"Trust me," she breathed. She then bit her lower lip and began to pull my t-shirt up.

Resisting, I stepped away from her. I truly didn't think I was ready, but at the same time, I didn't want to come off like Mr. Chicken. So, I forced myself to turn my back toward the pool and reluctantly pulled the shirt over my head. Wadding it up in a ball, I tossed it on the same chair that my jeans hung on. Deliberately turning, so that my back was toward the others, I muttered, "Might as well get it over with."

Julie stepped up to me, put her arms around my neck, smiled sweetly and gazed into my eyes. It was almost like being hypnotized. I was absolutely paralyzed by the adoring look she gave me. Suddenly, her smile turned quite mischievous. Julie then gave me a slight push backward, where strong hands waited to grab my arms and legs. The guys lifted me off my feet and then carried me toward the pool.

As they launched me out into the deep end, I barely had time to take in a breath. When I returned to the surface, I was not surprised one bit to find everyone laughing at me. While treading water, I found Julie's laughing eyes and in a mimicking voice, I exclaimed, "Trust me, she says!"

The cool water felt wonderful, so I was in no hurry to get back out. Instead, I swam to the shallow end. There, I waded and watched, as the other guys jumped in, also. The girls returned to their loungers, all except Julie. She came to where I waded and sat on the edge of the pool.

Dangling her feet in the water, Julie smiled down at me, but then it faded. "You know I'm dying to ask you how your meeting went with your…with Adam," she said, correcting herself. "But you probably don't want to talk about that now… Do you?"

"The meeting didn't go well at all Julie and…no…I really don't want to talk about any of that stuff now. Just as soon as you and I can be alone…I promise… I'll tell you everything."

Julie softly replied, "That's good enough for me, Dreamboat."

"Dreamboat?" I chuckled. *Girls and their nicknames,* I thought. *Good grief, Charlie Brown!*

"Better get used to it, Jackson," giggled Julie. "You're a dreamboat…And I'm not the only one who thinks so, either." She then slipped into the water, put her arms around my neck, and in a tone just above a whisper said, "But, for the rest of this week, you're *my* dreamboat."

I suddenly made a show of wildly looking around in all directions, to see who might be sneaking up on me.

Julie laughed, "What are you doing?"

"Last time we were like this, it didn't work out so well for me."

"Yeah, but you're already wet now."

"And you're not wet enough." I then picked her up and took us both under.

When we both broke the surface, Julie yelled, "JACKSON!"

"I know, I know…I'm a snot!"

Instead of trying to exact some revenge on me, Julie simply beamed and softly said, "Yes…you are."

Her eyes beckoned me to kiss her, so I did.

The afternoon was filled with more teenage laughter and high-spirited screams. The guys and I showed off by performing our most ridiculous dives from the board. Later, we put the girls on our shoulders and had chicken fights. For that game, Tony had to play referee because for the first time ever, Mike was a mandatory contestant. When a rest was needed, we crawled out of the pool and lounged in the sun.

Once again, Julie surprised me with some her boldness. She did it by instructing me to lie on my stomach on one of the loungers. Then, she began massaging suntan lotion into my back. Immediately, I relaxed and blocked out any onlookers. As her fingers worked their magic on my muscles, I moaned, "That feels so good. Where did you learn to give back rubs?"

"From Momma," replied Julie. "My first year in cheerleading, I strained muscles in my back. Momma used to give me massages before bed at night. I asked her how she got to be so good at it. She told me that giving a back massage is just like kneading bread dough." Julie then bent down and whispered softly in my ear, "You just have to put more love into it."

Again, Julie was taking me to a place I didn't want to go, but at the same time, I never wanted anything more. I pushed myself up and rolled over onto my side, so I could see her face. At that very moment, I couldn't believe what was going through my head...and my heart. I was about to open my mouth, but Julie put her fingers to my lips and subtly shook her head. She silently mouthed the words, "Not now." My girl then prompted me to roll back over onto my stomach.

When I closed my eyes and Julie resumed massaging my shoulders, I allowed my body to relax. *Help me, Lord, help me, Jesus,* went through my mind. Never had I experienced such profound pleasure by a pair of loving hands.

Marilyn Falkner had made periodic appearances throughout the afternoon to check on us. Just then, she came out and asked, "Do you kids mind if I join you, so I can get a little sun?"

Dave jumped up and offered his chair. "Take mine, Mrs. Falkner. I'll grab another one from the patio."

I could not help but smile at what was probably Dave's first gentlemanly act. I then allowed myself to relax again and Julie kept up her attentions to my back muscles. I rapidly became drowsy and was literally half asleep, but then Gail spoke, and I became immediately alert again.

"Jackson, I really don't mean to make you upset or anything, but...how did you get your scars?" she asked.

Julie angrily burst, "GAIL! YOU PROMISED!"

In a cravenly manner, Gail said, "I know, I know...I lied." Then, she attempted to ward off any hostile reaction I might send her way by batting her eyes and giving me the most sheepish grin.

When I looked at Gail, something loosened inside of me. I just couldn't get mad. Instead, I simply laughed at her not-so-innocent inquiry about what had always been such a touchy subject. It actually felt good to laugh about it.

Just then, I realized it wouldn't bother me to tell them. In fact, I wanted to tell them.

"They're from a beating I took when I was five years old," I explained. "I don't remember hardly anything about it. I sometimes get flashbacks, though, usually when I'm not ready for them. But then, I forget right away. The only thing I remember clearly is Adam standing over me, yelling, 'What've you done?' I also remember waking up in the hospital with my back hurting. I don't have too many memories of being in the hospital, but I've always been pretty sure about who put me there. That is, until today."

"We've been friends since the second grade," said Dave. "You've always had those?"

"Yep."

"But we've never seen those before," asserted Dave.

"I've never had my shirt off around you guys before."

Anne asked, "Does it hurt? Your back, I mean."

"No, not now, but I used to wake up with what the doctor called phantom pains. Boy, I used to scare Janet Wilson with those and later, my adoptive mom."

"How do you mean?" asked Julie.

"I used to wake up from bad dreams, screaming because my back felt like it was on fire," I replied. "But that hasn't happened for a year or so."

"You met with him today, didn't you? Adam Harris, I mean," queried Tony.

"Yeah, but it didn't help out any. I'm just more confused now."

"Why's that?" asked Gail.

"He told me two things today. He told me that he wasn't my real dad, he never was. And he told me it was my mom who gave me these scars. When he said that, I got real mad and left. I thought he was lying. But, to tell you the truth, I have no idea what to think anymore."

Just then, I noticed Marilyn abruptly get up from her chair and expeditiously walk into the house. To me, it looked as though she could have been crying. *Way to go, Landry*, I thought. *Idiot!* I didn't know if anyone else had noticed her state, so I waited a few minutes, then got up and excused myself from the group.

"Jackson!" called Gail, "I'm sorry! I didn't mean to…"

Seeing the worried look on Gail's face, I shot her a big smile and said, "Don't worry, I'm fine. I'll be right back."

I grabbed my t-shirt from the patio chair and pulled it on. Letting myself into the kitchen, I looked around and then called out, "Marilyn?!"

Almost immediately, Marilyn's trembling voice came from the living room. "I'm in here."

I walked from the kitchen to the foyer and then into the living room. There, I found Marilyn, sitting on the couch and wiping her eyes with a tissue. I went to her but didn't sit down – I didn't want to get suntan lotion all over their furniture.

"I'm sorry," I said. "I forgot you and my mom were once close."

Marilyn smiled through her tears and said, "Oh, Jackson, you don't owe me any apologies."

"Still, it was stupid of me."

"Not at all, honey. You just reminded me that your mom wasn't the only one hurt by the past." Then, Marilyn almost pleaded, "You know, I can help you with that stuff…if you let me."

Sometimes, it helps if you trust a stranger, screamed through my head. Marilyn Falkner wasn't exactly a stranger. But then again, she was.

"Okay," I agreed. "How do we do this?"

"Tomorrow…Can you get away in the morning?"

"Yeah, no problem."

Just then, Julie entered the room from the kitchen. "Everything okay in here?"

Marilyn smiled and replied, "Everything is fine, baby. You and I have a date tomorrow morning, with a very thoughtful young man."

The gang prepared to leave an hour before dinnertime. Since I was the last to arrive, the afternoon seemed way too short. So, when Julie asked me to stay behind for a while longer, I was more than happy to oblige. Since dinner was still a ways off at the Wilson's, plus the fact that I was in no hurry to return to the uneasy silence that permeated their household, I had no problem, whatsoever, spending a little extra time alone with my girl.

After the gang left, Julie and I lingered by the pool. I sat on one of the loungers, soaking in the late afternoon sun. I wanted to finish drying before getting into my jeans. Julie occupied the lounger next to me. She softly hummed along to the radio, which played, The Temptations' old, hit song, *My Girl*.

As I lightly tapped my fingers to the beat on the armrest of the chair, Julie reached over and covered my hand with hers. "You looked like you wanted to tell me something today," she said.

"Really? Like what?" – I was getting better at *the game*.

Julie chuckled and asked, "How am I supposed to know?"

Trying to be cool, I replied, "Well, you must've known something. You hushed me quick enough."

"Jackson, I did that because you looked like you were going to say something that I didn't want you to say, not while everyone else was around."

"So...what is it you didn't want me to say?"

Julie giggled and then exclaimed, "Darn you! Now you're just being a brat!" She then raised herself and turned sideways in her chair. "Come here," she coaxed.

Warning alarms were going off in my head, but I did as she wanted. We were sitting with our knees pointed toward each other. We leaned forward, resting our forearms on our knees and she held both my hands in hers.

In a tone just above a whisper, Julie said, "I think I already know what it is, but I'm just dying to hear you tell me."

"You really want to know?"

"Yeah...I do."

"Okay, you win." I looked deep into her eyes and in a soft, intimate tone, said, "I was going to tell you that...I love...the way you give backrubs."

Just one look told me that my words had sorely disappointed her. Julie lowered her eyes and looked almost like she was about to cry. My head was saying, *"You're about to be very stupid,"* while my heart screamed, *"TELL HER...NOW!"* Lifting her chin, so she could see my eyes, I smiled slightly and softly said, "Look,

I've been trying, really hard, not to tell you what you already know." My heart was seriously pounding its way through my rib cage, when I said, "I love you."

Julie's smile was so sweet when she replied, "I knew it. And I know you didn't want to tell me. I know you think it's going to make things harder this weekend. I've been feeling the same way. But, when you looked at me that certain way this afternoon, that's when I knew there's no way I was going to let you leave this town without telling you…I love you, too."

We both leaned in and then tenderly kissed. Of course, that was Marilyn Falkner's cue to come out and ask if I was staying for dinner.

I thought I was the one who would screw this up! I couldn't help but laugh when I replied, "No thank you. I'd better get going. I need a shower and some clean clothes."

"Do I get to see you tonight?" asked Julie.

"I'll call you. It's getting a little weird at the Wilson house and I would hate to make a promise I can't keep."

After Marilyn went back inside, we snuck another kiss. I then got up to get dressed. As I stepped into my jeans, I noticed Julie looking rather serious. "What's with the gloomy look?" I asked.

"Are you glad you told me? I mean, do you think we'll end up regretting it?"

"What, saying it or letting it happen in the first place?"

"Both, I guess."

"I'm too new to all of this, Julie. But I think I would regret it more if I hadn't told you. I don't want to go home thinking there was something I should have said or done while I was here. I don't want to leave here thinking I was just too scared to say it or do it. You know what I mean?"

Julie smiled, nodded her understanding, and said, "I think at the end of this week, we'll both know that even though it was just for a short time, we had something really special."

"Had?" I repeated, as I pulled my t-shirt over my head. "Don't you mean *have*? Just because I'm leaving at the end of the week, doesn't mean I'm going to stop feeling the way I do."

"This is going to get really complicated, isn't it?"

"I don't think so. I have to go now, but I promise to explain it to you later."

Just then, Julie seemed determined to keep me from leaving by throwing out an invitation. "The Twins are playing Detroit tonight," she stated. "Do you want to come over and watch with me?"

As I finished putting on my tennis shoes, I replied, "There are definitely worse reasons to come see a pretty girl." I then gave her a quick peck on the lips and made a move for the gate – I was trying to hurry.

Julie headed me off and beat me to the gate, but opened the latch for me and asked, "Are you nervous about tomorrow?"

"No, but ask me again in the morning," I chuckled. *Holy smokes,* I thought. *If it's this hard to get out of here at the end of the week...I'm screwed!* I then started down the sidewalk toward the street.

"Jackson?!"

Sounding a little impatient, I whirled around and replied, "What?!"

As Julie sauntered down to where I stood, she smiled that sweet smile of hers. She then put her arms around my neck and kissed me long and almost... fiercely. "That's just in case you don't get to come back later," she said. Then, like a girl well trained in the art of womanly wiles, Julie abruptly turned on her heels and sauntered back to her gate. Me? I just stood there, dumbfounded, watching the hottest little wiggle my young eyes had ever seen. Just before going through the gate, my girl looked back at me, smiling. "Later, Dreamboat...I hope." She then disappeared behind the gate.

I stood there frozen, thinking, *"Nothing short of the end of the world or the second coming of Christ could keep me from coming back here tonight!"*

Rejoining reality was like being hit by a bolt of lightning. I was jarred out of my stupor and had to force myself to start walking. As I shuffled along my way, I couldn't wipe the grin off my face. *"Yeah,"* I thought, *"I've definitely found my smile, Doc!"*

CHAPTER 24

The shower I took before dinner felt wonderful, especially as I incrementally decreased the rate of hot water. Cool showers had always been a great relief on hot afternoons, and I was in definite need of relief. However, the shower failed to get rid of a particular tenseness I felt. As I toweled myself off, my thoughts turned to Janet and Brad. When I had entered the house that afternoon, both had been in the kitchen. As I passed them by, nothing more than hurried hellos were offered by the three of us. Because of what I had overheard, while lying in bed the previous night, I knew there would be more serious talk between us, but I was glad they had allowed me to slip past and cool off in the shower first.

The upstairs bedroom was like a furnace, so I was sweating again before I could finish dressing. Even though I was in no mood for any kind of heated encounter with the two adults in the kitchen, I wasn't about to avoid them by hiding in the hottest place in the house. *Hopefully, I can make it to the basement without fighting,* I thought. *God, I hate this!* Leaving my outer shirt untucked and unbuttoned, I hurried down the stairs to cooler air.

Janet was busy getting dinner ready, while Brad sat at the kitchen table, balancing their checkbook. As I stood in the archway, which separated the hallway from the dining area, I looked apprehensively at the two of them. Neither gave any indication they knew I was standing there at all. Part of me wanted to just slip past them, but I also wanted to clear the air. Once again, my heart was in my throat. Not wanting to upset the delicate peace that seemed to have settled on the house, I thought I had better just leave them alone. *They'll talk to me when they're ready,* I thought. *Maybe, getting out of the house for the evening would be best.* Gathering a little courage, I asked, "Do either of you mind if I go to Julie's to watch the game tonight?"

Brad looked up from the bills he was studying and Janet turned from slicing a carrot. They looked at each other, nodded, then turned to me. Brad said, "If that's what you want to do, buddy, then it's okay with us." I didn't recognize it just then, but there was something else in the look he gave me, something resembling sorrow.

Without saying anything more, I attempted to slip past them to get to the coolness of the basement. But, before I could escape, Janet quickly turned and through her arms around me. As she held me close, I felt her tremble. "I'm so sorry for what happened last night," she cried. "Please forgive me. We can't let things go on like this. Are you ever going to be able to forgive me?"

Without hesitation, I replied, "Yes." Immediately, I felt the need to exhale, like a huge weight had just been taken off my chest. At the same time, I was unable to stop my own tears from forming. "Do you forgive me for coming back? I didn't know I was supposed to stay away."

Janet held me even tighter and then said, "Of course you didn't. How were you supposed to know anything? That outburst last night was because I have been missing you so much. And I know I will again when you leave. You just forget about that, you hear? You come see us whenever you want, whenever you can. We'll always be here for you! I love you, kiddo!"

I then felt Brad enfold the two of us in his strong arms. "Jackson, I am so sorry I said those things to you last night," he said solemnly. "It was stupid of me. Yes, you come see us whenever you want."

As we three held each other in that healing moment, I felt my heart loosen. I marveled at how their words and our embrace, almost instantly, made the world seem right again. *Of course they were upset,* I thought. *How could I be so stupid?! How could I have possibly thought that I was the only one who got hurt from my going away?!* It had been a bad assumption and one that I would never make again.

Janet broke the embrace first and immediately went back to cutting up carrots. "We have so much to tell you…when you're ready," she said, "but I don't think we should do it tonight. You have a date, right handsome?"

"I'll break it…for you," I replied, but prayed to God she would see right through my halfhearted offer.

"Very nice, sweetie, but I know Julie will never forgive you if you don't spend every possible minute with her."

"How do you know?"

With tear-filled eyes, Janet replied, "Because, if I was thirteen and you were the boy I wanted, I wouldn't." She then added, "I love you."

Only Janet could have come up with that kind of understanding, so I hugged her again and whispered, "I love you, too."

The basement was so much cooler than the kitchen. Compared to the upstairs bedroom, it was downright cold. Wanting to enjoy it, undisturbed, I plopped down in the easy chair and attempted to get some reading in before dinner. One of my goals was to finish reading the Louis L'Amour western that I had been laboring on before I left Mankato. I had just picked up where I had left off, when what sounded like a stampede emanated from the stairwell. Without looking up from my book, I knew it was Kurt and Danny. When they entered the den, they both delivered smart-assed greetings and then made for the pool table. Since reading was now out of the question, I put the book down, crossed my arms, and waited for the verbal assault to begin. I didn't have to wait long, either.

Wearing a Cheshire Cat grin, Danny said, "So, Jackson, we're having people over again tonight. You want us to invite Lori?"

"If you want," I replied coolly.

Danny exclaimed in genuine surprise, "Really?!"

"Sure, why not?" I chuckled. "I'll be at Julie's house, so go ahead."

Kurt laughed and then nodded in my direction. "Good one, twerp."

As they turned their attention to the pool game, I decided to forget about reading all together. Getting up from the lounger, I then ambled over to watch them play. Taking a seat on one of the tall billiard chairs, I noticed Danny giving me an apprehensive look.

"What?" I asked.

"It's probably nothing," replied Danny, "but I overheard Greg Dodson talking at work today. He was telling some of the other guys how he plans to make another play for Julie."

Genuinely amused at Dodson's chances, I chuckled and asked, "Did you wish him luck?"

Still looking bothered, Danny replied, "I didn't butt in, little brother. I just thought you should know."

"Danny, I'll be gone at the end of the week. What am I supposed to do about it? When I'm in Duluth, I can't stop him from doing anything."

"Jackson, I'm just telling you because he doesn't know you're here. He doesn't know about you and Julie, either. He might not wait until the end of the week to make a move."

"Thanks, but I'm really not worried about it." I then gave Danny a reassuring smile.

Kurt frowned a little and said, "Keep your eyes open, Jackson. Dodson is a spoiled ape. If he doesn't get his way, he might cause trouble."

Taking Kurt's words a little more serious, I asked, "Is he really that bad?"

Danny answered, "He fights like a moron, but I've seen him hit. When he connects, guys don't always get up real fast afterward."

"Danny, I think Jackson will be just fine," said Kurt, giving me a knowing wink.

Their warnings set me to wondering. What would I do if Dodson made a move on Julie while I was present? I truly wasn't afraid of him. In fact, I didn't feel one way or another about Greg. My worry was Julie. What would she think of me if there was an altercation between Dodson and me? I was fearful of losing my temper in front of her. It was a side of me I never wanted her – or anyone else for that matter – to witness.

After dinner I prepared myself to help Kurt with the dishes. Danny remembered he owed me a few favors, so he jumped in. "Your girl's waiting, so get outta here."

Giving Danny a quick thank you, I then hustled to the bathroom to brush my teeth and comb my hair. I also borrowed a splash of Brad's aftershave. When I emerged from the bathroom, Brad and Janet were curled up on the living room couch, watching pre-game highlights. When I walked in to say my see-you-laters, I took their closeness as a good sign. Whatever trouble they were having, seemed to be getting ironed out nicely. As I stood in the archway, Janet laughed at me. "What's so funny?" I asked.

"Kiddo, I can smell you from here. I think you need to wash some of that stinky stuff off. You don't want to choke the poor girl."

I immediately turned around, went back to the bathroom, and did as Janet advised. After dragging a washcloth across my face a few times, I went back for another opinion.

When I reentered the living room, Janet got up from the couch and came to where I stood. Putting her arms around me, she nuzzled my neck, tickling me a bit. "That's better, sweetie," she said. "Julie shouldn't know it's there until her nose is in just the right place." Janet then playfully nibbled on my neck.

Brad asked if he could drive me to Julie's, but I declined his offer. It wasn't that I wouldn't have appreciated the ride because it was still quite hot outside. I just didn't want to disturb whatever reconciliation was taking place between them on the couch.

The walk to Julie's didn't bother me half as much as not knowing what to expect from an evening with Gary Falkner. Janet had warned me about disrupting the special bond, which, according to her, exists between fathers and their daughters.

When I arrived on the Falkners' doorstep, I was extremely thankful that I was not covered in sweat. Shortly after ringing the doorbell, I heard Julie's slightly-muffled voice behind the door. She yelled, telling the entire household, "I've got it!"

The door opened and Julie stepped out onto the landing, closing the door behind her, but leaving it slightly ajar. Her hair was pulled back into a ponytail and she had a Navy-blue ribbon in it. She looked great in her Minnesota Twins t-shirt and white shorts. Her ensemble accentuated the fresh layer of sun she was sporting from our afternoon spent by the pool. "Hi," she sweetly said and then kissed me. Her lips tasted like strawberries.

"Hi," I said in return. "Hey, you taste good."

"It's my new lip balm," she said.

"Really?! Can I borrow some more?"

Julie giggled and said, "Later, the game is starting." She then leaned in and smelled my neck. "Mmm…that's nice," she said softly. "I like it."

Thank you, Janet!

While standing in the foyer, Gary Falkner greeted me much the same way he had previously – warm and genuinely. "Game time, Jackson," he reminded. "You have any predictions?"

"The Twins, of course, by two," I replied – Grandpa Mack had taught me to always go into a game with a positive outlook, even if I did think they were going to lose. That night, I wasn't overly optimistic about the Twins chances.

Looking a little put out by my conservative prophesy, Julie asked, "Only two?"

"We're struggling against Detroit this season and they have a home-field advantage," I rationalized. "But we're still gonna beat 'em tonight."

"I like it," said Gary. "You're an optimist!"

Marilyn then swept into the entryway. She greeted me with a hug and a smile. "Hi, you…Did you have a good dinner?"

"Yes Mmm…arilyn." I then chuckled for having to correct myself.

With a hearty laugh, Marilyn stated, "I'll break you of that yet!"

Giving her a sly smile in return, I asserted, "No ma'am, you won't."

Even Lisa greeted me warmly by putting her hand on my shoulder, as she said a simple hello. Afterward, the five of us shuffled off to their basement to watch the game in their spacious lounge. When we arrived at the bottom of the stairs, I saw that provisions for the game were already in place. Two large bowls sat on their coffee table, one with potato chips and the other was brimming with popcorn.

Lisa immediately ran behind the bar to get a pop for everyone. "Jackson, do you want a root beer or what?" she asked.

In my usual, smart-assed fashion, I replied, "I'll have a what."

Lisa gave me a confused look for couple of seconds before she caught on. In but a few moments, she came from around the bar, carrying pop for everyone. As Lisa handed me a root beer, she shot me a snotty look, but it soon turned to a smile.

I felt a little taken back by the gathering. There was no question about Julie and her dad being Minnesota Twins fans, but Marilyn had stated earlier she thought baseball was boring. As for Lisa, I had no idea what her interest might be. Leaning toward Julie's ear, I whispered, "What is all this?"

Julie whispered back, "Just go with it. It's new to me, too. I think Lisa has a crush on you and now, I guess Momma does, too!"

The game was scoreless for the first three innings. That's when most of our conversing took place. Late in the first inning, I noticed that Gary had developed a rather questioning look. It made me feel more than a bit self-conscious. Initially, my uneasiness was not caused by anything he said, but rather, the way he kept looking at me, like I was under a microscope. I wondered if it had anything to do with my intrusion on his father-daughter time. Finally, in the third inning, Julie's dad erased all concerns in my head. You could have knocked me over with a feather when Gary asked, "Jackson, are you related in any way to Brice Landry?"

"Yes, sir, he's my dad," I replied calmly.

Gary sat up straight in his chair, exclaiming, "What?! Are you kidding me?!"

"Do you know him, sir?"

"No, I don't, but I would love to meet him! He has some very interesting business philosophies that I'd like to hear more about. I read about your dad, not long ago in Minnesota Business Magazine. I was very impressed with the interview he gave. B & C Enterprises is the fastest growing business up there in the Twin Ports area. If he were to go public, that's stock I would buy in a heartbeat."

I looked at Julie's dad and nodded like I knew exactly what he was talking about. In truth, I didn't understand a word of it. Back then, Dad's business was just that – Dad's. He hadn't shared a lot of information with me, so I had no clear understanding of the actual size of the company.

Gary continued, "I noticed in some of the magazine pictures that your dad hires blacks." The comment was spoken as if in passing, but I picked up on the question attached to it.

"Yes, sir…Dad has some who drive deliveries and some who work in the warehouse."

Gary queried further, "But, none in the front office, right?"

"As far as I know, Mom and Dad *are* the front office, sir. I don't think they have but one other office person. And she's kind of an older lady."

Gary simply nodded his head in understanding.

The undertones of Mr. Falkner's inquiries were not lost on me. Back then, many of the younger set, at one time or another, had to deal with our parents' racist opinions. I remembered having to use a lot of patience with Mom, when she once told me that it would be okay if I dated a colored girl, but strongly advised that I not fall in love and marry one. In Mom's mind, interracial dating was perfectly acceptable, but she didn't feel society was ready for interracial marriages. I always disagreed with her in silence. I liked Dad's attitude the best. "What does black look like, Jackson?" For one simple reason, Dad treated all people with the same respect and dignity. To him, they *were* all the same.

Gary then pressed me for a little more information. "So, as an employer, your dad is color blind?"

Wanting to get off the subject, so I could concentrate on the game, I chuckled and replied, "Sir, my dad *is* blind."

Marilyn then came to the rescue. She scowled at her husband a little and asked, "Gary, can we talk about something else?" She then smiled at me and winked.

Yeah, I liked Marilyn Falkner just fine.

The Twins exploded in the fourth inning, scoring four runs. They led going into the fifth inning, four-to-nothing. That's when Marilyn called it quits on the game. She asked Lisa to accompany her upstairs.

"Aw, Momma, I wanna watch the game," whined Lisa.

"Of course you do, honey…Let's go."

Julie leaned over and whispered in my ear, "She doesn't even like baseball."

Detroit went on to score three runs in the sixth inning and in the seventh, the Twins gave up two more runs…and the lead.

Gary exclaimed, "Come on, guys! You're not supposed to give up the ghost until the ninth!"

"They'll come back," I said. "You'll see."

"I don't think so," countered Gary. "It's like you said, 'they're struggling against Detroit this season.' Anyway, I have some work to do upstairs. So, if you two will excuse me…" Without finishing the sentence, he got up from his easy chair and headed to the stairs. As an afterthought, Gary said, "Let me know if anything changes." He then stomped up the stairs and disappeared into the kitchen. Surprisingly, he closed the door behind him, giving Julie and me some greatly desired privacy.

Finding ourselves alone, with nothing but the TV for a chaperone, Julie didn't waste a minute letting me know exactly how she wanted to spend the rest of the game. Directly, she got up and dimmed all the ceiling lights. When she returned to the couch, her boldness continued. She positioned herself so that I had to cradle her in my arms. "Didn't you ask to borrow some of my lip balm earlier?" she teased.

"Why, yes," I replied. "I believe I did."

The Twins did nothing in the eighth inning, but I could not have cared less. Julie was taking me to paradise with soft, gentle kisses of strawberry delight. In the ninth inning, Rod Carew hit a sweet RBI double to tie the game. Julie and I quit making out long enough to watch the replay and smile at each other. "Cool!" I exclaimed. "Extra innings!" We then returned to our previous activity.

Julie and I made out until the bottom of the tenth inning. By then, we both felt the need to come up for some air. Julie needed to freshen up her lip balm and I, quite frankly, needed to rest my lips.

As I helped Julie up from the couch, I said, "I have to tell you something. I know about Greg Dodson."

Julie sadly replied, "I figured you might. I was pretty sure you knew, especially when I found out that Danny works with him. I was going to tell you about him, Jackson. I mean it."

"I'm not worried about it," I smiled. "I just thought you should know that he plans to try and get you back. Danny overheard him talking today."

Julie scrunched up her face and said, "Fat chance! He's such a goon." She then put her arms around me and asked, "Any questions?"

"None," I replied, then prepared my lips for another short exercise session.

We stayed in the basement until the beginning of the twelfth inning. The Twins and the Tigers were still locked in a tie game. It was now late. That is, late for a thirteen-year-old Romeo, so I decided I had better be on my way. I reminded myself that I would see Julie first thing in the morning. It made leaving that night a little easier.

Gary offered to drive me home, so I would get there in time to see the rest of the game. I was more than happy to take him up on his offer. I said my thank-yous and my good-nights, then piled into Gary's 1966 Corvette Stingray.

During the short drive, I noticed that he seemed uneasy about something, so I asked, "Are you okay, sir?"

"Jackson, I hope I didn't offend you with any of my comments or questions earlier tonight. I don't want you thinking I'm some kind of racial bigot."

Feeling more at ease with my girlfriend's dad, I offered, "Sir, my mom thinks she doesn't have any prejudices against blacks, either, but she does. I just don't think she realizes it. It doesn't matter to me. I still love her."

Gary mused, "Hmmm." Then, as he pulled in front of the Wilsons' driveway, he said, "I appreciate that and thank you. You're a pretty smart young man."

"Thanks for the ride, sir. And thanks for letting me come over to watch the game."

Gary chuckled knowingly and then said, "Well, I doubt you saw much past the seventh inning, but you, sir, are most welcome. See you soon, okay? Good night."

As I stepped in the side door, soft music oozed from the basement, which meant Kurt and Danny's get-together was still under full swing. I walked into the living room and found Brad and Janet riveted to the TV.

Brad exclaimed, "Have you been watching this? What a game!"

I asked, "Is it still tied up?"

"Yeah, and it's going into the top of the thirteenth inning," he said.

"It's pretty late, kiddo," said Janet. "You should have called, so we could come pick you up."

"Gary…I mean…Mr. Falkner gave me a ride home. That Vette of his is so cool!"

Janet just smiled and shook her head. She then patted the couch cushion next to her. It was my signal to join them.

When the Twins scored two runs in the top of the thirteenth inning to break the tie, we three cheered. However, when Detroit scored another run, we held our breath and crossed our fingers. With only one out in the bottom of the thirteenth inning, we were afraid the Twins would fail to fend off the Tigers. Fortunately, our fears were put to rest that night. The Twins held on and won the game by one run. Energetic high fives were given all around.

"I'll take that win!" exclaimed Brad. "What a great game!"

"Long game," corrected Janet. "I'm going to bed." She then turned and kissed my cheek. "Good night, you," she whispered.

"Good night, you," I repeated.

While watching Brad straighten some couch pillows, I considered talking to him about what had transpired at St. Joe's that afternoon. But, since the day was ending on such a high note, I chickened out. Even though the day started out a bit rough, there was plenty afterward to mark it as wonderful. I had spent the afternoon with Julie and my friends at the pool, Julie and I declared our love for each other, Brad, Janet, and I had made up before dinner, I had just spent a fantastic evening with Julie and her folks, and the Twins won! Why ruin it?! So, I decided to put all serious notions away for the night. *Tomorrow…I can talk to him tomorrow,* I thought.

After Brad and I said good night to one another, I continued to sit, motionless, in the living room. The music that emanated from the basement was soft and inviting. I was too keyed up to go to bed, so I decided to go check out what was happening in the downstairs den.

As I quietly descended, I hoped Larry Armstrong would be available for a game of eight ball. However, when I reached the basement, I found the pool table was vacant. Couples danced slowly to the Moody Blues song, *Nights in White Satin,* while others made out in various locations of the den, thus sending the room temperature soaring. The air smelled a sweet mixture of perfume, aftershave, and sweat. The lights had all been dimmed until the bulbs barely gave off enough dull-orange light to see by.

In the almost pitch-black atmosphere, I spied Lori Mudd. She was dancing with and making serious eyes at Larry Armstrong. *When did that happen?! So much for getting a game with Larry,* I thought.

Quietly, I made my way to the pool table and began to take a few shots. Unfortunately, the sound of a ball, when it fell into a pocket, was quite loud and disruptive, so I laid the cue back on the table and just stood there for a moment.

Watching Kurt and Danny, along with their friends, carry on as if I were not in the room, I suddenly felt invisible. It was as if I didn't even exist in their world. I mean, there I was, only a few feet from all of them, but no one even glanced in my direction, nor acknowledged my presence. I was a ghost. Right about then, reality hit me. Alarming thoughts raced through my head. *None of this is real! I don't belong here because I really don't exist in their world! Kurt and Danny aren't my brothers anymore and these aren't my friends! This isn't my family, and I don't get to live here anymore. I don't get to stay! I don't get to stay with Julie and the gang! I can't have this! No matter how much I want it…I can't have this!*

The weight of it all descended on me like a massive, falling boulder. I was crushed under the weight of my own thoughts. Things had been too perfect, and I had allowed myself to be blinded by the illusion of it all. Soon, very soon, I was going to have to leave Mankato. I would have to leave the wonderful fantasy behind. I had to return to Duluth and face reality, my reality.

Quite suddenly, I had the strongest urge to get out of that basement. So, I quietly, but hurriedly, made my way back to the stairwell.

Kurt must have seen something I didn't intend him to see. He called out, "Jackson, where ya goin'? You don't have to leave."

Ignoring his voice, I hurried out of the den. Up the stairs I went and into the kitchen. Once there, I paused and took in a few deep breaths, while I collected myself. Almost immediately, I heard footsteps coming up from the basement. Just as suddenly as my exit from the downstairs, Kurt and Janelle appeared in the kitchen. They both looked worried.

Janelle asked, "Hey, cutie, are you okay?"

I thought about her question for a second, then replied, "Not right now, but I think I'm gonna be. I'm going to bed now. You guys have fun."

Janelle gently took my arm and kept me from leaving. "What's wrong?"

I hesitated for a moment and then said, "You've been great." I then smiled at the two of them. "All of you have been great, but do you know what I have to do in a few days?"

"You're going home," answered Kurt.

"That's right. I have to leave again. I have to leave all of you. 'Home,' you say. That's hilarious. I've lived in Duluth for just over three years. That place feels like many things, but *home* isn't one of them. This place used to feel like home, it always did. But now, everything has changed. It's really hard, but I finally get it. I don't belong here...Do I, Kurt?"

Kurt didn't answer. With his hands in his pockets and his shoulders hunched, he just leaned against the counter and stared down at his feet. Janelle seemed to understand the moment better. She tried to pull me in and put her arms around me, but I resisted.

"Please, don't," I insisted.

With a hurt look in her eyes, Janelle queried, "Jackson?"

Pointing at Kurt, I explained, "You don't understand, Janelle. He's the big brother I don't get to have. Danny is the other one. In such a short time, you've become like a big sister, but I don't get to have you, either. The absolute worst part of all this is...I'm head over heels for Julie. But, like everything else here, I don't get to have her. I don't get to have anything here that I want. Like I said, I finally get it. I don't belong here because no matter how much I want it, I can't have it."

I then turned and intended to make my dramatic exit, leaving them to stand there and ponder my words. I wanted to get upstairs to the seclusion of the bedroom. Again Janelle stopped me. Imploringly, she said, "Don't be that way, Jackson...Please. I just started thinking of you as the little brother I never had. So, please don't tell me that it's all done and over with, not just because you're leaving in a few days. Don't tell me I'm never going to see or hear from you again."

My tears were trying to escape, but I choked back my emotions and was able to muster a reassuring smile for her. "You'll hear from me again. And, maybe someday, you'll see me again, too."

"Promise me," insisted Janelle.

Again I hesitated, so I could consider my response, but only for a moment. Then, shaking my head slightly and in just above a whisper, I said, "I can't promise you that. I can't do it. I can only tell you what I want, but I can't promise it'll happen."

Throughout the exchange between Janelle and me, Kurt refused to take his eyes off the floor. Like me, he was struggling to keep his emotions in check. Kurt accomplished it best by saying nothing at all.

Janelle looked as though she was deeply hurt, but then she smiled and stepped in to give me a hug. Allowing the embrace, I felt my insides get all twisted. As Janelle lightly rubbed her hands up and down my back, she softly said, "Just so you know, when you do leave, I'm going to miss you...a lot," Then, in a whisper, she added "I love you."

As I hugged her in return, my heart was in my throat. "I love you, too," I whispered. Then, turned and finally made my exit up the noisy stairs to the bedroom.

As I lay in bed, with my hands clasped behind my head, my mind churned away at a hundred miles per hour. *How could I have been so stupid?! How am I supposed to say good-bye now?! This very afternoon, I told Julie that I love her and now I have to get ready to leave?! What the hell was I thinking?! I've dug myself a real pit, now I have to figure out how to get out. Then there's Adam Harris. If he isn't my real dad, who is? Did my own mother actually try to kill me? What the hell did I fall into down here? This has all become like a real bad dream! Doc Elliot was right all along!*

Suddenly, I knew I could no longer trust my heart to do the right thing. At long last, it was time to start thinking clearly with my head. That night, I spent hours trying to decide what to do about my predicament. I knew in my heart what I should do, but I just wasn't sure I had the courage to go through with it. To say the least, there was very little sleep for me that night.

When Danny came to bed, I rolled over and played like I was fast asleep. I even snored a bit. After I heard his heavy breathing, telling me he was out for the night, I got up and went downstairs. I toyed with the idea of calling Mom and Dad, but it was way too late for that. So, I just sat on the living-room couch, mulling things over and over again inside my head.

When my mind finally began to shut down, it was close to two o'clock in the morning. I had successfully formulated a plan. It was based on what my thirteen-year-old mind *thought* was the best course of action. I was convinced I was going to have to do what was best, not just for me, but for Julie and everyone else concerned. I just wasn't convinced that I could see it through alone. As a matter of fact, I was positive I couldn't do it by myself. *Who can I trust to help me?*

I then decided not to do anything drastic. At least, not until I heard what Marilyn Falkner had to say.

When I finally felt myself beginning to get drowsy, I remembered that I had an early date with the Falkner women, so I decided I had better get some shuteye. I didn't want to take the chance of waking anyone by going up the noisy stairs in the wee-morning hours. So, I just stretched out on the couch, with my head close to an open window. I closed my eyes and listened to a languid breeze, as it rustled the leaves of mountain ash in the front yard.

Chapter 25

Wednesday, 16 August 1972

As agreed upon, I arrived at the Falkner's at 8:30 A.M. Even after the almost seven-block walk, I still wasn't fully awake. I had lost a lot of sleep the previous night and now wished that I was still in bed. My eyes felt like someone had thrown sand in them and the shower I had taken failed to help the slightest bit.

When Julie answered the door, the only greeting she offered was a rather unenthusiastic, "Morning." But then, she leaned in and gave me a quick kiss.

Taking a good look at my girl, I could tell she was as tired as I felt. Her eyes were a little puffy and not nearly as bright as I had become accustomed to seeing. The denim shorts and pale blue top she wore were nice, but not overly exciting. Even her hair seemed a tad dreary. Instead of pulling her curls back into a neat ponytail, she left them hanging loose and somewhat untidy.

"You didn't get much sleep either, did you?" I asked.

"No!" exclaimed Julie, scowling at me playfully. "Darn you anyway! I thought about you all night long!" She then broke out a smile, but it, too, lacked energy.

Julie then led me into the kitchen. There, I smelled fresh coffee brewing. It was probably the first time I actually wished I had the stomach for coffee. I had tried it once with Dad, but thought it was disgusting stuff.

Julie went to the stove and stirred milk that was heating in a pan. "I'm making us some hot chocolate. Or would you rather have coffee?"

"Hot chocolate sounds great. I need something to get my heart started this morning."

At that, Julie promptly dropped her stirring spoon on the counter, came to me, and planted another kiss on my lips. "Maybe that'll help," she said, then gave me another wry smile.

Chuckling, I admitted, "Yeah, that helps, but it also keeps me awake half the night."

We both laughed at the pure truth of it.

"Momma's putting on final touches," Julie explained. "She'll be down soon."

Knowing little or nothing of women's morning routines, I scrunched my nose and asked, "Final touches?"

Julie chuckled at my inquiry. "She's putting on her makeup."

"Your mom doesn't need makeup."

From the staircase behind me, Marilyn called out, "I heard that!" She then breezed into the kitchen and, to me, appeared to be the exact opposite of Julie and me. Marilyn looked and sounded wide awake and full of energy. Her hair was neatly brushed and sprayed in place. The little makeup she did wear was applied perfectly. Even Marilyn's ensemble seemed wide awake. The slacks she wore were lime green in color, as was her top, but with dark blue accents. She was so bright and shiny that it almost hurt my eyes.

Marilyn then hugged me, saying, "Hi you! That was sweet of you to say."

"Morning," I returned, wondering how a woman could look that good so early. *Where's the dimmer switch for that outfit?*

Marilyn poured herself a cup of coffee and then sat at the kitchen table. While Julie finished making the hot chocolate, Marilyn motioned for me to join her. She looked at the two teens in her kitchen and then said, "Neither one of you look like you slept at all last night."

Julie and I exchanged embarrassed smiles.

Displaying a knowing grin, Marilyn said, "Oh, to be that young again."

Just then, it dawned on me that Marilyn was perfectly comfortable with my attraction to her daughter and vice versa. *Why is she so willing to let me be with Julie, especially when everyone else warned me not to?*

Julie finished adding cocoa to the milk. She poured the hot chocolate into two heavy mugs and then joined Marilyn and me at the table. When she sat down next to me, I thanked her. "Careful, it's really hot," she cautioned.

Again I caught Marilyn smiling warmly at Julie and me. But then, her gaze went beyond us and she looked out the window directly behind our heads. It was almost as if she were preparing herself for what came next. After a long, silent moment, Marilyn asked me in a straight tone, "Are you ready for this?"

"Yeah, I think I am."

"Well then, let's go into the living room and get comfortable. Julie, I think you should hear this, too."

Julie looked at me and asked, "Do you want me there?"

A little shocked by her question, I replied, "Absolutely!"

The three of us then adjourned to the living room. Marilyn sat in her favorite Queen Anne's armchair, which was upholstered in blue velour. Julie and I sat close to one another on the couch. Julie didn't hesitate to curl up beside me, hook her arm through mine, and put her head on my shoulder. I thought she was going to fall asleep immediately. That very notion crossed my mind, too.

Marilyn chuckled, "You both look like you *really* need a nap. Well, maybe later."

I just smiled in return.

"Jackson, you have to let me tell this my way," Marilyn began. "Some of what I'm about to tell you may be hard for you to hear, but please understand that it's hard for me, as well. I still sometimes find it hard to believe that things turned out the way they did."

Marilyn then took in a deep breath and let it out. She wistfully gazed out the large bay window that looked out onto their front yard. Again, it appeared to me that she was preparing herself for some great difficulty.

Taking small sips of my hot chocolate, I waited patiently for Marilyn to begin. Sitting on the couch, with Julie resting on my shoulder, felt amazingly comfortable. No matter how hard the truth was going to be, I just knew Julie's warmth would give me the strength I needed. Fortunately, we didn't have to wait long for Marilyn to begin her tale. She started out slow, as if she were choosing her words carefully.

"Your mother's maiden name was Stevens. Her dad, your grandfather, was a construction worker. He helped build many of the houses in the newer neighborhoods in town. Your mom's family moved next door to us when I was in the first grade. I was so happy to see they had a little girl my age. Needless to say, we became great friends real quick.

"At the same time, there was another girl who lived in the neighborhood. Her name was Janet Lieferman."

I queried, "Janet Wilson now, right?"

"Exactly," replied Marilyn. "As you might imagine, the three of us became pretty-good friends. Much the same as Julie, Anne, and Gail are friends. Sharon was always the ringleader. She had a very outgoing personality. By the sixth or seventh grade, you could just tell she was going to be quite gorgeous, when she finished growing up. Her looks got her lots of attention from the boys.

"Adam Harris and Brad Wilson were classmates of ours. In high school, both competed for Sharon's affection. But, back then, Sharon had no romantic feelings toward either of them. Sharon was only interested in one boy, but he wanted nothing to do with her. Ironically, he was busy pursuing me."

Sleepily, Julie asked, "Daddy?"

"Yes, baby, your father. He was considered by all of us girls as somewhat of a prize at Mankato High. Julie, don't you dare tell him I said that!"

Julie's only reply was a drowsy-looking smile.

Marilyn was now talking in a comfortable rhythm and I was hanging onto her every word. I wasn't too sure Julie was catching everything, though. Her eyes were heavy lidded, and she looked as though she could drift off at any moment.

"During our high school years, things began to change between Sharon, Janet, and me. Janet was the first to split off from our threesome. I was spending a lot of time with Gary, Sharon was dating, but Janet wasn't doing much of anything. She was one of the smartest in our class, but…let's just say…boys didn't flock to her the way they did to Sharon. It became apparent to Sharon and me that Janet was unhappy because we weren't spending much time with her anymore. It's just what happens when boys start playing a larger part in a girl's life. I think even Julie has felt the pinch a little in the past year with Gail and Anne."

I looked at Julie and with her head still on my shoulder, she simply nodded her affirmation.

"Sharon and I remained close through our high school years. After graduation, we knew it was going to be more difficult to stay close because Gary and I were going off to college in the Twin Cities. Your mom's family couldn't afford to put her through college, so she stayed here and took a job at Falkner's Store, when it was still on Front Street. I can't prove it and he'll never admit to it, but I think Gary made that happen for her.

"During my first year at college, I got plenty of letters from Sharon. Plus, I got to see her on holiday and semester breaks. She seemed to have adjusted well enough, but she always talked about moving out to California. During my second year, she wrote and told me she met a Marine. He was doing recruiter duty here in Mankato. His name was Timothy Belanger and he was just the type Sharon was attracted to. He was good looking, very well put together, and just an all-around-good guy. If he had any faults, it was that he was kind of a heavy drinker. But, so was Sharon, for that matter. I think it's even likely that they met in a bar. They married in the spring of 1950. I was her maid of honor. Shortly after that, Tim was reassigned to some camp in California. Sharon was ecstatic to be leaving here. Gary and I married in the spring of 1954. I wanted Sharon to be my maid of honor. But she couldn't come because she was pregnant with your oldest brother, Derrick, and very close to her due date.

"Somewhere in the middle of all this, Brad Wilson and Janet Lieferman were dating before he went off to Korea. They married shortly after he returned. I was hoping somehow that Janet and I could be friends again, but life just kept getting in the way, so no attempt was ever made by either of us. They were busy with their sons, Kurt and Danny.

"Tim, Sharon's husband, was killed in a car accident, right after your other brother, Brian, was born. Sharon was absolutely devastated. She was so in love with that man. Initially, she wanted to continue living in California, but she couldn't find work that paid enough to live on. Gary and I offered to help, but she wouldn't hear of it. California was no place for a young widow with two little boys and no money. So, she was, more or less, forced to move back in with her folks, here in Mankato.

"I saw her shortly after she moved back and noticed a drastic change in her personality. She didn't seem to care about things the way she used to. She wasn't as outgoing as I remembered her to be. She was so very sad…all the time. I felt terrible because I knew she wanted so much out of life, but it appeared she wasn't going to attain any of her dreams. She started frequenting local bars and often left your brothers with her parents. There were stories floating around about how she would sometimes disappear on a Friday evening and then not reappear until Sunday. Her folks even threatened to throw her out if she didn't straighten up.

"Out of feelings of self-preservation, I distanced myself from Sharon for a time. She didn't try to contact me, either. I rationalized it as…we both just changed into vastly different people.

"Then, in December of 1958, when I was four months pregnant with Julie, Sharon came to me, crying. She, too, was pregnant…with you, honey. She told me that she knew who the father was but wasn't prepared to cause any trouble in that person's life. According to Sharon, he was a classmate of ours. She was scared because if word got out, too many people that we still cared about would get hurt. She never told me who he was. Sharon never believed it was his fault. She blamed herself. She said they coupled in a moment of weakness, when his marriage appeared to be ending, and she desperately needed to be with someone."

As I listened to Marilyn tell me of my mother's accidental pregnancy, a very powerful feeling came over me. An idea too crazy to believe entered my mind and took hold. *Jesus, no,* I thought. *Don't let it be!*

Marilyn continued with her story. "During that same meeting, Sharon told me Adam Harris offered to marry her and take care of her and the boys. She felt that marrying Adam was wrong, but it was the only thing she could do. She was in such a jam because her parents were getting ready to throw her out. So, Sharon and Adam married in January of 1959. They moved into an old house on east Madison Avenue. Working at the cannery, Adam didn't make a lot of money. Just the same, he tried so hard to make her happy. But all it seemed to do was make matters worse. Sharon felt indebted to Adam, but she wasn't in love with him. On one occasion, she even admitted to me that she could never love him that way.

"That July, Sharon went to St. Paul to be with her sister and to give birth to you. You were named after Adam's favorite president, kind of. Instead of Andrew Jackson Harris, Adam thought you would have an identity all your own if they named you, Jackson Andrew. Personally, I've always adored the name!"

With a tired smile, Julie chimed in, "Me, too!"

Marilyn smiled at Julie's interruption and then continued. "Shortly after you were born, Sharon apparently got restless again and refused to stay at home to raise her sons, like a good mother should. I tried to get her to see the damage she was causing, not only to herself, but to her entire family. That's when things got really bad for her. For a while, she tried being the dutiful wife and mother everyone thought she should be. But rumors of indiscretions kept floating around town. Adam refused to believe the stories and did his best to stand by Sharon. Once again, it just made matters worse. Sharon's self-esteem was at an all-time low. I believe she actually began to hate herself.

"I saw her in the fall of 1964. You and Julie were in kindergarten then, honey. It was early in the afternoon and she had already been drinking. She went on and on about how unhappy she was. She rambled on about how things would be so much better if she didn't have so many kids. I got real mad at her and chewed her out for having such a terrible attitude, but nothing seemed to get through to her. Sharon honestly made me believe that she *really* didn't care anymore. I left her that day thinking, 'I'm not coming back to see her, not ever.' But it didn't work out that way at all."

Marilyn paused to sip her coffee and gaze out the bay window again. I then noticed her eyes begin to tear up. I took it as a sign that she was about to come to the more difficult parts of her story. When Marilyn continued, she had a distinct tremble in her voice.

"In March of…1965, I got a frantic call from Adam. He told me something I just couldn't believe. He told me that Sharon had almost…almost beaten you to death in your bedroom. He told me what he had walked in on, when he got home

471

from work. He had called me from the hospital, where he'd taken you. From there, he begged me to go get Sharon. He wanted me to take her to the hospital, too, and get her into the psychiatric ward. He was afraid the hospital staff would call the police and get them involved. He wanted her under a doctor's care before the police found her.

"I drove so frantically that day and did as Adam requested. When I found Sharon at the house. It was like she was in a trance. There was blood all over your little bed and a bloody wire clothes hanger laid close by. Sharon sat, huddled like, with her knees up to her chest, in a nearby corner. She had a blank stare and there was nothing in her eyes that told me she even knew who I was. When I got her up and led her out to my car, she was totally docile, but she never uttered a single word. I tried to make her speak by asking her what had happened, but she wouldn't make a sound. I then drove her to Immanuel Hospital. A very nice technician helped me get her inside the ER. The attending psychiatrist was called and when he met with her, he ordered her immediate admittance into the psychiatric ward. While I waited for word on her, I looked for Adam."

As Marilyn wept and talked, my own lost memories began to flood in. I knew right then her story was true. As I remembered the horrible events of that day, I wasn't able to stop my own tears from coming. Julie looked at me and with worry in her eyes, squeezed my arm tighter. However, there was still more to Marilyn's story, so she pushed on.

"They already had you admitted into the children's ward. Adam was with you every minute. I was able to get the room number and as I hurried down to the ward, I heard you crying for your mommy. When I saw you on that hospital bed, I couldn't believe my eyes. Your back was bandaged, and they had applied cold compresses, too, which made you scream even louder. I just couldn't believe what my friend had done to her little boy."

Marilyn then lost control and broke down crying. As she sobbed, my memory kicked in again and fed me another flash from my past. "It was you!" I exclaimed.

Marilyn looked up at me, clearly alarmed.

"Friday night, when we first met, I just knew I had seen you before. Not recently, like at church, but long ago." My recollection caught both Marilyn and Julie by surprise.

Marilyn asked in an astonished tone, "You remember me from the hospital?!"

"Yes...I do. I remember now. I remember all of it. That day, she said it was my fault. I didn't know what she meant at the time, but I do now."

I then got up from the couch, leaving Julie to herself. I stepped up to the large bay window, giving the women my back – I didn't want them to see my tears. While setting my gaze on their front lawn, I began my recollection of that ugly day. "I was playing in my room, all by myself. Back then, I did that a lot. Derrick and Brian didn't want much to do with me. They weren't even home at the time. It was just Mom and me. I remember hearing her crying out in the living room, and almost yelling to herself. When I heard her, I got real scared. I thought Adam had come home and was beating her, the way he used to beat me with his belt. But, when I went to see what was going on, I got confused because Mom was alone.

"When Mom saw me standing there, her eyes got wild. For the first time ever, I was afraid of her. I almost thought it was someone else and not Mom at all. That's when she started screaming at me. 'It's your fault,' she yelled. 'It's all your fault.' I turned and ran back into my bedroom, crying. She came after me, but I had closed the bedroom door and tried to keep her out. She was so much stronger, so when she forced her way in, she knocked me onto the floor. Before I could get up and run, she grabbed me and literally threw me onto the bed. Then, she started hitting me. I rolled over onto my stomach and tried to get away, but she held me down. She then grabbed something and hit me some more. This time, the pain was different...you know...worse. It was too much. I kept screaming for her to stop, but she just...kept hitting me. I must have blacked out or something. The only thing I've remembered for years is Adam standing over me yelling, 'What have you done?!' It's the only thing I've remembered about that day. I've always thought he was the one who did it because of the beatings he used to give me and my brothers with his belt. Before that day, Mom never touched me in a bad way."

I then turned and wiped my tears away. Julie immediately came to me, with tear-streaked cheeks of her own. There, in front of her mom, we held each other close. In the midst of my tears, something changed. I was almost instantly able to get control because just then, a feeling of complete relief washed over me. I took a deep breath and gave Julie a reassuring smile. In just above a whispered tone, I said, "I remember. I remember it all! And it's okay." Leaving Julie by the window, I went to Marilyn, who was busy dabbing tears from her eyes with a tissue. Going down to one knee beside her, I said, "Thank you."

Marilyn put her hand on mine, smiled, and said, "You really do remember, don't you?!"

Nodding, I replied, "Yes, I remember it all and I'm okay. In fact, I feel better than I have in a long time."

Marilyn continued to smile, but then it faded. "That's good, honey, but we're not through. There's more."

I nodded at Marilyn, thinking, *"What else could there be?"* I then returned to the couch. There, Julie once again took up her position next to me. We waited a moment for Marilyn to wipe her eyes, blow her nose, and then settle back into her chair. Like the calm that follows a storm, when Marilyn began to speak, I sensed peace in her demeanor.

"I don't know how you're going to feel about this, but it was Adam and I who kept your mother out of prison. You see, honey…she was sick and needed psychiatric help, not a prison sentence. Adam and I talked to a friend in the District Attorney's office into helping us get any charges dropped. He was an old schoolmate of ours, too. I think he also once had a thing for your mom, so it wasn't hard to get him to sympathize. Adam gave all kinds of assurances that only the best care would be given to you boys. Sharon would not be allowed around any of you until she underwent extensive, psychiatric therapy.

"Your older brothers were sent to the sister of Timothy Belanger. When I last heard, they now live somewhere in Michigan. When you got out of the hospital, you stayed temporarily with Adam's sister. Adam was busy making arrangements to have you baptized Catholic. After that, he enlisted the aid of Father Michael to help get you situated into a Catholic foster home. Adam knew of a co-worker at the cannery who was already in the foster care system. He asked him for his help."

"That would be Linus Matson," I inserted.

"I didn't know his name," said Marilyn, "but I do know how Father Michael at St. Joseph's had a hand in convincing the family to take you in."

I simply nodded my understanding.

"Once you were put into foster care, Adam kept tabs on you the best he could, but from a distance, through Father Michael, I think. He got word that you were not doing well within that home and pressed the social services into finding a family better suited to care for you. He learned that Brad and Janet Wilson were also volunteers within the foster care program. He talked to Brad about the possibility of taking you in. I talked to Adam after church one morning. He told me that Brad jumped at the chance to take you in. Adam said that Brad seemed very eager to help. He said they even showed interest in the possibility of adopting you.

"You were transferred to St. Joseph's the Worker Elementary for your second-grade year and shortly thereafter, moved in with the Wilsons. Throughout that period, I continued to visit with Sharon, but only from time to time. She seemed to be making vast improvements, mentally, and eventually was able to return to a more normal life. She was staying with her parents at the time. She seemed to be perfectly okay with the fact she had lost visitation rights with you and your brothers. She didn't seem to have a problem with your brothers living in Michigan, either. However, when she learned that you were living with the Wilsons and of the possibility of them adopting you, she flew into a panic. 'NO!' she yelled, 'not with them! They can't have him! He can't stay here! He has to get away from here! If he stays with them, this town will destroy him!' She was adamant about it."

I briefly interrupted Marilyn by asking, "Were you the one who told her where I was staying?"

"Yes, honey…I am," Marilyn stated remorsefully. "I wish now I hadn't. Not long after, Sharon contacted me and told me everything was going to be okay. She was confident that everything was going to turn out for the best. I talked to Adam and he was unaware of anything unusual. He continued watching you from a distance. He even got sporadic reports from Brad, stating everything was good and you were adjusting quite well. Because I knew Sharon was still mentally unbalanced, I didn't pay too much attention to anything she had to say. I distanced myself from her again and from the entire situation. You must understand, Jackson, I had two little girls of my own to be concerned with."

I smiled and nodded to let her know that it was okay. Her smile in return was all the thanks I needed.

Marilyn then put a rather disappointed look on her face and said, "I simply assumed that one day I would hear adoption proceedings had taken place and you had become part of the Wilson family...permanently."

Once again, Marilyn paused to look lovingly at her daughter. When she continued, new tears formed in her eyes. "One day, in the summer of '69, that little girl sitting next to you came home, crying. She was so unhappy about a certain boy from school who had up and moved away for good. That's how I found out the Wilsons had, in fact, not tried to adopt you."

I looked down at Julie and saw more tears welling up in her eyes. It was now my turn to offer some support.

As I maneuvered to get my handkerchief from my back pocket, Julie cried hoarsely, "I hated that day. I'll hate that memory forever."

I handed Julie the handkerchief and then held her just a bit tighter. Afterward, I shared more information.

"The last time I ever saw my mom was shortly after I moved in with the Wilsons. I came home from school one day and there she was, talking with Janet in the back yard. I don't think she was actually there to see me at all. She didn't seem very interested in visiting with me and when I asked if she came to get me, she just said, 'No, Jacky, this is just a short visit.' She left me that day without even giving me a hug or a kiss. No explanations, either. She just gave me a wave... then left."

A silence then settled over the room. Like me, Marilyn appeared to be wrestling with some deep thoughts. When a few minutes had gone by, Marilyn looked directly at me. "Last year, just after the fourth of July holiday, I saw Sharon for the last time. She looked better than I had seen her in years. She was cheery and reminded me of her old self. I hoped things were truly turning around for her. But the very next week, her parents left town for a day. They went to visit friends in Albert Lee in the morning. When they returned that evening, they found Sharon lying on the couch. When they discovered an empty bottle of sleeping pills and half a bottle of vodka on the coffee table in front of her, they immediately tried to wake her. You already know the end of that story."

I had already gotten over the shock of learning about my mother's suicide, so I had no reaction to the newer details given. Still, Marilyn watched me intently, as if to test my tolerance level. After a brief spell, she stated, "Jackson, I want you to come with me now. There's something you and I should do together. Julie, you stay here please. We'll be back in a little while."

Julie asked, "Where are you going?"

Looking directly at Marilyn, I replied, "We're going to the cemetery, aren't we?"

"Yes, we are," answered Marilyn. "Can you do that with me? I think we both need to. We need to go say good-bye to her...for good."

Julie leaned over and kissed my cheek. "Are you gonna be okay?"

"I'll be fine, Jules." I then tried to give her my best, reassuring smile. "Your mom is right...I need to do this."

"We won't be gone long, baby," said Marilyn. She then looked directly at me and said, "I don't believe in long good-byes."

After Marilyn and I made the turn onto Baker Avenue, in her immaculately clean, white, Cadillac sedan, I stared out the side window. I thought about the newly resurrected memories that her story had brought back. Mostly, I thought about a terribly hard decision that I had just made. Marilyn retelling my mother's story had helped me more than I ever thought possible. Right then and there, I knew where I truly belonged. An awful sadness gripped my heart because there was absolutely no doubt in my mind anymore that Doc Elliot had been right all along.

As Marilyn drove, she snuck random glances at me. I didn't have to wait long to find out what she was thinking. "You're very intuitive, Jackson," she observed. "That's good. I hope it serves you well, not just in the future, but more so, while you're still here in town."

Trying to sound smarter than I actually was, I said, "You think I haven't figured it out yet, right?"

"Figured what out, honey?"

"Who my real dad is."

"You have to be very careful with that, honey. Who do you suspect?"

"I'm pretty sure I know who it is, but I'm not going to say anything. I mean, not until I know for sure. I don't know, maybe I'll never say anything. I know who

I belong to now, so why bother? I know that I can't make a mistake about any of this. Too many people have already been hurt over me. I don't want anyone else to get hurt, not because of me." I then went back to looking out the side window and while shaking my head, added, "God, what a mess."

After a few more blocks passed by, I turned and looked at Marilyn, but didn't say a word. She, too, gave me a quick glance before returning her attention to the task of driving. I then envisioned Julie in the future, looking exactly like her mother. I also thought how strange it was that I should have such a link to Marilyn, especially when I considered my attraction to Julie. Was it destiny that brought Marilyn, Julie and I together or was it divine intervention? Whatever cosmic energy was at work, I was thankful for it. For the first time in my life, I knew exactly where I belonged, and I had Marilyn to thank for it. With those thoughts in my head, I smiled at the mother of my girl, but she didn't see. Marilyn was too busy driving and appeared to be wrestling with thoughts of her own, so I left her to them.

To me, cemeteries had always seemed like creepy places. It was largely due to the many late-night, horror movies I watched, usually when I was supposed to be asleep. The thought of walking the grounds where dead, decaying bodies lay beneath my feet was enough to give me the heebie-jeebies. However, Glenwood Cemetery was anything but creepy. Neatly situated rows of headstones, made of polished granite and marble, were set against a canvas of manicured lawns and colorful gardens. The landscape was shaded wonderfully by numerous elm, maple, mountain ash, apple, and choke cherry trees. There, in the broad daylight, I thought the entire setting was beautiful. The look of the place alone helped me put away any foolish fears about visiting the dead.

Because Marilyn had trouble recalling the whereabouts of the grave site, I deduced that she had not come to visit her friend for an unknown amount of time. When she finally got her bearings, she drove us directly to the right section and parked just off the narrow, service drive. After we exited the Cadillac, we gave each other apprehensive looks. Marilyn then came around the sedan, took my hand, and smiled. "Let's go do this," she said softly.

Without saying a word, I took in a deep breath, let it out and then nodded.

Marilyn led me past many headstones and grave markers, until we were under an old maple tree. She then slowed down, released my hand and began reading grave markers. As she slowly walked down the line, I followed her closely and watched. When Marilyn finally found the marker she had been searching for, she stopped suddenly and faced the grave. I felt a small surge of uneasiness pass through me when Marilyn said, "Here she is." Then, while staring down at the marker, she added, "Hi, honey…I'm here with you…and I brought a special visitor."

At first, my thirteen-year-old mind thought it weird that Marilyn spoke out loud to the grave, but I also noticed her tone had nothing but love in it. I realized then that she honestly missed her friend, or at the very least, the memory of her in better days. I stepped up to Marilyn's side and, once again, took her hand. Instead, she smiled and put her arm around me. Together, we silently stood and looked down at the ground, which now covered the woman who brought me into this troubled life.

I was so weary from the lack of sleep; my mind unable to focus. I had no clear, let alone grievous, thoughts. To me, it was just grass that I looked at. I couldn't even access a decent memory of my mother. Then, Marilyn spoke and awakened me again.

"She deserved so much more than what this world gave her." Marilyn then inspected the grave marker, and with a disapproving look, said, "They're not doing a very good job with upkeep around here. I'm surprised I even found her. Just look at the way they are letting the grass grow over the marker."

Void of any clear emotion, I looked down at the humble, nondescript stone and then nodded my agreement.

Marilyn said, "Well, I brought some things with us, so we'll fix that, honey." Once again, her comment was directed at the grave. She then turned her attention to me and said, "You stay here and visit. I'll be right back."

Before I could utter a response, Marilyn traipsed off to the car, leaving me to look down at my deceased-mother's grave. I suddenly found myself wishing that I had worn different clothes that morning. Because Marilyn had earlier referred to our meeting as a date, plus the fact that I had no idea I would be digging around in the dirt at a gravesite, I wore slightly better pants than my usual blue jeans. Casual dress slacks and my dress shoes had seemed appropriate that morning, but now I was having second thoughts.

I squatted in front of the marker and tested the grass covering the stone. At the time, the only thing legible on the marker was her name, Sharon A. Harris. As I pulled at a handful of grass, I was confused by the last name, Harris. After listening to Marilyn's story and discovering that she never loved Adam, I thought it strange that my mother hadn't changed back to her maiden name.

The grass was loose enough, so I began to pull it back. I could see where moisture and dirt had discolored the stone, making it hard to read the dates. I brushed out the carved numbers and letters with my fingers, revealing her date of birth. I then went to work on the date of death. I had only to expose the first two digits when I was suddenly gripped by a terrifying realization. My mind raced, as the horror of it all descended upon me. I immediately lost my balance and fell forward onto my hands and knees. There at my mother's grave, the weight of it all was too much for me to keep inside.

When Marilyn returned from the car, I was still in the throes of grief. She spotted me, dropped the small basket of garden tools, and then rushed to my side. Kneeling down, Marilyn pulled me to my knees and into her embrace. There we remained for I don't know how long, as I let out half my lifetime's worth of disappointments and deep-seated pain. The whole time, Marilyn just rocked me in her arms, patiently comforting me while I got it all out.

When I thought I was done with it all, I stood up and helped Marilyn to her feet. Without uttering a word, I then walked over and retrieved the basket of garden tools. With tears still in my eyes, I went to work on trimming the grass away from the stone marker.

In a soft tone, Marilyn said, "Honey, I'll do it." She then tried to take the garden shears from my feverishly working hand.

"No!" I insisted, pulling my hand away. "Let me! She gave birth to me. I owe her for that. This is the only thing I'll ever be able to do for her. This is all she left me. So I'll do this now…because I'm never coming back here again."

While I worked, Marilyn kept her hand on my shoulder. The job didn't take long and when I had finished, I took the grass clippings and put them under a nearby hedgerow. Marilyn then knelt to place some fresh-cut roses from her garden on the grave. She then stood and with a slight tremble in her voice, said,

"Sharon always loved roses, but she hardly ever got them." She then turned to me and apologized, "I'm sorry, Jackson, this visit hit you harder than I thought it would."

Nodding at her, I said, "It took me by surprise, too, but I know why. When Brad and Janet told me about her death the other day, I convinced myself that her suicide had nothing to do with me. This morning, I listened to you and it still didn't hit me. I didn't understand that killing herself had everything to do with me. When I saw the date of death on her marker, it all just kinda…crashed in on me."

"What about her date of death?"

"15 July 1971…was my twelfth birthday."

Marilyn was aghast, "Oh, Jackson!"

I waited a moment and then said, "She waited until she knew for sure that I was gone. She waited until I belonged to someone else, someone not in Mankato. Once that was settled, there was nothing standing in her way." I wanted to cry again but fought through the bout in order to finish. "They left her alone on my birthday! They shouldn't have done that! She didn't want to live anymore, did she?! Why didn't she want to live?! Why didn't she want me?! Why did she give up on everything?!" I then broke down again for a short spell.

Marilyn hugged me close and spoke softly in my ear. "I don't know why she did it, honey. I've asked myself that question over and over again, but I can't come up with any solid answers, just a whole bunch of possible reasons. I do believe you're absolutely right about her not wanting to live anymore. I can't begin to know what she was thinking or why she wasn't a better mother. It's something you're going to have to take some time with. But, in the end, you and I need to put her behind us. We have to…let her go. She's gone now and hopefully…she's at peace. There aren't going to be any concrete answers for us, so we'll have to be strong and get past all of this. We have to just leave it all behind, you and me. I know that I won't have any real peace until I do. I imagine the same to be true for you, honey."

Just then, Patrick's words resounded in my head. *"I'll pray you find the truth of the matter and that it brings you peace."*

When Marilyn saw that I had recovered my wits, she asked, "Can we go over there and talk for a minute?" She pointed to a nearby wooden park bench that rested under the shade of an elm. We walked to it and sat down. Marilyn then looked as though she wasn't too sure how to proceed, so I decided to break the silence.

"Don't worry about me. I know now that I'm gonna be okay. Mom and Dad will make sure of it. Ever since I left Mankato, they've always made sure of it. I know I'm gonna get past all of this, too, just like you said."

Marilyn then spoke softly, like she was afraid of disturbing the nearby deceased. "I know you'll be fine, Jackson. I think, someday, you *will* be able to put it all behind you. You're so much stronger than Sharon ever was. I think you're going to have to be for what's coming. Before you leave town, there's still some hurt coming your way."

I didn't understand Marilyn's meaning just then, so I simply looked at her.

With a smile, Marilyn stated, "You're in love with my daughter. You're in love and probably for the very first time in your oh-so-young life. I know that it's Julie's first time."

Now I was the one who had to consider his words carefully. I hesitated some before saying, "Yes…I am. But I didn't plan on it."

"Of course you didn't," Marilyn said sweetly. "At your age, nobody does. It just…happens."

As she looked at me, I once again realized where Julie inherited her amazing smile. "When you leave," continued Marilyn, "I'm going to have a brokenhearted little girl on my hands for a while. Have you two talked about what happens when you leave Mankato? You know you're going to have to let her go, don't you?"

Her words cut like a knife, but I knew she wasn't trying to be mean. She was only trying to do what was best, not just for Julie, but for me, too. Marilyn was simply trying to get me to accept the truth of what was coming.

With my emotions trying to get the better of me again, I said, "I've thought about it a lot, especially in the past few days." My heart was in my throat, but I remained in control. I fortified myself and then said, "I'm going to do something. But I need your help."

I then laid out for Marilyn the plan I had formulated during the sleepless night prior. When I was through giving her specific details, she gave me an astonished look and exclaimed, "Jackson! Honey, are you sure that's what you want?!"

"It's not what I want at all. But I'm almost positive it's what I need to do. Please, don't try to change my mind because you can't. Nobody here can, not even Julie...not anymore."

Marilyn thought in silence and minutes passed. When she was ready, she offered me some very-helpful suggestions. More than Marilyn's words, it was her look that told me she would cooperate fully. There, in the middle of that cemetery, I made my final decision to actually go through with what I was sent to Mankato to do. Although I was resolved, I was also scared to death of the plan I was about to set in motion.

"You truly are as special as I thought you were, when we first met," said Marilyn. "I'm glad my Julie will have you in her heart forever. You'll be in mine, too."

With great sadness in my voice, I said, "She'll find someone else and then she'll forget all about me."

"It's true that someday, someone else *will* come along, Jackson. But a girl *never* forgets her first love...ever. I'm so glad it was you, honey." Marilyn then gave me another amazing smile and asked, "Do you think you're ever going to forget her?"

Angrily I replied, "Never!"

"And that's the way it works," said Marilyn softly. After a moment, she added, "Let's get out of here. Right now, I have a need to rejoin the living."

On the return trip from the cemetery, my mind was reeling with way too many thoughts. It was hard for me to know exactly what my next course of action should be. Suddenly, I remembered something from the cemetery that had struck me as strange. Putting on a puzzled expression, I turned toward Marilyn and asked, "My mom didn't change her name back after the divorce?"

"What divorce, honey?"

"Adam and her...They never divorced?"

"No, they never did. Adam didn't want to put her through all of that. He didn't believe she could handle it." Marilyn paused for a moment and then continued. "Even though she lived with her folks, Adam continued to support her, financially, as best he could." Another short pause, then Marilyn shook her head slowly and wistfully said, "God, how he must've loved her." She then tactfully changed the subject on me and asked, "Do you think you'll come back here someday?"

I thought about her question for a moment, then offered, "Maybe, but I think it'll be a long time before I do. I don't belong here anymore, do I?"

"No, honey, you don't. You once did, but it's all gone now. Do you see it?"

"Yes, and I understand it, too. I need to be with my mom and dad now. And they live in Duluth."

"Mankato is a good town, honey. It's got good people in it, just like everyplace else in the world. Only some of us are a little…screwed up." Marilyn chuckled and then looked at me thoughtfully. "Yours is a life spared, Jackson."

Immediately, I understood her words and silently nodded my agreement.

Then, almost pleadingly, Marilyn said, "I need you to listen to me, honey. I need you to promise me something. Someday, when you're ready, I believe you will come back. I have to believe that. I don't care how long it takes. If you do come back, you have to promise to come see me. Regardless of whether you and Julie are still talking, you have to come see me. Promise me, Jackson…Please? I have to believe I'm going to see you again, okay?"

For long seconds, I just looked at her. In that moment, it was beyond my comprehension, but I suddenly knew without a doubt, to Marilyn, I was important. So, nodding my head slowly, I said, "I promise."

Just then, I changed my mind about going back to the Falkner residence to be with Julie. Instead, I needed to make some important phone calls. "Could you please drop me off at the Wilson's?"

As if Marilyn already knew what was on my mind, she replied, "Sure thing. What do you want me to tell Julie?"

"Tell her that I'll call her later. Tell her I really need a nap, which, by the way, is the truth."

As Marilyn kept her eyes on the road, she just smiled and nodded.

When Marilyn brought the Caddy to a complete stop in front of the Wilson residence, I thanked her appropriately, climbed out and then watched her shiny, white, luxury car until it disappeared around the corner. Turning and taking a good look at the Wilson house from the driveway, my heart began to sink.

When I stepped in the side door, I called out, "Anybody home?!" I then stood silently, hoping no answer would come. When I was rewarded with no sound, I felt relieved that I had the entire house to myself. I immediately went into the coolness of the basement to make my telephone calls. Sitting in the big comfortable lounge chair, I took the phone from the end table and sat it on my lap. I then picked up the receiver but had to put it back down in the cradle because I couldn't decide who I should call first. Giving it some thought, I chose Joel. The last thing in the world I wanted was to hear Mrs. Brighten's, disapproving voice. So, When Joel answered the phone, I felt almost blessed by God.

"Hey Joel, can you talk? Yeah, well…I need your help with something…"

When I was through talking to Joel, I made my next call to Father Michael. I gave him the abridged version of how I had just spent my morning. I then asked him to pass on a message to Adam Harris for me. After that, I had to sit and listen to some of his pearls of wisdom, which almost put me to sleep. I was, however, able to remain patient and awake throughout his mentoring speech. More so than listening to his guidance, I simply listened to the sing-song lilt of his voice and smiled uncontrollably. Ending that call was extremely difficult, and I had a huge lump in my throat, especially when I heard Father Michael say, "Good-bye, lad. May the Lord bless you and keep you safe…always."

Before making my third and final telephone call, I paused to gather what courage I could. I needed to rehearse exactly what I wanted to say. I was extremely tired and somewhat overly emotional but knew that I needed to be totally coherent and resolute. When I was finally convinced I was ready, I took a deep breath, picked up the receiver, and then dialed. As I inserted my finger into each number of the rotary dialer, I almost did not have to look - the phone number was second nature to me. When I heard the voice at the other end of the line, I smiled because it was the exact voice I needed to hear.

"Good morning, B and C Enterprises. How may I help you?"

"Hi, Mom, it's me."

CHAPTER 26

"Hey, kiddo, didn't you hear the phone?!" Janet exclaimed, as she gently shook me awake.

"What time is it?" I asked groggily, still sitting in the big lounger in the basement. *Crap! I fell asleep!*

"It's around four-thirty," replied Janet, standing above me, chuckling. "Answer the phone. It's Julie."

I sat up hastily, attempted to wipe the sleep from my eyes and then grabbed the phone. "Hi, Jules," I greeted apprehensively, wincing at the potential trouble I had gotten myself into.

Without the slightest bit of annoyance in her voice, Julie replied, "Hey, sleepyhead, can you be ready to go soon?!" Her voice told me that she was in some great hurry.

"Where?"

"The gang wants to meet at Kresge's for a burger and then hit an early movie. Momma's going to drive us. So, can you be ready in say…half an hour?"

"I'll be ready," I said, still trying to wake up.

"Cool…Love you…Bye."

I couldn't help but laugh at the energy in Julie's voice, plus the abruptness at which she signed off.

Janet, who was giving me a knowing grin, asked, "Okay, where are you off to tonight?"

"Burgers at Kresge's, then to a movie with the gang," I replied, then realized I was still stationary. "Cripes! I gotta get moving! They're picking me up in thirty minutes!"

As I scrambled up the basement steps, I heard Janet laughing behind me.

Marilyn dropped Julie and I off in front of Kresge's Five & Dime as planned. We thanked her for the ride and agreed to meet her outside The Grand Theater, following the movie. As Julie's mom drove off, we waved and then stepped up onto the sidewalk. The temperature was still in the nineties, so we didn't wish to linger outside. I didn't even have to strain to see the heat waves coming off parked vehicles, smoldering in the early-evening sun. Almost burning my hand on the brushed metal door handle, I hurriedly opened Kresge's door for Julie.

Stepping inside was like going from a blast furnace into a refrigerated meat locker. Julie even commented that she was glad she wore long pants but wished she had also brought a sweater.

As we entered the diner, we looked around for signs of the gang, but we were the only souls there. So, we decided to claim choice seating at the counter. The eatery had no other customers because Mr. Steiner usually had the grill closed down at that time. Julie had explained that Ann and Gail called earlier and pleaded with him to keep it open. They even used my pending departure to grease that wheel. Since Kresge's would be closing its doors for good soon, Mr. Steiner was glad to accommodate our little group, if but for the last time.

Brenda was waitressing again. As Julie and I seated ourselves, Brenda gave me a suspicious look. "So, what are we puttin' horseradish on today?" she asked.

"Nothing...today," I replied coolly. "Two Cokes please."

While waiting for the others to arrive, Julie and I chatted a bit about how the morning went. I apologized for not coming back with her mom and explained to her how badly I needed the nap.

"Don't worry about it," chuckled Julie. "I fell asleep while you and Momma were gone. I didn't wake up until an hour before I called you. Momma didn't wake me up, either."

"So, we're okay then?"

"Yeah, we both needed the sleep. But I do feel a little robbed."

As Julie spoke, I noticed a sign for a photo booth on the opposite wall from the diner. Brenda was delivering our Cokes, when I grabbed Julie's hand and pulled her up from her stool. "Come with me," I laughed, then called to Brenda. "We'll be right back."

When Julie saw where I was leading her, she immediately understood. "Oh, yeah…Let's!"

The booth required a dollar in quarters, so I went back to see Brenda about getting some change.

Julie called after me. "Get enough for two sets!"

When I arrived with the quarters, Julie surprised me again by grabbing me and pulling me into the booth after her. It was cramped quarters, but we were able to sit side by side on the small bench facing the camera lens. She stopped me from putting the quarters in right away. "We have to rehearse first," she giggled.

"What? Don't we just have to smile?"

Julie shook her head and grinned. "Uh-uh, I want a couple of different poses, but one has to be like this…" She leaned in and kissed me.

When we were finished in the picture, a.k.a. kissing booth, we returned to our stools at the counter. Julie placed the two strips of four pictures in front of us. We then huddled over them, laughing at the different expressions we had put on our faces.

Julie asked, "Which set do you want?"

"Whichever one you don't, I guess."

"We can decide later."

Julie was about to put the pictures in her purse, when a teenage boy appeared out of nowhere. He plopped himself on the stool located to Julie's right. It only took me a moment before I recognized the guy as Greg Dodson. He looked basically the same as I remembered him, except his blonde hair was much longer. He had piercing blue eyes and like me, he had filled out some, but I still wasn't impressed or intimidated. I could see at a glance why a girl might find him attractive. That is, until he opened his mouth.

In a friendly-enough tone, Dodson greeted, "Hey, Julie, what's happenin'?"

"Hi, Greg," replied Julie, but sounded nowhere near as friendly.

Refusing to acknowledge my presence, Dodson asked, "Can I talk to you for minute?"

When Julie replied, the impatience in her voice was clear. "What's it about, Greg?"

"Well, can we go over there and talk in private?" Dodson replied, pointing at one of the vacant booths.

Chuckling sarcastically, Julie answered, "No, Greg, we can't. I'm with Jackson."

Dodson exclaimed, "Jackson?!" He then looked around Julie and eyed me up and down. "Harris? Is that you?"

"Hey, Greg," I said flatly and then nodded. I didn't bother to correct him about my last name. Because of his rude intrusion, my temper was already at a low simmer. That, plus I knew what he wanted to talk to Julie about. *Keep your cool, dummy,* I silently advised myself.

"Come on, just for a minute," Dodson pressed. "You don't mind, do you, Harris?

Julie was adamant. "I already said no, Greg. Now please go away and leave us alone."

I recognized the stress in Julie's voice and knew that she was becoming a little frightened. Still, I held my place. It wasn't time for any brash moves, yet, so I simply eyed Dodson coolly for failing to take Julie's more-than-ample hint.

Dodson then looked down at the counter, saw the pictures lying there, and made a quick grab for them. "You guys visited the booth I see, how cute. Oh, now there's a nice shot."

He was now truly obnoxious and my blood pressure was on the rise. *Stay cool, Landry, in case this really gets ugly. Keep your head, like Kurt taught you.* I was beginning to fear the situation would turn violent. It wasn't that I was afraid to fight Dodson at all. I just didn't want to do so in front of Julie.

"Give 'em back, Greg," Julie ordered, making a grab for the pictures.

"Alright, alright, don't get your undies in a bunch," Dodson insisted. The creep then handed Julie the pictures and she very quickly tucked them into her purse.

In a pleading voice, Julie asked, "Will you please leave us alone?"

"You guys claiming the whole counter for yourself?"

In a disgusted tone, Julie said, "Come on, Jackson. Let's go grab a booth."

As Julie pivoted around and prepared to stand, Dodson grabbed her arm, saying, "You don't have to run off."

It was the last straw. I immediately came off my stool and took up a defensive posture against the blond, knuckle-dragging Neanderthal, who was now attempting to manhandle my girl. In response, he let go of Julie and back peddled a few steps. I instinctively put myself in front of Julie, my thoughts getting wilder. *Aw, Christ! This is really gonna happen!*

Brenda had been watching the scene unfold, so she ran into the kitchen, calling for Mr. Steiner.

With a sadistic smile plastered to his face, Dodson attempted to bait me. "Yeah, Harris, come on…I dare you," he taunted. "Seems to me I owe you for the sore nose you gave me a few years back."

I just couldn't keep from firing back, "Most guys learn the first time, but if you really want to be a jackass about it, let's go."

Just when I thought there wasn't any way out of a public brawl, I was quite forcefully shoved to one side. At first, I thought it was Mr. Steiner, arriving in time to defuse the situation. To my great surprise, when I regained my balance, I saw that it was Julie who did the pushing. Astounded, I stood and watched as she fearlessly stared Dodson down, eyes glaring, her nostrils flared in anger.

Suddenly, red and yellow streams of ketchup and mustard hit Greg in the face and down the front of his shirt. Because Greg and I had been so focused on each other, neither of us noticed Julie grab the two plastic dispensers from the nearby counter.

His eyes wide with surprise, Dodson yelled, "STOP IT!"

I couldn't help but burst out laughing at the comical scene that unfolded in front of me. Julie kept accurately hitting Dodson with ketchup and mustard, while he desperately looked for a place to hide. For just an instant, I thought she might actually empty both bottles on him.

When Julie finally finished giving Greg his new paintjob, she looked at him defiantly and pointed her finger at his face. "Get away from me, Greg…And stay away!"

Of course, Dodson was at a severe loss. It was clear he didn't know what his next move should be.

Just then, Mr. Steiner and Brenda came hustling out of the kitchen. Dave, Tony, Joel, and Mike were also making their way into the diner. They all took one look at Greg and howled with laughter.

I calmly went to the counter, peered over it, and found Brenda's cleaning rag. "Please?" I asked, pointing to the rag.

While trying to suppress a laugh, Brenda handed me the already-wet cloth. When I tossed it to the teenage statue – Greg seemed frozen – I didn't even try to hide my smirk. He deftly caught it and immediately began wiping his face. I could tell he was positively mortified. There was also a very good chance that he was in a mild state of shock. I know at that very moment, I was! I actually felt some pity for him, but just a little. It reminded me somewhat of the scuffle we had in the third grade. Danny's words from that day resonated in my head. *"He had it coming."*

"The bathroom is that way, Greg," I said, pointing the direction out for him.

The now red, yellow, and somewhat-orange colored Dodson didn't hesitate a second. He took off at a trot in the direction I pointed.

Julie then came to my side, took my arm, and spoke softly into my ear. "Jackson, that's the way to the ladies room. The men's room is in the other direction."

I simply replied, "I know."

When the realization hit home, Julie's eyes sparkled, and her mouth opened wide.

It was only a few, short moments before an absolutely-seething Greg Dodson hurried past us again, this time in the opposite direction. "BUTTHEADS!" he yelled. Of course, his anger meant little to those of us who were now doubled over in laughter.

Thinking I was the culprit, Dave stepped up to me, laughing. "Oh man, I wish I had gotten here just a little earlier. I would've loved to have seen you give it to him."

"I didn't!" I exclaimed and then pointed to Julie. "She did!"

Julie smiled innocently and the guys laughed all the harder.

We did not see the bully again that night. He simply vanished from the five and dime. Shortly after his disappearance, the other girls showed up. We immediately took up the counter and ordered our burgers, fries, and drinks. We then filled the diner with our teenage laughter, while Tony got the Wurlitzer rocking with some decent tunes.

While the burgers cooked on the grill, Mr. Steiner paid us all a short visit. Apparently, he appreciated Julie's tenacity, too. "You did good, little lady," he said. "That will teach him to keep his hands to himself."

When Mr. Steiner disappeared back into the kitchen, Julie turned serious eyes on me and lost her smile. "Were you really going to take him on, right here?" she asked.

"Look, Jules, I hate fighting. I really do, but when he grabbed you, it kinda flipped a switch in me."

Snidely, Julie said, "My hero."

Picking up on her disapproval, I offered, "If it means anything, I liked your way of handling it better."

Smugly, Julie said, "That's because girls are smarter than boys." Then, she rewarded me with a smile.

I couldn't argue Julie's point, though, and was suddenly feeling like I had fallen down a notch or two in her eyes. It must have shown because she leaned over, kissed my cheek, and softly said, "Still, I've never seen any guy stand up to him the way you just did. It was pretty cool."

"It was stupid," I mumbled.

"Yeah, it was," giggled Julie, "but I know you were thinking of me, so it was cool." Julie then looked me in the eye and silently mouthed the words, "I love you."

Perhaps it was my imagination, or maybe just the romantic coming out in me, but that evening, Mr. Steiner's burgers never tasted better. Looking up and down the counter and taking in the entire scene, I was suddenly struck by the notion that after that night, I would never see the diner again. The gang and I would never sit at its counter, nor hear any of Mr. Steiner's good-natured jabs. The five and dime would be closing forever and I, too, would be going away. An era was coming to an end. The reality of it all made me sad, but just for a moment. The girl seated next to me had a strange ability to pull me out of whatever sullen mood I fell into. And she did it with nothing but her smile.

When the clock on the wall, which resembled an oversized Coca-Cola bottle cap, told us it was time to leave and start heading toward the theater, the guys and I paid for the food. Then, we all gave a special thank you, and said our good-byes to Mr. Steiner and Brenda, all before spilling out of the five and dime into the early evening heat. The Grand Theatre was only three blocks away, but because the heat hadn't let up much, it seemed an overly long journey.

That night, the movie we went to see starred Robert Redford, as *Jeremiah Johnson*. Even with the beard he wore for that role, the girls all agreed that he was – as they put it – "absolutely gorgeous."

Personally, I could not understand how any girl could be attracted to a much-older man. So, giving Julie a perplexed look, I asked, "Do you really think Robert Redford is that good looking? I mean, he's almost old enough to be your dad!"

"Yeah, I suppose," replied Julie. "But he's not my dad. Dad's good looking, I guess, but he's no Robert Redford!" Julie then laughed and afterward asked, "You think Mama is pretty, don't you?"

"Yeah, but..."

"Well, there you go," Julie rationalized. "When I get older, I'll be lucky if I look half as pretty as my mom. Do you think you'll look like your dad when you get older?"

As I pondered Julie's question, I looked at the sidewalk. After a few moments, I answered, "How am I supposed to know?" Even though I wasn't sure of anything, it still felt like a lie when I said, "I don't know who my dad is." Then, giving it all too much thought, I added, "Even if I did know him, I wouldn't want to be like him. I don't want to look like him. I don't want to act like him. In fact,

I don't think I want to be *anything* like him." I then took my eyes off the sidewalk and looked at Julie. She was no longer giving me her brilliant smile. Instead, she looked very sad. "I'm sorry," I said. "It's just that…"

Stopping me short, Julie said, "Jackson, don't…You don't have to explain anything. I know this morning was hard for you. Let's just let all that go for now, okay? Let's just have a good time tonight."

Smiling, I squeezed Julie's hand and simply nodded in the affirmative.

When our little gaggle finally arrived in front of The Grand Theater, we all hurried to get inside. After sending the girls in ahead of us, the guys and I purchased tickets at the window out front. We then scrambled inside to meet up with our dates. Almost immediately, we felt refreshed by the air-conditioned interior.

There was still plenty of time before the curtain rose, so we all decided to choose our seating before getting the necessary provisions, like pop, candy, and popcorn. We guys let the girls choose where they wanted to sit. In turn, the girls acted like a small committee. It seemed as though they couldn't quite decide on whether to sit in the very front row or the very back. To say the least, I was more than a little surprised, when they finally decided on the very back row.

There are rituals to dating. However, at the time, that's *all* I knew about dating. Unfortunately, Mom had not progressed me that far, yet. She and I were still working on opening doors, speaking clearly when spoken to, standing when a lady enters the room, etc. So, to say the rules of dating were still somewhat alien to me, would be like saying a two-year-old doesn't quite know how to drive an automobile. Still, when I was with Julie, there seemed to be a natural flow to things. To counter my awkwardness, I simply relaxed, plus occasionally watched Dave and Joe, hoping to learn a bit from their vast experience with girls.

It was during one of my observation periods of Dave and Anne that I saw him get up and ask her if she wanted popcorn. I was not about to be bested, so I asked Julie if she wanted anything.

"I'll take a Coke and, if you don't mind, maybe a small popcorn," answered Julie. Then, rapidly changing her mind, she said, "Better yet, why don't you just get a large popcorn and we can share."

Wondering how Julie could possibly be hungry at all, especially after the burger, fries, and Coke she had just consumed at Kresge's, I facetiously asked, "You sure you don't want any Junior Mints, too?!"

Julie giggled in return, "Now that you mentioned it, sure!"

After giving her a comical look, I peered down the row. The others were engaged in boisterous, but subdued, chitchat. That is, all except Joel. While everyone laughed and carried on, he brooded over something and I had a pretty good idea what that something was.

I caught everyone's attention and announced, "Popcorn run...You guys want anything?"

Gail and Nancy chimed in their orders, but Mike and Joel just shook their heads. Nudging Tony, I said, "Come help me carry this stuff, will ya?"

While making our way out of the row of seats, I suddenly noticed Joel following us. Tony asked him, "Change your mind?"

"Kinda," replied Joel.

As the three of us made our way back out into the lobby, Joel announced that everything was arranged for another baseball game. It was all set for early the next morning. When he spoke, I clearly picked up on his unhappiness. So, when the others weren't paying attention, I poked him and whispered, "Smile."

"I'll be alright," he said, but his look was way too serious.

Knowing the reason for his pouting, I scowled at him and shook my head.

Leaning in close, Joel whispered, "You gotta tell the others."

"No way, not until it's time. If you or I say anything, everyone will start acting like we're at a funeral. I don't want that. You said you would help. You said you wouldn't tell, not even Gail!"

"I know, I know, but it sucks." Joel then took in a deep breath and let it out. "Don't worry...I'll do what you want."

"Thanks man...I owe you...big time. Now, are you sure you don't want popcorn?"

Joel chuckled slightly and then said, "Alright, I'll have a popcorn...and maybe a root beer." He then had an afterthought. "By the way, we're short a few players for tomorrow, but I suppose we can still manage."

I thought about it for a few minutes and then, surprisingly, heard myself say, "Let's invite the girls to play."

"Are you kidding?!" exclaimed Joel. "They can't play. I doubt any of them know how! Besides, none of them would be able to hit the ball."

"Sooo...we'll make a new rule," I argued. "We can make it underhand pitch to the girls and overhand to the guys. That way, the girls don't end up being bored, just sitting in the bleachers."

Joel mulled it around in his head for a minute and then admitted, "Hey! That could work!"

When we returned to our seats and disseminated the popcorn, pop, and candy, we pitched the idea to the group. Of course, the girls were more than enthusiastic about being included. However, Dave shot me a rather pessimistic look and then laughed, saying, "Oh, God...This was your idea, wasn't it, Landry?"

Nevertheless, as I handed Julie a pop and a box of Junior Mints, I got big-time approval from her eyes.

The ball game agreed upon, we all settled in and waited for the curtain to rise and upcoming attractions to begin. While the lights were still up, I looked around and took in the old theater's décor. I also remembered some of the matinee movies I had seen there years prior. The Grand, like most of the buildings on front street, was built somewhere near the turn of the twentieth century. Its stage had seen many years' worth of vaudevillian acts, magicians, plays, and various concerts. When moving pictures became popular, The Grand became the perfect venue in Mankato to make that transition, as did The Town and The State Theaters. Sitting there, knowing I would probably never sit in The Grand's old seating, nor watch another movie on its large, silver screen, I was suddenly overcome with more sadness. As I snuck a look down the row of friends sitting with me, I immediately understood that it wasn't the theater that I would be missing at all.

Shortly after that night's feature began, I learned a few things about girls, air-conditioned movie theatres, and the advantages of sitting in the very-back row.

While munching on a mouthful of popcorn, I suddenly became aware that Julie had crossed her arms and was rubbing them a bit. "You cold?" I asked.

"Yes, kinda," Julie whispered, "I should have brought the sweater Mama told me to bring, but it was so hot out."

Taking the hint, I tucked our bucket of popcorn under my seat and wiped the so-called butter off my hands with five, flimsy, theater napkins. I then reached over and put my arms around Julie. The Grand's old-theater seating did not have armrests. That alone made things easier, when I pulled her toward me, nice and close.

"Better?" I whispered.

"Mmm…Much better," purred Julie.

Besides many other dating rituals I knew nothing about, I hadn't yet learned there is an art to keeping one eye on the movie screen, while paying attention to a girl with the other. Throughout the feature, I periodically caught Julie looking up at me. It was usually just after she applied a fresh layer of strawberry flavored lip balm. We would then make out, while I tried to keep at least one eye on the movie. Albert Einstein once said, "Any man who can drive safely, while kissing a pretty girl, is simply not giving the kiss the attention it deserves." That may be true, but at age thirteen, I had not studied Einstein's works. Besides, I really wanted to see that movie! Still, I rapidly learned that I truly could not do the one without failing miserably at the other. So, naturally, Julie ended up getting my undivided attention.

That night, after careful consideration and much contemplation, I came to a logical conclusion: If you actually plan on *watching* a movie at a theater, do not bring a pretty girl and do not sit in the back row.

When the movie ended and the lights came up, the gang and I stayed seated and waited for the departing crowd to die down. Personally, I think it was just another excuse to keep from leaving. I don't believe any of us wanted that night out together to end.

When we exited the theater, it was just after nine o'clock, but there was still a failing light in the night sky. The air was still, warm, and dry. There was no breeze to cool things off and I was glad of it. The theater had been a little too air conditioned.

"I thought I was going to freeze to death in there," complained Gail.

"I don't know what you're talking about," said Julie, giving me a clever smile. "Where I was sitting, it was nice and warm."

The others were being picked up by parents in front of the theater, also. So, we said our good-byes right there in front of The Grand. When Julie spotted her mom's Cadillac, we both made our way out into the street. When Marilyn brought the car to a halt, Julie and I climbed in the front seat together.

As Marilyn headed us toward the neighborhood, Julie talked excitedly. Her exuberant gestures made driving a challenge for her mom. I cringed a little, when Julie talked about the incident at Kresge's, involving Greg Dodson. But Julie bragged on me, like I was some kind of knight in shining armor. That is, right up until she stepped in with the ketchup and mustard.

"Julie, you didn't!" exclaimed Marilyn.

Julie and I just laughed and nodded our heads. Marilyn had a fake disapproving look for both of us before giving in and laughing, too.

"I see I'm going to have to talk to Mr. Dodson about his son's manners," threatened Marilyn.

"I wouldn't waste your time," I told her. "I don't think Greg is going to be bothering Jules anymore."

To that, Julie just smiled and squeezed my hand.

When we arrived at the Wilson's, Marilyn parked the car in front of the driveway.

"Thank you for everything you've done today," I said sincerely. I then turned to Julie and said, "I had a great time tonight. See you in the morning?" I then opened the door and stepped out.

"Oh, no you don't! You're not getting off that easy," replied Julie. "I'll be right back, Momma."

Marilyn just shook her head at her daughter and muttered, "Honestly, Julie, what am I going to do with you?"

As the two of us walked down the driveway, I noticed the house was quiet. I half expected to hear loud music coming from the basement. It was still relatively early, so I thought Kurt and Danny might have their friends over again. Instead, the only noise was that of crickets calling and frogs croaking.

Feeling rather pleased with how the day turned out, especially the evening, I said, "It's been quite a day. I feel different."

"How do you mean?" asked Julie.

"Your mom helped clear up a lot of things today. All that stuff has been bothering me for so long, but now it doesn't. Now I feel like I can really put it all behind me. It feels great." Smiling at my girl, I said, "Then, there's you, Jules."

"I've noticed that you're now calling me Jules. Nobody calls me that."

"I'm sorry. If you want me to stop, I will. But it fits."

"It fits?"

I then heard myself say, "Yeah, I mean, sometimes your eyes sparkle like blue diamonds. You know…jewels." When I saw that Julie's eyes had widened and become as big as fried eggs, I felt the blood rush to my face. Struggling to recover my dignity, I said, "I know, that sounded really retarded, didn't it?" I then chuckled to hide my embarrassment.

Julie accepted my explanation with grace. She simply smiled and said, "That's okay, Jackson. I just love the way you talk to me."

Even though the area was amply lit, we kissed at the bottom of the steps that led to the side door. I didn't care anymore about being under the watchful eye of Marilyn Falkner.

When the kiss was over, Julie turned slowly and began to walk away. Without turning to look at me, she called out over her shoulder, "Good night, Dreamboat…I love you."

As I watched her walk away, I just stood there, smiling. I then made a move toward the side door, but just as I was about to open it, Julie stopped and turned around. Wearing a clever smile, she asked, "Jackson, do you love me?"

I couldn't help but chuckle a little when I admitted, "Yeah…I do." I then ducked into the entryway.

When I entered the house, Brad and Janet were once again seated at the kitchen table, playing cards. They both looked up from their game and saw me standing there with a grin that I simply could not get rid of.

"Oh, God," said Janet. "I've seen that look before."

Brad asked, "How was your date, buddy?"

"It was great," I replied. "Tomorrow is going to be even better. We have all kinds of things planned."

Janet asked, "Like what?"

"Well, first thing in the morning, we're all meeting up early to play baseball, while it's still cool enough. In the afternoon, the girls want to go to that new roller-skating place. After that, Mike's parents are letting him have a small cookout."

"Wow!" exclaimed Janet. "That really is a full day." Then, she lost her smile and gave me a straight-forward look. "You took yourself quite a nap today. Are you having trouble sleeping at night?"

"I had a hard time last night, but it's okay now. I spent the morning with Julie and her mom. Marilyn told me all about my mother. She told me how the three of you grew up together in the same neighborhood. She even told me she missed being close friends with you."

Sarcastically, Janet asserted, "I'll bet she did. Anything else?"

"Yeah, she helped me remember that it was my mom who put me in the hospital, not Adam. She's the one who gave me these marks on my back. I even understand why it all happened. I feel better knowing it. I even know that Adam Harris really isn't my father. I realize now that all he did for years is make sure that I was taken care of."

Brad asked, "Jackson, did Marilyn tell you who your real dad is?"

Putting on a look of disappointment, I replied, "She didn't know. My mom never told her."

With a look that told me nothing, Brad nodded his head slightly, as if he understood my disappointment. Intently watching his eyes, I held my breath, but he said nothing more. I then turned my gaze to Janet and saw nothing there that helped me, either. A moment of silence settled over the room, so I waited.

After a bit, Brad picked up the cards lying in front of him, sorted them, and then prepared to make his first play. When Janet did the same, I knew we were done talking.

You're not going to do it, are you? You're not going to tell me that it's you. The thought raced through my head. Half of me wanted it to be him and the other half prayed to God my suspicions were false. I thought about coming right out and asking that all-important question, but just then, all I could say was, "I think I'll turn in. I've gotta big day tomorrow. Good night."

"Oh, wait!" exclaimed Janet. "Your folks called while you were out tonight. They said they're coming down early. They'll be here early tomorrow evening."

Acting genuinely surprised, I shot back, "Really?!"

"Yeah," said Janet. "They called to say they would be staying at a motor inn, but they would be here at the house sometime after dinner. Will you still be at Mike's then?"

"No," I replied flatly. "I'll be here."

"Jackson, your mom sounded funny over the phone," asserted Janet. "Is there something you'd like to tell us?"

"Like what?"

"Like, do you have any idea why your parents are coming down so early?"

Thinking quickly, I lied by saying, "My parents pretty much do as they please. Mom's been missing me. She gets that way."

"Well, it'll be a good opportunity for us all to spend a little time together before you have to go back," said Brad.

As I nodded in the affirmative, I nonchalantly agreed by saying, "Sure… Good night."

I then traipsed up the noisy stairs but stopped when I arrived at the top. At the far end of the room, the fan was drawing in outside air from the window, but it hadn't cooled the room much. I saw Danny lounging on his bed, with his back against the headboard. Sweat glistened on his bare chest and the frown affixed to his face told me he had been listening at the vent again. Acting like nothing was wrong at all, I simply walked to my bed and sat down.

Danny asked, "What're you doing?"

"What do you mean?"

He then pointed to my two large suitcases, which I had taken from their temporary storage location, so I could do some preliminary packing. I had meant to put them back but did not have the time.

"You're getting' ready to leave early…Aren't you?"

At first, I wanted to lie and assure Danny that I had no such plans, but there was no point in it. Danny would see right through my deceit; he always did.

"You've been listening again, haven't you?" I quietly asked.

Danny nodded.

After a short pause, I said, "Yeah, I'm leaving. I'm leaving tomorrow night."

"Why?" he asked.

"Because I know that I don't belong here anymore. It hurts, Danny...really bad. So, I have to get out of here. I don't want to stay anymore."

"Does it hurt so bad that you can't wait a few more days?"

I understood Danny's disappointment, but right then, I didn't care because I was somewhat angry with him. I was angry because of my suspicions, and they told me that Danny, as well as the rest of the Wilson family, had not been honest with me. So, instead of remaining on defense, I turned the tables on him and played a little offense. "Let me ask *you* something," I began. "How long have you known, Danny?"

"Known what?"

"That you, Kurt, and me aren't just foster brothers. We really are brothers."

The look of horror that spread across Danny's face, told me I was right, but it was his words that made it all too real.

In a hushed and desperate tone, Danny cried, "Aw, Jesus, Jackson! How did you find out?! You weren't supposed to know. Who told you?!"

Back then, I often felt there were time when I may have been too clever for my own good. In that moment, having Danny confirm that which I prayed was not true, was definitely one of those times. In a heartbeat, my head practically exploded, while I fought to get over the shock of the truth I had just stumble onto. My voice trembled a bit when I replied, "You just did. I kinda figured it out today when Marilyn Falkner was telling me about my mom. Tonight, I saw Dad's eyes when he asked if Marilyn told me about my real dad. I could tell he was hiding something. They both have been dropping hints about something important since I got here." I then pointed at the heat vent and continued. "I even heard them tell each other that that they owed me the truth. I thought they might tell me tonight, but they didn't. Jesus, Danny, why didn't they tell me?!"

"They won't," Danny sniffed. "They came close to telling you a couple times, but I don't believe they ever will, especially after you leave. They think it'll be easiest if you never find out."

"Why?" I asked.

"Well, now that you do know, what good does it do you? You still have to leave. Jackson, we don't get to be together." Danny then covered his head with his hands. In years past, he had always gone to great lengths to keep from crying in front of me. I always felt Danny prided himself on being the tougher, older brother. However, I could now tell that he was desperately fighting an emotional outburst of tears.

I said, "At least I now know the truth, but it should have come from them. Does Kurt know?"

Danny nodded his head and whispered, "Yeah, he knows. We've both known for a while now. I wish they had never told us. I don't know why they ever thought it would be any easier for Kurt and me." Danny then looked directly at me. The pain and anger I saw in his eyes were indescribable. "I hate him, little brother! I hate him for what he did. I hate them both for letting you go."

In the past, I had never seen Danny in such pain, but right then, I could see that his heart was as broken as mine. Together, we did our best to choke back our tears, but failed miserably. We didn't cry long, though. It just wasn't our way. It was enough that we both fully felt the hopelessness of the situation and understood that it was a total injustice.

When I regained control, I thought for a spell and then decided to collect a favor. "I'm getting ready to do something in the morning, Danny. It's already started, but I need your help."

Without thinking first, Danny volunteered, "What is it? I'll help."

I then gave Danny the details of my plan and didn't leave out anything. I was very specific about what I needed him to do. As I laid it all out for him, his eyes got bigger and bigger. When I finished, Danny changed his mind and tried to back out of it. He shook his head and said, "I can't...I can't do that."

My voice cracked, "You have to. You said you'd help. I need to do this, Danny, but I can't do it alone. Promise you'll help me and promise you won't tell. And you can't tell them I know about Dad."

Danny looked at me through tear-filled eyes. "Alright," he said hoarsely, nodding his head. "I promise."

That being settled, there was no further need for words. Danny immediately set his alarm clock above his bed. He then lay down on his stomach and buried his face in his pillow. Sometime after that, I know not when, he dropped off to sleep.

While I made preparations for the morning, I continued to fend off my tears. It took me another hour or so to do some more packing, plus do a little writing. Then, feeling quite drained, I lay down on my bed, thinking that I would not fall asleep at all that night. Once again, though, I was wrong. The lack of sleep from the previous night, coupled with the emotions I was now battling, completely exhausted me. I rolled over and looked at Danny's back. He lay on his side, motionless, facing the wall. I heard his heavy breathing and knew my brother was fast asleep. With renewed tears in my eyes, hoping he might even hear me, I whispered, "Good night, Danny...I love you."

Chapter 27

Thursday, 17 August 1972

Danny's alarm went off promptly at five o'clock in the morning. After hastily turning it off, so no one else in the house would hear it, Danny rolled over and looked at me. I was already awake and had been so for at least a half hour. Sitting up, with my knees pulled up to my chest, my chin resting on them, I simply watched my brother wipe the sleep from his eyes.

Danny asked, "How long have you been awake?"

"Not long. I've just been sitting here, thinking."

"Did you sleep at all last night?"

"Yeah…Actually, I slept pretty good…I think. I'm not sure."

"I'm sorry about last night, little brother. I'm sorry you found out about Dad the way you did. I'm sorry about this whole mess."

"It's alright. Sitting here, it's what I've been thinking about. I'm glad I know the truth. I don't have everything figured out, yet, but it's okay. Just don't worry about me, Danny, okay?"

"Yeah, well, I just can't stop wondering how everything got to be so shitty," he said. Then, as an afterthought, he added, "Damn it!"

"Mom and Dad were right," I admitted. "I should have stayed away. Then, none of this would have happened."

"How were you supposed to know? God, this is going to drive me nuts! Don't worry about you? Are you kidding?" Then, trying to escape the subject altogether, Danny breathed heavily, "I need more sleep."

When Danny rolled over and faced the wall again, I smiled at his back. Then, I got up and dressed. Suddenly, Danny bolted upright in bed. He looked as though there was an additional something he wanted to say but was also ready to change his mind.

As I tied my tennis shoe, I asked, "What?"

Danny paused momentarily and then asked, "How are you gonna get through today?"

I thought for a moment, smiled broadly, and replied, "Don't worry. I plan on having a blast."

Looking extremely troubled, Danny asked, "Do you really have to do this thing now?"

"Yeah, I do. It's the only chance I'll have, why?"

"It's just that it…it seems a little…retarded."

I chuckled a little and then said, "You see…I really *am* your brother!"

When I left the upstairs, Brad was in the main bathroom, getting ready for work. Janet was still in bed, snoring lightly. Running water from the faucet, plus Brad's weak attempt at humming an unrecognizable tune, provided the cover noise I needed to get down the creaky stairs undetected. Once I made it to the kitchen, I then quickly found a flashlight in the utility drawer. Grabbing my windbreaker from a hook by the side door, I then slipped out onto the landing.

At first, I stood silently, so I could test the early-morning air. It was very dark out, the first graying of dawn had yet to begin, and the air was still, warm, and humid. I immediately changed my mind about the windbreaker and hung it back on the hook, just inside the door. I quietly locked the door behind me and stepped down onto the driveway.

Making my way out onto Westwood Drive in the dark wasn't difficult. However, I had to let my eyes adjust some to the pitch blackness that takes place just before dawn. The closest streetlight was down on Moreland Avenue but was of no assistance to me. I thought about turning on my flashlight, but I didn't want to attract any undue attention, so I left it off. Once my eyes adjusted a bit, I took off at a trot.

As I plodded along, I saw interior lights come on in neighborhood homes. The lights were a sign that people were waking and getting ready for work. Much like my first evening in Mankato, I stayed out of sight as much as possible. While I worked my way around Westwood Drive and headed toward Baker Avenue, it wasn't hard to go unnoticed. Should a vehicle happen by, there were plenty of places for me to hide.

After a block or two, I slowed to a fast walk. As I slowed my breathing, I couldn't help but think about the task at hand. Danny was right to question the necessity of it, but it didn't matter to me. I just knew in my heart that I was doing the right thing. I had gotten involved with a girl. And she wasn't just any girl. To my way of thinking, Julie was *the* girl. We both knew it hadn't been a smart thing to do, but it didn't slow our hearts down, not one bit. *It's too late to save my heart,* I thought, *but maybe I can help Jules.* Regardless of how it all turned out, Julie had given me back my smile. It was the one thing I would take to Doc Elliot.

Preparing to do that which I was sent to Mankato to do in the first place, I marveled at how everything had changed for me in such a short period of time. So many wonderful things had taken place amidst the many terrible truths I had learned. Inside, I felt stronger than I had ever felt before, but was I strong enough to carry out my entire plan? Trying to relax, I focused on executing one piece of the plan at a time. In addition, for the first time in my life, I knew how it felt to think and see things with true clarity. When I first arrived in Mankato, I had no idea how I was ever going to say good-bye to it all. Now, as I walked in secrecy, during the early morning silence, I suddenly knew, without the slightest doubt, that I was going to be okay.

When I reached the fence line behind the Falkner residence, I stopped and listened. There was no sound at all, so I turned on my flashlight and headed down the pathway. Down the hill I went, into the woods, and toward the creek bed. Suddenly, I tripped and crashed loudly into a tangle of dew-soaked weeds. When I finished tumbling, I calculated that I was only halfway down the hill. Petrified, thinking that I had just given myself away, I lay quietly, with a mouthful of weeds, listening. *Way to go, dummy,* I thought, spitting the weeds out. *Why don't you wake up the whole neighborhood while you're at it!* To make matters worse, I had also accidentally blinded myself with the flashlight. Just then, wild thoughts, doubt, and fear entered my head. *What the hell am I doing?! Danny's right! This is really stupid! What if I run into a skunk?! That'll do more than ruin my plan…It'll ruin everything!*

Dawn was going to break soon, so I needed to hurry. Recovering my wits, I swallowed my fears, got up, regained my heading, and reestablished myself on the beaten path. As I continued down the hill, I found it difficult to get my bearings. To make matters worse, in the limited, artificial light, the woods looked incredibly eerie. Plus, my eyes still had not yet readjusted from the accidental blinding I had given them.

When I successfully reached the bottom of the hill, without breaking my neck, I looked in all directions for the huge, fallen cedar tree. I couldn't believe I was having difficulty finding it because Julie had showed me the way only a few, short days earlier. When I finally did locate the tree, I immediately went to gnarled roots at the base and began my search for the large, flat rock that covered Julie's secret, keepsake, cookie tin. Luckily, I found it with little problem. In truth, I tripped on it and almost fell into the weeds again.

Getting a good grip with both hands, I heaved the rock from its resting spot. I then quickly retrieved the old tin from its hiding place, thinking, *I love you Jules. I hope you'll understand.*

When I pulled a letter-sized envelope from my back pocket, there was a large lump in my throat. Working as fast as possible, I added the envelope to the protective plastic bag filled with Julie's prized photographs. I then returned the box and the rock to their resting place. The intended task completed, I then shifted my thoughts to getting back to the Wilson house. Getting out of the house undetected had posed no real problem. Getting back inside was going to be an entirely different challenge.

By the time I made it back up the hill, the dim, gray light of dawn was just beginning. My clothes were now drenched with sweat and early morning dew. Even my tennis shoes and socks were soaked. I was glad I had the presence of mind to wear my oldest clothes.

On the way back, I hid behind bushes and trees to keep from being spotted by passing cars. Once, I actually lay down in the grass, behind a low hedge, just to keep from being spotted by a neighbor, who was pulling out of his driveway. At the time, I thought I was quite cunning. But then, another thought hit me. *What am I hiding for? None of these people care if I'm out this early in the morning!*

Feeling like an absolute imbecile, I got my dew-soaked self out from behind the hedge and walked the rest of the way in the street. *Idiot!*

Once I made it back to the Wilson's, I saw that both vehicles were still parked in the driveway. Brad would be leaving for work soon, so I had to be patient and wait. I ducked behind the garage and sat on an old bucket that I had overturned. There, I waited for the telltale sound of the Corvair's engine to start.

While waiting, I mused about how my plan was coming together thus far. I wanted that day to go by at a snail's pace. I wanted to savor every minute ahead of me. I then thought about my last telephone conversation with Father Michael. I believed that I had successfully put his mind at ease that I was going to be fine. Of course, I looked forward to spending the entire day with Julie and my friends. Yes, everything appeared to be coming together nicely. *Now, if I can just get into the house without Brad and Janet finding out what I've been up to! Hopefully, before I catch a cold from these wet clothes!*

Just then, I heard the side door open and then close. Shortly after, the Corvair roared to life. I listened, as Brad backed it down the driveway. It was my cue. As soon as Brad hit Moreland Avenue, I came out from behind the garage. Danny was standing at the side door. In a hushed tone, he exclaimed, "Hurry up! She's in the shower!"

I ran to the door and we quickly got inside. Danny practically pushed me all the way back upstairs to the safety of the bedroom. It was hard to keep from laughing out loud at our antics. I was extremely grateful for the warmth of the attic bedroom.

Danny had grabbed a towel from the kitchen on the way up. Handing it to me, he said, "Here…Get out of those clothes and dry yourself off. We'll throw 'em in the dryer after Mom leaves for work."

"Remind you of anything?" I chuckled.

Danny met my gaze, then immediately laughed. "The day you fell in the creek. I had to take care of your wet clothes that day, too!"

"You never told Mom or Dad about that day, did you?"

"Are you kidding? They would have strung you up. Now be quiet! We're supposed to still be asleep."

Looking at Danny, I thought about how he would no longer keep me out of trouble. Another large lump formed in my throat.

As fate would have it, I was almost late to my very last baseball game in Mankato. Of course, it was because I had to wait for a girl. I had arrived at Julie's house early enough, but she wasn't quite ready. When we did finally leave for the ballpark, Julie simply took her sweet time. As we walked hand in hand, my mistake was letting her set the pace. Julie seemed in no, big hurry at all to get there.

Upon our arrival, Julie saw that we were somewhat tardy. Turning toward me, she apologized for making us late. "I'm sorry, Jackson, but I had to finish getting ready."

I've never seen anyone primp that much before, just to play baseball, I thought, but couldn't help smiling at the result. That morning, Julie looked like a breath of fresh air.

"Then, there were the calls I had to make to the other girls," Julie explained.

"What other girls?" I asked.

Giving me that clever smile of hers, Julie replied, "The other girls who showed up, wanting to play, too." She then giggled loudly.

I looked at the crowd of teens being systematically split into two teams. There were more people than Joel and I had figured on. There were six more than we needed, so we split them in half. That way, each team would have a slight bench of extras to rotate in and out of the game. Both teams agreed, regardless of the outcome, everyone would get to play.

To say that we did not play serious baseball would be a gross understatement. I've never laughed so hard during a baseball game, before or since. I don't think any of the guys had either. At first, some of the more serious ball players did not appreciate the handicap imposed on them by some of the girls. It was clear that most of our female company had never played baseball before. However, as the morning went on, I watched attitudes change. By the fourth inning, everyone was laughing and having a great time.

We watched Anne swing at a pitch with all her might, only to accidentally let go of the bat and send it flying toward the pitcher's mound. The bat missed Dave – who just happened to be pitching – by mere inches. As the bat safely passed by, Dave boldly stood his ground. Narrowing his eyes at Anne, he then smiled, laughed, and said, "I could take that personally, you know?"

Later, we watched Joel scramble from the outfield toward the infield and we all held our breath. He was after a short pop-fly hit by Tony. The grass was still wet with dew and when Joel tried to hit the brakes, he looked as though he had just stepped on a banana peel, like in some cartoon we had all seen before. He was literally sliding on one foot, trying in vain to keep from wiping out. Of course, Joel missed the fly ball and Tony ended up safe at first base. The rest of us in the dugout were falling off the bench, laughing hysterically. Tony would not be that lucky again.

Julie was next at bat and Dave gave her one of his lame-duck, underhand pitches. Surprisingly, Julie hit a solid ground ball toward third base. However, Doug Haines made an easy grab and threw it to second base, which was being covered by a pretty blonde named Kathy Lebowietz. She juggled the ball some, finally got it under control, but didn't step on the bag for the automatic out. Instead, she practically tackled Tony, who was running full steam for the base. Once again, there was more laughter. When it was explained to Kathy that she only needed to step on the bag in that situation, her embarrassment was evident, but also temporary. Kathy earnestly asked, "Really? Then, giving Tony a sly smile, she said, "Well, my way was more fun. Don't you think so, Tony?" She was absolutely beaming at him.

Yeah, I know that look, I thought, smiling at the revelation.

Kathy's comment got raised-eyebrow looks from everyone. That is, everyone except Tony. He looked positively stupefied.

At the time, I was on deck, getting ready to bat. So, when Tony came back toward the dugout, I gestured for him to come toward me. When he was close enough, I grabbed the front of his shirt, pulled him in close, and spoke in a lowered tone. "So much for keeping your dukes up." I then gave him my best Cheshire Cat grin.

Looking at Tony was like seeing my reflection in a mirror. Back when Julie first kissed me under the weeping willow, I imagine that my look closely resembled what I was now seeing on Tony's face. His facial features had a mixture of fear, drunkenness, excitement, and wonderment plastered all over the place. But mostly, it was fear. When I looked Kathy's way, I noticed she looked quite pleased with herself. There was no doubt in my mind about what was going on in that head of hers.

When I finally stepped up to the plate, I was still laughing. Waiting on the pitcher's mound, Dave had a knowing grin on his face. He stood there, nodding his head. I knew he was looking to gun me down, so I set my jaw, stepped into the batter's box, and waited for Dave to go into his windup. I watched, as Dave's first pitch, a fastball, blew right past me. To me, it appeared low and inside.

"STRIKE," yelled Mike.

I immediately stepped out of the batter's box and gave Mike a disapproving look but said nothing. I was having too much fun to start an argument at the plate.

At first base, Julie cheered me on. "Come on, Jackson! Bring me home!"

Now, there's an idea, I thought, smiling at the irony. I then stepped back into the batter's box and prepared myself for Dave's next pitch. I took a huge swing at a curveball but missed it by a country mile.

Again, Mike yelled out, "STRIKE!"

Dave only had the two pitches, a halfway decent fastball and an under-developed curveball. Having just swung at his curve, I somehow felt the fastball was coming again. I decided to crowd the plate a bit. As expected, the fast ball came, but it just about took my ear off.

"BALL," yelled Mike.

I now had a dilemma on my hands. I was behind in the count and I had just seen Dave's fast ball for the second time. Almost instinctively, I knew he was going to bring the heat again. So, I made a show of digging in and taking practice swings, like I was going to brutalize whatever came down the pipeline next.

Dave went into his windup and delivered the expected fast ball. As he released it, I immediately changed my posture and attempted a surprise bunt. Successfully knocking the ball down and heading slowly toward third, I launched myself toward first base. I caught everyone flatfooted, including Julie. "RUN!" I yelled.

At first, Julie looked like she didn't know what to do. But then, almost as if she had just been given a swat to her backside, Julie catapulted herself toward second base.

When Dave came off the pitcher's mound to make a play on the ball, he momentarily slipped and lost his footing. It provided me the head start I needed. Not only did I beat his throw to first base, I saw that it sailed over the first baseman's mitt. Rounding first base and heading toward second, I yelled for Julie to keep running. As I ran, I was also laughing my head off.

Tony had positioned himself at third base, so he could act as the running coach. He yelled and gave Julie the signal to round third and head for home. The throw to second was late, but enough to hold me up there. Now, Kathy Lebowietz had a dilemma on her hands. She didn't know whether to throw for home plate or just hold the ball. Mistakenly, she decided to throw for home. Unfortunately for Kathy, she took too long to decide, so Julie made it safe.

As soon as Kathy released the ball for home, I headed for third. With Julie safe at home already, the catcher caught the ball, then made an immediate throw for third. Dave tried to wave him off wildly but was not in time. The throw to Doug Haines was too late. I had slid headfirst and tagged the bag. I was now safe at third.

"HOLD THE BALL! HOLD THE BALL!" yelled Dave. "For crying out loud, let's don't give him a homerun off a bunt!" Dave then shook his head at me and grinned. "Landry, you suck!" he laughed. Immediately calling for a timeout, Dave motioned his entire infield to the pitcher's mound.

I didn't pay too much attention to their huddle. Instead, I was busy trying to get sand to run down the legs of my jeans. I shouldn't have slid headfirst. Tony stood there, laughing at me because he understood my problem. I had a lot of sand in my underwear and that's just bad. With all the girls present, there was no efficient way to get rid of it. I mean, you can't just drop your drawers in front of a bunch of hormonal-teenage girls. So, while I shook the sand out, it didn't take much brainpower for me to come to a logical conclusion – *No more sliding for you, moron.*

The huddle at the pitcher's mound broke up and everyone dispersed to their assigned positions. When Doug Haines joined me at third base, I got my head back in the game. The next batter on our team was stepping up to the plate. It was Mike's girl, Nancy Carter. In previous innings, she had effectively demonstrated that she knew absolutely nothing about swinging a baseball bat. *Great*, I sarcastically thought. *Two outs already and Nancy is at bat. The only way I'm gonna score is if I steal home.* Almost as soon as the thought entered my head, I made up my mind. *Why not?! Today, anything goes!*

I watched Dave closely and he looked over his shoulder back at me from the pitcher's mound. Right as he turned his attention back toward Nancy and prepared to go into his windup, I stepped off third base and took a huge lead. I was still watching Dave when I felt Doug Haines tag me from behind. When I turned to look at him, Doug was wearing a huge grin and showing me the baseball that he had not relinquished from the previous play.

Doug laughed, as he gloated, "You're out, man. You can go sit down now. Or better yet, take the field. That's the third out!"

I turned and looked at Dave. I must have had the most idiotic look on my face because he was doubled over, laughing at me. When the shock wore off and everyone understood how I had just fallen for the oldest trick in the book, we all had a good laugh.

In the sixth inning, I watched Adam Harris's Chevy pull into the parking lot. He stepped out of his clunker and positioned himself on the hood, so he could watch from across the field. At that moment, I was in the doorway of the dugout, talking to Tony, waiting for my turn at bat. Instead, I asked Sandy Maynard to stand in for me, so I could go talk to Adam.

When Julie saw me making my way out of the ballpark, she hurried after me. "Jackson, do you want me to go with you?"

"Sure, if you want."

Julie hustled back to the dugout and asked another one of our extras to stand in for her. She then grabbed her small purse and jogged to where I stood waiting. I took her hand and together we began to make our way around the ballpark. As we closed the distance to Adam, Julie's grip on my hand got a little tighter. She looked nervous.

"Relax, Jules," I said softly. "Everything's fine here. You'll see."

"Why is he here?"

"Well, in a roundabout way, I kinda asked him to come."

Julie's look turned to slight surprise, but she said nothing. We continued on in silence until we came to where Adam was leaning on his old clunker. This time, he made a show of stepping forward and extending his hand to me. Smiling warmly, he greeted us both, "Hello, Jackson. Hello, Julie."

I tried to remember if I had ever seen him smile that way, but nothing came to mind. For the first time ever, his greeting felt genuine. In return, I smiled, too, and gave him a solid handshake. "Hello, sir," I greeted.

Adam said, "Father Michael gave me your message, so I thought I better come see you play."

I could hardly believe that I was glad to see him, but I was. Continuing to smile, I said, "I'm glad you did. I'm glad you're here because I owe you an apology…"

Adamantly, my former dad interrupted, "No! Stop right there. You owe me no such thing, ever. It's me who owes you an apology. Much of what has happened to you is my fault."

"Thanks," I returned, "but I know better now. I know the truth. Julie's mom told me everything. And then, I actually remembered it all. It was Mom. It was her all along. Now, I just want to put it all behind me. But I know I wouldn't be able to do that unless I saw you first."

Nodding his understanding, Adam said, "You should put it behind you. Please, don't let any of the past stop you from being happy, now, this very day. The one thing I can tell you for sure is that it's going to take some time, Jackson. So, just be patient. I know that I haven't quite got over everything, but I still hope to."

I was amazed at how sincere his words seemed. Talking with Adam in such a civil manner, felt extremely alien to me, but at the same time, it was comfortable, like the required healing was already taking place. He then asked me a few casual questions about my parents and my life up north. As I shared the requested information with Adam, I felt more and more at ease around him. Adam appeared extremely pleased to hear about Mom and Dad. Then, I saw him struggle somewhat to keep his composure. So, I smiled at him and said, "I know you did everything you could for me. I know you did your best."

Adam shook his head and struggled with his words. "If I had done my best, you would still be my son. I see how well you are growing up and all I can think is…how I unknowingly gave up on a pretty good thing." Tears were now welling up in Adam's eyes.

I didn't know what to say. Prior to that instant, I couldn't remember a single tender moment shared with Adam. Suddenly, a very surprising notion took hold of me, so I asked, "Do you have some paper and something to write with?"

"I do," offered Julie. She quickly rummaged through her purse and produced a small note pad and pen.

Taking both from her, I wrote down my address, tore out the page, and handed it to Adam. "Will you write to me sometime? Let me know how you're doing, sir."

Adam smiled at my gesture and said, "My friends call me Adam."

"Maybe…someday…I can be one of them…sir."

Adam nodded his understanding and then stepped forward to extend his hand to me. "You take care, Jackson."

Once again, I took his hand and said, "You too, sir." Julie and I then turned to depart.

Suddenly, Adam exclaimed, "Oh, wait a second! I brought you something!" He reached into the window of his car and brought out a neatly-wrapped package. As soon as he handed it to me, I knew it was a book. "Father Michael told me you were a reader, so I thought you might like that."

I tore off the plain brown wrapping and discovered it was a rather thick book on the history of baseball. I smiled and said, "Books and baseball. My two favorite things in the whole world."

Acting a bit put out, Julie immediately shot me a raised-eyebrow look. "Oh, really?!"

"Oops," said Adam. "You might want to rethink that, son."

I didn't take offense to Adam's slip of the tongue. Instead, I just shared in the laughter. It was another first for Adam and me. After giving him heartfelt thanks for the gift, Julie and I said our final good-byes to him.

While we walked back toward the gang and the on-going game, I caught Julie smiling at me from the corner of my eye. "What?" I inquired.

"That was amazing!"

"Yeah," I agreed. "And the day is just getting started."

Chapter 28

When Marilyn Falkner dropped Julie, Anne, Dave, and I off in front of the roller rink, it was twelve noon. There, we met the others in our group. They were dropped off by some of the other neighborhood moms. As usual, Gail and Joel were the last to arrive. None of us were surprised that it was Gail's mom who dropped them off, either.

When I saw Joel, I imagined that Mrs. Brighten would use his absence to imbibe in some early afternoon cocktails, not that his presence dissuaded her at all. Given my circumstances, the fact that Joel was with us, instead of putting up with any of his mom's drunken antics, made me so much happier. Besides, when it came to planning that day's activities, Joel got a lion's share of the credit.

The roller rink was located on the south side of town on Madison Avenue. It was like nothing I had imagined. It was everything my friends said it would be and more. As soon as we entered, I was mesmerized by the psychedelic colors and flashing lights used to set the tone of the place.

Loud music blasted throughout the building from large speakers, which were suspended from the ceiling. I had never heard such a sound system before. Skaters had already taken to the large oval-shaped floor and were rockin' and rollin' to the music.

Aside from roller skating, there were pool tables, air hockey, and various pinball machines in an arcade area. A snack bar, filled with every type of junk food a kid could possibly want, was also available.

I was entranced by the entire scene. That is, until I felt Julie come up behind me. "Is your place in Duluth anything like this?" she asked.

"No way!" I exclaimed. "We don't have anything like this! This is so cool!"

We all quickly went to the rental counter to get our skates. Then, we found vacant benches to sit on, so we could quickly change from our tennis shoes to roller skates. Lockers were available for twenty-five cents, so we got one for the girls and one for the guys. The girls, of course, placed their purses and shoes neatly inside their locker. We guys just crammed our tennis shoes in the other, making them a tangled mess.

The skating floor itself was made of concrete and coated with a polyurethane covering that was aquamarine in color. The traction skaters got on that surface was amazing. I was used to skating on the old hardwood flooring of the Curling Club, which at times could get quite slippery. In addition, skaters at the Curling Club felt every blemish that old floor had in it. In contrast, the floor of Mankato's new rink felt smooth as glass. There were practically no defects to be felt at all. Having never skated in such a place before, I fell in love with the rink immediately.

Not wanting to stand out, I began that afternoon by hiding my skating talent from my friends. However, after observing them for a little while, I discovered that they were not without some skill themselves. As my friends went tear-assing around the floor, I observed that they all appeared to have spent some time on skates and were quite confident of their abilities. So, I dumped the angst, joined them, and simply began to enjoy myself.

At first, I just hung out with the guys and watched, while Julie and the other girls practiced various spins, twirls, and dance steps. None of what they performed was polished or refined, but it was definitely better than anything the guys were capable of. When we guys took to the floor, we basically just played tag and tested the skate guard's patience with our speed. He blew his whistle at us three times and then threatened to bench us for a while if we didn't slow down. *There's nothing like messing with a skate guard on a power trip, just because he has a whistle,* I sadistically thought.

Thirty minutes into that afternoon's session, the disk jockey announced that it was time to clear the floor for the first couples-only skate. The guys and I found a bench away from the girls and then searched the crowd until we located them. That couples-only skate was men's choice, so when Bobby Vinton came across the speakers, singing *Blue Velvet*, the guys and I made a beeline for our respective girls. I didn't even get all the way over to where Julie sat, so I could actually ask her to skate. Instead, as soon as she spotted me, she sprang up from her seat and met me on the fly. At first, we just skated side by side, holding hands. We had to practically yell at each other to be heard over the music.

"So, how do you like the place so far?" asked Julie.

"It's great! I love this floor. It's so much smoother than the old hardwood floor at the Curling Club."

"Do you skate much in Duluth?"

"Some."

Julie then looked somewhat longingly at many of the other couples who were dance skating. Much like ballroom dancing, the guys skated backward, facing their girl while on the straightaway. The couples would then use the momentum of a turn or curve to spin around gracefully. I watched the other couples, too, and knew I could hold my own against any of them.

"I think it would be so neat to skate like that," yelled Julie.

I coolly asked, "You want to try it?"

"What?!"

"Do you want to try to skate like that?" I enunciated.

"Sure! Do you know how?!"

I immediately executed a quick half turn to face her. Placing my right hand on Julie's waist and clasping her right hand in my left, I explained how I would lead her through turns. I started us off by showing Julie how to weave back and forth without getting our skates tangled. She learned quickly and in a very short time, was comfortable with the movement.

Julie exclaimed, "This is great! What else can we do?"

"Do you want to try a spin?"

"Yeah, show me!"

I guided Julie to the outer most part of the oval rink, so we would be out of the way of the other skaters. There, I explained and demonstrated the mechanics of using each other's momentum to help with the spin. Going very slowly, we tried it a few times. When Julie gained enough confidence, she announced that she wanted to try it at full speed.

On our first attempt, we got our skates tangled and went down in a heap. Laughing, we got up and tried it again. We went down a few times during that first couples-only skate, but I knew it wouldn't take her very long to catch on.

After the customary three slow songs were played, the couples-only skate was over, so everyone was allowed back on the floor. Julie stayed by me and asked me to continue my instruction. At one point during the process, Julie stopped abruptly and then led me to a nearby bench. "Just how good are you?" she asked. "Show me."

I hesitated at first and offered up a weak protest, but Julie just waved me off and repeated, "Show me!"

Reluctantly, I took off around the rink and performed a few spins and turns in rhythm with the music. Each time I passed where Julie sat, her expressions told me she was genuinely impressed. In fact, her approving looks motivated me to do something I really should not have tried. As I approached her again, I prepared to execute a double axel. I don't know why I attempted such a stunt. I had been practicing the feat all summer long. Biff had been coaching me, but I still hadn't landed one successfully. Nevertheless, when I was almost in front of Julie, I launched myself into the air and attempted to spin around twice. While still in the air, I realized that I did not have enough rotation. So, like all my previous attempts, I prepared myself for a very hard landing.

There was absolutely no chance for a recovery, so when I hit the hard surface of the rink, my skates immediately came out from under me. I hit the floor hard and wound up sprawled out directly in front of Julie. Of course, my failed attempt at greatness got plenty of laughs from her. To make matters worse, the skate guard's whistle blew loudly, just behind me.

"Hey!" the guard yelled, as I picked myself up and turned to face him. "No jumping with the rental skates," he scolded. "The axels aren't good enough and will bend or even break!" Then, he gave me a knowing smile. "That would have been pretty cool, though, if you had actually stuck the landing."

I just nodded at him and then turned to Julie, who was finally able to recover from her laughing fit. She smiled, shook her head, and said, "Yeah...what he said." Julie then giggled and added, "That's what you get for showing off." She then took my hand and led me back out onto the rink. Giving me a snide look, she said, "It just figures...Is there anything you're not good at?"

Trying to recover from my embarrassment with wit, I replied, "Yeah, knitting."

"What?!"

"Knitting," I repeated. "I suck at it!"

The next two and a half hours were spent showing off for Julie, as well as teaching her more dance-skate moves. I really enjoyed the couples-only skates. It was the first time I dance skated with a girl I actually cared for. It had almost the same feeling as when Julie and I first danced together in her basement. The thought reminded me how short my time in Mankato had truly been.

Julie and I didn't spend that whole afternoon just skating together. At one point, the whole gang got involved in a game of tag. The game itself may sound a bit childish, especially for teenagers, but tag on skates, on a crowded rink, is quite challenging. The only real obstacle to our fun was the Nazi-like skate guard. When he threatened to throw us all off the rink, we decided to quit and take a rest. At that point, Dave and Anne joined Julie and me on a bench.

"That's it, Jackson, it's official!" yelled Dave. "You are hereby known as Twinkle Toes Landry!"

As the four of us laughed, I couldn't hide the blood rushing to my face.

Kathy Lebowietz also showed up that afternoon. Just then, we four watched, as she and Tony skated past, hand in hand. I gave Julie an inquisitive look.

"I wonder how Kathy knew Tony would be here this afternoon."

"Maybe she just planned on skating this afternoon, like the rest of us."

"Is she coming to Mike's place afterward...like the rest of us?"

"Now that you mention it, I think she is!"

I could not help but laugh at how my friend was methodically being set up. It brought to mind how they all similarly conspired against me at Kresge's lunch counter the previous Friday. I then realized that incident had taken place a mere week prior. So many wonderful things had happened to me in such a short time. When I realized how rapidly it was all coming to an end, another lump formed in my throat. I quickly swallowed, took a deep breath, and masked it all with a smile.

The second part of that day was a complete success. Even Joel looked to be having a great time. It was exactly as I wanted it to be. Everyone was laughing and appeared to be having the time of their life.

When the afternoon skate came to a conclusion, we all quickly changed into our shoes and prepared to go outside. The neighborhood moms would be waiting to transport us all to Mike's house for a late afternoon cookout. As we headed toward the door, Julie took my hand and squeezed it.

"We have got to come back here tomorrow or Saturday, Jackson! I want to skate with you again before you leave. This was great!"

In return, I just gave her a big smile and then led her through the crowd of kids, out into the late afternoon heat.

The fare at Mike's cookout wasn't fancy, just hot dogs, hamburgers, potato salad, chips, and pop. Nevertheless, we teens devoured it like it was a prime-rib dinner. For convenience sake, and/or ease of cleanup afterward, we ate outside in the McDonalds' shaded backyard. The girls sat at a picnic table made of cedar. There, they excitedly recounted much of the day's funnier moments. We guys sat on folding chairs, held flimsy paper plates on our laps, and pretty much let the girls do all the talking. We were too busy stuffing our faces to add anything to their chatter.

When everyone had finished gorging themselves, we all pitched in and helped ensure that paper plates, cups, and napkins were properly disposed of in a large aluminum garbage can. We then sat around and digested the meal, while the girls kept up their verbal dueling. It was as if they were in a contest to see who could tell the funniest story. To the guys, it seemed all their stories' aim was an attempt to embarrass one or more of us. Their banter was at a fever pitch, when I overheard Nancy suggest to Mike that we all go to the basement to escape the heat.

After getting permission from his mom, Mike ushered the group through the house to the basement stairwell. Like a noisy heard of cattle, we all stomped down the steps, single file, to the waiting coolness of the McDonald's den.

Like most homes in that neighborhood, the McDonald house did not have central air conditioning. However, the basement den was refreshingly cool. Its layout was that of one big entertainment area. Large open spaces existed for those who cared to dance. A huge sectional sofa formed a conversation circle in front of a big RCA color TV. Additional seating was sporadically located along the stained, pinewood-paneled walls. The chocolate brown, wall-to-wall, cut-pile carpeting added a rich look and felt wonderfully comfortable under our stocking feet.

Music emanated from a lacquered maple Magnavox stereo console. Mike had no record collection that we could tell, so we relied on KDWB-FM Radio to provide the pop-music selections we wanted.

Since there was no need for Tony to man the record player, Kathy Lebowietz made a show of monopolizing his time. It was unclear whether Tony was uncomfortable with the attention he was getting or not. He seemed to be just going with the flow of it all. However, from time to time, his face did reveal some uncertainty. I simply watched, smiled, and wondered if similar looks appeared on my face, when Julie first ambushed me. *When a girl gets it in her head to go after a guy, God help him,* I thought.

Julie also watched the new couple with great interest. It became abundantly clear to me that she intended to help their situation along when she challenged the two of them to a game of couples' Twister.

The Milton Bradley Company's game, *Twister*, was challenging enough in its original formatted play, but couples' Twister added a degree of difficulty I had not yet experienced. Co-ed teams, competing against each other in a contest that not only tested flexibility, but teamwork, too. To us, it also created a unique recipe for a lot of laughter.

The large plastic mat was spread out flat on the floor. When I thought about the four of us occupying that mat, it suddenly didn't look very large to me at all.

As I looked at the rows of colored dots, which marked where players were to put a designated hand or foot, when told to do so, I felt my face get as red as that particular row of dots. *How in the world does she get me into these lunatic things?!*

Mike volunteered to man the cardboard spinner and called out instructions to us as indicated by the pointer. The four of us scrambled for whatever colored dots Mike called out. The object, of course, was to get our opponents into such a position, as to make them lose their balance and fall. When reaching for a left hand green or a right foot blue, the positions we had to contort ourselves into were sometimes, to say the least, very interesting.

As the game progressed, I wondered who was more embarrassed, Tony or me. Sometimes, when getting into the positions required to stay in the game, I was afraid my hand might accidentally brush against a certain part of either girl's anatomy. I was very self-conscience and had to wonder whose side Julie was actually on. It was almost as if she were trying to get me to fall first. Because of a certain amount of blocking moves she made, I wound up in a makeshift spider-crawl position, with Julie reaching over the top of my torso. At one point, her breasts were literally hanging in my face. The laughter was too much for me to handle. I gave up and let myself fall to the floor. Shortly thereafter, Julie conceded the game to Kathy and Tony. She then came and took her place next to me.

"That was…interesting," I said.

Julie laughed, gave me a kiss, and then said, "Thanks for being a good sport about it."

The next setup for Tony came when Anne suggested a game of Truth or Dare. When she began the game by picking on Mike, visions of Lori Mudd danced in my head. It was enough to make me want to leave before it was actually time.

As the game went on, I sympathized with Tony. He was quite deliberately being railroaded into a relationship with a girl that I wasn't even sure he even liked! He didn't seem too offended by Kathy's persistence, though, so I just played along and let the cards fall where they may.

At one point, Julie took a dare that netted me ten minutes of make-out time with her in a nice, dark closet. However, it was just my luck that when I took a dare, there was no making out involved. Instead, I had to eat a disgusting-looking concoction of leftover potato salad, beans, chocolate syrup, peanut butter, ketchup, mustard, pickle relish, root beer, and toothpaste. The dare called for me to eat at least three spoonsful. To say the mixture tasted differently to me, is like saying rose thorns make excellent safety pins. It was difficult, but I got it down without heaving. Now, it was my turn to torture someone. Julie pointed at Kathy Lebowietz, so no one was too surprised when I called on her and asked, "Truth or dare?"

I think everyone was even less surprised when Kathy responded, "Dare!"

Julie wanted desperately to whisper in my ear, but I gestured for her to hold her water. This was my show. "Okay, Kathy…Take Tony, go to the closet, and be indecent for the next fifteen minutes."

I no more than got the words out of my mouth, when Kathy leapt from her curled-up position on the sectional, grabbed Tony's hand and without hesitation, led Tony toward the dark closet that awaited them.

Just before disappearing through the doorway, Tony hit the brakes and looked back at me. "What do you mean by, 'be indecent?'"

I thought for a second and then replied, "Just think about what your mom would approve of, then do the opposite."

The entire room was suddenly wide-eyed. Even Julie gave me a surprised look. When the two disappeared behind the closet door, she exclaimed, "Jackson! That was bad!"

"Hey, you started this," I rationalized. "I'm just making them do what you were thinking."

Julie scowled at first, but then smiled mischievously, saying, "That's not fair, even if it is true!"

While we waited for Kathy and Tony to immerge from the darkness, interest in the continuation of *Truth or Dare* petered out. Instead, it became apparent to Julie and me that the other couples wished they were holed up in a closet somewhere. No longer needing a brick wall to fall on me to get a clue, plus knowing that the clock was rapidly ticking away crucial minutes, I wasted no time letting Julie know what I wanted. In turn, Julie sweetly let me know that we were on the same wavelength.

Chapter 29

It's strange, but even in the midst of anticipated anguish, friends can unknowingly keep it all at bay. That afternoon, I had a secret. Joel was the only additional party privy to it. Because the gang's laughter and immature game playing had been nonstop throughout the afternoon, I had lost complete track of time. But then, seemly out of nowhere, a feeling of absolute dread came over me. I hurriedly looked to Joel. When I saw him giving me his own look of despair, my heart immediately sank. He then nodded toward a large decorative clock that hung on the wall. When I saw that the time was six-forty-five, I almost gasped.

I had already informed everyone that my folks were coming into town that evening, so I would have to leave early to meet them. In addition, I still had to walk Julie home. So, giving Joel a nod, I stood slowly and announced that I had to get going. As could be expected, there were some moans and groans from the others. I then helped Julie from her seat. While she quickly gathered her things and prepared to leave, I watched Joel. He appeared to be struggling mightily to keep his poker face. We thanked Mike and said casual good-byes to everyone. Julie and I then went upstairs, with the gang calling after us, "See you tomorrow!"

Before leaving, Julie and I stepped into the living room, thanked Mike's parents for the cookout, and then took our leave of the McDonald residence.

As Julie and I walked out the door into the early evening heat, my heart was in my throat. There it stayed for the entire three-block walk to Julie's place. Thanks to Julie's banter, I didn't have to talk. I was very much afraid that my changing voice would fail me and possibly crack at a crucial moment.

Julie was still energized over the day's events. She talked excitedly about how everything seemed to fit into place. In her opinion, it was one of the most amazing days she had since I arrived in town. It was exactly as I planned it, but right then, my heart wasn't in the same place as hers.

When we arrived on Julie's doorstep, she turned those blue eyes of hers on me. "I know you need to go, but couldn't you come in…just for a little while?"

Struggling mightily with my emotions, I managed to keep it all together. I smiled and in a casual tone, replied, "Yeah, as a matter of fact, I can."

While in the foyer, Julie noticed her mom sitting on the living room couch, reading a magazine. Julie asked, "Is there anyone downstairs?"

"No, Baby…It's all yours," replied Marilyn.

Julie then led the way toward the kitchen. Before following, I looked to Marilyn for a moment. She simply looked up from her magazine and nodded knowingly. She then winked and gave me an understanding smile. Her gesture did not help me one bit.

When I got to the bottom of the stairs, Julie was already making herself comfortable on the large sofa. She softly beckoned me to join her. "I know you can't stay long, but…come here…just for a little bit."

I sat at the end of the sofa and prepared myself for what I knew she would do next. Positioning the two throw pillows against the arm of the couch, she angled herself across my lap and leaned against the pillows. With Julie looking deep into my eyes, it was extremely difficult to keep my composure. My heart pounded in my chest and the huge lump in my throat simply would not go down.

As always, Julie smiled amazingly. She teased me with soft, gentle kisses. But then, she stopped and said, "I've wanted to ask you something since yesterday. After everything Momma told you and everything you now remember, do you hate your mother for what she did?"

Her question hadn't actually occurred to me until just then, so I thought about it for a moment before answering. "No, I don't hate her. What would be the point?" I then paused for another instant, remembering my own blind rage, when I beat Darrin Anderson to a frazzle. "When she attacked me, I don't believe it was *me* she was hitting. I know what that's about. She was sick inside and she felt lost. I know how it feels to be that lost. So, no, I can't hate her. It'd be like hating myself…And I don't do that."

"Do you still feel lost?"

"No…Thanks to you and others down here, I don't."

I was now beginning to feel desperation set in. *You need to get out of here… Now!*

Julie kissed me and said, "I wish you didn't have to go so early. It was such a great day. I can hardly wait to see you again tomorrow."

"Did you really have a good time today?"

Julie's voice was so soft and sweet within my ears. "Yeah…I really did."

When I spoke next, it was just above a whisper. "That's good. That's the stuff I want you to remember."

Julie then leaned in and kissed me softly on the lips. As she did, I could no longer hold out and my tears began to flow.

Pushing herself slightly back from me, Julie asked, "Jackson…what is it?"

I gestured for Julie to move, so that I could stand. After doing so, I slowly reached into my pants pocket and pulled out a neatly folded piece of notebook paper. Then, choosing my words carefully, I handed it to her and said, "I need you to do two things for me, Jules. First, I need you to take this. If you call the number on here, I'll talk to you every time, if I'm home. If you use the address and write to me, I'll answer every letter; I promise. You take that now and use it if you want to. If you don't feel you can, then you know what to do with it." I then turned and headed toward the stairs.

The realization of what was about to take place was beginning to show on Julie's face, especially in her eyes. "What's the other thing you need me to do?"

It took every bit of will power I could muster to keep from breaking down, when I said, "I need you to come say goodnight to me."

When Julie came to me, tears began to stream down her cheeks. Bravely, she put her arms around me and with a trembling voice, asked, "I'm not going to see you tomorrow...Am I?"

I softly pleaded, "Jules, just say good night...Please."

Not fully understanding what was happening in that moment, Julie argued, "Jackson, we're supposed to have two more days together."

Before saying more, I took a deep breath and smiled. Then, I explained, "I didn't come down here looking for you, Jules. I came down here to find out some things. Well, I found them out. I know now that I don't belong here anymore. It doesn't matter that I want to stay with you, with all of you...I can't. I can't have what I want... and it hurts. So...I don't want to stay longer. I have to leave. I have to leave now... tonight. That's why my parents came down early." I took a couple of deep breaths to calm myself further and then continued. "You weren't supposed to happen to me, but you did. I don't regret any of it. I never will. I'm supposed to say good-bye to this town, but I know now that I can't ever do that...because you're here. I can't say good-bye to you, Jules. I don't know how. So, please...just say good night to me."

As if it were possible, Julie moved in and kissed me more tenderly than any other kiss I would ever remember. The tears running down our cheeks intermingled. I then felt her reach into my back pocket and pull out the handkerchief she knew would be there. Julie then backed away from my embrace and began to dry her eyes. Raising the handkerchief up, she gave me a weak smile and said, "You're not getting this one back, Dreamboat." She again wiped her eyes, forced a smile, and said with a trembling voice, "Good night, Jackson...I love you."

As Julie turned and headed back toward the sofa, I simply stood there and watched, smiling. She plopped down and looked lovingly at me through tear-filled eyes. I then turned to start up the stairs, but Julie stopped me one last time. With her voice still trembling, Julie called to me, "Jackson...do you love me?"

With my insides totally twisted into a knot, I hung my head. *Oh God*, I thought, *please don't do this.*

A huge part of me was now dying, so I desperately needed to get out of that house. Instead, I made myself stop and gather up what fortitude I had left. Turning toward Julie one last time, I smiled and replied, "Yeah...I do." I then bolted up the stairs, with one additional, but unspoken thought piercing my soul...*But probably only for the rest of my life.*

When I emerged at the top of the stairwell, I closed the basement door behind me. Momentarily leaning on the door to gather myself, I heard my very first love cry out mournfully to me, "JACKSON!"

Unable to hold on much longer, I stood there, shaking, with my heart feeling like it was in a vice, straining to hold back the on-coming dam burst. Marilyn was waiting by the kitchen counter. She rushed to me, threw her arms around me, and held me close.

Fighting desperately to regain control, I swallowed hard and then pleadingly said, "Don't leave her down there alone...Please. She needs to be held."

Marilyn's tears flowed, when she said, "I love you, honey. You take good care of yourself...Okay? Now, go on. Go quickly." She then opened the basement door and went to her daughter.

Before turning toward the foyer, I stood quiet for a minute, collecting myself.

Gary stood by the front door, holding it open for me. "Jackson, would you like a ride home, son?"

I sniffed once and smiled. "No, sir, but thank you. I've got friends waiting down the street."

Gary just nodded approvingly and said, "You really are something. You know that? You take good care of yourself." He then shook my hand and ushered me out the door.

When the Falkner door closed behind me, I stood on their walkway and readied myself for what I knew was coming next. It wasn't going to be nearly as hard as what I had just gone through, but I still needed to get my head straight. When I felt I was ready, I slowly walked to the end of Sunset Boulevard.

I heard them talking behind the pines before I could see them. Joel had kept his word and informed the gang about what was happening. I wasn't surprised at all to find them there waiting for me, just grateful.

As I rounded the corner, Anne was the first one to see me. "Jackson, you're leaving?"

"Yeah, I'm leaving tonight."

"Why didn't you tell us?" asked Gail.

"I just wanted one more great day with you guys before I left. I didn't think it would be all that great if everyone knew I was leaving early. If Julie had known, she wouldn't have had as much fun as she did today."

"Saying good-bye to Julie was a killer, wasn't it?" asked Anne. "How is she?"

"She'll be fine, I hope. Her mom is with her." Then, as an afterthought, I said, "Man, I don't ever wanna go through that again."

They all nodded their heads in agreement. For a tense moment, we stood there. An uncomfortable silence hung in the air, so I decided to break it. "Look guys, I really suck at good-byes, so…"

Anne immediately came forward and threw her arms around me. "We're gonna miss you and we're never gonna forget you. So, don't worry about that… ever." She then stepped back, wiping tears from her eyes. I was greatly surprised by her burst of emotion.

Gail was next to step forward. "I should kick you…ya know?!" She giggled, but then her face scrunched up and she began to cry. "Darn you, Jackson…it's not supposed to be like this."

As I hugged Gail, I forced myself to smile and say, "Take care…you little snot."

Kathy and Nancy were next in line, but there wasn't any real emotional attachment with those two. They did give hugs, though, voiced simple good-byes and told me to take care. I then heard Dave's voice behind me.

"Leave it to you, Twinkle Toes, to get the girls crying." His off-handed comment had the desired effect. We laughed and shook hands before he grabbed me and gave me a bear hug. "Take care, man. I expect to see you from the pitcher's mound again…someday."

"I'll still be able to hit your fast ball," I jabbed.

"Yeah, but not my curve," Dave countered.

"You got one of those?" I shot back.

Once again, we smiled at each other before I moved on. When I next looked at Mike, I no longer saw my shy friend. To me, he seemed somehow larger and more confident. Mike didn't say a word, he just smiled and then hugged me. There was nothing for me to say, except, "See ya." I then gave him a smile and moved on.

When I stood in front of Tony and Joel, I had a sudden rush of emotion because I actually remembered to use the moment. "Listen you two…I never thanked you guys for pulling me out of the creek. You know you saved my life that day…Don't you?"

"Hey man, we were just kids," said Tony.

"Yeah, we were," I said. "Still, I don't know when, or even if, I'm going to see you again, so I had to say something."

Tony hoarsely replied, "Got it." He then gave me a quick hug and patted me rather hard on the back. "Take care, man."

I don't know why saying good-bye to Joel was the hardest. It just ended up that way. Like me, I think he was tired of seeing good things come to an end. When I faced him, I saw tears stream down his cheeks. He appeared to be fighting to keep from breaking down. I guess I was, too. Speaking softly, I hugged him and said, "When you feel you have to leave this place, promise me you'll come north."

Joel clearly couldn't talk just then, so he merely nodded his agreement. I gave him one last good look before doing the same with the others. I then turned and began to walk away.

Gail then called to me. "Jackson, don't you want us to walk you home?"

When I turned, I didn't bother to hide my tears. I just shook my head and said, "No thanks…See ya." Giving them one last smile and a wave, I turned and hurried down the street.

Upon arriving at the Wilsons', the first thing I took notice of was Mom's station wagon parked in the driveway. Because I needed to see her and Dad badly, the car was a welcomed sight. Whatever happened next in that house, I took great comfort knowing that the two people I finally accepted as my parents would be with me. A mere two weeks prior, I could hardly wait to get to Mankato. Now, I was in an awful hurry to put that town behind me. I marveled at the thought of it all.

Because I had a pretty good idea about what awaited me just inside the door, I had to stop and take in a few deep breaths before entering. As I grabbed the door handle, I felt the rush of emotions welling up inside me again. When I entered, I wanted to be completely calm, so again I hesitated. Wrestling with the reality of how Doc Elliot had been so completely right, I had to bolster my resolve to do what I now felt was necessary. When I finally felt prepared, I slowly opened the door.

When I stepped into the kitchen, my nose was met immediately with the smell of fresh brewed coffee and cigarette smoke. The kitchen windows were open to let the smoke out, but it didn't help much. Even with a small, oscillating fan, which was laboring at full speed, the heat in the kitchen was almost unbearable.

Janet was the first to see me. "Here he is," she announced to all.

Mom and Dad had their backs to me, as they sat side by side at the kitchen table. With their backs to the wall, Brad and Janet took up the opposite side. When Mom turned in her chair to see me, I immediately searched her eyes, hoping to get a visual sign that would tell me how much trouble I was now in. Instead, her face lit up with a huge smile. She got up from her chair and came to where I stood. When she wrapped me up in her arms, I was amazed at how absolutely safe I felt.

"Hey, kid!" Dad exclaimed from his chair but stayed put.

Speaking softly in my ear, Mom said, "I've missed you so much."

Straining to hold back the rush of emotions that wanted to burst forth, I said, "Me too." I was never happier to see her than I was right then.

After that wonderful embrace, Mom pulled back from me a little, so she could see into my eyes. "Honey, what's been going on here? Are you okay?"

Whispering, I replied, "Not right now, but I will be, when we get home." I then tried to give her a smile, but I knew she saw through it.

With that worried look of hers, Mom then said, "We just got a call here from a Marilyn Falkner. She asked to speak to me."

"Really? What did she tell you?"

"We'll talk about that at the motel…Okay?"

Suddenly, I heard Janet's voice from across the room. "Jackson, your mom and dad tell us you're leaving us tonight." Her tone was almost sheepish.

Expressionless, I looked Janet in the eyes and simply replied, "Yes... I am."

Just then, I heard footsteps coming down from the attic bedroom. In a few moments, Danny appeared in the archway by the kitchen table. As he leaned against the arch, his look was somber, like he was waiting for my next move. Because I wasn't sure if Danny would keep to his word, my anxiety level went up a few more notches.

Mom asked, "Did you forget to tell Janet and Brad something? You promised me you would explain it to them."

I turned to Mom and said, "No, I didn't forget. I just didn't know how to explain this."

Brad then asked, "Jackson, has something happened to make you want to leave early?"

Again, my heart was beating fast. I was afraid of what would happen next. Still, I knew I would have to answer. So, taking in a huge breath, I let it out and then explained, "The other night, when you told me I shouldn't have come back... well, you were right. I know that now."

"Wait a minute," interrupted Dad. "Did you tell him that?"

"Yes...I'm afraid I did," replied Brad, his brow furrowed. "It's gets worse. At one point, we even told him that when he leaves this time, he shouldn't come back again. But...I thought we fixed all of that, buddy."

Dad erupted, "Are you kidding me?!" His anger was very apparent.

I left Mom and went to where Dad sat. Putting my hand on his shoulder, I said softly, "Dad, don't get mad, please. Brad's right...We fixed all of that." I then eyed Brad and Janet. "It isn't because of what you said that night or even that you were right. It's because of what I was sent down here to learn. I don't belong here anymore. I know that now. Even my friends here know I need to leave. I can't stay here anymore. It hurts too much right now, so I have to go...right now."

"Is that it?" asked Janet. "Is that your only reason for wanting to go so abruptly without telling us?"

Looking down in shame, I replied, "I didn't know how to tell you. You've been so great to me..."

539

"Bullshit!" interrupted Danny, almost yelling. "Don't do it, Jackson! Don't you let them off the hook! You tell them! You tell them now!"

"Danny, don't...please," I pleaded. I suddenly realized my clean getaway was about to become an impossibility. The lie wasn't going to work. Danny was about to ruin the whole thing. I wasn't able to stop the rush of tears welling up in my eyes.

"Oh, God," moaned Brad. "Danny, what did you do?"

"Danny hasn't done anything," I answered, my voice straining for control. "I figured it out myself."

"That's right!" Danny asserted, his anger clearly reaching a fever pitch. "My little brother is smart! He figured it out all by himself. He just tricked me into telling him what he already knew. I ended up accidentally telling him because you wouldn't."

"Wait a minute...Hold up," said Dad. "Jackson...What did you figure out, son?"

My brain was on fire. I was totally over my head and drowning in a situation I had no idea how to handle. I could not make myself answer Dad. So, I was more than a little surprised when I heard Janet answer for me. Her voice was strained, and she bent herself forward, as if she were truly agonized. "Brad is Jackson's real father."

Clearly shocked by what he had just heard, Dad exclaimed, "What?!"

"We wanted to tell you," continued Janet. "We wanted to tell you so many times, honey, but we couldn't. You've already been through so much, so we decided it would be best to just keep it from you." Janet then looked up and I saw that her eyes were filled with tears.

Dad's faculties were clearly challenged by what he was hearing. His voice boomed with anger, "I don't believe this! You told us you were willing to help him! Now it turns out you've been the problem all along?! Do you have any idea what you've done?!"

"Brice, please, calm down," urged Mom.

"Jackson...I'm sorry. I'm so, very sorry," sobbed Brad. "We didn't think we were ever going to see you again, which would have been best. But then, your mom

540

and dad called. I couldn't stand knowing you weren't doing well up north. I wanted to help in any way I could. I just wanted to see my son one-last time."

"You selfish bastard!" yelled Dad. "Didn't you think about how dangerous it was for him? Why didn't you tell us?! How's he supposed to deal with all of this crap now?!"

Until then, I had never witnessed the fullness of Dad's anger. Afraid of what might happen next, I turned to Mom for help. I hadn't seen or heard Kurt come up from the basement, but there he stood, close to Mom. His look told me he had no idea what to do, either.

"Brice, stop!" ordered Mom. "You're scaring our son!"

Tugging at Dad's arm, I pleaded, "Please, let's just go, okay?! Let's just go!"

As my carefully-made plan unraveled at the seams, I could no longer hold back my tears. Pandora's box was now open; there was no way to put back the chaos that had escaped. It wasn't what I wanted at all. I just wanted to gather up my belongings, load them into the car, and get out of town. I looked at Danny and could tell he was about to lose all control, as well.

With his entire body shaking, Danny sobbed and spoke. "Why did you do this? Why did you send my brother away in the first place?"

"I'd like to know the answer to that myself," asserted Dad. Despite my urging, he refused to let up.

With their heads in their hands, Brad and Janet wept. Neither offered an explanation. No one spoke for a minute or two. Just then, a thought came to me. Much like their refusal to tell me the truth, neither Brad nor Janet was going to answer Danny. Oddly enough, I somehow felt sorry for the two, so I decided to answer for them.

"It's because she threatened you…Didn't she? My mom threatened to tell everyone what you did. She showed up that one day, and it wasn't to see me at all. Was it? She heard you wanted to adopt me. So, she threatened to tell everyone that you were the one who got her pregnant. You were afraid of what the town would think of you."

Glaring down at his parents, Danny spoke in strained voice, "You coward! You gave my brother away because of what this town might think?!"

"No!" snapped Brad. "That's not it at all! I couldn't care less what the people in this town think of me! It was for Jackson! It's because of how they would have treated him if he had stayed here. Jackson, please, try to understand. This town would never have given you the chance you have now. They would have looked at and treated you like you were less of a human being. You wouldn't have any of the opportunities you have now."

Clearly out of control, Danny stormed, "What about me and Kurt? You didn't give us away. You didn't even try to fight for him. You just did what was easiest...Didn't you?!"

Brad pleaded, "Danny...Please!"

"I gotta get outta here!" cried Danny. "I gotta get outta here right now!" He then shook his head and ran for the front door.

In a weak attempt to stop Danny's departure, I cried, "Danny, no! Don't leave!"

"I'm sorry, little brother, but I gotta go!" Danny then bolted out the front door. I watched him for a moment, as he ran down Westwood Drive. Dad's voice then caught my attention, so I turned back toward the kitchen.

"I've heard enough," Dad announced. "Catherine, we're leaving...NOW! Jackson, make sure you have all your stuff."

Suddenly, we all heard the horrific sound of car tires screaming against asphalt, the unmistakable thud of something or someone being struck, followed by eardrum-piercing screams. In that same instant, a single thought registered in my head. *Danny!*

Almost by reflex, I wheeled about and launched myself out the front door. As I raced toward the intersection of Westwood Drive and Moreland Avenue, my thoughts were wild. *No! God no! Please, don't let it be!*

It took me mere seconds to reach the accident scene. As soon as I arrived, my blood ran cold. Danny lay motionless in the middle of Moreland Avenue. His left leg was twisted in a sickening fashion and blood oozed from lacerations to his face. The teenage driver who struck him was frantically knocking on the Milners' door, calling out for help.

In my Boy Scout troop, I had received some rudimentary medical training. I had even been awarded my first aid merit badge. However, right then, my mind was drawing a blank, so I couldn't make myself react. Feeling absolutely helpless, I knelt next to Danny. Luckily, Brad was right on my heels. He arrived seconds after me and immediately began rendering aid to his son. He listened for Danny's breathing and checked his pulse. I wanted to wipe some of the blood from Danny's face, so I mindlessly reached for my back pocket. It was then I remembered how ownership of my handkerchief had very recently been turned over to Julie.

Frozen in place, I was of no use. Suddenly, powerful hands grabbed me from behind and lifted me to my feet. Strong arms wrapped around me and moved me away from where Danny lay. It was Kurt, holding me in his signature, reverse bear hug. However, this time he wasn't squeezing the life out of me. He just held me from behind and kept me from getting in the way.

I was barely cognizant of his weeping and whispering in my ear repeatedly, "He's gonna be alright. You'll see…He's gonna be alright."

Looking around at the growing number of concerned neighbors, who gathered in the street, I wondered if anyone had called for an ambulance. Almost as if my thought had spurred someone into action, Tony Milner Sr. came rushing from his house, announcing to the throng that an ambulance was on its way.

Brad continued to kneel over Danny, monitoring him. "His pulse is weak, and his breathing is labored," he said forcefully. "Danny! Can you hear me? Stay with me," Brad instructed, but Danny was unresponsive.

Then, almost as if Brad had willed it, Danny stirred out of his unconscious state. He looked right up at me, then at his twisted leg. His eyes then rolled back in their sockets and once again closed, his head rolling to the side.

Thinking that my brother had just expired, I was suddenly gripped by sheer terror. "DANNY!" I screamed, while trying to escape Kurt's hold. But it was no use; Kurt held me firmly in place.

Just when I thought I was going to lose control, Mom appeared before me. "Honey, calm down," she urged.

"Jackson! He's just fainted!" yelled Brad.

I then felt Kurt's arms relax, as he transferred possession of me to my mother's arms. *This can't be happening,* I thought. *I can't lose Danny! I just can't!"*

My mind raced in countless directions. I thought I was absolutely losing my mind. Again, I called out to my brother. "DANNY!"

Mom then took my face in her hands and looked me in the eyes. "Please, honey, you have to calm down." She continued to talk softly to me, face-to-face, words so soft, but none that I would ever remember. She took my attention away from my broken brother, who lay sprawled out in the middle of the street.

Finally, off somewhere in the distance, I heard an approaching siren. As if a switch had been flipped, I came back to my senses. I was once again fully aware of my surroundings, but just couldn't keep from looking into Mom's concerned eyes. It was almost like a surge of electricity that coursed its way through me. Then and there, her eyes told me everything I would ever want to know. They answered every question I ever had about who I truly belonged to. I finally understood, from that moment on, that she was the woman who would forever be my mom. I belonged to her and she was mine. Slowly, I allowed myself to focus and regain control.

"Better now?" Mom asked.

In response, I simply nodded my head.

When the ambulance finally arrived, I stood frozen next to Mom. There, I watched in despair and with the utmost interest, as the paramedics prepared Danny for transport. They worked quickly, but it wasn't fast enough to suit me. I wanted them to magically heal my brother right there but knew that wasn't going to happen. During the entire wait, Mom continually reassured me by keeping her arm around my waist and occasionally rubbing her hand up and down my back. When Danny was finally loaded safely in the rear of the ambulance, Brad announced that he would ride with him to the hospital.

Mom maintained a watchful presence at my side until the ambulance sped off, with its siren wailing. She then grabbed me by the hand and led me back to the house, leaving the curious throng of neighbors to speculate how the accident happened. As we walked away, I could hear them all gabbing like a gaggle of geese.

When we stepped back into the hot, smoke-filled house, Mom made immediate preparations for leaving. Like a freight train, traveling in a singular direction, Mom hurriedly helped me finish packing. She appeared completely purpose driven and could not be derailed. Because most of my belongings were already packed – it was something I had incorporated into my plan – the task didn't take long at all. When we were ready, Dad carried, with ease, one of my large suitcases down from the bedroom. I had to wrestle tremendously with the other over-stuffed monstrosity.

At the bottom of the steps, I took note of Janet's condition. She sat silently at the kitchen table, nervously smoking a cigarette, looking as if she had no idea what had just happened or what to do next. Mom deduced that she was in some form of mental shock. So, she quite literally ordered Kurt to drive Janet to the hospital and to stay with her. Mom also informed him that we would lock up the house and follow soon after.

Historically speaking, I remembered how Kurt loathed taking orders from anyone. Nevertheless, right then, Kurt merely nodded his understanding, then went to Janet, took her arm, and helped her from the chair.

As Kurt led Janet to the door, she looked back over her shoulder at me. The pain in her eyes was unmistakable. I wanted to say something, but at that moment, I couldn't make my mouth work. I didn't know what to do. I suppose that, like Janet, I was in shock, too. I could scarcely believe how my world seemed to be falling apart.

When Kurt and Janet disappeared out the door, Mom turned to me, grabbed my shoulders, and held me at arm's length. "You know the way to the hospital… Right?"

I silently nodded in the affirmative.

"Jackson, listen to me. I know you're extremely upset, but right now, I need you to stay strong for me."

Having to be strong or having to do that which no one else would ever have to do, never failed to bring about sarcasm within me. *Me?! Be strong?!* I thought. *What else is new?!*

Chapter 30

The room at the motor inn, which Mom and Dad had already checked into, was located on the second floor. We entered it off an exterior concrete walkway, which also served as a make-shift balcony, or so I thought at the time. When we arrived at our door, I observed a rather tall, potbellied man, just a few doors down. He leaned against the thick, steel-piped railing, smoked a cigarette, and appeared a little too interested in our arrival. His dark hair was a tangled mess, and he wore nothing but a sweat-stained T-shirt to cover his torso. I took note of how he seemed to have as much dark, matted hair on his arms, shoulders, and back, as he did atop his head. To me, he was filthy and in dire need of bathing. The worst part of our encounter happened while I waited for Mom to unlock the door. The cooty-ridden Sasquatch smiled and showed me all five of his tobacco-rotted teeth. In a voice that sounded like he had gargled with gravel, he greeted, "Hello there!"

Mom finally got the door opened and led Dad into the room. Thoroughly repulsed, I politely smiled back at our temporary neighbor and then dragged my behemoth-sized suitcase through the doorway.

Upon entering, I looked around the room and immediately judged it harshly. It was garish, stuffy, and smelled like a twenty-year-old, dirty ashtray. Mom and Dad had forewarned me, though, so the less-than-pleasant accommodations were no big surprise. It was only going to be for the one night, so I wasn't too put off by it. Besides, I doubted that I would actually get any sleep. None of my normal concerns about motel rooms applied just then. To me, none of it mattered.

Mom and Dad had checked into the inn prior to coming to the Wilson place, so they had already claimed their pick of the two queen-sized beds. When it came to staying at motor inns with my parents, I was always left with the bed closest to the door or window.

Instead of leaving my suitcase on the floor for Dad to trip on, I hefted it onto the bed they had left for me. I then plopped down next to it and stared at the ceiling. My mind immediately went back to the hospital we had just left.

The emergency room at Immanuel Lutheran Hospital was not overly busy that evening. However, it still seemed to take forever to get word on Danny's condition. We all sat in the waiting room in silence. Brad and Janet smoked nervously together in one corner, with Kurt nearby. Mom and Dad stayed close to me on the other side of the room. I noticed and appreciated that they refrained from smoking themselves. Besides the hospital staff, there were few other people around.

An uneasy silence and separation existed between us and the Wilsons. It was terribly unbearable, and I wanted to leave immediately. In fact, right then, I wanted to be anywhere other than Mankato. I thought about urging Mom and Dad to take me away from there, but I already knew the answer to that request. So, I remained silent and just stared at the three souls sitting directly across from me. When I couldn't stand the atmosphere any longer, I used the cigarette smoke as an excuse and told Mom I needed to go get some air.

Leaving the air-conditioned lobby and stepping out into the hot, evening air was not more comfortable, but it felt so much better than the claustrophobia that had been gripping me in that waiting room. I walked to Marsh Street, leaned against a no-parking sign, and looked down the thoroughfare through vacant eyes. *Nothing has turned out as I planned,* I thought. Danny was lying in the hospital. I knew he was hurt bad and at that instant, I just knew it was entirely my fault. *I should've never come back. I should have known I wasn't supposed to come back. What good does knowing the truth do? I still don't get what I want. My brothers will be here. My friends will be here. According to Julie, she'll always be here, too, but I'll always be someplace else.*

Suddenly, I felt a hand come to rest on my shoulder. Startled out of my trance, I whirled around and found Kurt standing there. Being so deep in thought,

I hadn't heard his approach from behind. He just stood there looking at me through emotionless eyes. God, how I wanted to keep from breaking down in front of my older brother, but it was no use. It was all too much for me right then.

"I'm sorry," I sobbed. "It's my fault! I know it is! I'm sorry!"

Kurt immediately grabbed me and hugged me close. He then pulled back and held my face in his hands. He also held me with his intense, brown eyes. In a quiet, but forceful tone, Kurt said, "Jackson, you listen to me. You didn't do this. It's not your fault. You hear me? None of this is your fault. This was done by them!" For effect, he pointed an accusing finger back toward the hospital. "And they didn't just do it to you...little brother."

It was the first time Kurt ever called me that. Startled at what had just come out of his mouth, I stopped crying immediately.

"That's right...You're my little brother, just like Danny is. Nothing is going to change that, not even you leaving us again." He then paused momentarily, as if he were thinking about what to say next. Seeing that I had regained control of myself, Kurt released his grip on my face and looked down at the ground before continuing. "The doctor came in, just after you left. Danny's going to be okay, just like I said he would. His leg is broke pretty bad, but they can fix that. He also has a mild concussion. But if I know that thick head of his, he'll be fine." Kurt paused again to let out a quick chuckle. "I know you're probably thinking that because you have to leave again, we don't get to be brothers. I was thinking the exact, same thing for a while. The grownups really screwed up this time. So...you, Danny, and me will have to figure out how this is going to work."

I could hardly believe the words coming out of Kurt's mouth. It had always been Danny who made the biggest show of accepting me as a brother. Just then, I didn't quite know what to think of Kurt's sincerity.

"We have to stay in contact, Jackson," continued Kurt. "It's too important. Just because things seem really messed up now, doesn't mean they'll always be that way."

Thinking clearly again, I quickly suggested, "When you go to the Twin Cities to look for that girl, maybe you could also come a little farther north."

"Yeah...I can do that," he replied. "There will always be phone calls and letters." As he talked on, I nodded my agreement. "Jackson, don't let all this take you down. Go home with your mom and dad…Be happy. They're good people. You gotta good thing going there, so don't waste it by getting hung up on all this crap down here." He then motioned with his head for us to head back toward the hospital. As we began to walk, Kurt gave me one last thing to think about. "I know it's probably going to take you some time, but someday you're going to have to forgive Dad and Mom for not keeping you. When I first found out about you, I talked to Dad about it, long and hard. I happen to believe he's right about one thing. Mankato is a small town. There are people here, stupid people, who would never give you a fair shake, just because of your mom. You're not going to have to deal with any of that now." Kurt stopped us one last time and said, "I know it sounds weird, but Mom and Dad love you very much. And that's all you really need to remember."

I didn't realize it at the time, but that brief moment with Kurt outside the hospital would become one of my most cherished memories of him. His resolve about us being brothers was absolute.

When my mind came back to the present, inside the room at the motor inn, I became aware that Mom was watching me closely. I was heartsick over the day's events. The sound of Julie calling out to me resounded in my ears. The vision of Danny's broken body lying in the street came to my mind's eye, too. The thought of having to live so far away from my two brothers made me absolutely ill inside. There was much more, but I didn't want Mom to see any of it. So, I got up, opened my suitcase, took out necessary articles I needed to prepare for bed, and adjourned to the bathroom. When I was ready, I came out and moved the suitcase off the bed and put it as far out of Dad's way as possible. Dad had turned the TV on, so he could listen to the late edition of the evening news. Sitting up in bed, I made a show of appearing to be interested.

Mom wasn't fooled one bit. She left Dad's side, grabbed a couple of pillows from their bed, then walked over to my bedside. Motioning me to scoot over, she then positioned the pillows against the old, wooden headboard. As we sat crossed-legged next to each other, Mom put an arm around me and pulled me in close. Prior to that evening, there had been no such closeness between the two of us. Right at that moment, it was exactly what I needed. Then, Mom spoke. When she did, her voice was very soft in my ear. "I told you earlier that I got a call from Julie's mom… Remember?"

"Yeah, I remember."

"She told me that I had a very special young man for a son, like I really needed her to tell me that." Mom smiled and squeezed me a little harder before continuing. "She also said I shouldn't leave him alone tonight because he's going to need his mother. She said, 'He needs to be held tonight.' Was she right?"

Mom's words were like a glorified message, telling me it was okay to let go. So, for what seemed like the umpteenth time that day, the dam burst. I buried my face in Mom's chest and cried over my shattered heart. "It hurts, Mom!" I sobbed. "It hurts so bad!"

"I know it does, honey," said Mom. "I won't lie to you. It's going to hurt for a while, too. But it won't always. It'll get better…someday."

While I let all my pain out, Mom waited patiently. She gently rocked me back and forth, slowly stroking my hair with her fingers. I then felt Dad join us, as he sat beside me and gently rubbed my back. When I finally had no more tears left, I caught my breath and strained to turn off the waterworks. We three sat there quietly for long minutes. I was the first to break the silence. "I'm never doing that again," I muttered in a hoarse voice.

"What aren't you doing again, honey?" asked Mom.

"Falling for a girl that way."

Mom gave out a soft chuckle and then said, "Oh, honey, that's just not true. You'll fall for a girl again. You just wait."

"No way."

"I'm afraid it's just what happens to handsome, young men like you. Some very nice girl is going to recognize that huge heart of yours and decide she wants it. And you'll give it."

"Not if it ends up feeling like this, Mom."

"It's not always going to feel like this. I'm not going to tell you it gets easier, either, because it may not. Then again, someday, it might be the easiest thing you do. Nobody knows for sure, but there is something I do know. You've had a very bad day. I know what your heart wanted, but things didn't turn out the way you thought they would down here. Listen to me please; you will always have my love and your dad's. You're *our* son now and we aren't ever giving you back or giving you away. I couldn't bear to lose you." She then held me tighter until her arms gave out.

As well, Dad put his two cents in. "I may be a little stiff with you from time to time, Jackson, but don't ever doubt how much I love you. I hope you understand how much we want you. We want you to know and *believe* that your future is with us because, quite simply…it is. I hope, more than anything, that you want that future because we'll *always* want you. And, until the day we die, we'll always be there for you."

The only thing I could think to say at first was, "I do want it, Dad. I learned that while I was here." A momentary silence took place before I remembered to add something I would never hold back from them again. "I love you both… very much."

Before calling it a night, Mom gave me one last thing to consider. "You're going to have to find it within you to forgive the Wilsons. It may take you some time, but you're going to have to find a way." To that, I just nodded my head in agreement.

I truly don't remember sleeping at all that night. I do remember lying there in bed, replaying almost two weeks' worth of memories, like a movie projector inside my head. Of course, Julie dominated my thoughts. I just knew that I would be forever haunted by a pair of piercing blue eyes, raven curls, amazing smile, infectious laugh, and a voice with such sweet energy. I was convinced she could never be equaled, duplicated, or replaced. As far as I was concerned, my heart was destroyed for life. Such were the dramatic thoughts of a thirteen-year-old rookie.

I rolled over on my side and faced the other bed. I watched Mom, as she quietly slept and couldn't help but smile at the noisy lump of covers lying next to her. Dad snored louder than any train that ran through the old neighborhood. I wondered how Mom actually slept at all when he was letting loose like an unmuffled John Deere tracker. I rolled back the other way and gave much thought to Kurt and Mom's words about forgiving Brad and Janet. Truth be told, I knew I still loved them too much not to forgive them. I just didn't want to give in to it, yet.

I also wondered about the future Dad spoke of. *Will it be a good one? Was Mom right? Will I really give my heart to another girl? Will Kurt, Danny and I find a way to stay brothers, or will I simply drift out of their lives again?* At the time, I didn't understand that my age was my biggest ally. I was unable to grasp the idea of having years and years ahead of me to discover the answers to all of my questions. Deep into the night, I contemplated the possibilities that lay ahead of me, but also wished the sun would hurry and make its appearance.

That last morning in Mankato, Friday, 18 August 1972, I hurried and got the car loaded, just as quickly as I could. I wanted to be on our way as fast as possible. The early morning was a decent seventy degrees, but the morning weatherman forecasted the temperature would be a blistering ninety-five by early afternoon. I looked forward to feeling the cool air coming off Lake Superior again.

As I maneuvered my two suitcases around inside the back of the station wagon, so everything else would fit, too, I marveled at how I was actually looking forward to returning to my life in Duluth. Football season would begin soon, and I was anxious for practices to start up. I felt it would go a long way to helping me get over everything that was going on inside of me. Two weeks prior, I had been so excited about arriving in Mankato, but things had not turned out at all the way I wished. Now, I just wanted to leave and never come back. Doc Elliot had been right all along. There truly was nothing for me in that small town. Since I had finally arrived at that same conclusion, there was no reason to linger any longer than necessary.

When Mom finished getting us checked out of the room, we got in the car and prepared to leave. I was already saying a final good-bye to Mankato in my head but felt my heart sink when Mom suggested we round up some breakfast first. There was a roadside café just a few blocks from the inn, so we settled for eating there. I was too keyed up at the time and thought I wouldn't be able to eat, but when we stepped into the diner, I immediately changed my mind. The smell of bacon, sausage, and other fried food hit my nostrils and my stomach growled from hunger.

During breakfast, Mom suggested we go to the hospital and see Danny before leaving town.

I was adamant. "I don't want to, Mom. Let's just go, okay?"

"Jackson, you have to go see him and say good-bye," insisted Mom.

"Mom, no…Please?!"

"Honey, if you don't do this now, everything here is just going to follow us back home. Remember what Doctor Elliot said, 'Say your good-byes.' Believe me, honey, if you don't, it will just turn into regret later."

Dad came to my rescue and I felt a glimmer of hope. "Catherine, maybe we shouldn't push things here. Maybe it would be best if we just leave. I mean, geez, don't you think he's been through enough?"

Mom was now unwavering in her assertion. "No, Brice, he has to do this. They may not have done right by him, but I want our son to be strong. And I want him always to do the right thing. It has to start here and now. Jackson, make yourself do the right thing here. You'll be so much better off if you do. Besides, I'm the only licensed driver here and I know which way the car is headed when we leave this diner." To drive her point, Mom gave me the slyest smile I had ever seen from her.

Chuckling, Dad turned toward me and asked, "Now, how are you going to argue with logic like that?!"

The thought of seeing Danny lying in that hospital bed had been unbearable, but after listening to Mom's words and letting them sink in, something loosened inside of me. I suddenly knew she was right. I had to see Danny. I had to say good-bye to him and if possible, say good-bye to Kurt. I then smiled at Mom and gave her the nod.

"Good!" exclaimed Mom. "You help your dad go pay the check, while I go call Janet."

Upon arriving at the hospital ward, a kindly nurse informed us that Danny was still – as she put it – "out of it." He had spent a good deal of the night in surgery and was still somewhat under the influence of the anesthesia. In addition, because of his concussion, Danny wasn't allowed to sleep too much. He had to be periodically awakened and checked on. The nurse advised that we shouldn't expect too much from him.

When we walked into Danny's room, Kurt, Janelle, and Carrie were already present. Brad and Janet were nowhere in sight. I exhaled and relaxed, but only a little.

Mom then tapped me on the shoulder and said, "Dad and I will wait in the hallway. Take your time, honey. We're in no hurry here." She then led Dad out of the room.

As soon as they were gone, Janelle and Carrie came to get their hugs.

Janelle asked, "You're leaving us today?"

I simply nodded my answer, gently brushed past her, and went to the left side of Danny's bed. He was asleep, so I put my hand on his chest. I didn't really care if he slept just then. I would've been happy to whisper my good-bye to him and then leave before he woke up. However, at the touch of my hand, Danny's eyes fluttered open. When he was able to focus and recognize me standing there, he gave me one of his charming smiles. "Hey, little brother," he greeted in a hoarse voice.

"Hey, Danny."

I checked out the IV needle, which was inserted into his left hand. His face was bandaged, but not well enough to completely hide the road rash on his right cheek. I then looked down at his casted leg, which was in traction. After assessing his injuries, I looked back into his eyes and said, "You look like crap."

Danny laughed a little, then grimaced. "Oh, God, don't make me laugh. It hurts too much."

I kept trying to think of something to say, but all I could manage was, "I came to see you, Danny, then we're leaving for home."

Without saying a word, he nodded his understanding and then closed his eyes again. I wondered if there was anything else I should say. At first, I couldn't think of a thing. I just stood there, with my hand resting on his chest. Then, I remembered why Mom insisted on bringing me to the hospital. Danny and I had never used warm, fuzzy words around each other before, it was the same with Kurt. But just then, I knew I couldn't leave without telling my brother something imperative. So, even though his eyes were closed, plus I was almost positive he had drifted off to sleep again, I leaned in close and whispered, "I love you, Danny."

He didn't open his eyes. Instead, a smile appeared on Danny's lips. He then reached up with his uncluttered right hand, messed up my hair, then pulled my head down to his chest, pinning it there in a makeshift hug. When he finally let me up again, I saw his face was all scrunched up and tears were drawing a slow trail down the sides of both temples, but he didn't utter a word. With my heart in my throat, I turned toward Kurt and the girls. I was becoming desperate to leave before I started to cry, too.

"I gotta go," I announced softly.

Janelle was the first to close the distance between us. She hugged me close, kissed my cheek, and with a tear-filled smile said, "See ya, cutie. Take care. Don't forget to write me."

Carrie stepped in next. Holding me close, she said, "Good-bye, Jackson. Come back soon and see us…Okay? I'll miss you."

When Carrie released me, I looked to Kurt. With his back to me, he faced the only window in the room. His arms were crossed, and he was slightly hunched over. From behind, he appeared to be looking at the floor.

"Kurt, you gonna say good-bye this time?" I asked.

Kurt didn't speak a word, nor did he move. He just stood there with his back to me.

God, this is so hard, I thought. *Damn it, he's gonna do it to me again!* Remembering how he wouldn't say good-bye in 1969, my emotions began to get the better of me and I became angry.

"You chicken shit!" I cried, then started toward the door.

In a flash, Kurt wheeled around and grabbed me. He pulled me in close and held me in a vice-like embrace. He never said a word, just held me and cried. After what seemed like a very long moment, he finally released me. He then turned toward the window again. Janelle went to him and put her arms around him.

I watched the two of them for an instant before turning to find Janet leaning in the doorway. Like the rest of us, her tears were apparent. I slowly walked to where she stood, slipped my arms around her waist, laid my head on her shoulder and while she stroked my hair, I broke down one-last time.

Struggling to find my voice, I finally managed, "I still love you. I still love you both. You have to tell Dad for me. He has to know I still love him. But right now…I just don't know why."

Janet enfolded me in her arms and cried, also. She too struggled, but managed to whisper, "We'll always love you, kiddo." Then, taking my face in her hands, she looked into my eyes and whispered, "Now, go be happy…Okay?" She gently kissed my forehead, delivered her last hug and then gently shoved me out the door.

As I shuffled down the hallway to my waiting parents, I felt Janet's eyes on me the entire way, but I didn't look back. I simply went to Mom, who put her arm around my shoulders. Dad took my other arm and allowed me to guide him down the crowded corridor. That day, we three walked out of that hospital and for the very-first time, I looked forward to beginning my life all over again.

EPILOGUE

When I arrived back in Duluth that summer in 1972, a body might assume that I was a pretty screwed up teenager. But I was determined to not let that be the case. Because of my misadventures in Mankato, I discovered a strength within me that was not present beforehand. Of course, Mom and Dad were afraid that emotional setbacks would rear their ugly head. In all honesty, there were very few, if any at all. After hearing the details of the visit, even Doc Elliot was somewhat amazed. He had his concerns about how I would deal with the newly-discovered truth. During our last session together, I was able to convince him that not only was I okay, but I had found what he sent me to find – my smile. Looking back on it, I think I just made a conscious decision that I wasn't going to let any of my Mankato past destroy me. Besides, Kurt had given me all the assurances I would ever need. I was positive things were going to work out just fine. I just needed to allow myself time to adjust to the changes – something I was becoming quite efficient at doing.

For the remainder of that summer, I took it somewhat easy on myself, so did Mom and Dad. Expectations of me were held down some and I was allowed that necessary time to get over whatever they felt might be tormenting my mind and heart. Prior to school beginning, I read books, went fishing, exercised, and prepared myself for the coming football season. I relaxed and took it one day at a time. Of course, I thought of Julie every day. Mostly, I thought of her when I was alone, which was practically always. When I was fishing or taking one of my many, long hikes through the hillsides of Duluth, I would sometimes imagine Julie right there with me. It was like preparing for a possible future, when she would travel north, just like she told me. There, on the shores of Lake Superior, I would show her my world.

Just before the beginning of the new school year, something inside me gave way. One day, Mom answered the doorbell to find Jerry Campbell and a few of the neighborhood guys crowding the steps. They were getting up a game of baseball and came to see if I would play. Mom told them I might not be up for it. Imagine her surprise, when I scooted past her, while she was still in the doorway. With my bat and glove in hand, and the guys chattering excitedly, I hurried down the walk. But then, I thought to stop, turn, give Mom a smile, and say, "Bye…See you at dinner." I watched, as her mouth, which had been gaping in astonishment, changed to an approving smile. Yeah, I may have been feeling a little sorry for myself, but it was nothing that a good game of baseball couldn't cure.

Decades have passed since that summer and, just like everyone else on the planet, my life has moved steadily forward. I am older now, but don't feel old. Still, when it is quiet, I do take some time to look back on the people and events that helped mold me into the person I am today. Grandpa Mack was ever so wise, especially in his teachings about the heart being the storage place for the people we will love forever.

My relationship with Mom flourished after that trip. She loosened up her stiff-as-a-board ways and became a lot less ridged. Whenever Mom wanted hugs and kisses, they were given freely by me. It rapidly became an everyday thing with her. I was never shy about telling her I loved her, either. She remained attentive, but didn't hover over me like an old, mother hen. Of course, she continued to worry about me, but when it was time for me to experience new things, she displayed great courage and allowed those many learning events to take place. When some girl had me completely baffled, which, like most young men, was a cycle that seemed to have no end, she became that person I could talk to. When my heart was broken, Mom was always the first to recognize it and seemed to know exactly how to console me.

Dad and I constantly redefined our relationship. He did his level best to support me in all my endeavors. However, we had to come to an understanding. Ours was never going to be a traditional, father-son relationship. Instead, we got creative and found things both of us could enjoy together. Reading was at the top of that list. He loved sitting in his favorite easy chair while I read to him. Over the years, Dad and I went through piles of novels, business periodicals, and political tell-all books. It surprised me how his favorite reading material seemed to be Hollywood autobiographies. To tell the truth, I sort of liked them myself, but only because I saw how he truly enjoyed them. Later, I learned that whatever material I read, was nowhere near as important as the fact that we were spending quality time together.

Whenever I had trouble with the girls I dated, my parents never made light or poked fun at me about it. I witnessed some of my friend's parents make that mistake with them. In doing so, they inadvertently caused a lack of trust and later, lack of communication between themselves and their children. I once asked Mom and Dad how they kept from making that mistake with me. Dad put it quite eloquently. "Jackson, your mom and I learned, that summer of 1972, your heart is nothing to trifle with. It's been our responsibility to protect and nurture it. I hope we've done a good job." They both always preached, "Enjoy a girl's company, Jackson, but for God's sake, be careful you don't give that huge heart of yours away too freely."

As within all families, there were minor hiccups along the way, but only here and there. Nevertheless, Mom, Dad, and I never doubted our love for or commitment to one another. We remained close always. Shortly after retiring, Dad's heart gave out. Mom passed two years later. I think she just missed him and decided it was time for me to go it alone again. They have been gone many years now and, of course, I still miss them terribly. I visit and personally care for their graves whenever I am in town. Continually hearing their words of love and wisdom in my head, they have become the two angels who walk with me daily.

Over time, I have learned that as we go through the years, friends and loved ones move in and out of our lives almost uncontrollably. It pains me how I've lost so many friends to the years. It was not a conscious decision made by any of us. Nevertheless, because life moves at such a frantic pace, we simply let each other fall by the wayside. It is sometimes due to the shortage of hours in a day, coupled with a difference in geography. Careers and child rearing is another example of how we lose contact with those who mean the world to us. After loss of contact, the decay of time causes the most damage. Oftentimes, we just don't see a roadway back to one another. We make bad assumptions and think the other has simply forgotten about us. We fail to reach out and reconnect. For many of the above, lame rationalizations, my friends from the old Mankato neighborhood are lost to me now. We grew up apart and our lives simply went in different directions. Nevertheless, I find that I was never able to remove any of them from my heart. Now, because my life is no longer as hurried or hectic, I wish for that roadway back. But the pragmatist and realist in me say there isn't one. So, for now, as I have always done, I'll leave them all in God's hands. I believe Grandpa Mack would approve.

Julie Falkner became somewhat of a constant in my life. That is, because she was my first love, she holds a special place within my heart. It is a place that all healthy, heterosexual men know about. She truly was the one who flipped the switch. How was I ever supposed to forget the wonderful way she awoke this scared, little boy's heart? And, after that two-week stint of being hooked up with the prettiest girl I would ever know in Mankato, well, you get the picture.

Just after school began in the fall of 1972, Julie went to her hiding place and dug up the old, rusted, cookie tin. Inside, she found the envelope I left for her. She immediately climbed up on the fallen cedar tree, sat down, and read the note I had enclosed:

> Hey Jules,
>
> If you're reading this, then I know you've come to put me back into the box. Don't ever worry about it. I'm not sure, but I kind of think it's what you're supposed to do. I'll never forget you and the great times we had while I was there. I'm even pretty sure that I will love you forever.
>
> Yours always,
> Jackson

It definitely wasn't Shakespeare, but I thought it was pretty good, especially for a broken-hearted thirteen-year-old. How do I know Julie retrieved her keepsake box in that manner? In the first week of October that year, I came home from school, feeling under the weather. I had contracted my annual fall cold. As I stepped into the kitchen to greet Mom, I found her grinning from ear to ear, waving an envelope back and forth. She handed it to me and when I saw the sender's name and address, I simply smiled back at her. Giving Mom an absent-minded wave, I retreated to the privacy of my bedroom.

Upon entering my room, I dropped books on my desk and then carefully opened the envelope. As I extracted what I can only describe as extremely feminine stationary, something metallic spilled out of the envelope and dropped to the floor. When I bent over to pick it up, I discovered a small silver medal. It was attached to a delicate, silver chain. It was Julie's Saint Christopher medal. I stood there and examined it for a moment before I remembered it came with a note. Even with my cold, I was able to detect Julie's perfume on the parchment. She must have given it quite a blast.

Holding Saint Christopher in one hand, I reclined against the headboard of my bed. I turned on my reading lamp and commenced to savor every word Julie wrote:

Dear Jackson,

Nice try, Dreamboat, but you're not getting rid of me that easy. I found your letter when I went to get the Saint Christopher medal for you. I may not be able to be with you, but at least that little part of me can be. Keep him with yours, will you? I was sorry to hear about Danny's accident. I wish I could have been there for you, just like I wish I could be with you now. I've decided to hold you to your promise. You know the one you made to me that night in our basement? I really need to hear your voice again. Please call me — NOW!!!

All My Love,

Julie

There were two lines of Xs and Os at the bottom of the page. And, in case I had forgotten it already, she also included her phone number.

That evening, I drove Mom and Dad crazy. I added a two-hour, long-distance charge to our phone bill. Of course, they were patient, tolerant, and understanding. Well, they were for that phone call anyway.

It was fabulous to hear Julie's voice again. Remembering Kurt's advice about how to handle phone calls with girls, I once again let Julie do most of the talking. However, we did settle one important issue during that call. We both agreed to never say good-bye to one another. Julie promised to write and occasionally call. I made her the same promise.

Much like Kurt and the girl he corresponded with for years, so did Julie and me. The cards, letters, and pictures she sent became some of my most cherished keepsakes. Years went by before Julie and I saw each other again, but the details of that reunion are not pertinent to the telling of *this* story. The important thing is that it happened. But, like everyone else from Mankato that I've lost to the years, I inevitably had to include Julie. We never said good-bye. We simply got too busy with our adult lives and communication stopped. She lives on the east coast now and has a family of her own. In the nineties, when I realized that I no longer belonged in her world, I bowed out. I simply keep her memory wrapped in love and tucked away. I thank God – and Julie – for the part she played in my life.

After my visit, that summer of 1972, Brad and Janet tried to make a go of their marriage, but they failed. The two called it quits and divorced in 1975.

Shortly after the they parted ways, Brad fell ill and was diagnosed with a heart condition. In the fall of 1980, while driving his prized Corvair at a high rate of speed, he lost control of the vehicle and drove off the county road he had been traveling on. The little coupe rolled several times and was reduced to little more than a pile of scrap metal. Brad was declared dead at the scene. Later, the coroner's report stated that he had suffered a massive heart attack. I did not travel down to Mankato to attend the funeral. Surprisingly, no one honestly expected me to show. It was not that I didn't care about him, either. In truth, I was rocked by the news. I just felt the need to mourn him privately. The years have now shown me the wisdom hidden within his unorthodox decision to let me go. He was right all along. Life with my adoptive parents afforded me so many opportunities I would not have otherwise had. I never actually questioned Brad's love. So, like the many others who have preceded me in death, I love and miss him to this very day.

Janet kept working at the hospital. She never remarried and after she retired in 1997, she moved into a retirement village in Florida, something she had always wanted to do. I stayed in contact with her, more so after the death of my parents. As I grew older, I never bothered to ask for explanations from her about the past and why they gave me up. But there was one question that always nagged me. So, during a weekend visit, when I was in my thirties, I initiated a conversation with her.

"Janet, shortly after moving in with all of you, my mom came to see you. I know she wasn't there to see me. Is that the day you learned I was Brad's son?"

"Yes, yes it is," replied Janet. "Has that been bothering you again?"

"Not so much," I returned. "But it kind of begs another question?"

"So...ask away, kiddo," – Janet never ceased calling me that.

"Okay...After finding out the truth, how could you have ever loved me?"

"Oh, honey, there are parts of the answer that are easy and other parts that aren't easy at all. You see, I always knew you were Sharon's son. Even though we two quit being friends, while we were in school, I was never truly comfortable with my behavior toward her, especially after learning that my life was panning out better than hers. I just couldn't allow myself to get involved with her; too much bad water under the bridge and all that. So, when Brad gave me the news that he wanted to help Sharon and Adam by taking you in, I felt it was the one way I could help her without getting too involved. I guess I felt it would be like babysitting and nothing more. I'll tell you this, though, I sure didn't count on you stealing my heart the way you did. So, you see, when Sharon told me about her, Brad, and how you were their son, it was too late. I couldn't stop loving you if I tried. Of course, I was mad as hell at Brad for a long time, but because of you, I was finally able to forgive him. After you were adopted, plus the way things turned out that summer, when you were thirteen, I found that I could no longer love him. I tried, Jackson, but it was no good. After you learned the truth, he was no longer the man he once was. I knew he broke your heart and that is something I could never forgive. I haven't been able to forgive myself, either."

After that conversation, I spent years trying to convince Janet to forgive Brad and herself. However, it remained heavy on her mind, right up to her death in 2011. I know that to be true because when I did call, she always wanted to talk about it. I always wished that she would just let it go. In spite of what happened that summer, so very long ago, I always maintained a deep love and appreciation for her and all she ever did for me.

Initially, Kurt and I managed to stay in contact. He still lives in Mankato and is now retired from teaching at Mankato West High. For years, he was also their wrestling coach. He never made that journey to the Twin Cities to find Gwenn. Instead, he married Janelle.It happened during my sophomore year in college. Seven months after the wedding, Janelle gave birth to my first niece, Kimberly. Even though others made comment, I did not then and still do not care about the math discrepancy, as it pertains to my niece's birth. She was conceived and raised in love. That is all I have ever cared about. Once my professional life took off, and I began traipsing all over the globe, communication with Kurt became strained. It has incrementally lessened through the decades. I now reach out once or twice a year, just to make sure he is still alive and doing well.

My continued relationship with Danny was my biggest family-related challenge. He was devastated by the totality of the family breakup. Danny just couldn't deal with how his entire family had been torn apart. So, he retreated to the false comfort of a booze bottle and for years to follow, remained under its influence. Kurt and I labored, emotionally, but we never gave up on our brother; it was to no avail. We lost Danny in 2009. He never conquered his addiction and simply wasted away. As usual, I tried to blame myself for not doing enough to help my tormented brother. Kurt and Janet simply told me to knock it off. None of what happened to any of them was my doing or my responsibility. That may be true, but oh how I miss Danny's boyish grin and charm.

Although it took me quite a few years, I finally returned to Mankato and have continued to periodically revisit the small town. I have marveled, not by its resiliency to survive hard times, but rather, how it has flourished and grown. What once was a dying and decaying Front Street in 1972, is now healthy, renovated, remodeled, restored, and prosperous again.

Since I didn't get to finish growing up in the old neighborhood with my brothers and friends, I intentionally stayed away from it for decades. Only recently have I wandered those streets of my childhood. I expected to find it run down and neglected. I was extremely happy to discover how it, too, has flourished. None of the old families I remember live there anymore. Of course, many of the elderly have died. Some families moved far away within this great nation of ours. Still, others have simply moved out of the neighborhood, but remain somewhere within the town. In their place are new families. They do a wonderful job keeping the neighborhood warm and inviting. Children are nurtured and fiercely protected by a cooperative of involved and dedicated adults.

St. Joseph the Worker church has also undergone revitalization efforts. It now looks and feels fresh and new. When I'm in town, I visit the church and like to sit in that same pew where Father Michael found me, so many years ago. He has been gone for some time, but when I sit quietly and clear my mind, I can still hear the wonderful lilt of his Irish voice. And when I do, I cannot hold back the smile that comes forth.

The campus of Mankato West High has changed exponentially. It has been remodeled and added onto over the years. Although new grandstands were built, people still line West Pleasant Street in the fall to watch the Scarlets' home football games. In the spring and summer, they watch youth baseball games on the other side of the street, for the ball diamonds are still there and well maintained.

The railroad tracks, which ran through that entire area of town, haven't existed in decades. Where once steel rails and tarred-wooden ties lay, now extends miles of asphalt covered nature trails. Town's people can be found walking, running, or biking at all times of the day and into the early evenings.

The south end of town, at the top of Madison Avenue and beyond, has been totally industrialized. Shopping malls, strip malls, motels, restaurants, taverns, and many other businesses too numerous to mention, now exist.

Mankato is now predominately a college town. It plays host to four separate campuses and has, in the past, been voted as the most young-people-friendly town within the state.

When I think of Mankato now, I am reminded of a Hemmingway quote: "Sometimes, great beginnings can also make for great endings." Of course, Ernest was speaking of storytelling, but I've always thought of that quote as a wonderful metaphor for life itself. Even today, I keep a fantasy locked away about possibly moving back to Mankato, after retirement. I doubt that I will ever actually make that move, for I and my family, including my grandchildren, live close by each other elsewhere in these United States. Nevertheless, from to time, I still indulge myself in such wonderful daydreams. I have listened to many people, who wish they could return to the place of their childhood. Conversely, I have also heard from some who never left their birthplace, but wish they had. Because I have grown into a man of almost too many different worlds, it is now difficult for me to pinpoint my exact feelings on the subject. Because I have lived and worked all around the world, I have learned to be happy in so many different environments. So, it has now become quite difficult for me to say I have strong feelings at all, one way or the other.

People think my early brush with death was the first, true turning point in my life. I say it's just one of many things that led up to that August in 1972. I arrived in Mankato that summer, a poor, little rich boy who couldn't find the forest for the trees. But, thanks to the love and patience of some very special people, I returned to Duluth a very different person. I became confident and willing to accept my fate, not as a form of punishment for a crime I didn't commit, but rather, for what it truly was – one of God's many blessings.

In the fall of 1972, when I returned to St. Jean's for my eighth-grade year, I was very apprehensive about what lay in store for me. I was still nursing a broken heart over Julie. In addition, I was resolutely convinced there was no way I would ever give it to another girl, only to have it shattered again by fate. Initially, my expectations for happiness were slight. Seeing my favorite teachers, playing football that fall, then basketball in the winter, were the only things I felt confident about.

Even when I was welcomed back by many of my schoolmates, there was still a certain amount of angst for me to deal with. In my heart, I just knew I was not anyone's pick. Once again, there would be various, weekend parties and social gatherings taking place. As much as I wanted to be included in those soirees, I was positive no invitation would come my way. I counted on being left out again and would have to spend my final year at St. Jean's the loner I had always been. However, much to my surprise, I soon found that I wasn't the only one to do some growing and maturing over the summer.

One day, in the second week of the new school year, I caught Sarah Caskey following me, as I walked down the hall after math class. I was going to my locker to store some books and retrieve others for my next class. As I turned the dial on the combination lock, Sarah leaned against the adjacent locker to my right. "Hi, Jackson," she greeted cheerfully.

I kept my eyes fixed on the lock, but muttered a flat, "Hi, Sarah."

While her fingers nervously tapped on a three-ringed notebook, she asked, "Did you have a good summer?"

Acting as though her presence were of little consequence, I replied, "Not bad…How about you?"

"Me? Except for one thing, I had a great summer!"

"Really? What was the one thing?"

"You didn't call me like I wanted you to."

I looked up and saw disappointment in those fantastic eyes of hers. I also noticed that she was biting her lower lip. I replied, "No, I didn't, did I? Sorry about that. I was…pretty busy all summer."

"It's okay. I understand. I was pretty busy, too."

Since her tone had brightened some, I went back to trying to remember my locker combination. As I scrambled the tumblers for the umpteenth time, Sarah slipped an envelope in front of my face. I stopped working the lock, took the envelope, and asked, "What's this?"

"It's an invitation to my party this weekend."

"Really?"

John K. Lanphier

"Yeah, really. I'm inviting everyone, but I wanted to give you your invitation first."

Of course, I was speechless. I just looked at her and tried to read what I saw on her face. I could not.

Sarah then smiled, leaned in, and softly said, "You'd better be there, Jackson."

Her words almost reverberated in my ears. *Now, where have I heard that before?* But a sincere, "Thanks," was all that I managed to say.

As Sarah began to walk away, she tossed a very sweet, "You're welcome," over her shoulder.

I was now gawking in Sarah's direction and got the impression that my attention was exactly what she had been after. She leisurely walked a short distance down the hall, but suddenly came to an abrupt halt. Casually turning around and giving me a very-sly smile, she said, "Oh, and Jackson? Don't be late." She then stood there, absolutely beaming at me.

Whoa! I know that look!

The End

570

CPSIA information can be obtained
at www.ICGtesting.com
Printed in the USA
LVHW081729170922
728624LV00015B/877